D

and four Ma**g**_____ **fighters** were closing on them. By now the enemy's sensors would have revealed the Gamant ship's vulnerability.

"Damn it," Cole muttered.

"They'll be in firing range in ten seconds. . . . *Five, four, three, two . . .*"

They all braced themselves, sucking in a final breath as though it would help. Ten more seconds ticked off like centuries of agony. The Magisterial fighters swooped down to within shouting distance. Cole peered out the forward portal at the silver wedges which had now formed a semicircle around them. "What the hell are they doing?"

Rudy just shook his head.

"Cole checked monitor number two. It showed their fellow Gamant ship equally dead in space, shields gone—*but alive.*

"I don't understand," Rudy growled hoarsely. "Why aren't they firing?"

Cole started when the green communications light on his console flashed, demanding a response. A glacial chasm of terror suddenly yawned before him as understanding came at last. *"Oh, my God, they want us alive!"*

KATHLEEN M. O'NEAL'S
POWERS OF LIGHT TRILOGY:

AN ABYSS OF LIGHT

TREASURE OF LIGHT

REDEMPTION OF LIGHT

REDEMPTION OF LIGHT

KATHLEEN M. O'NEAL

DAW BOOKS, INC.

DONALD A. WOLLHEIM, FOUNDER

375 Hudson Street, New York, NY 10014

ELIZABETH R. WOLLHEIM
SHEILA E. GILBERT
PUBLISHERS

First Printing, May 1991

1 2 3 4 5 6 7 8 9

In memory of Tedi

The nightmares haven't stopped yet, Ted. I still wake up in the darkness and listen to hear if you're crying. I reach out to see if you're warm enough, to see if you need another pain pill. And then there's the terrible moment when I close my fist on air, because I realize you're gone.

We haven't been able to pick up your toys. Mike can't seem to get warm anymore. There aren't very many people who understand.

But there weren't very many people who ever understood you, Ted. They never opened themselves up to share the love you gave so unselfishly to anyone who'd let you. They never saw the strength or gentleness in your eyes. They never saw your bravery—even in the last days when it was so hard, when you couldn't walk anymore and the pain kept you awake all night.

We miss you, Ted.

It's very cold here without you. I hope you're warm, wherever you are.

I still worry.

ACKNOWLEDGMENTS

When the hours got long, the Wild West Deli in Dubois provided a much needed escape, not to mention the best coffee and sandwiches in four states. Special thanks go to Melinda, Roxanne, Kellie, and Gnat for their patience with the bleary authors who often stumble through their door and talk in half sentences.

Sheila Gilbert, as always, provided brilliant comments on the original manuscript. To all the readers who wonder what makes a superb editor, I can tell you: She has the uncanny ability to see more deeply into the strands of plot and the hearts of characters *than the author does*. It's a rare talent. Occasionally disconcerting. Always received with much gratitude. Thanks for taking the time, Sheila.

W. Michael Gear spent too many breakfasts with his elbows on the kitchen table while his eggs got cold, discussing gravitation and genocide, neurophysiology and heartbreak. For all those wonderful mornings and for understanding why the holocaust stalks my dreams with such vengeance, I owe him more than I can ever tell him.

THE SACRED BOOK
OF THE INVISIBLE GREAT SPIRIT

Micah made a golden calf that could dance. He named it Sesseng gen Pharaggen. He placed it in high mountains upon which the sun never rises. It stood over the living waters on the way which leads through the Great Gate to the Light everlasting.

He knelt before it and clutched his hands in prayer. "I am ready, God. I have armed myself in the armor of Light. I took shape in the cycle of the riches of the Light, giving form to that which is never begotten. Now, God of Silence! Hear me!"

Micah wept and his warm tears struck the red earth like lightning.

"I beg thee, lead Rachel out of the bitter tree. Establish her in the holy light on high, in the Silence unattainable, before the wicked archigenitor can roast us all in the flames that never die . . ."

One of the Secret Books of the Egyptian Gnostics. Manuscript reported stolen from the Coptic Museum, Old Earth, 2008. Mutilated, vandalized fragments found on Giclas II, 4789. Document almost certainly corrupt.

PROLOGUE

The Year of the Epitropos, 5426.

The call came like a bare whisper of wind through his mind.

For a time he fought to deny it, to shove the disturbance away and return to his dream of leaf-strewn meadows high in the sunrise-painted mountains. The tang of pine-scented breezes still lingered in his senses. He struggled to keep the vision, concentrating on the sight of shimmering mist twining ethereal fingers through the dark branches over his head. His beautiful wife, Ethnarch, sat beneath the overarching limbs, smiling up at him lovingly. Peaceful. So peaceful.

But the voice intruded again—harsh with buried anxiety.

"Great Master, forgive me, but we must talk."

Magistrate Mastema reluctantly woke and peered into the softly lit room in which he floated. Blurred images swam around him, twinkling and unfocused, as though seen through newborn eyes. The silver glow of the lights threw an icy mantle over his green chair and desk. His enormous library lined every wall. The information disks and rare books gleamed, sealed in stasis for his timeless slumber. A mustiness clung to this long unopened vault deep in the heart of his home world, Giclas 7.

He stretched, feeling the supreme comfort of the pillar of weightlessness upon which he floated. As he inhaled a deep breath, the call came again, wandering like a homeless waif through his thoughts.

"Mastema, please? I'm desperate."

"I'm awake," he murmured, barely audibly. His long unused vocal cords ached from the effort. "How . . . how long has it been?"

"You've slept for two millennia, Great Master."

"Two?" He paused contemplatively, wondering at the changes that must have occurred in that long span of time. "And who are you?"

"I am the current ruling Magistrate, Gibor Slothen."

Mastema nodded. Each of the Magistrates served for at least a millennia before being granted a Peace Vault where he could dream eternally. Disturbing one of them was considered a grievous crime unless demanded by the direst circumstances.

Mastema heaved a bitter sigh. "I see. Have you contacted the others?" Pilpul and Maggid had slept even longer than he, thousands upon thousands of years.

"No. Not yet. I'd hoped that you and I, alone, could resolve the problem."

"A prudent move." Mastema blinked, trying to bring his eyes into focus. He could see four of his six limbs wavering in a blue wash around him. They felt numb, as though not really his. "Unless we're on the verge of the abyss, I'm not sure Pilpul would understand. She was always a contrary sort, more concerned with her own pleasure than the salvation of galactic life.

"I assume we're at war?"

"Yes, and have been for over a decade. If you'll search your neural templates, I'm sure you'll find memories of a cultural group called Gamants. Their insanity is to blame for this catastrophe."

"Gamants?" He sighed deeply. "Yes, unfortunately, I do recall them."

Gamants were a bestial group of human dissidents. Under his administration, they'd been collared like dogs on the planet Earth. But despite his precautions, they'd managed to escape to wage a devastating war against him. "Do you know, Slothen, that I've successfully managed to forget those animals for centuries? Well, never mind. I'd hoped a few millennia under the whip would have lessened their ardor for oblivion. Apparently not. Go on."

"It's a long story. Gamant unrest increased a few years ago, just after the Gamant leader Mikael Calas requested we forcibly move his people to the planet Horeb—a barren wasteland at the very edge of the galaxy."

"He *requested* relocation?" Mastema shook his head disbelievingly. During his time, Gamant leaders had deliberately scattered their people to the solar winds, hoping the diaspora would assure their survival. They'd always been too canny for their own good. "Didn't Calas realize that once we had them in one place, we could do with them as we wished?"

"I don't believe it concerned him. He claimed God instructed the relocation in a vision. He was only eight years old, Magistrate, but now he's become an annoying twenty-year-old. At any rate, it was certainly to our benefit, so we initiated the program. Shortly after the massive relocation began, Gamants revolted suddenly and bitterly. Currently, we're in the midst of another full-scale Gamant Revolt—just like the one you faced millennia ago."

"All right. I understand. I take it that Gamants have managed to obtain weapons?"

"Yes. Weapons and ships. Twelve years ago, we cornered and destroyed most of the Gamant Underground fleet. But instead of surrendering, the lunatics started converting minor vessels—freighters, frigates, and star-sails—into war machines. They've amassed an impressive new fleet."

"Clever. Who's the military genius behind it?"

"We suspect a dissident named Baruch, but we're not certain. They're using those vessels to wage a devastating hit-and-run war against us. We've had no choice but to respond in kind, and you know how much time and funding a war requires. Our redistribution program is in shambles. Several nonhuman species have grown tired of the lack of food and military protection. Entire solar systems have risen against us, refusing to meet their quota of goods for the communal programs. They've even begun to attack and loot our military installations. To make matters worse, Palaia Station is nearing perihelion with Palaia Zohar and our own people are scrambling to keep the station in stable orbit outside the singularity's event horizon."

"Zohar, yes, I remember."

Mastema caressed his brow. Palaia Zohar was the black hole companion to the star around which the enormous bulk of Palaia Station orbited. It revolved in fifty-six year cycles. At the end of each cycle, the station complex came perilously close to the hole's gravity well, requiring some fancy navigational maneuvers to escape the overwhelming gravitational pull and tidal effects.

"I assume, Slothen, that you've initiated selective sterilizations to 'encourage' Gamant cooperation?"

"We've killed them by the thousands, but they breed like sewer rats. I believe there are more Gamants in the galaxy now than twelve years ago—though I estimate we've easily killed a hundred thousand revolutionaries in that time.'

Mastema let his blurry gaze drift over the tarnished silver ceiling. His vision had cleared some. He could make out the individual colors of the book bindings in the library. "Have you tried taking hostages?"

"Yes, years ago, when I first realized the course history might take, I had fifty thousand of the animals captured on Horeb and transferred to the station here. We constructed a series of ten satellites and set them into orbit around Palaia, then incarcerated our captive Gamants on them. As a shield, you understand. I thought that the Underground would think twice before attacking Palaia when they knew that we could, at their very first movement in our direction, destroy fifty thousand of their families and friends."

"Prudent move."

"Yes, it's kept the Underground from attacking us directly, but they're stirring up havoc everywhere else. I'm afraid Giclasian rule of the galaxy hangs in the balance, Master."

"I gather, then, that you're aiming your war efforts at genocide?"

"I've considered the matter carefully and I think it's the only way to end the Revolt once and for all. Do you object?"

Mastema thought about it. There'd been a time when he would have, long, long ago, before the first Gamant Revolt—before he understood the peculiarly violent and unpredictable behavior of the subspecies. But after the atrocities he'd witnessed in that initial rebellion, his sympathy for them had vanished. "No. Not really. Oh, there's a part of me that balks at such complete measures, but Gamants were a cancer in the galaxy even when I ruled. It seems they've metastasized and are spreading their disease through the body of civilization.

But hear me clearly, Slothen! You'll have to do it delicately, in secret, or all the bleeding hearts in the galaxy will add to your problems. Have you thought about trying . . ."

Mastema ceased in mid-sentence. A dark shadow blackened the face of the library. Through his cloudy infrared sensitive vision, he saw a deep glimmer of heat swell from the shadow's center, boiling out in a golden blur.

"What . . . *Who are you?*" he gasped in shock.

Slothen responded curiously, "I don't understand."

"Gibor, I'll contact you later. I have an intruder in my vault!"

"But that's impossible. Your vault is two hundred miles beneath solid rock. No one could penetrate—"

The dattran connection went dead.

Mastema panicked and mentally tripped his vault switch to notify the guards outside his door that he needed immediate aid. The golden blur flared and crystallized into a human-shaped figure. With unnatural grace, it walked forward to stand no more than two feet away. The sweet scent of roses swirled through the room.

"Who are you?" Mastema demanded again.

"Surely you remember me, Magistrate."

Mastema began to deny it but stopped. Where had he heard that soft, infinitely gentle voice before? Through his tear-dusted vision, the amber figure seemed to shimmer like polished crystal beneath a brilliant noonday sun. Memories stirred, emotionally traumatic yet visually indistinct, like the recollections of birth buried deeply in the souls of every living creature.

"Identify yourself!" Mastema commanded. *Where are the guards? Why haven't they entered to protect me?*

The crystalline figure smoothed a hand over Mastema's rest pedestal. "Think back, Magistrate. Long ago, almost three millennia now, you called me Milcom. It was I who gave you the Tablets of the Law inscribed with the Treasures of Light."

Mastema battled his sleep-drugged tri-brain to find some semblance of meaning in his memories. "The what?"

"Light, Magistrate. *Pure Light.* You remember the stories, don't you?"

"No. No, I—"

"Then let me remind you." Milcom threw back his caramel-colored cloak to put his hands on his hips. "In the beginning, the Most High was all there was: pure indivisible Light. He withdrew a part of himself to spawn the dark void of creation. Then He plucked a handful of jewels, vessels of light—sometimes called celestial sapphires—from his throne and cast them into the Abyss. He sundered one of the gems with His breath, then took the broken vessel and inscribed in black fire on the halves the figures of the Law which govern the workings of all things. Those figures are the Treasures of Light."

Frightened, Mastema shouted, "You talk in riddles! Speak to me straightforwardly, or be gone with you!"

Milcom crossed shining muscular arms over his broad chest. "Please, try, Magistrate. I know the constant dreams of this vault obscure true memories more with each passing year, but you must think. The last time we talked, we stood in a meadow on the newly constructed Pharaggen Mountains on Palaia Station. The false sunset you'd created to simulate planetary rotation worked marvels; it sent flames through the drifting clouds. You talked proudly of how you'd conquered savagery. I called you a fool. I told you the only Truth in this universe is that opposites are everlasting. *Remember?*"

Mastema squeezed his eyes closed. What did this being want and how had it gotten into his locked vault? He fought the feeling of violation and fear to search his memories. Such a long time. He would have been young, having barely risen to the rank of Magistrate. The Treasures of Light? Figures? What did that mean? Equations? A small tendril of fear wound through him. *Where are my guards?* Was his security system down? Or had this strange intruder done something to prevent his mental order from being accepted by the com unit that constantly monitored his brains?

Mastema fought to sit up, to force his eyes to give him a sharper image. He accomplished a small victory: he could see the figure pacing a short distance away, strolling thoughtfully before the ancient leather-bound books in the library, as though contemplating the titles. The very nonchalance of the action sent Mastema's nerves into a frenzy.

"How did you get into a secured area? I *demand* that you leave this vault immediately!"

Milcom stopped. Mastema saw the hem of the being's caramel-colored cloak sway gently back and forth as though it had been set to dancing by his sudden halt.

Milcom turned to face Mastema. "I am created of undying fire, Magistrate. I don't take orders from creatures made of stardust. You used to know that. Now, please, time is short and we must discuss the future of this universe, but until you recollect who I am, I'll be wasting my breath."

Mastema sent a frantic message through the system, ordering the com to return the gravity so he could physically try to escape. When nothing happened, he lost control and shrieked, "Com? Return gravity. *Return gravity!*" Still, he remained chained atop his weightless pillar. He struggled with his withered body, so numbed by centuries of serenity.

The golden man swept across the room and Mastema caught a new scent, bitter and dry, like the stench of fear-sweat that clung to the ruins of ancient destruction—just as soon, the fragrance of roses masked it.

Terrified, Mastema quavered, "What do you want?"

"I came to warn you, Magistrate."

"Warn me?" Mastema blinked hard and his vision cleared a little more. He could make out a face, amber and glowing as though from an inner fire. The image caught at his throat like a strangling hand—because, God forbid, it did seem familiar.

"The Law I gave you allowed you to find and collect the sapphires in this galaxy so that you could use them to build worlds, to feed billions, to power your starships—and to gain the prestige you sought so desperately. *I* gave you the sword to damn all your enemies to oblivion. And so you did—except for Gamant enemies. And why?" Milcom held up a condemning finger. "Because you let one critically important divine sapphire escape your clutches."

"But . . . I don't understand. Why would that fact influence the course of history?"

Milcom's brilliant eyes sparkled like suns. "Gamants have a different use for the sapphires, that's why. They utilize them as gateways to God."

"Don't patronize me! There is no God."

Milcom's pointing finger coalesced into a shaking fist. *"Verily, verily I say unto you, Magistrate, that single drop of heavenly dew will plunge your empire into the eternal pit of darkness unless you capture it."*

Mastema's heart throbbed. The tone, the archaic speech pattern . . . glimpses of the past abruptly flitted through his mind: He saw himself young, terrified, staring wide-eyed over simple, magnificent equations delivered out of the air by a being of pure gold. He saw himself locating thousands of quantum black holes, *schethiyas* in the Giclasian language, and sending out tugs to retrieve them. They'd constructed a special containment vessel—Palaia Station—and moved the center of government there for added protection. The very foundation of his galactic empire had risen upon those tiny power plants.

Fear pounded a hard fist into Mastema's stomach. He swallowed convulsively. "Milcom. Yes. *Yes, I remember.* It's been a very long time, but . . . Milcom. Milcom. What have I done that you would come here? I kept my part of the bargain!"

"Yes. Indeed, you did," Milcom agreed softly. "You caged Gamants so brutally they couldn't wait to slit your throat. You did well, Magistrate. I didn't come to torment you about our bargain." In a magnetically tender voice, Milcom continued, "On the contrary, I came to help you—to give you the head of the Gamant leader on a silver platter, if you want it. It's the only way to stop the Revolt."

"Calas is a twenty-year-old youth. I can't believe he's the real threat. There must be another Gamant, a military genius, who's responsible for this fiasco that Slothen faces."

"The boy is the real danger, for he wears around his neck the *Gehenna* gate, Magistrate—a special sapphire. Millions of Gamants have died protecting it, passing it down through the centuries from one leader to the next. And when Mikael stands in the mountains on high and opens that gate, all that you and yours have built will come crashing down." A hazy smile adorned Milcom's glowing face. "He'll destroy you."

Mastema fought to control the quaking of his six limbs.

The last time he'd dealt with Milcom, he'd gained an empire and lost everything in the galaxy that meant anything to him: his wife, beautiful Ethnarch, with whom he spent all his dreams, his children, his home. . . . The wounds inside him would bleed forever.

"Come, come, Magistrate," Milcom said impatiently. He walked the book-lined room, fluidly graceful, cloak fluttering behind him. "You know very well that the fist of survival often gets dirtied with blood and marrow. Do you want Giclasian rule of the galaxy to collapse? Would you like to have your home world destroyed and Palaia Station taken over by Gamant fanatics? Do you know what they could do with the resources there?"

"They could turn the singularities into weapons and destroy every civilized system in the galaxy."

"Of course."

Mastema steeled himself and gazed up into that sinfully magnificent alien face. It seemed to glow brighter, casting a glimmering amber halo over the vault. "What do you want?"

"I ask nothing, Magistrate. I offer *everything*."

"You never give without expecting your pound of flesh. Tell me your demands."

Milcom hesitated for a long time, as though considering what could be said safely. Then, in a violent gesture, he lifted a shining hand to the invisible heavens. Mastema saw the whirling maw of blackness spin out from the wall to swallow the library. A rush of warm wind flooded the room. Mastema choked on the scents of darkness and decay.

Terrified, Mastema screamed, *"What do you want?"*

Milcom stood resolutely still, his chin tipped as though contemplating the rippling arc of the black vortex. Power encircled him like a thrumming electromagnetic aura. Mastema's flesh prickled from the impact. After an eternity, Milcom quietly responded, "I want you to save yourself by finding that sapphire."

"How?" Mastema weakly inquired.

"You must do two things. First, you must go to the fields of Anai and seize Cole Patrick Tahn, a former captain in your own fleet. Second, you must find Mikael Calas. Then you must bring both men *alive* to Palaia

Station. If you fail to deliver either one, Mastema—you are lost."

"What are you talking about? Are you telling me that all Giclasians will die if I don't?"

"No, Magistrate." Milcom's voice caressed him like a lover's warm hand. "I'm telling you that this entire universe will die."

Milcom started to step into the whirling vortex and Mastema shouted, "Wait! Tell me more!" He reached out to the golden alien with a trembling hand. "I need to know more about this . . . this divine sapphire that Calas has."

Milcom bowed his head and shook it slightly. "No," he answered and his voice seemed to echo through the room. "You know far too much already." Then he walked into the roiling night of the Void. For a split second, Mastema saw a flash of cerulean blue, and the light of what seemed a hundred torches wavering in the wind.

The Void spun closed.

In that same instant, four guards burst through Mastema's door, eyes wide with wonder and fear. These soldiers had undoubtedly been standing guard their entire lives and never expected him to wake, to call out to them. They looked stunned. They wore heavy armor over their six-legged blue bodies, and each held a rifle across his chest. Mastema waved them over with a weak hand.

In a dreadful voice, he murmured. "Call me a physician. I have urgent business to discuss with Magistrate Slothen. We have to find the best captain in the fleet to handle this."

CHAPTER 1

"Well?" Captain Amirah Jossel demanded tersely. "I was ordered to abandon a critical mission around Calistus and appear here for a psych evaluation, Doctor. We've done that up nicely over the past three days. So why the hell am I still here?"

She fixed Doctor Hans Lucerne with a fiery gaze. He paced the hospital floor, uneasily flipping through the pages of her psychological report while she got dressed. "You're still here, Captain, because you're sick. It's a good thing Slothen saw fit to order you in." He was a middle-aged man with thick black brows and wavy salt-and-pepper hair. A shaggy mustache draped down over Lucerne's upper lip.

Jossel's smile ridiculed his words. "I've never felt better in my life, Doctor. I'm just having some minor problems adjusting to the tension of the past several months. I'm—"

"The hell you are."

She bristled and he straightened to give her stare for stare. He'd gone over and over the data in her report and still remained mystified as to the source of her mental disturbances. But one thing he did know—she was deeply ill and the stress of this top secret mission that Slothen had just given her could well send her over the edge.

Jossel looked him up and down distastefully, as though trying to decide whether or not to court-martial him. Not that she could—he outranked her. Jossel just had a knack for making people's skin crawl. She was a tall woman with long blonde hair. Her button nose rode over full lips. She would have been beautiful, Lucerne had to admit, if she could ever get rid of that impaling glint in her turquoise eyes that made people wriggle as if she'd skewered them with a dull lance. Her caustic tone of

21

voice didn't help much either. Typical, though. Brusque, impatient habits inevitably came to a woman of her military prestige and talent. She'd been personally curried by the Magistrates in Academy and since getting out had distinguished herself as a superior officer. She'd won medals that Lucerne had never even heard of and he'd been a physician on Palaia for thirty years.

Lucerne turned away while she took off her hospital gown and tugged on her uniform pants. Around him, Palaia's finest hospital pulsed with the hum and buzz of sophisticated equipment. Antiseptic scents twined through the small examination room like pernicious serpents. Two other beds lined the opposite wall, both empty. Through the far door, a gray-haired nurse in a white form-fitting jumpsuit entered and jangled a table of silver instruments and vials of blood.

"Explain, Doctor," Jossel ordered. "I think I'm just so goddamned tired of war duty that my mind is playing tricks on me. What do you think is wrong?" She sat on the edge of the examination table and reached for her uniform shirt. The golden captain's bars on the epaulets sparkled with an unnatural brilliance in the stark glare cast by the lustreglobes that blanketed the ceiling.

"It could be the war duty," Lucerne answered honestly. "You've had some tough missions in the past two years. But I doubt that's the source of the problem." He folded his arms as ominously as he could. His gray sleeves shimmered like gossamer mist at sunrise. "How long have these 'flashbacks' been bothering you?"

"They're not 'flashbacks,' " she corrected impatiently, lifting a condemning brow. Lucerne fought the urge to squirm. "Flashbacks are memories. These are . . . well, I don't what they are. That's *your* job. But they're not scenes from real time. They're fantasy images. We're sitting in the same wing where most of those images take place and I don't see any interconnected net of lights or a Devouring Creature of Darkness either." A tiny shiver went down her back before she tightened her muscles to kill the fear response.

Lucerne noted the action and vented an exasperated sigh. "For the sake of argument, let's call them flashbacks. They certainly have the characteristics of confused memories. Your grandmother is always there, correct?"

She slipped her shirt over her head, then tucked it into her purple pants. Bitterly, she answered, "Yes."

Lucerne ran a hand through his salt and pepper hair. He had to tread lightly with her or she'd undoubtedly get up and stalk out before he'd gleaned even half the information he needed to relieve her of command of her ship. The very thought made him swallow convulsively. Unconsciously, he glanced toward the ceiling, seeing the winged battle cruiser in his mind. The *Sargonid* floated vigilantly in orbit around Palaia Station. What would her crew do if he succeeded? They had a reputation for irrational loyalty to their captain. Would they mutiny? Try to break her out of the psych ward? It was a possibility he'd have to take up with the military advisory council *if* the time came—which was unlikely after his last conversation with Magistrate Slothen. Slothen, too, seemed irrationally loyal to Jossel.

"Let's go through it one more time," Lucerne said. He lifted the report and shook it emphatically. "Most of the flashbacks begin with you hearing your grandmother shouting at you that the savior is coming, then you smell the metallic scent of blood. You're covered with it, your uniform is sticking to your body in clammy folds. The halls are pitch black. You're supporting your wounded grandmother, dragging her through smoke-filled corridors here on Palaia, and you're being pursued by a 'Devouring Creature of Darkness.' From everywhere you hear voices, mostly speaking in the Gamant language. An unknown man yells at you to hurry. Explosions rock the building. You see Magistrate Slothen. You shout at him, begging him to help you. Your grandmother changes into a huge serpent and wraps around you, squeezing the life from you. But the serpent still speaks with your grandmother's voice. It screams at you over and over, but you can't understand what it's saying. You kill the serpent, cutting off its head. Is that the extent of the images?"

Jossel shrugged. "Pretty much. Sometimes I see the sparkling net of lights burst from my grandmother's face to engulf us both. Occasionally her face turns into . . . into a man's face—or a Giclasian's."

Lucerne frowned. For a moment he'd thought she was going to give him a name. "Do you know the man?"

"No, no, not for certain. He seems to be a collage of different great military officers throughout history."

"For example?"

Irritably, she waved it off. "I can't tell you. I don't know who they are. They're just—familiar."

"And these are all recent developments? Since your psych evaluation last year? They must have something to do with your scorch attacks on Gamant—"

"Not . . ." Jossel hesitated, her mouth ajar. "No. The images first started coming when I was fourteen."

Lucerne leaned forward in stunned disbelief. *"What?"* She unquestionably knew the penalties for withholding such information from Palaia's medical staff. If he reported the cover-up, the military advisory council could take away her command and throw her into the brig, or worse, for years. Jossel lifted her chin defiantly and Lucerne squeezed the bridge of his nose. He asked simply, "Fourteen, huh? Was that a traumatic year for you?"

"Not especially. My parents had been killed the year before during the Pegasan attack on Rusel 3, my home world. But the shock had worn off by then. I'd say I was a fairly normal youth going through the throes of puberty."

"You were living with your grandmother, weren't you? When the first flashback occurred, I mean?"

Jossel pulled long blonde hair out of her shirt and quietly walked to the foot of the examination table to retrieve her cap. She twisted the purple bill anxiously. Her beautiful face had contorted so much at the mention of her grandmother that Lucerne felt the intensity of her emotion throbbing in his own breast. He smoothed his fingers over the tangled black briar of his mustache, contemplating the implications. The nurse across the room mumbled something that sounded profane and hurriedly left the room. Lucerne took advantage of the opportune distraction and stared absently in her direction, hoping Jossel would settle down in the interim. The woman had an almost violent aversion to discussing her grandmother. "Captain, I have administered your annual psych evaluation every year for the past ten years. Why have you never reported these incapacitating flashbacks—"

"They're not incapacitating!" Jossel swiftly swung

around to stand nose to nose with him. "My duties have *never* suffered because of the 'flashbacks'!"

Lucerne stood resolutely still. Beneath her stony exterior, he thought he perceived a twinge of very real fear. She must realize his reasons for probing her personal history so thoroughly. Did she know he'd already requested she be relieved? She might have guessed it. One corner of her mouth twitched uncontrollably, though she fought to suppress it.

"Captain—" he thumped the psych report in his hand and tried to speak gently, "—the last time you had one of these attacks, your own officers had to help you off the bridge of the *Sargonid*. Your second in command, First Lieutenant Jason Woloc, reported that you were raving. If I'm ever to cure you of these flashbacks, you must help me!"

Jossel's smooth freckled cheeks vibrated with the grinding of her molars. After a moment, she dropped her gaze and adopted a letter-perfect "at ease" position. Her blonde hair glinted with a silver sheen in the light. "I meant, Doctor, that the flashbacks have never affected me seriously until recently."

"*How* recently?"

She shook her head as though aggravated by his questioning. "Doctor, why can't you just use the mind probes, trace the neural circuitry of the disturbances, and alter the dendritic connections to eliminate the flashbacks?"

Lucerne fidgeted. That was a hell of a good question. They'd advanced so far in medical science—especially with the astounding leaps in the past three months—that not even death was final anymore, not if they caught the situation quickly enough. "Captain, we've known since your entrance into Academy that your brain is organized and constructed differently than other human brains. Very much like Gamants' brains, actually." Seeing her hot glare, he hurriedly continued, "I'm not accusing you of having Gamant blood, Captain. We've found that same recessive trait in humans with no Gamant ancestry whatsoever—as is your case. But that's not the issue here. The reason we can't locate the source of your mental disturbances is that you seem to have a—" he threw up his hands, "—a *compartment* in your brain that is

impervious to probing. We don't know why it exists, but
I—"

"Where is it located? What part of my brain?"

"In the hippocampus. You have some other interesting
anomalies there, too: Upside-down dendrites, misaligned
pyramid-shaped cells, there's even some neurofibrillary
. . . uh, scar tissue."

Jossel's turquoise eyes narrowed. She remained silent
a moment, scanning the white walls and beds in the hospital. "Scar tissue? From what? I was rarely sick when I
was young and I never suffered a severe impact to my
skull that I can remember."

"We don't know why. We've never noted it before.
Which is truly a surprise since Magistrate Slothen himself
has insisted on being present at every one of your psych
evaluations since you entered the service—and he *knows*
the neuro systems of humans. Anyway, it appears to be
a progressive phenomena. I suspect that the scar tissue
expands each time you have one of these flashback
events. The tissue seems to respond to endogenous
events to form a stronger and stronger fence around the
compartment. It acts almost as though it were programmed to lay down scar tissue to *protect* the area
where the flashbacks originate. Very peculiar. Now, Captain, let's get back to my former question. How long
have you been seriously plagued by these attacks?"

"Doctor Lucerne," she challenged. "If I remember my
neurobiology course work correctly, all of these specific
anomalies, the upside-down dendrites, etc., suggest
schizophrenia. Are you saying that I'm—"

"No, no. I wish I could make that diagnosis." Indeed,
he did. He'd have no problems getting her into an institu-
tion if that were clearly the case. "Other than the flashbacks, you show no behavioral symptoms of such a
disease. I simply mentioned those facts to try and explain
why we are unable to probe and eliminate your disturbances. *How, long, Captain?*"

Indignantly, she asked, "Are you recommending I be
relieved of command?"

Lucerne pretended not to notice that her nostrils had
begun to flare with her suddenly rapid breathing. Her
face remained inscrutably blank. He clamped his teeth.
Angrily, he lifted the psych report and slapped it down

on the examination table. "I made that request three days ago, Captain. Magistrate Slothen himself denied it. He said that other than *one* fainting spell on the bridge, he saw no clear evidence of instability in your evaluation. He also told me that you were being assigned to a secret mission and would be coordinating some difficult strategy and tactics in the Anai system and then you and your crew would be heading for the Gamant planet of Horeb to aid in containing the insurrection that's raging there. He—"

"Horeb is a quagmire of dissent and insanity," she affirmed sourly. "Slothen's patience with that idiot governor who's ruling the planet has finally run thin."

"Captain, do you know how Slothen defended you?"

"I've no idea, Doctor."

"He said he was certain the reason you'd 'fainted' on the bridge was because you'd had no sleep for sixty hours. He assured *me* that exhaustion and stress were the root of your delusions and I was to drop the matter immediately!"

"Good for him." She bowed her head and laughed deprecatingly, as though in derision of her own fears of being relieved of command.

Lucerne's mouth pressed into a tight white line. Damn her. She knew as well as he did that she wasn't capable. Though she wouldn't say so, he suspected the flashbacks had grown so numerous and so vivid that when they struck she couldn't distinguish between fantasy and reality. The woman needed to be institutionalized before she hurt herself—or worse, someone else.

Jossel gruffly tugged her purple cap down over her forehead. "Can you give me something to help with the flashbacks? Something to lessen their intensity?"

He shook his head. "Not without impairing your ability to make quick command decisions. Drugs might kill you faster in a critical moment than the flashbacks."

"I see. Well, then, I'll manage." Briskly, she started for the door.

"Will you?" He shouted furiously. "You think you can handle anything by sheer force of will, don't you? Well, for all our sakes, I damned well hope you can." Lucerne lifted a finger and stabbed it at her. "Because if one of these *seizures* strikes in a desperate moment of battle, you're just liable to get yourself, every member of your crew, and very likely a lot of other people killed. Do you understand what I'm saying? It is my medical opinion that you are unfit for command, Captain!" He slowly lowered his hand and stared Jossel hard in the eyes. "I strongly recommend that you march into Slothen's office and respectfully request to be relieved. You need at least a month in a rehab center. The flashbacks won't go away. It's just going to get worse, Captain! *Don't fool yourself!* If I had the authority, I'd—"

"The ruling Magistrate has pronounced me fit, Doctor. I suggest you save your talents for someone who needs them." Jossel strode past him in a blur of purple uniform and fluttering blonde hair.

"You're going to get somebody killed, Captain! You hear me?"

She didn't so much as flinch. She stamped out the door and vanished down the hall before Lucerne could even begin to curse her. He put his hands on his hips and tensely headed for the door himself.

He slammed a fist into the wall before he exited the examination room.

CHAPTER 2

The magnificence of autumn splashed the mountains of Kiskanu, throwing an irregular crimson and gold patchwork quilt over the densely forested slopes. Fluffy clouds drifted lazily above. In the slanting rays of sunset, their edges gleamed with a marmalade fire.

Cole Tahn lifted another crate and carried it across the landing pad to the growing pile beside his triangular silver fighter. A tall, slim man with brown hair and piercing blue-violet eyes, he had an oval face and a straight nose. His camo jumpsuit clung to his muscular body in sweaty patches. He'd been feeling strange all day, jumping at every sound. His gaze roved the forests, as though expecting something unseen to grab him suddenly. He'd worn another millimeter off his pistol grip from the number of times he'd reached for it in panic this afternoon.

"What the hell's the matter with you?" he growled harshly at himself. "There's nothing there."

He set the crate down and wiped his brow on his sleeve. People hustled around him, loading the freighters, laughing and talking. Four ships, freighters and fighters, sat in a neat row along the perimeter of the field. In the fiery light, they seemed drenched in liquid silver. A small square office took up the far left side of the pad. Inside that office, he knew Rudy Kopal manned the scanners, watching the skies for any sign of the enemy. But the knowledge comforted him little. He'd never really gotten along with Kopal, which made it hard to trust him. "You're being an ass. Stop it. If anything happens, Rudy'll give you plenty of time to get to your ship and get out of here."

He kicked the crate lightly to relieve some of his frustration. It was probably just Kiskanu that set him on edge. The old Gamants who survived on this isolated

world had strange mystical beliefs. They boasted that
they spent day and night drawing runes on cold stone
floors in candlelit rooms, trying to command the powers
of God and angels to bring the Mashiah so he'd wipe the
Magistrates from the face of the galaxy. A strange place,
the planet's agricultural and mineral riches went largely
unused, except by the Underground which paid hand-
somely for the supplies.

Cole's gut tightened at the thought of the Magistrates.
He forced himself to kneel down and begin untying the
ropes that bound the crate. He took his Wind River
fighting knife and pried the lid off the top, then hastily
stacked the petrolon canisters in the fighter's tiny cargo
hold and surveyed the haphazard work. Canisters leaned
precariously atop one another. As soon as he lifted off,
they'd fall into a jumbled mess. If one of his crew had
done such a job, Cole's throat would have been raw for
days from chewing the soldier's butt. Gruffly, he punched
the hold console to shut the door and leaned back against
the silver hull. The wind that brushed his moist face was
warm and redolent with the dry spicy smells of autumn.

The trucks bearing the last supplies had already come
in and soldiers worked tirelessly to transport the crates
to the ships. Mechanical loaders churned about like great
four-armed beasts, while people scurried around their
legs hauling smaller petrolon boxes and the precious special gifts that the members of the starship crews had
requested.

His gaze landed on Carey Halloway. She stood a short
distance away, orchestrating the resupply process. Second in command of the battle cruiser, *Zilpah*, she was
strikingly beautiful. Her perfect body rippled with toned
muscles beneath her formfitting black jumpsuit. Auburn
hair fell in straight silky locks to her shoulders, accenting
her emerald green eyes and pale translucent skin.

Despite the dread that lingered in his mind, Cole found
himself smiling as he watched her. She stood, hands
propped on her shapely hips while she yelled at Lieutenant Joshua Samuals and Corporal Lu Zimmern, dressing
them down for slovenly work. Carey poked a hard finger
into Samuals' chest and his shoulders hunched more with
each passing second. Tahn cast a surreptitious glance at
his own hold and cautiously slid sideways, covering the

door with his broad back. He'd been the object of Carey's
wrath too many times to look forward to it. He struggled
with himself, but he couldn't help it, he laughed. Too
loudly. Carey turned and scowled. He smothered his
smile and pivoted around to fiddle aimlessly with an
empty crate. Birds chirped in the trees, their songs blend-
ing in a bright symphony.

Carey dismissed Samuals and Zimmern and walked
over to loom over Cole. He got to his feet to face her.

"Well, you sound more cheerful," she commented.
"No more doom and gloom prophecies?"

"If you're subtly asking me how I feel, the answer is,
still bad. I've just decided not to show it for a while."

"Good. The last time you grabbed for your pistol, half
my loading crew hit the ground and scrambled for
cover."

"That's because your lovable personality keeps them
all jittery."

Carey grinned and leaned back beside him against the
fighter's hull, amiably propping an elbow on his shoulder. Sunset dappled through the trees, setting her beautiful face ablaze with a lavender aura. Being close to her
eased some of his anxiety. Down through the long years
of fighting and running, she'd never let him down. In the
early days, he'd longed to have a more intimate relationship with her. But a captain in the Magisterial fleet didn't
court his second in command; it made for poor ship
morale. And now it was certainly too late. He doubted
that Jeremiel, Carey's husband, was ever really out of
her thoughts.

Cole lowered his gaze to stare at the golden leaves that
blew around his feet, piling against his boots. He'd been
thinking about his friendship with Carey a great deal of
late. Their friendship and their mutual past. When he
did, he saw himself standing tall on the bridge of a ship
that had died long ago, his purple uniform crisp, the
pulse of power throbbing in his veins. Carey sat at the
nav console in front of him, her cool, green-eyed gaze
pinning him. He wondered now why it had taken them
so long to throw off the shackles of that insane existence.
Since they'd left the Magisterial service and joined the
Gamant Underground, they'd been on the run constantly, hiding wherever they could, frightened every

minute that they'd be captured and returned to the horrors of the government's mind probes. But he'd never been happier.

Carey looked at him askance. "Are you worried about Horeb? Is that why you're so jumpy?"

"I'm probably just tired." He playfully kicked her boot and laughed when she kicked him back, hard.

"Tired and worried about Horeb."

"All right," he granted irritably. "I'm worried about Horeb. The planet has split down the middle, Mikael's and Sybil's rebel forces are apparently starving in their ditches, and our ragtag fleet is woefully inadequate to tackle the four battle cruisers that Governor Ornias demands constantly guard the planet. But we're going to attempt a rescue anyway! Anybody with sense would be worried."

"We've no choice, Cole. The Magistrates have stepped up their battle against Gamants. We have to get those people off Horeb and to Shyr or they'll be dead in a few months."

Cole squinted up at a white bird that soared through the darkening skies; its wings flashed mauve as it dove. The Underground had searched for ten years to find a planet where they believed the remnants of Gamant civilization would be secure. Since that day four years ago, they'd been diligently, secretly, stocking Shyr with food and animals, tools and weaponry, so that as the Underground rescued the remnants of Gamant civilization from their war-torn planets, they'd have a home to go to. The time had almost come to initiate a rescue on Horeb.

He gave Carey a surreptitious appraisal. She'd picked up a golden leaf and contemplatively twirled it in her fingers while she scanned the slopes. In the deepening rays of dusk, the mountains had taken on a mottled cloak of shadows.

"Incidentally," she quipped, "did you hear what the old Gamants here on Kiskanu told Rudy this morning?"

His gut twisted suddenly, as though a warning fist knotted inside him. "No."

"They tapped an illegal dattran stating that Governor Ornias has ordered all children under the age of seven rounded up because he believes some ancient prophecy about the coming of the Redeemer."

"Well, that's wonderful news. Was that supposed to ease my anxiety?"

"Kiskanans say the order is the final sign."

"Sign of what?"

"The coming of the true Mashiah."

He massaged his brow condescendingly. "When will these backward barbarians get it into their thick skulls that God is a bastard? Gamants will only see salvation when each and every one of them picks up a rifle. This religious hocus-pocus . . ."

He stopped when a bright blue light sprang from Carey's chest, penetrating the black fabric of her jumpsuit. He recoiled. "Goddamn, what's the matter with that thing? It's been going crazy all day!"

Gingerly, Carey tugged on the golden chain around her neck and pulled the *Mea Shearim* from her suit, letting it rest over her heart. The blue ball emitted such a brilliant cerulean light that Cole had to lift a hand to shield his eyes.

"It seems to have an affinity for conversations about Horeb. Have you noticed? It only flares when—"

"I've noticed," he said gruffly. Every time they'd discussed the planet or proposed operations concerning it in the past week, the *Mea* had gone wild. "Do you think that means something?"

She lifted a shoulder. "Maybe God wants to talk to me about strategy?"

"Well, for your sake, I hope not. Epagael's strategies usually result in death and devastation for Gamants."

"I'm not a Gamant."

"No, but you're married to one. Which, as I understand it, is worse. Isn't there some prohibition against Gamants marrying 'foreign' women? I seem to recall some nonsense about how the woman will be devoured by the flames of the Lord and the man will be stoned to death. I wouldn't talk to God if I were you. It's too risky."

"Why, Cole," she said, a brow lifted with interest. "I'm shocked. Have you been reading Gamant religious treatises?"

"Don't be snide. I have ears, don't I?"

"Ah, you've been eavesdropping again."

He opened his mouth to defend himself but lifted a

brow instead. "It's not as though it requires any talent in a battle cruiser, Carey. You just have to walk the halls."

"Do they often talk about Jeremiel and me on the *Orphica*?"

"Too damned much for my taste. Every time we lose a battle, some superstitious sonofabitch knows exactly where to lay the blame."

She grinned. "Foreign women, eh?"

"You think it's funny? I don't. I hope like hell that the Horeb campaign goes well. If not, they'll more than likely hang you up by your heels and perform some unpleasant torture ritual to exorcise demons from your soul."

Cole squinted at the *Mea*. Jeremiel had given it to Carey only two days before they'd left on this mission, and that had been a month ago. He'd called it a good luck charm. For a decade the device had been dead. It hadn't glowed at all. But the moment Cole and Carey had boarded their vessel and flown out of the landing bay into the star-strewn blackness of space, the thing had burst into brilliance. Now, as he looked at the device, he thought that perhaps it hadn't been dead at all—just waiting. He quelled the tingle that crawled over his skin.

"I wish you'd take that damned thing off, Carey."

She eyed him speculatively. "Scares you, does it?"

"Damn right."

She picked up the chain and let the *Mea* swing freely. White swirls eddied across the azure surface. Her smooth cheeks had taken on a rosy hue, as though the flaring of the necklace sent a flush of adrenaline through her system. "I've considered taking it off, but I can't seem to convince myself to do it. Ever since I put it around my neck, I've felt oddly . . . attached."

"That's called fear, my dear."

"No, it's more like a feeling of premonition."

"Yeah? I've been feeling the same thing all day. The question is, a premonition of what?" Again his eyes drifted to the dense forested slopes and he felt a desperation that verged on panic.

She shook her head. "I don't know. But I've been having very strange dreams, filled with war and pain." Her nostrils flared as though she smelled the coppery odor of bloody corpses penetrating these gorgeous autumn mountains.

"Then why the hell don't you take it off?" he demanded too sharply.

"I want to talk to God. Always have. So I can call him a bastard to his face."

"Well, that ought to convince Him to help Gamants." Cole squinted at the *Mea*. Whenever he looked at it, he had the queer feeling that he'd just stepped over the edge of a precipice. "Well, just for your information, it brothers me deeply that you wear a primordial black hole around your neck."

A gust of wind swept the landing field, peppering their faces with sand and swirling dead leaves fifty feet high before scattering them across a steep hillside.

"We're not sure that's what it is," she pointed out.

"We're pretty sure."

Immediately after the globe had started to flare, they'd taken it and subjected it to a series of tests. Weight: Four billion tons—though the *Mea* felt feather light. Outer containment vessel: Cooled beryllium ions organized into a series of spherical concentric shells. The ions slipped around the shells in a liquidlike phase but rarely diffused. Yes, indeed, he strongly suspected a singularity lurked at the heart of the *Mea*. But he hadn't figured out yet why it seemed to have no mass. Perhaps the hole existed in some alternate universe and they saw it through the gate?

Carey tilted her head and studied the device curiously. "Jeremiel's original analysis on the *Hoyer* twelve years ago supports your thesis. I remember him telling me about it. In fact," she smiled amiably, "he told me to be careful. Even though I'd worn the device before and nothing happened, he said it could flare to life at any time and I should be prepared."

"Prepared for what?"

"Having God call for a chat."

He rubbed his chin testily. "I see."

"If the *Mea* is a singularity, it lends credence to a lot of the ancient legends about it. The great Gamant philosopher, Sinlayzan, called *Meas* 'thunder stones.' He believed they were related to the gate of the world, the *loka-dvara*, through which a soul might pass to the beyond."

"Well, that's crystal clear, isn't it? The 'beyond'? There's no telling where that damned thing could take you if you let it. If it were mine, I'd blow it out a hatch."

"Would you?" she asked, amused. In the dwindling light, her auburn hair took on a brassy gleam which highlighted her pearlescent complexion. "The device that allowed Yacob, one of the fathers of the People, to talk to God? You know it's said that he went to sleep on a stone at the place where heaven and earth opened on to each other and Epagael came to him. Gamant zaddiks, holy people, say that at one time the sky sparkled with thousands of *Meas*—they called them Indra's net. But the Magistrates collected them all and—"

"Forget the legends. Doesn't it bother you that it only shines when you wear it? It's like the thing's calling to you in particular."

To make his point, he reached out and bravely clasped the blue globe in his hand. The glow died, leaving the *Mea* dull, gray and lusterless—as though the "gate" had been locked and bolted against him. As soon as he released it, the blue aura rekindled, pulsing like a beacon.

"For God's sake, Halloway. For centuries the Magistrates have been trying to access the parallel universes predicted by mathematics. Has it ever occurred to you that this quaint, archaic necklace might be the key?"

"It has occurred."

He spat a disgruntled subvocal curse. "Oh, I get it. You like the idea of getting sucked into a black hole. And to think that for twenty-five years I've thought you had good sense." He made an airy gesture of self-reproach.

She adopted a thoughtful pose. He grimaced. Her stance accentuated the swell of her breasts and the curve of her hips. He crossed his arms and drummed his fingers on his biceps. In all the years she'd been married, he'd never lost that deep feeling of attraction to her. Of course, that was mainly because he loved her—as more than a friend—though he rarely admitted it even to himself. For a period of three years after they'd joined the Underground, he'd tortured himself over it, vacillating over whether or not to tell her about his feelings. But he knew that such a declaration would have forced her to make a decision between him and Jeremiel and he'd be damned if he'd do that to her. Worse—he wasn't sure he could handle her decision.

Carey kicked him playfully. "But what if God has some critical information on Horeb that we need to know? Don't you think we ought to ask?"

"Why don't you ask me if I'd like to be captured by the Magistrates just to see if they've forgiven me?"

"You think it's the same risk?"

"Pretty close. Though the *Mea* might be worse. I . . ."

The words died in his mouth when he saw Rudy Kopal burst out of the office.

He grabbed Carey's arm hard. *"Something's wrong,"* he shouted as he ran wildly toward Kopal. From the corner of his vision, he saw Carey whirl, crouching.

"Cole! Get down!" she screamed.

Rifle fire shredded the peaceful beauty of Kiskanu, flares of violet crisscrossing the forests. Cole hit the ground rolling and came up with his pistol leveled. Through the scope, he spotted over a dozen Magisterial marines rushing through the trees. Their purple uniforms sent a flush of terror through him. He opened fire, slashing down through the onslaught. *Goddamn, how did they get on the planet without the scanner detecting their approach?* Unless . . . unless they'd been here all along. Trap? But how could the Magistrates have known the Underground would come to the Anai system?

An explosion rocked the field and black clouds of smoke billowed out of the gray office building to darken the sky. Underground soldiers dove for cover in ships or behind piles of crates. Cole slithered along on his stomach to take shelter behind the landing gear of the closest ship, Kopal's fighter. The half-filled hold gaped open, but the entryway was closed. *Hell of a choice.* He'd have to expose himself for a full five seconds to access the entry console on the hull.

The pad had come alive with the sounds of shouting and racing feet. On the far side of the field, where Rudy's team fought, an eerie luminescent web of lavender laced the sky. In front of the office, three Giclasians lay dead, their six-legged, balloon-headed blue figures

sprawled hideously. On his right, Cole saw Josh Samuals'
team fanning out. Flooding toward the line of ships, their
pistols whined through the warm autumn evening. The
coral rays of sunset glittered in Samuals' blond hair. A
crackle of violet blasted a supply wagon in front of Josh
and a burst of petrolon fragments impaled the air. Samuals hit the ground hard, covering his head with his arms,
but his vulnerable right leg took several hits of shrapnel.
Blood splashed the crates. Josh struggled to stand, but
fell again, shrieking in pain.

A glint of blue caught Cole's attention and he turned
just in time to see an enemy marine's foot slide behind
the adjacent ship. He quickly brought up his pistol and
triggered it. A shrill scream echoed and a rifle beam shot
in from Cole's left, lashing the landing gear in front of
his face.

He lunged for the opposite side of the gear and trained
his scope on the dense tawny underbrush in the forest.
Four, five, six. . . . He switched his pistol to wide beam
and panned the entire area. The garish flash reflected
from the drifting clouds like waves of lavender lightning.
In the brief lull, he lunged to his feet. Flipping open the
control panel on the side of the ship, he closed the hold
door and began inputting the main entry sequence. Shots
flared around him, one flashing from the hull of the
fighter. The gangplank descended with agonizing slowness. Just as Cole started to leap inside, he heard a series
of screams and shouts from behind him. He dodged
behind the plank. Four members of Rudy's team had
been caught in the center of the landing field. They took
the concentrated fire of a dozen rifles from higher up the
mountain slope. Bodies writhed hideously beneath the
wide-beam fire.

The hum of ships powering up washed over the pad.
One fighter lifted off in a blast of dust and dry leaves,
then shot away into the sunset-washed skies, piercing the
mauve clouds like a silver dagger.

Carey. *Where was Carey?*

Frantically, he searched the last place he'd seen her.
He spotted her, two ships down, closer to Kopal than to
him. She'd dragged a wounded sergeant—Stacy Lepin?—
over to the gangplank of a freighter and was struggling
to haul her inside. But before she could make it, the

ground beneath her feet quaked so violently it threw her backward. A lurid burst of purple light engulfed her, blinding Cole.

"Carey?" he shouted, thoughtlessly standing up. Hit? Had she been hit? A furrow lanced the ground beside him. He jumped sideways and wildly returned fire. Two Giclasians went down, their bodies decapitated.

Frantically, he spun. Carey lay on her back in front of the freighter. Blood soaked her chest. Spatters of it created a horrifying pattern across her beautiful pale face. *Oh, God . . .* Despite the insane shrieks and rifle blasts, she didn't move. Cole's heart pounded so painfully, he couldn't breathe.

Insanely, he ran out onto the field, legs pumping. He had to get to her, to drag her to safety. Lying in the open as she was, she'd be a prime target!

Rudy Kopal ran toward her, too, and Cole saw Kopal briefly reach down, trying to grab her *Mea*, but a shot slammed the ground beside him and Rudy lunged forward again, intersecting Cole's path. He grabbed Cole's arm and viciously hauled him back toward the fighter, *Trisagion.* "Don't be a fool! We've got to get out of here!"

Cole raged, "I can't leave her! Let go of me, damn it!"

"Listen to me! We can't afford to lose both of you!"

Lose. . . ? *"NO!"* He couldn't let himself believe. . . . He struggled to throw off Kopal's iron hand, but Rudy held him tight. "For God's sake, Kopal, she's your best friend's wife!"

"There's nothing we can do for her! Come on, we have to get out of here!"

"No, damn it, let me—"

"She's dead, Tahn! Dead, do you hear me? DEAD!"

Blood drained from Cole's head. He stared at Rudy as though he'd just heard his own eulogy uttered. No, it couldn't be. How could he live without. . . . In the background, over Kopal's shoulder, purple uniforms dotted the slopes like ants. There had to be hundreds.

"Hurry!" Kopal shouted. Gripping Cole's sleeve, he flung him into a shambling trot toward the fighter's gangplank. They ran inside and Cole numbly dropped into the pilot's chair. Rudy took the copilot's seat. Three levels of computer screens displayed different colored information over their heads. In shock, Cole carried out the pilot's routine automatically, rapidly hitting all the right patches to assure lift-off.

"Ready?" Rudy asked, his eyes blazing with fear.

"Ready. . . . No, wait!"

Through the portal, Cole saw the remnants of Samuals' team trying to get to them. Using the line of ships as cover, they ran an obstacle course of fire. One woman went down under the flares, her body cut in half, the torso thrown into the center of the field. But three made it. As they raced up the plank, two bursts of rifle fire struck the ship. Tahn activated the shields. They snapped on in a translucent wave even as he was sealing the ship.

"They're in! Go, go, *go!*" Rudy ordered.

Tahn punched the acceleration switches and the ship shot upward, skimming the tops of the trees before swooping into the star-strewn skies.

Rudy suddenly jerked forward, eyes searching the console. "Oh, Mother of God," he whispered hoarsely.

"What's wrong?"

"Didn't anybody recharge this ship?"

From behind, a gasping voice blurted, "We were . . . going to do that . . . once we got loaded."

"What the hell are you talking about, Kopal?" Cole demanded.

"It means, Tahn, good buddy, that we'd better come out of vault on the money and within Jeremiel's reach, or we'll be sitting ducks when they come through after us."

Adrenaline and a near-hysterical sense of futility flushed Cole's system. He slammed a fist into the control console. "Is anybody after us yet?"

Rudy gazed hard-eyed at the screens. "Not yet, but I wouldn't suggest dallying." His fingers danced over his computer console. "Coordinates for vault are in the system. Twenty seconds to initiation. Do you want me to . . ." He paused suddenly. "I lied. Four fighters and . . . what the hell is that? Starboard!"

Cole whirled to stare out the side portal. Softly, he said. "A goddamned battle cruiser. We were set up, Kopal. Give me readings. Can I—"

As if in response, a blast rocked the fighter, throwing

it sideways. Warning sirens blared through the command cabin. Someone started crying, a soft suffocating series of sounds.

Cole lunged for the weapons patches. "Rudy, give me energy readings. If I return fire, will we have enough—"

"*Negative*. We're just going to have to pray the shields hold."

Another blast slammed their fighter, shuddering through the ship. Tahn leaned forward to check his monitors. "We're up to speed. Initiate vault."

Rudy tapped in the sequence. A long tunnel of luminescent yellow formed, purple wavering around its edges. They hurtled down it, going faster and faster. The ship lurched when the stars disappeared.

"We're safe," Kopal whispered. "For now."

Cole leaned back in his chair, breathing hard, wondering idly who the captain of that cruiser had been. The man had pulled off a nearly perfect ambush. He . . .

Cole stared hollow-eyed at the ceiling. The ship had gone quiet. In the ablative silver paneling overhead, he saw his jaw quiver and clamped his teeth to steady it. A weight like the condemning hand of God crushed him. *Oh, Carey . . . Carey. . . .*

When the universe ended, the silence would be no more terrible than this.

CHAPTER 3

The white command cabin of the fighter spread in a twenty by fifteen foot oval around Cole. The stench of dirty uniforms and stale sweat stung his nose. He squinted out the side portal. In the past two weeks, a nightmare feeling of terror had swept him up, the panic so strong he could barely endure the cramped environment of the fighter. He coped with it by spending hours staring out the portal. He'd learned the technique of self-abandonment long ago in a light cage on Old Earth. The Pegasans had tortured him endlessly. He'd escaped the agony by searching deep inside until he found his soul, then he took it and put it within the sheltering walls of the cathedral of Notre Dame, a place so hard and impervious, their probes couldn't hurt him. Since the Kiskanu attack, he'd done the same thing with the vault. His mind existed in the midst of that terrible darkness, a place so cold and timeless that thoughts of Carey's death couldn't reach him.

Cole absently fingered his new growth of dark, heavy beard. None of them had had the luxury of a shower or shave, and the last time he'd looked in the mirror, a stranger's face had stared back, the blue-violet eyes piercingly empty.

"Tahn," Rudy said. "We've got five minutes before we exit vault. Are you ready."

Cole nodded without turning. Behind him, he could hear the soft voices of the crew. They rang with such a hushed fear and urgency that his mind seemed to act like an echo chamber, resonating with memories of other desperate times.

. . . And again he heard Carey's voice on that terrible day so long ago just before they'd scorched the Gamant

42

planet of Kayan: *"What the hell are we doing, Cole? What the hell are we . . . whatthehell . . ."*

Rudy's chair creaked and Cole opened his eyes to stare back out at the utterly black womb that held them. The path he and Carey had walked since that day had been sinuous and steep. She'd married Baruch. Cole had become the captain of an Underground vessel. He'd made the right decision when he'd betrayed his government—*because it had betrayed him first!* In the past twelve years he'd discovered the true extent of the Magistrates' war against Gamants and it made him so ill he could barely endure the thought that he'd willingly participated in those efforts for so many years.

Carey . . . Carey . . . only she had understood.

"Initiating exit," Rudy informed.

Cole swiveled around to his console. In the process, he caught the wide-eyed looks of Franzia, Uro, and Rangor who sat silently in their chairs at the rear of the fighter. His heart pounded. He felt their fear more intensely than his own. Three levels of computer screens flashed different colored information to him. He checked them fleetingly. Rudy threw him a worried glance. Kopal's brown curly hair stuck to his forehead in damp wisps, accentuating the pointedness of his nose and the deep olive tones of his skin. His gray eyes bored into Cole.

Rudy input the exit sequence. Under his breath, he asked, "Are you with me, Tahn? I can't pilot this ship by myself if we run into trouble. Do you want me to—"

"I'm with you."

Rudy nodded, but he continued to glance up periodically, evaluating.

Cole stared at the chronometer, watching it slow. The numbers flashed in green—the color of Carey's eyes. His memories displayed them for him, warm, calculating, that hint of a smile around the edges. He could feel the muscles knot in the pit of his stomach. *Goddamn it.* The crew had gone silent. He forced his mind back. "What's our location, Kopal? How close are we going to be to the *Zilpah*?"

"If Jeremiel's had the luxury of staying stationary, we

should exit very close. But if he's moved and those Magisterial fighters come out—"

"Count on it," Cole interrupted. He glanced out the forward portal. A tunnel of luminescent yellow had formed as they hurtled out of vault. Purple licked around the edges like waves of violet flame. Haggardly, he said, "I suggest we all prepare for combat."

A brief flurry of activity clattered around the command cabin, people scrambling to brace themselves in their seats. The *Trisagion* didn't even have enough energy left to make the EM restraints operable.

"Here we go, folks," Rudy informed.

The saffron tunnel vanished and the stars burst to life, streaking the skies like pearlescent blue-violet tubes. The Moran gas nebula gleamed, a fuzzy splash of white gauze against the black velvet background.

"We're in the right place," Rudy murmured tautly. "But where's the fleet?"

Cole forced a swallow down his tight throat. He reached up and hit the communications patch. "Fighter *Trisagion* to *Zilpah*, do you read?" He waited a short interval, then repeated, "*Trisagion* to *Zilpah*, mayday, mayday. Anybody out there? Our coordinates are one-forty, twenty-two, by three. . . . Baruch, for God's sake, if you can hear us, we're in deep trouble out here, Repeat, our coordinates are one-forty, twenty-two, by three. Over."

Behind them, a single blip flared. Cole's eyes narrowed. "Tell me that's not a battle cruiser, Kopal."

Rudy vented a tight breath. "The mass readings indicate it's one of our fighters. Must be Zimmern."

An audible sigh of relief reverberated around the cabin, punctuated by nervous laughter. Cole hit the communications patch again. "*Trisagion* to *Hullin*, do you read, Zimmern?"

A pause. "Zimmern here, Captain Tahn. Where's the fleet?"

"Baruch must have been forced to leave. Listen Lu, we're expecting unfriendly company. *Trisagion*'s low on energy. If you can get to us before any Magisterial vessels appear, I want you to cover our backs for as long as you can, but if things look bad—get out. Make a run for it.

Try to find the fleet and report on the attack in the Anai system. Tell Baruch . . . tell him Carey's dead."

In a bare murmur, Zimmern responded, "Aye, sir." Several seconds elapsed before he continued, "What will you do if we have to—"

"Manage the best we can. *Just go*."

"Affirmative, sir. Good luck. Zimmern out."

Tahn cut the dattran and swung around to Rudy. "What's our energy status?"

Kopal filled his cheeks with air and exhaled loudly. "Damn near zero."

"How long can we sustain thrust at current levels?"

"About ten minutes."

"Oh, well, that's lovely." Cole leaned back and massaged his forehead. "That's *just* lovely."

On the second overhead monitor, five more ships exited vault, then six, seven, eight. He saw Rudy glance at the readings. "Fighters. No cruisers."

"Oh, I feel better." An unpleasant chuckle of futility escaped Cole's lips. He bowed his head and shook it. He'd always imagined death's preamble would be terrifying, but he only felt a sweeping sensation of unnatural calm. *What idiot ever said life was the merciful gift of God? Some ridiculous prophet, no doubt. Clearly, death is the gift.* There'd be no more insane battles, no more wrenching feelings of hopelessness, no more necessity to watch precious friends die.

Rudy swiveled around in his chair and gave Cole a broad grin. Cole's eyes narrowed suspiciously. In that soft drawl that marked his upbringing on the planet of New Savannah, Kopal said, "Just because I'm in the mood, Tahn, I want you to know something."

"What?"

"I never really liked you."

Cole lifted both brows. "A frivolous point, I should think, at this particular moment."

"Spurious, not frivolous."

"Did you think I didn't know?"

"Didn't matter. I—"

"Well, what'd you bring it up for?"

Kopal drummed his fingers on his white console. "I thought I owed it to you to tell you."

"You Gamants have a very peculiar sense of honor."

Kopal grinned halfheartedly. "Maybe, but it was weighing on me. I could never understand what Jeremiel saw in you. You're arrogant, offensive on the best of days, and a blackguard at heart."

"It was the arrogance that Baruch *liked*," Cole assured him, pointing a finger. The constant past tense didn't seem to affect either one of them.

Rudy gave him a wry smile. "Wouldn't doubt it. Jeremiel's always had questionable tastes." He heaved an audible sigh. "On the other hand, I suspect you've saved forty or fifty thousand Gamant lives in the past ten years. You're a brilliant military tactician, Tahn. For that, I'd like to thank you."

Cole swiveled in his chair and met those gray eyes. A warm and authentic gratitude stirred in their depths. "I never liked you much either, Kopal . . . until now." He leaned forward and extended a hand.

Rudy took it in a strong grip and shook, all the while holding Cole's gaze.

They both went deathly still when the ship gave a final lurch and then sailed into a quiet drift pattern. The interior lights flickered, backup generators kicking on to maintain the life-support systems.

Rudy squeezed Cole's hand hard one last time and turned to inspect the monitor to his right. "Shields dead. Thirty minutes of air left."

"What an optimist you are."

They exchanged a resigned sideways glance and both straightened in their seats, leaning over their controls, valiantly pretending some defensive action still existed to be taken. In the background, Kelly Rangor prayed, a sweet and high sound, her voice filled with tears. Someone else joined in. The soft drone of sacred words swirled through the ship.

The Magisterial vessels formed up in an inverted flying wedge and swung around, surrounding Zimmern's fighter. Cole clenched a fist in his lap. *Come on, you goddamned Gamant God, give your Chosen People some help for a blasted change.*

As though to spite him, violet beams lanced out, three vessels concentrating fire. The *Hullin* lunged sideways, shields flaring, absorbing, redistributing energy. In a mad attempt to slip out of the wedge, Zimmern fired back wildly and applied reverse thrust, shedding V. The Magisterial fighters shot forward, pitching headlong toward the *Trisagion*. Four ships veered off, heading back for the *Hullin*. The remaining four continued forward, closing on the *Trisagion*. By now their sensors would have revealed the ship's vulnerability. The fighters descended like vultures on a dying rabbit.

"Damn it," Cole murmured. He folded his arms, straining at his own impotence.

"They'll be in firing range in ten seconds. *Five, four, three, two . . .*"

They all braced themselves, sucking in a final breath as though it would help. Ten more seconds ticked off like centuries of agony. The Magisterial fighters swooped down to within shouting distance. Cole peered pensively out the forward portal at the silver wedges which formed a semicircle around them. "What the hell are they doing?"

Rudy just shook his head.

Cole checked monitor number two. It showed the *Hullin* dead in space, shields gone—*but alive.*

"I don't understand," Rudy growled hoarsely. "Why aren't they firing?"

Cole started when the green communications light on his console flashed, demanding a response. A glacial chasm yawned in his chest to swallow all his sensibilities. *"They want us alive."*

Rudy's eyes widened. "And we don't even have the energy to initiate a destruct sequence? Oh, God."

Cole listened to the nauseating rush of blood in his ears. The possibility of capture stood as the single greatest horror of every Underground soldier, but the horror ran especially deep in Cole. The Magistrates would want to make an example out of him, lest other human captains get any treasonous notions. They'd probe him until only a bare husk remained of his mind. Almost as though he were contemplating a stranger's fate, he wondered if they'd ship him to the neurophysiology center before or after they court-martialed him. He grinned at the irrelevance of the question. Calmly, he reached down and slipped his pistol from its holster on his hip. He gripped the weapon comfortingly as he checked the charge level.

Kopal watched him through dark somber eyes. "Planning on leaving this show early?"

"I can't let them take me alive, Kopal."

"No. Don't suppose you can. Well, *Baruch atta Epagael*." A tinge of amusement rang in his voice as he praised God. "Judgment Day has finally arrived."

Cole frowned. "Was that supposed to be insulting?"

"Not even slightly. It's you and me, Cole, old buddy. I can't allow myself to be captured, either. I know too much about Underground operations. My brain could betray the entire movement." Rudy laced his fingers over his stomach. "How shall we do it?"

"I'll handle us both . . . if you want me to."

Rudy gruffly rubbed a hand over his mouth. "Well, make it good. I hear the Magistrates have recently developed some remarkably effective revitalization machines."

"Don't worry. At this range, there won't be much left for them to work on."

Rudy sighed and squinted at the flashing green light on the communications panel. "What do you think they want?"

"Our surrender. Among other things. They'll order us to prepare to be boarded and probably promise us something ridiculous like sanctuary in exchange for our cooperation."

"You think we ought to talk to them?"

"Not particularly. Do you? I doubt that they'll . . ."

A brilliant splash of light washed space. Cole whirled breathlessly in his chair. The Magisterial fighters around Zimmern's ship exploded in a hurricane spray. The sudden violent impact of a blast sent the *Trisagion* hurtling, the nose of the ship slanting down. The crew tumbled out of their seats, bashing into each other and piling against the back wall.

Cole struggled to get his feet under him, but the massive g force made him dizzy. "What the hell's—"

Rudy whispered, *"Jeremiel!"*

A flush of adrenaline seared Cole's veins, sudden hope nearly suffocating him. He shoved off the wall to get a view out the forward portal. Two more Magisterial ships vanished in a blaze of white. And beyond, in the blackness of space, a scatter of over a hundred vessels lit the sky. Three battle cruisers plunged headlong toward them, cannons firing on full, blasting every Magisterial vessel in sight. Around the edges, fighters dove and fought, swerving drunkenly.

Cole spun to look out the left side portal. Two Magisterial fighters had escaped. They plummeted downward, picking up speed to vault.

"Goddamn it, Jeremiel," he warned harshly, noting three Underground fighters disengage to pursue. "You can't let them get away. They'll report the exact location of the fleet and then we'll—"

A burst of light ignited the heavens. Cole threw up his arm to shield his eyes. The blast rocked the *Trisagion*, tossing it about like a wayward rag doll. When he lowered his arm, the Magisterial vessels had vanished. Only an expanding blaze of shimmering ivory limned the blackness.

The communications panel flared green again. Cole pulled himself up and made his way forward by grabbing onto things to counter the tilted position of the ship. He hit the com patch.

"*Trisagion* here."

"Cole?" Jeremiel's deep, confident voice penetrated the cabin. "Sorry it took us so long to get here. We were called in to deliver med supplies for that virus that's ravaging Jotaya. Where's the rest of your flotilla?"

All the anxious agony about Carey that had vanished in the battle came back, smothering Cole like a black sheet. He dropped into the pilot's chair and braced his elbows on the console. "We have injuries aboard, Baruch. Please have med techs standing by in the landing bay. Our wounds on the *Trisagion* are minor, though. I think Zimmern's crew got hit worse than ours."

"Understood. We'll have people waiting. Where's the rest of the—"

"Jeremiel," Cole said and bowed his head to stare numbly at the dials and patches strewn over the command console. He aimlessly rubbed his fingertips over the cool white petrolon, wishing suddenly that he weren't one of this man's best friends—knowing such things were easier to take from coolly impersonal strangers than sympathetic confidants. "We were attacked in the Anai system. Ambushed. They were waiting for us. I don't know how they knew we'd be there, but . . ." He forced a deep breath into his constricted lungs. "Carey's dead."

A long and terrible silence blanketed space. Cole closed his eyes, the nightmare feeling of terror filling him again. He propped both fists against his forehead and tightened them until his hands ached. "Copy, Baruch?"

"Copy."

Another pause, then Jeremiel said in a too quiet voice. "I'll meet you in the bay. Baruch out."

Cole's hand shook as he reached down to cut the connection.

"Blessed Epagael," Rudy muttered under his breath to keep the crew from hearing. "I hope Jeremiel can stand it. When Syene died, he fell apart."

Cole nodded. Syene Pleroma. He remembered her death with crystal clarity, as though each image had been etched in marble. He'd been fighting for the Magistrates at the time. The government had captured Syene Pleroma and a half-dozen officers had repeatedly raped her when she refused to give them any information about Baruch. Cole had been called in later. He remembered his shock when he'd walked into that blood-spattered apartment. The living room had looked as though a bomb had blasted it. Furniture lay overturned; broken glass shimmered like tears on the green carpet. Syene must have fought like a tiger when she'd realized the trap. They'd set her up to believe she'd be bargaining with Major Johannes Lichtner, buying him off so he'd pull the Magisterial troops out of the Gamant section of town and leave it safe at the critical moment when the Underground cruisers combined fire to blast all the government's military installations on the planet of Silmar. In reality, she'd been bait to lure Jeremiel's forces into a huge net where they couldn't maneuver.

Cole had fought with Lichtner. In the whirl of fists and feet, Pleroma had lunged for the window, trying to escape, and Lichtner had fatally shot her.

Cole hadn't found out until later that Syene had willed herself to live until Jeremiel found her. She'd died in Baruch's arms.

Yes, Jeremiel had fallen apart. And he'd only known Syene for three years—he'd been married to Carey for twelve.

Cole swiveled around in his chair and met Kopal's gaze

squarely. Rudy looked as though he'd swallowed something sour. "Let's get prepared to be towed, people. Pick a chair and get braced. We should be under the *Zilpah*'s power any moment."

CHAPTER 4

Jeremiel wiped sweaty palms on his black uniform as he strode down the long white halls of the *Zilpah*. His boots thudded dully against the gray carpet. Arranged in herringbone patterns, the corridors intersected each other at about thirty foot intervals. Here and there, holos of planets dotted the walls, providing brief splashes of color. His breathing came fast and shallow. Tall and broadshouldered, he had deeply set blue eyes and wavy blond hair. His reddish-blond beard and mustache formed a neatly trimmed mantle below his patrician nose.

He rounded the corner and pounded a fist into the transport tube patch. While he waited, he absently returned the salutes of crew members who passed. Though the *Trisagion* and *Hullin* had just been hauled aboard, the troubled looks the crew gave him told him they'd already heard. With a critical battle for Horeb in the offing, they'd be worrying, wondering what he'd do. He couldn't let himself think about it yet—not until he knew all the details of Carey's . . . *Say it. Go on. You're going to have to discuss it in a few minutes. Dead. She's dead.* . . .

In the silent recesses of his soul, a muted voice screamed, *No, no, she can't be.*

The tube arrived and he stepped inside. "Level nineteen."

Deck numbers flashed in blue over his head as the tube descended. In this momentary isolation, the tightness in his chest seemed like a block of dry ice—heavy, stinging. He tipped his chin heavenward, staring at the bright lustreglobe panels in the ceiling, telling himself not to feel anything.

The tube stopped and the door snicked back. He strode down the corridor, turning left at the intersection and coming to stop before the landing bay door. "Come on," he whispered roughly to himself. Cole and Rudy would be tired and anxious to tell him everything so they could hurry to their cabins and get some rest. He fought to quell the panic that fired his veins. Already his mind had begun spinning images of what it must have been like. A lethal shot would have taken her either in the chest or—or the head. *No! Don't imagine it! For God's sake, stop! Just stop it.* He struck the entry patch.

Before him was a broad, white-tiled room, measuring two hundred square feet. The seventy-foot ceiling gave the bay an even larger feel. The fighters sat like black-scarred silver daggers on the floor. Med techs raced to and fro, rushing antigrav gurneys from the ships and into the emergency bay tubes to take the injured to the hospital on level six. Rudy and Cole stood outside their fighter, battlesuits grimy and stained, talking to the dozen transportation technicians who questioned them.

When Cole turned and his gaze touched Jeremiel's, he said something to Rudy and excused himself from the group. He walked forward slowly, his steps sluggish. His brown hair draped around his face in dirty strands. His gaze struck Jeremiel like an iron bar in the stomach. Cole's normally sharp blue-violet eyes had gone dull and lifeless.

He walked up beside Jeremiel and said, "I told Rudy we'd meet him in conference room 1900."

"All right."

Jeremiel turned and led the way out of the bay into the hall. They walked side by side in silence, neither daring to speak yet. Jeremiel could see how tired Cole was—how carefully and wearily he placed his feet. When they got to the room, Jeremiel hit the patch and waited for Cole to enter.

A table and six chairs took up most of the space. Along the walls, holograms of galactic nebulas hung, their white and gold gaseous images unsettlingly hazy. Cole sat on the edge of the table and propped a boot in the seat of a chair. His pale face looked wooden, his new beard dark against the sallow background of skin. He pressed his lips together tightly, as though struggling against a deadly disease which was eating him from the inside out.

Jeremiel pulled out a chair and sat down, leaning his elbows on the table. "Tell me how you are, Cole. After Kiskanu and the battle, if you're too tired—"

"No, let's get this over with, Jeremiel. Once it's done—it's done. They came out of nowhere. At least a hundred Giclasians. We were loading supplies when they hit us. Carey . . ." Cole's voice floundered. He took a deep breath and Jeremiel steeled himself. "Carey took a—a hit . . . in the chest, I think. Rudy got a better look than I did."

Jeremiel nodded once. Voices called out from his memories. Syene's little girl laugh blended hauntingly with Carey's deeper tones. Both tightened around his throat like deadly ropes. His wounded mind played horrifying tricks. Carey's face appeared and swirled around, superimposing itself over Syene's on that snowy day long ago on Silmar. Brown hair faded into auburn. . . .

The conference room door snicked back. Rudy walked in and briefly met their gazes before striding over to stand between where Cole sat on the table and Jeremiel's chair.

"You're sure she was dead?" Jeremiel asked in a surprisingly steady voice.

Rudy sank back to rest a shoulder against the wall. "Yes. No question about it."

Jeremiel felt all the blood drain from his face.

Cole lunged off the table and lumbered to the rear of the room, his face turned away, staring at the red and green swirls of the holo of the Loggerhead Nebula.

"How many could have survived and been captured?" Baruch inquired.

Kopal lifted his hands uncertainly. "I don't know. I guess maybe ten. I think everyone else—"

"Any of those people could reveal the exact location of the fleet if they're probed. We're going to have to move fast. How many officers may have survived?"

Cole turned around and pinned Jeremiel with a haunted look. "Every officer is accounted for except one. The last time I saw Josh Samuals, he had a shrapnel wound in his leg. If he managed to take cover—"

"He could be alive." Jeremiel steepled his fingers over his mouth for a moment. "Samuals knew at least the fundamental details of the Horeb mission. If he was captured, they would have probably taken him to Palaia. He would have been considered too valuable to leave his interrogation up to any regional neuro center."

Rudy shifted his weight to his left foot. "You think we should try to send somebody in? It would be a suicide mission, but I think we could find a volunteer. Neither Samuals nor the volunteer would make it out, but maybe we could get to Samuals before they put him under the probes."

"Don't be a fool, Kopal," Tahn accused. "Leave aside the fact that Palaia is invulnerable and the suicide mission volunteer would probably be captured and make things worse for us—if we make any moves now, if we *breathe* wrong, the Magistrates will tighten their security net around Horeb and we'll never get those people off that hellhole! The solution is to step up the Horeb mission. Since we have to get the fleet out of here anyway, *let's hit Horeb now, before it's too late!*"

"Are you crazy?" Rudy shouted. "We're not ready!"

Jeremiel listened to their stormy interchange for several more minutes, but he barely heard the words. In the back of his mind he could hear Carey calling his name, over and over—*as though she were alive.* Simultaneously, the logical part of his brain whispered, "She's dead. Accept it. She's not coming home this time."

He gazed up soberly at Cole, who'd grown red-faced and seemed on the verge of violence. Rudy looked just as bad, fit to burst at the seams. They were tired, both of them.

Jeremiel shoved himself out of his chair. "Go and get some rest. Consider Cole's suggestion of stepping up the Horeb mission. We might have to. I'll schedule a strategy meeting for 09:00 tomorrow morning."

"All right," Rudy responded tiredly. He started toward the door then stopped beside Jeremiel. Rudy clamped a strong hand on his shoulder. Kopal smelled so pungently of old blood that it made Jeremiel feel hollow. Traces of the stain spilled over the white threads on Rudy's cuffs. Red blood, not blue. Human. *Which friend? Friends?*

"Rudy, if you have time, please put together a list of casualties for me. I'll need to inform the families."

"I'll make time." He patted Jeremiel's shoulder and briskly left. The door closed behind him.

Tahn stood at the far end of the room, a fist pressed to his lips as he stared intently at the floor.

"Cole, after you've had some dinner and sleep, I'd like to talk to you more . . . about Carey."

Tahn sucked in a halting breath and held it. He nodded. "Let me know when you're available."

"Tomorrow night. I'll be—ready—by then."

"Understood," Cole responded softly.

Jeremiel put his hand against the exit patch and the door slipped open. Voices echoed down the corridor, discussing the damage sustained by the *Trisagion*. He exited quietly.

* * *

Something moved inside her like a tangle of serpents twisting around each other in some perverted mating spectacle.

She choked, fighting to swallow the welling of blood that surged up her throat. *Swallow. Swallow, damn you!* But the tide flooded up too quickly. She felt herself drowning, unable to get any oxygen, as though a wall of warm water had engulfed her and deluged her lungs. *Move! Roll over, you cowardly bitch, or you're going to die! Move!*

But her muscles wouldn't respond. She couldn't feel her body from the neck down. *Spinal damage. . . .*

Panic seized her mind and poured a hot torrent of adrenaline into her system; it seared her veins like molten metal.

And then she heard voices.

Not Gamant. Enemy.

CHAPTER 5

Cole Tahn wandered around the guest quarters he'd been assigned. He'd just showered and dressed in a tan jumpsuit. Brown hair bordered his cheeks in wet wisps. The wall chronometer over his bedside table read 0:300 hours. Trying to sleep had been folly. He'd tossed and turned and when finally he'd drifted into a half-conscious state, he'd relived every moment of the Kiskanu battle. When he'd seen Carey go down for the hundredth time, the web of blood crisscrossing her beautiful face, he'd jerked awake, panting into the chill darkness.

Worse, he'd started thinking about the recent advances in Magisterial medical technology. They'd only heard rumors, but. . . .

Every light in his cabin gleamed now. The bright white glow drove out some of the anguish that suffocated him. A small room, it spread ten by fifteen feet. The bed sat in the back, next to the desk which supported a com unit. His gaze riveted on the cursor, which flashed rhythmically green as quickly as his damnable heartbeat. A table and two chairs nestled against the right wall near the entry. Stark and foreign, the only thing in the environment that he owned was a bottle of hundred year old rye whiskey he'd found in their resource scavenging last month. It glimmered like honey on his bedside table.

He ran a hand through his damp hair. He'd gone over and over the details of the battle until he felt physically ill. "Rumors. Just goddamned rumors. You can't be sure." *No, but if the Magistrates have developed a technique which allows them to revitalize tissue if they recover the corpse within half an hour after death. . . .*

His gut corkscrewed.

Picking up his cup of taza from the table, he sipped it while he thought. If they'd gotten to her immediately, they'd have taken her to Palaia—but what part? Neuro-physiology division, probably. But maybe the military prison on the other side of the capital city of Naas. That way she'd be within easy reach of Slothen's ruthless grasp. He frowned at his taza. The brew had gone stone cold. It left a glacially bitter flavor on his tongue. He set the cup back down and started across the room, zeroing in on the bottle of rye.

"That's exactly what you need. A stiff belt to muddle your sense of responsibility." *Yes, indeed, if you're going to resign from the fleet and beg for a fighter, there's no sense in burdening your conscience with questions of duty*.

When his fingers gripped the cool bottle, his gaze drifted to the com unit over his bed. Baruch had said to wait until tomorrow night, but the knots in Cole's stomach wouldn't let him. Reaching up, he turned the volume down low, input cabin number 261 and softly called, "Jeremiel. Are you awake?"

In less than a second, a tired voice responded. "Of course, Cole."

"Are you interested in company?"

A long pause as if Jeremiel couldn't decide, then, "Come. I'll be waiting for you."

"On my way." He cut the communication, clutched his bottle to his chest, and quickly exited into the hallway.

Turned low to simulate nighttime, the corridor gleamed with a muddy white light. He passed no one on his way to the transport tube. Once inside the narrow compartment, he ordered, "Level two," and watched the deck numbers flash in blue above the door as he ascended.

When the tube stopped, he stepped out and strode down the hall, turning left at the first intersection of corridors and stopping at the second door on the right. He lifted a hand and palmed the com patch. "Jeremiel. It's me."

The door opened. Cole cautiously stepped inside. Only one light gleamed, a lustreglobe over the table. It cast a soft snowy glow over the room, glinting off the ancient books in the bookshelf over the table. Large for a battle cruiser, the room occupied a twenty foot square. A table and four chairs took up the left wall, next to the door that led to the latrine. In the back, a double bed sat, gray blankets rumpled. Another blanket, blue and white striped, lay on the seat of one of the desk chairs. Cole glanced at Baruch. The man had a tough, inquisitive expression on his face, but Cole knew him too well. Jeremiel had been having a hard night. Deep lines etched the flesh around his blue eyes. Had Baruch slept in the chair rather than chancing the dreams that sleeping in his and Carey's bed would have spawned?

Two desks with glowing com units sat side by side along the right wall. Jeremiel stood over the second unit, his hand propped on the top of the monitor. A litter of crystal sheets, com disks, and a golden locket were scattered across the desktop. The sight of the necklace made the ache in Cole's chest intensify. He'd given it to Carey for her thirty-fifth birthday—eons ago, just after they'd joined the Gamant Underground.

"Sorry, Cole," Jeremiel offered, seeing what had caught his attention. "I didn't think . . . that's where she left it." He reached for the locket, as if to get it out of sight.

"No, it's all right. Please, leave it."

Jeremiel let his hand hover over the necklace for a moment, obviously trying to judge from the look on Cole's face whether that was the best maneuver or not. He pulled his fingers back. His blond hair and reddish-blond beard gleamed in the soft light. He wore casual clothes, an ivory-colored shirt and black pants.

Cole walked quietly to the table and set the bottle down, then disappeared into the latrine to grab two petrolon glasses. He filled each full and handed one to Jeremiel, ordering, "Here, drink this."

Jeremiel took the glass and one of his bushy blond brows arched. He held the glass up to the lustreglobe, watching the light dance in the liquor with amber brilliance. "That's a healthy dose."

"I hate to get drunk alone."

"I know that from past experience, but I'm not sure I want to keep you company tonight."

"Yes, you do. You just don't know it yet."

Jeremiel cocked his head quizzically. "Generally, I trust your judgment." He took a sip of the rye. "Did you come to talk about Carey or Horeb?"

Cole wondered how he could ask so calmly, as though they'd be discussing the relative merits of chocolate ver-

sus vanilla iced desert. For two weeks Cole had been
absorbed with his grief, hearing Carey's laughter, seeing
the sparkle in her emerald eyes, feeling the warmth of
her touch that last day on Kiskanu. In the past eight
hours, Jeremiel had undoubtedly been remembering,
too, and with an anguish even more wrenching than
Cole's own. Yet Baruch could stand here like a marble
statue, staring emotionlessly at Cole.

"I came to talk about Carey."

For several seconds, Jeremiel just stood. "Go on. I'm
listening."

Cole surveyed the holos of mountain scenery that
Carey had loved so much; they covered every wall. The
largest, a four by five foot picture of the Tetons on Old
Earth lit the wall near the entry. The craggy pinnacles
glowed lavender in the fading rays of sunset. Snow
frosted the steep slopes, flowing into every crevice like
pearlescent milky icing. He ambled over and stopped
beneath the magnificent peaks. "I'm worried."

Clothing rustled. "About the new medical techniques,
you mean?"

Cole turned and appraised Jeremiel severely. "I should
have guessed that your thoughts would have been running along the same lines as mine. Yes, that's what concerns me."

"It doesn't matter."

Cole's mouth gaped in shock. "What the hell—"

"Even if she is alive, there's nothing we can do about
it right now. Horeb must be our first priority and the
war effort can't spare either you or me . . . and there's
no one else I could ask to risk his or her life to go to
Palaia and find out."

Cole moved forward to stand face-to-face with Baruch.
They stared intently at each other. "Let me go. Give me
a fighter and I'll take the risk. I—"

"I can't. You're too important to the Horeb mission."

"*Listen to me!* If she's alive, she could endanger the
entire Underground movement! The woman knows every
detail of our operations." Cole took a tense breath.
"Including the location of Shyr. No Gamant will be safe
anywhere if she breaks."

"*If* she's alive. We've no way of knowing. We have to
pretend she's dead and continue—"

"Goddamn it!" Cole raged. He slammed his half-empty glass down on the table. The crash sounded as loud as a mortar blast in the sudden silence. "What's the matter with you, Jeremiel? This is your wife we're talking about! Not some stranger!"

Jeremiel shook his head and turned his back on Cole.

"She's not dead, Jeremiel. I don't *feel* her dead. Do you? Is there a hole in your soul? If she were dead, I'd know it."

Baruch closed his eyes. "I can't base military judgments on our emotional inadequacies."

"I'm just one man, Jeremiel. Let me go. From a prudent strategic point of view, somebody should cover the possibility that she's alive. *Let it be me.*"

Jeremiel's mouth tightened. He finished his whiskey and set the glass on the table. Very quietly, he walked back to Carey's com unit and picked up the golden locket. Slowly he turned it over and over in his hand. "Let's discuss other things for a few minutes. I had dinner with Rudy three hours ago. We discussed Horeb."

Cole exhaled silently, not wanting to let it drop—doing it anyway. "Is he still being an idiot?"

"No, he's changed his mind. He says he'll be ready to vault day after tomorrow."

Cole leaned back in shock. Kopal had been acting as stubborn as a witless mule. "What did you do? Threaten him? I thought he was dead set against stepping up the Horeb mission?"

"I convinced him it wouldn't take more than a week."

"*One* week?" Cole squinted and eased down into a chair by the table. "All right. Why don't you feed me the same line you fed Rudy? Just so I'll know how to answer in case somebody slaps me in the head and demands I explain this insanity."

Jeremiel paced methodically in front of the table. His ivory shirt now showed signs of sweat around the collar and beneath the arms. "We'll go in fast, hit them hard, and load up the refugees. We should be able to offload them on Shyr by the first day of Sivan."

"Uh-huh." Cole rubbed his bearded jaw. The only way they could complete the Horeb mission in a week was if they met scant resistance from the planet's guardian cruisers—which would require a miracle. "You think those four Magisterial battle cruisers are going to scream and run when they see us coming with all of our freighters and starsails, is that it?"

"Pretty close."

Cole made an airy gesture of self-reproach. "I'd be intrigued to find out why. Could you fill me in on the magical tactics we're going to employ?"

Jeremiel pulled out a chair and sat down. His hard eyes glittered like sapphires. "I told Rudy you'd agreed to go in early—on a sabotage mission."

Cole reached for his whiskey and took a stiff drink. He blinked dubiously. "And Rudy bought it?"

"Completely. He knows your talents."

Cole bowed his head and laughed. "I see. And just what am I supposed to sabotage?"

"We'll discuss the details later. Let's talk about what happens after we successfully free Horeb."

Cole examined Jeremiel curiously. The light shone in a fiery sheen over the perspiration drenching Baruch's face. Was he afraid Cole might say, "No, thank you. I like to pick my suicide missions myself?"

"What happens?" he asked bravely.

Jeremiel took Carey's locket and gently laid it on the table. It sparkled like spun gold. The back of the cameo was face up, the engraving glimmering: *To my best friend. For never openly declaring mutiny. Love, Cole.* An ache of longing for her welled deep inside Cole. He hastily finished his whiskey.

"The trip to Shyr lasts a month minimum," Jeremiel explained coolly. "Once we load the Horebian refugees and make vault, Rudy and Merle can handle the final elements of off-loading people, setting up villages, bringing in the remaining supplies: seeds, farm equipment, more stock—"

"I get your point." Cole fiddled anxiously with his empty glass, shoving it back and forth across the black tabletop. So Jeremiel had been clandestinely planning on rescuing Carey all along—good. They had a better chance if the two of them went together. But if the fleet lost both of them. . . . "Would it do any good for me to remind you that you're too valuable to risk and you should obviously let me go alone?"

"No." Baruch leaned back in his chair.

"Let's talk seriously. I know Palaia Station better than you do. I've been there several times. You've never been there."

"Irrelevant. It's a two person job. Neither of us can do it alone."

Cole draped an arm over the back of his chair and briskly massaged the muscles at the back of his neck which had already tied themselves in knots of anticipation. "All right, I'm with you. Let's discuss this brilliant sabotage mission I'm supposed to pull off before we go after Carey. Any more word on how Mikael and Sybil are doing on Horeb? The old Gamants on Kiskanu said they'd heard that Ornias had ordered all the children under seven rounded up because he feared some rumor about the coming of the Mashiah. They said it was the final sign. Do you know what that means?"

Baruch reflectively smoothed his fingers over his reddish beard. "Yes. It's a very old prophecy. . . ."

Two hours later, Jeremiel watched his door slip closed behind Cole's broad back. He slowly walked to the table to refill his glass. He picked up the bottle of rye, then set it down again and went to the drink dispenser on the wall. He keyed in for a strong cup of taza. As he reached for the cup, his hand shook. He gripped it in both hands and watched the steam rise in a fragrant veil to curl around his face.

Even if he and Cole both survived the Horeb battle, neither of them had any idea how to break through Palaia's defense net. The space station was shielded by an infinite series of electromagnetic shells. For over twenty-five years, Jeremiel had been trying to crack the puzzle of Palaia. Doing it now would take a miracle.

But it didn't matter.

He had to find out if Carey was alive.

He sipped his taza and fought the ache that constricted his chest like the icy hand of God.

CHAPTER 6

The Governor's Palace On Horeb

Governor Ornias and his new Minister of Defense, Fenris Midgard, briskly walked the long atrium that connected the palace with the Detainment Center. Windows lined both sides of the hallway. Beyond them, misty rain fell in silver veils over the ridges that surrounded the palace like a fortress, changing them from ruby red to a deep dark purple. He despised this filthy wasteland. If the Magistrates weren't paying him five billion notes a year to govern it, he'd be somewhere far away. *Somewhere decent.*

They turned a corner and Ornias caught his reflection in the glass. He looked himself up and down and smiled admiringly. A tall man with sandy hair and lime green eyes, his elaborately braided beard accentuated the perfect oval of his face. His gold silk robe glimmered like flame in the murky light. Let those other Magisterial fools don hideous uniforms, he preferred the sensuous luxury of satins, silks, and velvets.

"Governor," Fenris said as he restlessly balled his fists and tucked them into the pockets of his purple uniform. A short, thin man, he had graying brown hair and a nose as long and thin as a spear point. "I know Magistrate Slothen's demand that we find Calas was urgent, but I assure you these rebels we captured in the last battle are a stubborn lot. I've used every technique I know, including the probes, and not one of them has revealed any critical information about Mikael Calas' location. The only thing I got was that they're planning a food gathering mission in the high latitudes in the next few days. Should I—"

"I'll take care of that, Midgard. I have a special unit to

handle such missions." Yes, indeed. He'd trained them himself, using the probes to erase any and all elements of compassion and guilt from their young minds. The soldiers in the Brandish Unit averaged between sixteen and eighteen years of age and felt guilt only when they failed him. He smiled gloatingly to himself, proud of that piece of ingenuity.

"Yes, sir. I apologize. I don't understand why I've been unable to break even one of these—"

"Of course you don't," Ornias informed him irritably. Midgard had only been on Horeb for two weeks. He knew nothing about the reality of this squalid existence. "You don't know Mikael Calas. He trains his troops well. Your problem, Fenris, is that your methods of information gathering are too sophisticated."

Fenris hurried to keep up with Ornias' longer stride. "I don't understand, sir. What else—"

"Just wait, Midgard. You'll see. I've had the prisoners moved to an isolated area of the Detainment Center."

Fenris looked at him askance, but said nothing.

Ornias sniffed disgustedly. Midgard annoyed him. The man had no ethical elasticity. How could anyone so narrow-minded have survived this long in the realm of Magisterial diplomacy? He grunted to himself and turned the final corner, stepping down the dark stairs that led to his private interrogation chamber. Dank odors of mildew and rat droppings breathed from the stairwell. Midgard's boots clacked hesitantly behind him.

Ornias stopped before the door at the bottom and struck the communications box, calling, "Sergeant Horner? This is Governor Ornias. Please release the latch."

The door creaked open. Ornias stepped aside and extended a hand for Midgard to enter first. The minister nodded and stepped into the cold, foul-smelling room. The soft gasp that floated out made Ornias chuckle. He stepped inside and shut the door.

Within the ten by fifteen foot room, six rebels dangled a foot off the stone floor, their wrists and ankles bound in iron shackles. Rancid odors of urine and vomit clung cloyingly in the air. Ornias smiled at the four gray-suited planetary marines who guarded the room. Most refused to meet Ornias' eyes. Good. The more they feared him, the better he liked it. From the corner of his vision, he saw Horner grinning maliciously. The bestial little man had porcine yellow eyes and a head almost as square as a brick; he shifted eagerly from foot to foot. Black hair hung in dirty strands over his acne-scarred forehead. The filthy little marine adored torture, worshiping Ornias for his expertise in the matter.

Ornias quickly passed by Midgard and went to the cabinet on the wall. He pulled out a crystal decanter of Cassiopan sherry and poured himself a glass.

"Would you like some sherry, Fenris?" he asked.

"No" A swallow went down Midgard's throat. He hadn't taken his eyes from the prisoners. Dark clots of blood matted their filthy clothing to their bodies. Two were women, four were men. One of the men had a jagged rent in the black fabric over his chest. Beneath, a hideous wound oozed with pustulation.

"*Governor*," Midgard whispered tautly. "That man needs medical attention."

"Yes, I'm sure he does." Ornias took a refreshing sip of his sherry, watching Fenris. A dark gleam of horror had entered the minister's eyes.

Midgard's nostrils quivered. He pulled his thin body straighter, glaring. Ornias swished the sherry around his mouth. The sweet honeylike flavor caressed his tongue like a silk scarf over skin.

Midgard exploded, "Governor, I don't believe the Magistrates would approve of such barbaric—"

"If I waited for them to approve of everything I did, Minister, we'd all be dead and Horeb in the hands of Mikael and Sybil Calas."

Ornias crossed the room to the array of ancient and modern torture devices that covered the wall opposite the prisoners. He preferred the ancient methods of information gathering: thumbscrews, racks, flayers. Terror was the only truly effective means of discouraging dissent. Couldn't Midgard see that?

Shackles jangled behind Ornias. Someone moaned. He sipped his sherry and strolled back to stand before the female leader of the group. Thin and willowy, with long brown hair, her left breast spilled from her torn black uniform. Ornias gazed appreciatively at the dark nipple.

The muscles of her shackled arms tensed, setting the iron jangling again. She fixed him with hate-filled eyes.

"Sira Ben," Ornias cooed pleasantly. "I've always wondered what you were like. Captain Jonas told me that before they captured you, you killed thirty of my marines." He cocked his head, and smiled his respect. "It saddens me to see a woman of your beauty and obvious talents tortured like this."

Her sepia eyes gleamed like a hungry wolf's. She spat at him. Ornias artfully dodged, but rage flared in him.

"Dear Sira," he warned. "You mustn't antagonize me. I'm annoyed enough with your silence as it is. Would you like me to kill each of your compatriots before your eyes? Would that teach you manners?"

Her face tensed.

"Really, Sira, if you just answer one of my questions, I'll release you. *Where is Mikael Calas?*"

She snorted derisively and then had the gall to laugh out loud. Chuckles spread down the line of prisoners, rising to a roar which reverberated from the cold stone walls.

Ornias smiled, too, as he waited for the tirade to end. A crimson pool of blood had formed at Sira's feet, spreading more every time she moved. He noticed with interest that a persistent trickle dripped from her right boot. Surely her wounds would have clotted by now . . . unless Horner had been tormenting them. He glanced surreptitiously at the ugly little man.

Striding past her, Ornias looked up mildly at Ibn Ezra—reportedly Sira Ben's lover. "Ibn," he said, extending a manicured hand to Sira. "She refuses my offer. What about you? Where is Calas? Hmm? We thought he was with your battalion, but obviously we were mistaken. *Where is he?* Answer but one of my questions truthfully and I'll release you and all of your friends."

Ezra, a heavily muscled, dark-haired giant of a man, stared down with icy contempt in his black eyes. The shreds of his camo uniform revealed deep gashes crusted with old blood. "Truth, Governor?" he whispered. "What do you know of truth?"

"Are you trying to be profound, Ibn? I'm afraid I haven't much patience for such worthless diversions." Ornias took a long drink of his sherry. Horner snickered blasphemously in the background. "I hear Sira is your lover, Ibn? Is that so?"

Ezra glanced in panic at the woman beside him. "No."

Ornias grinned sardonically and waved a hand at one of his guards. Horner shoved through to trot up beside him. The short, evil looking little marine licked his lips eagerly.

"Aye, Governor, what do you want me to do?"

Ornias cocked his head and smiled at Ezra. "Kill the woman," he ordered.

"NO!" Ezra screamed as Horner opened fire. Purple light splashed the room with a lurid burst of color. Ezra gasped as Sira's blood splattered him in hot red gouts. The giant squeezed his eyes closed and his massive chest heaved with sobs.

"Governor!" Midgard exploded. His face had gone ghost white, jaw quivering in disbelief. Sweat matted the strands of his hair to his head like thick gray-brown strings. "I cannot believe—"

"No, I'm sure you can't. You're a man of limited imagination, Fenris."

"I won't stand by and witness—"

"Then, please go. You're becoming a nuisance."

Midgard fairly ran for the door, slamming it behind him. Ornias sighed and lazily strolled down the line. The sibilant hiss of his low laughter filled the room like the prophetic rustle of a burial shroud waving in the wind. Most of the prisoners clamped their sweaty jaws and turned away.

Ornias gazed up into the face of the youngest prisoner. A gorgeous girl of perhaps fifteen or sixteen, she had huge black eyes and thick wavy brown hair. Ornias tilted his head admiringly as he examined her. With a good washing and an expensive gown, he might be able to use this one.

"What's your name?" he asked softly.

She kept quiet.

"Dear girl, do you realize I hold your life in my hands? I'd rather not kill you. *Has Calas retreated back to the safety of the polar chambers or is he still in the wilderness?"*

She closed her eyes and leaned her head back against

the gray stone wall. A transparent sheen of perspiration glimmered from her slender olive throat.

"You believe in the coming of the Mashiah, don't you, dear? Yes, I'm certain you must. I do," Ornias lied. Only an idiot could believe such simplistic hogwash. "You don't have to tell me about Calas if you don't want to. Instead, you can save your life by talking about this savior baby. We've heard so many rumors about him. You've heard those rumors, haven't you, dear? What's the child's name?"

The girl's mouth quivered with repressed tears. "I don't know. None of us do. We're waiting for the sign to tell us."

"Sign?" Ornias scoffed. He chuckled maliciously. "What's your name, girl?"

'Ruth.'

"Ruth? There, that wasn't so hard, was it?" He leered at her, then called over his shoulder, "Peron? Hark? Please release Ruth. Take her to my personal chambers."

Terror tensed her pretty face. Ornias reached up to stroke her cheek seductively. "Don't worry," he whispered silkily. "You'll be well cared for. I'll see you tonight."

She fell into Peron's arms when he unlocked the shackles. Her arms, which had been chained over her head for an entire day, thumped against her sides like dead meat. She whimpered as Peron carried her from the room.

"So?" Ornias said mildly to the remaining prisoners. "Which of you would like to live? Surely someone in your rabble suspects the identity of this savior baby. What names have been suggested?"

None of the rebels responded. Some stared at the ceiling. Other had their eyes closed.

"What names?"

A low chant began, something ancient, powerful, the words unknown to him: *Adoneinu Malkenu yarum hodo, Adoneinu Malkenu yarum hodo. . . .* Each rebel picked it up and their whispers rose to a roar which reverberated thunderously from the stone walls.

"Who is this savior child!" Ornias demanded at the top of his lungs, but his voice was drowned in the rebels' din. *"I must find that child!"*

Enraged, Ornias stomped to the exit. By the time he

reached the door, the chant had died and an oppressive silence draped the center. The rebels watched him through devilishly glittering eyes. He stopped briefly and shook a fist angrily.

Horner grinned like a fanged dog.

Ornias surveyed the shackled prisoners distastefully, then he flicked a hand in irritation. "Kill all these little Gamant bastards," he ordered as he stepped through the door and into the long white hallway outside.

CHAPTER 7

Sybil pushed a mass of brown curls over her shoulder and rested her head on Mikael's bare black-furred chest. He tenderly stroked her side, gazing down through heavily-lidded brown eyes. His black hair and beard framed high cheekbones, full lips and a rounded nose. He'd returned from his military mission exhausted and aching because he'd lost half his team—Sira included. She'd been one of their closest friends.

Sybil had listened to him talk for hours about the debacles of the mission and how Ornias seemed to have intensified his efforts to drive them out of the polar chambers—then he'd fallen silent, more disheartened than she'd ever seen him. It made Sybil's throat go tight. The governor had scouted out each of their hundreds of entrances and exits to the honeycomb and now had them heavily guarded; he'd managed to pen them inside the subterranean chambers for the first time in ten years—or so he thought. What Ornias did not know was the extent of their cached supplies, nor did he have the slightest grasp of the intricacy of the internal maze beneath the ground. There were other ways out. Old and obscure, but there, hidden in the tumbled war-torn corridors. They'd find one that they could open. And if Ornias succeeded in breaking through the human fortress that guarded the depths of the polar chambers, he'd have one hell of a time finding the inhabitants, for they'd scurry like rats through the narrow chambers.

Sybil stared hollowly at the flickering candle that gleamed on their bedside table. It threw wavering golden light over the beautiful room. Hexagonal, their bedchamber was thirty feet in diameter. Rich paisley rugs of turquoise, mauve, and caramel covered the floors and walls like irregularly strewn magic carpets. The soft light

71

flamed in the gold and silver stitching that laced the edges of the designs. Small tables and a desk clustered along each side of the hexagon. Crystal vases and ancient paper books adorned niches carved into the walls.

They'd only broken into this chamber on level forty a few months ago. When Mikael had first learned of her pregnancy, he'd searched for the most remote room in the entire polar chambers structure—to keep her safe. The day they'd smashed the seal and burst through the door of chamber 231, everyone's eyes had widened at the stunning opulence. The beauty still took her breath away. They'd left the place exactly as they'd found it, except for cleaning and straightening. It still intrigued her that each rug and table covered hidden niches filled with ancient supplies of food and ammunition. What had King Edom feared so terribly? Something as malignant and creeping as Sybil did now? Had he had an opponent as ruthless as Ornias?

Mikael broke the silence, softly whispering, "Salome says her uncle intercepted a message on his dattran that hinted that the Underground might be planning a rescue mission for Horeb."

Sybil tightened her grip around him, hugging him fiercely. Surely, he couldn't be suggesting they should hide their heads in the snow and wait? "It may never come. We have to attack Ornias' palace immediately. He captured too many of our people in the last battle. The children alone are reason enough. And we can't just leave Sira—"

"I know, Sybil. I'm tired. Forgive me." Mikael tenderly caressed her arm. Candlelight danced in the dark depths of his eyes. "It's just that our paltry one thousand men, women, and children seem like a handful compared to Ornias' twenty-five thousand trained Magisterial soldiers. And . . . there are also rumors that Slothen is dispatching another battle cruiser for Horeb. Not as a 'peace-keeping' vessel," he said mockingly, for everyone knew the four cruisers that currently circled Horeb did nothing at all—except ferry important diplomats and retrieve supplies from the planet's surface. "They're supposedly sending the vessel to provide direct military support for Ornias' actions against us."

Sybil sat up in bed and looked at him fearfully. A

wealth of brown curls tumbled over the bodice of her shimmering white nightgown. "Why would Slothen suddenly decide we were that important? In ten years of fighting the only action he's ever taken to hinder our attacks against Ornias was to kidnap all the Gamants he could and take them to places unknown."

Mikael's face took on a haunted slackness. "It's as though he's heard the stories about the coming of the Mashiah and is—"

"You think he would care? Why? Gamant legends are totally meaningless to Giclasians."

Mikael tilted his head uncertainly. The reflected candle flame glittered in the tangles of his dark beard. "Perhaps, we can't be certain. From a military perspective, he should take into account the rallying of Gamant spirits if the savior child does appear. If I were him, I'd do everything I could to stop that event." In a gesture filled with desperate hope, he reached over and put his hand on Sybil's swollen belly, then he closed his eyes and she could tell his lips moved in a silent prayer. When he'd finished, he lifted his hand to pull the *Mea* from beneath the sheet. He held it up so that it swung like a pendulum. The glowing blue ball on the end of the golden chain had been revered for centuries as the sacred gate that allowed Gamant holy people to speak directly to Epagael, to God. "I wish we had help, Sybil. Any help! The Underground, God, Metatron. . . ." His voice faded to nothingness.

For two years after they'd been sent back to Horeb, Mikael had awakened almost every night in a cold sweat, crying out for Metatron, though he rarely discussed it anymore. The angel who had so faithfully guided Mikael in his youth had stopped coming right after their arrival— as though Horeb were hell and angels could not descend into the vile wretchedness. Sybil suspected that Mikael believed God had abandoned him for some wrongdoing. That couldn't be true. Mikael had always done the best he could.

Sybil gripped the *Mea* and tugged it up to place it against Mikael's forehead, then she put her head against the ball and kissed him. His eyes softened in understanding. In a dream long ago, Sybil had seen them do that— *they'd been standing on a grassy hill looking down over a bloody battle. Men and women screamed in agony, writing as they died under purple lances of power from ships that swooped through the yellow skies. She and Mikael had held the* Mea *between their foreheads and kissed and a war had ended. The sounds of battle and pain had ceased.*

"Have we gotten any word on Uncle Yosef or Ari?" Mikael asked.

"Yes, Yitsa said they left four days ago. You know how they are. They're probably wandering around like kids in a new playground, searching for the *genizah*."

Mikael smiled faintly. "Probably. Sometimes I think they have too much interest in those books your mother found twelve years ago."

"I don't know. Deep down inside of me I think they hold the key to destroying the Magistrates. Mama said they talked about the construction of Palaia Station." Sybil's stomach always ached when she talked about her mother. The last time she'd seen her mother had been on Palaia Station, twelve years ago. Rachel had appeared out of nowhere, hugged Sybil, assured her she loved her very much, and vanished. Sybil had never stopped missing her. Secretly, she thought her mother was dead— though she'd never been able to say it aloud. "If we can get our hands on those books, maybe we can find a way to break into Palaia and defeat the government."

"And free the Gamant people for all time." Mikael's gaze drifted over the ivory and crimson carpet hanging on the wall beside them. In the candlelight, it gleamed like swirled wine and cream. "I hope we do it soon. Ornias' new proclamations terrify me. His insane demand that we turn over all children under the age of seven smacks of madness."

"Yes, Ornias' proclamation has turned everyone here into shuddering idiots."

"Did you hear what Lin told me?"

Sybil shook her head. Long brown curls fell back over her face, creating a silken veil. Poor Lin ish Kriyoth. His infant son Jehudah had been captured in the last battle. Lin had lost his wife only two months before. He'd gone nearly mad with grief and terror.

Mikael inhaled a deep breath and expelled it hard. "He said Ornias has been leaking rumors that he's going to line all the children up in the palace gardens and shoot them. But I can't believe it. Granted, he's killed thousands of adults in recent years, but children? The Magistrates have held his brutality at bay for years. I can't believe they'd let him—"

"Ornias doesn't need their permission. He thinks he's cornered us. Now he has to draw us out into the open so he can finish us off. If he does that, the Magistrates won't give a damn about the methods he uses. Twelve years ago he initiated a major slaughter of all the Old Believers in the capital city of Seir, including children." She twined her fingers tightly in the sheet over Mikael's heart. She could feel the organ pounding furiously beneath his warm skin. "And maybe Slothen has changed his policy. Did you think of that? Maybe that's why that new battle cruiser is coming, to give Ornias a free hand in squelching our rebellion. *We've got to get those babies out.*"

Mikael stroked her back. "I've already started making plans. Tomorrow I'll select the assault team. I was thinking about assigning Jonas, Yehud, and Dara as leaders. What do you—"

"I'm going, too."

His arm muscles hardened. "No, you're not. You're not capable now, Sybil. If we get into trouble, you'll never be able to move fast enough—"

"I don't want to be part of the actual assault team. I'll serve as lookout. I'll hide up in the rocks and signal you if anything looks bad."

"No! For me, please, stay here where you and our son are safe. *For me?*"

Sybil tenderly squeezed his hand. "It's for our son that I must go. Mikael, while you were away, I had dreams about attacking the palace and you . . . you get hurt." Tears swelled in her throat. She'd loved Mikael since she'd been a child. She couldn't bear the thought of raising their son without him. "In the dream, I'm not there, Mikael. *I'm not there.* I have to go with you."

The candle flame flickered and spit suddenly, throwing ghostly shadows over the rugs and across Mikael's taut face. He pulled her hard against him and nuzzled his cheek in her hair. Too many of her *dreams* had come true for him to ignore this one.

"Let's wait and talk about it tomorrow," he murmured. "I can't think straight tonight." He placed his hand on her stomach again. His large fingers felt warm through her white gown. He caressed her skin softly and Sybil felt their son kick as if he felt it, too. "We can't risk Nathan."

The unspoken words: *because he might be the promised Redeemer foretold eons ago in legends* hung like a shroud around them. Nathan's birth would coincide with the prophesied year. To further fulfill the prophecies, their son would have to sweep the Magistrates from the very universe and set up God's promised kingdom in their place. Nathan? The Mashiah? The very thought terrified Sybil. She sent a silent prayer to Epagael, begging Him to bypass Nathan. But if God chose to lay so heavy a burden on their son, she prayed for Him to let Yosef and Ari find the *genizah*. Nathan would need all the help he could get.

CHAPTER 8

Lights flashed, green and red. They came close in a rush, then dissolved into wisps of nothingness before abruptly flaring again. The foul odor of alien sweat filled the stark room so powerfully that it was suffocating. Carey Halloway fought to keep from vomiting.

"Now, Lieutenant," someone said in a bland mechanical voice. "You're feeling better, aren't you? Does your chest still ache?"

She whispered, "No." Vague memories of pain and battle and med units welled. Her last memory of Kiskanu was hearing Cole frantically shout her name.

"Good. Very good. See if you can concentrate on what I'm saying. We know you committed treason over the planet of Tikkun. We found that out from the loyal soldiers you abandoned on the planet's surface. Answer my question. Where is Cole Tahn?"

Carey fought to open her eyes. Her lids fluttered. *Good.* She still had partial control of her voluntary muscles. She glimpsed her reflection in the silver helmet suspended over her head. Drenched strands of auburn hair clung to her temples and cheeks. Her skin gleamed as whitely as eiderdown in the sun.

"Go to . . . hell," she managed thickly. Her tongue didn't quite work. In the dark recesses of her mind, she remembered that the anesthesia they gave before neuro work slowly paralyzed the body and confused the mind while it was being absorbed. Once it had fully entered her system, her brain would work perfectly. The knowledge brought panic. How long could she hold out against them?

"We'll find him whether you help us or not, Lieutenant, but the longer you fight us, the more pain you'll

77

suffer. Do you understand what I'm saying? You don't want us to hurt you, do you?"

She laughed, but the sound came out a gravelly moan. Her mind spun images of all the loyal crew she and Cole had safely put down on Tikkun. So they'd lived? Were they still all right? Her heart fluttered. "*Hoyer* . . . crew," she asked. "Status?"

The voices dropped to whispers. Someone said, "She wants to know what happened to her crew." Another voice responded, "I don't see any harm in telling her. In fact, it might help her memory."

"But I don't think that's wise. She might . . ." The words faded into an incomprehensible drone.

Carey seemed to float, rising out of the cold white chair to drift aimlessly through the air. To her right, she saw a long table laid out with instruments. Three Giclasians prowled the corners, their six-legged bodies writhing like bright blue snakes as they talked. Two wore white coats. One had on a strange uniform—deep purple with gold tassels across the front. On the far wall, a com screen flared in amber, ready to visually project whatever memories the probes touched.

"All right, Lieutenant." The harsh tone brought her back with a jerk. "I've been authorized to tell you about your crew. They're dead. We had no choice but to probe them thoroughly to find out what happened over Tikkun. The neuro work damaged critical centers of their brains. Euthanasia was mercifully administered six weeks after their rescue."

Rescue? *They'd murdered the* Hoyer's *crew.* If Cole ever found out, it would kill him. He'd taken every precaution to insure his crew wouldn't be tainted by his treasonous actions.

Carey groaned in rage and lunged forward, fingers feebly groping for the Giclasian killers. For a split second, she saw a ruby red mouth gape to show needle-sharp teeth, then someone shouted, "Put her down! Give her more anesthesia! Quickly!"

"She's human, Mundus! It's dangerous to give her more."

"I don't care, I said *do it.*"

Her fingers still groped, arms wavering unsteadily as she tried to grip Mundus' throat. Feet padded softly across the floor. She heard the ring of metal clashing against metal. Then the horrifying scent of chemicals stung Carey's nostrils, and a moment later she felt as though her very blood was on fire. She gasped desperately, writhing in her chair. Then, suddenly, her body went cold and still.

But her mind seemed to instantly grow clear—crystalline in its perceptions. Her eyes had frozen open. The silver helmet suspended over her head looked immensely large, the probes inside insidiously pointed. She heard the erratic breathing of the doctors, the low hum of the machinery. Somewhere far away, the shrill clacking of alien laughter sounded. Down the hall? Or in an observation room next door?

A chair squealed as Mundus dragged it across the floor to sit down beside her. His balloon-shaped head glimmered a ghastly azure in the light. He leaned over, lowering the probe helmet onto her head. A terrifying nightmare of smothering threatened to overwhelm her.

She battled the sensation, forcing it down by analyzing it. She tried to trace its source down the infinitely complex neural circuitry. When had she felt this way before? Years ago, in another life. Horin 3. They'd been called in to aid the local planetary forces in suppressing a civil war. Carey's ground troops had been ambushed. The clarity of the memories transfixed her. She could see and feel everything. Her fighter had been hit, the entire tail section slashed off. She'd crashed into the winter dense forests. She'd been lying facedown in the wreckage. A cascade of debris along with the dead body of Sem Nunes had fallen on top of her, his two hundred pounds pressing the air out of her lungs. Blood dripped from his wounds to soak her uniform with hot stickiness. She'd struggled to get up, but couldn't. Her broken ribs ached as though afire, and she couldn't catch her breath. Smoke had rolled through the command module and she'd heard the crackle of the flames coming closer, closer.

"Carey?" Cole's voice exploded in her memories. Metal squealed as he shoved it out of the way. He'd rolled Nunes off and knelt, his handsome face wild with fear as he got his arms under her shoulders and knees. She could hear the fear in his voice as he shouted, "Carey, can you grab onto me?" She'd gripped his

sleeves like a lifeline and he'd thrown all of his strength into dragging her from beneath the debris, then he'd carried her out of the burning wreckage into the glacially cold starlit night. Cole . . . always Cole . . . encouraging, soothing her fears. Her captain—and her friend. Warm feelings of love and respect flooded through her mind.

Someone spoke quietly in the far corner, barely audibly, but it resounded like cannon fire in her ears. "Don't be an idiot. *We* trained the woman in how to resist mind probes. We can't—"

"We just need to override that conditioning. It'll take time, perhaps weeks, but eventually we'll wear her down. Just like we did the *Hoyer* crew. We'll get the information, I assure you."

"We don't have time, Doctor. Slothen *wants* Tahn. He's waiting right now, and he hasn't much patience. For that matter, neither do I."

"Interrogation takes time, Councillor. We'll work as fast as we can. You don't want us to kill our source, do you?"

Councillor? Carey struggled to look at the man. A member of the Magistrates' military advisory council? Fear returned. Why such a bigwig? And why did they want Cole so badly? After all these years. . . .

A violent shudder attacked Carey's limbs as the new flood of drugs seeped into her body. The lustreglobes on the ceiling seemed to move toward her, growing huge in her field of vision, like a dozen falling moons, tumbling, tumbling down on her. She fought not to cry out.

"Relax, Lieutenant Halloway. You're all right. How are you feeling?"

She said nothing.

"Come, come, Lieutenant. *Carey,* we're your friends. You can talk to us. Tahn is fighting with the Gamant Underground. Isn't that correct?"

"Dead," she lied. "He's . . . dead."

"Please, don't make me hurt you. I don't like hurting my patients."

"Lying bastard," she managed to whisper. "Filthy goddamned . . . bastards."

The doctor shifted positions. His chair creaked. Carey felt a prickle like electricity crawling over her body. Then the probes descended deeper, eating into her brain like the tiny teeth of a million ants.

Memories welled as the probes stimulated the neural circuitry. She saw her mother's round face, white and delicate, smiling at her as she sorted fruits from their own orchards, green apples and mono-strawberries. The sweet fragrance of orange blossoms filled the air. Other scenes flashed, mostly battles, filled with mortar blasts and anguished cries. Blood spattered her mental screen. She jerked in her chair, wondering about Horeb. Were Cole and Jeremiel there yet? Had they rescued Mikael and Sybil? Then Jeremiel's face formed and her fears faded. Tall and handsome, his blond hair shimmered in the slanting rays of afternoon light that dappled through the trees on Garotman 2. The look of love in his blue eyes warmed her. She smiled at him, noting the slightly different color of his eyes. A dozen years before, on Tikkun, he'd been tortured, his right eye burned out. After Rudy and the remnants of the Underground fleet had rescued them, Jeremiel had undergone a painful transplant. Only she could tell the slightly darker color of his left eye. Carey let herself drown in the gentleness of her husband's touch. They'd been stretched out in a meadow of wildflowers, talking, laughing with each other. The feel of his hand entwined with hers fulfilled some deep need in her. She rubbed his calloused palm affectionately over her cheek.

An excited voice intruded, "*There.* Yes, that's it, Lieutenant. Very good. Tell us about Commander Baruch. Where is he now?"

Terror wrenched her. She threw all of her strength into lurching forward in her chair and screaming, "*NO!*"

CHAPTER 9

Yosef Calas, a short, pudgy old man with a round face and soft brown eyes, glanced down at the yellowed map in his hands. The herringbone lines indicated dozens of libraries on this level. The ancient Kings of Edom apparently had a passion for books. Yosef pushed up the spectacles on his nose and scrutinized the jumbled clutter in the corridor in front of him. Red dirt and massive slabs of debris clogged all the halls on level eleven, making it difficult to know precisely where they were at any given moment. The place looked like a caved-in bomb shelter. They'd already passed hundreds of numbered rooms, and a honeycomb of adjacent passageways jutted off from this main one. If they lived a thousand years, they'd never be able to check every possible *genizah*. Yosef tilted his head to examine the warped ceiling. It could tumble down and squash them flat with only mild provocation.

Ari Funk came up behind him and peered quizzically at the map. "What are we stopping for?" An extremely tall old man, Ari's thick gray hair draped around his head like an abused mop. He had a withered triangular face with hollow cheeks and a crooked nose—the remnant of too many well-deserved blows.

"Ari, do you think—"

"Shh!" Funk hissed, casting a worried glance at the roofing.

Yosef's mouth puckered. "It's wooden—*just like your brain*. It can't hear us."

"You've always been a skeptic." Ari accused, grimacing at the ceiling.

Yosef looked Ari up and down disparagingly. Tipping the map sideways so his friend could see, he asked, "Do you think we're in the right place?"

"We must be." Ari draped an arm over Yosef's shoulder to tap the ancient crystal sheet. "Remember, we passed room 600 about ten minutes ago."

"All right, let's go on, then."

They trudged forward, passing room 613. Yosef's steps slowed. A curious tingle climbed his spine as he gazed at the ancient scripted numbers. Most of the other doors had lost their identification long ago, casualties of Ornias' numerous attacks on the polar chambers. Only dust-imprinted substitutes remained to taunt the inquiring. But this room seemed miraculously untouched. He glanced down at the map. The square for this room had been darkened in. From years of experience, he knew that meant this chamber had once been sealed.

Ari demanded, "What's wrong?" as he poked Yosef in the kidney with a skeletal finger.

He shook his head. "I don't know. Apparently this room was sealed just after King Edom first moved into the polar chambers over a thousand years ago. But it doesn't have the bricked up surface that the other sealed rooms did. Remember?"

"I remember. So maybe Edom opened it up again for some reason. Does the map say it was a library?"

He shook his head. "No."

"Then let's go on. Room 703 is the next square marked 'library.'"

But Yosef continued to study the door, unable to pull his eyes away. The lamp Ari carried trembled so badly that he couldn't get a good look at the edges to see if they'd ever been cemented shut. The wavering flame cast the two men's shadows like drunken sailors over the dusty white walls. Yosef turned and lifted a bushy gray brow. Funk might well set them afire before the roof had a chance at them.

"Will you hold that thing steady," Yosef chastised. "I'm starting to feel like I'm being followed by an army of ghosts."

Ari lazily examined the multiple images. "That's because you're senile. The vision center of your brain's dead."

"Give me that lamp," Yosef ordered. "You take the map."

He shoved the map at Ari's bony chest and they made

an awkward switch. Yosef clamped both hands around the base of the lamp and waddled forward again. Chunks of blasted walls towered around them like gargantuan sentinels.

"Wait a minute." Ari turned the map upside down and blinked curiously. "Did you see this?"

"See what?"

"Right here. The writing is terribly faded, but this looks like . . . like it lists this whole area as King Edom's private chambers."

"Let me see." Yosef squinted at the letters Ari underlined with a dirty finger. "Might be. What difference would it make?"

"What difference? You are senile. Don't you remember Rachel saying the library she found when she was here with Adom was just down the hall from Edom's bedchamber?"

Yosef blinked, trying to remember. He did forget things too often these days, but at the age of 327 memory had become a prerogative, not a necessity. His thoughts drifted to Adom, Horeb's former Mashiah, and a forlorn smile curled his lips. The gangly good-looking boy had been the kindest, purest soul he'd ever met. Yosef exhaled hard. Adom had been a casualty of the planet's violent civil war—killed by Rachel Eloel to take the heart out of his followers. Adom and Rachel had taken refuge in the polar chambers just before the war began. And, yes, now he recalled. Rachel had said that was when she'd found the rare books on galactic history that Mikael and Sybil still searched for—just down the hall from Edom's bedchamber.

"*Of course*, I remember," Yosef admonished indignantly. He waved an arm to accent his certainty.

"Well, then, let's get going. Maybe seven-oh-three is the place."

Yosef gingerly slid around a precariously tilted slab that blocked half the forward passageway. His protruding belly skimmed the grime off the salb. The red dirt made a ghastly slash across the tan robe covering his navel. He brushed at it halfheartedly. They'd been searching this level for days, ever since Sybil had left on the food mission. By now, both of them looked like they'd been crawling through muddy ditches.

Ari ducked and came through the opening after Yosef. Blackness met their searching gazes. Yosef lifted his lamp higher and walked forward a short distance. A massive spiky array of boards and rocks completely cut off the route, stabbing at them like defensive swords. A more narrow corridor opened to their left.

"Well, what are we going to do now?" Ari asked, disgruntled.

"Can we get to seven-oh-three by going down this corridor and around?" He held his light up for Ari to study the map.

"The lines are so faded, I can't tell. But it looks like we don't have any choice."

Yosef started slowly down the narrow passage, placing his feet cautiously. Almost no debris cluttered this hall, though a fine mist of gravel and sand covered the floor like a gauze shawl. Yosef's boots squealed as he walked.

"Yosef—stop."

He turned. Ari had crouched on the floor to gently blow dust away from a splotch on the dirty white tiles. Yosef went to investigate, hovering over his oldest friend. "What is it?"

Ari shook his head. "I don't know, but it looks like—like blood."

Yosef bent down and touched the reddish-brown smear. It flaked off on his fingers. Queasily, Yosef wiped it on the hem of his robe. Looking around, he spotted two more splotches. He quickly turned to follow them out.

"Ari, come look at these. See the spacing? How regular it is?"

Ari bent low to see better. "Yes, almost as though someone stepped in a pool of blood and then ran when their boots were still wet."

A sick pang lanced Yosef's breast. He looked up at Ari and they exchanged a glance of silent dread. Yosef continued down the hall. More crimson stains marred the tiles, weaving as they neared the door on the far left—as though the perpetrator had raced away on unsteady feet.

"Yosef, wait a minute. Let's look in here first."

Ari had stopped before the first door on the right. Yosef brought the lamp back and held it up while Ari jarred the door open with a loud shriek. They both stepped inside and Yosef's eyes widened in amazement.

The large room must have measured thirty by forty feet. Magnificently embroidered tapestries covered the walls. Colors of jade and rose dominated the forest scenes. Strange, foreign animals pranced playfully across the weaves. High-backed chairs adorned one side, carved of brilliant ruby-red wood. And straight ahead a broad bed nestled against the wall. Its pink velvet canopy gleamed with a saffron hue in the flickering light of the candle flame. Tousled quilts and pillows lay in a rumpled mass over the sheets—as though slept in only yesterday. The faint fragrance of sandalwood clung to the room. And beside the bed, on the left, a small pack lay open, revealing lacy feminine undergarments.

Yosef's knees went weak, as though the soles of his feet felt the rhythmic pounding of other boots walking this quiet ghostly room. "Ari, this place feels *familiar.* As though I've been here before. Maybe in my dreams."

"More like nightmares," Ari corrected. He took the lamp from Yosef's hand and bravely stepped forward, going to gaze reflectively at the bed. "You think this is the place?"

Yosef wiped the perspiration from his deeply wrinkled brow. "You mean where Rachel and Adom spent their last night together? Yes. I–I think so."

Funk bent over the bed, throwing back the blankets to examine the sheets with an experienced eye. After several seconds, he leaned closer, going over every inch of the fabric. Finally, one of his silver brows arched. "No, can't be."

Yosef blinked. "Why not?"

"No *'evidence.'* You know on their last night they'd have—"

"What's the matter with you?" Yosef shook a fist. "Is that *all* you think about? Come on, you imbecile! If this is the king's bedchamber, then we can't be far from the *genizah.* Hurry!"

Ari tried to walk away from the bed without losing sight of the sheets. In defeat, he grumped under his breath and gave up, striding for the door. Yosef gripped his arm and shoved him outside.

"You're an old lech, do you know that?" Yosef accused, glaring hostilely.

"You've never been scientific."

"I don't know why I continue to associate with you. You embarrass me every day of my life!"

Ari grinned slyly. "You've been associating with me for over three hundred years. Habits are hard to break."

"Especially bad ones. Give me that lamp!" He tried to take it from Ari's hand, but Funk fought belligerently. At last, Yosef jerked with all his might, tugging it from Ari's protesting fingers. The candle wavered so violently, it almost went out. "Let's go," Yosef ordered as he stamped away down the hall.

"Where are we going?"

"You're the one with the map. You tell me. Are any of these rooms listed as possible libraries?"

"No," Ari responded morosely. "But maybe we ought to check them all, just to be sure. Sometimes things aren't listed on maps."

Yosef stopped before the first door on the left and opened it. A bare chamber met his gaze. Four white walls and no furniture. "Well, this isn't it. This one's empty."

Ari walked ahead, to the second door on the left and shoved it ajar. A small frightened gasp escaped his lips. "Oh, Yosef . . ."

"What is it?" He hurried forward as fast as his ancient legs would carry him.

Ari pushed the door back and stood aside, anguish on his withered face. Yosef passed by and almost reeled from the sight. He fell back against the door frame, panting, his stomach threatening to empty itself. A huge gray screen curved two-thirds of the way around the small room. Below it, lying on his side, the corpse of a man sprawled in a long-dried pool of blood. He'd been dead for years. The flesh of his skull had shrunken miserably, pulling tight across the mouth to reveal every tooth; and the eyes . . . the eyes had desiccated, leaving shriveled pits in the orbs. Straggles of long blond hair clung to the scalp. They shimmered a pale gold in the flickering candlelight. Yosef's gaze riveted to the man's chest. A knife still protruded from it, wedged between the ribs.

Blood spattered the corpse's torn ivory robe in a rich crimson starburst. Yosef stared in horror. *Adom.*

"Let's go, Yosef," Ari murmured softly. "There's no reason to stay here."

"Wait," Yosef whispered miserably. The boy had been so gentle, so innocent. Everyone had loved Adom. That had been his downfall. Ornias, then acting as Horeb's High Councilman, had used the masses' adoration for Tartarus like a finely honed blade to slice out a place of wealth and power for himself. He'd begun a massive campaign to slaughter Old Believers and institute Adom's God, Milcom, as the one True God. Not that Ornias cared about God. He'd done it to lure Jeremiel Baruch to Horeb so that he could capture him and turn him over the Magistrates for five billion notes. The plot had soured in the end. Tahn had scorched about ten percent of the planet before Jeremiel stopped the attack. The fire storms set off by the attack had ravaged nearly the entire surface of Horeb. None of it had been Adom's fault. The poor boy.

Yosef pushed his elderly legs forward and knelt. Taking his finger, he drew the Gamant triangle over Adom's heart and then formed his hands into the same sacred gesture. Quietly, he prayed, "Epagael, full of mercy, who dwelleth on high, cause the soul of Adom Kemar Tartarus which has gone to its rest to find repose on the wings of the Shekhinah, among the souls of those as holy and pure as the firmament of the skies. May his soul enjoy eternal life with the souls of Avram, Yeshwah and Sinlayzan, Sarah, Jekutiel and Rachel, and the rest of the righteous men and women who are in Paradise.

"Amayne." Yosef squeezed his eyes closed. How strange that another Rachel, Rachel Eloel, had killed Adom. The celestial Rachel had been the protective mother of the People. Some even speculated that she was the feminine element of Epagael Himself. But others said just the opposite, that her essence twined eternally with the wicked Aktariel's—the prince of the pit of darkness.

Behind him, he heard Ari reverently echo, "Amayne."

Yosef opened his eyes and gazed once more on the corrupted corpse. Reaching out timidly, he stroked the boy's ragged sleeve in a gesture of tenderness. "Rest easy, Adom."

He grunted as he got to his feet and walked into the hallway. Even after all these years, Yosef's soul ached for the blood of the innocent shed for all of Horeb. Ari put a warm hand on his forearm and squeezed gently. "I'm glad you thought of that," he said. "I was too shocked to—"

"I know." Yosef patted Ari's hand and started forward. "Let's see if we can't find the library. It must be along this corridor somewhere."

His gaze slid sideways every time he passed one of Rachel's bloody footsteps. He had to take two for each one of hers.

Ari softly noted, "She must have been running with all her heart."

"Yes. She loved Adom. I'm sure the task of murdering him to save Horebian citizens almost killed her. She was never the same afterward."

"No, she changed dramatically, but that was more than Adom. After she and Tahn rescued Jeremiel from that death camp on Tikkun, she disappeared. Do you remember the times before the relocation ships forced us off the planet? Rachel would go away for months at a time and no one knew where she went. Then she'd come back and her eyes would seem hollower, like she'd lost part of herself."

Yosef exhaled hard. "I remember."

"During those dark days, I thought she only came back to talk to Jeremiel, as though the two of them shared some dreadful knowledge that they feared to reveal to anyone else."

They walked straight down the passageway and edged beneath the tilted slab again. Yosef took a deep breath and gazed once more on room 613. "Ari, let's try this one first." He shoved on the door. It refused to budge. He threw all his weight into it and finally it jolted open.

A treasure trove of antiquities met his searching gaze. "Oh, my God, Ari!" Yosef shoved the door open farther and gingerly stepped into the small room. He coughed and waved a hand at the dust that plumed up into his face.

Ari pushed up behind him, bumping Yosef so that he

had to take two lunging steps forward. "This must be it," Ari whispered in awe. "The *genizah!*"

"Don't get your hopes up," Ari warned. His bushy gray brows lowered. "This could be just one of the hundreds of libraries that King Edom set up."

A velvet-thick layer of fine reddish-gray dust covered everything—the dilapidated couch to his left, the sagging bookcase on his right, the tiny black table and chair shoved against the far wall in the back. Stacks of precariously piled paper books encircled the table or were scattered about the room.

"Look at this," Ari said.

Yosef turned to see Funk kneeling and pointing. Swirling patterns marred the dusty floor, as though the hem of someone's robe or cloak had swept the loam of centuries into ripples like waves.

Cautiously, they both edged forward, following the weaving path through the heaps of fallen books. Here and there, Yosef made out toe prints left by the careful steps of bare feet. Small, delicate feet. A woman's feet.

One of the fallen books lay open along the trail. Yosef bent forward and frowned down at the writing. Many of the pages had crumbled to dust; others existed as large brittle flakes of paper. He shoved his spectacles up and squinted at the words. Unknowingly, he whispered them aloud:

> ". . . *blue beasts came in droves . . . took us to . . .*
> *Lord only knows what would have happened if we*
> *hadn't . . . the secret lay in their energy source.*"

"Sounds like they were talking about the Magistrates," Yosef whispered.

"Bah!" Ari grumped. "If they were, they'd have said blue *bastards,* not beasts."

He leaned over Yosef's shoulder and coughed in his ear. Yosef elbowed him in the stomach. "Will you back up? What are you trying to do, drown me?"

Yosef shoved Ari's shoulder, making him step away so Yosef could straighten up. Gruffly, he wiped the beads of spittle out of his ear. "Blast you, Ari, have you no manners?"

Ari ignored him and began plodding along the swirling

path. The footprints were clearer ahead, etched into the dust as though pressed into moist clay. Ari hunched over a book composed of some strange sticky substance. In the gleam of the candle, the pages shimmered like golden gauze.

"The Secret Halls of Giclas?" Ari whispered in astonishment. He swung around to pin Yosef with owlish eyes. "That's the heading on this page!" He gently picked up the book and read:

> "*During the month of Uru, First Magistrate Mastema lectured to the Hall of Science on 'Phase Transition Dynamics in Clouds of Trapped Ions . . .'* "

Ari lowered the book and cast a disgruntled look at Yosef. "What the hell do you think that means?"

Yosef shook his head. He wiped clammy palms on his dirty tan robe. "I don't know, but I think maybe we should collect as many of these books as we can and take them to Mikael and Sybil."

"Why don't we just bring them back here? That would be easier than carrying—"

"I . . . I just have the feeling we might not make it back. Don't ask me why. I don't know. Hurry, let's gather all the books on the Magistrates that we can find."

Yosef hobbled around, selectively grabbing books from the floor. After he'd loaded six in the crook of his left arm, he waddled to the black table and slumped down onto the chair, waiting for Ari to fill his arms.

Heaving a sigh, Yosef idly turned around and started reading the first page of the black leather-bound volume that lay open on the table.

> "*Yea, though I walk through the valley of the shadow of death. . . . The final attack has come. Horeb lies a barren waste. Thirty-two million dead. Milcom—Aktariel, I'm sure now—says we must press ahead.*
> *I haven't the heart.*"

Yosef gasped. Adom had worshiped Milcom. How old was this journal? Old, very old. Did this imply that Adom truly had seen the golden glowing God he'd

claimed, that Milcom had seduced others long before
Adom was born—*and that Milcom was in fact the wicked
Aktariel who, for centuries, had been proclaimed the
Deceiver?* Yosef's gaze skipped around through the jour-
nal entries:

> *"Doubt consumes me.*
> *I have only a questionable source . . . a fallen*
> *angel of immense beauty with a soothing voice and*
> *the power to convince frail humans of anything.*
> *I can't go on."*

Overhead, a low rumble echoed like a deep-throated
growl. Yosef clutched the white fabric over his throbbing
heart and struggled to get to his feet. Ari's eyes grew as
wide as gray saucers.

"What's that?"

"An attack. . . ."

The sound grew louder, increasing to a violent roar.
The room shuddered as though tormented by an earthquake. Books cascaded out of the sagging bookcase,
slamming to the floor. Yosef grabbed Middoth's journal
and the other books he'd collected and lunged toward
the door.

"Come on, Ari!" he shouted as he staggered across
the vibrating room. "We have to get to the lower levels!"

Ari grabbed Yosef's arm and they helped support each
other to the door. In the hall outside, a fetid gush of air
blasted the boulders and debris, whirling dust up like a
deadly sandstorm in the deepest deserts.

Yosef rushed forward, but stumbled and screamed in
fear when a dark shadow grew out of nothingness, swelling to monstrous proportions before his eyes. Like a huge
black demon, it loomed over them. Repellent odors of
darkness and decay filled the hall.

"Dear God," Ari quavered. *"What is it?"*

The blackness hugged the walls as it hurried away—
slithering toward the chamber where Adom's corpse lay.

CHAPTER 10

Ornias glumly marched across the palace gardens. The thudding footsteps of his ministers and soldiers pounded behind him. The lush vegetation glistened wetly in the storm. Beads of rain clung to the emerald leaves of the trees, sparkling like tears in the flashes of lightning that lit the afternoon sky. Didn't it ever do anything but drizzle on Horeb? He hated it. Tahn's scorch attack over a decade ago had thrown so much dust and debris into the atmosphere that the clouds rarely parted for more than a few minutes at a time now. Ornias tilted his head to glare at the brooding gray sky. Cold fingers of wind gripped the hood of his amethyst velvet cloak and jerked it from his head. Rain sheeted his face. He cursed under his breath and pulled his hood back up, holding it in place. The gale set his gold embroidered hem snapping around his legs.

Blast! He was in a bad mood. He'd been unable to sleep all night long. A dream—a powerful dream—had been tormenting him for days. Every time he drifted off, a warm pool of glittering gold swallowed him and an alien being appeared. The creature's amber features seemed to be chiseled from pure light. It called itself an angel and *threatened* him if he didn't do as he was told!

An involuntary shiver traced up his spine. "Dreams aren't real, fool. Get a hold of yourself. It's just your unconscious reinforcing a decision you made weeks ago." He cast a surreptitious glance over his shoulder anyway, just to make sure a hooded man of pure gold wasn't standing there scrutinizing him.

The "angel's" message wouldn't leave him. It kept repeating in the recesses of his mind: *You must kill all the children. You can't let a single one escape or the true Mashiah will rise up and crush the life from you.*

"Stupid things, dreams."

He sidestepped a flailing branch that swept the cobble-stoned path he walked. Ahead, he could see Sergeant Horner and a dozen other marines encircling a large group of bawling brats. A few adults stood around the edges. The children huddled together for warmth, their cries carrying on the wind like the howls of the damned echoing from the pit of darkness.

"Governor," Fenris Midgard said tightly as he sprinted to catch up with Ornias. "Who are these children? Why are they here?"

"Captives from the last battle, Minister." Ornias grinned at Midgard. Rain had matted the man's graying brown hair to his pale cheeks and forehead, highlighting the suspicion on his face. His purple uniform clung in clammy folds to his thin body.

"Why are they here?" Midgard demanded.

"We're searching for the Mashiah, Minister," Ornias clarified amiably.

"Surely, you're joking, Governor. You can't believe—"

"No, of course not. But *they* believe, Minister. Don't you see? If we can find and kill this child, Mikael Calas' superstitious followers will consider it the end of the world." He grinned in anticipated triumph. Yes, Calas' followers would fall apart. Their faith in Mikael's and Sybil's leadership would crumble like the pages of a thou-sand-year-old manuscript.

"But—but," Fenris sputtered. "How will we know which one is the supposed Mashiah? Surely these people won't just point him out."

Ornias gave Midgard a condescending look, then hur-ried forward to stand outside the circle of soldiers. Wind set his amethyst cloak billowing. Children shrieked, reaching out to the closest adult, begging to be held. They'd been standing in the storm for hours and they looked like drowned, dirty-faced rats.

Ornias glowered menacingly at the few Gamant adults who stared in his direction. "If they won't point the child out, Midgard, then we'll be forced to take more sweeping actions to ensure the baby's demise. Of course, we'll advertise and stage the executions at just the right moment. No sense in wasting such a priceless opportunity to lure the Calas family into our hands."

Fenris' jaw hardened. His chest puffed with anxious breaths. "Gamant children are protected under the Treaty of Lysomia, Governor! You have no authority—"

Ornias smiled coldly. "I do what I please on Horeb, Midgard. If you don't like it, you're welcome to request reassignment."

"I'll do that immediately, Governor!" Fenris stated flatly as he nodded vehemently. "Yes, indeed I will. And I'll inform the Magistrates of your brutal, illegal behavior here."

Ornias laughed long and loud. "I suggest you talk to Slothen himself, Fenris. I hear he has his own problems with Gamants rioting on the ring of satellites he's erected around Palaia. I'm quite certain he'll understand my methods here."

Midgard's mouth puckered, "Have you heard, Governor, that Magistrate Slothen has dispatched a battle cruiser to Horeb?"

Ornias paled slightly. Was this some kind of last-ditch ruse by Midgard? Slothen had no reason to send in another cruiser. "What for?"

"The message came in only an hour ago. It didn't specify the reason, it only instructed that we make arrangements to greet Captain Amirah Jossel."

"*Jossel?*" Ornias shouted before he caught himself. That brutal, efficient witch generally served as Slothen's hit woman. She had a reputation for coming in fast, striking with deadly accuracy, and letting someone else pick up the pieces of slag.

A small grin of triumph lit Midgard's face. "Yes. I'm sure *she'll* be especially interested in your illegal activities here!"

Fenris backed away. Ornias watched him stalk across the gardens, clearly heading to the palace's communications center. Ornias signaled Horner. The ugly little marine immediately shoved through the crowd to get to him.

Horner saluted sloppily. "What is it, Governor?"

"You remember the unfortunate accident that Major Winfeld had last year?"

A cruel grin twisted Horner's mouth. He gripped his gray rifle tightly. "Aye, sir. Who's being a nuisance this time?"

Without deigning to look around, Ornias said, "Our brave Minister Midgard wants to see the battlefront up close. It's unfortunate that he won't be coming home."

Horner chuckled nastily and saluted again. 'Yes. Unfortunate, all right."

Ornias pretended to study the crying children while he secretly watched Horner trot after Midgard; the marine caught the zealous minister at the corner of the palace entrance. Gripping Fenris' arm tightly, Horner escorted him in the opposite direction—toward the space dock.

CHAPTER 11

The landing bay spread in a cluttered two hundred foot square around Cole. He wiped clammy palms on his black battlesuit and absently looked around. Stasis cabinets lined one wall, providing quick access to emergency parts and tools. Around the perimeter six fighters gleamed. Beneath the bright glow of the lustreglobes, they created triangular pewter smears against the white walls. One fighter sat in the open before the bay doors. Baruch stood beside it, giving curt hushed orders to the crew; he stood stiffly, fists clenched at his sides. The two women of the command team nodded nervously, worried by the strange, vaguely hostile tone in Jeremiel's voice. The pilot, Rivka Leso, a short woman with close-cropped red hair and bright green eyes, kept glancing at Cole.

He ignored the proceedings to check and recheck his equipment. For the hundredth time, he flicked the switch on his belt tran to make certain the unit worked, then carefully scrutinized the charge in each of his two pistols. He frowned glumly at his false ID papers. *Sonny Flaum?* What the hell kind of name was that?

He scratched at his beard and mustache which created a dark brown mantle over his face. He grunted irritably. Why was he so damned fidgety? He'd played spy for the Magistrates dozens of times. But it had been years ago. And he knew that top level espionage required a person with a superior lack of morals. He'd sprouted so many useless scruples in the past twelve years that this mission might just kill him. For days he'd walked around his cabin and studied himself grimly in the mirror, thinking dismally, *You* accepted *this mission? What a brave moron you are!*

He hoped to God one of the captains of those five cruisers circling Horeb would remember the training session in the Wocet system last year. If none of them did, Jeremiel's plan might just fall to pieces.

Baruch strode across the bay, a taut look on his handsome face. His blue eyes seemed as piercing as coherent beams. Sweat stained the collar of his black suit. "Are you ready, Cole?"

"I went on hara-kiri mode yesterday. Of course, I'm ready." He anxiously pulled his pistol half out of the holster, then shoved it in again.

Jeremiel studied the action. "You're certain you don't want to back out?"

"Don't be ridiculous. I'm perfect for this job. Where else could you find someone with such scant mental capacity?"

Baruch smiled faintly. "Remember, if everything goes well, you and I will be on a ship headed for Palaia in about seven days."

"That's what keeps me going, Baruch." He held Jeremiel's gaze. A flicker of desperation lurked just beneath the cool, calculating surface. It echoed with a powerful resonance in Cole's own soul, like the taunting wails of the sirens.

"You've got the palace and desert chambers floor plans, right?"

"I've got them." He tapped his breast pocket.

"Good. The *Sargonid* just made orbit around Horeb. We don't know her orders, but we assume she's there regarding the planetary revolt Mikael's leading. Ornias has undoubtedly requested an immediate meeting to discuss suppression—"

"And Amirah Jossel's commanding the *Sargonid*? I hope she's as dynamic as her personality profile suggests. I could use a few days of spirited debate. But even if she's an idiot, she's good looking. That'll be some consolation." Cole toyed with the fasteners at his neckline. His collar suddenly felt like a noose.

"Is there anything else you need from me?" Baruch asked.

"No."

Jeremiel scrutinized him, eyes logging every feature, as though it might be the last time they saw each other. It made Cole feel as if he clung by his fingertips over the gaping maw of a fire-breathing Arcturian flame cat.

He laughed with grim amusement. "Don't look so confident, Baruch. You'll give me a swelled head."

Jeremiel glanced over his shoulder at the soldiers by the fighter. The bay had gone quiet. The command team waited pensively. Rivka, the pilot, kept shifting from foot to foot. "As soon as you complete stage one, tran Rivka and she'll get the message to us. We'll be no more than a day away."

"Understood."

"Don't take any unnecessary risks."

"My passion for martyrdom died long ago. I won't."

Baruch lifted a hand and placed it warmly on Cole's shoulder. He went on issuing instructions, but Cole barely heard. Jeremiel's stricken face held his attention. Like a man drained of his lifeblood by a fatal internal wound, Baruch's skin had paled to a ghostly white. Cold sweat dotted Cole's arms as he listened to the buried fear in that deep, hurried voice. Every day they'd bent over the dattran together, seeking any word that Carey lived. But there'd been none. In response, Cole's dreams had sketched horrifying pictures of Carey lying alone and dead in the cold subterranean chambers on Palaia. Or worse, alive but with no mind. Night after night, he'd awakened with his heart racing and his sheets coiling in drenched folds around his waist.

"I get the picture, Baruch," he interrupted gently. "Don't worry, *nobody's* going to capture me." Expressively, he patted the pistol on his right hip, then turned to gaze seriously at the fighter. Rivka had started marching back and forth before the nose of the ship. "I'd better be going."

Jeremiel reluctantly dropped his hand. The cooling units kicked on and a puff of chill air waffled their black sleeves.

"If I haven't tranned Rivka in two days, forget about me, hit the planet hard."

"Affirmative. Just make sure you—"

"And then get to Palaia." Cole straightened and leveled a stern gaze at Baruch. "If Carey's alive, she can't possibly hold out against the probes for more than a few days. I know. I've been under them and the techniques are a great deal more sophisticated now than they were thirty years ago."

"I'll get there as quickly as I can," Jeremiel responded in a quiet voice. "Take care of yourself."

"Affirmative. Tell Merle I damn well plan on coming back and finding my ship in one piece. If I don't, she's in for some disgusting punitive duty that's beneath her dignity."

"I'll tell her."

With that, Cole headed briskly for the fighter. His boots pounded a hollow cadence against the white deck plates. He climbed into the cramped command cabin and slipped on his jet suit and pack. Gripping his helmet, he sat down, securing the EM restraints while the pilot and copilot dropped into their seats. Cole's two assistants, Sergeants Keynes and Ward, both young and black-haired, gave him grave looks as they secured their restraints.

"Keynes?" Cole said. "This is going to be tricky. I want to go over the sequence of actions you're to undertake at least a dozen times in the next few hours."

Keynes adjusted his holster and nodded. "Aye, sir. That sounds like a good idea. Ward and I are ready, but—"

"Captain," Rivka Leso said as she powered up the ship. "We're going to exit vault in the midst of those cruisers and dive for the planet on full thrust. We'll drop you and your team about ten miles from the military governor's palace."

"What's our jump window?"

"Ten seconds. Then we expect to be under fire. We'll draw them away from you for as long as we can. If we escape, we'll wait for your signal before we make our second pass."

A sick qualm twisted his stomach. Leso would be dodging the combined fire of at least two cruisers. He and his team would have to go through free-fall for a mile before they could power up their jets or those cruisers would spot them immediately and blow their whole little show. "We're prepared."

He leaned his head back against the white wall and watched the bay doors open through the fighter's rectangular front portal. Space gleamed like a sequined black blanket as they edged out.

CHAPTER 12

Clouds drifted in smoky veils over the luminous face of the full moon, but no ships marred the heavens. Sybil took the chance and inched closer to the crest of the ridge. Using the erratic flashes of moonlight, she scrutinized the city that lay in the valley below. A few lustreglobes twinkled, flickering over lavish three-and four-story government buildings. Quietly, she lifted her rifle and scoped out the grounds of the governor's palace. She spied dozens of children, dressed in rags, shivering from the cold. Three dead babies sprawled a short distance away, their bloody corpses stacked precariously. Armed guards surrounded the living children. Their rifles glowed a malignant silver in the dim glow that lit the rainy palace gardens.

Sybil thought she caught a glimpse of Marcus' team moving through the deep shadows on the other side of the city. She rolled over on her back and slithered down the slope. Childish whimpers rode the wind. They cut her to her soul.

Carefully guarding her swollen belly, she inched into a rocky niche sheltered from the storm. Mikael pulled himself forward on his elbows and worriedly searched her face. "How many?"

"About fifty or sixty. Ornias has moved them into the gardens."

He dropped his head to stare blindly at the damp red soil. "Blessed Epagael, he has them standing out in the open? Then this is certainly a trap."

Sybil's gut tightened. The frosty light captured Mikael's still image like an ancient black and white snapshot. Black hair hung in drenched strands over his cheeks, accenting the gauntness of his handsome face.

Sybil looked away. They'd found out only hours ago.

A sixteen-year-old woman had burst into the polar chambers, waving her arms, shrieking madly, "They're doing it! Did you see? Did you hear the screams? Ornias is killing our babies—just like he said he would! *Our babies!*"

Sybil touched Mikael's shoulder. "Let's wait."

"And let more of our children be shot down before our eyes?"

"But if it's a trap, waiting is better than—"

"No, it isn't. Even if the twenty of us die, it's better than sending a message to Ornias that he can kill our children while we sit by and cower in fear." He shook his head sullenly. "We can't wait, Sybil. You said so yourself. We may have help coming from the Underground, but it could just be another rumor. There've been so very many in the past years. And this is a good maneuver. It just might work regardless of what Ornias has planned."

"It might," she agreed softly. But doubt gnawed at her. She reached out to take his hand. "I love you, Mikael."

He threw her a morose smile. "Don't worry, I'm not going to let myself get killed if I can help it."

"I know you won't."

She released his hand and anxiously fidgeted with her rifle, clicking the safety off and on, off and on. Throughout the labyrinth of rock, men and women waited. She saw an arm move a short distance away. A head shook farther down the line. The twenty in their group were true survivors—children of the Horebian holocaust who'd magically been missed by the Magistrates. They all shifted, ready to move. The sound of their breathing rose to pound against Sybil's ears like the howl of a cyclone just before it strikes the world deaf and blind.

For the briefest of moments, the soft rays of predawn broke through the storm clouds to fall like an opalescent blue shawl over the jagged parapet.

Mikael turned to her, dark eyes wide. "Ready?"

"Yes."

He swung around to face the others. "You all know what you're supposed to do? Dara? Shoshi?"

Nods eddied down the line. Mikael crawled forward.

They all followed him out onto the rain-slick rocks of the ridge crest and began dispersing into strike units.

When they stood alone on the windswept summit, Mikael gripped Sybil's arm hard. "Promise me you'll stay here. So help me, if I find you down in the midst of the firefight. . . ." His hard tone softened. "I couldn't fight if I thought you and Nathan were in danger."

"I won't set foot off this ridge," she guaranteed. *Unless you're in trouble, Mikael. Only then.*

Their sleeves billowed in the gale. He alternated between searching her eyes and watching the sky for enemy ships. "If you see anything suspicious, fire one long burst and one short and we'll retreat."

"I understand. Be careful."

He dropped his hand to gently caress her swollen belly, then slowly backed away and trotted down the slope. Sybil watched him until he disappeared into the dark shadows of the city streets. For a time, she let her gaze drift over the rolling clouds and the red and gold lights of the gaudy palace.

She angled to slip into a curious rock formation that overlooked the city. It was shaped like a spired castle and the rain hadn't yet penetrated the niche. Easing down to the dry red sand, she propped her rifle over her knees and leaned against the cool stone. Her back ached miserably. She tried to ignore it. She peered through a crack at the city below. The children had huddled together, sharing each other's warmth. Their cries carried on the wind, high and shrill. Through her scope she saw a little girl of maybe four lift her arms pleadingly to one of the guards. He shoved her into the mud. The girl tumbled across the ground and cried louder.

Sybil's fingers knotted around her rifle. She thought she could hear the guard laughing. "Laugh now, bastard. In an hour, you'll be dead."

A curious stir touched her womb, an agonizing throb, as though her son, too, had witnessed the event and he was crying out in pain.

Sybil kept her finger braced on the trigger guard of her rifle and dropped her left hand to rub her belly soothingly. "It's all right" she whispered. "Don't worry, Nathan. Very soon, we're going to leave this place. We're going out there to find the Great Gate. We're going to find that naked singularity and when we do, we're going to pass through it into an endless ocean of peace and tranquillity. Your father told me, *buzina*. I know it's true because an angel named Metatron told him. And your grandmother . . . Mama mentioned the Great Gate, too, a long time ago when she didn't think I'd understand."

Sybil regripped her rifle. Thoughts of her mother made her feel ill. When Rachel had come to visit her at Palaia, she'd been different, crying at odd moments, talking to herself, screaming and slamming her fists into walls until they bled. Sybil remembered wanting to run away from that stranger who looked like her mother.

Through the bars of light that shot through the clouds, Sybil could see patches of the sea. They shone a dark crimson. The Sea of Blood had been created when Captain Tahn had attacked Horeb. Under beam cannon fire, the rocky red ridges of the vast deserts had melted into glassy pools.

Sybil jumped when a wretched scream pierced the silence. It rose like a banshee's wail, wafting on the rain-soaked wind. Sybil froze for a split second, then quickly bent over her rifle and stared through the scope, searching, searching. A platoon of purple-clad Magisterial soldiers herded six members of Marcus' team in from the perimeter; they had their hands clasped behind their heads. Sybil held her breath, silently counting to ten.

Fiery apocalypse burst loose over the city.

The captured Gamant team hit the ground, taking advantage of their captors' surprise to roll and kick out viciously, forcing a hand-to-hand battle and scrambling for any dropped weapons. Rifle fire lanced the heavens. Dara's group broke from the rocky terraces around the governor's palace and rushed the front gate, diverting the guards who held the children. At the same time, Shoshi's attack unit raced for the children, driving them before them in a shrieking wave, while Mikael's forces provided flanking fire.

When Sybil saw Mikael's and Shoshi's people retreating without a single loss, she thought her heart would burst. But she stayed put, listening to the pounding of her heart, counting the dead lying in bloody heaps throughout the palace gardens, wondering which friends they'd mourn tonight.

A slight hum touched her ears. Sybil glanced up in horror as dozens of ships dropped like ghostly daggers out of the cloudy sky. Lunging forward, she fired the warning shots and watched as the ships hurtled downward toward Mikael and Shoshi, firing to cut off their escape. Mikael shot vainly into the swarm of ships, covering for his people so they could dive for the rocks.

"No! *No, Mikael! Run!*"

Sybil grabbed her rifle and scrambled out of her rocky sanctuary, feet slipping on the wet, shining sandstone. She saw Mikael drop to his knees as two dozen Magisterial soldiers darted from the underbrush to surround him. Why hadn't they killed him? Sybil ran with all her might. When she got within range, she dropped to one knee and braced her rifle against an upturned boulder. Sighting through the scope, she switched to wide-beam and fired, and kept firing, watching the purple-suited enemies die beneath her hands while Mikael's group fought and scattered.

Purple arcs lanced the ridge crest around her, exploding rocks. Sybil kept firing, covering Mikael's retreat. Something slapped her shoulder and she fell backward, landing hard against the ridgetop. For a moment, she lay stunned, not sure what had happened. She concentrated on the cool patter of rain against her cheeks.

And from somewhere faraway, she heard a voice. It came faintly at first, as though unreal. A deep woman's voice, brittle with tears and love. It echoed from the red cliffs.

"*Sybil, forgive me. I couldn't warn you.*"

"Mama? Mama, where are you? I need help, Mama." Sybil felt blood rise up her throat to bubble on her lips. She coughed and stared in terror at the flow of red that ran from her mouth across the stone. "Mama, I'm hurt! Help me? I think . . . I think I'm dying." She put one trembling hand over her belly and lifted the other to the red-tinged heavens. "*Mama! He's your grandson! Help him!*"

But her strength faded and her hand dropped like a lead brick against the sandstone. She tried to focus her hazy vision on the clouds. They glowed a deep coral in

the first rays of the risen sun. Around her, a widening
pool of blood spread and she felt the hot flow soaking
her shoulder. The last thing she saw was a dozen enemy
ships diving out of the sunlit heavens. From somewhere
in the distance soldiers screamed in intergalactic lingua.

Like a skilled assassin, a curtain of blackness crept
over her, swallowing the world.

CHAPTER 13

Captain Amirah Jossel stepped out of her shuttle and down to the soft red sand of Horeb. Afternoon light pierced the heavy cloud cover in pale blue luminescent shafts. Red and gray banded bluffs jutted up around the palace, forming a blocky fortress. She'd been here once before, or rather she'd flown by, twelve years ago. It had been her first assignment on a military energy ship, a clandestine forces vessel ordered to scout the heavens for primordial black holes. They'd thought they'd found one near Horeb. The reflected gravity waves they'd picked up had looked extremely promising. But the political situation on the planet had been so volatile that they'd put aside any attempt to retrieve the precious commodity. Amirah looked up when a mean-faced little planetary marine trotted around her ship and saluted halfheartedly.

"I'm Sergeant Horner," he greeted her stiffly. "I'm supposed to take you to the governor's council chambers."

"Good afternoon, Sergeant. Thank you for meeting us."

She took a deep breath of the rain-scented air. Lightning struck one of the jagged peaks in the distance and thunder rolled over the ridges in a deep-throated growl. She waited for her security team, Lieutenant James Tolemy and Sergeant Chris Richert, to step out of the shuttle behind her.

"Very well, Horner," she said. "Please lead the way."

The ugly little man spun sloppily and stumbled sideways before catching himself and walking off. Amirah scowled. Drunk? Tolemy, a medium-sized man with graying black hair and a beard and mustache, lifted a disapproving brow. Amirah met his eyes and expelled an annoyed breath, giving him her best "I haven't the vaguest idea" shrug.

They passed through a beautiful garden. Imported oaks from Old Earth and Sculptorian maples dotted the expanse, framing dozens of flower beds. The sweet scents of roses and daffodils carried to them on the cool breeze.

When they reached the palace doors, Horner hiccuped rudely as he input the entry sequence into the com patch. Amirah could smell the odor of whiskey on his breath. She stifled the urge to dress him down. *It's not worth the effort. Whatever happens here, within five days you'll be leaving this wasteland anyway.*

Horner turned and gave her a suggestive grin. "The governor was expecting you three hours ago, Captain. He's going to be angry that you're so late."

Amirah smiled threateningly. "His emotional inadequacies are not my concern, Sergeant."

Horner opened his mouth to say something else, but at her stony glare, he wisely snapped it closed and darted through the door, shepherding them down the long corridor.

Pink marble arches rose in Gothic magnificence a hundred feet over her head. Stained glass windows filled every niche, each portraying a different image of the governor. She recognized many of the poses: Washington crossing the Delaware on Old Earth, Colonel Sarah Myers staking the first colony on the moon, Pleros of Antares 3 delivering his infamous "Limited Rights" speech which slashed the civil freedoms of his people and resulted in the massive Plerosian Revolts of the third millennia. She shook her head, disgusted. Ornias seemed to have a rather high opinion of himself. She'd never met the man, but the stories she'd heard raised her hackles. Allegedly, Slothen had destroyed several files which confirmed Ornias' nefarious background as thief, embezzler, and murderer. The reasons for Slothen's actions were a little vague. The "purgation notes" on the files cited "galactic security" considerations.

Tolemy and Richert followed behind her, mumbling profanely about government waste and mismanagement. As she turned a corner down a new hall, she grunted in distasteful agreement.

Plush Orillian velvet carpets tufted the floors. The geometric designs interlaced colors of ebony and carnelian, dusty rose and mauve. Etched mirrors lined the entire corridor. She glanced at her reflection as she walked. At the age of twenty-nine she possessed a trim athletic figure. Muscles bulged along her thighs and arms, stretching the fabric of her formfitting purple uniform. Five feet nine inches tall, she had pleasing shoulders which narrowed to a tiny waist—absurdly tiny a man not worth remembering had once told her. Her wavy blonde hair was cut straight over her eyebrows and fell in waves to the middle of her back. She had a delicately-shaped mouth and a light scatter of too-large freckles over her button nose. The bane of her childhood, they'd finally started to fade when she'd turned twenty-two. Of course, by that time, it didn't matter anymore. Men avoided her like a leprosy victim. She'd already been awarded her own command and had received the Giclasian Gold Leaf, the Crossed Bars of Mars, and the Naassene Silver Cross. Few men had the internal fortitude to try and court her.

She hadn't the time for them anyway. But loneliness certainly stood as the single greatest curse of command. Too often of late, she wandered sleeplessly around her cabin, wishing she had someone, anyone, to talk to, to confide in about the insanity that wouldn't let her sleep— the insanity that now affected even her waking hours.

The flashbacks had become her constant companions. Fortunately, a few seconds into each of the events, she could distinguish it as unreal and force herself out—except at night in her dreams where the visions seemed to be growing more and more powerful, taking over her entire unconscious world.

And other problems plagued her. There was more to this Horeb mission than Slothen let on, for example. Her orders had been crisply urgent: *Retrieve Calas no matter the cost. Immediately return to Palaia. Top priority. All other priorities rescinded.*

She frowned at herself. Actually, she did have someone on the *Sargonid* she could trust—Jason Woloc, her second in command. But she couldn't talk earnestly with him about her fears. Their professional relationship was too delicate to chance such confidences. He loved her. She'd known it for over a year. But she didn't feel the same way about him. And besides, a captain couldn't seriously date one of her officers. It stirred up gossip and charges of favoritism, which made for poor ship morale.

Still, she liked Jason a great deal. Perhaps in another time and place. . . .

"We're almost there," Horner said and pointed to the huge, intricately carved wooden doors at the end of the hall. "Best be careful how you talk to the governor, Captain. He's got connections everywhere. He's big with the Magistrates."

Tolemy cleared his throat in a disgruntled manner and hooked a thumb at his pistol, then pointed at Horner, silently requesting Amirah's approval. She shook her head and mouthed, *"Mine."*

Horner caught the exchange and his pig eyes narrowed threateningly. "You battle cruiser martinets—" he began.

Amirah pushed by him, reaching to pound a fist on the communications patch outside the huge doors. "Captain Amirah Jossel to see Governor Ornias," she called.

A honeyed male voice answered, "Just a moment, Captain."

Amirah ground her teeth while she waited, checking the walls and ceiling for hidden "eyes." "Jim," she ordered her security chief, "stay here. My orders are to meet with the governor alone." Yes, strange orders, indeed. Slothen had also instructed her to take no more than two officers for her security accompaniment. A contingent she thought grossly inadequate given the war situation on Horeb and the threat of Underground intervention.

Tolemy and Richert lined out on either side of the door, standing with their arms crossed and scowling disdainfully at Horner. One of the doors swung open and Amirah stepped through it into the council chambers.

As the door closed behind her, her gaze drifted upward involuntarily. The domed octagonal chamber was fifty feet in diameter. Pink and gray marble columns rose splendidly on each wall, providing an exotic frame for the rare paintings Ornias had collected; their ancient pigments shone darkly in the murky light penetrating the windows. Here and there, a priceless vase sat atop a sculptured table, or a Cassiopan emerald clock ticked in perfect time.

Governor Ornias stood twenty feet away, beneath the awe-inspiring frescoed dome which pictured an ancient battle; Soldiers fired at each other, blood spattering the azure heavens. Ornias had a crystal glass of amber liquid clutched in his manicured hand. Tall, with sandy hair and a tightly braided beard, he had strikingly cold lime green eyes—like a snake, she thought. The golden threads embroidering his long amethyst robe glimmered when he moved. He smiled admiringly at her.

"I'd no idea you'd be so attractive, Captain," he said silkily.

"And I'd no idea you'd be so incompetent, Governor," Amirah parried. "I've reviewed your files quite thoroughly."

His smile faded into a grimace. She straightened and locked her hands behind her in an at-ease position. Ornias' gaze brazenly drifted over the swell of her breasts.

"Yes, well . . ." he said in a faintly amused tone. "Everyone has a right to their opinion. I must say, your reputation has preceded you. I'm honored to—"

"Enough of the 'pleasantries,' Governor. We have business."

"You're as subtle as your reputation suggests, Captain. I suppose such arrogance goes hand-in-hand with being a great war hero. Despite your manners, however, I would like to get to know you better. May I get you a glass of sherry first? Or something else, Captain?

Amirah gave him one of her best loathsome looks. "No, Governor. I expect this to be a short meeting."

"Indeed? I'd anticipated a lengthy discussion about Horebian affairs." Ornias turned abruptly and walked away from her to stand before the broad windows. Outside, dark clouds roiled, rain falling in wavering misty blankets. The red ridges glimmered a bright orange beneath the flashes of lightning that split the heavens. "And just what, pray tell, are you supposed to tell me, Captain?"

"Magistrate Slothen wants Mikael Calas, *alive and well and immediately*. If you are unable to bring him in within the next two days, I've been put in charge of the cruiser forces orbiting Horeb and I've been instructed to use all the resources at my command to attain his capture."

Ornias leisurely paced the black, rose-strewn carpet. "And why does Slothen want Calas alive? It seems to me it would be a great deal easier to deliver him to Palaia

Station in a less formidable state. That boy's become quite a nuisance, Captain."

"I'm well aware that he's grown into a first-class soldier, but if you can't corner him, I'm certain my people can."

"Are you?" Ornias smiled dubiously. "Do you know I've lost more than twelve thousand marines to Calas' uncanny military strategies?"

"I do," she answered unswervingly.

The Governor tipped his chin like a king examining a truant servant. "I've been trying for years to capture Calas, without success. Just how does Slothen expect me to suddenly—"

"Find a way."

He uttered a soft sound of angry disbelief and shook his head. "In two days? May I enlist your cruiser's weaponry to blast his polar hiding place to dust? We have him cornered there at this very moment. Only yesterday we—"

"I'm not authorized to use cruiser weaponry unless you have failed through conventional methods. However, I can assign several more platoons to your planetary marine corps if you deem it necessary."

"That would help. But really, Captain, this is ridiculous! You're placing me in an impossible situation. Even with more soldiers, I seriously doubt—"

"*Nonetheless*, you have two days."

A dark suspicion stirred in Ornias' eyes. He cocked his head inquisitively and paced before one of the ancient paintings. "Slothen seems terribly anxious to have this completed, Captain. Is there something you've failed to tell me?"

Amirah ground her teeth. In the dim light streaming through the windows, Ornias' robe gleamed extravagantly. It set her on edge. "Nothing that we've confirmed, Governor."

"Uh-huh." Ornias caressed his beard thoughtfully. "And what have you heard that's unconfirmed?"

"We have unverified reports on the low dattran bands suggesting Baruch may be planning an assault on this planet."

Ornias' face paled suddenly, as though an icy finger had traced his spine. His lime green eyes narrowed.

"Why haven't I been notified of such a possibility before now?"

"It's just rumor. Nothing to worry about yet."

The governor's arrogance and bluster seemed to fade before her eyes. She kept her amusement hidden. Everyone knew that he and Baruch were old enemies. A dozen years ago, Ornias had betrayed and sold Baruch to the Magistrates for five billion notes. In a still unexplained maneuver, Baruch had captured the ship destined to take him to Palaia, the *Hoyer*, under the command of Captain Cole Tahn, and escaped. Certainly if Baruch captured Ornias, the governor's death would be a slow one.

While she waited for Ornias to muster the courage to discuss the issue further, she let her thoughts drift to Tahn. A highly decorated officer, his brilliant military strategies were still taught in Academy. During the early days of her training, she'd had a terrible crush on him. In the holo lectures on tactics, he'd been so handsome, so utterly confident and in control—he'd quickly become one of her greatest heroes. She'd memorized nearly every element of his career. Arguments still raged as to whether he'd died in the fighting over the planet of Tikkun or now lived in hiding amid the Underground. She believed the former. A man of his superior valor and loyalty didn't just decide to switch sides one day.

Ornias lifted his sherry and smoothly finished it to the last drop. "Well," he said airily. "It seems I have no choice but to apprehend Calas immediately. Please give me as many additional soldiers as you can, Captain. We'll storm the polar chambers immediately."

"I already have platoons on standby. Let me notify my security chief to order them down to the planet." Amirah stalked to the door of the council chambers and gave Tolemy the news, then she marched back. "In an hour, you'll have an additional one thousand soldiers to launch your attack. I do hope that will be enough, Governor."

Ornias stiffened. "What does that mean?"

"It's very simple. If you are unable to capture Calas in the specified amount of time, my orders are to relieve you of command and transport you back to Palaia Station for disciplinary action."

Ornias laughed incredulously. "That's ludicrous. Who

else could the Magistrates possibly find to govern this barren wilderness?

"Military appointments are not my jurisdiction, Governor. *You have two days.* I'll expect a report from you by 08:00 day after tomorrow."

She turned in crisp military fashion and headed for the door. Stopping before the exit patch, she turned halfway around and leveled a scorching examination. "Please don't force me to tran you, Governor."

Ornias lifted a brow. A slow hot smile came to his face. "Don't threaten me, Captain. I've contacts in places you've never even *heard* of."

"Undoubtedly. Gutter hooligans are not my jurisdiction either."

She hit the patch and exited into the hallway without waiting for his response. Her security team fell into line behind, matching her quick steps. Horner tried to dart in front of her, but she gruffly commanded, "It won't be necessary for you to escort us, Sergeant. We know the way."

Horner grumbled resentfully, but obediently stopped. Amirah marched around the corner and down the hall of the Gothic arches. Two rods of sunlight shot through the stained glass windows, lancing the plush carpets like golden spears.

The farther she strode the more angry she grew. Ornias' comment about his "contacts" rankled—for it was certainly true. Under her breath, Amirah cursed, "Goddamned pompous sonofabitch."

"What happened?" Tolemy inquired. "We couldn't hear a thing from the hall."

Richert fell farther behind. She glimpsed him staring in awe at the gorgeous magenta peaks of the arches.

"Let's just say the governor is as anxious as we are to complete this mission."

"He'd better be—if he wants his neural pathways to stay in their current configuration."

Amirah laughed softly, shaking her head. Her thoughts drifted to what she'd have to do if Ornias couldn't comply. She and Woloc had planned in detail how to attack the polar chambers utilizing a cannon barrage. But a large number of innocent civilians would die that way. She got so wrapped up in the alternate strategies that she barely heard the gasp from behind. A scream rang out, then four almost simultaneous shots.

Amirah spun, her hand grabbing for her pistol, but she'd barely made it halfway around when a man hit her and knocked her to the floor. A hard, muscular arm closed around her throat and she felt the barrel of a pistol press into her back.

"Don't make any sudden moves, Captain," a cool male voice instructed. "I've no intention of killing you unless you give me no choice. Understand?"

"Yes."

A black-clad arm reached around and relieved her of her pistol. Silently and expertly, he patted her down and removed the knife from her thigh sheath. Then her attacker jerked her to her feet and hurriedly shoved her into a dark narrow passageway that jutted off from the main corridor. She staggered, sucking in a stunned breath when she saw Tolemy and Richert. They sprawled twenty feet apart, dead. Two unknown men lay toppled over her team. Wide crimson pools of blood spread around them like fiery lakes.

"Hurry, Captain," her attacker whispered in her ear. "We haven't all day."

He rushed her so quickly, she stumbled over her own feet and fell against the pink marble wall. In a flash, she knew this might be her only chance to save her own life. She lifted her leg and whirled around, leveling an expert kick—

Her assailant immediately countered, thrusting up with his arm to tumble her backward. She rolled and scrambled to her knees. He leveled his pistol, a hard glow in his blue-violet eyes. Brown hair clung in damp wisps to his forehead. Very handsome, he had a straight nose, thin lips, and a heavy dark brown beard that shrouded most of his face. He bent forward slightly, panting, grimacing in pain—and she noticed the stain of blood permeating his black jumpsuit over his left thigh. Vague recognition tugged at her memories. Where had she seen him before?

"Easy, Captain," he commanded softly. "Get up, *slowly*."

Amirah complied, pushing to her feet.

"Clasp your hands behind your head," he ordered. "And march."

Cautiously she turned and headed down the narrow hall. When they came to an intersection of corridors, he ordered, "Stop. Get down on your hands and knees. There, see that block of marble? Good, shove it to the right."

Amirah pushed hard, putting all of her strength into moving the huge block. It made a gravelly scritching noise as it opened. A black hole looked back at her, foul odors drifting out.

"Inside, Captain. Quickly. And don't get any ideas. I'll be right behind you. And my aim is damned accurate at five feet."

She quietly slithered in on her belly and felt him follow. Water splashed beneath her hands. Her panting echoed from the walls as though magnified by some hidden source. She slid back against a cold stone wall and watched a tiny blue handglobe flare in his palm. It cast an azure gleam over the plain gray walls of the subterranean passageway. Without taking his eyes from her, he reached out and pushed the block closed.

Vile odors rose from the gurgling water. She glared, realizing he'd forced her into a sewer channel. Undoubtedly dozens of them laced the rocks beneath the palace. And where did they come out? Had Governor Ornias—fool that he was—failed to post guards on each exit tube? Or had this skilled assassin killed them all?

Using his pistol barrel, he motioned for her to crawl. "Hurry, Captain, straight ahead. We've a long way to go to get to the abandoned chambers of the legendary Desert Fathers."

Amirah scrambled through the malodorous filth. Only the dim bluish light of his globe lit the pathway. She glanced back at her assailant constantly, waiting for him to drop his guard. If he'd just take his eyes off her for a split second, she could take him.

For fifteen minutes, they splashed through the channel, then he suddenly shoved her back against the wall and ordered, "Stay very still."

Amirah malevolently eyed his pistol. His aim never wavered as he backed away a few feet and levered another block open a crack. Wan sunlight penetrated the dark, falling in a gray rectangle over his torn black battlesuit. She could see the nasty wound on his thigh, the blood pulsing with his heartbeat. He briefly touched the com unit on his belt, then regripped his pistol with both hands. *Who had he signaled?*

"All right, Captain, outside," he ordered. "Easy."

She crawled forward and ducked beneath the stone, emerging into a misty rain shower. He followed, instantly grabbing her purple sleeve and jerking her back against the palace wall. Her head cracked the stones painfully.

He twined his fingers in her purple sleeve and forced her in front of him, as though using her as a shield. "See that cleft in the ridge ahead?" he demanded. "The one that cuts the sandstone like a lightning zigzag?"

"Affirmative."

"When I count to three, you're going to run with all your heart for it. Clear?"

"Yes."

"One, two, three . . ."

She lunged forward. His racing steps echoed behind her, squishing in the sand as they darted into the cleft. Slamming an arm across her back, he forced her facedown into the soft wet grains that filled the crevice. She felt his pistol pressing into the base of her skull.

"Damn you!" she spat. "Who are you? What do you want?"

"Right now, I want you to pretend you're on an Academy training mission. You're going to have to slither on your stomach for about half a mile—and you're going to have to do it fast. Crawl straight ahead and slip down into that crevice that opens off to your left. It'll be just barely big enough to give you the space to maneuver. Now, hurry, I suspect Governor Ornias or some of his henchmen have already found the prizes we so untidily left."

Like a snake into a gopher hole, she slid into the crevice and scrambled forward. Once every five or ten minutes, he instructed her to turn down a new passageway. They seemed to get narrower and narrower, until finally she couldn't breathe. The terrors of claustrophobia clamped ghostly fingers around her throat.

"How much longer?" she asked. "I can't stand much more of this."

"That makes two of us. Confined spaces remind me too much of cages—though I'll take solid rock to light bars any day. We're almost there. Just a few more minutes."

She forced her weary body forward. Light bars? He'd been captured before? By whom? When? *Why did he seem so familiar?* Even his voice struck a chord of recognition in her memories.

After another fifteen minutes of dust clogging her lungs and making her cough and grunt, the hole widened. She poked her head out into a diamond-shaped corridor—and saw her chance. Before her captor could utter any further instructions, Amirah kicked out with all her strength, slamming him in the shoulders. He cried out angrily as she dove into the corridor and ran blindly through the darkness. The faint glow of his handglobe spurted suddenly and she could see the dark tunnel that veered sharply off to the right. She lunged for it.

"Captain!" his angry voice echoed. She heard his booted feet pounding the stone as he pursued her.

Then the faint light of the globe died and the sounds stopped. A sullen stillness gripped the halls.

Only her hand against the cold stone told her when she'd reached another intersection. Heedlessly, Amirah rounded the corner, then slid silently down the new corridor, trying not to pant, trying not to make any sound at all. For what seemed an eternity, she moved a step at a time, listening intently to the blackness. She edged through an eerie shroud of invisible webs that netted her face and throat. She scratched at them, pulling them away from her eyes. No more passageways converged with hers and she grew panicky. *He saw the first turn you took, Amirah. He may have heard the second. He's probably in this corridor with you.*

She halted.

A breath of cool wind permeated the tunnel. Amirah trained her ears on the hush. Nothing. *Where are you? What do you want?* She allowed herself a deep breath. None of it made any sense! Why capture her? Was this some Gamant plot designed to keep Mikael Calas safe? Did they plan an exchange?

She leaned her head back against the wall and exhaled a long quiet breath. Her survival depended upon seeing her pursuer before he saw her—or, in this pitch blackness, on hearing him. Even after twelve years, she could hear the voice of her clandestine operations professor at Academy, Jones Yura, lecturing, "Assume the bastards are waiting for you to make the first move. Don't. Frustrate the enemy. Make them impatient. Force them to get hasty. Then. . . ."

Before she'd even finished the thought, she heard a slight, almost inaudible whisper of breathing—or was it just the constant wind that swept this corridor? It was a sizzle, a hissing . . . like a . . .

Serpent! Dark. Dark! Narrow corridor. Smoke. She smelled smoke!

"Amirah!" her grandmother shouted and wept. "Don't let them do this to you! Remember who you are! Don't be a pawn for them!"

Movement. Vague, insidious.

The Devouring Creature of Darkness crept closer, like a huge black shadow, blacker than the darkness itself.

Amirah screamed hoarsely and ran through the stone passageways like a madwoman. Where was her grandmother? What was happening. Grandmama was always with her when the serpent—

"Captain!" a man yelled. "Don't run!"

"Leave me alone!" she shrieked back and ran with all her might.

Before she could find a new corridor to race down, something heavy struck her from behind. *Dark! So dark!* Amirah clawed and fought as though she'd forgotten all the hand-to-hand skills the military had taught her.

"Stop it, Captain!" the man said. "Don't make me kill you! Our plan works whether you're dead or not! Stop this!"

The cold barrel of a pistol jammed into her stomach. She blinked the stinging sweat out of her eyes.

And realized where she was. Horeb.

Her security team had been ambushed. She'd been kidnapped. Kidnapped . . . *yes, forced out of her home and bodily dragged to . . . to—where? What had she been thinking?* Her hands twitched uncontrollably.

A deep voice whispered to her from the ebony quiet. *"Don't move, Captain Jossel."*

A blue handglobe flared and she stared into the eyes

of her captor. He had her pinned to the stone floor, his
pistol now pointed at her face. His blue-violet eyes sparkled demonically in the dimness as he pushed off of her
and got to his feet unsteadily.

He clutched his wounded leg with one hand and gestured with his gun with the other. "Come on, Amirah,
walk. We've lost a lot of time. You don't mind if I call
you Amirah, do you? I'll call you Amirah anyway, so
you may as well not object."

Weakly, she got to her feet. "And what shall I call
you?"

"Nothing for the moment. Head down this corridor
and take a left at the first intersection."

She walked, watching the blue light of his handglobe
reflect with a violet sheen from the red walls. The sounds
of their breathing and footsteps reverberated down the
tunnel. A dry spicy scent clung to the stone, like cinna-
mon mixed with cloves. Dead ends often met her when
she turned the wrong way. At other times, rockslides and
broken doors thrust up like sharp fangs from massive
holes in the floors. Had someone in the distant past tried
to blast a way out of these chambers? Why? To escape
some terror within or an enemy penetrating from without?

"Turn right at the next intersection," her captor
instructed.

She did and halted abruptly. A three-pronged corridor
met her searching gaze. "Which way now?"

He eased cautiously forward and pushed her aside so
he could see her dilemma. Backing a few steps away
from her, he braced a shoulder against the wall and
pulled a map from his breast pocket. He scrutinized it a
few moments, eyes only leaving her for an instant at a
time. He finally breathed a subvocal curse, then whispered to himself, "Goddamn it, Baruch. What the hell's
this?"

"Baruch?" she spat repugnantly. "I should have known
you were part of his filthy band of murderers."

"Really? What tipped you off? Just my charm or something else?"

"Your charm was enough. *Who the hell are you!*"

His handsome, dirt-streaked face fell into stern lines.
"We're friends," he said carefully. "You can call me
Cole."

They stared at each other for a timeless moment, then her heart did a triple step, building to a violent crescendo where it slammed against her ribs. *Cole. . . ? Light bars?* He'd been captured during the Pegasan invasion of Old Earth. Captured and imprisoned in a six-foot-square light cage for several months. They'd tortured him endlessly. When Magisterial forces had defeated the invaders, and released him, he'd crawled out of his cage, his sanity not quite intact, they'd said. The Magistrates had promoted him, lauding his "superior valor and indomitable will." Machinelike, her mind replayed scenes from the training holos in Academy—powerful scenes of a tall, brown-haired officer dressed in a crisp purple uniform lecturing before a tactics class, younger, more serious. No beard had obscured his face then, no lines had etched his forehead.

Softly, she murmured, *"Cole Tahn."*

He pinned her with piercing blue-violet eyes. The impact of that gaze struck her like a spectral fist in the dark. Her scalp prickled.

"Good work, Amirah. I'm sure you and I will have a lot to talk about over the next few days. We can start by reminiscing about Magisterial strategy regarding Gamant affairs."

She wiped her sweaty forehead on her sleeve. "I doubt it."

He reached down and unclipped her com unit from her belt and handed it to her. "Before we can began any pleasant dialogues, you're going to need to tran your ship. Tell them you're being held hostage."

She watched him remove his own unit and set it for a peculiar form of scramble. Insuring what? That the *Sargonid* wouldn't be able to get a fix on the origin point of her garbled message? *Or was he altering the transmission's focal frequency to make it appear that it came from somewhere else?*

"No. I don't think I will, Tahn."

He took a step back and leaned heavily against the wall, taking a series of deep breaths. Their fight in the corridor had undoubtedly torn holy hell out of his wound. He was hurting.

After several seconds, she pressed, "If the Underground is going to attack Horeb, why do you need me? My ship will fight just as well without me."

His glare hardened until it seemed chiseled from stone. "Better, I'll wager. Now, switch on your com unit, Captain. Your message is simple: *I'm being held hostage by terrorist forces. I'll contact you later regarding the ransom.* Understand?"

She refused. Contemputously, she quipped, "I'm the stubborn type. I guess you'll just have to kill me."

"I'd rather not if you don't mind." He thrust out his hand, demanding her com unit back—and emphasized his request by clicking off the safety on his pistol. She tossed the unit at him and prepared to lunge. . . .

But he stood defiantly still and let it fly by; it landed with a clatter on the rocky floor. His pistol aim hadn't wavered. "You're really not very likable, are you, Amirah?"

He walked away and knelt in front of her com unit to key in an unknown sequence. Lazily, he commented, "I'd have preferred your ship to have an authentic voice print, but this will have to do."

She watched him send the message and anger and futility rose with a fiery vengeance. She shook her fists at him. "This is ridiculous! My second in command will search every—"

"Yes, Jason Woloc," Tahn rapped his knuckles irritably on his knee. "I'm sure he'll want to blow up half the goddamned sector to get you back. At least, I certainly hope so."

Amirah shifted uneasily. His voice had a knowing quality, as though he suspected she and Jason had a secret relationship. "What the hell are you implying, Tahn?"

"Woloc loves you, doesn't he? He's requested transfer four times in the past two years. I admired the wording of his last attempt, 'Captain Jossel is an officer of superior ability; however, I am unable to concentrate under her command.' "

Amirah squelched the urge to shout. "How do you—"

"You're a very attractive woman, Captain." Tahn's eyes took on a hard questioning gleam. "I'll bet serving on the *Sargonid* is a living hell for him. Sitting in front of you every day, close enough to touch you and not being able to must tear him apart. Why didn't you give him the transfer, Amirah?

She slowly leaned back against the wall and wet her dry lips. She'd asked herself the same thing a thousand times.

CHAPTER 14

Sybil concentrated on the faint consciousness that washed the edges of her mind. Strong antiseptic scents clogged her nostrils—mixed with smells of infection and the coppery sting of fresh blood. People moaned around her. Over her head, a hazy flicker of flame danced, warm, caressing, weaving through her disconnected thoughts like a golden thread.

"What happened?" a vaguely familiar voice asked. *Doctor Plutonius.*

Mikael responded tautly. "Our attack went bad. They ambushed us and followed us back to the chambers. Reinforcements came in today."

Sybil tried to call out to Mikael, but her voice had grown cold and still. The doctor's scalpel glittered brightly in the candlelight. Hazy reflections sparkled through the darkness of the polar chambers.

"Yosef?" she heard Mikael murmur. "Those books you found. If anything happens to me, get them to Baruch. I don't know how you'll do it, but—"

"We'll do it," Yosef assured. Through her wavering vision, Sybil could see him. His round face and bald freckled scalp gleamed in the candlelight.

Sybil felt a skeletonlike hand squeeze her forearm and she heard Ari whisper, "Don't let them get you, Sybil. We all need you and love you."

Weakly, she tried to reach out to him, but her hand barely moved. Ari reached down and gripped her fingers tightly, before kissing her on the forehead. "Save your strength," he murmured lovingly.

"Please go now, Uncle Yosef," Mikael demanded frantically. "We may not have much time."

From the concave blue shadows that swallowed her, Sybil watched Mikael's face drop closer again. She focused on him, on the black wisps of hair that clung wetly to his cheeks. Then the doctor's movements drew her attention away. Plutonius bent over her, dropping his hands out of sight near her chest.

"If I save the child, I may lose Sybil, Mikael. I hope you're ready for that."

"Save my wife, doctor. I don't yet love the child."

"*You* may not love this child," Plutonius informed gruffly, "but your followers do, Mikael. They're calling this baby the Mashiah and singing his praises at this very moment. A crowd of five hundred have gathered in the far chambers. They're praying for the *child's* survival."

"I don't care!" Mikael said with hushed violence. Sybil saw the quick flash of a gray pistol barrel. "You'll save my wife, doctor!"

"Yes," Plutonius sighed tiredly. "Yes, of course, I will."

The pains inside Sybil grew to a staggering weight. Stunning in their endurance. Then everything in the world went stark and quiet. Cold seeped from every pore of her body, setting her to shivering.

Vague, dark voices exchanged whispers. The shrill whine of rifle fire penetrated the mists that enveloped her, coming from far away. Flames shot up in Sybil's mind. Her flesh rebelled, writhing. She groaned.

"Blast!" the doctor hissed. "This is the hardest Governor Ornias has ever hit us and we've barely enough anesthesia to keep the injured from getting up and walking away from the operating tables! I can't afford to give her anymore."

Explosions rang through the labyrinth, shuddering the table beneath Sybil, but she didn't know if they were real or imagined.

"Dear God. They're getting closer."

"Shut up!" Mikael ordered. "Keep working."

In a blur of dusty black battlesuit, Sybil saw Mikael kneel at her bedside. He smelled pungently of sweat and battle. Scents she'd known since childhood and found comforting. Lovingly, he murmured, "Sybil, listen to me. Can you hear me! You're hit in the lung. Doctor Plutonius is going to try and save it. If he can't, he'll remove it. I know you can feel the instruments inside you. But you have to be very still."

Instruments clinked together. The room spun nauseatingly, getting darker, darker, and she suddenly felt as though she'd stepped inside of herself. She could see her own heart contracting and expanding, see the shredded pinkish-white of her lung clotted with dark blood. In the midst of it all, a shimmering blade moved as though alive. Her mind went dark. Sightless. As blind as God. Consciousness seemed to flutter around her, aware of itself, but of nothing else. She struggled to pull it back inside her head. Terrible. So terrible to feel herself separating.

"Hold on, Sybil. *Don't leave me!* I need you so much. I love you . . . I love you. . . ."

Mikael repeated the words over and over. Murky feelings of his touch against her cheek and hair penetrated her haze, and delicately she felt her mind tie to her body again, a whisper of warm sensation. Mikael gripped her hand tightly.

"The baby's coming."

A hard pounding of military boots echoed.

"Get out of here!" Plutonius said. "Save yourself, Mikael. The people need you. For God's sake, go! Get away from here. I—I'm sure I can leave these lungs a moment to pull your son. He's so tiny, he shouldn't—"

"No!" Mikael ordered sternly. He set the candle down on the floor. "I'm staying. Keep working. Tell me what to do and I'll bring my child into the world myself."

Plutonius gave Mikael soft hurried instructions.

Pain. So much pain. Waves and waves of it. Black chaos possessed Sybil's soul, timeless and absolute, like a diamond clawed demon scratching out the eyes of everything bright.

Shouts. People running. Piercing bursts of rifle fire. . . .

"Oh, God. Blessed God!" Plutonius shrieked. "They're just outside the door! They're here!"

A tiny angry wail stirred the darkness. "So's my son, Doctor. He's here, Sybil. He's here and he's beautiful."

She opened her eyes and could make out a hazy image of Mikael holding the baby tightly against his breast. Cautiously, he walked forward and held the bloodstreaked child up for her to see. "See? Here he is Sybil. Nathan. Nathan *buzina kaddisha.* My son. Our son."

In a blinding flash, the *Mea Shearim* around Mikael's

neck flared to life. Plutonius inhaled sharply and backed away.

Through her pain-dusted vision, Sybil saw the *Mea's* cerulean halo spread like wildfire, engulfing her son in an azure ocean. Nathan's pale face shone as though reflecting the shadows of a towering ice cliff.

And for a moment, for the briefest of moments, Nathan's unfocused eyes seemed to clear. He stared wide-eyed at the *Mea* as he reached a tiny bloody hand for it, seeking, seeking.

"Oh!" Plutonius whispered hoarsely. "Look at the boy's face. *Look at his face!* It glows as though afire. It's true! He is the blessed redeemer!" Plutonius fell to his knees and prostrated himself before the child.

"Get up," Mikael ordered. "Finish operating on Sybil."

"No, no, she's not important anymore. The boy . . ."

Sybil saw only a black whir of Mikael's boot. Plutonius tumbled across the floor and cried out. Mikael leveled his pulse pistol at the doctor's head. Sybil blinked tiredly. So tired. Mikael cut a strange figure. In one hand, he clutched new life. In the other, he fingered the trigger of death. Nathan waved his blood-streaked fists hostilely, peeping his upset.

"Get up, Doctor!"

"Don't shoot. I'm getting up. See me? I'm—"

Shouted commands. More rifle fire. The shudder of mortars. A roar of dozens of men shouting.

"Calas! Halt!" a brutal voice shouted. "Move and you're dead!"

Mikael barely responded. He slowly extended his pistol and dropped it to the floor. It clattered away. Slowly, he turned halfway round and held up his son. "I'm not going anywhere, Sergeant. Get up, Plutonius. Damn you, get up quickly!"

The words swirled around Sybil, deep, cool. A breath of wind touched the candle flame on the floor. It flickered wildly. But in her wavering vision she saw something else—something black and huge, like a gigantic living shadow. It loomed over her and she caught the horrifying scents of decaying vegetation and stale darkness. She tried to sit up, to run. But she couldn't move. "Mikael?" she mouthed—but no sound came.

The Darkness moved. But not toward Sybil. It went

to envelop her son, folding around Nathan like a black demon from the depths of oblivion.

A ragged scream pierced the room and she saw Mikael jerk backward suddenly, away from the Darkness. He fell onto her bed.

Rifle barrels, dozens of them, appeared over her.

CHAPTER 15

Rachel Eloel sat beneath a pomegranate tree on the sandy shores of Lake Kinnaret, her arms wrapped around her drawn up knees. Across the shimmering water, a tan ridge rose like an impenetrable wall. A dust devil whirled along the heights. She tipped her chin up to the warm, olive-scented breeze. Her beautiful heart-shaped face and huge black eyes shone so perfectly in the sunlight, they seemed fashioned from painted alabaster. Strands of long black hair danced before her eyes. She brushed them away with a numb hand. Anger and agony twined into an incapacitating poison in her chest.

Sybil, my baby, forgive me.

She sat for a long while in silence, listening to the sounds of this peaceful place: birds cawed high overhead, animals bleated and neighed, laughter crept out of the confines of the city a quarter mile away.

Why did she always ache? She laughed bitterly at the question. All she'd ever done was ache. No, she chastised herself, not always. She still woke on some nights, feeling content and happy, and reached out for her husband Shadrach. Her body remembered his warmth against hers and constantly craved it—and for those brief moments, her mind forgot that he'd been killed by Ornias in the temple holocaust a dozen years and an eternity ago.

Rachel scooped a handful of sand and let it trickle through her fingers, forming a peak on the shadow-dappled ground. From the moment Shadrach had been killed and she and Sybil had run away from Seir, the capital city of Horeb, seeking refuge from the Mashiah, she'd been drowning in suffering. Jeremiel had come to Horeb and organized the war against the Mashiah. Rachel had been sent back to Adom's palace to gain his confidence so that she could murder him when Jeremiel's first attack came. And she had . . . murdered him. When Rachel closed her eyes, she could still see Adom gazing up at her, long blond hair tumbling around his broad shoulders, blood on his lips, a gaping knife wound in his chest. In his eyes she saw all the boyish innocence, the tenderness and love, that had ravaged her heart, and his last words rang like claps of thunder in her soul: *"It's . . . all right, Rachel. I know you just wanted to end the suffering . . . too."*

Smothering rage and the bile of disillusionment struck her. What had all that agony had been for? Had it helped her when she stood before the throne of God and stared in terror at the black whirlwind across the River of Fire? Had it given her courage or knowledge when she'd challenged His infinite wisdom by hurling accusations that he wasn't good or powerful or all knowing?

No. Epagael had thrown her out of heaven. She'd tumbled through the utter darkness of the void to find herself in the ice cave near the polar chambers—freezing to death. *And then Aktariel came and saved me.* She remembered the way his golden light had flickered like diamonds from the ice-encrusted walls. He'd taken her in his arms and warmed her hypothermia-ravaged body with his own, stroking her hair. *"Sleep, Rachel. . . . Don't worry. I won't let anyone hurt you. Not even God."*

Involuntarily, she shivered. She felt so alone and frightened. Even the whisper of the warm wind through the tree over her head seemed to sizzle malevolently. After going down to Tikkun with Cole Tahn and witnessing the horrors of Block 10—the babies piled into trash bins, children shot down ruthlessly by laughing guards, men and women working like hollow-eyed draft animals, their bodies as emaciated as skeletons—she wondered if she would ever be able to find goodness anywhere in this universe again?

Horrifying scenes from the past flitted through her mind like windblown sparks from a campfire. Deep in her heart, she longed to see this universe happy, triumphant, the way God had promised her forebears it would be if they were good and just, and followed His path of Truth.

But that would never be. She'd searched and searched

the multiple universes, struggling to find a way of *making* it happen.

And she thought maybe she had . . . though she prayed Aktariel hadn't guessed yet. She had too many details left to take care of. If he discovered her actions, he'd certainly stop her.

From the corner of her eye, she caught sight of a tall man walking toward her. Brown hair flowed down over the shoulders of his coarse camel-colored robe. His long beard was buffeted in the wind, pressing back around his throat. He had a straight nose and large dark eyes. He took his time, meandering along the shore, tenderly touching every goat he passed, as though he feared for their peace of mind.

The sight leavened her spirits a little. As he neared, he gave her a small, apologetic smile and sat down on the sand beside her, gazing out across the water to where birds soared and dove, their wings flashing golden in the sun.

"Ha Notzri," Rachel said plaintively, "why do you follow me?"

He shrugged and retrieved a piece of driftwood, fiddling with it in his broad sun-bronzed hands that radiated more power in their gentle movements than their owner understood. His eyes seemed to grow in size, highlighting the length of his nose and the fullness of his lips. "I'm sorry."

"Do you wait for me?"

He nodded, a little ashamed. "Yes." He pointed toward a grove of trees that dotted the banks of the glimmering lake. "Two days a week, I sit there, and I watch this spot, hoping you'll come back."

Rachel shook her head. She'd tried to avoid him, coming at night, coming before dawn, not coming at all. But this place with its calm peacefulness drew her like a thirsty beast to water. She couldn't stay away—but neither could she risk talking to him. She'd seen his fate in other universes and knew how dangerous he was. She'd often wondered what would have happened to him in her own universe if he'd had a friend worth the name. Not the pathetic, cowardly fools whose bravest moment had been to wring their hands and howl when he'd died. In this universe, he was nothing more than a carefree fisher-

man, living most of his life in the tiny boats that rocked
across the lake. *But he could be more if she encouraged
and guided him.* . . . And the very fabric of the multiple
universes would heave and shred beneath the weight of
what he would feel compelled to do.

"Why do you wait for me, Ha Notzri?"

He gazed at her through dark eyes that glowed with a
haunted light. "Because, I–I think I need you." He
tapped a hand against his chest. "I feel it in my heart.
Where do you come from, Rachel?"

"Far away," she said coolly and gathered her white
robe in her hands, starting to rise to leave.

He reached out and put a hand on her shoulder, stopping her. "Please, Rachel, I beg you, talk to me. Just
for a few minutes. That's all."

"I can't, Ha Notzri. It's bad for both of us. I've told
you that before."

A forlorn look came over his face—so forlorn it made
Rachel waver in her decision. What would a few minutes
hurt, if she talked to him only about unimportant things?
If she let him do most of the talking and just listened?

He seemed to sense her softening resolve. He smiled
radiantly. "You'll stay? I'm so glad. Every time we
speak, my heart soars. You've taught me so much,
Rachel. I've been thinking for a year now about what
you said about evil."

Foreboding chilled her spine. She sat down hard in the
sand. To him, it would have seemed a year since he'd
seen her last. To her, it was a month, and no months.
Eternity couldn't be marked. *But she'd said nothing!* She
was always excruciatingly careful not to discuss anything
that might change the course of the future in this universe. Rachel glared at him, noting the simple dignity of
his face, the breadth of his shoulders. "What did I say?
Tell me?"

"You don't recall?" He smiled teasingly, but it faded
at the utterly serious look on her face. He dropped his
gaze.

"Tell me."

He hurried to answer, words pouring out in a rush.
"We were talking about silly things, the water system
and how far the women had to carry buckets, about when
the dates ripened. I brought you a flower, a little blue

thing that grows in the deserts. You laughed, but you had tears in your eyes." He hesitantly reached out and touched her hand where it rested in the sand, caressing her fingers. Had it been any other man, she might have pulled away, but she knew his intentions were the same as with the goats, to soothe a pain he didn't quite grasp, but somehow felt just the same. "I asked you why beauty made you cry."

He paused and Rachel's heart pounded. *What? What did I say?* "And?"

"You said—" He gave her a shy smile. "—I memorized the words, 'Do you think the beauty of a wildflower pales when your heart is broken, when your child is crying from hunger? Do you think despair clouds every sunset?' I told you that I thought he who suffered in the flesh had ceased to sin and therefore suffering was salvation."

Rachel heaved a sigh of relief. She hadn't told him anything, not really. The wind flapped the white sleeves of her long robe. The scents of the lake, fish, and moist grass salved her weary spirit.

"That's not quite right, Ha Notzri," she bravely ventured. "You see, I remember, too. You used the Romans as an example. You said, 'Perhaps redemption can only be bought with a price of blood, but we should thank God that it can be bought at all.' "

"Did I?" He grinned sheepishly. Brown locks danced over his face. He pulled his long hair forward and knotted it, then tucked it into the back of his tan robe. "That sounds more profound than I recall. I only remember your words. Mine seemed unimportant by comparison."

For an instant, his heavily-lidded eyes seemed deep dark holes. Rachel studied the way his jaw had clenched. He dropped his gaze to examine the twig of driftwood.

"Why did my words about the flower bother you, Ha Notzri?"

"Because," he said, and his voice sounded pained, unsure. "It has a bearing on God, doesn't it? I mean, if you believe that despair clouds the beauty of every sunset, then you think suffering is more prevalent than happiness. And you have to ask why God made it so."

The hollowness in Rachel's breast seemed to boom. She said nothing.

He pressed, "Why do you think He did?"

"You tell me."

He shifted, rolling to his side to gaze up at her eagerly. Whitecaps had formed on the lake behind him, undulating across the surface like swirls of frosting. "I took a trip. I went down to Khirbet Qumran, to talk to the mystics there. They told me something I thought you'd be interested in. I've been studying it so I could tell you."

"What?"

Eagerly, he slid closer to her. "They're a strange group, but they have beliefs that I think make sense. For example, do you know that they believe the creator God is wicked? And that, therefore, everything He made is wicked."

He gazed up at her with childlike innocence, reminding her of Adom. Her soul ached. His eyes seemed less haunted, less filled with hidden anguish at times like this.

"But if they think the Creator is wicked, whom do they worship?"

"This is the part I really wanted to tell you about," he smiled excitedly and dropped his piece of driftwood, standing it up like a pillar in the sand. "They believe there is a higher God. One who's composed—if that's the right word—of immeasurable Light, pure and indescribable, perfect and imperishable."

"They believe the Creator and the Treasury of Light are different? That is interesting."

His eyes widened. "You call it the Treasury. . . ."

Ha Notzri halted, turning around quickly at the soft sound of footfalls in the sand behind them. The sweet scent of roses filled the air and Rachel closed her eyes knowingly. *His* image danced on her closed lids, beautiful, awesome.

"Hello," Ha Notzri said, a little afraid. "I see you're back again, too. Welcome, friend."

A pause ensued and Rachel could feel Aktariel's eyes boring into the back of her head. Ominously, he said, "I've been searching for Rachel. It didn't occur to me she'd be here with you—*again*. Would you excuse us, Yeshwah? I need to talk to Rachel alone."

The sound of that deep, infinitely kind voice sent a shiver through Rachel. Ha Notzri reached out and caressed her hand a last time before saying simply, "I hope to see you again, soon. Thank you for talking with me. I'll try to learn more while you're gone." Then he rose and ambled away down the shoreline, heading back to his clump of trees where he would, no doubt, keep watching them, wondering who and what they were.

"Rachel," Aktariel said reproachfully. "How many times must I tell you it's dangerous for you to—"

"You *don't* have to tell me."

She cast a glance over her shoulder. The gusting wind pressed his blue silk robe flat across his broad chest, outlining his perfect muscular body. The sight of him like this—without his magnificent glow—always made butterflies sprout wings in her stomach. He had taken to dropping his glow whenever they were together because he knew the human appearance made her more comfortable—or perhaps more *malleable.*

"Even the smallest things," he continued, "things you think are completely irrelevant, may alter enough of this past that you could—"

"*I know, Aktariel.*"

"Do you? Do you also realize that if the course of this universe changes all the others in the Void will be affected, too? Every choice Ha Notzri makes as a result of your discussions affects a billion billion alternate universes. Those changes could 'catch' like wildfire across the Void—*setting flame to the entire weave.*"

Sullenly, she picked up a small rock and threw it hard, sending it splashing into the lake. She knew the risk. "How are things in my universe?"

"Worsening every moment. Cole Tahn just captured Amirah Jossel. We haven't much time. We—"

"Is Tahn going to survive?" She turned to stare up at him.

Aktariel's mouth tightened. He smoothed the sand with the toe of his sandal. "Hard to say."

Gracefully, he walked around to stand before her. His blond curls fluttered in the breeze, highlighting the deep tan of his perfect oval face and dark brown eyes. The wind whipped his long robe around his legs until the silken fabric crackled. She held Aktariel's powerful gaze and all her miseries swelled to unbearable burdens. Rachel closed her eyes and braced her forehead against her knees.

A long silence ensued between them. She listened to
the bleating of the goats as they greeted Yeshwah, then
she turned her head to stare at the grains of sand still
trickling to fill the impression left by his tall body.

"Rachel, you only torture yourself by coming here. I
wish I'd never shown you this place."

She rubbed her forehead against her knees, concentrating on the softness of her white robe while she gathered the courage to ask the question that gnawed her
soul like a ravening beast. "I assume that Nathan's been
born?"

Aktariel came forward and eased down beside her.
"Yes."

Rachel's emotions welled up with a violence that startled her. A sob caught in her throat. "*I can't do it, Aktariel. Do you hear me? I can't! She's* my daughter. *He's*
my grandson."

He casually smoothed his blue silk sleeve and evaded
her eyes. The gesture condemned as surely as the crack
of a judge's gavel. When he looked back up, his brown
eyes glimmered. "It's up to you," he responded gently.
"You know the stakes. You know that individual lives
are meaningless in the overall scheme of things."

"Yes, but . . . Sybil's been hurt so much. Can't we
just—"

"No. I wish we could. We haven't the luxury of ending
the suffering for a select few in that universe. It's either
all or nothing."

"The thought breaks my heart."

"Interfering with the patterns of either Sybil's or
Nathan's destiny could kill our plans. To change what
Epagael has wrought, we must move precisely, one step
at a time, or all our work will have been for naught. This
is a house of cards we're building, Rachel. Any wind
could knock it down for good. But I'm sorry that it has
to be this way."

He tenderly brushed the long waves of black hair that
fell down Rachel's back. She pulled away, sliding across
the sand to brace her back against the cool trunk of the
pomegranate tree. Aktariel dropped his hand and dug
his fingers into the sand, but his eyes stayed on her—measuring, evaluating. From her new angle, his blue robe

seemed almost to blend with the background of the cerulean sky.

"Aktariel, I have a question for you."

"What is it?"

"It's about Epagael and the Treasury of Light."

"Epagael *is* the Treasury of Light." His tanned brow furrowed. "At least, insofar as the Treasury concerns us."

"What does that mean? Maybe they're two sides of the same coin, different but one. Ha Notzri just told me that the mystics at Qumran—"

"Oh, I see." He leaned back on his elbows and stared out across the lake. The herd of goats frolicked near the shore, baaing as they playfully chased each other. "That's the other problem with you coming here. Let's get this straight, Rachel. Yeshwah may have been one of the fathers of the Gamant people in your universe, but he's not in this one. He knows nothing of the nature of the Void. The teachings of this time period are fascinating, I'll grant that. The Qumran mystics, especially, have touched the rind, but they have no understanding of the true foundation of reality."

"What do you mean, they've touched the rind?"

"The *reshimu,* the residue of light left in the universe when God withdrew to spawn the void of creation. Some mystics, very diligent ones, can transcend the bonds of their own ego consciousnesses and melt into the background radiation. Those rare individuals sense the patterns in the maze of chaos. But what they touch isn't the Treasury, Rachel, it's a filmy counterfeit."

Rachel frowned up at the red pomegranates clinging to the branches over her head. They looked ostentatiously scarlet against the jade green leaves. "I'm not so sure anymore that you're right," she challenged. "Do you know I've wondered if perhaps you and Epagael aren't just a strange alien species? In my jumps to alternate universes I've seen . . ."

Aktariel laughed softly. "Aliens? That's actually not a bad way of putting it. Especially when you're describing God. He is alien to everything in this universe."

In a fluid move, he stretched out on his back and laced his fingers behind his head. Above, hawks glided unhindered on the warm air currents. "Let's talk about it.

After this past week, I could use a good intellectual discussion."

Rachel studied him suspiciously. Usually when he agreed to such conversations it was because he'd been planning them all along. "In the beginning all that existed was Pure Light, correct?"

"Correct."

"The Light withdrew a part of Itself to spawn the dark Void. But in the Void a residue of Light remained, the *reshimu*—like the perfume that continues to scent the bottle long after the contents have been emptied."

"Pretty much. It would be better to say that *Epagael* withdrew a part of Himself. Go on."

"Epagael shot a minute part of Himself into the Void and creation began."

"Not exactly," he said. His brows lowered thoughtfully. "Creation did not begin until the vessels of light burst. You remember why they burst?"

"They were tainted by the *reshimu*."

"Exactly." He retrieved Yeshwah's driftwood twig from the sand and gestured with it. "Without the fullness of God, the light that had been trapped in the Void soured, became a shadowy remnant of the original substance. When Epagael threw the vessels filled with Pure Light into the Void, they picked up the taint and burst forth, scattering through the Void in a massive flood."

"And developed a consciousness of their own?"

"Oh, yes. The consciousness of this universe—because it's denied the fullness of reality—is very different from God's consciousness. It's chaotic and violent. That's why it fascinates Epagael so."

"And we experience that chaos as suffering."

"We do."

"Adom told me once that for every moment the creation continued to exist, chaos sent more tendrils twining through the body of the universe like a malignancy. He said that not even entropy could kill suffering."

Aktariel's gaze went hollow as though he again saw Adom's innocent face and boyish smile. Rachel dropped a finger to the sand and drew a spiral. *Circles within circles. That's the way the fabric of the Void works.*

"The culmination of entropy," Aktariel responded, "will only clear that universe for another infusion of divine light. And because the *reshimu* will have grown even more rancid by the end of time, the fresh vessels of light will burst immediately. I fear greatly that the new beings condemned to live in such a foul universe will suffer even more terribly than we do now."

"More?"

Aktariel inhaled a breath and let it out slowly. "Yes. We must force Epagael to reabsorb all those tormented consciousnesses, so that he can actually *feel* the suffering and understand how terrible it is."

"Does He have the compassion necessary to understand?" When she'd stood face-to-face with Him, she'd seen no signs of such merciful tendencies.

Aktariel bowed his head. "I believe that He does. And perhaps His personality will grow and change—like a child's does when faced with the horrors of life."

Sounds from the lake drifted up to them: an ass braying; a man cursing; laughter from the boat filled with fishermen that rocked lazily along the edge of the azure water.

"You sound as though you mean God will become someone else."

He looked at her through eyes filled with so much sorrow that she felt wounded by that gaze. "God is God—regardless of who He is, Rachel."

A curiously empty sensation invaded her. "You mean God's personality is irrelevant to–to His station or . . . what?"

He cocked his head and gave her a bare smile. "To His essence. The essence of Pure Light stays the same, it simply tastes different."

"Has that ever happened? Has Epagael's personality ever metamorphosed completely?"

Aktariel blinked contemplatively. "If I answer that for you, will you answer a question for me?"

Her pulse started to throb. "What?"

"Rachel, whatever else you believe," he said sincerely, "I'm sure you understand that I'm fighting for the salvation of trillions. You're not sabotaging my efforts by playing God in other universes . . . *are you?*"

"I don't know what you're talking about."

He pursed his lips and vented a disbelieving sigh. "Don't lie to me, Rachel. I can't bear it. I know you've seen Nathan's future and are deeply hurt by it, but you must understand—"

"I *do* understand. Don't preach to me. You know I hate it."

He turned away and studied the way the sunlight glinted from the lake. "Yes, forgive me. But we're so close to the end. You don't have to play on my side— I've never demanded that of you. *But I beg you, Rachel, please don't work against me! I don't have the time to follow you around correcting what you've interfered with!*"

Rachel angrily got to her feet and pulled her *Mea* from beneath her robe. She lifted her hand to the beautiful crystalline skies and a black whirlwind spun out of the air, gouging a hole in the tawny hillside. The warm winds of eternity whipped the tree branches.

"Who was God before He became Epagael, Aktariel? I want to *know*."

But before he could answer, she stepped through and vanished into the darkness. The Void spun closed behind her. And she ran with all her heart.

CHAPTER 16

Carey inhaled a shallow breath. Voices echoed around the small white room, harsh and angry. The drug permeating her body magnified the doctors' emotional tones until each alien note clashed like an out of tune piano. She shifted slightly, straining against the EM restraints to find a more comfortable position. Her right leg had gone numb. How long had she been under the probes this time? Ten hours? Fifteen? The helmet still hugged her skull, molding to her head like a cool silver burial shroud. A hollow, aching sensation filled her, as though the probes had drowned the fire in her spirit. Yet she kept fighting, diverting them. Every time they touched a dangerous memory, she quenched it by deliberately saturating her mind with so much hate and rage that the neurotransmitter environment obscured the memory.

Mundus shook wormy strands of hair away from his blue balloon face and irritably slapped a palm against his side. "I say we bring in one of her companions and use the tandem technique. What was that boy's name? The one with the leg injuries?"

Axio gasped. "Are you sure you want *that* one? He's dangerous! We've captured hundreds of the Gamants who are tearing the satellites around Palaia apart. Why not use one of them?"

Carey opened her eyes a slit and gazed at Axio, Mundus' assistant, the anesthesiologist. He clenched three of his hands nervously. Both doctors looked overwrought, sweat shining over their blue faces. Had Slothen threatened them with punishment if they didn't discover Cole's whereabouts in the next few days? The intensity of their efforts certainly suggested it.

Carey's gaze drifted over the room. They'd moved things around—part of the psychological technique to

142 Kathleen M. O'Neal

keep her disoriented. The long table with instruments
now sat to her left beside a desk strewn with crystal
sheets. She faced the door and the rectangular windows
which framed it. Six physicians in white coats stared in,
watching her through blank clinical eyes. Five were
Giclasian. One was human, a roly-poly little man with
white hair, a pointed beard, and ears that stuck out from
his head like glued-on shells; he peered in warily, occasionally scribbling in a notebook.

"Let's check with Doctor Creighton," Mundus insisted.
He moved to the window and hit the communications
switch. "Creighton?" Mundus called. The human looked
up from his notes. "Since Lieutenant Halloway is being
so recalcitrant, we were thinking it might be wise to bring
one of her companions in and subject him to intensive
probing to encourage the lieutenant's cooperation. Does
that suggestion meet with your approval?"

A companion? Who else had survived the Kiskanu
attack?

"Yes," Creighton noted distastefully. "The *Sargonid*
should be circling Horeb right now. If Jossel can't capture Calas, no one can. The sooner we discover the
whereabouts of Tahn, the sooner we'll all be able to
return to important work. Proceed."

Carey's auburn brows drew down over her nose. They
wanted Cole and Mikael? Why? They had nothing in
common—except things in the past. Cole had been the
one to pick Mikael up off Kayan just before the *Hoyer*
had scorched the planet. Carey recoiled from memories
of how worried and gut-sick Cole had been at the sight
of the terrified little boy in the landing bay. He'd taken
care of Mikael as though he were his own son. But what
did they have in common now?

Mundus turned and commandingly waved a hand at
Axio. "Go, retrieve the one with the leg injuries."

"But that one's dangerous, Mundus. He punched
Technician Hio in the stomach!"

Carey smiled. Pride for the unknown comrade filled
her. She and Cole had taken great pains to train every
Underground soldier in the techniques of resisting mind
probes. Anger served as one of the best, discomfiting
Giclasian doctors and drenching the human brain in
adrenaline, which hindered the progress of the probes.

Axio continued in a taut voice, "Are you sure we can't choose the woman with the respiratory—"

"I said bring the man! Difficult subjects like Halloway usually calm down once they share their comrades' memories. *Bring him.*"

Axio bowed at the waist and left the room hurriedly. The door closed with a soft clack. Carey ground her teeth. The tandem technique involved witnessing each other's memories? What would that accomplish that ordinary individual probing couldn't? She fixed Mundus with a hate-filled glower. He wandered around the room, picking up instruments and slamming them down, kicking at table legs and frowning menacingly. Finally, he strode over and reached behind her chair for something she couldn't see. He glared as he held out the *Mea* in his blue hand.

"What is this, Lieutenant?" He lowered it to swing like a hypnotic pendulum over her chin. The glow had vanished. She blinked wearily at the gray lusterless ball.

"A necklace . . . idiot."

His ruby red mouth quirked contemptuously. "We've had it analyzed, Lieutenant. For a simple 'necklace' it has some curious properties. For example, the electromagnetic shells which compose the globe itself seem to spiral down into nothingness, like a vortex focusing on infinity. Were you aware of that?"

"No," she lied. She and Jeremiel had discussed the object extensively. "What does that . . . mean?"

"I'm asking you."

"I don't know."

Jeremiel suspected it was a rotating hole. The theory supported all the ancient stories of the Gamant zaddiks who claimed they'd traveled through the Mea *to the throne of God.* Rotating black holes were different from other types in that the singularity at the center was not a point but a ring. Hypothetically, if you approached the ring at an oblique angle, thereby avoiding infinitely curved space-time, you could pass straight through into another universe. *Heaven, perhaps.*

"Look, Lieutenant," Mundus growled testily. "We only have a limited amount of time to gain the information we need from you. If you don't start cooperating, you'll simply be eliminated. Do you understand what that means?"

Carey laughed grimly. The fools. She'd already been dead once. Did they think threats of murder could frighten her? *Imbeciles. Goddamned buffoons.* She laughed harder.

The door snicked back and Carey opened one eye to see Axio push Josh Samuals into the room on an antigrav gurney. Propped up on his elbows, Samuals looked worse than she did. His blond hair stuck to his round face in wet curls. Sweat beaded across his hooked nose. Heavy bandages enveloped both of his legs. He glanced at Carey and their eyes met. He looked as frightened as a scalded cat. *Goddamn, they've been putting you through the wringer, too, haven't they, Josh?*

Mundus strode arrogantly across the room and lowered the probe helmet onto Samuals' head. A brief shudder rippled through Josh's body. He leaned back weakly against the gurney and stared at the ceiling.

From the corner of her eye, Carey glimpsed Creighton standing up. He leaned forward, studying the room pensively. His purple uniform bulged around his fat little body.

"Mundus?" Creighton called. "Switch the screens, so they can view each other's memories."

Axio complied, turning the luminescent three by five foot white screen near Samuals' first, so that Carey had a clear view of it. Then he walked across the room and hit the button to turn Carey's. She tried not to breathe while he stooped over her. Axio smelled oddly from the chemicals he dealt with, like a dead carcass putrefying beneath a searing sun.

"All right, Creighton, they're ready," Mundus informed.

The fat man waved a hand negligently. "Good, please stimulate the cerebellum at the same time you're probing areas 1178 of the amygdala and 213 of the hippocampus."

Mundus' lavender eyes gleamed in anticipation as he strode across the room. He smiled at Carey. If she'd been able, she would have reached up and slapped that cocky smile off his face. In the harsh light of the lustreglobes, his blue skin had an ethereal silver cast.

Mundus reached out to the helmet control console. She heard two clicks. A second later, chemicals tingled in her veins and the probes began moving, biting into her brain like tiny stingers. Carey heard Josh moan softly. Images flickered to life on the screen over his head. She watched in reluctant fascination. Like a faulty hand-operated projector, the scenes moved erratically, sometimes in slow motion, other times in fast. *Good. Fight, Josh. Don't let them get anything coherent.*

When the probes stimulated her cerebellum, the three-lobed structure at the back of the human brain, Carey felt ill, motion sick. The room whirled. The doctors' faces slid at her from the edge of her vision, hideous and bug-eyed. She gripped her chair arms to fight the rising nausea. A wealth of images tumbled through her mind: playing with her brother Tim when she was nine; hiding in the tall green grass while her parents argued in the house; practicing hand-to-hand combat aboard the *Hoyer*.

Her eyelids fluttered. She saw Josh's memories flashing on the screen. They mixed eerily with her own, twining, taking her thoughts down certain lines through association. Josh's eyes were riveted to the screen over her head, as though caught in a strange absurdist film. Their memories seemed to lead each other along. When Josh thought of family, she did, too. When she forced her thoughts to meaningless days of lying in the sun outside of Academy, his thoughts reflected the same train. It dawned blindingly what they were doing and Carey squeezed her eyes closed, refusing to look at Josh's screen.

"Open your eyes, Lieutenant," Mundus ordered. "Shall I force you? You know I can. The last time the anesthesia made you sick for days. Remember? *Open your eyes.*"

She didn't respond.

A brief flurry of activity clattered around the room, metal scraping against petrolon, hushed voices raging irritably. Finally she heard Mundus whisper, "Forget her. We'll concentrate on the other one. He's already given us a great deal."

A hot flood of adrenaline flushed her system. What did Mundus mean? Had Josh broken?

She felt the probes stimulating memories of Jeremiel and she made a deep-throated sound and drove her memories elsewhere . . . *elsewhere*! To Academy. Yes, yes, Academy and listening to boring lectures about metabolic mapping of the neuro systems of the amygdala. She concentrated on Professor Vol's face, his thin gray hair, his mouth. . . .

"Is that the bridge of the *Zilpah*?" Mundus asked Josh in an insidiously kind voice.

"N–no!" Samuals stuttered.

Carey jerked her eyes open, staring at the screen which portrayed the *Zilpah* so clearly. Jeremiel sat in the command chair, a serious look on his handsome face as he studied the forward monitor; he caressed his reddish-blond beard thoughtfully. Josh's memories moved about the bridge, focusing on Carey where she sat at the nav console just in front of Jeremiel. She had her head cocked, a brow lifted.

Moran system. Two months ago. They'd been hiding amid the gas clouds, trying to get a fix. . . .

"Mundus," Creighton commanded from the observation room. "Freeze those scenes. What star system is that?"

Panic ravaged Carey's brain. Was the fleet still there? "Don't, Josh! *Don't!*" What else had Samuals told them? He hadn't revealed any data about the Horeb mission, had he?

Samuals moaned and thrashed on his gurney. She saw his arms flailing against the EM restraints. From her skewed perspective, they twisted like eels out of water.

"Easy, Lieutenant Samuals. Everything's all right. We've already got that scene logged. There's nothing you can do about it now. Relax, relax," Mundus soothed, but Josh continued to thrash wildly; his voice rose to an anguished scream, and he swung aimlessly at Mundus.

"I warned you he was dangerous," Axio hissed.

Mundus angrily flicked a hand and the anesthesiologist ran around behind Josh and hurriedly administered more drugs. In seconds, Samuals went limp, his wide blue eyes staring blankly at the ceiling.

Carey stopped breathing. He looked so pale, so quiet. One of his hands twitched for a few seconds, then fell still.

"There, Lieutenant, very good. Are you feeling better?" Mundus asked.

No answer.

Mundus frowned. "Lieutenant Samuals? Are you feeling better?"

Axio's blue face slackened at the same time that his lavender eyes went wide. "No, he can't be . . . I was in a hurry to put him under, but . . ." He raced from behind his anesthesiology console and to the general med panel. His white coat flared behind him like the wings of a giant bat.

"Oh, it can't be! I didn't give him that much!"

Mundus spun, aghast, and shouted, "Get a revitalization team in here. Quickly!"

Carey stared at Josh. A serene, almost thankful expression adorned his round face—as though in the last moments, he knew something had gone wrong—and the knowledge eased his torment.

She lay quietly, watching Creighton. He angrily tapped the end of his laser pen against the window. The soft ticking sound reminded Carey of an old style clock.

Unconsciously, she used it to tally the seconds. On the count of twenty, four Giclasian technicians burst into the room. They shoved a multilegged revitalization unit in front of them. Positioning it over Josh's limp body, their hands flew over the control console, powering it up.

Carey closed her eyes. *Please, Epagael, let him die. Be merciful.*

She listened to Mundus' despotic instructions. Feet pounded ominously around the room, instruments clashing with resounding clangs. Each moment passed as though millennia. And finally, she heard Josh gasp. A flurry of relieved cries sprang from the group of doctors. Someone laughed giddily.

And Carey's soul withered to nothingness. Josh started to cry, a soft suffocating sound.

Carey swiveled her head to stare at the spiderlike revitalization machine that held Samuals in its grasp. It would be there from now on, she realized, until Slothen had the information he sought.

The Magistrates weren't going to let them die.

CHAPTER 17

Jeremiel sat alone in his cabin, staring at the crystal sheet that lay atop the black table. He lifted his cold cup of taza and drank it absently.

> *Magisterial flotilla in Moran and Tonopah systems. Am monitoring movements. Will report more when possible.*
>> *Captain Simeon Lakish*

He prodded the sheet with his finger. A hollow ache pounded in his stomach. Lakish was the commander of a freighter that formed part of the Underground's clandestine forces branch. His ship, the *Derekh*, performed average trade transactions while keeping an eye on Magisterial movements throughout the Orion arm of the galaxy.

The government's invasion of both the Moran and Tonopah systems could mean only one thing:

"An officer has broken."

He massaged his brow, trying to suppress the terror and hope that swelled like storm clouds inside him. Any captive from the Kiskanu attack, regardless of rank, could have revealed the Underground fleet's former location in the Moran system, but only Samuals or Carey would have known about the secret operations in the Tonopah system where the Underground actively sowed dissent among the Magisterially sanctioned planetary councils.

He sat back in his chair. The lustreglobe above his table threw a flickering light over his black battlesuit and his stern face, accentuating the red in his blond beard. Cole's bottle of rye whiskey still sat on the table, untouched since their last meeting in this cabin. In the

148

background, Billie Holiday sang "Good Morning, Heartache." The pain lacing Holliday's beautiful lilting voice stabbed clear through him.

Carey had given him that disk for their first wedding anniversary. Knowing his passion for Billie's music, she'd searched every port where they'd docked, until she'd found this rare piece. He remembered the joyous smile on her face when he'd opened the present.

He shoved his taza cup around the table. "Doesn't mean Carey's alive," he softly chided himself. "It was more likely Samuals."

His looked around the room. Everywhere he saw Carey: her books, her music disks, the ivory gauze sleep shirt that still lay beside their bed. He hadn't been able to pick it up. He doubted he ever would.

His heart had gone on defensive mode, shutting itself off, aching numbly, as though torn from his body but not completely severed. In his mind, she wasn't dead. Her presence haunted him every moment, as though she sat next to him always, during strategy sessions, when he had dinner, and especially when he was alone in their cabin. *She was there.* That part of her that he kept safe inside him, still advised, still argued vehemently over elements in his plans that she disagreed with, still gazed at him with all the love and respect they shared. He found himself reaching for her in the night and when he touched only cool sheet, he pretended it was her hand and clutched it tightly. He'd even caught himself talking to her aloud, discussing her objections to his plans, parrying with every other possibility he could conceive of.

In his mind, she wasn't dead.

Only his heart cried out that she was, and he should get a hold on himself and learn to live with the truth.

But he'd isolated his heart. Just now it couldn't claw at him the way it would after the Horeb battle . . . and for the rest of his life.

He rubbed his arms to warm them. He'd been deliberately neglecting the thermostat. The ship automatically shut down the temperatures at night, but he relished the cold. It worked on him like a slap, keeping him alert—sane.

Tipping his chair back on two legs, he braced his head against the white wall and squinted at the dark overhead panels. "How are you doing, Cole?" If Tahn didn't seize Jossel on her initial visit, he never would. And *if* he managed that, then the hard part would begin.

The waiting tore at his gut. They'd anxiously been keeping track of the five cruisers circling Horeb. None of them showed the slightest apprehension. They'd adopted no special formations, completed no practice maneuvers, nothing. Why not? Surely, if an officer from the Kiskanu attack had broken under the probes, Palaia would have warned the Horebian cruisers about the impending Underground assault. Wouldn't they? If not, *why not?* If he knew about the Underground's plans, Slothen should have already dispatched twenty more battle cruisers to Horeb. Had the aging Magistrate deployed his cruisers so widely that he couldn't get them to Horeb quickly?

Jeremiel couldn't depend on that.

Methodically, he ran his thumb around the smooth edge of the black tabletop. He ground his teeth, mind clicking off the questions that had begun to mount. Too damned many things didn't make sense.

First, for years Jeremiel had wondered why Slothen hadn't simply authorized a major battle cruiser attack to destroy Mikael and Sybil's forces from space. Mikael and Sybil had been bold and brilliant in several of their attacks on Ornias' forces—but to initiate them, they'd had to leave the safety of the polar chambers. And each and every cruiser in orbit would have known precisely when, where, and how many people Gamants were taking to ambush Ornias' soldiers.

Why had Slothen always refused to allow his cruiser captains to give such data to the military governor of the planet? Ornias was an idiot, true, but not incompetent. Unquestionably, he would have used the information with stunning results, quelling Mikael's and Sybil's operations and very likely killing both of them years ago. Did Slothen want the Calas family alive?

Second, why would Slothen send Jossel in the first place? With four cruisers already acting as "peace keepers" around the planet, why didn't the government simply send a dattran to Abitha Stein in command of the *Hammadi*? She was in charge of military activities around Horeb. Stein may not have had the glory associated with her name that Jossel did, but she had a reputation for cold efficiency that went unmatched.

No matter what Slothen intended, whether to finally authorize more government troops on Horeb or to employ cruiser firepower, Stein or *any* of the captains already on assignment around Horeb could have handled it. Barely a thousand Gamants clung to life on that barren rock—the auxiliary crew of one battle cruiser armed with mobile cannons could have laid waste to every hiding place of every Gamant on Horeb.

"What game are you playing, Slothen?"

Something deep. Ominous. Something with very high stakes.

"It's as though Slothen has been waiting for a particular event in which Jossel will play a key role—a role no one else can fill."

And Jossel seemed to have no past. He'd contacted every clandestine source available, requesting information on her early life, but all to no avail. Oh, the general overview was well-known: Born on Rusel 3. Parents killed when she was thirteen. Went to live with grandmother. Grandmother mysteriously disappeared. No traces ever found. No siblings. Father had been a government employee in the Records division. Jossel had entered Academy at the age of sixteen—very young, very brilliant. Slothen had paid personal attention to her. More so, it seemed, than to other young, brilliant cadets; The Magistrate had personally reviewed each of Jossel's test results for coursework and demanded to be present during her annual pysch evaluations to *"monitor her progress."* Whatever that meant.

Strange, indeed. Jeremiel knew of no other cadet who'd been singled out at such a young age and treated so specially.

"Has Slothen been currying you for a particular mission, Jossel? Against who? Gamant leaders like Mikael and Sybil? The Underground? Gamants in general? *Who?*"

Unfortunately, he had to admit that the special treatment could have simply been because the woman was indeed a magnificent commander and Slothen had apparently recognized her potential very early.

Jeremiel's room com buzzed. He reached up to the

unit over his table and hit the access patch. "Baruch here."

"Commander?" Shira Gaza, his new second in command, called. "We've just received a Clandestine One message from Captain Kopal. Do you want me to send it through on the aura or pipe—"

"Pipe it through, Shira. Baruch out."

He got up and hurried across the room to his desk com. Clandestine One meant that Rudy had logged and sent the message on a one-burst narrow beam for Jeremiel's eyes only. Rudy's taut face formed. Unease pulsed through Jeremiel as he listened:

"Rivka checked in—just before her ship was destroyed by the *Hammadi*," Rudy informed gravely. "Tahn's got Jossel. I suggest we initiate Operation Kawwanah. Kopal out."

The image faded and Jeremiel braced both hands on the table. Grief for the loss of Leso and her crew made his breathing shallow. *But Cole had Jossel!* He hit the visual button on the unit and watched as the bridge formed. Shira swung around in her chair. Her short ebony locks gleamed in the bright glare. A tiny woman, she had a triangular face, a pug nose, and blazing brown eyes.

"Shira," he ordered. "Clandestine One back to Kopal and Wells simultaneously. Ready?"

"Aye, Commander. Go."

He checked the wall chronometer over his bed and gazed confidently into the com. "Good morning, Rudy and Merle. As of 0:500 hours, Operation Kawwannah is in effect. Please line out and await further instructions. Baruch out."

Jeremiel's eyes landed on Carey's gauze sleep shirt. He remembered the morning she'd taken it off and tossed it beside the bed—just like she did every morning.

He reached down to caress the shirt. "Live for me, Carey. *Live!*"

CHAPTER 18

Cole suppressed the groan that pressed against his teeth. The pain from his wound had grown to staggering proportions. Though a clean flesh wound, the torn muscles burned and throbbed with jackhammer intensity. At least, the bleeding had stopped—unless he moved suddenly, which he valiantly tried not to do.

He slowly made his way around the broad red cavern, opening boxes and pulling out clothing, food, and ammunition. Just as Jeremiel had said, this chamber contained everything he'd need to survive in comfort for the next several days. The faint scent of spices clung to the air, as though centuries of holiday feasting had occurred here. The rounded chamber stretched fifty feet over his head and measured at least seventy in diameter. A long wooden table surrounded by twenty chairs filled the center of the room. Dusty crystal goblets and plates adorned the woven place mats. He'd lit a fire in the hearth on the far wall when they'd first arrived, hours ago. The flames crackled warmly, the light the fire generated flickering across Amirah Jossel's strained face. She sat on the faded ocher rug before the fire, knees drawn up, arms grasped around them. Anger reflected with startling potency in her gorgeous turquoise eyes.

Cole gingerly knelt and ripped open another box, continuing to watch her surreptitiously. She'd brushed her long blond hair behind her ears, revealing the smooth line of her jaw. His gaze lingered on the fire-dyed curves of her body. A beautiful woman indeed. The holo prints Jeremiel had obtained had been pale in comparison to the real thing.

Cole brushed away the box's fluffy packing material. A sigh of relief escaped his lips when he saw the contents. A dozen dusty bottles of wine and several containers of food concentrates lined the bottom. *Anesthesia, thank God.* He piled food into the crook of his left arm and grabbed a bottle of wine. As he limped past the table, he grabbed two crystal goblets.

"How about some dinner?" he asked as he knelt on the opposite end of the ocher rug, five feet away from her.

She didn't move, but the tiny lines around her eyes tightened. EM restraints bound her ankles, but he'd left her hands free.

"I know you're hungry," he remarked. "It's been ten hours since our last meal."

Silence.

He twisted the cork out of the bottle and tried to blow the dust from the goblets. When that didn't work, he used the cuff of his sleeve. Filling both glasses, he carefully placed one within her reach, halfway between them. The dancing firelight flickered in the maroon liquid—and in Amirah's hair. She looked almost frail, like a willowy porcelain doll.

He tugged his gaze away, annoyed by the sensations her beauty stirred in him. Powerful sensations he thought he'd forgotten. He hadn't been alone with a woman—except Carey—in years. Oh, he'd tried dating some of the women in the Underground, but the cultural and historical differences between them seemed to be as divisive as a brick wall. Maybe that's why he'd grown to love Carey so much. She was the only woman in the world he could really talk to anymore. His stomach went queasy. *Don't think about her, you fool. What are you trying to do, kick your own guts out?*

Sitting cross-legged, he took a long drink of the rich, earthy claret, letting it caress his tongue. "Not bad. Try it."

Jossel lifted a brow and glared.

"Feeling pretty bad, huh?" he asked. "Well, starving won't help. You need to keep your strength up, so you can waylay me when I drop my guard."

He picked up a food container and tossed it toward her. It landed beside her boots. When she didn't automatically grab for it, he threw another one. This time, as he intended, it hit her in the thigh.

She gave him a heartlessly unflattering look, picked up the bottle and threw it back—*hard*. It slammed his arm.

He grunted and sat down with an unpleasant jolt. "All right, starve. See if I care."

From this angle, he could make out the faint splotches of freckles that sprinkled her button nose. Her lips pressed tightly together in anger. Defiantly, she edged across the floor and retrieved the bottle of concentrate, commenting, "You're right. If I'm going to kill you, I have to keep my strength."

He grinned. "I knew you'd agree. Try the wine. You'll like it."

"How do you know what I'll like?" She reached for the goblet, jerking it back. Wine spilled down the sides of the glass, trickling over her thin white fingers.

He suppressed a smile and opened one of the food containers. Waving it under his nose, he tilted his head uncertainly. "But I suspect you won't like this." He sipped the contents. The sour lemonlike flavor made his mouth pucker, but it tasted refreshing. He took a long drink. "It's not as bad as I thought. Ever had Sculptorian limes?"

"Once."

"Did you like them?"

"No." She pulled off the lid on her container and gingerly sipped. A shudder went through her. "Just as I thought. It's terrible."

He shoved to his feet and walked back to the crate, searching through it for other selections. Finding three different types of food concentrates, he carried them back and knelt a short distance in front of her, setting them down. "Maybe one of these will suit you better."

Backing away, he circled wide and went back to his own dinner. Suspiciously, she reached for the bottles he'd brought and opened one. Sniffing it, she eyed him dubiously, then tasted it.

"How is it?"

"Good." She glowered. "Thank you."

Cole grinned. The authoritative hate in that look undoubtedly made most people scream and run. He liked it. "What's it taste like?"

"Oh, a little like . . ." Her magnificent turquoise eyes softened with fond memories. "Giclasian apple cider."

"It's been a long time since I've had Giclasian cider. But I remember how delightful it was." His heart ached. He and Maggie Zander used to sit beneath the trees outside of Academy and share bottles while they laughed. He missed Maggie. Sometimes, in his dreams, they still loved each other. Thank God for dreams. Scenes of her death battled to rise—*locks of blonde hair twining through the bars of the light cage . . . her extended hand.* . . . Cole forced the images away by gulping his lemon-lime concentrate.

They finished their dinners in silence, glancing warily at each other. Cole tossed away his fourth bottle of concentrate and refilled his wine goblet. Lifting the bottle, he asked, "Can I refill yours?"

"Do." Cautiously, she leaned forward, meeting him halfway.

He complied. For the briefest of moments, their eyes met over the bottle—close, intense.

Cole slowly backed up. "You have an impressive record," he commented, making conversation. "What battle were you involved in to win the Naassene Cross? That's quite an accomplishment. They don't give that medal to just anybody. I never won one."

"Actually," she said in a strangely resentful voice, "you did—through a lot of other people."

"How's that?"

She shrugged. "I used your tactics in the Kirinyi battle. That's how we won."

He looked surprised. The fact that someone continued to study those tactics disks he'd so painstakingly put together made him feel odd. "Well, I'm glad to hear they're still good for something."

She frowned at her wine, finishing half the glass before she spoke again. "You're brilliant, Cole Tahn. Didn't you know they still taught your tactics in Academy?"

"No."

"Of course, they do. Good God, the Marco and Antares Minor maneuvers are classics. When I was trapped in the Jaron system, outnumbered ten to one, the Marco—"

"Wait a minute," he objected. "I *lost* the Antares Minor battle!"

She nodded heartily. "I know. You made a stupid error."

"What error?" he thundered indignantly. "I didn't make *any* goddamned errors!"

Jossel looked him over from head to toe and stretched out on her side on the ragged rug. "Well, forgive me, your highness, but I'm compelled to point out that you damned well did!"

He blinked incredulously and poured himself another glass of wine. His pain had lessened slightly. He could actually take deep breaths now without bracing himself in case he fainted. As he started to set the bottle down, she extended her glass. He refilled it.

"All right," he agreed. "I'm game. Let's discuss the details. I had Baruch surrounded, boxed tight in the asteroid belt around Antares Minor, outnumbered five to one. We took potshots at each other for three days while we negotiated his 'surrender.' " He lifted a finger and pointed it sternly. "I had no way of knowing that he was secretly evacuating his crews. He used blasted inertialess pods to get his people out of the four ships he stationed as decoys. Then he—"

"Then," she enunciated sharply and pointed a finger back, stabbing it like a dagger at his heart. "He set the matter/antimatter engines of those ships on time delay for merge and ran the rest of his fleet for the light vault like 'bats out of hell,' as you put it in your report. You shot three of the bats down before you realized the trap." Her eyes glittered triumphantly. "The entire asteroid belt, including fifteen Magisterial vessels vanished in the explosions."

He felt the same sinking feeling of defeat twist in his gut that he had seventeen years ago. "Right. No one sane can predict what Baruch will do. *You* should know that by now. The man's a lunatic." He gulped his wine.

Amirah casually watched him over the rim of her glass. He could see the speculative smile that curled her lips. "You were brilliant," she praised. "Flawless in your calculations and positioning of vessels. Stunning in the way you orchestrated the battle, keeping Baruch boxed and unable to effectively fight back."

"So?" he growled. "What did I do wrong?"

As she lifted her wine to take another sip, her hand swayed. Tipsy? He grinned at her.

She grinned back, but it was a predatory expression. "Mass readings."

"What?"

"You didn't take any. You were always magnificent in your tactics, but you were an idiot when the situation demanded subtle appraisals of your enemy's strategy." She flicked a hand nonchalantly. "But that's your career in a nutshell, isn't it?"

"Wait just a goddamned—"

"If you'd grasped anything about Baruch, you'd have known he'd pull something like that—and you'd have scanned each Underground vessel to begin with, taken periodic readings during the course of the battle, and guessed that he was evacuating the crews from those ships."

"The hell I would have!" he roared. "Mass varies every time you fire a shot! You can't assess—"

"I've done it," she said smugly. She leaned forward, getting closer to him. Her blonde waves brushed the rug, glimmering like strands of the purest gold in the wavering firelight. "*It works.* That much mass shows."

He glared thoughtfully at her, trying not to notice the way her new position accentuated the curves of her body. Silently, he ran a few mathematical calculations through his head, just to see. When the figures started appearing, a twinge of unease rose.

"Uh-huh." She nodded as though reading his mind. "See?"

"It *might,*" he granted, roughly swirling the wine in his glass.

She laughed softly and when he looked up at her, he saw the glint of warmth in her eyes. "Don't be so arrogant. I'm right and you know it."

"Me—arrogant? Don't *you* be so smug," he accused, reluctantly laughing with her as he shook his head. "You've had years to study that maneuver. I only had days."

"I know." Her smile faded into a somber look. Quietly, she said, "I've always wondered what you were really like. The great Cole Tahn. A legend. Brilliant. Handsome. And a traitor."

"Or a patriot. Depends on how you look at it."

"A patriot?" she scoffed. "Patriots don't betray the people who depend on them." Her face went stony—devoid of all emotion. His gut responded by roiling defensively. "Do you know what happened to the crew you abandoned on Tikkun? They trusted you, Tahn."

His shoulder muscles crawled. "No. What happened to them?"

"The Magistrates probed them until their minds were completely gone, then they administered euthanasia. Mercifully, quickly—but they killed your crew. You condemned those people to death. *You did.*"

She uttered the accusation in her professional "captain's" voice, in control, just reporting—but when she abruptly rolled over onto her stomach and began fiddling with the torn cuff of her purple sleeve, he could see her utter disdain for him. The firelight painted her strained face with a wash like thick amber resin.

"Disappointed in the legend?" he asked.

"Yes. All my life, I've believed you were innocent." She tapped her chest with a stiff finger. "*I* have defended you repeatedly against people who charged you'd gone over to the other side. Evidence of what a fool I am."

He finished his wine, but the liquor had little effect on the wrenching ache that throbbed in his chest and completely drowned out the pain of his wound. A dozen faces of officers he'd respected flashed across his mental screen. Rich Macey, Carlene Millhyser. In his memories, he heard their voices, their laughter, could still see the love and trust in their eyes when they'd spoken to him. Good officers. The best soldiers in the fleet. Dead. "Do you know what the Magistrates were doing on Tikkun, Amirah?"

"Neurophysiological experiments on Gamant dissidents. They were researching—"

"They were murdering, *murdering* men, women, and children. Innocent civilians! I saw the bodies of hundreds of dead babies thrown into trash bins. I *witnessed* the ruthless murder of children!" His voice had risen to a violent crescendo as his memories replayed scenes of horror. . . . *Dawn. A line of people standing before a ditch: naked, pitifully starved, hands bound behind their backs. Old women and little girls. A series of crisply uniformed soldiers stood on the opposite side of the ditch, rifles aimed . . . violet slashes of light, whimpers, the red soil running with blood. . . .*

Cole's gaze impaled. "I turned against a government that betrayed me, Amirah. I thought I was fighting for righteousness, damn it! Not the Magistrates' right to mercilessly torture human beings because of their cultural beliefs."

Rage seethed on her face. "You turned against your crew!"

He stifled the urge to shout at her. In a very soft voice, he said, "Amirah, I put those people down on the planet to keep them safe. I did it specifically so they wouldn't be tainted by my actions. I didn't think the Magistrates would take it out on them, not if I—"

"You betrayed them."

"No," he defended. "I did everything I could to make sure they wouldn't suffer because of my treason. I'd been involved in the *Annum* incident—which I'm sure you're aware of—where the Magistrates also probed the crew to death. I put the *Hoyer* crew down to protect them from that. I just . . . just didn't know the twists and turns the future would take. I betrayed a brutal *inhuman* government—not my crew."

"It's the same thing!"

He ruthlessly slammed a fist into the rug. Red dust puffed in the firelight. "And you called *me* an idiot. What are you, some sort of empty-headed fanatic about the government?"

Her cheeks vibrated with the grinding of her teeth. "You know as well as I do that the government and the people are inextricably—"

"No, they're not! A man can disown a political movement without disowning the people who compose it, Amirah."

"No." She shook her head vehemently. "If he betrays one, he betrays both."

Cole forced his agitated nerves to calm, and kept his voice steady. "Indeed? If the Magistrates ordered you to kill your crew, Amirah . . . would you?"

She made a disgusted sound. "They wouldn't. And what does that have to do—"

"*Wouldn't they?* If your crew were composed of

Gamants, Amirah? They might. Yet Gamants are techni-
cally citizens of the government, too. Would you obey
that order?"

She blinked suddenly, as though he'd slapped her.
"No," she whispered.

"Really? So, there are times when betraying your government is good. Is that right? When the Magistrates
give you an unjust order, *it's your duty to the* people *to
disobey it, correct?*"

A bruised expression came over her face. "Let's talk
about something else. I—I was wrong . . . when I said
you couldn't betray one without betraying the other."

Cole suddenly felt confused. Her beautiful face had
taken on a taut, haunted look that he didn't understand.
What nerve had he touched that wounded her so deeply?
But he had no ardor to push the discussion; it made him
sick to his stomach. "All right, Amirah. We've explored
my past. Let's discuss yours. Tell me why you refused to
grant Jason Woloc the transfer he requested? And don't
tell me you're unaware of his feelings for you; I can see
it on your face."

She toyed with her empty glass, moving it erratically
over the faded geometric designs in the rug. The fire
crackled, spitting suddenly. In the burst of flames, Cole
saw his shadow blend with Amirah's on the far wall.
Sparks whirled out of the hearth to flit over their heads.

"What do you know about Lieutenant Woloc?" she
asked sharply.

"Not much. His official record—he's quite an officer.
You should be very proud of him."

"What would make you think he has feelings—"

"Oh, for heavens sake, Amirah." He waved an arm
for emphasis. "I know crew psychology. Any officer who
requests as many transfers as he has is hurting. He's trying to escape a situation where he thinks he's failing himself, his duty, or his captain. And the wording of his
requests . . ." He cocked his head knowingly. "Those
were written just for you, you know? His way of telling
you his feelings without making any demands, his way of
pleading with you to let him go before he embarrassed
either of you."

Her facial muscles tensed. "People get over—"

"No, they don't. You're not that naive. Unless you

were trying to fool yourself? Were you? Did you want to keep him around to bolster your own ego?"

Her breast heaved with impotent rage and the look she fixed on him made him shift to guard his vitals. "I wouldn't do that to him. I like Jason Woloc."

"But you don't love him."

"That's none of your business, Tahn."

"You're a curious one, Captain. I don't understand you. You don't love him, but you can't let him go. Why the hell not? Can't you admit to yourself that you love him? Too proud? Afraid he's going to try and dominate you on the bridge? *What?*"

She turned away to glare at the fire shadows crawling over the hearth walls and Cole grimaced dourly at himself. Why did he have to challenge her so ruthlessly on this subject? What was he doing? Punishing her for feelings about her second in command that he couldn't come to grips with himself? *She's wrong, you're not an idiot. You're a bastard.*

"Tahn," she said tautly, "is your strategy to use Jason's feelings for me against me? To kill him and my ship?"

He met and held her gaze. "If I can."

She tried to lift her glass but clumsily knocked it over. It thudded dully on the rug. Carefully, she regripped it. Her anguish was all too visibly revealed on her face.

Cole pushed to his feet and walked stiffly away to the opposite side of the room, where he slumped down against the red sandstone wall and folded his hands in his lap.

He watched her in silence for an hour, until she rolled into a fetal position on her side, buried her face in her dirty purple sleeve, and fell asleep. Her breathing had fallen into deep, rhythmic patterns. The glowing coals in the hearth cast ruby reflections over her wavy blonde hair which spread in a silken veil over the rug.

He vacillated, castigating himself, then decided he wouldn't wake her to put EM restraints on her hands until he decided to sleep, too. In the meantime, he thought about Jeremiel and the fleet. They'd be very close to Horeb by now—if Rivka had survived to send word that Cole had achieved the first stage of their plan. But she must have. He could almost sense Baruch's pres-

ence, like a looming tidal wave on the horizon. Silently,
he prayed those Magisterial cruisers would fall for the
trap they'd been endeavoring to set with Jossel's capture.

She moaned as though hearing his silent meanderings
and stretched out her bound legs.

Cole readjusted his shoulders against the wall and studied her. Her beautiful face had tensed, nostrils flaring
with quick breaths. Dreaming. He gingerly pressed his
fingers against his wound, testing the sensitivity. It felt
better. Maybe he could sleep. If he could find a position
that didn't. . . .

Jossel sat bolt upright. Cole jumped but didn't rise.
Her turquoise eyes had a glazed look of abject terror, as
though she were staring at demons crawling out of the
depths of the pit of darkness.

"No. Don't. . . ." she murmured and began sliding
backward as quickly as her ankle restraints would allow,
knocking over her dinner goblet and thrashing through
the mound of empty food containers.

"Amirah?" He got to his feet and walked cautiously
toward her.

She didn't seem to see him at all. She screamed and
flopped on her stomach, using her elbows to haul herself
swiftly toward the door.

Cole pulled his pistol but hadn't the slightest idea what
to do with it. She was clearly asleep. Or experiencing
something much worse. Her facial expression hinted at
the latter—too much terror, too real. Delusion? Flashback?

"No, Grandmama, no!" she wept in a child's voice,
soft, so pathetic it made Cole hurt deep down. *"Hurry!
We have to hurry! It's coming! . . . It's almost here! . . .
What does that mean, 'nahash'? I don't know what a holy
serpent is, Grandmama! What is it?"*

Her next scream sent a jolt like electricity through
Cole. He ran headlong for her. She seemed to be trying
to fend off some unseen creature. She lashed out with
her fists and feet, all the while sobbing insanely and staring wide-eyed at nothing.

He knelt ten feet from her. In a soft, unthreatening
voice, he said, "Amirah? Amirah, wake up. I don't know
where you think you are, but you're not there. You're
on Horeb. You hear me? You're on Horeb with Cole
Tahn. Wake up, Captain. Everything is all right. You're

in no danger . . . for the most part." He felt compelled
to add that last. He kept talking, trying to bring her out
of it as gently as he could.

Jossel's wrenching sobs turned into muted little girl
cries that sounded like a mewing kitten. Cole shook his
head. Had she regressed in her dreams to an earlier
time? What terrible thing had happened to her, he
wondered?

"It's all right, Amirah. Don't worry. You're not in any
immediate danger. You got that? You're twenty-nine and
doing fine. You're currently the most respected captain
in the entire Magisterial fleet." Her muscles started to
relax, long legs sagging firmly against the floor. "That's
it, Amirah. Come out of it. You're healthy and safe.
You're—"

"Hardly . . . safe, Tahn," she said weakly. She lifted
her dirty purple sleeve and wiped the tears that streaked
her face. Wet blond strands of hair had glued themselves
to her temples and chin. "Thanks . . . now get the hell
away from me."

"My, you're gracious. What was that all about?"

"Just a bad dream."

"Didn't look like a dream. It looked like a delusion.
Had it before?"

She fixed him with her old predatory gaze that let him
know she was indeed feeling better. "Why would that
concern you?"

"I just wanted to know if I should expect similar conduct in the future. And I have other reasons." *Good
ones, Captain. You just exhibited a brand of delusional
behavior that I'm very familiar with. Too damned familiar. After bad battles, my dreams still creep with things
that go bump in the night.*

Jossel sat up and wrapped her arms around her knees.
"I've had it before. Why don't you help me out and tell
me what I said."

His eyes narrowed speculatively. She was inquiring in
earnest. "You don't remember?"

"Sometimes I do. Sometimes I just get parts. Almost
always the same parts." She let out a shuddering breath
and blinked away the final tears in her eyes.

Cole judiciously lowered himself to the floor to sit
cross-legged facing her. "Well, the most interesting part

of the event was the sound of your voice. You seemed young, ten or twelve, maybe. You were talking to someone you called 'Grandmama.' You told her you didn't understand what 'nahash,' or the holy serpent was. Then you seemed to be struggling bodily with something or someone. I didn't know which. Most of the other things you said were just exclamations of fear." He frowned thoughtfully at her. "You understand any of that now that you're awake?"

She twisted her hands in her lap. "No. None of it."

"How often does this happen?"

Amirah wet her lips and in the marmalade light of the fire, Cole saw her mouth tremble. She shook her head and meditatively whispered, "Nahash, holy serpent . . . *don't be a pawn.* . . ." Her voice faded.

"Another phrase from the delusion? Do these events only hit you after battles? Or at other times?"

She lifted her head and gazed at him with a penetrating intensity. "You're not exactly my type of confidant, Tahn. You don't mind, do you?"

He lifted his hands apologetically and got to his feet. Backing away, he pulled the EM restraints from his pocket. "I don't mind. Not if you don't mind that I need to bind your wrists to your ankles and attach both to the wall by the fireplace so I can get some badly needed sleep."

Amirah sighed and awkwardly scooted on her fanny back toward the fireplace. "You force me to do some very undignified things, Tahn," she commented. She stopped by the old iron ring that extended from the wall. Fireplace utensils had undoubtedly graced it originally, but now it stood empty.

Cole grinned wryly. "Please turn around and extend your hands, Captain."

CHAPTER 19

Rachel lifted a hand to shield her eyes against the brilliant glare of the noonday sun. She stood high atop a tan ridge overlooking a bustling community of white-robed men. They scurried like ants far below, chanting sacred songs as they worked. Fear charged her body. *Playing God.* . . .

"I know what I'm doing, Aktariel."

She fought back an overwhelming sense of desperation as she gazed down upon the chanting holy men. They seemed ethereal amid the rising waves of heat that blanketed the land.

"No," she murmured to herself. "The time is wrong. Maybe later."

She lifted her hand and a black whirlwind spun out of nothingness. She slipped from one void to another, skillfully covering her trail. But her heart withered under the knowledge that no matter how good she'd become at manipulating the interfaces, she'd never be better than *he* was.

She hurried, stepping in and out, backward and forward in time, until she almost lost her way amid the multiple planes of darkness and light.

* * *

Jason Woloc sat tensely in the command chair aboard the *Sargonid,* eyes focused on the huge forward screen where Horeb rotated like a gleaming orange ball, two-thirds light, one-third dark. A medium-sized man with a round face, large hazel eyes, and a crooked nose, Woloc had closely-cropped honey blond hair. His purple uniform stretched over his muscular chest, revealing the breadth of his shoulders and the trimness of his waist.

The bridge was forebodingly quiet around him. Amirah's message had left them all teetering between rage and terror. Especially him. Twice in the past hour, he'd been on the verge of grabbing a fighter and flying hellbent to search for her himself.

He sucked in a breath and forced his mind to concentrate on the bridge. The oval room was composed of two levels and eight officers staffed the consoles. The captain's chair with its massive array of controls and com links occupied the upper level. Below him, officers sat in twos at the four niches that adorned the perimeter of the oval. Thirty screens ran in a three-hundred-and-sixty-degree ring above them. At a glance, he could determine the status of any section of the ship. He noted absently that the second level mess hall was still undergoing repairs.

"Sir?" Orah Pirke, his redheaded navigation officer, called. His high cheekbones and dimpled chin gleamed with a sheen of perspiration. "I've got Engineer Rad on com. He says they've tied down the general origin point of the captain's message."

"Put him on."

"Aye, sir. Screen four."

Jason swiveled his chair around, gazing hard at the mini-screen on the wall to his right. Rad's face formed. His flat features looked pale beneath the harsh lights of Engineering. Short black hair covered his head like a five-day stubble of beard.

"Where, Rad?"

"We've gotten mixed signals, sir. There seem to be three possible origin points: Horeb, the planet Sinai, and the asteroid belt that hovers between the tenth and eleventh planets. Sinai seems the most likely."

Jason caressed his smooth chin. A soft anxious murmuring had broken out among his bridge officers. The world of Sinai was a poisonous gas mote, holed like Swiss cheese. "Are you certain, Rad?"

The engineer nodded firmly. "Aye, sir."

"Did you get a precise fix on the point of Sinai?"

"Negative. The cracks and cavities of that ball of dust make it impossible to tell. If they're holding her deep inside, the message could have bounced a thousand times before it escaped."

"Any word on the ransom yet?"

"Negative."

His stomach felt as though a hundred scorpions were spiking him with their stinging tails. "All right, Rad. Thanks. Keep me informed. Woloc out."

He cut the link and stared speculatively at his bridge officers. "Well, what do you think?"

Pirke swung around in his chair and lifted a shoulder. His red hair gleamed with a brassy tinge. "Sinai's a perfect hiding place. If she's there, it'll take hours of probing with our best equipment to find her."

Gever Hadash, the com officer, massaged her lean weasellike face and shook her head. Long brown hair cascaded over her shoulders. "I think it's a ruse, sir." Her green eyes sparkled calculatingly. A small hand-held distortion device would have been enough to confuse the signal. How could they have gotten off Horeb?"

Jason frowned at the forward screen. His thoughts ran rampant, trying to decipher the conflicting possibilities. "What about that fighter the *Hammadi* destroyed? Could it—"

"Negative," Pirke declared, shaking his head with certainty. "It never landed."

"But," Hadash pointed out, "the fighter could have been a diversion to draw our attention away from a tiny vessel slipping away from the other side of the planet."

Jason's pulse started to race. "How could such a ship escape the scanners of five cruisers?"

"Unknown," Hadash granted with a shrug. "But if we were bunched at the time, it could have."

"Run a check on the locations of every Magisterial vessel during the two hour interim between when Governor Ornias found the bodies of Richert and Tolemy and the time we received the captain's message."

"Aye, sir." Pirke began inputting the request.

In the meantime, Hadash eyed him severely. Her lean face seemed even more feral when she concentrated like that. "You realize, of course, that it'll take two cruisers to adequately search the nooks and crannies of Sinai. Three would be better. Even then, it'll take hours."

"Approximately how many?" Jason asked.

Hadash guessed, "With two cruisers? Four or five, at least."

"And with three cruisers?"

"Maybe two hours."

He rubbed the back of his neck, trying to work out some of the knots in the muscles. A tension headache pounded behind his eyes. "Well," he began, but stopped when Pirke whirled back around in his chair, eyes narrowed. "What?"

"At approximately sixteen hundred hours, when that fighter dove between us and the *Marburg*, a narrow opening existed on the other side of the planet that aimed directly at Sinai. Gever's right. A small ship could have escaped."

Jason leaned forward pensively. "Hadash, get me Captains Williamson and Stein. Two cruisers searching Sinai will . . ."

The com aura snapped on in a golden halo around Hadash's head. Her eyes went vacant, staring at the ceiling. Jason waited. After a few seconds, she swiveled around in her chair.

"Governor Ornias requests visual with you, sir."

"Put him on. Let's get this over with."

The governor's tanned face formed, a smug smile curling his lips. His sandy hair gleamed with a saffron tinge from some hidden light source. Dressed regally in a viridian silk robe shot through with silver threads, he stood in his council chambers. Pink marble columns framed his image.

"Good evening, Lieutenant Woloc."

"Good evening, Governor. I assume you have not apprehended Calas yet?"

Ornias grimaced. "Indeed? Well, you're *wrong*. I have both Calas and his wife. Sybil Calas is severely injured. I'm sure with your superior equipment you can have her walking and healthy in two or three days. When may we transport them?"

Jason's jaw went hard. The Magistrates had ordered the *Sargonid* to return to Palaia the instant they'd apprehended Calas. The orders had a Priority One rating, which meant no other emergency could supersede them.

"Regarding Calas' wife, Governor, can you sustain her for six hours?"

Ornias lifted a brow. "I thought the Magistrates were in a hurry, Lieutenant?"

"Yes, Governor, that is correct. However, the kidnapping of our captain has added a twist to this—"

"I'm well aware of your problems, Lieutenant Woloc. However, you must understand that every instant I hold Calas in my palace, the tensions on Horeb rise. His fragmented band of brigands is certainly planning a rescue attempt. I won't be held responsible if they succeed."

Ornias paced gracefully around his magnificent chamber, casting evil looks at Jason. The gold filigree outlining the frescoed dome gleamed with a fiery radiance over the governor's head. Something about the manicured primness of the man affected Jason like a foul stench in his nostrils.

"I understand, Governor. However, if you could sustain Ms. Calas for a few hours, it would give us the chance to—"

"Perhaps we don't understand each other, Lieutenant," Ornias said tautly. "Mikael and Sybil Calas are now *your* responsibility. Why can't you take them aboard and then search for your captain?"

Jason's fingers tightened over his chair arms. There'd be no point in telling this pompous military appointee that orders obliged him to leave as soon as Calas set foot aboard the *Sargonid*.

"Please ready Calas and his wife for transport, Governor. We'll reroute one of our supply shuttles to pick them up."

Ornias gave him an oily smile. "They'll be ready."

The screen went dead.

Jason ground his teeth. His officers stared at him questioningly. *Oh, Amirah, forgive me.*

"Pirke," he ordered. "Set course for Palaia. Hadash, contact Williamson and Stein. I'm certain they'll carry out the search for Captain Jossel with the same diligence we would."

"But, sir!" Pirke objected.

Jason lifted a hand. "We've no choice, Lieutenant. Hadash, go on."

"Aye, sir," Gever whispered forlornly as she swung back around to her console.

Jason watched Pirke's fingers inputting the course to Palaia and sank back in Amirah's command chair. He could feel the gentle contours of her feminine body

imprinted in the petrolon cushions. They molded around
him, slightly different from his own, as though her body
pressed warmly against his.

He clamped his jaw against the pang of desperation
that struck him.

* * *

Yosef wiped clammy palms on his camo jumpsuit and
peeked around the edge of a crate marked, "Inert." Ari
slumped in the shadows on the ground behind him. In
the past two hours, Ornias had tightened the security on
the loading dock until they could barely breathe. They'd
sneaked in when several of the guards had run to gaze
out at the sudden din surrounding the palace. But they'd
come back. Planetary marines in gray uniforms swarmed
all over now, rushing through the maze of crates and
supplies that crowded the landing field. Misty rain
drenched the red ridges, shimmering like liquid wax on
the marble columns of the palace. Four Magisterial vessels surrounded the magnificent rectangular structure.

Yosef turned around. "Ari, those ships are still there.
What do you think they're doing?"

Ari blinked owlishly. His gray mop of hair stuck out
at odd angles, frizzing in the rain. "What ships?"

"Name of God!" Yosef hissed in irritation, pointing at
the palace. "You looked at them ten minutes ago. Do
we need to jump start your brain cells again?"

Ari shoved to his feet and hobbled forward. The pack
of books he carried on his back made him look like a
hunchback. His brown suit had mud clinging in lumps to
the legs. He peered intently through the veils of mist.
"Oh, those ships." He sighed gruffly and started to hob-
ble back to his place.

Yosef grabbed Ari's arm and swung him around. "*Why*
do you think they're there?"

"It probably has something to do with that missing
captain."

"What missing captain?"

"Jossel, or whatever her name was, from the *Sargonid*."

"Where did you hear that?"

Ari waved a hand dismissively. "From that stupid loading dock worker who was slithering around earlier. He

was whispering to his companion about it. I . . ." Ari drifted off, eyes going vacant. He grimaced and massaged his butt, frowning as though deep in thought. "Do you know," he asked indignantly, "that my tailbone hasn't hurt this much since Agnes wanted to try that twisted Kama Sutra position back in—"

"Oh, for God's sake! What did that stupid worker say about Jossel?"

"What worker? Oh . . . Oh, nothing much. Just that she'd been captured by a terrorist force here on Horeb."

Yosef eyed Ari askance and reflectively played with the folds of skin hanging slackly over his throat. "There are no terrorist forces here. Unless you call Mikael's rebels terrorists. Do you think maybe Jehu or Sammy escaped the chambers?"

"No. Those planetary marines rounded up everybody important."

Yosef nodded. He and Ari had witnessed the forced evacuation. They'd hidden in the rocks outside the chambers and watched the ship that came to pick up Mikael and Sybil, then they'd slipped off to join the refugees rushing into small ships to flee. Except they'd headed their ship for the spiny ridges that surrounded the palace. Yosef's knees still ached from climbing through the rocks.

He leaned a little farther out from behind his crate and surveyed the dock again. Some sort of shift change was in progress. Marines scurried back and forth, muttering obscenities, whispering behind their hands as they scrutinized the Magisterial soldiers in purple uniforms who roamed the interlocking rows of supply stacks.

"If a captain got kidnapped, then maybe Jehu did escape?"

"Bah!" Ari discounted. "Even if he had, he couldn't have gotten here early enough to nab Jossel. That stupid worker with no teeth said she'd been missing for six hours."

Yosef's eyes widened as a Magisterial soldier joined up with a planetary marine and walked straight for their row. "Somebody's coming!"

Ari scrambled to his feet and ran on his tiptoes down the row, turning the corner into a dark dead-end alcove formed by crates piled ten high. Each container had a red triangle marked conspicuously on the outside. "Now you've done it," Ari blamed. "Look what you've gotten us into!"

"Quit complaining. Pry the lid off that crate on the ground."

"But we don't know what's in there."

"*Who cares?* Do it!"

Ari reluctantly jerked his knife from the sheath on his belt. Manically, he pried at the lid. The crate opened with a shriek.

"Help me," Ari ordered and Yosef trotted forward, hefting with all his strength to lift the heavy lid. The blasted thing weighed a ton. What was it made of? Uro-lead?

"Hurry! We have to get inside!"

Ari tucked his knife back in its sheath and made a basket with his hands. Yosef jammed his foot in it, levering himself up. By the time he got halfway there, however, Ari's arms waffled so wildly that Yosef ended up toppling into the crate headfirst. The tubular, tightly packed canisters that stuffed the bottom of the crate jangled when he hit. Ari swiftly scrambled over the lip and fell on top of Yosef. He pulled the lid back over them. They lay in contorted positions, panting.

"Will you get off my face!" Yosef insisted furiously, slapping at Ari's skinny butt.

"Shh! They're coming."

Yosef stopped in mid-swing, listening to the sound of booted feet on hard stone.

"Yes," one of the officers said in a deep voice. "These are the crates. Get them loaded into the shuttle quickly. First Lieutenant Woloc identified them as top priority."

A hesitation. Yosef heard someone's boots clicking as the man approached. The crate tilted suddenly.

"Goddamn it, Corporal! Put that down!" the deep-voiced officer commanded. "Doesn't that governor of yours teach you anything important? You could blow up half this planet handling those crates roughly. You see those red triangles? That symbol signifies a very special and very touchy explosive compound."

Yosef watched Ari clap a hand to his sweating forehead. His lips moved in what had to be a silent prayer. Warily, Yosef glanced at the canisters from the corner of his eye. In the past few seconds, they'd grown a malignant personality. He could feel them grinning at him.

"Don't tip that crate at more than forty-five degrees, Corporal, or you'll—"

"Well, why didn't anybody tell me before?"

"Just be careful!"

The thudding of retreating boots vibrated through the crate. The remaining man cursed under his breath. In a few minutes the growl of a loader moved closer and their crate gently lifted.

Ari craned his thin neck to scowl murderously at Yosef. Carefully avoiding the canisters, Funk reached down and tried to twist Yosef's ear off. It took a concerted effort not to scream or thrash about. In defense, Yosef thrust a skeletal finger into Ari's crotch. Funk jerked, gray eyes going wide. He let go of Yosef's ear.

The loader carried them for a period of about fifteen minutes, then gently set them down. A series of new scents and sounds penetrated their container. Foreign voices, all speaking intergalactic lingua, issued quiet orders. Metallic clashings and hollow thuds rang out. Finally, someone gently shoved their crate over a smooth surface until it banged softly against a wall.

They strained so hard to hear any word or movement that when the door slipped closed, it sounded thunderous. A blanket of dark silence descended.

Yosef gazed up at Ari. He couldn't see him, but he could hear Funk's labored breathing. The shuttle moved. They felt it rise off the ground. G-force pushed them back against the crate wall as the ship shot forward.

"Good God," Ari whispered morosely.

* * *

Aktariel stepped out onto a barren ball of red dust. He propped his hands on his hips and scanned the windswept wasteland. Anxiety and exasperation combined into a fine hot brew inside him. He had critical business to attend to. He couldn't afford this search!

"Where are you, Rachel," he asked through gritted teeth. *"What are you doing?"*

A dust storm tormented the distant plains. Red spires bobbed over the sun-drenched land, twining and colliding. In a furious movement, he gripped his *Mea* and concentrated. He hadn't time to trace her path! There were too many possible universes to search!

His jade green cloak flapped like wings as he strode back into the void.

CHAPTER 20

Carey slumped wearily in the probe chair. The lights shimmered with a starry radiance in the facets of the instruments on the silver table in front of her. The EM restraints gave her scant room to shift positions to ease the discomfort in her legs and lower back, but she struggled against them regardless. Every nerve in her body screamed at her to move.

In most of the galaxy, they'd call this torture. It would be against a thousand treaties. But not on Palaia. In this secret government bastion Slothen can order anything he wants and no one will know.

The helmet still rested on her head. She blinked wearily at the catheters they'd inserted in her abdomen to remove body wastes. More slithered from her throat and arms—feeding her, giving her air whether she wanted it or not. Sometime during the night, they'd removed Samuals. Probably taking him to the hospital. He'd screamed for hours, pleading for mercy, telling them everything he knew.

From the edge of her vision, Carey could see the windows on either side of the door. No Giclasian monsters marred the raised seats. They'd all vanished in the early hours of the morning. Idly, she wondered what time it was now, 0:400? Mundus had swiveled her chair around so she could no longer view the chronometer. She faced north, overlooking the last place Samuals had lain. Scratch marks from his frantic fingernails still gouged the wall.

In the deep dark recesses of her soul, a voice whispered, soft, reassuring in its deep tones and she shuddered, closing it off, forcing Jeremiel's confident face from her thoughts.

"Don't dream," she roughly commanded herself. "Stop it!"

They'd left her hooked up to the probes for a specific reason: at some point, she had to sleep. When she did, the dreams came unbidden, and the monitors recorded every scene in intimate detail. Her only defense lay in falling into deep dreamless sleep for a few minutes and then jerking herself awake. It kept her exhausted. Three times in the past day, she'd sobbed insanely and deliberately. Anger no longer worked. They'd expertly drained her of rage. Now only wrenching expressions of grief and despair kept the probes out of her most dangerous memories.

But how long could she wield the bitter explosions of anguish before their jagged edges sliced her resistance to nothingness? How long before she, too, surrendered to the sweet oblivion promised by the probes? Samuals had broken far sooner than she'd expected. It terrified her.

How long can you hang on, sweetheart? The crew on the Zilpah *are convinced you're a tough bitch. Are you? Dear God, let Jeremiel and Cole be far away when I go.*

Surely, they'd already have taken defensive action, just in case any of the officers had survived the Kiskanu attack. Did they suspect she might have? A trembling began in her hands. She clutched her chair hard. If Jeremiel or Cole suspected, they'd both be wild with fear and near desperation. If she could only find a way of killing herself, she could free them. . . .

"No, Lieutenant, that won't be necessary."

The kind voice echoed through the room, as soft and beckoning as an extended hand. Haggardly, she blinked at the far wall. A shadow wavered, huge, as though cast by some hunching monster from the deep.

In a sudden burst of light, a man of crystalline beauty appeared. He wore a jade cloak cut from the finest velvet. Within his pulled-up hood, a magnificent golden face glowed. The angles of his features were sharp, as though chiseled from pure light.

And she knew where she'd seen him before . . . *on the bridge of a dying starship when the very survival of Gamant civilization hung in the balance.* As he walked toward her, Carey's heart seemed to stop.

"Angel," she whispered. The sound of her hoarse

voice frightened her. Had she cried out so much in the last session?

"Yes, Lieutenant," the man of light answered gently.

He loomed over her, looking down through eyes as compassionate and concerned as those of God Himself. He threw back his hood. Hesitantly, as if worried about her response, he extended a golden hand and caressed her face. The fingers felt so warm and tender, they sent a tingle through her weary, weary body.

"Why are you here?" she croaked.

"To help you."

"Can you get me off Palaia?"

He lowered his brilliant gaze to pensively study the multitude of tubes that webbed her. Curiously, he prodded the petrolon lengths. "In all the ways that count, Lieutenant."

"What does that mean?"

"I can't physically take you away. I'm sorry. Your presence here buys time for Jeremiel and Cole. Time they desperately need."

"Then how—"

"If you'll let me, I can give wings to your soul."

Carey eyed him anxiously. "How?"

With the tenderness of a lover, he removed the *Mea* from around his own throat and draped it around hers. Then, strangely, he reached around to the chest of drawers behind her. He brought back Jeremiel's *Mea*. It flared suddenly in his hand. The sudden flash of stunning blue light made her gasp in awe. A cerulean gleam sparked across the room, touching everything like a flaming sapphire wash of St. Elmo's fire.

Carey whispered, "Why? Why do you need—"

"I'm not sure I will," he responded softly. A forlorn tone echoed in his voice. "But I might. And mine will work just as well for you, since you'll want to go through the seven heavens."

Gently, he brushed drenched auburn hair from her pale face, lifted Carey's new *Mea*, and pressed it against her forehead.

"Let me show you the way to God, Lieutenant," the angel whispered intimately. "Close your eyes."

Carey basked in the warmth of his smooth fingers against her forehead. The last time she'd seen him, he'd saved thousands of Gamant lives—and foreign women, too. She was loath to trust anyone, yet she did as he instructed and let her eyes fall shut.

"Yes, that's it, Carey. Clear your mind of thoughts. Now go deeper, very deep, seek that one place inside of you that always listens."

For what seemed hours, she followed his guiding voice. Whenever she took a wrong turn, his confident tones corrected and soothed, showing her how to back up and retrace her steps—until finally she entered a strange silent place. It had a peculiar feel, safe and warm, like a protective womb of light. She felt oddly as though all her waking life were nothing more than the echo of this eternal brilliance.

"That's it, Carey. Stay there. Can you still feel the press of the *Mea* against your skin? Good . . . good. Now I want you to imagine a tunnel, a tunnel of pure light that shoots out from you to connect with the Mea."

Carey concentrated and the tunnel seemed to form out of nothingness, swirling like a fiery vortex.

"Yes, very good. Now walk, Carey. Just walk . . . from here . . . to the gates of heaven. Come, I'll take you as far as I can."

He stayed close beside her, his green cloak swaying with his graceful movements as they traversed the tunnel. They talked about little things, the cyclones of light that eddied beneath their feet, the glitter that fell in a shower from overhead. At times, his amber body seemed to blend with the tunnel until only his green cloak existed. The sparkling vortex spiraled upward, upward. She could not keep from glancing at him. She'd always believed the stories of the ancient Gamant zaddiks about angels and God—strongly suspecting they were alien beings from another universe.

A cool wind brushed her hot face and she saw a gaping black void widen before her. It devoured the tunnel of light.

Carey took a step back.

The angel gripped her arm supportively. "It's all right. The Darkness only seems to conquer the Light. It's a brief illusion through which you must pass. But I can't go in there with you."

Fear tingled along her limbs. "What is that?"

"The path to God. Are you brave enough to seek Him out?"

"Me? Brave?" She smiled disparagingly at herself. "How do I get there?"

He pointed down the throat of the Darkness. "Walk straight ahead. Don't let the images you see frighten you. The void holds the imprint of all the faces of the creatures who've ever ventured on the path of illumination. But they're not real. They can't hurt you."

She expelled a taut breath, thinking about God. All the old Gamant stories rose in her memories. "I've dreamed of this, you know."

The angel's amber eyes flared, glowing so brightly she could barely continue to hold his gaze. "Yes, I know. What will you say to Him?"

Carey folded her arms. Was she dreaming even now? A cold tickle of fear tingled around her hairline. Perhaps her brain had found the key to truly avoiding the probes: Dreams that weren't based on memories. Could she control it? If so, she could gain a reprieve for her exhausted body.

She turned and tilted her head curiously at the angel. "I think I'll ask Him why He takes such poor care of His Chosen People."

The angel bowed his head for a long moment. "I'd hoped you would."

He touched her hand warmly, then he slowly walked back the way they'd come, calling, "If you have any problems, ask to see the archistrategos Michael. No matter what the lesser angels tell you, you have the right to take your case for entry to a higher judge."

"Who are you? Who should I say sent me?"

But he only lifted a hand in farewell. Carey watched his green cloak waver through the deluge of gold until it vanished. She turned to face the whirling Void of Darkness.

From the depths of her memories, Cole's voice chided, *"Oh, I get it. You like the idea of getting sucked into a black hole. And to think that for twenty-five years I've thought you had good sense."*

"Anything's better than the probes, Cole," she sighed as she resolutely forced her feet forward.

CHAPTER 21

The thunderous swell of hundreds of voices penetrated Mikael's mental haze and woke him. Cold wind gusted over his face. Blearily, he opened his eyes. They had him chained to a pink marble pillar on the broad third-floor balcony of the palace. An oval structure, tiny blue and gray tiles shimmered in the floor. A table and two chairs sat framed by two more columns on the other side of the balcony. Mikael struggled to get his shaky legs under him. An overwhelming headache pressed behind his eyes. He remembered the fight, the beating Ornias' marines had given him when he'd tried to stay with Sybil. Where was she? And his son? . . . His tiny baby son.

He locked his knees and stood up straighter, forcing his legs to hold him. From far below, a frightened din rose. Mikael turned, suddenly feeling as though ants were crawling in his guts. In the gardens, a hundred Gamants stood in the rain in blood-spattered rags. They gazed up at him through wide inflamed eyes. People reached out to him pleadingly; hope and adulation creased every face. Battalions of purple-suited soldiers surrounded them, rifles clutched tightly.

"Well, well," a smug silken voice said from behind Mikael.

He tried to turn to look, but the chains prevented him. Not that he needed to see. That voice haunted his dreams. Mikael fixed his gaze on the masses wailing below. "How long have I been unconscious, Governor?"

The sibilant rustle of satin carried as Ornias came to stand beside him. Dressed in a maroon robe with a broad ivory sash around the waist, he seemed a kingly obscenity from another time. His sandy hair and braided beard looked darker in the slate-colored light streaming across the balcony.

"About eight hours, Mikael Calas."

"My wife. Where is she?"

"She's right here in the palace. She's sleeping peace-fully after her ordeal. I had my doctors give her a seda-tive to calm her down. I'm afraid she was quite upset by my orders."

The unspoken words, *"orders to . . ."* hung like a deadly lance suspended above Mikael's heart. "There's no need to play games with me, Governor. What have you done?"

"Nothing yet. I've been waiting for the right moment. You may not have to witness it, though. I understand the shuttle dispatched by the *Sargonid* has just arrived at the landing field. They were very anxious to get their grubby hands on you."

Ornias walked across the balcony, admiringly stroking each pink marble pillar that he passed. When he got near the edge of the structure, a foul rumble of hatred erupted from the crowd. People shook their fists and screamed profanities. A few, very few, threw themselves down on the wet grass, pleading for mercy.

Ornias turned to ask incredulously, "Do the idiots think I might save them?"

Mikael just closed his eyes. The governor's scornful chuckle made his blood run cold. The mob shrieked louder.

"Annoying, aren't they?" Ornias observed. "Well, no matter. They won't be around long enough to cause me much more worry."

Fear-sweat soaked Mikael's torn black jumpsuit, run-ning in cold rivulets down his chest and sides. Terror did something to a man's scent, turned it acrid and unpleas-ant. His own smell stung his nostrils.

Ornias folded his arms. Conversationally, he said, "You know, I thought for the longest time that these fools believed *you* were the promised Mashiah." He shook his head in mock self-reproach. "Silly of me, I know, but I . . ."

His voice trailed away as a clamor of thudding boots and shouts echoed in the palace. Sybil's hoarse cries pen-etrated all the others: "No, no, give me my baby! Leave him alone!"

Mikael thrashed in his chains, screaming, *"Sybil?"*

Ornias lifted a hand and a hush seemed to magically fall. The storm winds billowed in his maroon robe. To someone inside the palace, he commanded. "Bring the woman and the child. Set them here before me on the balcony."

Mikael watched mutely as six marines pushed Sybil out on an antigrav gurney. Plutonius and another man, a doctor from the insignia on his purple epaulets, brought Nathan. His son was wrapped in a blue blanket.

"Plutonius?" Mikael gritted.

"I'd no choice!" The nostrils of his flat nose quivered. Someone had given him a purple uniform to wear. The pale dome of his bald head shone like iridescent ivory, making his cold green eyes seem to blaze. "They'd have killed me, too, if I hadn't agreed to help them!"

"You filthy traitor," Mikael whispered weakly.

Nathan started crying. And almost as though God had heard, a searing white flash of lightning split the dark sky, followed by a rumble of thunder which trembled through the blasphemous palace. Mikael's chains jingled.

Plutonius gasped as the sun slashed through the thick blanket of clouds and a shaft of gold lanced the balcony, falling on Nathan like a luminescent spear.

The soldiers shuffled backward, bumping into each other in their haste. Nathan wailed shrilly, flailing his tiny fists in anger.

In a bare whisper, Mikael heard Sybil say, "Epagael, please!"

When she turned to gaze at him he felt as though Yehoshua's ghost had risen from the blood red soils of ancient Earth and stormed across the stars to come to him. Sybil's eyes burned like suns made to stand still in the heavens. "What's happening, Mikael?"

He shook his head.

"You imbeciles!" Ornias' insidious voice broke the spell. The shaft of sunlight vanished in a crack of lightning and thunder. He waved a fist at his shoulders. "What's the matter? Haven't you ever seen sunlight through the clouds? Morons! Have you all become Gamant converts? Doctor Aijalon, *bring me that child.*"

The elderly soldier walked forward and laid the boy in Ornias' manicured hands. The governor looked up at

Mikael, then his gaze slid to Sybil. A foul smile twisted his lips.

"So this is your savior," Ornias quipped. He turned to Plutonius and glared. "Are you certain this is the child the rebels are calling Mashiah?"

"Yes . . . oh, yes." A difficult swallow went down Plutonius' throat. He backed away a step.

"Scares you, does he, Plutonius?" Ornias shook the baby. Nathan squealed. "Yes, he is a fierce savior, isn't he? My very bones quake at the thought that he might lift his pitiful little hand and call the wrath of God down on all of us." He roared with laughter.

Icy sweat traced lines down Mikael's chest. "Ornias!" Mikael shouted. "Stop this charade. Let him go. He's just a baby. He's no threat to you!"

"Isn't he?" Calmly, Ornias strolled to the edge of the balcony and gazed down at the milling crowd. He scowled. "Really, Calas. Couldn't you have provided me with a more imposing savior? It's hardly worth my effort to crush a pathetic little wisp of flesh like this."

"Ornias! What do you want from me? Tell me what you want!"

"You're no longer of any use, Calas." Ornias stroked his braided beard reflectively. "And maybe crushing the child will be impressive. After all, the title of 'baby-killer' has stood more than one great leader in good stead."

"Stop it, Ornias! *Let him go!*"

The governor pulled Nathan from his blanket before raising him over his head, displaying the boy to the crowd. Rain soaked the baby in cold sheets. "I give you your savior!" Ornias shouted.

The throng roared, *"Mashiah! Mashiah! Mashiah, save us!"*

"Your savior!" Ornias repeated. "I hold him in my hands! What shall I do with him?"

Mikael thrashed wildly in his chains, shouting, pleading, threatening until his vocal cords ached. But his words were lost in the wailing crash of screams that burst up again from the crowd: "Save him!" "Let us have him." "Don't hurt him!"

But across the balcony, the Magisterial soldiers spat, "Kill him." "The brat's the cause of all this." "Murder the little bastard. That'll take the fight out of these rebels!"

Ornias lifted a brow at his marines. "Bloodthirsty louts, aren't you? I suppose the baby frightens you, too, eh?"

In tones deep with mockery, he lifted his voice to the crowd, chanting ancient phrases, a prophecy every Gamant knew, words that announced the beginning of the end of Creation and had been burned into their souls from birth:

"Rejoice, sons and daughters of Seir!
Shout aloud, Gamant people!
See now, your King comes to you.
His cause is won. His victory is gained!"

Ornias fell into uncontrollable laughter, greatly amused by the irony of his words. He lowered Nathan and hugged him to his chest in bogus affection. Nathan grabbed a handful of Ornias' maroon robe and stopped crying. He stared up through sightless newborn eyes, as though seeing beyond this day to a calm and serene future. Ornias' face tightened. His laughter burst forth again, but this time it sounded forced.

"He will banish the bow of war!
He will proclaim peace for the nations.
His empire shall stretch from sea to sea,
from the River of Fire to the ends of the universe."

He lifted Nathan again, callously jerking the baby's fingers away from the maroon robe.

"Ornias," Mikael called. "Don't do this! I beg you. Kill me, but—"

"Don't be foolish," Ornias purred. "Your life means nothing. But this boy's . . ." In a velvet smooth move, Ornias spun around and pulled a pistol from a guard's holster.

A wretched scream rent the murky day. At first Mikael didn't recognize that horrified voice. But, then, in shock, his gaze shot to Sybil. She'd pushed herself up on her gurney, bracing herself on her elbows. Long, blood-matted brown hair fell in waves over her wounded chest. She shook all over, as though possessed by a deadly palsy. She wailed and wailed, screaming a garbled word which could have only been Mikael's name.

He responded by insanely screaming, *"NO! NO! Governor, please! Stop! Don't do this!"*

Before the sound had died on Mikael's lips, Ornias gripped Nathan by his tiny arm and flung him over the balcony railing. For a terrible, terrible moment, time stood still. Nathan seemed to hover, his tiny form silhouetted against the deep crimson of the storm-soaked cliffs, his naked body shimmering in the rain.

Ornias aimed his pistol.

A white fire, like a stiletto's blade, plunged between Mikael's ribs. His heart seemed to labor, throbbing as though it would burst. He bent forward, trying to catch his breath as he watched his son fall. The crowd below gasped and a wild howl of disbelief and anger rose.

Then . . .

From nowhere, everywhere, a single note, like the blare of a trumpet rang out. It began low, hanging in the misty air, then built to a shattering climax that slashed apart the very foundations of the palace. Ornias' gun wavered.

Mikael gasped as a gaping black hole swirled out of nothingness, swallowing his tumbling son before Nathan struck the ground. The crowd in the garden scattered. Covering their heads, they ran for the trees, the palace, any shelter. And through the maw, Rachel Eloel walked, her long ebony hair whipping about her shoulders. She wore a shimmering ivory robe and her eyes blazed like midnight moons.

The marines on the balcony screamed and fled, racing into the palace. The clacking of their boots across the marble floors pounded like the staccato of discharging rifles.

Ornias dropped his pistol and stumbled backward, slamming into the railing. *"Rachel?"* he whispered in utter terror.

She stepped out of the void and picked up the pistol. The black maw spun closed behind her. For several moments, she simply turned the pistol over and over in her hand. "Yes, Ornias. Did you think I'd died? No. I've been waiting for this for years."

"Guards!" Ornias shouted wildly. "Guards. . . ?"

But no one came.

In a weak tear-choked voice, Sybil called, "Mama? Mama, I missed you so much. Where's my son? Where's Nathan?"

Rachel swiftly went to Sybil and hugged her tightly as she stroked her tangled brown hair. "I missed you, too, baby. Forgive me. I've been preparing a way for you and Mikael. Save your strength. Tomorrow is going to be worse. Epagael isn't finished with us yet."

"Rachel?" Mikael said. "Can you get these shackles off me? The guards were stunned. They'll be back. Please. We have to hurry." He shook the hands chained over his head.

Ebony hair blew around her face as she shook her head. "No. I can't."

"Why not?" Mikael shouted in rage and fear.

"Because you must get on that battle cruiser, Mikael."

"You're turning me over to the Magistrates?" he demanded in unreasoning terror. *"Why?"*

Her dark eyes softened and she looked away, out to the shimmering veils of rain that caressed the maroon ridges. "It's necessary."

"But they'll kill him!" Sybil screamed. "Mama, let him go! Free him!"

Rachel didn't respond. She lifted her gaze to Ornias. A smiled curled her mouth—a frightening expression frosted with madness. As though walking on clouds, she moved forward. "Do you remember, Ornias," she questioned in a soft threatening voice, "when you marched Sybil and me to the square? I can still smell the stench of the thousands you crowded into that public gathering place. Do you remember when you ordered the guards to open fire on us? People ran insanely, trying to get away." She lifted her pistol.

Ornias wiped his clammy palms on his maroon robe. "Rachel, listen to me. I'm rich and powerful. I can—"

The first shot sliced off Ornias' left hand. Blood gushed from the severed arteries, spilling like a thick crimson river across the balcony. He howled in shock and gripped the railing to support himself. *"Oh, dear God!"*

"I remember, Ornias," she continued in a caressing voice. The sleeves of her ivory robe buffeted in the wind. "I remember the cries of the children buried beneath the mound of dead. Children I knew were dying and there was nothing I could do to help them."

Mikael stiffened, bracing himself as she aimed at

Ornias' eyes. But out of nowhere a deep voice boomed:
"Rachel, no! NO! We can't risk it!"

She gazed wild-eyed up at the lightning torn sky. "He deserves it!"

Another black whirlwind was borne on the clouds, it hurled downward, sweeping away everything in its rush to get to Ornias. Seeing the line of its descent, Rachel defiantly lifted her pistol and jerked the trigger. The shot went wild, missing Ornias and blowing a hole in the balcony railing. Marble splinters blasted into the cool air. Ornias dove and scrambled on his knees for the interior of the palace. But the black tunnel followed, swooping down to suck him up.

In speechless horror, Mikael watched Ornias spiral away. He tumbled down, down into the blackest Sheol, the deepest Pit of Darkness, getting smaller and smaller. . . .

Rachel clenched her fists and fired insanely into the sky, screaming, "YOU PROMISED ME! What have you done with him? You told me he was mine! You promised!"

The clouds roiled violently, spinning into a dark cyclone. From out of the eye the voice came again: *"What have* you *done with that child? Where's Nathan?"*

Mikael's knees trembled. His gaze darted from Sybil's ashen face to the stunned crowd hiding amid the trees below. Had the universe gone mad? He felt as numb as a sleepwalker trying to escape a terrible nightmare on leaden legs. "Rachel?" he called again. "Help me? *Free me?"*

She looked up and her face twisted as though she wanted to, but the voice echoed again, stern, commanding: *"Don't try it, Rachel. Mikael* must *get on that cruiser and you know it. Don't force my hand!"*

Rachel swallowed hard and hesitated before violently throwing her pistol to the floor. In the gardens below a sustained din of horror and awe rose, gazes shooting from the voice in the clouds to Rachel's mad and distraught face. She spread her arms imploringly. "Don't you ever keep your promises? Just this once—"

A huge hand formed out of the clouds, reaching down to her.

In the palace, a series of shouts could be heard along with the sound of people running. Rachel ran to Sybil and kissed her daughter. "Do what you must. I'll see you soon."

"Mama, where's Nathan!"

"You mustn't ever ask again. Trust me. If everything works out, you'll *know*." She straightened up and backed away from the cloud-carved fingers. A new chasm whirled open in the palace and she raced for it to disappear into the dark mists. A chill wind gusted around the balcony, whistling through the pink arches.

Mikael went rigid when ten Magisterial soldiers flooded through the doors. The insignia of the battle cruiser *Sargonid* plated their purple sleeves. Somber light fell across their rifle barrels, creating bright charcoal blazes.

When the commanding lieutenant turned to Mikael, he suddenly felt very tired. He and Sybil seemed to be caught up in the mad plan of some demon. He leaned his head back against the pink pillar and stared sightlessly at the storm clouds. "What the hell is happening to us?"

* * *

Carey walked through the eye of a dark whirlwind. Cool fragrant winds ruffled the sleeves of her black jumpsuit, setting her auburn hair to dancing around her face. She inhaled a deep breath of the sweet air and squinted at the black waters boiling beneath her boots.

"The center of the ring singularity?" The possibility fascinated her. She concentrated on memorizing every facet of the experience.

Soft indistinct sounds eddied across her path, muted voices, the clatter of cartwheels on stone, a horse screaming in fear. Her *Mea* cast a subdued cerulean gleam over the darkness. Sometimes, when she seemed to get off the "path," the *Mea's* gleam faded to almost nothingness. Only when she turned in the correct direction again did it flare brilliantly.

Her thoughts drifted as she walked, wondering what Jeremiel and Cole would be doing now, trying to feel her body back in the probe chamber on Palaia. How would Mundus and Axio respond when they found her catatonic? At least, she assumed that was how she would appear. The older Gamants spoke laughingly about the month just prior to the fateful battle against the Magistrates on the plains of Lysomia. Zadok, the story went, had gone through the *Mea* and stayed away for so long his troops believed him dead. They'd allegedly even prepared his body for burial. It shocked everyone when he awoke on the burial display platform and shouted irreverently at the hundreds of wailing people who filed before his coffin. He'd gone on to lead his people to a crushing victory over the Magistrates. God, he claimed, had revealed the strategy to him.

Carey stopped walking when a figure loomed out of the blackness, huge, riding a strange dragon-headed beast with flaming membranes wings. Carey dove sideways, rolling madly to get out of his way as he thundered past, his black cloak flapping in his hurry.

She panted in fear. *Real? Or illusion?*

The angel's words came back. *". . . The Void is filled with the faces of all the creatures who've ever ventured on the path of illumination. They're not real."*

She crouched in the darkness. Another face formed a short distance away, a blonde woman. She knelt in prayer. Tears streamed down her face. Carey struggled to hear the words she spoke, but her cries came too softly. In a burst of light, the image vanished.

Carey blinked, frowning. A faint graying had appeared in the distance, like a smoky pinprick in the rippling blanket of space-time. She stood and started walking again. Her *Mea* blazed almost blindingly.

As she got nearer to the light, a small man waddled toward her. Bald and immensely old, he had a hooked nose, black eyes, and bushy gray brows. He wore a coarse homespun brown robe. He contemplatively watched his feet as he walked.

Carey heaved a sigh. How could she ever get to the throne of God when illusions kept distracting her? She bowled forward, striding straight at the little man. When she stood no more than three feet away, he looked up suddenly and his black eyes jerked wide.

"Blessed Epagael," he murmured. "You're a new one. I thought I'd seen every face in this void."

Carey cocked her head, intrigued. None of the other illusions had spoken to her. "Do you see me?" she asked.

A hand went to his heart. He scrutinized her intently

for a few moments, then edged forward and prodded her arm with a stubby finger. "Good God, you're real." He stared breathlessly at her. "Who are you?"

"Carey Halloway. Who are you?"

He formed his hands into the sacred triangle and bowed gracefully. "Zadok Calas. I used to be—"

"*Zadok?*" she all but shouted the name. He flinched. "You're dead! You've been dead for over a decade."

"Yes, I know. But despite that, I feel pretty healthy."

When she didn't return the sacred triangle, he uncomfortably dropped his hands. A curious expression creased his withered face. "You're not Gamant," he guessed.

"No."

"Then why are you here? Why are you following a pathway to a God you don't believe in?"

"But I do believe in Epagael. Besides," she said wryly, "an angel sent me. Apparently, I need to talk to God."

Zadok gave her a sidelong look. "Which angel?"

"I haven't the slightest idea."

"You didn't ask?"

"I asked. He wouldn't say."

Fear crept into the old man's black eyes, darkening them like nightfall. He nervously crushed the fabric of his brown robe. "Well, that worries me."

Carey read his suspicions on his withered face. Too many times in the past she'd slouched around a strategy table listening to old men in prayer shawls accuse Jeremiel of being possessed by the Archdeceiver. "Because you think it might have been Aktariel who sent me?"

"Yes."

"What difference would it make? Isn't talking to God always good? And anyway, maybe it wasn't Aktariel. Why would the Deceiver want *anyone* to hear the Truth straight from God's mouth?"

"That, my dear, is a good question. And one I can't answer. But Aktariel's ploys often follow contorted routes."

Carey nodded agreeably. "I've read enough Gamant history books to believe that. However, I'm still going to talk to God, Zadok. Nobody's going to stop me. I'd like you to come with me. I've many things to tell you about what's happened to Gamants since your death. But not if you're worried about being tainted by my—"

"About Gamants? What do you know about Gamants?"

"Quite a bit. I'm second in command of the Underground battle cruiser, the *Zilpah*."

Zadok lifted both bushy brows. "The *Gamant* Underground? When did Baruch start allowing non-Gamants to serve?"

"When he married one."

Zadok's eyes went over her carefully. The darkness behind him fluttered like black windblown flame, as though reflecting his astonishment. "You're Jeremiel's wife?

"Yes," she responded, silently daring him to say anything about "foreign women."

Zadok heaved a resigned sigh and affectionately took her arm. "Why didn't you tell me that immediately? I wouldn't have felt such reservations if I'd known. Epagael wouldn't allow Jeremiel's wife to be deceived by Aktariel."

Carey's brows lowered. She gazed down at the elderly hands that caressed her arm so tenderly. Zadok had a light of glowing certainty in his eyes. Did he know nothing of the terrible fate of Gamants in her universe? And if he didn't, why had God kept such things from him? "I can see we have a very great deal to discuss, Patriarch."

"I can't wait. Here, let me show you the way. I know this path rather thoroughly. I doubt Epagael will let me cross the threshold into the first heaven, but I can take you that far."

"Why can't you enter the first heaven?"

"Oh, it's a long story, I'm afraid. Epagael gave me a choice of heaven or helping my people in your universe. I chose the latter. The price was permanent exile here in this cold wasteland."

Carey's eyes narrowed. What possible justice could be served by condemning the greatest Gamant patriarch to the darkness of the Void for eternity? "But you haven't helped them, Zadok, have you?"

"Oh, yes," he fervently exclaimed. "I've spoken to Mikael several times, through his *Mea*, of course."

"When was the last time?"

He cocked his head uncertainly. "I don't know. The

Void is timeless. But it seems like only a few days ago. What year is it?"

"It's 5426."

He stopped as though stunned. "I . . . I don't understand. Are you sure? Mikael was still a boy the last time we spoke. But Epagael assured me—"

"Then he lied to you."

Carey strode toward the graying patch in the distance. New scents drifted on the wind: trampled grass, flowering jasmine, a fragrant tang like freshly cut wood.

Zadok puffed to keep up. "What are you talking about? I thought Gamants were safe on Horeb?"

"No, Zadok. They've never been worse off. In the past decade the Magistrates have slaughtered them by the hundreds of thousands. Horeb is one immense death factory."

His ancient face paled. "But why didn't Epagael tell me?"

"Maybe he doesn't want you to know."

He glanced sideways at her and retrieved her arm again, forcefully tugging her forward toward the light. "There must be another explanation. Let's go find out."

* * *

Jason Woloc paced anxiously before the huge forward monitor on the bridge. Over the past several hours, his purple uniform had gotten damp and uncomfortable. His officers sat rigidly in their control niches, their eyes glued to the screen. The *Marburg* and *Hammadi* circled the planet Sinai, probing it. At the same time, the shuttle *Aretz* sped toward Jason's cruiser, a silver needle gleaming in the brilliant wash of sunlit space. As soon as it arrived with the Calas family, they'd immediately be obliged to head for Palaia Station.

His gut knotted.

He'd been desperately hoping that either Williamson or Stein would find some trace of Amirah before he had to leave.

"Sir?" Gever Hadash called. Her weasel face pinched as the com aura snapped on in a golden halo about her head. "I have Captain Williamson—"

"On screen, Lieutenant."

He futilely straightened his purple sleeves and sucked in a deep breath. Mikos Williamson's face appeared. His bald head gleamed. A short man, he had a bulbous nose and slanting blue eyes that always made Jason brace himself for the worst. Williamson leaned forward in his command chair. "Good afternoon, Lieutenant."

"How are things going, Captain."

"Not well, I'm afraid. Something strange is happening on Sinai. We're noting curious density fluctuations in the gas mote—as though the entire planet is on the verge of phase change. The instability has slowed our search considerably. And you will recall, Lieutenant, that Slothen recently ordered my ship to deliver food to the starving war victims of Delores 2. I do hope this search doesn't delay us much longer or we're going to have multitudes dying there."

The man's haughty tone cut like shattered glass. Jason stiffened. Williamson had never liked Amirah. She'd outsoldiered him in one too many critical battles. Professionally, Jason asked, "Do you think the disturbance is natural or artificial?"

Williamson ran a hand over his shiny scalp and lifted a shoulder. Behind him, people rushed around the *Marburg*'s bridge, checking com screens, whispering urgently. "You think those terrorists might be causing the flux? Well, it would take some sophisticated equipment, but it's possible. When are you leaving orbit?"

He glanced down at Pirke. "Orah?"

"Approximately fifteen minutes, sir."

"You copy that, Mikos?"

"Yes," Williamson nodded. "Well, we'll keep searching for as long as we can. But if this planet gets any wilder we might have to call it off. You understand that?"

Jason nodded reluctantly. "I do. I appreciate your help, Mikos."

"Keep it in mind the next time the *Marburg*'s in trouble, Lieutenant. Williamson out."

The screen went blank and Jason went to ease down into Amirah's command chair. *Amirah's. . . . Even if I live as long as Slothen himself, this will never be my chair. Never.*

His mind played glimpses of memories: Amirah smiling at him across a strategy table, her long blonde hair shimmering over her shoulders; Amirah praising his "brilliance" in the Jaron debacle—but it had been her brilliance that had extricated them from that impossible trap. He could still feel her soft touch on his arm when they'd both walked off the bridge together after forty hours without sleep and only scanty meals eaten in haste. She'd invited him to her cabin for a strong belt of whiskey. He'd gone gratefully. They'd talked. Laughed. Nothing more. But something in her beautiful eyes that night, something warm and joyous, had left him floundering. From that moment forward, his heart had pounded hollowly whenever he met her unexpectedly in the corridors. Sitting in front of her at his nav console on the bridge had become an exercise in self-chastisement. He constantly had to remind himself of his duty.

"Sir? Shuttle *Aretz* has docked."

He propped his elbows on his knees and nodded. "Take us out of orbit, Pirke."

The ship lurched slightly as it pulled out of Horeb's gravity well and sailed toward Palaia.

CHAPTER 22

Amirah fiercely rubbed her hands together to get the circulation back. Tahn had removed her restraints a half hour ago when he saw how deeply the bands had cut into her flesh. Raw red furrows crisscrossed her wrists.

She leaned back against the wall by the hearth and stretched out her legs. Mud and things-she'd-rather-not-think-about still clung to the hem of her purple pants. The banked glow of the fire threw ruby reflections over the ceiling. They danced as though alive. But she barely noticed. Her eyes rested on Cole Tahn. He leaned over the table, examining the maps he'd spread out. In the azure light cast by the handglobe in his left palm, the dusty crystal goblets shimmered with a prismatic brilliance. His brown hair, handsome face, and black jumpsuit had a thin coating of red dust from wandering around the cave. For the past fifteen minutes he'd been examining her curiously.

"What the matter?" she demanded.

"Well, I was thinking. . . ."

Just the tone of voice set her on edge. But the wry, speculative glance he threw her made it worse. "About what?"

"I was wondering how shy you are? But I don't think I know you well enough to tell."

She brushed dirty blonde hair over her shoulder and lifted a brow insolently. "Oh, you're astute."

Slowly, he limped around to sit on the edge of the table. "Tell me something? If I were to suggest being naked together, what would you say?"

She let her eyes strategically land on the most vulnerable places of his anatomy. "I'd say you might just get your goddamned guts kicked out."

He shifted restively. "Maybe I put that the wrong way.

What I mean is that after crawling around in those sewer channels yesterday, I can barely stand being close to myself and I thought—"

"Having been close to you, I can understand that."

Tahn scratched his dark beard expressively and gave her one of those bland looks that implied she was being an ass, but he was too polite to say so in public. Her eyes slitted. "As I was saying," he continued. "I was thinking maybe I'd take a bath—you don't have to, of course."

"They have a bath here?"

"Yes. Just down the hall. At least it's listed on the maps. I don't know if it's still running, but we could see. Would you like to bathe?"

She ground her teeth, evaluating. Would he leave her alone? If he gave her even a moment of privacy in the bath, she might be able find something to waylay him with. "I would," she said and shoved to her feet.

He studied her as she brushed off her uniform. "Good. I take it, then, that you're not timid?"

"I'm about as timid as a charging Klimona havelina, Tahn."

"Glad to hear it. Because you realize, of course, that I can't let you out of my sight. Not even a second."

She propped hands on her hips and caustically said, "I've studied your life thoroughly. I don't remember any data on voyeur inclinations."

He laughed. "Don't you? Good. That means that planet's ransom I paid to keep the Iesu 2 event out of my record worked."

She frowned until the piece of information clicked into place. "Oh, yes. Iesu 2. The place where you were arrested for brawling in the stripper's joint. I remember. Second Lieutenant Hatfield reported that you smiled all the way to the jail cell. He claimed you were inordinately pleased with yourself for breaking all four bouncers' jaws in less than twenty seconds." She pursed her mouth disgustedly.

Tahn's brows went up. "And just when, pray tell, did they put that into my record?"

"After the Tikkun affair. The Magistrates wanted a precise psych-history of Cole Tahn. They probed everyone who'd ever served with you."

His smile waned. She saw his jaw muscles jump. "I see."

Tahn straightened. Amirah straightened. She felt a little like they'd just squared off for hand-to-hand. The pistols adorning his hips left no question as to who'd win.

"They did it for the good of the fleet, Cole."

"Sure. Right. Slothen had everyone's best interests in mind." He picked up one of the dirty place mats and slammed it down in frustration. Dust puffed up, sparkling in the firelight. "Come on, let's go take a bath."

"I'd appreciate it."

He gestured toward the crates lining the far side of the wall. "There's clean clothing in that box next to the food concentrates. Why don't you go select something less fragrant to wear?"

"Gladly."

Keeping her distance, she walked around him and went to kneel before the open box. She pawed through the multicolored robes and finally found one that looked to be roughly her size. Pale gold silk, it felt as soft as fur against her fingertips. She clutched it to her breast and slowly stood up.

"Good, Captain," Tahn praised. "Now, if you don't mind, I'd like to do the same. Please step away from the box."

She did so and he cautiously came across the room and indiscriminately jerked a red robe from the array. He tossed it over his shoulder and pulled his pistol. Holding the handglobe in his left palm and the gun in his right hand, he ordered, "Please go through the door and take a left. Keep walking straight until I tell you to turn. Got it?"

Amirah nodded and walked out the door. Turning left, she headed down the diamond-shaped corridor. His boots clicked in a slightly uneven cadence behind her. The halls smelled sweetly of crushed herbs and spices. She wondered if the stones had picked up the fragrance from the very pores of the men who'd traversed these corridors for centuries.

Over her shoulder she asked, "How much do you know about the Desert Fathers who used to inhabit this labyrinth?"

His deep voice seemed to echo in the confined space.

"Not much. Just that they swore vows of chastity and poverty and they were heavily involved in the civil war here a decade ago."

"When you scorched the planet?"

"Yes." The word came bitterly, uttered as though a profanity.

"They broke the Treaty of Lysomia, not you. Duty required that you—"

"Duty?" He let out a low disparaging laugh. "What is that, Captain? And to whom do you owe it? The Magistrates? Or the civilians you're theoretically 'protecting'?"

"Both."

"Really? And when the Magistrates put you and your ship in the position of having to choose one or the other? Which would you choose? Incidentally, you're going to want to take a right at the next intersection of corridors."

She let the question dangle and turned right. Who would she choose? Her conscience assured her she'd choose the people. But . . . would she? She owed everything to Magistrate Slothen. It would take a miracle to convince her he had made an error in judgment.

Halfway down the new hall, a wall of warmth rose. Mist filled the air, sparkling like a cerulean gauze shawl in the light of Tahn's handglobe. A green curtain draped over a door at the far end.

"I think we've found it," she commented.

"I take it you're not going to answer my question?" he challenged.

"I'm not in the mood for another argument." *If I can just get through that curtain first, then when you enter, Tahn, I can pivot. . . .*

"Amirah. Stop."

Reluctantly, she did, turning around to glare at him. "What for?"

He edged by her and went to the curtain, pulling it back to check the room. Mist flooded into the corridor. He gestured her inside with his pistol barrel. "Easy, now. I want you to go in and stand by that urn."

What the hell was he? A godforsaken mind reader? Every time she thought she might have a chance to take him, he countered the move before she initiated it. Well, she'd have to find a way of distracting him. All she needed was a split second and she could level a fatal kick. An image of him lying dead on the floor appeared in her mind—and she felt a twinge of regret. She sort of liked him.

She entered the room and went to stand by the urn, a three-foot-high ceramic masterpiece crusted from top to bottom with rare Lytolian sapphires and rubies. They gleamed wetly in the diffused blue light. A small chamber, perhaps twenty feet in diameter, a hexagonal jade-tiled tub filled the north wall. A spout poured a constant river of water into it. Around the perimeter, a stone bench had been hacked from the wall. It protruded like a pouting lip. Chests and crates packed the space beneath it.

Tahn surveyed her position, then cautiously entered and let the curtain drop closed. He braced a shoulder against the wall and set his handglobe down on the bench. "Check that crate behind you. According to the floor plan, it should contain 'supplies.' "

Gingerly, Amirah knelt and dragged it from beneath the bench. She opened it and pulled out two towels sealed in a waterproof transparent sheath, and a bar of soap. Ripping them open, she tossed the towels to the bench and held the soap to her nose. "Hmm. Horebian wild jasmine," she judged.

"Yeah? How do you know?"

"They sell it in all the dingy shops in the Sculptor sector. It's supposed to have aphrodisiac qualities."

"Indeed? Ever tried it?"

She threw the soap down with a smack and turned to examine him. "Oh, getting insulting, eh? Punishing me because I wouldn't answer your question about duty? Well, for your information, I didn't know how to answer it, that's why I didn't."

He propped a boot on the bench and rested his pistol on his knee. His mouth quirked into a half-smile. "I figured that was the reason. I just wanted you to think about it—for when it happens."

"You're an arrogant sonofabitch, you know that?" she asked and grimaced when his smile widened. "I'm going to undress. You don't mind, do you?"

"Not at all."

Amirah slipped off her boots and tucked them beneath the bench. Then she pulled her shirt over her head and tossed it on the floor. She had to tug on her pants to peel them off. Standing in only her lacy underwear, she glanced up. Tahn stood watching her with a faltering intensity. His handsome face had slackened, going utterly serious.

"My God, you're beautiful," he said in soft anguish. He briskly massaged his forehead.

"You're the first man to say so. Thanks," she answered honestly and wondered just why she'd done that. She never mentioned her dismal history with men to anyone.

Tahn's face screwed up disbelievingly. "Then, maybe it's just me. You'd be doing me a great favor if you'd get into that tub so I can start breathing normally again."

In the azure gleam of the handglobe, a warm glint flared in his blue-violet eyes, making Amirah extremely nervous.

To defuse the magnetic sense of attraction, she jerked her underwear off with military brusqueness and threw it into the growing pile on the floor. Grabbing up the bar of soap, she tested the water with her toe before stepping into the tub and sinking up to her neck.

The water felt so warm and soothing, every aching muscle in her body seemed to heave a sigh of relief. She ducked her head beneath the surface to wet her hair. Long blonde strands moved around her shoulders in serpentine wisps. From the edge of her vision, she saw Tahn ease down onto the bench, pistol propped on his thigh.

She took the bar of soap and washed her long legs, then lathered her hair. He watched in silence for a time before saying:

"So, tell me about yourself?"

"What do you want to know that you didn't find in my records? And by the way, how do you get access to confidential personnel files?"

He gave her a disagreeably amiable smile. "The same way we get access to cruiser flight plans. You were born on Rusel 3, correct?"

She scowled cynically. "Yes. My parents died when I was thirteen. They were killed in the Pegasan attack."

"Indeed? We have more in common than I'd thought. My parents died when I was six."

"I remember." It had happened during the Carinan

invasion of Delphinus. Tahn had managed to escape his
bombed home and hidden in the dense underbrush
around the house. He'd witnessed his parents' murder.
Carinans had a barbaric custom of ripping out the intes-
tines of their victims and watching them die in slow
agony. Cole had listened to his mother's screams for
hours. When Magisterial forces sailed in and drove out
the Carinans a week later, Captain Juan Moreno of the
battle cruiser *Quillon* had found a half-mad little boy still
clinging to the decaying corpse of his mother. "She needs
me!" Tahn had reportedly screamed over and over. Moreno had talked to Cole for two hours, trying to convince
him his mother was dead and there was no longer any
need to guard her. The boy had still fought like a tiger
when Moreno forcibly dragged him away.

Tahn shifted, propping his foot on the bench. "Did
they put you into one of those wretched government
orphanges?"

"No. Unlike you I had a living grandmother. She
raised me."

Pleasant memories of Sefer Raziel possessed her.
Amirah could still see her, sitting in her rocking chair on
the bright sunlit porch of their tiny home. The rocker
creaked on the rickety floor as Sefer snapped the freshly-
picked green beans that made a mound atop her apron
and chanted the old stories to a young Amirah. She could
still see the numbers engraved on her grandmother's
forearm and the deep scars that crisscrossed her face like
a hideous web. When she'd once asked Sefer about them,
her grandmother had laughed ominously: "Your father
would probably turn me in to the Snoopers if I were to
tell you, darling. But someday . . . maybe I can tell you.
I don't know. We'll have to see what happens to the
galaxy." Amirah had loved that thin old woman, loved
her with all her heart. Despite all the years since her
grandmother had vanished, Amirah still ached for her.
When the memories dimmed and Amirah looked up
again, she found Cole watching her through kind eyes.

"She must have been quite a lady," he observed
gently.

"She was very good to me."

"Is she the one who taught you to fight?"

"Other than the government, you mean? Yes. To fight

and to seek Truth." She smiled pleasantly, but beneath the veneer, an idea occurred to her. "Grandmama used to say, 'There are a thousand paths that lead to the orchard of Truth, Amirah. Find yours.' "

A startled frown lined Tahn's forehead. "Do you know that that's—"

"Gamant theology? Oh, yes. She was a Gamant."

He lounged back against the wall indolently. His face was expressionless, but he peered at her as though a hazy blanket had fallen between them and he couldn't quite make out her features anymore.

Her Gamant ancestry was her own secret hell, but telling Tahn about it might confuse him and make him tend to trust her more. Some of her earliest memories were of her mother screaming and shaking her for repeating Grandmama Sefer's stories in public. She'd adored those wild colorful tales. But Lucan Jossel, her mother, had fully converted to the atheism of the Magistrates—and of her husband, Johan. Lucan feared that if his high-level government friends knew of her Gamant blood, they'd ostracize her. As a result, she punished Amirah severely whenever she caught her whispering such things to her childhood friends.

Tahn blinked curiously. "Why did you tell me that? That information certainly isn't in your personnel file."

"No. My father worked in the government records office. Whenever anything came in which hinted at my mother's ancestry, he simply purged it. That left a clean slate for me."

"Convenient." From this angle, his straight nose and the firm line of his bearded jaw seemed chiseled from stone. A steely glimmer lit his eyes. "Why would your mother forsake her Gamant heritage to marry a—"

"Because during the last Gamant Revolt, my grandmother left for several years—I don't know where she went—and my mother was sent to a Magisterial Right School. They corrected her thoughts."

" 'Corrected,' " Tahn scoffed. "I've always thought that was an interesting way of putting it. So they erased every shred of Gamant culture and history from her brain, huh? And your father found that attractive?"

"I guess. My mother was very beautiful and intelligent. Papa had good reasons for loving her."

"Can I ask you a personal question?"

"I doubt it, but you can try."

"How can you . . ." He stopped, as though trying to find a better way of putting it. "Doesn't it hurt you every time you're ordered to attack Gamant civilians?"

She fumbled with her soap. It did. But she'd suppressed the emotion for so long she'd almost conquered it. In the early days, she'd often thought about what Sefer Raziel would do if she could see her granddaughter now. Grief taunted just below Amirah's control. She splashed anxiously at the water. "Do you practice picking at people's wounds, Tahn, or does the talent come naturally?"

"If my question wounded you, then you've answered it."

"I don't like attacking any civilian populace. But orders—"

"—Are orders. Yes, I used to think the same thing. Fortunately, I grew up."

She shoved suddenly to her feet. Water cascaded in silver streams from her body. "It's what you grew up into that's disturbing: a traitor and a criminal."

He kept his gaze riveted on her as he stood and slowly walked down the length of the bench to retrieve a towel. He brought it back and warily extended it. She gauged his positioning and the aim of his pistol, wishing to hell he'd drop his guard for just a goddamned moment. She jerked the towel from his hand.

Tahn backed away, going to lean against the wall again. Amirah got out of the tub and dried off, then slipped her pale gold robe over her head and smoothed it down over her hips. The blasted garment clung to every curve like the thinnest of glimmering spiderwebs.

Tahn vented an admiring sigh. "That's almost worse than seeing you unclothed. You look like a goddess straight off Mount Olympus."

"Mount what?"

"Never mind. I'm obviously the historian here. Why don't you come over here and sit down where I can keep an eye on you." He indicated the place on the bench with his gun.

Amirah seethed at the "historian" comment, but she walked forward and slumped down on the indicated spot.

Tahn carefully bound her hands first, then her ankles, in
EM restraints.

He backed away cautiously. Unclipping his belt, he
dropped it on the edge of the tub. The gray gun in the
holster glowed dully against the jade tiles. He relinquished the pistol in his hand, too, placing it on top of
his belt, then he undid the fasteners on the front of his
black jumpsuit and peeled out of the sleeves.

Amirah drew her feet up onto the bench and propped
her bound hands on them. She watched Tahn intently,
waiting for him to get more than three feet away from
his weapons. Even bound, at close range, she might have
a chance. His broad muscular chest with the thick mat
of dark hair stirred sensations she loathed, but she continued to watch his every move. After a few moments
her mind began to wander and then run headlong down
the road that led away from all the "Thou Shalt Nots . . ."
her grandmother had ever drummed into her brain. Not
to mention the Magistrates; they frowned on officers frat-
ernizing with the enemy.

He kicked off his boots and Amirah watched him step
out of his suit completely. Her eyes focused on the
wound in his thigh. The shot had taken him just below
his pelvis, ripping a gash through the muscle. A broad
redness of infection encircled the wound. It must have
hurt like hell. He gingerly stepped into the water and
winced when the hot liquid spread over his injury. Steam
spun a silken veil around him.

"So," she demanded, "tell me about yourself."

Tahn had one eye squeezed closed, no doubt fending
off pain. The other eye focused on her. "Why?" he
gasped. "You know me better than I know myself."

"I doubt it. I know nothing about the past twelve years
of your life. What happened after you joined the Gamant
Underground? How did it *feel* to commit treason?"

He reclined in the tub and very slowly extended his
legs. After several seconds of adapting to the heat of the
water, he breathed out a sigh of relief. "Bad at first. For
years I'd marked the boundaries of my identity by the
reflection of myself I saw in my crew's eyes. It was a
good life, by and large. Every time I felt lost or lonely,
I had simply to look at my officers to know again who
and what I was. Do you do that?"

She snugged her shoulders more solidly against the wall. Her gold robe whispered against the stone. "I'm not on the stand anymore. You are. So treason is lonely, huh?"

He lathered his wound and smiled—but it was the sort of expression that made Amirah curl her toes over the edge of the bench. He continued, "Magisterial life had left me unprepared for a fiercely independent people like the Gamants. Maybe you'll understand this better than I did. Gamants don't care in the slightest what status you've attained in the past. They judge you based upon the positive qualities they see in your soul. Either you measure up as worthy of their respect or you don't."

"And you didn't?"

"Not at first. Most of them hated me. My crew and I had been responsible for the deaths of hundreds of thousands of their people, you see. Excuse me, *your* people." He briefly ducked his hair. "How many of your people have you killed, Amirah?"

The sweet scent of jasmine wafted on the mist. Her hair had begun to dry and fall about her shoulders in long ringlets. "So how did you survive the Underground's hostility?"

"You don't like it when I call Gamants your people? You must have had difficulties growing up. Did you spend all your time running away from yourself? Or is this a recent survival strategy?" She glowered hotly, but he met it with equanimity. "To answer your question about how I survived the Underground—I had a friend to help me."

She pulled back at the caressing tone in his voice. "Oh, a woman."

"Does that bother you?"

"Why would it?"

"I don't know. It's just that you sounded jealous and it made my heart go pitter-patter."

She massaged the muscles at the back of her neck. "Good God, you don't even have to work to turn somebody's stomach. I think it's your grin mostly. Do you practice that in the mirror?"

He couldn't help smiling at that, even as he began to lather his chest. Blue-tinged fog swirled near the ceiling, diving down toward the tub like thin transparent fingers.

"Not very often anymore. The Underground keeps me too busy."

"Baruch's a slave driver, huh? Tell me about him? Do you know him well?"

He turned toward her and the shadows mottled his wet face, highlighting his cheekbones. He laid a hand on the jade tiles near his pistols and lifted his chin inquiringly. "Why do you want to know?"

"Is he as brilliant as they say?"

"Jeremiel is not a topic for discussion, Amirah."

"Why not?"

"Because I plan on letting you go when you've served your purpose. I may openly banter about my past and yours, but I won't endanger him."

He stood up and she got to her feet, too. Tahn's shoulder muscles tensed. "Do sit back down, Amirah." He pointed to his pistols. "You wouldn't want to get me nervous."

She made an awkward gesture with her hand, then angrily slumped back to the stone bench. "I'm hardly a threat! I was going to grab the towel off the bench and hand it to you."

"Thanks just the same."

He reached over and picked up one of his pistols just for good measure. With his free hand, he gripped his injured leg and gently levered it over the edge of the tub. His foot hit the wet tiles awkwardly. Off-balance for a second, he grabbed for the edge of the tub and dropped his aim. Amirah leapt in a lightning fast move.

Her balled fists caught him in the chest. The force slammed him back against the wall. She dove forward, hands raised for the killing punch to his throat . . . but he spun out of her way and landed a brutal kick to her shoulder. It knocked her backward and she tumbled into the pool.

She tried to swim away, but her bound feet and hands made it almost impossible to move at all. He dove after her. In a swift violent move, he grasped for her throat. She slammed both knees into his wounded thigh. He cried out, but his fingers kept groping for her face. Amirah spun under the water and knocked his feet out from under him. He tumbled sideways, sending a silver crested wave over her face—then he lunged. He jammed

a knee in her chest and forced her beneath the water.
She held her breath as she struggled in his iron hands,
vaguely surprised by his overpowering strength. She'd
fought hundreds of men in training classes and hand-to-
hand competitions—but she'd never had her limbs strait-
jacketed. She'd never felt so helpless.

"Captain!" she heard him shout. His angry voice
wavered through the layers of water. "Stop it! Don't
make me hurt you! Amirah, for God's sake! Stop this!"

She writhed like a fish out of water, flopping, kicking,
trying to break his hold, but he held her fast. The certainty of defeat sapped her strength. She'd gambled and
lost. God Almighty, she was going to get Jason and her
crew killed if she didn't escape! Her ship . . . her ship.
Goddamn you! Fight! She kicked Tahn weakly, but the
wall of water felt as thick and impenetrable as lead. Her
legs moved so slowly she thought they'd never reach his
side. Her air ran out in the midst of the battle and she
gulped water into her lungs. The sensation terrified her.
She coughed and inhaled more water. Her chest burned
as though afire. She struggled to get to the surface, but
obviously he didn't recognize the difference in her tactics.
He fought her, keeping her face pressed resolutely
beneath the shimmering blanket of death. Just before
she lost consciousness, she glimpsed his panicked face
through the rippling water. . . .

An indeterminable amount of time later, she came to
and found him giving her old-fashioned artificial respira-
tion. His lips felt hot against hers. She groaned weakly
and he brusquely rolled her to her side. He'd unbound
her hands, but they flopped uselessly against the cool
floor. The gush of water that drained from her mouth
seemed massive. She had trouble catching her breath.
Her lungs didn't want to inflate.

"Lie still," he ordered.

He rolled her onto her back again and slipped a hand
beneath her head, then covered her mouth with his own
and breathed life into her. Her eyes fluttered, taking in
his nakedness, tracing the lines of his shoulder muscles.
So handsome. . . . Mist floated like a glittering halo
around his head. Her chest expanded a few times and
she feebly turned away.

"Enough," she whispered hoarsely.

He gazed at her hard, as though judging the truth of that assertion by the strength he saw in her eyes. Some of his dread left him. He let out a long exhalation and ran a hand through his drenched brown hair.

"You had me scared. You didn't come out of that nearly as fast as you should have."

"Weak . . . weak lungs. Smoke damage."

It had happened the day her parents died. She'd run screaming through their flaming house, listening to the raid sirens wail through the streets outside. Somehow, she'd gotten lost in her own home. The wall of smoke and fire had been so thick, she couldn't see.

Vainly, Amirah tired to raise herself on her elbows, but her strength failed. She fell back to the hard stone floor. A swimming vision of jade tiles and stone walls wove a queasy pattern. She fought the nausea. A moment later, powerful arms slid beneath her shoulders and knees and she felt herself being carried down the hall.

Amirah awoke, lying in Tahn's arms, her head pillowed against his broad chest. She felt better, though still feeble. She blinked lazily at the flickering flames in the hearth. Carnelian flashes of light glinted in the silken folds of his red sleeves.

"What are you doing?" she inquired weakly. "Let go of me."

"You won't like it if I do. The last time I tried laying you on the floor you stopped breathing."

So he'd been holding her ever since? She scowled up at him, but inside her gratitude stirred. Firelight flickered over his face, deepening the hollows of his cheeks and dancing in his eyes—magnificent blue-violet eyes that melted her soul. *What the hell's the matter with you? He just tried to kill you!*

"I'm fine . . . now. Let me go."

"All right, but take it easy."

He loosened his grip, giving her the freedom to escape while still guarding himself. Anxious to be away, Amirah sat up too suddenly. She wobbled sideways, crashing into him. He swiftly grabbed her again, holding her up. The action brought their faces no more than three inches apart. Amirah's heart did a flip-flop. Her glance took in the way his clean brown hair and beard sparkled in the firelight, and rested for an instant too long on the wry twist to his lips. The twist faded, going deadly serious.

He bent and kissed her.

The logical part of her brain told her she ought to pull away, but her body sent traitorous signals to keep her there. A tingle rushed through her, bewildering, frightening. His mouth moved expertly, striking fire along her every nerve. She instinctively kissed him back. And for a timeless moment she let herself drown in the sensation of his strong arms around her and the passionate, leisurely way his lips moved. She'd dated in Academy, like everyone else, but no man had ever kissed her like this. His closeness comforted like a rifle in her hands in a desperate battle. She felt safe for the first time in too many years to remember. But . . .

He clutched her more powerfully against him and she wrenched herself away so violently, she sprawled across the floor like a dead squid.

Their gazes met . . . like those of two people staring at each other over dueling pistols. He was breathing as hard as she was and an odd glint sparkled in his eyes.

Amirah hesitated, suddenly uncertain. Then she shook her head and feebly rolled onto her side. The stone floor smelled dusty and cool. "You have a knack for making me commit embarrassing acts, Tahn."

He grinned and slowly extended a hand, offering to help her up. "And I'm worse once you get to know me. How are you feeling?"

Amirah reached out and took his hand, letting him pull her upright. His fingers felt large and strong in her grasp. She held them securely. "Too good for either one of our best interests," she commented honestly.

"Affirmative, Captain."

They talked long into the night and Amirah found she could discuss almost anything nonclassified with him. She never felt awkward, or at a loss for words as she often did with other men. Cole let her talk about herself and the daily annoyances aboard the *Sargonid*. He sympathized with her personnel problems and offered solid experienced advice. They veered away from any personal issues, like Jason Woloc or Jeremiel Baruch, and by the

time evening had worn on into early morning, Amirah
felt unpleasantly happy. She turned and gazed worriedly
at him.

"What's wrong?" he asked.

"I like you."

He smiled reproachfully. "Well, don't worry. In another day you'll think I'm intolerable. Most people do."

"That's comforting," she said, and meant it.

CHAPTER 23

Just out of the shower, Jeremiel stood before the mirror over the table in his cabin, fastening the cuffs of his clean black battlesuit. He had one hour before he had to be on the bridge to initiate the exit from light vault.

He glanced around the disarray of crystal sheets strewn over the table, desks, and floor. Several piles leaned precariously against the walls and created a barricade around Carey's gauze sleep shirt beside their bed. He'd gone over and over every detail of the Horeb battle until he prayed he'd ferreted out each possible pitfall, but so much depended upon things he couldn't be certain of. If the Underground fleet emerged from vault on top of five bunched cruisers, a lot of Jeremiel's people would die before they could slip into vault again.

He shook his head tiredly. The game he played had few reliable rules, except those imposed by the laws of physics. Because his ships utilized singularity drives for power generation and time dilation, warping the space around the vessels to literally create a hole in space-time, they could drop directly out of vault on top of an enemy—but not when that enemy orbited a friendly planet. The gravity waves shed by his fleet would pulverize Horeb's populace. That critical fact meant they had to emerge a safe distance away. Unfortunately, that distance gave the enemy cruisers about fifteen seconds to spot them and prepare for battle before Jeremiel could fire a shot. For two days, he'd been living contingency plans in his sleep, running first one, then another.

He smoothed his sleeves down and gazed hard at himself in the mirror. Black smudges marred the skin beneath his bloodshot blue eyes. His mouth had a cynical twist to it, as though he already tasted the bitterness of battle.

He took a few swipes at his hair and beard with Carey's brush, then started for the door. He stopped when the glint of her golden necklace caught his eye. It lay coiled on the edge of the table, half covered by a crystal sheet.

Gently, he reached out and picked it up. It swung like a glimmering pendulum in his hand. He remembered the day Cole had given it to Carey.

They'd been standing in a circle of people at her birthday party, laughing, feeling joyous. He and Carey had been married for less than a year, but even then, he couldn't remember what life had been like without her. The seventh level lounge roiled with a riot of happy people dressed in civilian clothes. Gowns of amber and mauve dotted the gathering like gems. Soldiers in the Underground rarely had a chance to relax and dress up, but when they did, they celebrated to the hilt. Bottles of champagne passed among the group like rifle charge packs before a fight.

Cole had shouldered his way through the crowd and into their circle, the necklace in his hand. "Here," he'd said warmly. His gaze had gone over Carey as though she were a priceless treasure. "This is the one you liked, isn't it?"

She'd seen and admired the piece of jewelry in a tiny shop on the planet of Trekow. Cole held out the rare ancient locket and Carey's green eyes widened. She reverently took it from his extended hand. "My God, this cost a fortune. We must be paying you too much to captain that leaky vat of grease."

Cole had lifted a brow. "I might take back that inscription."

Carey eyed him suspiciously and turned the necklace over, reading, "To my best friend for never openly declaring mutiny. Love, Cole."

She'd stared at the words as though memorizing them before she turned to embrace Tahn. They'd held each other for several seconds and Jeremiel had watched Cole's face change, going from that wry offhand affection to something much deeper. Tahn had closed his eyes and nuzzled his cheek against Carey's auburn hair before hugging her fiercely and backing away.

"Well," Cole had said softly. "Happy birthday. I have

to get back to my ship. Merle never gives me more than an hour at a time off."

Carey had nodded understandingly, but her strained smile clearly stated that she'd rather he stay for the rest of the party. "Are you sure?" she'd asked. "I wish—"

"No, I . . ." Cole had glanced at Jeremiel, then lowered his eyes. "I have to go. Drink enough champagne for both of us."

"I will."

Smiling awkwardly one last time, Cole had walked away, filtering through the crowd, occasionally stopping to swap lies with someone before he exited the lounge.

Jeremiel had never mentioned to Carey that he suspected Cole's love for her went beyond friendship. He feared that out of some strange sense of loyalty to him, she might unconsciously alter her close relationship with Cole.

Jeremiel gripped the necklace tightly and put it in his pocket. "I'd never do that to you, Carey."

Neither Cole nor Carey had ever truly blended into the Gamant structure, though Carey had managed to sink deeper because Jeremiel eased the way with constant explanations about cultural taboos, unique behavioral patterns, or lengthy lessons in Gamant psychological history. But Cole and Carey shared too many moments of togetherness from another world for either to ever feel complete without the other near.

He absently lifted and tossed a crystal sheet across the table, watching it flutter down onto a new pile. In the past five minutes, a burning fear had gripped him. "Stay alive, Cole. *Do you hear me?*"

He exited into the quiet hallway, briskly heading for the bridge.

* * *

Magistrate Mastema sat in his private compartment aboard the tiny transport vessel and peered out the portal at the scattered lights of Naas, the capital city of Palaia. They glimmered like strewn jewels in the predawn light. The sight brought him such delight he could barely contain it. On the outskirts of Naas the Engineering Spires pierced the sky like lavender spikes. The station's alternate control room was hidden there, deep beneath the soil.

He'd been the original architect and supervisor for the actual construction of the station complex. He'd had to create a hollow vessel which could hold a changeable number of primordial singularities ranging in size from a few billion tons to several trillion. The trick came when he set the Reissner-Nordstom charged holes into synchronous orbit inside the station. Ounce for ounce, the electric fields generated by those holes were enormously more powerful than average gravitational fields. Mastema's genius had been in displacing and focusing that energy into a protective net of electromagnetic shells around Palaia. No one could penetrate their shields from without, which is why Slothen had wisely set the Gamant-filled satellites in orbit just within the outermost shell boundary. That way, the ruling Magistrate had explained, no fanatic could blow them up and they were instantly vulnerable to the slightest manipulation of the shields. From the main control room on Palaia, anyone could vaporize the satellites at the push of a patch—and the Gamant Underground certainly realized it.

Mastema leaned closer to the portal, watching the broad plains pass beneath his ship. Trees and brush dotted the expanse. It was a masterpiece of workmanship. After he'd completed the containment vessel, he'd coated it with a thin veneer of foamlike petrolon. Mastema had used the protein molecules which formed the outer wall of the gigantic Giclasian Sulfolobus bacteria as a structural template; by coating the protein layer with petrolon, then using ion milling, his engineers had carved out a superbly patterned swiss cheese underlayer upon which the beautiful valleys and mountains of Palaia sprouted.

"Please fasten your restraints, Magistrate. We are preparing to land," the toneless mechanical voice of his pilot, Dybbuk, informed.

Mastema leaned back in his chair and hit the EM patch. The energy net snugged around him like an invisible blanket. As the ship gently set down, pale morning sunlight filtered through the portal to drench Mastema in a rosy veil. His white robe glimmered as though strewn with pink diamonds. He sighed appreciatively and struck the patch to release his restraints.

Two Giclasian medical technicians, Osman and Querido, entered his private room and immediately began chattering, their blue limbs spinning in a blur to get Mastema onto an antigrav gurney and covered with a warm pink and blue striped blanket. Weak from the centuries of slumber, he still couldn't walk under his own power. The techs attached protective defensive nodes to his gurney. Once outside, they'd activate them and a transparent energy shield would engulf all of them as they moved to the safety of the nearest building.

The side door of the ship opened and a ramp descended. Outside, hundreds of soldiers formed a perimeter within the rectangular landing pad to keep back the civilians who'd gathered. A cheer of adulation went up when his technicians pushed his gurney out into the morning sunlight. Mastema's skin prickled when the nodes activated and the protective shield snapped on around them.

Osman pushed him very quickly, heading toward the broad door ahead. Soldiers lined out around them, trotting forward at double time. Mastema waved four of his hands at the crowd and reveled in their shouts and cheers for him. Had Slothen staged this, he wondered? Or had the populace simply come of their own accord once they'd heard of this impending arrival? Regardless, it made him feel very welcome.

Mastema reclined atop his antigrav as they entered the doorway to the main governmental headquarters. He passively watched the white walls and staff go by as Osman shoved him down first one passageway, then another. Nearly every species in the galaxy paraded through these corridors. Though most passing by were Giclasians, he spotted several Orillians with their transparent bloblike forms, Rossians with hard green carapaces covering their multilimbed forms—even a few humans. If the galaxy weren't in such a mess, he would have felt a great sense of accomplishment, because it was this integrated wholeness he'd been striving for from the beginning when he created Palaia and the Union of Solar Systems.

Osman, Querido, and two soldiers accompanied him

into the transport tube that ascended upward to floor forty-five. When the door slid back, Mastema found himself in a ten by ten foot square outer office with lavender walls and stark white furniture. The Giclasian secretary behind the desk immediately stood and bowed with all of his limbs extended in a fan display.

"Greetings, Magistrate. I am Topew, Slothen's assistant. Please let me know if I can in any way make your stay here more comfortable."

Mastema smiled. "That's very kind, Topew. Thank you."

"Magistrate Slothen is expecting you, sir. Please continue down the hall to the end and the guards will admit you. I'll notify Slothen that you've arrived."

"Very good."

He flicked a hand at Osman and Querido. They shoved him down the corridor. Two human sergeants in purple dress uniforms guarded Slothen's office. When they saw Mastema coming, they saluted crisply and hit the patch to open the door. Osman pushed Mastema inside.

Slothen rose from behind his desk and bowed reverentially. "Master Mastema, welcome home to Palaia."

"Home, yes." Mastema turned to Osman. "Leave us. I'll call you when I'm ready to go."

Osman and the rest filed out and the door slipped closed.

Slothen remained standing, watching Mastema frown at the office. Fifty feet square, the room had a high arching ceiling with lavender walls and carpet. Slothen's desk sat like a round hunching turtle before the windows. Holograms of galactic solar systems hung at Giclasian eye level, seven feet off the floor. Beautiful. The technology had advanced so much since Mastema's years that he felt if he reached out he could close his fist on a handful of stars.

"Mastema, let me inform you that our forces on Horeb have captured Mikael Calas. He is, at this very moment, on his way to Palaia."

"Good work, Slothen. What about Cole Tahn?"

Slothen threaded his fingers through his blue wormlike hair. "I'm afraid we have no idea of his whereabouts."

"I take it your people ruined the operation in the Anai system?" Mastema's face creased with contempt.

"Unfortunately, Master, there are fourteen inhabited planets in that distant system. It took us time to isolate the ships which belonged to the Underground. We had our best people working on it."

Mastema grunted his displeasure. In the huge windows that overlooked Naas, he could see his reflection. His withered balloon-shaped head gleamed like polished azure in the bright saffron light streaming through the panes. Flashes of rifle fire from the plains drew his attention. Above them, fighters dove through the lemon-colored skies. "What is that, Slothen? Battle? *On the station?*"

Slothen turned to look. "No. Just training exercises, Master. Threats from the Gamant Underground have forced me to keep our troops on Palaia constantly war-ready."

"Slothen, I can think of no way the Underground could penetrate our shielding. However, it's a prudent measure on your part. Especially given the level of angst among our galactic citizens. I ordered my staff to let me listen to selective bands on the ship's communication system. I was shocked to hear freighters and fighters alike discussing the rumors of an impending Underground attack on Palaia." He sighed in agitation and scrutinized Naas. The city spread in a perfectly ordered hexagon around the central governmental complex. Mirrored buildings thrust up like spears, interspersed regularly with crimson thypan trees, or grassy parks and fountains.

Gracefully, Slothen sat down in his chair and smoothed his fingers over a mound of crystal sheets on his desk. "The Underground and all Gamant planets have rallied against us, Master. It seems rumors of the coming of the legendary Gamant *Mashiah* have bolstered their spirits. In the planetary rebellions, they're throwing themselves at our troops in suicidal waves."

"The Mashiah? You mean Mikael Calas. But if we have him—"

"No, not Calas, though I thought so at first, too. It's a child, apparently. We don't know his identity, but the rumors of his birth have spread like wildfire through the Gamant forces. The level of galactic fear is rising. Already Gamant civilians have launched attacks on the loyal Magisterial populaces of a variety of planets and stations, screaming, 'Mashiah! Mashiah!' ''

Before Mastema could comment, Slothen continued, "Please keep in mind as well, that Palaia Zohar is on its final approach. Already the gravitational pull is enormous. Our engineers are working overtime to keep the station in stable orbit."

"What does that have to do with this unknown Gamant Mashiah?"

Slothen's wormlike hair writhed and twisted in agitation. Mastema felt his own wriggle in response. "Master, there are legends—we've been aware of them for centuries—of this Mashiah opening a Great Gate to the Light Everlasting through which he destroys us and saves his people. Zohar seems to be the logical corollary to the Gate."

Mastema felt his pulse race. In his memories, a golden alien whispered, *"Verily, verily, I say unto you, Magistrate, that single drop of heavenly dew will plunge your empire into the eternal pit of darkness unless you capture it. When Mikael stands in the mountains on high and opens that gate, all that you and yours have built will come crashing down . . . he'll destroy you."*

Mastema laced his fingers together anxiously. "Slothen, how long until the situation with Zohar grows critical?"

"We reach perihelion in four days."

"Then that's undoubtedly when the Underground troops will level their assault. Are you prepared for that?"

"Yes. We are. We have a very special weapon, Master. It's been years in the developmental stage, but as of a few days ago, we believe it's perfected."

"And what is this weapon?"

Slothen got up from behind his desk and grimaced at the rifle fire blazing in the distance. Against the lemon-colored skies, his azure skin had a greenish cast. An eerie light had invaded his eyes. "I need to show you. You would doubt it if I simply told you about how it works. Let's finish our discussion here and we'll go next door and I'll let you judge its efficacy for yourself."

"All right. I'll wait. In the meantime, tell me when Calas will arrive?"

"Three days."

"Good. I want the boy delivered to me the instant he sets foot on Palaia. And keep searching for Tahn. You *must* find him soon or we're all doomed. Do we understand each other?"

"Yes, Master. I don't fully understand the correlation you see between Calas and Tahn, but I trust your judgment implicitly. Is there anything else you'd like to know before we—"

"No, I want to see this weapon first, then we'll discuss the rest of our strategy."

Mastema reached down to the com unit on his gurney to signal Osman, but Slothen's voice stopped him.

"Master, there's one other thing I need to tell you." Slothen folded four of his arms over his stomach and chest.

"What is it?"

"The military governor of Horeb, the planet where Mikael Calas was captured, mysteriously appeared here in our hospital yesterday. It's very strange. He claims he was standing on the balcony of his palace when a whirling maw of blackness opened up and swallowed him. The next thing he knew, he was here. I don't know what to make of it."

Mastema's face slackened. He peered disquietingly at Slothen. "What does he know of Calas and Tahn? Have you questioned him??

"No, sir, not yet. He was raving when we found him. He's still under sedation. We're regrowing one of his hands, which was sliced off in the fighting on Horeb. Should I set up a meeting with him for you?"

"Immediately! I want to see your weapon first—then Governor Ornias."

Mastema signaled his medical staff. Slothen's door slipped open and Osman and Querido entered, standing stiffly at attention. Mastema tugged his striped blanket up to his thin neck and cocked his head. "Let's go, Slothen."

"Yes," Slothen affirmed as he strode toward Mastema's gurney. "The viewing room is just next door."

* * *

Aktariel emerged into an ancient city. He left the vortex open behind him, letting its cool winds flutter his plum-colored robe. Magnificent buildings covered the grassy rolling hills that spread in a multishaded green blanket into the distance. He tiredly leaned a shoulder against one of the Appian arches and studied the graceful sweep and soar of the aqueduct.

"*Rachel*," he whispered tautly. "Where are you?"

In rage and fear, he shouted, *"And where is that child?"*

His voice echoed from the hills, coming back to him sounding more desperate than he'd thought. He could sense a growing pattern in her jumps: Persia and Palestine, Crimea and Regus—aqueducts and artificial lakes.

"We're so close, Rachel. *How can you do this to me?*"

If he only had the time, he'd unravel the tangle she'd woven so skillfully. But he didn't! He tramped back into the void.

CHAPTER 24

Mikos Williamson sat stiffly in his command chair aboard the *Marburg*. A short man with a bald head, slanting blue eyes, and a crooked nose, the captain's bars on his shoulders shone with a fiery luster against the purple fabric of his uniform. On the forward screen, Sinai blazed with a blue-green sheen beneath the fires of the system's sun. He could see the *Hammadi* paralleling their movements, searching the opposite side of the planet. They'd been orbiting Sinai for damned near eight hours straight. His butt hurt. His stomach growled. But he couldn't leave the bridge, not when they were in the midst of a blue alert. Damn it. He didn't even *like* Amirah Jossel. In fact, he despised her. The hotshot on the block, she'd shown him up in more than one battle. *Him!* A seasoned war veteran. He still fumed about it.

"This search is ridiculous," he grumbled to himself. The *Marburg* had important business to take of. The people on Delores 2 needed the supplies his ship carried.

Irritated beyond reason, he plucked nervously at the loose green thread in his chair seat. Looking down at the lower level of the bridge, Williamson could see that all his bridge officers seemed equally unhappy with the current situation. They didn't particularly adore Jossel either. Once every few minutes, somebody expelled an exasperated breath or muttered a curse. On the data screens that bent in an amber and green strip around the ceiling, Mikos could see all the information coming in from Sinai. The damned planet seethed like a tangle of gaseous maggots in a rotting corpse.

He grumbled distastefully and called to his navigation officer, Vela Kerr. "Vela, have we gotten anything coherent yet?"

She swiveled around in her chair to gaze at him

through dark eyes. A medium-sized black woman with a short kinky halo of hair around her beautiful face, she had full lips and a narrow, aquiline nose. "If you mean, have we detected any evidence that Captain Jossel is being held prisoner in this ball of fuming hydrogen—no." She crossed athletic arms over her ample breasts. "If you ask me, sir, I think we're on the proverbial wild goose chase."

Mikos rubbed his chin and spat a string of blasphemies to himself. "We're chasing geese while the victims of war on Delores 2 are starving. Wonderful." He drummed his fingers on his knee. "If the terrorists used a distortion device—"

"They could have signaled us from anywhere. Yes. We've already checked all the possibilities. The signal was sent on such a dispersed beam that it echoed from every solid object in this system. Sinai, Horeb, and the asteroid belt that hovers between the tenth and eleventh planets reflected the most strongly. For the life of me, I can't figure out why Woloc didn't dispatch at least one cruiser to search the belt. We could probably have eliminated one or more of the possibilities by now and saved time in the long run."

"I suspect, Lieutenant, that Woloc was endeavoring to assure our safety. Terrorists are clearly in this area. Two cruisers together can fend off nearly any attacking vessel, but if separated—"

"*Maybe* terrorists are involved, sir." She lifted a brow challengingly.

"What are you talking about?"

Vela tapped a thumb against her left bicep. "Well, consider the details: Jossel is attacked in broad daylight in the middle of a major government complex, her security team is killed, she's captured, and no one sees a thing? Either the person who did it is a goddamned magician—or it never happened."

"Never . . ." He hooked blunt fingers around his chair arms and bent forward pensively. "You think this is a ruse? By whom? Governor Ornias? Well, he's certainly not above such things, but—"

"Not necessarily Ornias, sir. This could be some sort of Magisterial exercise to test our strategic abilities."

He blinked harshly. "An exercise? Why?"

She shrugged. "I'm saying it's possible. You'll recall that the Magistrates pulled a stunt very similar to this in the Wocet system almost a year ago."

"Yes, that's true." He meditatively fingered his ear. Jossel had bested him on that one, too. Maybe that's what this was, a test to see if he'd fall for the same bait? Name of God! That would give the military advisory council an almost flawless excuse to court-martial him. "Blast! Do you think Jossel cooked this up with the MAC and is monitoring all of us!" The very thought grated like sandpaper on his eyes.

On the forward monitor, red flares of gas shot out from Sinai, piercing the blue-green haze like veins of blood. At the very edge of his vision, he thought he caught movement, as though a dark serpentine shadow slithered across the floor to his left. He swerved around in his chair, staring breathlessly, but only the white bridge walls and and gray carpet met his probing gaze. In the far reaches of his mind, he thought he heard a voice whispering urgently. An uneasy feeling crept through him. He physically shook himself to get rid of it. *Too damned long without a solid meal.*

His com officer, Sung Toktaga, turned to him. A petite Oriental woman with long black hair, she had an oblong head and delicate features. "Regardless of whether or not this is a test, sir, I think Vela's right. Somebody ought to be searching that asteroid belt. Those rocks are small and uncomplicated enough that one pass would probably be enough to eliminate that area."

Williamson stared intently at the forward screen, watching the gases that cloaked Sinai shift and flare as though they'd caught fire. An actinic marmalade burst roiled into space. The voice in his head seemed to grow stronger, pushing him.

"Yes," he heard himself muse quietly. The word startled him. Had he meant to say that? He nervously chewed the insides of his cheeks. It did make sense to search the belt. If Jossel and the MAC had orchestrated some sort of strategic test, then he'd save himself by having fathomed the flaw in the game plan. *Damn Jossel!* In all the battles where she'd taken the glory, she'd pulled some trick to win. The memories gnawed at him.

And Jossel always accepted her medals and praise humbly, never lauding herself, giving all the credit to her crew. It irritated Williamson until he wanted to wring her neck. He viciously picked at the loose thread on his chair again.

Impulsively, he commanded, "All right, Vela. Take us out of orbit. We'll go search that asteroid belt and then return here. Toktaga, contact Captain Stein and tell her we'll be gone for an estimated six hours."

"Understood, sir." Her hands darted over her console and the com aura glowed to life around her head.

The stars emerged as they left the flaming splendor of Sinai and sailed out into space. The elliptical galaxy, NGC 147, dusted the heavens. At this proximity, individual stars in the midst of the feature shimmered brilliantly. Williamson felt suddenly irritable. As though he'd been maneuvered into something he didn't quite feel comfortable doing, though he couldn't for the life of him figure out why not.

* * *

Mastema cast a quick glance at Slothen who sat in a chair beside him in the dark. Gibor seemed unaffected, as though he'd seen this same display a thousand times. Mastema clamped his jaw tightly and reclined on his gurney, hands crossed in his lap, gaze focused intently on the holographic film that played out in the center of the room before them. The clarity of the projection left him amazed. It could have been real and happening now. . . .

A young blonde girl, perhaps thirteen or fourteen years old, slumped in a probe chair with her eyes wide open. She wore a pale blue robe, long and flowing—the kind old Gamants considered orthodox. Slothen paced in front of her, talking softly, reassuringly. The child nodded and smiled at Slothen affectionately. She seemed calm, except for the constant twitching of her small hands that lay palms up on her thighs.

"Good, Amirah," Slothen praised. He patted her cheek. *"You're doing fine. Now please shove the probe helmet off your head and stand up."*

"Yes, sir." Amirah stepped out of the chair and tripped obliviously over the edge of a rug. She caught her balance and stood rigidly, apparently completely unaware of her surroundings. The only thing she seemed to see was Slothen.

"All right, Amirah. Wake up now. There, that's good."

The child shook long blonde hair over her narrow shoulders and gazed at Slothen curiously. *"Are we finished for today, Magistrate?"*

"Almost," Slothen assured gently. *"Are you anxious to see your grandmother?"*

Amirah's pretty face beamed joyously. *"Oh, yes, sir. She didn't want to come, you know. She hates Palaia Station. I don't know why."*

Slothen put a hand on Amirah's back and guided her to the center of the small, strangely empty probe room. Only the probe chair and helmet took up space in the far corner. *"Wait here, Amirah. I'll get your grandmother for you."*

"Thank you, sir."

Slothen left the child alone in the room and the lights dimmed to near nothingness. Amirah wrung her hands nervously, looking around, obviously unable to see in the sudden blackness.

A few seconds later, the door through which Slothen had excited opened and two guards shoved an elderly Gamant woman with scraggly gray hair and seething eyes into the room. Blood soaked her long white robe in lurid patches. *"The savior is coming!"* the old woman shouted at her brutal guards. *"You'll see! He'll kill you all for the way you've treated Gamants!"*

Amirah cried out and put a hand over her mouth as she gazed in horror at her grandmother's injuries. *"Grandmama!"* she screamed and ran to the old woman. Slipping an arm around her grandmother's waist, she held her up and tried to drag her to the probe chair. *"Oh, Grandmama, what did they do to you?"*

A din of Gamant voices, like a frantic platoon overrunning an enemy position, rang out over the room com. Then Slothen's voice rose above the others: *"Now, Amirah. Hurry."*

The child's eyes glazed. She weaved on her feet, stumbling as though the very room had turned upside down. . . .

Slothen froze the holo—
He turned to Mastema with glittering lavender eyes. "She's living the programming now. She thinks the battle has begun and the room is shaking."

Mastema's brows lowered in fascinated understanding. "She has no idea what's happening to her?"

"No. None."

"Go on. I want to see the rest."

Slothen struck the patch to start the holo again—

Amirah grabbed her grandmother ferociously and pulled her to her feet, dragging her across the room toward the door as fast as she could.

"Amirah!" the old woman screamed. *"What's the matter? Put me down!"*

"No, Grandmama, no!" Amirah wept uncontrollably. *"Hurry! We have to hurry! It's coming!"*

The old woman struggled to wrench her wounded body out of the child's wild, clawlike grip. They struggled against each other, but the old woman's injuries left her too weak to break free. *"They're doing this to you, Amirah! Let me go!"*

"What? I don't understand. Hurry! Grandmama, please, before it gets us! It's almost here!"

The old woman tore free from Amirah's grip and tumbled to the floor. She lay panting, staring up at the ceiling. *"Filthy demons!"* she cried out. *"What have you done to my granddaughter? Slothen? You* nahash! *The holy serpent is coming! You hear me? He'll wipe you and your government from the face of the universe!"*

Amirah threw herself to the floor beside her grandmother and started jerking viciously on the old woman's injured arm. Her grandmother sobbed in pain and tried to shove her granddaughter away. *"Stop it, Amirah! Don't let them do this to you! Didn't you hear a word I just said? We'll be free soon! Don't let them do this to you!"*

Amirah shook her head violently in confusion. *"What does that mean, 'nahash'? I don't know what a holy serpent is, Grandmama! What is it?"*

Abruptly, the door slipped open again, throwing a rectangle of amber light across the dark room. Slothen entered, a pistol in his hand. The old woman slid backward on the floor, weeping, cursing viciously—but the child simply stared blankly at the open door.

Slothen stopped the projection again—

"Jossel doesn't fully see me. She sees only a shadow of me. This image has changed in her mind over the past several years. She's separated me from the shadow, made us two distinct entities. It's a bad sign. It means that the compartment we so painstakingly erected to protect the trigger is breaking down.

"What does that mean about the trigger? Is it faulty? Can we rely on it?"

"If the barriers remain intact, we can rely on it. If she breaks through them, there's no way of knowing. It may continue to work. It may not. We erected an additional safety mechanism in case it happened sometime accidentally—hopefully it will work if she breaks through the programming deliberately, too. But, as you'll soon witness, when we tested her resolve as a child, we chose the perfect subject—the only person in the world Amirah Jossel has ever loved."

Mastema shifted to get more comfortable on his gurney. The frozen image of the old woman seemed to peer directly at him, hateful, deadly. "Turn it on again, Slothen I want to know the full story here."

"Yes, Master."

The holo came to life—

Slothen walked forward and put the pistol in the child's limp hand, folding her fingers around the grips. Once she felt the weight of the weapon, Amirah lifted the pistol expertly. Slothen smiled, baring his needle-sharp teeth. They gleamed in the light streaming through the door. *"She called me* 'nahash,' *that means serpent in the Gamant language, Amirah. Yes, do you understand? Serpent."*

The child nodded and her face contorted against something too terrible to be borne. She screamed jaggedly and fell to the floor on her knees, the pistol still clutched in her hands.

Her grandmother crawled across the floor and enfolded Amirah tightly in her arms, pulling her to her blood-soaked chest and rocking her tenderly. *"Shh, baby! Don't cry. I don't know what they've done, but you must remember who you are. Don't be a pawn for them!"*

Slothen backed away toward the door. Just before exiting, he whispered, *"Serpent, Amirah—'nahash.' "* Darkness fell over the room.

Amirah sobbed in wild despair and fought madly, insanely, shrieking and trying to get away, but the old woman managed to hold her fast.

"No, Amirah! It's me! It's Sefer—Grandmama! I love you, baby. Stop this! Don't let them . . ."

Amirah jerked one arm free, lifted the pistol and triggered it. The shot severed her grandmother's head. Blood splashed Amirah in hot red gouts and she screamed and screamed.

Slothen cut the holo completely. The room went dark until he turned up the lights. His blue forehead shimmered in the glare. "What do you think?"

Mastema fingered his withered chin. The lavender walls suddenly seemed too bright, too stark. He swallowed convulsively. "It might work. Now I understand why you wanted her in the hands of the Underground. That's certainly where *he* would be—*if they know who he is.* When are you sending the armada to Horeb for cleanup duty?"

"They were dispatched days ago."

CHAPTER 25

As the *Marburg* approached the tumbling rocks of the asteroid belt, Williamson heaved a sigh and got out of his chair to pace the carpet of the upper level. The three-sixty screens glimmered. He studied the activities of each level of the ship. Deck four mess was scurrying to determine the cause of a dispenser malfunction. Engineering had suffered a minor inexplicable fire in one of the com units monitoring the singularity drive maintenance section. The flames had been quenched, but Engineer Tulem reported continuing efforts to determine the cause. He'd dedicated five of his twenty member crew to the project.

Williamson rubbed a hand over his moist bald head and squinted at the details. Curious. One of the engineering techs had noted "swelling blackness hovering over the com unit" just before it burst into flames. His heart started to throb suddenly, even before he heard Vela Kerr scream:

"Captain!"

Williamson glanced at her, then rapidly followed her gaze to the forward screen. Twenty, no thirty, ships dropped out of vault from different directions to form four flying wedges that streaked through the belt. He dove for his command chair.

"Shields on full! For God's sake, Kerr, get us out of here. We've got to have maneuvering room!"

"I can't!" she shouted back. "We're surrounded!"

The deck shuddered beneath Williamson's boots, building to a violent gut-raking quake that shook all the hope out of his soul. Gouts of violet fire spun from the invading armada. Combining their firepower, they poured every erg into the *Marburg*. Stunned and desperate, he shrieked, "Return fire! Target that cruiser!"

Cannon blasts flashed from the *Marburg*, lancing the big silver ship. But his own shields began to waver, fluctuating wildly under the concentrated attack. Individually, these petty craft could do nothing to him! But when orchestrated in concert, they could kill him and his entire crew in less than a heartbeat.

"No, no!" Toktaga yelled shrilly. Dark hair fringed her forehead. "We've been ambushed!"

The lights on the bridge flickered. Consoles flared, overloaded, and went dead. Shields three, four, and five vanished, leaving the entire port side vulnerable. Williamson's shocked brain could barely take it all in. His lips moved spasmodically with soundless orders.

Kerr spun around in her chair. "What are we going to do? *Captain!*"

"I—I don't—"

"We've got to escape this formation or we're dead, damn it!"

"I—we . . . *Ram that cruiser!*" he shouted in a flash of illumination, coming half out of his seat. *"Full speed ahead!"*

She lunged to comply and the g-force slammed Williamson back into his chair. He clutched the arms as his ship hurtled headlong through a flickering obstacle course of freighters and starsails. Violet beams continued to rake the *Marburg*.

Williamson watched mutely as shields one and two buckled and collapsed. His body tingled with numbness. *If he'd only stayed close to the* Hammadi, *he and Stein could have concentrated fire and blasted these petty ships to kingdom come. . . .*

He sucked in a sharp breath. The head-on shot that whirled from the enemy cruiser lanced Engineering and split his ship in half. Reaction mass boiled out across the blackness of space.

He barely heard himself scream.

* * *

Relief drenched Jeremiel when they exited vault and saw only three cruisers. "Sound battle stations, Eli," he commanded.

"Aye, sir," his communications officer input the order

and a flurry of activity swept the bridge, officers checking
energy readings, reconfirming calculations already laid
into the ship's computers. Blue alert flared on the overhead monitors.

Jeremiel braced himself as the *Zilpah* shot toward the
two cruisers orbiting Horeb. One of those vessels had
reacted with stunning swiftness. Already cannon fire
splashed his shields in blasts of purple. But on every
monitor he saw his own ships dropping out of vault,
forming up to box the planet. When enough had appeared, he scrutinized his bridge crew.

He noticed the frantic movements of Shira Gaza's fingers over her nav controls. She'd taken over Carey's
duties—and had gone very pale in the past few minutes.
Unaccustomed to the responsibilities of being second in
command, her brown eyes had tensed as though she
expected some monster to rise up and swallow her whole.
Her nervousness put the entire bridge crew on edge. An
engineering navigator by training, Gaza had never before
seen battle from the stunning vantage of the bridge—but
she was the best he had. She'd started to sweat profusely.
Her short ebony locks fell around her triangular face like
charred weeds. In the back of Jeremiel's mind, he wished
Carey were here.

"Gaza, target that closest cruiser. Fire."

Her fingers danced over her console and a beam of
violet shot out from his ship. She missed. The shot
glanced off the shields of the cruiser on the right and
slammed the planet. A burst of dust and debris plumed
on the planet's surface. Jeremiel's heart lurched. *Had she
hit any population centers?*

"Retarget, Gaza," he ordered tautly.

"I'm sorry, sir. I must have—"

"*Fire!*"

Sweat beaded on her face as she struggled to comply.
She made small anguished sounds under her breath. Jeremiel caught the horrified look Eli Gustav shot him. She'd
been his communications officer for fifteen years. Tall
and whip thin, she had a birdlike face with a beak nose
and dark eyes. A mass of red curls framed her narrow
face. She glanced repeatedly from Jeremiel to Shira
Gaza.

Beams lanced out again, this time striking both cruisers

dead-on. The starsails and freighters, all of which had now exited vault, added their power. The enemy's shields wavered in violent swirls of purple.

On the monitor to his left, Jeremiel could see Rudy's ship and thirty-odd supporting vessels pounding the cruiser that had been circling Sinai. Thank God those cruisers had fallen for their bait and separated. A brilliant wash of white illuminated the asteroid belt. Jeremiel could make out Merle's cruiser and several freighters streaking the star-strewn background beyond the system, turning to get into the fight again. Her contingent must have come out of vault seconds before they did. And that's why that Horebian cruiser had responded so rapidly. The enemy captain must have caught the beginning of the asteroid belt fight and immediately gone to battle stations.

"Commander! That cruiser on the left is dispatching fighters," Shira shouted, voice breaking under the strain.

"Easy, Lieutenant," Jeremiel said coolly. "Forget the fighters. Concentrate on those cruisers."

"But our smaller vessels—"

"—Will have to take care of themselves until we've neutralized the central threat."

Two dozen daggers of silver burst from the enemy's bays, darting and dodging the fire of the oncoming flotilla. The inertia of the Underground fleet kept it on a nearly straight line heading, making it easy for the fighters to outmaneuver them. Two starsails flared and died.

"Look!" Gaza thrust an arm out at the forward screen.

The cruisers around Horeb sailed closer together and combined fire, striking the *Zilpah* with a blast that shivered the ship's bones. Eli clutched wildly for her console to keep from falling out of her seat. Shields five and six wavered, fluctuating, redistributing energy.

Jeremiel's throat tightened. *Good move.* Those captains had ordered the fighters to engage the smaller ships, compelling his support forces to fend for themselves. Which left the *Zilpah* on its own, facing the combined firepower of two superior vessels.

Shield three failed. Shira slammed a fist into her com. Her mouth gaped open in horror. "Oh, my God! We're open! *We're open!*"

Jeremiel manipulated the *Zilpah* so that the aft shields

took the brunt of the attack. "Eli? Get on the auxiliary weapons com. Reroute and take over the guns. I want you to finish the attack. Target the cruiser on the left. Gaza, in another twenty seconds we're going to be at point blank range. Calculate a course so we can match with Merle and be ready to combine fire. Understood?"

"Yes, sir," she responded shakily.

Eli lurched from her seat, fighting the gut-twisting deck shudder to work her way to the com unit three niches over. She fell into the seat and began working the controls.

One of the Underground freighters miraculously hit an enemy fighter; it exploded. Bits of silver tumbled like ice crystals through the silent blackness of space.

Jeremiel glanced down, anxiously studying his chair control console. The temperatures of every shield had soared into the critical zone. If one of those cruisers didn't give soon. . . . He cut the power to shields one, two, and four, leaving the *Zilpah* open to any attack from behind.

"What are you doing?" Shira shrieked. "Those fighters—"

"Shut up!" Eli growled. "He's giving us more power for the weapons."

The planet loomed up at them like a huge ruby red ball shot from a cannon.

"Now, Eli. Fire!"

She poured every available erg into the cruiser on the left. The ship frantically tried to move, lunging sideways, trying to put a starsail between the *Zilpah* and herself, while still combining her fire with the other vessel's. The starsail, as though on cue, dove out of the way.

Merle swooped down from above, her guns flaring. She angled to meet Jeremiel's vector and they combined firepower. A brilliant splash of light flared just as they soared over Horeb. Jeremiel swiveled to gaze at the opposite screen. They'd holed the cruiser's hull. Atmosphere, debris, and bodies boiled into space in a sparkling torrent.

"Shift your fire to that other cruiser, Eli," he ordered. "Shira? Initiate course correction. Bring us back around."

"Yes, sir." Her hands fumbled over the controls.

On the surrounding monitors, Jeremiel saw his surviving starsails and freighters following behind in a flood. Around Sinai, a Magisterial cruiser sat dead in space, listing sideways. Rudy's contingent streaked the dark starry heavens in the distance, hurtling to match with him and Merle.

Jeremiel watched tautly as the remaining Magisterial cruiser sped out of Horeb's orbit and accelerated for vault.

He pounded the air with a hard fist. "Get back on com, Eli. Contact Kopal and Wells. We'll never get regrouped fast enough to catch that vessel before they make vault. We're going to have to get Horebians loaded and out of here as soon as we can before reinforcements arrive."

"Aye, sir."

A few seconds later, Rudy's drenched face appeared on the forward screen. His brown hair hung in limp wet strands over his forehead. Smoke filled the bridge of the *Hashomer*. In the background damage teams raced to contain the fires.

Jeremiel's eyes narrowed, gut tightening. "You all right, Rudy?"

"Nothing we can't handle." He put a fist over his mouth and coughed. "I talked to Merle. She's fine. She lost seven freighters. I lost a dozen starsails and four freighters." He coughed again. "What are we going to do about that cruiser that's boosting for vault?"

Jeremiel ground his teeth. "Let her go. We've got more important things to think about. Once you get your damage under control on the *Hashomer*, grab a shuttle and rendezvous with me here. You and Merle and I need to have a strategy session."

"Affirmative. Give me two hours. Kopal out."

The screen faded back to the star-streaked ebony sky. Jeremiel studied the lacy patterns of the galaxies, seemingly crocheted into lumpy bluish chains at their speed. He sank back in his chair. A hollow sensation of premonition crawled up his spine.

Too easy.

Those cruisers had fallen for the Wocet trap as though they'd had no information about the Underground's impending attack on Horeb at all.

Maybe he'd been wrong about the officer breaking?

Maybe the appearance of the Magisterial flotillas in the Moran and Tonopah systems had been pure coincidence?

Ludicrous.

Slothen was up to something. The government had just let the Underground destroy four of their cruisers.

A diversion? A soak-off maneuver? What?

He pulled in a deep breath. "Get me Captain Wells, Eli."

* * *

Ornias lay on his back in his hospital room, drugged and drifting in and out of consciousness. Memories of the terrors on Horeb charged his dreams. He saw again the deadly look on Rachel's face and heard the whine of the pistol when she'd cut off his hand. Then he found himself hurtling endlessly through a vast black sea which washed over him in glacial waves.

Cold, so cold. He shuddered and unconsciously tugged at his blue blanket, pulling it up over his chest. His maimed hand, being held tightly in the stim unit beside his bed, ached suddenly and violently. It burned as though set aflame.

"I'll find you, Rachel," he promised. "I'll find you and kill you for doing this to me."

Anger filled him, but fear came, too. How had she walked out of the air onto that windy balcony? And whose voice had come from the clouds? Did he really remember that, or had he just been dreaming?

His body felt light, rising unwittingly off the bed, and he found himself floating in a glimmering golden haze. Flickers of light played across his closed eyelids, moving, forming half-coalesced images of amber eyes and glowing faces before melting away.

"It never happened," a soft, kind voice assured. *"You never saw Rachel. There was no voice from the clouds."*

Ornias peered through the golden mist, looking for the man who spoke. "But it seemed so real," he challenged.

"You were delirious. That little beast, Horner, betrayed you. He drugged your wine just before you stepped out onto that balcony."

"Why?"

"Mikael Calas' rebel forces paid him two million notes."

Ornias grumbled to himself. Horner had no loyalty beyond what he got paid for. Still, he didn't recall drinking wine. Nor did he recall Horner being anywhere in sight.

"You're a liar! Why are you—"

"Because the patterns of time have been altered by Rachel's rashness. I have to put them back—if I can. You'd have been coming to Palaia anyway—but you'd have come through conventional means."

Stinging tendrils crept through Ornias' brain, as though someone tampered with his neural pathways. He fought back, struggling in the belly of the haze. "Who are you!" he demanded. "What do you want?"

Fiery golden arms swept him up and rocked him violently as though in the grasp of a storm. He felt himself being flung from one area of the glittering sea to another, and all the while his mind seemed to be playing tricks on him. As if molded from clay, the memories of Horner came back to him. And he saw himself climbing into a shuttle and fleeing Horeb and the terrible battles that raged in the skies overhead. Who had piloted the ship? Oh, yes, yes, Jiva Haro. He could see her smooth young face smiling at him. Yes, of course. That's how it had happened. . . .

CHAPTER 26

A tiny sliver of light penetrated through the crate lid, landing across Yosef's face like a burning slash of moon-glow. He glanced sideways at Ari. His oldest friend slumped in the corner. He had his long legs crammed against the wall. In the diffused light, his straggly gray hair shimmered like icy twigs.

Another bang sounded, followed by a shrill scraping. Someone laughed.

Yosef pressed his ear to the crate wall, listening for any sound which might tell him where they were. After they'd left Horeb the first time, they'd landed once for a brief interval. "Puddle jumping," Ari had called it. Their shuttle had settled again about a half hour ago and now soldiers swarmed all over, shouting orders, unloading crates.

"Hey!" someone shouted loudly.

Yosef jumped.

"Private Row? Jerry? Come here. I need help with this last crate."

"On my way, Sergeant Nelson."

The sharp clip-clopping of boots against the petrolon deck sounded. The hold bounced slightly as two men stepped inside. Yosef could hear their heavy breathing.

"Let's clear some of this junk out of the way so we can slide the crate to the edge of the hold, then the lifter can grab it," Nelson said.

Something squealed as it was pulled across the floor. A dull thud reverberated. Then Yosef saw Ari's eyes go wide as their crate began moving in a zigzagging pattern. Grunts and gasps pierced the air.

"Goddamn," Nelson cursed. "When the hell did they start making this stuff so heavy? It used to be feather-light."

"I don't know," Row said through a strained groan. The crate edged forward another foot. "Maybe they're using a new chemical compound. Or maybe the slime bags on Horeb put something into it they shouldn't have. I don't care how many armed guards you put around them, you can't trust Gamant laborers. They'll do anything they can to kill the lot of us."

"Well, at least we finally caught that boy that's been causing all the problems. Maybe now things will—"

"What was his name?"

"Calas. Mikael Calas."

Yosef and Ari exchanged a dread-filled look. They'd captured Mikael? Oh, dear God. And what of Sybil and Nathan? Yosef forced a swallow down his dry throat.

"He's Zadok Calas' grandson. You must remember the stories about that old warhorse? Quite a soldier, he was. Beat the Magistrates lots of times when the odds were a million to one against him."

Row snorted derisively. "You sound like you admire the old murderer, Nelson. That's all he was. A clever old murderer with delusions of godhood."

Yosef leaned heavily against the crate wall. Ari's withered face took on an aura of pure hatred. Yosef tried to smile reassuringly, as though it didn't really bother him that these strangers talked so about his brother, but Ari knew differently. Yosef fiddled aimlessly with his collar, trying not to succumb to the welling pain this unknown man had wrung from his heart.

Nelson paused. "Well, everybody's got a right to their opinion, but I sure as hell respected the old codger. My granddad fought against Zadok in the last Gamant Revolt. He had a lot of respect for Calas. Called him a 'goddamned miracle worker.' And meant it half-affectionately. But I'm glad we caught his grandson, too. Maybe things in the galaxy will calm down now."

"I doubt it," Row quipped. "Gamants are too stupid to know what's good for them. I think we're going to have to grind them out of existence before they'll swallow their pride and give up all their antiquated separatist beliefs to live like civilized people with the rest of us."

One final long groan of exertion came and the crate stopped moving. Yosef looked up. Through the tiny crack in the lid, he could see the brilliant glare of a hundred lustreglobes. Dozens of boots cracked against the floor outside. The voices he heard carried to him with a slight echo, as though the room gaped as broadly as a cavern. His mind searched out every time in his life he'd ever been in such a room and he—

He nearly fainted. He gripped the fabric over his heart and breathed hard. *The landing bay of a battle cruiser?* No, it couldn't be. Ari must have realized where they were, too, for his eyes widened.

"There," Nelson groaned. "The lifter can get it from here. How about some lunch? We're fifteen minutes late for mess right now. I don't know about you, but I'm half-starved after all the work this morning."

"Lunch sounds great."

"Yo! Savon!" Nelson called. "Let's give these people a lunch break!"

A soft din of approving voices responded. The sound of boots retreated. The noise in the bay died away to nothing. Yosef sank back against the wall, wiping the beads of perspiration from his forehead.

Ari watched him through slitted eyes. "I think we ought to go find that little ass first thing. I'd like to toss him one of these canisters as a gift."

Yosef shrugged. Only Ari would understand how the conversation about Zadok had hurt him. "Forget about him. Start thinking about Mikael. I wonder where they'll be keeping him? In the brig?"

"Probably." Ari smoothed a hand over his pointed chin. When he spoke again, a tightness had constricted his throat. "Or he could be in the probe room next to the hospital. You should be prepared for that, Yosef, in case we find him . . . not—not well."

Yosef squeezed his eyes closed momentarily. "Hurry. Let's get out of here so we can go look. Maybe we can stop any medical procedures before they get underway."

Ari nodded and adjusted the pack of books on his back before crawling forward. He gently shoved up on the lid, then slid it sideways and peeked out owlishly. Finally, he threw his long spidery legs over the lip of the crate and tumbled over the edge. A sharp crack sounded when he landed. "Name of God!"

"What's the matter?" Yosef asked, scrambling up to peer out into the white, starkly lit landing bay. He had to stand on his tiptoes to glimpse Ari because Ari was lying prostrate on his stomach on the white tiles of the bay floor. He'd obviously missed stepping on the nearer floorboard of the shuttle.

"Did you hurt yourself?" Yosef hissed accusingly.

Ari groaned and pushed up with his arms. "I broke my skull!"

"Good. Then you won't mind this." Yosef carefully lifted two of the finger-length canisters and held them upright in his left hand while he climbed out of the crate and eased down to the bay floor. Even the cans bore the ominous red triangles.

"Here," Yosef said, thrusting one of the canisters at his friend. "Take this. Put it in your pocket."

"My pocket? What for?" Ari took one between two fingers, glaring at it in case it did something sinister. He got to his feet. "Are you crazy? One wrong move, one trip in the hallway, and we could blow out this side of the cruiser."

"That's the point," Yosef answered as he slipped his into the breast pocket of his robe. "Who'd dare threaten a man with one of these in his hand? Now, come on, we've got to get out of here before they come back."

Yosef waddled forward, heading for the exit. The landing bay stretched in a two-hundred-foot square. Two fighters sat anchored against the far wall. Cartons, crates, and boxes filled every niche, stacked three and four high.

Ari speeded up when they neared the exit. He pushed Yosef back against the wall while he gazed out the tiny window to scrutinize the hallway beyond.

Yosef stood quietly for several minutes, then began to get suspicious. Ari had started to sweat. Tiny rivulets traced down his cheeks to soak his collar.

Worried, Yosef asked, "What's wrong? Is there somebody out there?"

"Yeah," replied Ari. "A gorgeous redhead. I love these formfitting purple uniforms."

"Get away from that door!" Yosef twined his fingers in Ari's sleeve and gruffly jerked him backward. "What's the matter with you? We're supposed to be finding Mikael and you're ogling women?"

"You know nothing about espionage. I wasn't ogling. I was spying. There's a big difference. You have to be extremely careful and extremely subtle or they catch you and crush your gonads with pliers."

Imperiously, Ari headed for the door on the other side of the bay. Yosef threw up his hands and waddled after Ari's stalking figure. When they reached the door, Ari quickly jumped out into the hallway. "Come on, Yosef. Hurry it up."

Yosef peered up and down the empty white corridor and sighed in relief. "Why did you jump out like that? What if somebody had been in this hall?"

"I would have startled them, that's what, and then I'd have to disarmed them. And once we get our hands on a gun we can do anything. We can put these canisters in strategic locations, take over this ship, and free the galaxy, and then when we're finished saving the universe we can go home and drink beer."

Yosef glanced up sullenly. Ari's gray mop of hair made him look like a deranged palm tree in winter. "I swear to God, sometimes I think your brain is possessed by a dead politician."

He halfheartedly shoved Ari's shoulder as he strode down the hall, his thoughts focused mainly on Mikael. Nothing made any sense. Why would they capture Mikael and put him aboard a battle cruiser? Why not just kill him if they wanted him out of the way?

Ari stepped out ahead of Yosef, sliding cleverly along the wall until he could see around the corner. "Okay, it's clear. Come on."

He stepped into the next corridor. Yosef followed and ran smack into two Magisterial corporals who had just entered from another connecting passageway. The corporals stopped, staring curiously at them.

From the corner of his mouth, Yosef accused, "Clear, eh?"

Ari lifted his long arms over his head. He walked forward like an ancient mechanical robot, a step at a time. *"Klaatu barada nikto!"* he said.

The blond with the flat nose whispered, "What language is that, Chuck?"

The brown haired one shook his head, "Got me. Look, old man, what are you doing here? This is a secured level of the ship. No visitors are allowed in the weapons division."

Ari continued his stiff-legged walk and Yosef help-lessly followed. What did Ari hope to do? Get close enough strutting like a demented mongoose to disarm them? Oh, Lord, what a thought. Already Yosef's gonads ached.

When Ari was no more than five feet from the con-fused soldiers, he repeated, "*Klaatu barada nikto.* That's girl talk. It means 'Take me to your leader.' "

Chuck propped his hand on the butt of his holstered pistol. *"Who are you?"*

Ari puffed out his chest proudly. "I'm Ari Funk and this is Yosef Calas. We're from Tikkun originally."

"Calas?" Chuck's dark eyes fastened on Yosef. He smoothly pulled his pistol and gestured with it. "Down the hall, both of you. I'll *take you to my leader*, all right. Move!"

Yosef put up his hands and trudged forward. Ari joined him, a wide grin on his face. Leaning sideways, Funk whispered, "Now we've got them. Just wait until we get to the bridge."

"You idiot! When we get to the bridge, they're going to kill us!"

Ari pursed his lips disdainfully and patted his front pocket where the hypinitronium rested. "Not with these, they won't."

Chuck called from behind, "Turn right and go through those big double doors."

Yosef rounded the corner and gasped when the doors to Engineering loomed up like square white barricades. "Oh, my."

"Wait a minute!" Ari protested. He swung around and glowered at the two soldiers. "I thought we were going to talk to somebody important. We want to see the acting captain!"

Chuck's right eye twitched in irritation. "Move, old man. I'm taking you to my *leader*, the ship's chief engineer."

"Bah!" Ari sliced the air with a fist. "He's not good enough. Do you know who we are?"

Chuck gripped his pistol tighter and pointed it at Ari's head. "No, but I guarantee we're going to find out. Now, *move!*"

Yosef grabbed Ari's sleeve and flung him forward. Ari

grumbled as he walked through the doors into a round tri-level chamber. Duty stations perched like wire birds' nests on each level. Yosef's gaze was drawn upward. He counted the men and women, tallying nineteen.

An ugly man with short stubby black hair and flat features straightened up from where he'd been bent over a console. His purple uniform stretched tightly over bulging muscles. He clasped his hands behind his back and stepped forward, examining Ari and Yosef the way he might check out bad computer programs.

"Who are these men, Corporal Gregor?"

Chuck jammed his pistol into Ari's back and said, "They claim their names are Funk and Calas. But we don't really know, Lieutenant Rad. We found them wandering around the weapons division alone."

Rad circled Ari like a cat playing with a mouse and Yosef cringed at the gleeful look on his oldest friend's face. Whenever Ari got that look, it usually portended some dim-witted action. Rad's eyes narrowed. "You're obviously civilians. What were you doing in the weapons division?"

Ari lifted his gray brows and grinned. In a casual move, he reached into his pocket and pulled out the deadly canister, holding it up so everybody in the room could see the red triangle. Soldiers gasped and stumbled over each other retreating to the far reaches of Engineering.

Rad's face went stiff. He didn't move a muscle. In a painfully quiet voice, he asked, "Do you know what that is, old man? You'd better give it to me before we all end up—"

"Bah!" Ari blustered. "Hand over your weapons! You first, Rad! Then collect them from everybody else in here."

Rad laughed. "Don't be foolish. We can kill you fifty times over before you hit the floor! *Give me that vial.*" He took a menacing step forward.

Yosef intervened. "If we hit the floor, Lieutenant, you won't have to worry about confiscating that canister." He reached into his own pocket and pulled his canister out. "Or this one either, for that matter."

Rad's hand quaked before he dropped it to his side.

CHAPTER 27

Ornias crushed the hem of his white sheet in annoyance as he watched the nurse fly around his dark hospital room. Giclasians moved with such a windmilling of arms and legs that they seemed to be blue blurs. Only this morning, they'd moved him into this fifteen by twenty-five foot long private room. It sported a tiny window on the far end, the lavender drapes drawn closed, and a monstrous tangle of stim equipment beside his bed. His maimed hand was tucked inside one of the sockets on the unit, being regrown. On the wall in front of him was a portrait of the current Sculptorian president. The woman's gray sagging flesh, bulging ant eyes, and triangular face set Ornias on edge. Did they think that having a half-dead witch staring down on patients improved their mood? *Giclasian logic.*

"There," his nurse piped in her shrill voice. She pushed her blue wormy hair back over her ears and smiled—baring her teeth like a dog about to attack. Ornias drummed his fingers on his sheet.

"There *what?*"

"You've been fed and medicated and your room is straightened nicely. I think you're ready to see Magistrate Mastema."

"Of course I'm ready. Get on with it."

She'd told him when she first came in that she was in a rush to prepare him for a visit from the elderly Magistrate. For the life of him, he couldn't figure out why Mastema would want to see him. Did it have something to do with his actions on Horeb? Surely they weren't going to reprimand him after he'd captured Calas? The imbeciles. They might. He peevishly plumped his pillow and sighed.

The door slipped open and two guards pushed Mastema in on an antigrav gurney. The Giclasian had a face like a blue withered prune. His ruby red mouth formed a circular wound on his face. But those eyes! They gleamed like fiery lavender pits.

Without taking his gaze from Ornias, Mastema waved to his guards. "Leave us."

"Yes, Magistrate," both guards chimed simultaneously and scurried from the room. The door closed with a soft thump.

Ornias stretched languorously, faking relaxation. "What did you want to discuss with me, Magistrate?"

Mastema cocked his balloon head. "Your experiences on Horeb, Governor. You'll be glad to know that our vessel, the *Sargonid*, is currently on its way here with Calas. Unfortunately, another of our cruisers, the *Vajda*, reports they fought a devastating battle with the Gamant Underground over Horeb."

Ornias glowered. "They lost, I take it."

"Quite so," Mastema breathed, but a peculiar look invaded his eyes—as though that fact didn't disturb him very much. He irritably restraightened his red and gray striped blanket over his squirming legs.

"But even after the *Sargonid* left, there would have been four cruisers circling—"

"There was nothing they could do. Captain Amirah Jossel had been captured by terrorist forces and the cruisers had split up throughout the system to search for her. The Underground fleet dropped in directly out of vault and started firing."

Ornias contemplatively caressed his bearded chin. The terrorist maneuver had to be a subplot of Baruch's military strategy to free the planet. How else could he convince five cruisers to split up when they'd already been suspecting an Underground assault? Despite his anxiety at being on Palaia, he was suddenly heartily glad he wasn't on Horeb. Had Baruch captured him, he'd be mincemeat by now.

"Tell me, Governor," Mastema asked. His eyes glowed with a haunted light. "How did you get to Palaia?"

Annoyed at the stupidity, Ornias responded shortly. "In a shuttle. How else?"

Mastema leaned back on his gurney. "But I thought . . .

That is, Slothen said that when the doctors found you lying on the floor in the hospital, you said a whirling maw of blackness had descended on Horeb and swallowed you up then delivered you here."

Ornias' lime green eyes narrowed condescendingly. "*What?* Is this some sort of poor joke?"

Mastema stared. "You don't remember?"

"Remember *what?*"

"The voice that came out of the clouds to talk to you before you were thrown into the void?"

"What voice? This is all gibberish!" Ornias accused at the top of his lungs. What were they trying to do? Convince him he was crazy and therefore unfit for service? Well, it wouldn't work! He needed that five billion a year to keep paying off that marvelous little planet he'd purchased in the heart of the Giclasian system! "What is the meaning of this nonsense, Magistrate? My experiences on Horeb were very simple. One of my own marines betrayed me and slipped a drug into my drink just before Mikael Calas' forces stormed the palace. My hand was severed in the fighting and I passed out. One of my loyal servants loaded me into a shuttle and flew me to Palaia."

Mastema's gaze darted over the dimly lit room as he whispered to himself, "What's he doing? Why would he bring Tetrax to Palaia and then . . ."

His voice faded away when a dark smudge welled in the corner. Ornias cried out and struggled to back away, but his maimed hand was glued tight inside the stim unit. He screamed as the shadow grew into a monstrous looming darkness that engulfed half of the room. In the heart of the darkness, a golden gleam shone like a torch flame.

Mastema's eyes took on a faraway emptiness. He nodded obediently several times. "Yes. Yes. We've taken care of that."

The shadow vanished in a sooty blur. Gasping, Ornias slowly lowered the arm he'd thrown up over his face. "What was that?"

Mastema lay still, panting, his eyes riveted on the place where the darkness had stood. "We've work for you here on Palaia, Governor. You know Gamants better than any non-Gamant in the galaxy. We need someone to subdue the growing revolts on the satellites. Your new duties will include a substantial raise in salary and a promotion. *General Ornias*, are you interested?"

Ornias raised his brows. The old coot was a lunatic. He'd undoubtedly rigged this little display—*that's why they moved me into this room!* He examined every possible place a projector could hide. Behind the witch's picture? Or perhaps in the huge tangle of stim equipment? Mastema observed his efforts in deep silence, waiting for a reply. Ornias hesitated. He'd worked for insane people before—take Adom Kemar Tartarus for example. The boy had been daffy as a mad Orillian tiger. *But I worked it to my benefit.* Yes, in fact, he'd learned quite well how to manipulate lunatics to his own best interests by using their delusions against them.

"How *much* of a raise in salary, Magistrate?"

Mastema vented a long exhalation. "Say another billion a year?"

"Make it two and I'm yours."

Mastema looked old and very weary when he nodded to seal the bargain. "You'll have to start immediately. I'll arrange for our doctors to create a mini-stim unit for your hand so that you can travel. You're needed in the field, General."

CHAPTER 28

Amirah sat at the long table sipping a bottle of apple-flavored food concentrate. Her ankles and wrists both wore' EM restraints and ached fearfully. Her pale gold robe spread around her feet in shining folds. The line of three candles adorning the tabletop reflected in the crystal goblets to throw rainbow patterns across the place mats. She traced the geometric designs with her finger, occasionally glancing up at Tahn. He moved stiffly around the perimeter of the cave, brushing dust from the ancient runes engraved in the walls. The handglobe in his left palm glowed with an azure brilliance when he lifted it to inspect the strange symbols.

They hadn't spoken in hours and Amirah had begun to feel the weight of the silence. Dread for her ship and crew had nearly suffocated her. Her mind kept spinning horrifying pictures of the *Sargonid* with a holed hull, atmosphere boiling out into space in a silver mist. Or worse, Jason lying dead in a decompressed hall. She clenched her fists and fought back her overwhelming anxiety. At least when Tahn talked to her, she forgot some of her worry. She finished her concentrate and looked up. He turned halfway around, just to make sure of what she was doing, then went back to his runes.

She peered inquisitively at the curious drawings lit by his globe. She couldn't see them very distinctly from this far away. "What are they?"

"I haven't the slightest idea. The way they're arranged, they seem to be some sort of ordered sequence. Letters, numbers, concepts . . . I don't know."

Staring at him, she noted how his shoulder muscles bunched. The red silken fabric of his robe rippled with his tension. In the past several hours, they'd found each other anything but "intolerable." The strain of their attraction for each other felt as threatening as a gun barrel against Amirah's temple. Cole must feel the same way. He'd been diligently avoiding her for the past two hours.

Carefully, she lifted her hand and pointed to a number of disparate drawings. "If those were arranged in a contiguous order, I'd be tempted to call them mathematical symbols."

"So would I."

"How old do you think they are?" she asked.

"The thick patina that's built up would make me think two millennia or more, but—"

She blinked. "Before the advent of the Desert Fathers?"

"Maybe."

"Who lived here before they did?"

"I don't know for certain. I remember some talk about the wicked Kings of Edom, but who they were or what they did is a mystery to me. Ask Jeremiel when you meet him. I'm sure he knows far more about them than I do."

Amirah restrained her panic. "Will I meet him?"

Tahn eyed her evaluatively. "I think so."

She held his gaze, and her heart clutched up. Meeting Baruch would undoubtedly mean her ship had been beaten, perhaps destroyed. Hatred and desperation washed through her. She tucked her bound hands in her lap.

Instinctively, Tahn seemed to grasp the unsettling emotions she was experiencing. His stony expression softened. "The *Sargonid* could escape, too," he pointed out realistically.

Amirah nodded tersely and turned away in a whirl of gold robe, glaring at the door.

Tahn approached her, his steps muted by the rugs. For several seconds he said nothing. Then, "I know the fear you're feeling. I'm sorry."

"Are you? Then let me go." She turned and glared sternly. "No? I thought not. The only thing you're sorry about is that you're stuck here with me instead of being up there with your ship. You do have a ship, don't you? Didn't they make you a captain in the Underground fleet? Baruch's a fool if he didn't."

Tahn nonchalantly braced a hand on his pistol. "I have a ship."

"Worried about her?"

He shook his head. "Not especially. I've always had the suspicion that Merle's a better captain than I am. My ship's in good hands."

"Is he your second in command?"

"She. Yes. Merle's deserved her own cruiser command for a long time. There've just never been enough ships to go around. But maybe after this battle. . . ."

The words faded when he saw the animosity he'd roused. But she could easily finish the sentence for him: *if we capture any Magisterial vessels.* Amirah shook her bound fists, wanting to hurt him back, needing to despite the growing depth of attraction she felt toward him. "You like female navigation officers. Why is that? You promoted Carey Evan Halloway faster than any officer before or after her."

His bold eyes raked her. "Because she deserved it. She was the best damned second in command in the fleet. You should know that."

Ah, a wound.

Amirah laughed condescendingly. "Indeed? Scholars have always speculated you had something going with her," she lied. But he wouldn't know that. Could she taunt him into dropping his guard? "Wasn't she really your quaint concubine aboard the *Hoyer*? The theory's always been that you promoted her for her extra-military talents."

Cole straightened slowly, standing at an angle like a man getting set to throw a punch. "Feel better?" he asked. "One hurt for another? We both know that Halloway's superb record demanded every promotion I gave her. I apologize for the crack about getting Merle a ship of her own. I wasn't thinking."

The words sapped some the wrath that had been sustaining her sanity. It left her empty and aching. She wanted to slam her fists into something—preferably him—or weep to relieve her feeling of total impotence. She turned back toward the table to stare at the dusty crystal goblets.

Tahn shifted uncomfortably. The firelight played like whips of amber in his dark hair. Amirah gloomily stared at the rainbow reflections cast by the faceted goblets. Why couldn't she hate him? Silently, she railed against herself for being taken in by his charm, his warmth.

She braced an elbow on the table and propped her forehead against her fist. Closing her eyes, she quietly observed the amber reflections of candle flame dance over the insides of her lids.

Watching Amirah, Cole pursed his lips against the sympathy she called forth in his own heart. "Amirah," he began. "I know what you're—"

"How long will it be, Cole? If your side wins, when will they come to get you—us."

Despite the granite-hard look on her face, he strongly suspected she was smothering herself in guilt—feeling desperate for the safety of her ship and crew. And he knew only too well how it felt to run and rerun images of your crew's probable deaths through your mind. It felt goddamned bad. "It could be an hour or another two days. I don't think it'll be longer than that."

She shoved aimlessly at the closest place mat. "And what are you going to do with me if my side wins? Have you thought about that? What if your people never come for you?"

"My life will get a whole lot easier."

"I doubt it. Woloc will turn this planet upside down hunting for me. He'll *find* you, Tahn. If it takes—"

"He won't have to waste his time searching for me." He patted the pistol on his right hip. "You see, I can't possibly let him find me."

She glanced down at his gun. "You'd commit suicide rather than surrender? Don't be a fool. If you agreed to cooperate with the government, they might negotiate!"

"A deal?"

"Of course!" She leaned forward. "If you gave the Magistrates a list of the names and whereabouts of all the Underground's clandestine bases, they'd set you free and there's no telling what sort of wealth—"

He interrupted her with a boisterous laugh. How naive she was! Did she really believe that? He glared at her. Yes, apparently she did. Amazing. The Magistrates would probe him until he was brain-dead, then they'd kill him at a public execution just for spite. But the other side of the coin made him laugh even harder. *Him* bargain with the Magistrates? After what he'd seen on Tikkun? *After what they'd done to his crew?* The only contact he wanted with Slothen was to feel the Giclasian's blue throat beneath the blade of his Wind River knife.

He walked forward and braced both hands on the edge of the table, staring down at her. "You're a Gamant, Amirah. I doubt your head will understand what I'm about to say, but I'm sure the blood in your veins will: I'd rather sell my soul to Aktariel than bargain with the Magistrates. At least I'd know the game plan with the Archdeceiver. The government changes policies so swiftly one can never be sure."

"I'm not a Gamant," she whispered.

"Someday you've got to stop running away from yourself. Can't you see that the government's plan for your people is genocide?"

"That's not true!" she defended hotly and slammed her bound fists into the table. "Only two months ago, Slothen ordered us to drop food to the starving multitudes hiding in the forests on one of the satellites orbiting Palaia!"

Cole was momentarily silent, assessing possibilities. The Underground had heard rumors that Slothen's iron fist policy on the satellites had blown up in his face, but they'd no specifics. "The Gamants on the satellites are rioting? Is that what you're telling me?"

Pink flushed her cheeks, as though she knew she'd revealed some critical bit of data and was silently chastising herself for the error. She drew her bare feet up on her seat and rested her cheek on her knees, turning away from his probing gaze. Blonde hair shielded most of her face.

Cole walked around the table and pulled out the chair in front of her. As he sat down, he noticed her chin quivering. Fear for her ship, or just the urge to use those deadly fingers on him? Both, probably. Goddamn, he wished he didn't like her so much. No, it was more than like—but he couldn't admit that just yet.

"Let's discuss Gamant affairs, Amirah."

"I don't have anything to say to you, Tahn."

"We hear so little in this part of the galaxy. How many Gamants are on the satellites?"

She gave him a menacing look. The ramifications of hundreds of Gamants rioting in the pristine environment of Palaia's perimeter were enormous. If they could get someone inside, to organize and lead the factions. . . .

"Have the Magistrates set up *research* facilities for them, Amirah? Hmm? How many innocent civilians have they murdered in the name of 'scientific advancement'? I'll bet Slothen even tells his constituents that the studies are good for Gamants. They help civilize the *beasts*. Do you believe his propaganda?"

Her turquoise eyes burned with malice. "Some of it's true."

"*Some* of everything's true. Have you visited the research centers, Amirah?"

"No."

"But you've undoubtedly heard what happens in them. How—"

"Those are lies!"

He held that hate-filled gaze. Her fanatical loyalty to Slothen intrigued him. Where had she gotten that? It didn't come naturally to cruiser captains, he could vouch for that. "Are they? For the sake of argument, let's say they're not. How would you feel if your grandmother were there?"

"There's no point in discussing this, Tahn. The government would never allow the sort of brutality the rumormongers are pushing."

"Uh-huh." He braced an elbow on the table and ran a hand through his hair. "When you get back to a com terminal where you have access to clandestine files, look up Neurophysiological file 19118. Then look up the data on the disposition of Colonel Garold Silbersay. Check out the reports on the experiments undertaken on the planet Jumes just before I was ordered to scorch it. Look up the data on Tikkun. If those files still exist, I think you'll discover some things that will make you ill. They made me so sick I . . ." He massaged the knots in his shoulder. "Well, you know that story."

"Not really." She curled her delicate toes down over the edge of her chair seat, squeezing so hard the nails went white. Her breathing had quickened and her freckles seemed to stand out more clearly. "For the sake of argument," she taunted, "why don't you tell me about Tikkun."

"You think you can take it?"

"I can take anything, mister."

So, he did—from the molestation and rape of female children by Magisterial officers to the mass murders of "useless" subjects. He recounted the horrors in graphic detail. He told her of the ruthless slaughter he'd witnessed of women and children at the ditch. He told her of walking across a barren field in Block 10 with the camp commander, Major Johannes Lichtner, and Cole's voice grew deep and sharp with hate. He fairly spat the words, "My security officer, Rachel, jumped. I jumped. Because small explosions sprang from the ground, shooting wisps of dirt high into the air. Lichtner's guards laughed, they *laughed*, Amirah."

Her chest rose and fell swiftly beneath her clinging robe. Her beautiful face had gone progressively harder as she talked. "What were they?"

He steepled his fingers over his mouth. "Gases released by decaying bodies. Lichtner claimed he had thirteen thousand Gamants buried there."

Cole lifted his eyes to study her. She shook her head disbelievingly, but her eyes betrayed a worried woman. In a smooth move, she got to her feet. Her bound ankles made it difficult to stand, but she balanced herself.

"I don't believe you," she said in a low, savage voice. "You're so practiced at lying, Tahn, that you can't even—"

Angrily, he shoved his chair back. It squealed across the stone floor. He hadn't realized until now how much he'd perspired while telling her the story. The pungent scent of his own sweat encircled him. "Why would I lie to you? I've no reason to."

"Because you're trying to use my ancestry against me. You're tying to force me to—"

"*I don't give a damn about your ancestry!* The prisoners on Tikkun were innocent civilians, Amirah! The Magistrates rounded them up and subjected them to experiments which destroyed critical centers of their brains. They claimed—Lichtner claimed—the neurobiologists had discovered some physiological anomalies in the temporal lobes that explained why Gamants are 'irrationally' aggressive. Something to do with the rewards system. I don't know if that was true." He paced, reliving the wrenching memories. Her hands knotted in front of her.

Cole quietly said, "You shouldn't be worried about me using your ancestry against you. Worry about the Magistrates. If they find out, you'll be locked up in some very unpleasant—"

"You're a liar!" she raged. "A liar and traitor! You'd say anything to make me—"

"I'm telling you the truth! You're just too blinded by the official propaganda. . . ."

He barely noticed her subtle shift, as she turned sideways ever so slightly, her bound hands disappearing for a split second. The blow came out of nowhere, taking him in the chest. Amid the white flash of pain that blasted through his skull, he stumbled and she spun, leveling another double-fisted slam at his lower back. He dove out of the way, rolling to knock her feet out from under her—but the impact sent his pistol flying out of his holster to land several feet away. She tumbled across him and landed a hard elbow to his gut. He punched her in the solar plexus and wrenched her bound hands up above her head. She bashed him in his wounded thigh with both of her knees. He straddled her, holding her legs firmly between his while simultaneously pressing her hands to the floor over her head.

She let out a close-mouthed cry of rage.

Panting, he observed, "I thought we'd established that I'm better at this than you are."

"Get off of me!" she shouted in rage.

"I'm going, just relax."

Carefully, he got up and slumped to the floor a few feet away. He grabbed up his pistol and pointed it at her menacingly. His chest ached as though someone had plunged a burning sword between his ribs. A trickle of blood ran warm and sticky down his belly. Gingerly, he probed the area with his fingers. It hurt so badly he thought he'd faint every time he took a deep breath. "Goddamn it," he muttered. "I think you broke one of my ribs."

"Good! I hope the bone punctures a lung and kills you." She swiveled her head to look at him and he saw for the first time the tears on her lashes. He cocked his head, wondering if the pain had torn them from her iron hide, or if the discussion about Gamants had affected her after all.

"Oh, you're a real sweetheart," he observed. "I take back all those amiable and sympathetic thoughts I've been having about you. When I'm dead and there's no one to feed you, I'll bet your conscience twinges."

He probed again and winced. The pain flared every time his heart beat. "Goddamn it," he repeated, more weakly this time. Slowly, he got on his knees and staggered to his feet.

He swayed as he made his way to sit on the edge of the table. Casting a glance heavenward, he called, "Did you think I was serious in my dreams last night, Jeremiel, when I said I liked this woman so much I half-hoped you'd win the battle and forget about me? Well, I'm wide awake now, and damned ready to be rescued. Are you listening, Baruch? I don't have any med supplies down here. Not even . . . ." He accidentally took a deep breath and bent double. ". . . Not even any godforsaken painkillers."

Amirah sat up. He tried not to notice how the firelight accentuated the tears in her slit eyes.

But when Amirah glanced at the door, Cole quickly warned, "Don't get any ideas. Even if I can't breathe, I can still shoot." To reinforce his words, he leveled his pistol at her middle. "Why don't you come over here, Amirah. Sit down next to me and we'll have a pleasant chat while I bleed."

She painstakingly crossed the floor, moving her bound feet in tiny steps. Her robe billowed around her long legs like a cloud of gold. "How bad is it?"

The touch of authentic concern in her voice made him laugh. "Oh, I think you can be proud of that kick. Yes, indeed. I'd give you a score of ten." In Academy, a ten was the highest rating you could get for a single move.

"A ten would have killed you immediately," she corrected.

"Okay, a nine."

She halted about five feet away, standing tall and straight. The draft that penetrated the cave from the hallway fluttered blonde hair about her shoulders in gorgeous disarray.

"Sit down, Amirah." He gestured forcefully with his gun.

She eased into a chair. "Where does it hurt?"

"Right now? Everywhere. But I suspect once things settle down it'll mostly be my upper half."

"Do you need a doctor?"

He squinted at the irrelevance. "Probably. What difference does that make?"

She leaned forward with deadly geniality. "Free my hands. Let me call my ship. My hospital staff is the best in the fleet. I *guarantee* your safety! As the captain of the *Sargonid* I give you my word that you'll be—"

"Oh, my dear Amirah." He bowed his head and smiled indulgently. "You're so naive. A captain's guarantees mean nothing unless the Magistrates back them, and in my case I'm quite sure they'd override you. But don't get me wrong, I appreciate the offer. Did you mean it?"

"Yes." She twisted in her seat so she could brace her shoulder against the chair back. With her hands bound, almost any position felt uncomfortable. "Did you mean it when you said you liked me?"

He grinned. He almost answered, *that was ten minutes ago. I've changed my mind since then,* but the guarded, waiting expression on her face made him choke back the comment. Instead, he sighed, "Yes, Amirah, I meant it. I like you more than I'd feel comfortable telling you."

She hastily stood up. "Take off that robe and unbind my hands! I want to look at your ribs. I can't set them here, but I could wrap them so they'd shift less."

He pulled back suspiciously. "First you break my ribs, then you want me to take off my clothes? You certainly know how to win a man's heart. No, thank you. I think I've had all of your touch I can stand in a day. But there is something you could do for me."

"What is it?"

"I'll remove the restraints from your feet—but remember, this pistol has a full charge."

She sat down again and lifted her feet up to him. He took the key out of his pocket and waved it over the thin bands. They broke open. Amirah's slipped them off and set them on the table.

"Very kind of you," Cole commented, taking them back and tucking them in his pocket. "Now, if you please, could you get me a bottle of wine? I daresay I'm going to be needing it sooner than I thought." *Like five minutes ago.*

She walked across the room and rummaged through one of the crates to pull out a dusty bottle of alizarin. Bringing it back, she set it on the table and opened it, then filled a goblet for him and set it within his reach.

Cole switched his pistol to his left hand and retrieved the wine with his right. "Please sit down again, Amirah."

She sat.

He took a healthy swig of the earthy-flavored concoction, praying it would dull the pain without dulling his wits too much.

"Cole?"

The nausea had begun, sending foul messages to his brain. He gulped his wine. "What?"

"What you said about Tikkun—was any of that true?"

"All of it, I'm afraid. It still gives me nightmares."

She reached up and poured herself a glass of alizarin. "Let's talk alternatives. Are you able? Is it possible that Lichtner had gone rogue? That the Magistrates knew nothing about his operations in Block 10?"

"Seriously doubtful. The doctors employed at the camp were top quality, straight out of Palaia's science departments."

"For example?"

"Oh . . ." He searched his memory, trying to recall the names of some of the physicians he'd seen in the 19118 file. He'd read it in great detail after Rudy Kopal had picked them up off Tikkun. "Jonathan Creighton, Ranold Hyde. Several others that I can't remember."

She stopped with her glass halfway to her lips. "My God. You're sure Creighton was one of them? He's in charge of the entire Hall of Sciences at Palaia now."

"Makes sense. They promote swine like him."

Sweat rolled down his face, stinging in his eyes. He blinked ferociously to keep his vision clear. Refilling his goblet of wine, he guzzled it down, then refilled it again and drank half the glass. His position on the table had caused one of his legs to fall asleep. He tried to sit up straighter and gasped, squeezing his eyes closed against the pain. A shudder attacked him. He willfully controlled it. When he opened his eyes, he found Amirah staring at him worriedly.

"I'm not dying," he assured her, forgetting for the moment that she'd hoped for that.

"No, you're going into shock. Let me help you, Cole. Please?"

He wondered why he hadn't thought of that. She was right, damn it. He grabbed his pistol and pointed it at her. "No, but thanks for the tip."

In agonizing slow motion he slid off the table and stood on weak knees. "Please go over and stand by the fireplace. I'll be right behind you, so don't get brave."

She went. He followed, every step a white lance of fire through his chest. By the time they reached the hearth, he could barely stand. "Sit down," he ordered. "I hate to do this to you, but I'm afraid in a few minutes I may not be able to keep as close an eye on you as I should. I think I'm bleeding pretty badly internally. I don't know how long I can stay conscious."

She stretched out on her stomach and obligingly brought up her feet, bringing them as close to her bound hands as she could—obviously anticipating his instructions. She knew the prisoner-of-war routine. Every officer did. But why she was making it easier for him was an intriguing mystery.

"No," he said regretfully. "That would be safer, but I don't know how long I may be out. In that position you'd be in agony in an hour. Sit up and put your back against that ring that protrudes from the wall."

"You never did operate by the book," she commented as she slid backward.

"Not when I could avoid it."

Cole knelt and cuffed her hands to the ring, then guardedly cuffed her ankles together, waiting every moment for a kick he doubted he could counter. When he'd finished, he felt sick. Breathing had become agony. He tried to stand and reeled sideways, landing hard on the floor. Pain shot through him in hot waves.

"Tahn, why don't you tran your ship? Tell them you're in trouble."

He sat gasping. "I can't take the chance that such a communication . . . might be picked up by your people.

Besides, when the battle is over . . . if things go well for my side, they'll tran me. Until that time, it's too risky to send any sort of message."

Patiently, an inch at a time, he edged back to lean against the wall. Cold, he felt so cold. He shivered and held his broken rib while he extended his legs. His boots grated on the rough sandstone floor. The wine had finally soaked into his veins. His head felt pleasantly light though his body still burned like a blazing torch.

His gaze drifted back to Amirah and he soothed himself by watching the firelight dance with a brassy brilliance in her hair. *Oh, you're a prize. Feeling desire when you haven't even got the strength to breathe.* Idiotically, he smiled at her. "You're very beautiful, Amirah" he said. "And I do like you, too much."

He brought his pistol into his lap and leaned his head back against the wall, closing his eyes. If he could just sleep for a little while, escape the pain, build up his strength. . . .

Three hours later, Amirah sat quietly, watching the green light flash on Cole's belt com. His people had been trying to contact him for over an hour. But he'd been lost in a nightmare world, talking in his sleep, reliving battles, moaning. He frequently called for two people, Maggie and Carey. And Amirah knew both names. Maggie Zander—his love in Academy. She'd been killed during the Pegasus Invasion of Old Earth. Captured and imprisoned in a light cage only a few feet from Cole's, reports stated that Zander had reached out to Tahn with her last ounce of strength, trying to touch him before she'd died. The other was undoubtedly Carey Halloway. The way Tahn called her name made Amirah ache. He must love her. When Amirah had thrown out the taunt about a relationship between them earlier, she hadn't even suspected it might be true.

But it gave her a useful piece of knowledge.

Cole groaned and, illogically, Amirah clutched up inside. She ought to be hoping he'd bleed to death. But instead she was praying he'd be all right. His brown hair and beard both glimmered damply in the ruby glow of the coals in the hearth. Had his stories about Tikkun really been true? She'd been chasing them around her

mind. He *didn't* have any reason to lie to her—at least
not that she could fathom. But if the Magistrates had
committed such heinous crimes on Tikkun, the rumors
circulating about their experiments on the satellites
around Palaia might be true. And if they were true. . . .

"No. They can't be."

She closed her eyes as images of Sefer Raziel rose.
The bright sunlight streamed down through a rent in their
porch roof, striking her grandmother's withered face
where she sat in her chair. Sefer squinted against it, rocking back and forth in the shaft of light. The sweet scents
of newborn grass and early morning dew clung to the
cool breeze. Amirah sat cross-legged on the porch, her
doll sleeping in her lap, listening intently to the stories
Sefer told about the first Gamant Revolt, about the terrible things the Magistrates had done to *their* people.

Every muscle in Amirah's body contracted against the
word. But she still missed Grandmama and her strength.
She'd guessed when she got older that Grandmama
hadn't simply vanished, that she was dead. Or else Sefer
would have come home. She would never have left
Amirah alone if she could have helped it. Tears rose in
Amirah's eyes. She'd loved that kind old woman. . . .

A quick pounding of running steps sounded in the hall.
Amirah jerked her head up. Voices echoed. Three men
and four women entered the cave, all dressed in black
battlesuits, all carrying rifles. The man in the lead, a tall
blond with a close-clipped reddish blond beard and hard
blue eyes appraised her warily as he swiftly hurried to
Cole's side. He slung his rifle, then knelt and examined
Tahn, noting the dark mat of blood that soaked his red
robe and pooled on the floor at his side.

The blond ordered, "Chaim? Get a gurney out of the
shuttle. Notify the ship to have a med team waiting in
the landing bay."

"Aye, Jeremiel." The corporal sprinted away. His
steps reverberated down the stone corridor.

Amirah swallowed hard. Her ship . . . Jason. . . . She
clamped her jaw to keep it still. The questions seared
her insides. "Jeremiel *Baruch?*"

He glanced briefly at her before carefully picking up
Cole's wrist and checking the pulse. "Yes, Captain Jos-

sel. I see you've been well cared for, but I can't say the same for my friend. What happened?"

"He provoked me," she said straightforwardly, "so I broke his ribs."

"Uh-huh." Baruch gave her a disparaging look. "I'd congratulate you, but I'm not particularly pleased about it."

"Tahn didn't like it much either."

"I'll bet. How long has he been unconscious?"

"Three hours."

The conversation seemed to rouse Tahn. He muttered something unintelligible. Baruch affectionately squeezed his shoulder. "You're safe, Cole. Sit still. A gurney's on the way."

Tahn's eyes fluttered open. When he recognized Baruch, he tried to straighten but fell weakly back against the wall. "What happened? How many did we lose? Are Merle and Rudy all right?"

"They're fine. We're all fine," Baruch assured, looking uneasily at Amirah. "We'll discuss it later."

Cole looked at Amirah, too, and a faint smile came to his lips. To Baruch he conspiratorially whispered, "She tried to kill me."

"Did she?" Baruch inquired. "I can't imagine why. You were your usual charming self, weren't you?"

"Some people don't appreciate my magnetic personality. The next time you try to talk me into being alone with a beautiful woman for days, remind me to say no."

Baruch gently touched the blood on Cole's side and responded, "It was a terrible strain on you, I can tell."

Cole winced. Baruch smiled. Their eyes gleamed with warmth for one another, like long lost friends reunited after years of worrying about each other. Amirah watched with interest. Baruch and Tahn had been vehement enemies for fifteen years. They'd killed each other's friends, blown up each other's ships. When had all that hatred faded? The thought of Baruch and Tahn together set her head to pounding. If they were the good friends they seemed, then they must be working in close concert in the Underground. The two most brilliant military minds in the galaxy joined? Terrifying.

A soldier rushed into the room, pushing an antigrav gurney. Baruch stood up and moved out of the way, letting him get it into position, then Jeremiel helped lift Tahn to the stretcher. Cole's face pinched as he gritted back the pain. The soldier pushed him out of the cave. Most of the security team followed. Two women stationed themselves outside the door.

Amirah shifted, bringing her knees up. Baruch peered down at her intently, taking in her golden gown and face. "I'm sorry about all this, Captain," he said. "Let me assure you first of all that your ship is safe. We never had the chance to engage the *Sargonid*. It was gone before we arrived."

All the terror and anxiety that had weighed on her for days vanished in a hot rush, leaving her trembling with fatigue. *Oh, Jason, Jason, good work.* "Thank you for telling me, Commander."

Baruch came forward, warily sidestepping her legs and kneeling at her side. He took an EM key from his side pocket. "I imagine your hands went numb hours ago. Let me get you out of these."

CHAPTER 29

*In order that the mind of Darkness, which is the eye
of the bitterness of evil, might not be destroyed, I
took off my garment of light. I put on another garment of fire. I went down to chaos to save the whole
light from it.*

**The Paraphrase of Shem (VII, 1)
350 A.D. Arcane document presumed
to be from the original Nag Hammadi
Library of Old Earth. Discovered in
archaeological excavation on *Aurea
Catena* in the year 5065.**

Aktariel stood on the crest of a ridge overlooking a
valley of tan rolling hills. The scent of thyme wafted on
the warm breezes, bathing his face in ancient memories—
memories of a time when the scattered ruins below had
housed thousands, and voices shouting "Hosannah!" had
sundered the azure heavens. Now, only the marmots and
birds frolicked amid the desolation, perching on the ragged teeth of tumbled walls.

He braced a shoulder against the sandstone ledge
beside him and studied Rachel. She knelt at the crumbled
entrance of the Valley Gate, her long black hair fluttering in the wind; but her eyes focused on the silted-in
city beyond, as though she could see past the dross of
centuries to the resplendent fortress of old. And watching her, Aktariel, too, could almost hear the plaintive
calls of the milk and date vendors, the baaing of goats
and joyous laughter of the children who'd raced so freely
through the narrow winding streets once-upon-a-time,
millennia ago.

It had taken him days of searching to track Rachel

down. But despite how frantic he'd been, when he had, he couldn't bear to disturb her. He'd been watching her since long before sunrise, seeing her erect the Kingdom of God stone by stone in her soul, not out of mourning songs and the wails of the bereaved—as he himself did— but the way she longed to see it, out of sunshine and laughter, light and warmth.

"Oh, Rachel. How can faith still lurk in your heart after the horrors you've seen?"

He bowed his head and shook it uneasily. This quest was undoubtedly tied to her meanderings through the multiple universes, but how? What did it have to do with Nathan? He *had* to find out.

He started down the hill, maneuvering his sandaled feet around rocks and spiny bushes. His plum-colored robe whipped in the wind until his billowing sleeves belled. How long had she searched the voids to find this place? She must have hunted for a long, long time, for this vein of the future existed in only two arteries out of the billions upon billions. What had she hoped to find? Truth? A clue which would reveal a different path than the brutal one they currently followed?

"Don't you think I've searched for another way, Rachel? If I couldn't find it in billions of years, how could you expect to in twelve?"

He tramped quietly to stand behind her. The wind flattened her jade robe across her breasts and stomach. Her waist-length black hair fluttered over her back. She tensed ever so slightly and lifted her head to gaze up at him. Tears streamed unheeded down her beautiful heart-shaped face. She did not seem surprised by his presence or resentful that he'd followed her here. He gazed down at the rock clutched in her hand, a fragment of one of the fallen stones that had formed the gate. She'd clutched it so tightly for so long that her nails had left crescents in the soft surface.

"Why do you do this to yourself, Rachel? You could have simply asked me and I'd have told you this city wasn't built of angels' hair high in the clouds."

"I wouldn't have believed you."

Her voice sounded husky, as though she'd held Yerushalaim to her breast and wept all night for its loss.

"Here," he said tenderly and extended a hand. "Come with me. Let's talk."

She glanced at his hand. "I don't need your help. I can stand by myself."

He inclined his head agreeably and closed his fist on the warm fragrant air, pulling it back. As the end drew nearer, she grew more bellicose and belligerent. He understood her fears. Terror had become his own constant companion, like a splinter of cold steel working its way deeper into his heart every moment.

Bracing against the wall, she got to her feet and tucked her fingers into her pockets. He hesitantly grasped her elbow, waiting for her to object, but when she didn't he silently led her up the Hill of Gulgolet. Just why he chose that one, he couldn't quite say. Perhaps because it tasted of defeat so vile he hoped it would make her forsake that tendril of faith that stubbornly twined through her heart.

"Let's sit down at the top, near that boulder." He pointed and she obligingly allowed herself to be led into the cool shadows of the overhanging rock where they sat.

Aktariel leaned back against the gritty stone and basked in the olive scented air. A small grove of trees encircled the rim of the hill. In the distance a series of earth-colored, corrugated knolls humped like camel backs along the horizon. Rachel leaned back beside him, pressing her shoulder against his. The closeness felt comforting. He reached down and took her hand. She tensed, but didn't jerk it away. Bringing it to his lap, he stroked it intimately as he gazed out over the world. Ancient ruins dotted nearly every high place.

Rachel broke the silence. "How did you find me?"

"It wasn't easy. You've become very adept at hiding your colors in the tapestry of Creation. I had to trace every strand that bore your shades. Why are you doing this, Rachel?"

The wind set her long hair to dancing about her beautiful, tear-swollen face. She brushed the fluttering ebony strands behind her ears. "I needed to see this—for myself."

"Were you frightened that I wouldn't understand this quest of yours?"

"What do you know of my quest?" she challenged bitterly.

"Oh, a great deal more than you suspect." He smiled and patted her hand. "I once searched the voids, too, looking for hope, for another way out, for any sign that God intended to keep his promises to your forebears."

She fumbled with the slender blades of dead grass that sprouted beneath the cool rocky overhang. "But you never found it?"

"It doesn't exist, Rachel."

"That breaks my heart, Aktariel." She bit her lip and stared out across the undulating hills. Birds soared on thermals high above, darting through the cloudless blue. "Our universe may be terrible, but there's so much beauty and serenity in some of the others. I'd hoped that somewhere the seeds of salvation lay dormant."

And awaiting a tiller to work the soil and stir them to life? Was that what she'd been doing? Sifting through the universes to find the most likely version where Nathan could change the course of history? Yes, of course. Which *had she chosen?*

He forced down the panic that surged through him. "Ah, we're back to the old arguments. All right, Rachel, even if the seeds could be made to sprout, how much beauty is enough to counterbalance the pain and anguish? If God truly loves us, why does He make the good things so hard to find? Why does He hide His omnipresent Light under so many bushels?"

"Maybe he doesn't hide it. Maybe evil is an illusion. Maybe our perceptions are too limited to see the pervasive Good."

Aktariel lifted her hand to gently kiss the slender fingers. "Then what a poor Creator He is, to have made us with such a terrible flaw that we see suffering where there isn't any, that we feel deprived of His Light when it's really all around us. You and I both have watched millions die horribly, pleading to God for mercy." He hesitated, watching her fill her palm with sand. She clutched it tightly, as though it were the first handful to be cast into the grave of a loved one. "It's a terrible thing, Rachel, to die of thirst in an ocean of Love, Goodness, and Beauty. If God were all-powerful, he could correct our myopia with the wave of His hand. He doesn't. Why not?"

"I don't know," she responded softly.

"Epagael could have made a perfect universe filled with infinite choices. He didn't. He could call all this back right now and remake it so that it was perfectly ordered, so that we felt no suffering and existed in absolute bliss with our free will intact. He won't."

She tugged her hand away from him. "Don't preach to me, Aktariel. I can't bear it."

He lowered his fingers to draw interlocking triangles in the dirt. "I didn't mean to. I only wanted you to think. Those old arguments which presuppose an all-good, all-powerful, and all-knowing deity are quite simply false. God is none of those things. He hasn't been since he spawned the Void of Creation. The original genesis of dichotomy lessened Epagael, condemning Him as much as it condemned the consciousness which grew in the Void. He will forever be an outsider to our experiences here—until we *make* Him understand."

Her brow puckered as she carelessly creased the hem of her jade robe. "I've no argument with that premise, Aktariel. Of course, we must make Epagael understand."

"Where is our disagreement, then? I don't comprehend what you're doing. You and I both know that your interference with Nathan's death may well send all of our carefully laid plans tumbling down around us. Why would you take such a risk?"

Rachel twisted sideways, turning her back to him. The wind set her raven hair to dancing before his eyes.

As he waited for her answer, his gaze drifted over the hill. Voices, old and impassioned, rose up from the very earth. Every stone here spoke to him, crying out from a blood-drenched mouth. *"Repent! Repent! The Kingdom of heaven has come!"* Not one grain of sand, not one blade of grass on this mount had been spared the shower of blood that had poured from the slaughtered.

He lifted his eyes to the rocky tor a few feet away and again he heard the stamping of hooves, the screams of frightened horses. . . .

A scorching afternoon. The hill filled with crosses. People pushing and shoving to get out of the way of the

*bronze-suited cavalrymen who formed a cordon around
them, herding them forward with lances and shouts, forcing them to look upon a sight no member of the faithful
could bear: A Mashiah of flesh and sinew, who'd prayed
for salvation and died in despair. Weeping echoed over
the valley below. When darkness fell and the stars emerged
in a shimmering blanket, jackals roamed the hill, jumping
and tearing at the feet of the victims until the coral rays
of dawn revealed bare gnawed bone.*

Aktariel rubbed his eyes. God had not helped his Chosen People that day. There'd been no angels plunging
out of heaven, swords in hand, to free the writhing savior—though hundreds had waited, their gazes piteously
glued to the sky. A flood of pleading repentant voices
had washed this hillock clean of sin. And Epagael had
heard. He'd witnessed the horrors, searched the pitch-
black eyes and sun-burned faces, and irritably turned his
head.

Rachel frowned at the jagged ruins in the valley below.
"I would take the risk, Aktariel, because of this place."

"What do you mean?"

"I came here because I thought . . . I thought I might
find the twelve guardian angels floating over the twelve
sacred gates, with all the peoples of the Earth lying prostrate at their feet. I thought I might see the footprints of
the true Mashiah in the soil by the Valley Gate."

Aktariel toyed with a palm-sized rock that rested at
his side. He picked it up and tested its weight. The heavi-
ness of absorbed blood made it seem a chunk of lead.
"The New Yerushalaim will never exist, Rachel. None
of the parallel universes have the requisite foundations
for it."

"*How can you be so sure?* If we go back and influence
minor things in the tapestry, won't—"

"*No!* No, Rachel. Please, listen. You and I—no matter
what our powers—can never fulfill the promises Epagael
made to your forebears. Only He can do that, and He
won't. Surely this city is proof of that."

Aktariel reached out and laid a hand on her shoulder,
turning her around so he could stare into those midnight
eyes of hers. "You *cannot* remake any of the parallel
universes to fulfill your dreams. You understand me? the
strands in the tapestry are too complicated, Rachel. Nei-

ther you nor I can ever see enough of the picture to reweave it without taking dire risks that we'll create more suffering than Epagael already has. The few times that I've tried, I've only made things worse."

"But—"

"No buts. Judgment Day is almost here. Let's handle it the way we'd planned. The Great Gate that leads to the Light Everlasting is almost—"

"How soon?"

"When in Darkness the Judgment takes place."

Gruffly, she challenged, "What does that mean? You never tell me enough to allow me to make decisions for myself! Why is that? Don't you trust me?"

"I don't trust anyone, Rachel. I can't afford to. I've been so close before and never been able to—"

"But you told me that our destinies are interconnected, that our paths have twined and missed for millennia. You said that we were part of each other and that neither of us would be whole again until we were together. How can you *not* trust me?"

"When the time comes and the Great Gate opens, then I'll trust you. Why won't you trust me? . . . *Where is Nathan?*"

She swiftly got up and looked at him through haunted eyes. "If you had the time, you'd search every universe to find my grandson and kill him, wouldn't you?"

"Yes," he answered honestly. "I would. Because he can't do it, Rachel. Nathan *cannot* bring about the New Yerushalaim!"

"You don't know that!" she raged. "You can't know it! If we—"

"Rachel, listen to me! If you and I succeed, maybe—maybe!—*we* can bring about the New Yerushalaim!" He put a hand into the warm sand and pushed up to stand face-to-face with her. Her jade robe buffeted around her legs. "But not Nathan by himself. It's too complicated! *Think about this!* Wherever you left him, Nathan has already had enough time to have thrown a spark into the fabric of Creation. Your rash action may have killed even *our* chances of creating the New Yerushalaim!"

CHAPTER 30

Jason Woloc walked briskly down the long white hall on level six, heading toward the hospital. Turned low for nighttime, the lights gleamed with the strength of moonglow, reflecting eerily in the silver bulkheads. At each intersecting corridor, chronometers flashed the hour in blue. He crisply turned left and waded through a group of off-duty officers. He heard scraps of conversations—someone cursed the ragtag brigade of Gamants on Ingle 7 who'd managed to corner three thousand Magisterial soldiers; someone else blamed the event on the Magistrates' hard-line policy against dissidents. An argument arose. Jason noted the woman who defended the Gamants; Lis Sherwood, sergeant in the security division. He made a mental note to discuss the issue with her. She clearly needed some guidance about governmental reasons for using force.

Ahead, at the end of the hall, were the broad double doors of the hospital. Jason growled softly, angry at the problem he faced. When he'd tranned Slothen just after retrieving Mikael and Sybil Calas to tell the Magistrate that Captain Jossel was still unaccounted for and no demand for ransom had yet been tendered, Slothen had been patently unconcerned. The Magistrate had promised to take Amirah's predicament into consideration as soon as possible, but he wanted Mikael Calas now. Slothen had specifically demanded that Jason relieve Calas of the *"special necklace he wears around his neck."* The device, a small gray ball on a thick golden chain, now rested in Jason's cabin.

All the bizarre orders made his gut ache. He'd never been good at grasping the undercurrents that stirred galactic politics. If only Amirah were here, she'd under-

272

stand. Yes, she had a knack. . . . *Think about her later, not now.*

He strode headlong through the double doors and into the broad rectangular room, perfunctorily returning the salutes of the armed security personnel stationed at every exit. The hospital spread fifty by a hundred feet. Beds lined the walls, but only one held a patient—Sybil Calas. Locked in a silver med unit, her brown hair twisted in luxurious curls across her pillow. Beside the bed, her husband and Doctor York Hilberg stood, talking pensively. Hilberg glanced up as he saw Jason enter the hospital. A small slump-shouldered man with a bald head and a flat nose, he had brown eyes that most people described unflatteringly as "beady."

"Lieutenant," Hilberg greeted. "Our patient is doing well."

Jason glanced at Sybil Calas' sleeping face and nodded. An attractive young woman. "It's a lung wound, I heard."

"Yes. She'd lost a lot of blood, but we have her count almost back to normal now. She's lucky to be here. On Horeb it would have taken her months to heal—if at all. With our tissue regrowth equipment, she should be back to normal in a couple of days.

"Good. Do your best for her, Doctor."

Jason turned to Mikael Calas. Twenty, with jet black hair and a black beard, he had the sort of eyes that made men flinch—sharp as a hawk's, hate-filled. Someone had given him a tan jumpsuit to wear; it heightened the breadth of his shoulders and the narrowness of his muscular waist. Jason addressed the boy respectfully. "Leader Calas, may we talk? There are some questions regarding your apprehension on the planet that remain to be resolved."

Calas tenderly stroked his wife's hair before stepping away from the bed to follow Jason across the room to a table and four chairs. Calas tiredly took a seat and Jason eased down across from him. The boy's meticulous gaze seemed to take in everything, the size of the room, the number of guards, Jason's damp uniform, calculating his chances to the nth degree, no doubt.

"What is it you want to know, Lieutenant?" Calas asked coolly.

"First, let me inform you that you are considered to be a prisoner of war. You do not have to answer any questions unless you want to. However, be aware that the Magistrates will view your cooperation very favorably. It might lessen the severity of what awaits you on Palaia."

Calas chuckled disparagingly. "Lieutenant, please. I know Slothen. I spent eight months under his probes at Palaia when I was seven years old. Nothing will lessen the severity of what he has planned for me. Whatever information he wants, he'll get in the fastest way he can—probably through torture—so let's not play games. What do you want?"

Jason braced his elbows on the table and laced his fingers. Torture? Calas was obviously unaware of Palaia's sophisticated probe facilities. Torture was utilized only in rare circumstances now—usually with primitive alien species who had no recognizable neuro systems. "Where is Governor Ornias? We were unable to locate him."

Calas' dark eyes glittered. "I don't know."

"You didn't kill him?"

"No."

"Is it possible that your forces kidnapped him? We were also unable to find the Minister of Defense, Fenris Midgard. We assumed they might be together. Captured or in hiding."

Calas lifted a shoulder. "I can't tell you. Governor Ornias devastated my forces. His marines came into our polar chambers and indiscriminately killed men, women, and children. He broke every stipulation in the Treaty of Lysomia, Lieutenant." Calas paused and his hard eyes narrowed. "I'd assumed he did that at *your* command, or your captain's."

"My captain was ordered to assist the governor in any way necessary to apprehend you, Leader, including providing additional ground troops—but no one was authorized to break the law." Jason paused, nervously pleating his sleeve—at least not that he was aware of. Wouldn't Amirah have told him if such unusual orders had come down? "We're also curious about your child, Leader. It's obvious that your wife gave birth quite recently. Where is the baby?"

"I don't know that either." A tight expression came

over his young face, as though the images in his mind horrified him.

"Leader, the events of the past few days are very confusing. If your child has been captured or taken hostage by hostile forces, please let us help you get him back. The Magistrates will certainly want to—"

"I don't know what's happened to my son, Lieutenant."

Jason gritted his teeth. Was the boy going to be no help at all? He looked up harshly. Calas' dark eyes gleamed defiantly in return. How could someone so young look so old and fierce? Had he seen so much terror in his short life? "I see. Well, on another front, then, are you aware that our captain, Amirah Jossel, was taken hostage by terrorist forces on your planet?"

Calas shook his head. "No."

"Could you tell me what forces might have been responsible?"

"No. My forces certainly weren't, and I know of no other organized resistance efforts on Horeb."

Jason relaced his fingers and conscientiously scrutinized the two guards who laughed quietly near the door. "I wish you'd be more cooperative, Leader. We can't afford—"

"Lieutenant," Calas sighed gruffly and shifted in his chair to fold his arms. "Has it occurred to you that Ornias' forces may have been responsible for your captain's disappearance?"

Shocked, Jason stammered, "Wh–why would you suggest that?"

"Because it's exactly the sort of thing he'd do. If he thought he could gain some advantage from kidnapping Jossel, he'd surely have done it and blamed it on me."

"What evidence do you have to suggest something so—"

"Look," Calas held up a hand for silence. "I know of several ministers sent to Horeb by Slothen to keep an eye on Ornias who mysteriously vanished. Major Winfeld, Colonel Vahr, and even, I suspect, Midgard. They each undoubtedly stumbled onto one of Ornias' nefarious activities and he eliminated them before they could report on it. What you have to determine is whether Ornias could have benefited by capturing Jossel. If so, you'd better turn this ship around and go hunt through all of the governor's secret passageways."

The hair at the back of Jason's neck prickled. He'd read some of the Clandestine One orders Amirah had received regarding Horeb, though they were sent under "Captain's Eyes Only" clearance. She usually showed him such things because she trusted him. She trusted him. . . . Slothen's orders had stated that Ornias be removed and returned to Palaia for disciplinary action if he couldn't capture Calas, *"or if in the opinion of the captain, the corruption of the governor's administration warrants such measures."* Though certainly Amirah wouldn't have mentioned the latter to Ornias. Would she?

Jason's palms had started to sweat. He pulled them off the table and wiped them on his pants. If she had told Ornias, what would he have done? Ordered his forces to apprehend Calas no matter the cost and then disappeared with Amirah—holding her as his ace in the hole in case his marines failed? The pieces fit together too damned neatly. Maybe that's why the terrorist signals seemed to come from so many places. They'd been sent from Horeb, probably in some secret underground passageway, just as Calas suggested. The beam would have bounced off every rock face.

"Leader, do you know the locations of any of those secret hiding places?"

Calas nodded calmly. "All of them, I think."

"Could you provide me with maps?"

"Maybe." Calas tipped his chair back on two legs and his dark brows lowered. He looked like a wolf on a blood trail. "If you can pay the price."

Jason sucked in a breath, expecting the worst. "Leader, surely you're aware that with our probe facilities, we can gain the information anyway. It would just be quicker and easier on all of us if you—"

"The probes don't work on me, Lieutenant. Perhaps you'd better check your files more thoroughly. When I was seven, Slothen threw every barrage of probe equipment at me that he had." His gaze drifted over the ceiling panels and finally landed on his wife. A brief expression of grief creased his features. "The doctors at the time speculated that I had some peculiar ability to selectively seal off parts of my brain."

"How?"

"By shutting down the production of neurotransmitters to the sections they were probing." Calas smiled grimly, triumphantly, as though truly amused by the fact.

Jason's eyes narrowed. If true, it was an amazing talent. The probes depended upon the presence of neurotransmitters to get an accurate electrochemical analysis of neural circuitry. Without the normal transmitter environment, the probes read only a jumbled muddle. Some humans had learned this fact and could hinder the probes by willfully drenching the brain in other chemicals, particularly those created by strong emotions. But it was, at best, a delaying tactic. Eventually the emotional outbursts exhausted the patient and the probes proceeded. *Whether Calas really has the talent he claims is irrelevant. He'll be a hard case under the probes and Amirah may not have the weeks it will take to break him.*

Jason's blond brows drew together. "What's your price, Calas? What can I give you to secure your help in this matter?"

Calas stared hard at Jason, his dark eyes flashing. "I want a guarantee from you. When we get to Palaia, I don't care what you do with me, but I want my wife safe. I know there's a small community of Gamants from Horeb on Satellite 10. Some of Sybil's childhood friends are incarcerated there. Send her there *without being probed first.*"

Jason drummed his fingers on his leg while he thought. Slothen might go for it. The Magistrate had only requested that Mikael Calas be delivered anyway. Sybil's knowledge might be considered redundant. "We are currently in vault, Leader. I'll have to exit to contact the Magistrates for permission to accede to your demands." *The Magistrates will probably court-martial me for doing it, but if they agree to the deal I can transmit Calas' maps to Williamson and he can immediately begin searching that area for Amirah.*

"How long will that take?"

"I'll initiate an exit sequence immediately. We should have an answer within the hour." Jason reached for the com unit on the far side of the table. He input the bridge access. Orah Pirke's face formed, red hair framing his pale cheeks. "Lieutenant Pirke, I have some critical information that must be transmitted to the Magistrates. Please initiate vault exit."

Orah frowned disbelievingly. "But, sir, Slothen said he wanted Calas delivered immed—"

"I'm well aware of that, Lieutenant. We'll only exit for a short time, then we'll be on our way again."

"Aye, sir." Pirke nodded stiffly. "I'm initiating the sequence."

"Thank you, Orah. Let me know when you've opened a tran to the Magistrates."

He cut the connection, and looked back at Mikael Calas. The youth's eyes had narrowed, waiting. His face relaxed slightly when he felt the gentle lurch of the ship as it fell through the vault exit membrane.

Jason felt light-headed with anticipation as he stood. Calas stood, too. Jason extended a hand and Mikael warily reached out to take it in a strong grasp.

"Thank you for talking with me so honestly, sir," Jason said. "I'll let you know the outcome of our dattran as soon as . . ."

He stopped, dropping Calas' hand as Sergeant Qery raced into the room practically bowling over the two security guards at the door. A minor din broke out as Qery shoved past them to run headlong across the room.

Jason strode to meet Qery halfway. "What's wrong?" he asked in a hushed voice.

Qery saluted quickly. A tall wraith with blond hair, he had huge freckles across his face. "We don't know what happened, sir. Apparently we picked up two stowaways in one of our shuttles that set down on Horeb. They're in Engineering now, holding Chief Engineer Rad and two of his staff hostage."

Blood drained from Jason's face. "Where did they get weapons?"

Qery lifted his hands helplessly. "They used two vials of hypinitronium to convince the engineering staff to turn over their guns. Now they have a stockpile of rifles and pistols, along with the vials."

Jason rubbed a hand disbelievingly over his face. "Who are they?"

"Unknown. They demand to talk to you, sir."

Jason started across the floor. "Set up a visual com

outside of Engineering. Organize a security team and a special forces unit. Have them meet me there in fifteen minutes."

'Aye, sir," Qery saluted and pivoted to race away at full speed.

Jason wet his lips, pulse pounding like a kettle drum in his ears. He noticed Calas watching him intently as he strode out of the hospital.

* * *

Zadok slowed his steps as they neared the gray hole. The utter blackness of the Void swam and eddied around him. The opening seemed wide enough for two. Would Epagael allow him to leave for the first time in over a decade? His blood surged with excitement as he hurried forward. Carey Halloway followed behind him and stepped through the hole onto the grassy plains of the first heaven.

Zadok lifted his arms in relief and triumph as he inhaled deeply of the springtime air. "I'm through!"

Halloway came up beside him, her cool green eyes surveying the place as though searching for enemy soldiers. "Why do you think Epagael decided to let you pass?"

"He must need me for something."

"Something to do with Horeb, I'd wager."

Zadok's dark eyes narrowed. "Perhaps." The terrifying things she'd told him on their journey through the Void had left him deeply worried. But could they be true? A holocaust on Tikkun? Mass murder on Horeb? Gamant rebellions sparking across the galaxy as people frantically tried to hide from Magisterial tyranny? He could believe the latter. He'd led enough of those rebellions to know what desperation did to Gamants. But he couldn't quite believe the rest. Epagael would have told him. Epagael would have shown him how to guide Mikael to avoid such brutality. And if He hadn't—God had reasons.

Zadok examined Halloway again. Though wary, she seemed intrigued and delighted by everything. Her gaze caressed the splashes of orange poppies fringing the meadow, the gigantic oaks waving in the cool breezes, the fluffy clouds drifting through the azure skies. Her formfitting black battlesuit highlighted her tall feminine body and auburn hair. A hard, calculating glint shone in her emerald eyes.

Zadok tugged her black sleeve. "Come. Let's get to the gate and find out what's really going on."

He hobbled along a dirt path through the wildflower strewn meadow. Epagael's reasons for allowing him entry must revolve around her. But what could this tall, athletic woman have to do with the survival of Gamant civilization?

They walked past a jumbled pile of rocks and she said, "Zadok, would you mind if we sat down for a short time? I'd like to talk to you more before we challenge the gatekeeper."

"I wouldn't mind at all. These blasted knees have been bothering me for centuries."

He waddled over to a low boulder and sat down heavily. She stood beside him, propping a boot on a rounded rock and bending forward to brace her hands on her knee. She inhaled deeply of the fragrant flower-scented breeze.

"My God, it's beautiful here. More beautiful than I'd have ever dreamed. Providing, that is, that I'm not dreaming." She smiled wryly.

A white-tailed deer with two spotted fawns trotted out of the trees in the distance. Bounding through the tall grass, they paid Zadok and Carey little notice.

"You're not dreaming,' Zadok assured her. "And all the heavens are beautiful. Each has its own sort of splendor. Wait until we get to the seventh heaven, Arabot, you'll be amazed by the majesty of the music."

"How do we get through the gates? Doesn't the potential entrant have to prove his or her worthiness by answering some obscure questions?"

"Yes—often, very obscure. I'm sure Sedriel is thinking up something ridiculous at this very moment."

"Well, I'm certainly grateful to have met you, Zadok, because I don't know any of the secret signs or words to gain entrance."

Zadok rubbed his wrinkled throat and grimaced. "Yes, I've been wondering about that."

"What?"

"Why the angel who spoke to you didn't simply pass you through to the seventh palace. Certainly he had the power to do that. I've had to do it the hard way for years because the angels are crotchety enough not to have wanted to help me. But you. . . . I don't understand. Why did he bring you through the Void of Authades?"

She ran fingers through her auburn hair. A cool gust of wind rippled across the meadow to flap their sleeves. "I don't know. Unless he knew you were there and wanted you and me to talk first. You're one of my husband's greatest heroes. Many times over the past twelve years I've heard Jeremiel lament that things would have been different if you'd lived. Maybe the angel thought you could help Jeremiel through me."

Zadok forced himself to smile. "Perhaps. How is Jeremiel?"

Carey's face tightened and Zadok could see the love and fear for her husband. He reached out to touch her forearm sympathetically and together they watched an eagle lilting on the wind currents high overhead; its flight was a silent symphony.

"Jeremiel is fine. He almost died on Tikkun twelve years ago, but—"

"Almost died? What happened?"

"Oh, it's a long story, some of which I've already told you. You'll remember we talked about how Cole Tahn scorched Horeb? The attack had set off a series of devastating fire storms that rolled over the planet, killing everything in their wake. After Jeremiel took over the *Hoyer*, he struggled to rescue as many of the survivors as he could by bringing them aboard the cruiser. Later, the *Hoyer* was ordered to go to Tikkun to aid in suppressing the riots that had flared across the planet. Jeremiel had no choice but to comply, or he'd give away the fact that Cole Tahn was no longer in control of the cruiser. In the meantime, Jeremiel found out that the Magistrates had grown suspicious of the situation aboard the *Hoyer* and had dispatched five cruisers to surround the ship when it got to Tikkun. He knew his only hope of saving the Gamant refugees aboard was to put them down safely in the remote regions on Tikkun. But he had to check out the situation on Tikkun before he felt secure in doing that. At gunpoint, he forced Tahn down

with him to examine one of the 'research installations'
the Magistrates had set up on the planet. Jeremiel was
captured by Major Johannes Lichtner and severely tortured. Lichtner made him run between two lines of soldiers with flame wands. One of the witnesses claimed
that Jeremiel's skin seemed to boil as he staggered to the
end.'' She hesitated as though the telling gave her pain.
''Jeremiel received third degree burns over eighty percent
of his body. Had it not been for the fact that Cole and
Rachel went down to rescue Jeremiel, I'm sure he'd be
dead.''

Zadok clenched a fist. Jeremiel had been fighting
nearly his entire life to protect Gamant people and culture. And Zadok remembered all too clearly how tenderly, respectfully, Jeremiel had held him as he'd died
on that long-ago rainy day on Kayan. His desperate
hatred of the Magistrates grew.

''I thank Epagael that you and Cole Tahn joined the
Underground.'' Affectionately, Zadok reached out to
squeeze her shoulder.

Carey smiled and patted his hand, then her brows lowered in thought. The arching branches of a maple waved
behind her, silhouetting her still form. ''I don't know
how to ask this without offending you, Zadok.''

''Oh, I've been offended by the best. I'm sure I'll survive. What is it?''

She tilted her head back and frowned at the lacy puffs
of cloud sailing over the tops of the trees. ''It's about
Epagael. Why would he condemn you to such a terrible
fate? Confinement, alone, in that dark void must have
been horrifying.''

He expelled a long breath. ''It was. Sometimes I
thought I'd go mad. But it gave me the chance to talk
to my grandson. You see, with my body dead, Epagael
couldn't send me home again. I had no receptacle to
return to.''

''But if God is all-powerful, couldn't he have fashioned
a new receptacle? If He'd truly wanted you to guide the
Gamant people, why—''

''I've wondered that myself.'' Zadok brushed the
grains of sand from his coarse brown robe. ''In fact I've
been thinking about it for centuries. I think the answer
lies in the definition of omnipotence. I don't think it

means God can do anything He wants. I think it means He has control over all the power that's available to Him."

"And what isn't available to Him?"

"Oh, for example, that infinitesimal part that we possess. I don't understand it either, really. But I do know there are some things He cannot do. In the last Gamant Revolt, for example, Epagael could not have stopped the war Himself. That's why I had to travel through the heavens to talk to Him face-to-face to learn the victory strategy."

She smoothed her boot sole over the gritty rock and the lines in her forehead deepened. "Does that mean, as well, Zadok, that Epagael only has a limited amount of goodness, truth, and beauty?"

He lifted a shoulder. "I don't know. Shall we go and ask Him?"

"Do you think He'll tell us?"

"He's always been honest with me. I have the utmost confidence in his desire to help Gamant civilization survive." Zadok grunted to his feet and affectionately took Carey by the arm. "Come, let's go wrestle with the demon so we can be on our way to the second heaven. There's no telling what sort of foolishness Sedriel will use to delay us."

They tramped through the sweet smelling grass of the meadow and climbed a low tree-covered knoll. Birds chirped and fluttered in the boughs that curved over their heads. When they broke over the crest, Zadok heard Carey's low intake of breath. He looked up to see the enormous rapier-thin arch of the first gate gleaming gloriously in the sun. Against the arch, Sedriel lounged in lazy disarray. Dressed in a champagne-colored robe with a regal crimson sash around his waist, his crystalline features glimmered like polished golden teardrops. His brilliant white wings stroked the air to fend off the iridescent swarm of gnats that clouded around his head.

As they neared the gate, Sedriel haughtily declared, "You're late, as usual, Zadok."

"What do you care?" Zadok taunted. "You don't have anything else to do."

Sedriel's magnificent amber eyes narrowed. "Careful, Zadok, you're in enough trouble as it is. That wench, Rachel, is playing with fire and doesn't even know it."

Zadok felt suddenly hot. He looked up in horror at Carey. "I—I don't understand. I told Jeremiel to kill Rachel Eloel. *He didn't?*" Rachel—Aktariel's hand-maiden, the promised Antimashiah of legend. He'd read her name on the sacred Veil that stretched before the throne of God, the Veil where all events of creation were recorded.

Carey's eyes turned steely. "No. He believed at the time that Aktariel was fighting on the side of the Gamants, against the Magistrates."

Zadok closed his eyes in utter despair. "Oh, my dear God."

Sedriel smiled lecherously at Carey. "Oh, I can't wait until you tell Epagael that. Not that you'll have the chance. Neither you nor Zadok can pass through the gate."

"Why not?" Zadok demanded. His voice echoed around the hills, startling the birds into silence.

"Because Epagael hasn't called you, that's why. I can't even ask you any questions unless He approves and He hasn't, so the issue is closed. Go back to Authades." Sedriel shooed them away and rudely turned his back.

Zadok lapsed into infuriated silence. He turned to Carey. "See, I told you he was insufferable. Now, look here, Sedriel, this woman was sent by an angel. You may refuse me passage, but she certainly has the right to enter!"

Sedriel made a disgusted noise and glowered over his shoulder. "*Which* angel, Zadok?"

"Well, I—I don't—"

"He didn't give me his name," Carey interrupted. "But he looks very much like you."

Sedriel flapped his wings indignantly. "We all look alike to you ignorant humans. You can't even tell each other apart. How can you expect to distinguish between angels?"

Carey propped her hands on her hips and whispered conspiratorially to Zadok, "You're right, he is an arrogant sonofabitch."

"*I heard that!*" Sedriel snapped. He spun around. "After this, I'll never let you through this gate again, Zadok, I don't care how many questions you answer correctly!"

Zadok grimaced at the angel's stiff stance. "This is a new style for you, Sedriel. You look like you swallowed a broomstick."

Sedriel's gaze darted questioningly over the landscape, then he scowled. "Was that a comment on my allegiances!"

"What? Oh, I get it. Witches and all that. I simply meant that—"

"It's immaterial to me what you meant! Now, go on, get out of here before you really make me angry and I call fire and brimstone down from the heavens to burn you to a crisp—or . . ." He scratched his neck uncertainly. "Or something equally colorful."

Zadok mumbled an ancient profanity about angels' mothers and threw up his hands. "I'm sorry, Carey, but if Sedriel won't allow us to pass, then—"

"I'm going through that gate," Carey said challengingly. Her pearlescent complexion had turned a rosy hue. "Whether this humanoid likes it or not. I *will* talk to Epagael. I haven't come all this way for nothing."

"Humanoid!" Sedriel raged. He flapped his wings so violently the breeze knocked Zadok backward two steps. He had to lean into the gale to keep standing.

"Oh, hush, you flaming beast! She doesn't understand the ritual. Carey," Zadok explained, "if Sedriel says we cannot pass, then I'm afraid we've no recourse but to go somewhere and earnestly pray to Epagael for Him to hear our pleas."

A steely glimmer lit her eyes. She cocked her head threateningly. "No. I demand to speak to the archistrategos Michael."

"Michael's busy," Sedriel proclaimed imperiously. "Now, go away."

"I demand an audience with him. I have that right, don't I? To take my case for entry to a higher judge?"

Sedriel's face puckered into a pout. Suspiciously, he demanded, "Where did you hear that?"

"From the angel who sent me."

"Well, he certainly hasn't been around in a while. We changed that ruling centuries ago. Take my word for it, in this day and age, each gatekeeper is the final decision maker. Now, leave, I haven't all day to waste on you two insignificant wretches."

Carey lifted a brow and smiled icily at Zadok. "He called me a wretch."

"You should have heard what he called me the last time I was here: a pusillanimous mortal born from a putrid white drop."

Carey laughed, but it was a low, deadly sound that made Zadok's eyes widen. In a sudden move, she charged forward and landed a solid body kick to Sedriel's left kneecap. As Carey pulled herself upright again, Sedriel let out an enraged howl and stumbled sideways, grabbing the arch to steady himself.

"She—she . . ." Sedriel stuttered in shock and rage and finally wailed, "She *struck* me, Zadok! She struck an *angel!*"

Flabberghasted, Zadok didn't know what to say. If he hadn't already been dead, he'd have been worried. He extended a hand to Sedriel's writhing form and grimaced at Carey. "Look what you did? How could you do that?"

"Training," she responded glibly. Grabbing Zadok gruffly by the sleeve she physically hauled him through the gate with her.

Zadok stumbled along the dirt path of the second heaven, craning his neck to watch Sedriel squirm and rub his shattered kneecap. He shrieked, "You can't do this! Come back before I tell Epagael!"

"Damn it!" Carey cursed. "I wish I had a pistol!"

Zadok's mouth gaped. "My dear, you have the wrong attitude about heaven."

"No, Zadok. It's just that I haven't got anything left to lose. I may well be dead right now, for all I know. If I'm not, it's because the probe doctors decided they might be able to bring me out of my catatonia through other methods. That means they're saving my body for worse things." She wet her lips and squinted through the brushy barricade around the grove, watching Sedriel. He was still wailing. "My only hope—and the hope of the Underground, I fear—is to get to Epagael and ask him what the hell's going on."

Zadok's voice floundered. *Her body was under the probes? Blessed God.* "I didn't realize—"

"It's all right, Zadok." She looked over her shoulder. "Get ready to run. That blasted angel just staggered through the arch and is heading straight for us."

Zadok scanned the skies, waiting for retribution from a higher source. On the horizon, clouds drifted, their edges dyed a pale coral in the slanting rays of the afternoon sun. Shadows dappled the soft grasses like broken and irregularly strewn slate tiles.

"*Zadok?*"

The rich baritone rumbled through the skies and he saw the archangel Michael soaring over the tops of the trees. His milky wings reflected the color of the leaves, shimmering with a viridian hue. He circled the arch of the first gate, surveying the damage, then swooped down to land before them. His golden robe fell in waves around his feet. Zadok noticed Carey shaking her head in disbelief. Of all the angels, Michael was unquestionably the most awesomely beautiful. Sunlight glimmered like snow crystals from his eiderdown feathers. He looked so achingly perfect that for a moment neither of them could speak.

Sedriel hobbled up from behind, breathing like a pneumonia victim. A gentle breeze stirred his champagne-colored hem and sleeves, rippling in his wings like the invisible caress of God. Carey's face slackened as though the majestic vision of the angels side-by-side overwhelmed her.

Sedriel snapped his wings closed and charged, "Now, see here, Michael, these oafs have challenged my right to keep them out of the first heaven! They demanded to speak to you. I told them you were busy, but this—this *woman* attacked me!"

"Oh, hush, Sedriel," Michael said wearily. He turned to Zadok and Carey. "Why are you here, Zadok?"

Carey stammered, "I–I need to speak with you—privately, Lord Michael."

"You? I'm surprised. Very well."

Zadok watched as they went to stand beneath a towering oak. Carey's lips moved, but no sound carried across the meadow. Michael listened with his head bowed, nodding on occasion. Rays of light filtered through the branches to mottle Carey's serious face with hazy patches of burnished gold. When she reached a certain point in her explanation, Michael lifted his head suddenly. "Describe him to me."

The archangel paced erratically. He and Carey exchanged a few more quiet sentences. Sedriel hobbled forward, favoring his injured left knee, and tilted his head, trying hard to decipher the hushed words.

"Can you hear what they're saying, Zadok?" Sedriel inquired hopefully.

"I wouldn't tell you if I could."

Sedriel looked irked. He sneered and flopped a shoulder against a lush green tree.

A few minutes later, Michael strode across the grass and brusquely ordered, "Get back to your gate, Sedriel. These people have urgent business with Epagael."

"But—but," Sedriel spluttered. "*I'm the gatekeeper!* And I don't think they should be allowed—"

"Get out of the way!"

Sedriel closed his mouth and obediently stepped aside. Zadok cast a quick glance at him. The arrogant angel sighed sulkily and flicked a hand. "The Archistrategos authorized your journey, Zadok. Get out of my sight."

CHAPTER 31

Cole awoke in the broad white infirmary aboard the *Zilpah*. His eyes fluttered opened and closed. He glimpsed a bedside table and pitcher of water, plus the glaring overhead light panels. A silver med unit encased his chest. He could feel the probing of the surgical stimulators that knitted bone and directed tissue regeneration; they burned like tiny snakes slithering through his lungs. He groaned.

"Hurts, eh?" a familiar voice called.

Cole opened one eye to see Kopal staring down at him. Rudy had an arm braced lazily on the med unit. His black jumpsuit and brown curly hair both looked freshly washed. He lounged forward to squint. "I met Amirah Jossel. Five foot nine, a hundred and twenty pounds."

Cole could instinctively feel a jab coming. "Are you hinting at something?"

"Me? No, I was just hoping to hear some of the details of your glorious mission. Like why you let her break your ribs?"

Cole slitted his eyes. It felt good having Rudy around again to torment him. "Why are you annoying me, Kopal? Did Baruch give you the day off or something?"

Rudy shook his head and drawled softly, "No. Matter of fact I've only got ten minutes. I just wanted to say thanks. You did a damned fine job down there."

"Hurts to admit, doesn't it?"

"Only a little. So . . ." He grinned broadly. "Why'd you let her break your ribs?"

Cole cavalierly rearranged his white sheet. "At the time, it seemed preferable to my neck."

Rudy's expression twisted with repressed mirth. "From the way Jossel's been acting, I thought maybe you'd developed some bizarre new courtship ritual. I was going to ask for lessons."

"What do you mean 'from the way she's been acting'?"

"You haven't heard?" Rudy tilted his head appreciatively, as though lauding some talent Cole didn't know he had. "Jossel's deeply concerned about your health. She's been asking about you constantly."

"She's probably concerned about her hand-to-hand efficiency," Cole quipped casually, but a spot of warmth expanded in his chest. "Tell her I'm fine and I'm sure she'll be so disappointed she'll calm down."

"I don't think so. She tackled the last mess tech who delivered her dinner and demanded to know how you were."

Cole frowned. Amirah possessed no flighty qualities at all. Especially aboard an enemy cruiser, she'd be walking a careful tightrope. "Yeah? What did the tech do to her?"

"Nothing."

Cole frowned suspiciously. "She really tackled a mess tech?"

"Uh-huh." Rudy smirked.

From out in the hallway, Cole heard Jeremiel's voice as he talked quietly with one of the doctors. Rudy continued to loom over the med unit, grinning, until Jeremiel strode across the room and appeared at his side. Baruch gave Cole a confident smile, but he looked dead tired. Dark purplish smudges shaded the area beneath his eyes. His blond hair was matted against his head.

Jeremiel's gaze took in Kopal's smirk and Cole's curious expression. Propping his hands on his hips, he inquired. "Are you two getting along?"

"As well as we ever do," Kopal answered. "He was telling me about this new courtship ritual he developed, and I—"

"Goddamn, Baruch," Cole interrupted. "Will you give this man something to do so he'll quit bothering me?"

Jeremiel scratched his reddish beard, as though assessing the hidden variables. To Kopal he muttered, "You told him she tackled the mess tech, right "

Rudy nodded. "I hope you approved the visit she requested. I'd hate for any more of your crew to get headlocked over Tahn's condition."

"I approved it. She'll be here in half an hour."

Rudy chuckled and wisely backed away. "I'd love to watch, but I have to be getting back to my ship. I'll see you both later."

Jeremiel watched Rudy go and then took his place, bracing an arm across the silver beast that encased Cole's chest. Almost immediately, Baruch's teasing smile faded into a deadly serious frown. His evaluative gaze went over Cole in detail. "How are you?"

Cole twisted slightly, testing the ache in his chest. "Give me two days. I'll be ready."

"The doctor said four. I don't want you to—"

"The doctor is referring to the time necessary to completely heal that rib. I can heal on the way. In two days the bone will be fundamentally knitted. That's all I need."

"And your leg?"

"Feels better than it has in years."

Jeremiel expelled a worried breath through his nostrils and picked up a mini-com unit from the bedside table. He absently input data, then cleared it and started again. Cole studied him with growing nervousness. Around them, the hospital throbbed with a soundless intensity. Jeremiel's bushy brows drew together. "Immediately after we set you down on Horeb, we got word from Lakish that Magisterial flotillas had invaded the Moran and Tonopah systems."

A torrent of cold tingled through Cole's body. For the cruisers to get there so soon, they must have gotten the information from . . . "You think she's alive?"

Jeremiel clenched the mini-com in a hard fist. Cole could see pain and hope vie on Baruch's bearded face. *Like a man watching a precious loved one slowly eaten up by a terrible disease.* "Maybe. Could have been Samuals."

"Doesn't matter. I assume you've already selected and programmed our fighter?"

"Yes. It's ready. There's one more detail I want to discuss with you, though." Jeremiel poked the mini-com awkwardly, striking it like a tiny punching bag.

"What is it?"

"Jossel." He looked up and his blue eyes glittered.

"Go on."

Jeremiel tossed the mini-com back to the bedside table. "I've already talked to Rudy and Merle. Horebian refugees are currently being loaded onto their cruisers. We also captured the *Hammadi*. She's still in good shape. Merle is orchestrating the repair process. We're setting all the surviving Magisterial crew down on the planet on the Abaddon Islands. We're leaving enough food and supplies for four months—though I suspect the Magistrates will pick them up far sooner."

Cole tugged restlessly at the sheet. The Magistrates would do the same thing to the *Hammadi* crew that they'd done to the crews of the *Annum* and the *Hoyer*. The thought of Amirah ending up mindless made his stomach knot. She'd find out in a hurry how right he'd been about the Magistrates. He had the urge to slam his fists into something.

"What I want to know, Cole," Jeremiel inquired solemnly, "is whether or not you think we should put Jossel down there with them?"

"Do we have a choice?"

"I think so. She might be useful as a bargaining chip if we get into trouble on Palaia. She also might be a nuisance or dangerous. You've been with her. What do you think?"

Cole gripped handfuls of his sheet and crushed the fabric in anxious fingers while he considered. With enough time and the proper coaxing, he might be able to teach her to see the Gamant side of galactic politics. She had all the requisite intelligence and *ancestry*. Not that she'd ever leave Magisterial service, that would be too much to hope for, but he might grasp enough to develop a positive sympathy. And she'd be spared the certain probe-death that those left behind on the Abbadon Islands would face. "Do you know she's Gamant?"

Baruch's face darkened. "No."

"At least a quarter. Her grandmother was full-blood, I think."

Jeremiel slowly dropped his hands to his sides. "She *told* you her grandmother was Gamant? Why?"

"I'm not sure. I think she'd given herself up for dead and didn't believe it mattered anymore."

Baruch's eyes shone dangerously. "More likely she was supposed to tell you that."

"What are you talking about?"

Jeremiel clenched his hands into fists and tucked them into the side pockets of his black battlesuit. "The woman has no past. I've combed every obscure Magisterial file to locate information on her parents or grandmother, and none exists."

"Her father worked in the Records division. She says he purged all the incriminating data."

Jeremiel cocked his head. "I doubt it. Thirty years ago, Zadok Calas managed to slip insiders into that division. Those people were killed the instant they attempted to delete any data relating to Gamants. The government monitors the Records Office more heavily than it does Defense."

A numb sensation crept up Cole's shoulders. "That makes me think that perhaps the deletions were 'allowed' by the Magistrates—and . . . damn it, why didn't it occur to me before . . . maybe the Magistrates have something to do with the delusions Jossel suffers."

Jeremiel leaned forward pensively. "What delusions?"

Cole waved a hand. "It's a long story and she'll be here soon. In the time we've got, though, do you know what the word 'nahash' means?"

Jeremiel seemed to stop breathing.

Amirah paced around her stark cabin on level ten, waiting for the security team Baruch had promised would take her to see Tahn. In anticipation, she picked up pet-rolon glasses and threw them on the floor so she could kick them across the room. The dull thudding noises they made against the walls eased her stress level. She'd cursed herself over and over, wondering how in the name of God she could have let herself get into a situation like this—a situation where she was completely impotent. Her fate lay totally in the hands of hostile strangers. *Her fate!* A Magisterial captain! Self-hatred throbbed in her veins. And she was terrified about what might be happening on the *Sargonid*. Was her crew safe? How was Jason handling her absence? Undoubtedly superbly, but still she feared for them.

The room was at most a ten by twelve foot rectangle, with a bed in the back and a tiny table and two chairs near the entryway in the front. The door to the latrine stood open on the left wall, equidistant from the bed and the table. Holos of battle scenes adorned each wall, ships blasting each other apart, men and women carrying out ground actions—even a scorch attack in progress.

She'd showered and dressed in the purple Magisterial captain's uniform the quartermaster had delivered. It irked her that they could reproduce the latest official style in such detail. Even the captain's bars on her shoulders showed the delicate scrollwork around the edges which the fleet had adopted only eight weeks earlier. How did they know such things?

"Because they have an inside contact somewhere, that's how."

She occupied herself for a few minutes by thinking how good it would feel to kill the informer, then futilely threw up her arms and stalked to stand before the mirror over the table for the gillionth time. Clean blonde hair fell in waves over her shoulders, shimmerimg with a silver hue in the brilliant white light. She grimaced at how clearly her freckles stood out against the too pale background of her skin. Her button nose and full lips looked bloodless.

"You look like hell," she accused. She kicked one of the chairs. It banged against the table and made her feel better.

"Goddamn it, you're being a fool. Think! Think like a Magisterial captain! What are you going to do?"

She shook her fists at the ceiling just as her door com buzzed. A male voice penetrated the cabin: "Captain Jossel? This is Corporal Poimandres. I'm here to escort you to see Captain Tahn."

"On my way," she announced sternly and ran for the door. Hitting the patch to open it, she looked out into the faces of two young, dark-haired soldiers dressed in black jumpsuits, one a corporal, one a private, both carrying rifles. She stepped into the hallway.

"I'm Corporal Poimandres, ma'am, and this is Private Valentin. Please follow me."

"Lead the way, Corporal."

He started down the corridor and she fell in line behind him. Valentin unslung his rifle and brought up the rear. Knowing his aim rested between her shoulders, the hair on the back of her neck stood on end. They marched to the transport tube and entered. Amirah idly watched Poimandres strike the patch for level six. The tube ascended smoothly, deck numbers flashing in blue over the entry.

When the tube stopped, she followed them down a long empty corridor. She saw the "Infirmary" sign posted over the door at the end of the hall. When they got there, Valentin accessed the entry patch. The door slid back.

"I'll take you in, ma'am," Poimandres explained. "The captain's expecting you."

"Thank you, Corporal."

Valentin stayed outside, guarding the exit. Poimandres led her into a broad, white tiled room with beds lining the walls. A variety of emergency medical equipment huddled in the far corner like a lanky tangle of silver and gray arms. Four levels of computer screens filled the wall near the security officer's desk. He looked up at her as she entered, then shot a glance at Baruch, who hovered over a bed with an attached med unit. Baruch caught the glance and turned. Seeing her, he said a few soft words to Tahn, then came toward her.

He stopped a few feet away, formed his hands into the sacred Gamant triangle, and bowed respectfully. Amirah stubbornly refused to return the ancient symbol of greeting. Why had Baruch done that? It affected her like a splash of cold water. Had Tahn told him about her Gamant heritage? Of course he had. Any good officer would have revealed every shred of information gathered on a clandestine mission. The thought sat like a lump of ice in her belly.

"How are you, Captain?" Baruch asked.

"As well as can be expected, Commander."

"If there's anything I can do to make you more comfortable, please let me know." He paused and pointed to the bed with the med unit. "You'll find Captain Tahn over there. Please excuse me, I have business to attend to on the bridge."

"Certainly."

Poimandres headed across the room and stationed himself at the foot of Cole's bed in an "at ease" position.

Cole called, "I'm not dead, you'll be disappointed to know."

"So I heard. Maybe I do need hand-to-hand lessons from you, after all."

She quickly strode across the floor to stand over him. His brown hair framed his face in curls, highlighting his straight nose. He'd shaved his beard, leaving a clean jaw.

He looked at her sideways. "You're looking well."

She smiled reluctantly—angry with herself for being glad to see him. "So are you. How's your chest? It was just one rib, wasn't it?"

"One was enough, Amirah. The doctor says I should be out of here in two days. Incidentally . . ." He lowered his voice to a conspiratorial whisper. "Did you really tackle the mess tech?"

Her jaw went hard. "You didn't flatter yourself about it, did you? You're thoroughly conceited. You've never gotten over being the greatest captain in the fleet, have you? For your information I 'tackled' that technician because he provoked me."

"The brute. How did he do that?"

She gave Cole a dubious look and leaned against his med unit to scrutinize the dirt under her fingernails. "I think it was the tone in his voice more than anything else. I asked him about your condition and he told me he wasn't at liberty to reveal such information to a Magisterial *snake*."

Cole's smile faded. A brief flicker of fear went over his face before he pulled himself out of it and tilted his head apologetically. "Jeremiel will see to it."

"That's not necessary. I doubt that technician will ever get his baritone voice back. The squeak should be punishment enough."

Cole gazed at the foot of his bed. "Poimandres?"

"Yes, sir?" The youth leaned around the unit to peer at Tahn.

"Would you mind leaving us alone. No, don't worry, Captain Jossel isn't going to break any more of my ribs. She's aiming lower these days. I'll take full responsibility for relieving you."

Poimandres gave Amirah an unpleasant appraisal but nodded and backed away. "I'll be over by the door, sir. Just yell if you need me."

"I will, Corporal. Thank you."

Tahn waited until Poimandres was out of earshot, then

he said, "Why don't you pull up a chair and sit down.
There's one over by that next bed."

"What for?" she asked hesitantly. His expression told
her he had unpleasant news to deliver.

"Because I asked you to."

She pulled over the chair. Sitting down, she crossed
her arms tightly. "What is it?"

His handsome face tightened. "I wanted to talk to you
about a promise I made."

"To me?" She mentally searched her memories, trying
to figure out when he'd ever . . . A weightless feeling
like free-fall overcame her. She forced a disdainful laugh.
"You didn't think I really believed you'd let me go after
you'd used me, did you? How's Baruch going to do it?
Public execution? Or is he the quiet type? I'd prefer a
quick secret hustle into a vacuum tube."

He looked up at her and her heart slammed against
her ribs sickeningly. "I'm afraid you're going to live—
but I'm not sure what's ahead is preferable. Baruch asked
me if I thought it would be better to put you down on
Horeb with the remnants of the *Hammadi* crew, or . . .
or to take you with us."

Amirah swallowed past the lump that had risen in her
throat. "Destination?"

His face turned bland. "I can't tell you that, but I
recommended to Jeremiel that we take you."

She sprang unsteadily to her feet, chest heaving.
"Why? So you can use me against someone? Like you
planned on using me against my crew? *Goddamn it!* You
used to understand—"

"Listen to me! Do you want to end up a vegetable?
That's what they'll do to you if we leave you on Horeb,
Amirah. Just like they did to *my* crew. And the crew of
the *Annum.* They'll probe you until you're brain dead!
You know it—and so do I."

In angry indignation, she taunted, "You're interested
in my welfare, eh? Well, that does ease my fears."

His voice came out soft. "Amirah, I don't know what's
going to happen on this journey, but I can practically
guarantee you that you'll die fighting, not under some
helmet in a cold neuro lab."

She glared. "It's such a comfort, Captain, to have you

deciding what's best for me. *Just like you did for the*
Hoyer *crew.*"

Tahn stared at her numbly, as though she'd kicked out
his guts. "We'll be leaving day after tomorrow."

She felt like ripping the med unit off him and slamming
a boot into his chest. Unfortunately, she knew Poimandres would splatter her blood all over the hospital if she
tried. Spinning on her toes, she headed for the door.

Six hours later, in the middle of the night shift when
the hospital thrummed with silence, Cole leaned back
against his pillow. He couldn't get Amirah out of his
mind. Her voice, gruff and commanding—filled with
anguish—echoed around his memories, coming back
sounding like his own . . . an eternity ago in another life.
He could still remember how badly his fists had ached
from slamming them into the walls of his own cabin. A
prisoner on his own ship, he'd been frantic, almost
insane, to get away.

"So's she."

He closed his eyes and watched the afterimages of
Amirah's desperate face dance in the darkness.

CHAPTER 32

Jason Woloc sprinted down the long corridor, heading toward the huge double doors that led to Engineering. His six member security team followed on his heels. The swift beat of their boots pounded against the carpet like hoofed animals racing over rain-soaked earth. Three men and two women from the special forces division hovered over the portable com unit set up outside the double doors. Already their purple uniforms showed sweat around the collars. Jason sucked in a deep breath as he slid to a halt before the tense gathering.

Aryeh Patora, his chief of special forces looked at him from troubled brown eyes. A medium-sized woman with a bowl haircut, straight brown locks framed her oval face and turned up nose. "Our culprits seem to be two old men, First Lieutenant," she informed him. "We must have picked them up from Horeb, though how is still a mystery. They were found wandering around down in the weapons division. Two of the engineering staff, Fontaine and Itro, escorted them into Engineering at gunpoint. After that, the two old codgers pulled their canisters of hypinitronium and threatened to blow up the ship. They collected everybody's weapons, then forced all but three officers out of Engineering. After that, they sealed the entire section up tight."

"Who's left in there?"

"Rad, Fontaine, and Itro."

Jason glowered at the white double doors. Officers shifted around him, waiting for orders. He searched his memories, trying to recall what other commanders had done in similar situations—but the number of ships the Magistrates had lost to terrorists was so minimal the data was almost nil. Panic touched him. He struggled to think like Amirah. What would she do? Just drawing a mental picture of her soothed him.

"How well did they seal Engineering? Can we get in through any of the maintenance access tunnels?"

Patora shook her head. "No, the two old fools apparently knew what they were doing—almost as though they'd been coached."

Jason glanced up suddenly. "Coached? You don't think this is part of a larger plan, do you? Perhaps these old men are members of the same terrorist group that kidnapped Captain Jossel? Can we assume that this action represents the 'ransom' call we've been expecting?"

Jason stood resolutely quiet as the pieces started falling into place. If a terrorist group had miraculously managed to intercept a Magisterial dattran stating that the *Sargonid* was on route to Horeb with orders to retrieve Calas, they'd certainly have set in motion a counterassault. Capturing Amirah, then getting aboard the cruiser and demanding custody of Calas in exchange for Amirah would make perfect sense.

Patora shrugged. "Unknown, sir, but I'd say that's a good guess."

"Can we gas Engineering?"

"Maybe. Depends on the extent of their knowledge of how the ship works. From where they're sitting, they could counter our efforts with the punch of a reroute patch."

"Do we know our invaders' names?"

"They've refused to talk to anyone but you."

Jason ran a hand through his hair and straightened his purple shirt. "All right, Lieutenant, let's see what they want."

"Aye, sir."

Patora stepped forward to the pedestaled com unit and established the connection. She called, "First Lieutenant Jason Woloc is here now. Please hit the red patch on your console."

Jason walked forward and Patora edged out of the way. An old man's face formed. He was bald with a round face, freckled scalp, and old-fashioned spectacles clinging precariously to his fleshy nose. In the background, Jason could see Engineer Rad standing with his hands up. Another old man, very tall, with a gray mop of hair, held a gun on him.

"Gentlemen," Jason began, "I'm First Lieutenant Woloc, currently in command of the *Sargonid*. We've no wish to harm you. Please lay down your weapons and—"

"I'm sorry, Lieutenant," the first old man said. He tilted his head in a kindly way, as though gently reprimanding a child. "We can't do that. Engineer Rad has informed us that from these controls on my left—" the screen panned right to show Jason the master override console, then panned back to frame the old man, "—we can control any part of the ship we want. Please don't make any moves to enter this section, or I'll be forced to hurt your crew and I'd rather not do that."

"Who are you?" Jason asked tersely. He'd unwittingly clamped his fingers over the edges of the com unit, holding it in a clammy death grip.

"You can call me Yosef."

"What do you want, Yosef?"

"Two things. First of all, we'd like you to transport the Calas family down here to Engineering. After that, we'll talk more. Please hurry, Lieutenant. We'd like to see Mikael, Sybil, and Nathan within a half hour."

Nathan? "I take it your presence here represents a rescue attempt, then?"

"We'll talk more after we see you've met our first demands."

Jason stared somberly at the screen. Certainly Gamant terrorists. From the Underground? There'd been rumors that Baruch's forces had planned a full-scale attack on Horeb. But no one believed the Underground commander would do something so suicidal, not with four Magisterial cruisers orbiting the planet. Had the government's intelligence been wrong? Had Baruch planned a clandestine mission all the time? *Oh, Amirah, I should have guessed.*

"Yosef," Jason asked. "Are you part of the Gamant Underground?"

Yosef started to respond, but the other old man behind him shouted, "Of course, we're part of the Underground. What a ridiculous question. Tell the *gunzel* we want to make a deal. The Calas family for Jossel."

Yosef squinted over his shoulder, a look of utter disbelief on his withered face, but when he turned back he nodded and said, "Yes, Lieutenant Woloc. That's what we want to do. You deliver Mikael and his family to us and we'll signal our people on Horeb to release your captain."

So she is on Horeb. Jason tensed, his worst fears rising. Slothen had demanded Calas be delivered to Palaia immediately. Would he approve of such a deal? Blessed God, what if he wouldn't?

He propped a fist against the screen. "I'll need to discuss this with my officers, Yosef."

"That's fine, Lieutenant. But you'd better deliver the Calas family to us within a half hour—or else we'll be forced to do something unpleasant." He gestured to the override console.

"I understand, Yosef. I'll be in contact. Woloc out." He cut the transmission and straightened to face his assembled officers. People stared back, their faces eroded with hatred and worry. "Suggestions?"

Patora leaned heavily against the wall. "Can we use Mikael and Sybil Calas against them? What do you think they'd do if we refused to turn them over?"

"I don't know, sir," Qery, who'd come in behind him, said. He spread his long legs into an "at ease" position. In the bright glare, his freckles blotched his face like haphazardly strewn spots of melted brown crayon. "It'll be risky. I suspect those old men were sent on this mission because they're expendable. After all, they have to be pushing three hundred and fifty. They might just blow the hell out of us if we look at them the wrong way."

Patora lifted her brows. "Delivering Calas might buy us time. And if we can stall for a while, I *will* figure a way of getting into Engineering and eliminating the threat."

Jason put a hand on Patora's shoulder. "If we comply and let them contact their people on Horeb, it will take at least two days for a ship to get here with Captain Jossel. Is that enough time?"

"Probably. We also might get an additional benefit out of this, too. If one of our cruisers around Horeb picks up Yosef's message, they might intercept Yosef's friends before they can escape the planet."

Jason nodded heartily. Hope swelled like a hot fire inside him. "Or if they can't, at least we should have reinforcements coming. And maybe, if we time this maneuver right, we can set a trap and capture the whole lot of terrorists the instant they set foot aboard the *Sargonid*."

"Damn right!" Patora grinned, her brown eyes gleaming in anticipation. "I'm sure we can."

Officers nodded around him, bolstering his spirits. A round of soft whispers began, people planning, coordinating.

"Qery," Jason said. "See that Calas and his wife are brought down immediately. Assign a med tech to keep Mrs. Calas healthy. We don't want any charges of brutality or negligence leveled against us when this is over."

"Understood, sir. But who's Nathan?"

"Unknown. Just bring Mikael and Sybil."

"Aye, sir." Qery saluted and sprinted away.

Jason turned to Patora. "Aryeh, call a meeting with all your best explosives and chemical warfare specialists. We have to construct a foolproof ambush with a series of backup lairs just in case they penetrate the first round."

"Aye, sir. While they're working on that, I'd like to organize a special search unit to determine how to break into Engineering."

"Good. Let's get on it, people!"

*   *   *

Sybil slept within the confines of the silver monster that encased her upper half, dreaming . . . dreaming. . . . From somewhere far away, the ring of deep masculine laughter pierced her current dream.

She felt herself being pulled away, drawn down the dark throat of a whirling tunnel until she emerged in the midst of a broad desert. She stood on the shores of a metallic green lake. The sweet scent of some unknown flower wafted on the hot wind. A wall of cave-pitted rock rose behind her, shimmering surreally in the heat. Before the caves, a gaggle of white-robed men, very young and very old, bent over a crude aqueduct. The narrow covered canal that rose upon stone arches carried no water. Was it new construction?

Sybil walked slowly toward them, curiously examining

their labors. Rather than taking water from the lake, the aqueduct stretched high up over the rugged plateau behind the caves. Was the lake poisoned, Sybil wondered, or too salty to drink?

She watched with interest when an old man with gray hair and a long beak of a nose strode into the gathering, waving his arms and shouting. "You silly fools! Let me look at it. Go away and come back in an hour." Men flew away, chattering. A tiny boy of maybe six trudged at the old man's heels, beaming like a sacred lamp.

The child's high voice carried on the wind, "Why don't we use bricks instead?"

"We can't use bricks," the old man gently chastised. "We have to use stones if we want the arches to last. Water is too hard on bricks."

The boy nodded obediently and then followed the older man down the line. Sybil smiled. The child had coal black hair and the blackest eyes she'd ever seen. His white robe flapped and billowed in the wind, pressing tightly across his narrow chest. He ran to keep up with the longer stride of his teacher. In the glaring golden brilliance of the sun, his pudgy face gleamed.

"Paquid?" the boy called as he ran. "How much grade do you have to have over each stadia to keep the water flowing?"

The *Paquid* raised a brow appreciatively. "You're smarter than I thought." He stopped and knelt down. A loving smile curled his lips. He waved the boy forward. "Come here, Caius Nathanaeus, let me show you this."

The boy raced forward and threw himself at the old man's feet, smiling up eagerly; he put a hand on his teacher's knee and softly kneaded the white fabric.

The *Paquid* lifted his little finger and ran his thumb over the length of the second joint. "You see this, Nathanaeus?"

The boy nodded, eyes wide. "Yes."

"What is this measurement called?"

"One *uncia*, sir."

The old man smiled and patted the boy's obsidian colored hair. "Yes, very good. You're learning quickly. I remember when your Roman mother first brought you here. All you did was cry. But you're almost a man now, aren't you?"

Nathanaeus ducked his head shyly. "I am growing pretty good, sir. But I don't remember my mother."

"I know. You were just a baby. To answer your question, you must have six *unciae* of drop for every hundred feet of canal to keep the water flowing. You remember that, boy. No aqueduct will work without that knowledge."

Sybil smiled at the innocent joy that shone on the child's face. On the wind currents, high over the rocky parapet, black birds circled each other, rising higher and higher into the pale blue sky. The men who'd fled to the caves laughed happily. So peaceful. Sybil inhaled and exhaled the first relaxed breath she'd taken in months. A place like this could only exist in a dream.

Nathanaeus smoothed his tiny fingers over the stone arch before him. "I won't forget, *Paquid*. I want to do this, when I get bigger and stronger. To build. . . ."

His voice faded, mouth dangling open as another boy, bigger and older strode from the caves. Tall for his age, the boy had dark brown hair and huge brown eyes, but his body looked wasted and thin. When the breeze flattened his white robe against his chest, Sybil's heart throbbed. He seemed nothing more than a withered branch.

Nathanaeus stood up and whispered, "Who is that boy, *Paquid*?"

The old man turned to look. "Ah, that is a new member of our community, little one. A sad boy. He ran away from home. He claims a bright golden angel came to him in the middle of the night, grabbed him by the hair, and dragged him here to learn the sacred ways of the Teacher of Righteousness with us."

"What's his name?"

"Yeshwah."

The hot breeze gusted, setting whirlwinds to roaming the shores of the green lake like wayward ghosts, but young Nathanaeus didn't notice. He squinted at the new boy, cocking his head in deep thought.

Sybil studied the tall willowy child, too. He had to be about twelve, but his expression bespoke a longer, harder life. The raw flame in his dark eyes made it seem that everything he gazed upon had already been devastated— that he'd pierced the veil of time and glimpsed a ruined world where no one ever laughed, where no birds ever soared in the skies, or sang in the trees. Sybil lifted a hand to her aching throat, for she, too, had seen such desolation, in a real universe just a heartbeat away.

Nathanaeus licked his lips nervously as he wiped his sun-blackened hands on his white robe. "Can I go play with him, *Paquid*? He looks like he needs playing badly."

The old man laughed good-naturedly and ruffled Nathanaeus' black hair. "Yes, you go. But be kind to him. He has a wound inside him that may never heal—not even with all our knowledge about bodies and souls."

Nathanaeus leaned forward and quickly kissed the *Paquid's* cheek before racing away toward the older boy.

And from a distance, Sybil heard her name being called. *Sybil? Sybil?* The scene faded into a tan wash of nothingness as Mikael's deep gentle voice penetrated the dream. She found herself in the white hospital again. A medical technician pushed her bed across the floor. Mikael walked at her side, his strong hand upon her drenched hair.

"What's . . . what's happening," she croaked.

Mikael shook his head uncertainly. "I'm not sure. No one will tell me anything except that we're being moved."

* * *

Soft cries permeated the night as Arikha Anpin ran through the dark woods on Satellite 4. A tiny woman with black hair and blue eyes, she wore only a set of loose white pajamas. She ran awkwardly, in the midst of a group of twenty-two Gamant women who'd been kidnapped from their homes on Giclas 9 at midnight, barely dressed, in bathrobes and slippers, dragging children by the hands. Magisterial soldiers in crisp purple uniforms urged them forward with shouts and guns, driving the women and children like a herd of beasts up a hill and down a deeply eroded ravine. A little boy of maybe four slipped and fell against the rocks. He burst into cries of agony, holding his ankle. Before the child's mother could reach him, a soldier trotted up and calmly shot the boy, then shouted, "Move. Move! All of you! We told you to watch your feet! We told you not to fall or you'd be left behind. Now get moving!" Only the searchlights from the two fighters overhead lit the darkness. Snow fell lightly, frosting the branches and Arikha's long dark hair.

One fighter swerved right, leaving the women in darkness and a series of floodlights came on at the foot of the hill. They illuminated a line of soldiers. A major stood nervously off to one side, hands shoved deeply in the pockets of his long purple overcoat. Beside him, a general fairly pranced as the women came down the hill. Tall, with sandy hair and piercing lime green eyes, he had a cruel mouth. Arikha stumbled through the darkness toward him.

"You've just arrived, Major Rasch," the general explained professionally. "I wanted you to see what a routine liquidation of new prisoners looks like."

"New prisoners, General? But I thought our primary duty was to flush out the rebel nests and eliminate them. Why are we bothering with harmless women and children who've only been here for a few hours?"

The general turned menacing green eyes on Rasch. "We want the rebel nests to know we'll stop at nothing to get them. We want them to be worried about what we'll do to their families if they don't surrender as we've demanded. Terror has legitimate uses, Major. We'll discuss it more later. Here come the prisoners."

The general lifted his hand, and the soldiers knelt in firing position. Safety switches clicked off, sounding like perverse grasshoppers in the weeds.

As Arikha and the rest of the women and children flooded down to stand in a line before the general, Major Rasch reached up and gripped his superior officer's hand, staying it.

"Please wait, General Ornias." Rasch's middle-aged face looked pinched. In the dim light, his bald head shone like a polished silver bullet. He strode forward to stare at Saaydya Deo, a young blonde woman with wide blue eyes. Her tiny daughter of three, Temnath, clutched her legs tightly. Arikha's heart pounded sickeningly. She and Saaydya had been friends since kindergarten. Saaydya patted her daughter's platinum blonde curls and held her head high, meeting Rasch's probing gaze. "Are you a Gamant?" the major asked incredulously.

"Yes."

"But Gamants are usually dark-haired—"

"We're Gamants!" she cried fiercely. Pride and defiance oozed from every line of her oval face, but Arikha could see her knees shaking violently through her pale blue bathrobe. "You can take everything else away from us," Saaydya whispered hatefully. "But not that. *We're Gamants.*"

Colonel Rasch's gaze wavered and fell, as though he deplored the fact that with that admission there was no way he could save them. Tiredly, he stepped away and went back to stand beside General Ornias. "Let's make this quick and clean, General," he requested tersely.

Ornias smiled, but the expression cut like a blade. "We can't stand any milksops in our ranks. Try to get hold of yourself, Major." He stepped out in front of his soldiers and lifted his hand, then slashed down hard. Flares of violet shredded the darkness. Screams rose to a din of horror as women and children toppled like thin saplings in a windstorm. Arikha tried to run, but two dead women fell over her.

Lying pinned beneath the corpses, Arikha tried not to breathe. She watched Rasch in silent horror; the major writhed and jumped with each renewed burst of fire, his face withering.

When the firing stopped, a wretched groan shattered the stillness. An old woman and Temnath Deo had been wounded. The woman, elderly with black hair, wailed miserably as she pulled herself inch by inch, gripping the grass to try and escape. Temnath clawed up out of the mound of dead that had tumbled over her and peered hauntingly at Rasch. Blood streaked her pale face and matted her blonde hair; she seemed ethereal, like a mortally injured angel at the end of time.

A small groan escaped Rasch's throat. He waved his arms frantically. "General. Quickly! Kill them."

Ornias leisurely took a rifle from one of his private's hands and panned the area, slashing the old woman and Temnath in half. Arikha wept. Ornias straightened and handed the rifle back to his underling. He looked up gloatingly at Rasch—as though *proud* of his actions and the efficiency of his team.

But Rasch's eyes were turned away. A pitiable expression creased his square face as he watched the river of blood running down from the slaughtered to stain the white, white snow. He took a stumbling step sideways as the river slithered toward his polished black boots. "General," he said quietly, "may I speak to your troops?"

"Of course, Major. They'll be your troops tomorrow."

"Thank you, sir."

Rasch hurried to the firing squad who still knelt, preparing to shoot anything that moved. Arikha swallowed her tears and kept still.

Rasch wiped sweat from his forehead and faced the squad. "You are soldiers fighting in a desperate cause," he said in an unsteady voice as he walked down the line. "I know this duty is onerous. But you mustn't feel conscience stricken. The Gamant threat to galactic security increases everyday. We seek not a temporary security but a permanent one. These operations are a necessity. I commend each of you for unflinchingly carrying out your duties. You are honorable men, performing an essential function. . . ."

Arikha's sobs broke loose again, soundless, stomach wrenching. Did these soldiers believe him? Yes, she could tell they did. Blood drained from the slaughtered woman on top of her, flowing down in a hot sticky stream to drench her white pajamas. She lay motionless for another fifteen minutes, until General Ornias came over to Rasch and cut his speech short. "That's enough, Major. Our soldiers are well aware of their duties to the government. Come, we've work to do back at military headquarters."

Arikha watched in terror as the soldiers filed by and got into their ships. Lights flared and swerved over the dead as the fighters turned, then swooped up and away over the dark tops of the trees.

Arikha pulled herself out from under the corpses and crawled away through the snow into the trees. The general had said there were rebel nests on Satellite 4. She had to find them—to tell them what had happened here in this dark, dark forest. She got up on trembling legs and staggered through the dense forest shadows, hunting.

CHAPTER 33

Amirah wandered around her cabin, slamming her fists into walls, kicking chairs and anything else that didn't move out of her way. The gray blankets on her bed lay in a tumbled heap, half on the mattress, half on the floor. Only the light from the latrine illuminated the room, casting a bright rectangle over the table and chairs near the entryway.

For the first time since she'd almost died in her parents' fire-engulfed home, she felt completely helpless. She hadn't eaten or slept well since her capture and it was beginning to take its toll. Her tired legs trembled as she walked to the mirror by the table and tipped her chin up, gazing hard at herself. The reflection startled her. Framed in a mass of blonde hair, her turquoise eyes had the same desperate look as a caged animal's. Lines of strain etched crow's feet around her eyes and across her forehead. She looked so overwrought that it depressed her. No wonder the guards outside the door cringed when they had to deliver messages.

Folding her arms tightly, she crossed to stand before the holo of the scorch attack that adorned her wall. The planet spun amidst a violet haze of dust and debris. In the upper left corner, a Magisterial battle cruiser floated, purple beams from its cannons streaming down to slash the lush forests in carefully calculated patterns of devastation.

"Gamants are morose," she muttered, eyeing the holo malignantly, wondering about the identity of the vessel and who'd commanded it during that scorch attack. "What reason could Baruch possibly have for adorning the guest quarters with pictures of devastation? It's like keeping a wound raw by ripping the scab off every time it heals."

But Gamants were like that—*she knew*. Her grandmother had burned the words, "In remembrance lies redemption," into her brain. Every time Amirah had tried to interrupt a story of the miseries of Gamant history, Sefer had grabbed her by the chin, glared into her tiny face, and said, "This isn't something you can forget, Amirah. *Now, repeat the story I just told you!*" She recalled clearly the pain and the fear—not understanding why Grandmama found such things so important—while she tried to recite the story. Sefer always coached her in the parts she'd missed. Then Grandmama would pat her affectionately and praise her for being so smart.

And for a brief moment, the last rays of the wintry sunset on Rusel 3 splashed down over the small bed where Amirah lay drowsily gazing out the window. The sky glimmered a pale green, the winds whirling sunlit dust up to the thin transparent clouds. She'd been seriously ill for a week with Janus fever and felt tired to her bones, so feeble she could barely lift her head from her pillow. *"Ninety percent die,"* she'd heard the doctor whisper yesterday—just before Sefer had bodily thrown him out of their house.

Sefer sat at Amirah's bedside, as she had, day and night, since the onset of the illness. Only the creaking of her rocking chair against the cold plank floor fought for dominance with the sizzling of the wind against the windows. The old woman had been talking for days, telling her to stay strong, that she'd been born under the House of Ephraim and . . . "Not a single Gamant in history with that honor has ever died without putting up a fight. You feel that strength deep down in your soul, Amirah? God put that there so you'd be able to survive no matter what happened. All the women in our family have it. And don't you forget it."

Amirah remembered the dizziness that had swept over her when she turned to smile up into her grandmother's scarred and withered face. Sefer had patted her arm lovingly. "You're going to live, Amirah. I know it. God won't let you die."

The buzzing of her door com made Amirah jump. The memories burst like soap bubbles on a hot day.

"Captain Jossel?" A deep voice penetrated her room. "It's Commander Baruch. May I see you?"

She sucked in a halting breath. "If I said no, Commander, would you go away?"

A pause. "Probably not."

"Then come in."

She dropped her hands to her sides and spread her legs defensively as the door opened. He stood tall in his black battlesuit. He had a thick stack of crystal sheets beneath one arm. He defiantly stepped inside and the door closed.

"What do you want?" She demanded straightforwardly.

His broad chest expanded as he took a deep breath. He gestured to the table. "May I sit down?"

"This is your ship, Commander. I think you can sit wherever you want to."

"Thank you." He eased into a chair, and put his papers down on the table. They looked like a great white block against the black background. His gaze never left her. "How are you?"

She vented a disgusted laugh. "Terrible. Why do you care?"

"I want you to be as comfortable as possible. I know this is hard—"

"Well, that's great. Why don't you give me a rifle so I can kill every soldier aboard and then I'll feel much better?"

He leaned back in his chair and stared at her hard. "Having been captured by the enemy before, I understand that sentiment."

Amirah tilted her head dubiously. She'd researched his military career thoroughly, from his birth on Tikkun to the last battle he orchestrated in the Asad system. "You? Captured? I don't recall any records of you ever being apprehended by us, Commander."

"There aren't any records. Cole took care of that rather efficiently when he blew the hell out of Block 10 on Tikkun."

She started, remembering all the horror stories Tahn had told her about that installation. Why hadn't he mentioned that Baruch had been incarcerated there? Or that he'd *blown the hell* out of the place? Magisterial historians had always assumed the installation had been damaged during the Underground's clash with government cruisers. "You were captured by Lichtner?"

"Yes." His blue eyes glimmered like Lytolian sapphires—hate and old anger visible beneath the shroud of professionalism.

Amirah started to walk to the table, but her knees went weak before she could make it. She caught herself and stiffened them, but Baruch noticed.

"Captain," he said quietly, "sit down. Can I have my physician prescribe something to help you sleep or—"

"I don't need anything from you, Commander," she responded wearily, and purposefully paced in front of the table, passing in and out of the rectangle of light streaming from the latrine. "What did you want to see me about?"

His handsome face etched with wariness. "I've been doing some research. On Sefer and Zakuto Raziel."

Amirah's steps faltered. Fear rose hot and blinding. But that was silly—no condemning records existed. The only thing Baruch could have accessed would be birth and tax records and a few incidental reports. Amirah braced a hand against the wall to steady herself. "And?"

"I want to talk to you about them."

"Sorry. I don't discuss them. I didn't even know my grandfather—he died before I was born—and my relationship with my grandmother is private."

He stretched his long legs out across the carpet and crossed them at the ankles. He looked around the room, noting her disheveled bed, then his eyes came back to her, wide and blue and unsettlingly piercing. "I'd been looking in the wrong place, in the Magisterial records. When I checked the Gamant Archives, I found some very interesting documents. Did you know that records existed?"

Off-balance, she responded, "I didn't even know Gamants had archives."

Baruch carefully put a hand against the stack of sheets he'd brought and shoved them forward, to the edge of the table. Amirah studied them pensively.

"These are yours," he explained. "I thought you might be interested in your family history. Your grandparents were courageous, loyal soldiers in the last Gamant Revolt. Your grandmother in particular. Did you know she served as a spy in the Underground and was stationed on Palaia?"

Amirah drew in a sharp, surprised breath. Her grandmother had always been reticent about discussing her
own personal life and so it didn't shock Amirah with the
impact it might have. Still, she felt a hollowness that this
stranger knew more about her beloved grandmother than
she did. "No," she said simply.

Baruch continued, "For three years, she lived in constant danger, trying to maintain her cover. She allowed
herself to be captured and put in the Relocation Camp
just outside of Naas, hoping she could work her way into
the domestic service of the camp controller's home—a
human from Giclas 7 who had intimate contacts with the
Magistrates. It took a year of life in the regular camp—
where she was repeatedly tortured—before she worked
her way into Controller Heydrich's service as a laundry
woman. For two years she passed information through
the camp to the Underground outside the walls. The data
she provided was essential to Zadok Calas' victory on
the plains of Lysomia. Without Sefer's information, the
strategy Zadok received from Epagael would have been
useless."

Amirah's stunned mind pulled up Sefer's deeply scarred
face, her dark eyes shining like jewels. So that's how
Grandmama had gotten the number on her arm and thick
ridges of white tissue that crisscrossed her face and
hands. When Amirah had been young, she'd rubbed her
fingers over the scars constantly, asking endless questions—none of which her grandmother had ever answered.
She'd have liked to find those men who'd hurt Sefer, so
she could slowly and expertly kill each one.

Amirah scuffed a boot on the carpet to create some
sound in the silence. She could hear the passion and
heartache in her grandmother's voice when she related
stories of the war—of course Sefer had never told her
about being a spy. And no wonder Amirah's father had
been so desperate to wipe away any taint of Gamant
ancestry from his wife's and daughter's lives. "What happened in the end?"

Jeremiel put a hand on the stack, as though laying it
on a cherished holy book. "She was discovered. Heydrich
beat her almost to death, raped her, and gave her to the
camp soldiers. She scrambled to survive their brutality

for six months before Calas won the war and all prisoners were released."

He kept quiet for a long time, looking at Amirah, his eyes filled with speculation—as though assessing how she, a Magisterial officer, could have come from such loyal Gamant stock. "Your grandmother was a very great lady, Captain."

"I know that, Commander. She was my best friend during the hardest year of my life."

He got to his feet. Standing only three feet away, he looked taller than she'd remembered, more imposing. "Do you know what happened to her, Captain?"

Adrenaline rushed through her. "No. Do you?"

Baruch's handsome face was bland, but his eyes flashed. "No. Sefer's clandestine contacts on Rusel 3 reported that Magisterial soldiers surrounded her house on the 20th of Tishri, 5411. You and Sefer were dragged out forcibly and shoved into a small transport vessel and taken to Palaia. No one ever heard from Sefer again." He paused ominously. "Do you remember that day, Captain?"

Amirah shook her head violently, on the verge of an inexplicable outburst of panic. *What the hell's the matter with you?* She shouted, "I don't believe it ever happened, Commander!"

Baruch watched her intently, assessing her taut face and twitching hands. *Why did her hands always twitch when she thought about Grandmama?* Scenes flashed in her memories . . . strange . . . dark, so dark . . . Grandmama's terrified face staring at her, screaming. . . .

Amirah gasped suddenly and bent double. Pain ravaged her like a dagger repeatedly thrust into her heart. She crumpled to the floor, landing hard on her knees, and began sobbing uncontrollably. *What's the matter? For God's sake, get up!* her logical side raged, but she couldn't. She felt like her soul had been ripped from her body. More images stirred in the back of her mind, like malignant tendrils of disease—*but she fought them down! Fight them . . . fight!* After several seconds, her sobs subsided into bare breathless whimpers.

She heard Baruch move. He knelt in front of her. He looked as stern as an avenging angel straight out of Sefer's colorful old stories. "You can't control them, can you? Are they getting worse? More frequent? More vivid?"

So Tahn had told him about her delusionary episodes. God . . . She stared at the gray carpet, refusing to answer.

Baruch stood up again. "Why did the Magistrates want you in the hands of the Underground, Captain Jossel?"

She laughed bitterly. "Don't be ridiculous."

He walked a short distance away to stand in the rectangle of light. It frosted the side of his face, leaving his eyes in shadow. "One or more of our officers survived the Kiskanu attack—and broke under the probes at Palaia. Don't ask me how I know, I just do. The Magistrates had accurate inside knowledge of our attack plans for Horeb. Yet they sent you no reinforcements, Captain. And they ordered you down to Horeb with a security contingent of *two*. They sacrificed four battle cruisers to let us capture you." He strode briskly back and knelt again, staring at her so penetratingly she felt she'd been bludgeoned. *"I want to know why."*

Amirah sat stiffly. He'd made it sound so logical, but the premise was ludicrous. Slothen would never throw her to the dogs, unless he had no choice. And if the government had known any critical details about the impending Underground attack, it had a choice. Slothen would have notified her. Baruch was up to something else. What was he doing? Fishing for information about Kiskanu survivors? His wife had been at the Kiskanu battle, hadn't she? She bowed her head and laughed disparagingly. Of course. Cole had talked endlessly about Carey Halloway in his sleep. Both Tahn and Baruch must be worried sick that Halloway had been captured and sent to Palaia's neuro department. And that was what Baruch was fishing for—data on his wife.

Amirah stared back into Baruch's seething blue eyes and tried to figure out how to use that against him. "Buck up, Commander. If your wife's been on Palaia for the past two weeks, there's nothing left of her for you to worry about."

His face remained bland. "You seem to know all about the probe's capabilities, Captain. Good. I want you to think about something. Maybe you and your grandmother were taken to Palaia that day fifteen years ago.

Maybe you were put under the probes. You were very
young, your brain very malleable. It wouldn't have taken
much effort to mold your neural pathways and instill an
insidious program somewhere inside. Your grandmother
was a known Gamant hero. Using you against Gamants
would have been the perfect irony for Slothen. I don't
know what's inside you, Captain. But I strongly suspect
the time bomb has a word or phrase trigger that could
set it off at any moment."

Baruch backed to the door and palmed the exit patch.
Stark white light flooded the room. He stood silently in
the entryway, watching her. "I'm ordering you sedated
and taken to the brig where you can be monitored constantly, Captain. Get prepared." He left.

Amirah slumped backward on the floor and let her
gaze drift around the dim room, landing briefly on each
of the holos. The conversation had drained every ounce
of her energy. She felt weak and angry. The things Baruch had said had started a chain reaction of outrageous
questions in her mind—which he'd undoubtedly intended.
An insidious program? *In the compartment that no one
could probe?* Had Slothen kept it safe that way? So that
not even his best professionals could accidentally set off
the "trigger?"

"Don't be a fool, Amirah. Baruch is using your flashbacks against you. That's all. It's an attempt to make
you so unsure of yourself that he can manipulate you for
his own ends."

Amirah's eyes wandered to the thick stack of crystal
sheets he'd brought. She pushed up and walked around
the table to the drink dispenser to order a strong coffee.
Did you make up these documents, Baruch? What purpose could it serve to create a family history for her?
The only way to find out was to read them. And she'd
have to do it fast—before the security team came to take
her to the brig.

Pulling the cup from the machine, she braced herself
with a sip and went to the table. She sat down and
pushed the stack around to read the title page, *"A Con-
cise History of the Lives of all Sighet Medal of Honor
Winners."*

"You won the Medal of Honor, Grandmama?"

A bitter bile rose in Amirah's throat. Baruch was

clever. Did he think this would bind her more closely to the Gamant cause? "Well, you're wrong, Commander. Even if this is true, I'm not my grandmother. I'm a Magisterial officer."

But her fingers trembled as she opened the book and began to read.

CHAPTER 34

. . . And God said, "If I see that the justice of the world has become abundant, I will be long-suffering toward them. If not, I will stretch out my hand and I will grasp the inhabited world from its four corners and I will gather them all together to the valley of Jehosaphat and I will wipe out the human race and the world will be no more."

And the prophet replied, "Lord, if this was your intention, why did you form man? You said to Avram our father, 'I will surely multiply your seed as the stars of the heaven and as the sand along the shore of the sea.' And where is your promise?"

God said, "Come here, Ezra. Die, my beloved! Give back that which was entrusted to you."

The Greek Apocalypse of Ezra
Circa 150 A.D. Old Earth Standard
Document housed in Arnobios
Museum, Ophiuchus 7.

Rudy strode headlong down the corridor to conference room 1819 aboard the *Zilpah*. His clean black battlesuit had already become clammy with sweat and Jeremiel had only tranned him twenty minutes ago. He shouldered past three engineering techs and pounded a fist into the entry patch in front of the conference room. The door snicked back.

Breathing hard, he stepped inside. Jeremiel sat on the right side of the white rectangular table, hands clasped in his lap, and Tahn slouched on the other side. Both of them gazed at Rudy, waiting for an outburst from him, he suspected.

He calmly pulled out the chair at the head of the table

and eased into the seat. He turned to Jeremiel. "Let's look at it logically, *unemotionally*. You're telling me that you believe two men in one fighter can get by the dozen cruisers generally docked at Palaia, manage to break through the EM defense shells, locate one captive in a maze of hundreds of guarded government buildings, grab that captive without anybody noticing, get back to their fighter, exit the defense shells—after the entire god-damned universe will be up in arms about the first breach—and slip by the cruisers and every other vessel in the vicinity that will have been assembled to guard the station. Have I got it all, or did I leave something out?"

"That's about it," Tahn said curtly, and he had the nerve to grin.

Rudy massaged his forehead. "What are you going to do about the three thousand soldiers Slothen will have to greet you when you set foot on Palaia?"

Tahn gestured airily. "Make do as best we can."

"You two are being idiots!" Rudy accused. "We don't even know Carey's there, let alone alive!"

"She's there," Tahn stated flatly. He'd slouched deeper in his chair, and braced an elbow carelessly on the edge of the table. "Once they realized who she was, they'd have been too terrified of Slothen's wrath to take her anywhere else."

Rudy ground his teeth and focused on Jeremiel. "Listen to me, friend, *if* she's alive, the chances of you succeeding are ten million to one. You're throwing away your life and Tahn's at a time when Gamant civilization needs you desperately!" He tightened his hands into fists and shook them futilely at the ceiling. "You know you're too valuable to send on this mission! Let me find somebody else. I can have a hundred volunteers for you to choose from before you—"

"No." Jeremiel said mildly. "I won't ask anyone else to risk their lives on this mission."

"But you're taking Tahn? At least—"

"He'd play hell trying to leave me behind!" Cole blustered. He straightened up in his chair and looked vaguely like an officer for a change. "Listen, Kopal, your duty is to get every Gamant you can off Horeb and to Shyr as quickly as possible. You don't need me or Baruch for that task. And if everything goes well on Palaia, we'll meet you at Shyr within a week of your arrival."

Rudy glared unforgivingly at Cole, but directed his question to Baruch. "You're dead set on this, Jeremiel? There's no way I can talk you out of it?"

Baruch's black jumpsuit rustled with his movements. He rubbed his fingers over his reddish-blond beard. "With you commanding the *Hashomer*, Merle on the *Orphica*, Eli in charge of the *Zilpah* and Michel Jaroslav taking over the *Hammadi*, the fleet will be safe."

"So you're content to get yourself killed for nothing!"

Jeremiel's blue eyes tightened. "No. Jossel will be the key. None of those cruiser captains will see a single fighter as a threat—especially not with Jossel's face on all their com screens. Her story will be that she was captured and escaped and is coming home to report . . . she knows the secret codes to get into the docks. She knows the most recent layout of Palaia. We—"

"Uh-huh," Rudy scoffed. "Jossel's the key." He slammed a fist into the table. "She's not even sane! You have no idea how she'll act under pressure! She might just damn well fall apart. Or worse. If you're right about her programming, you could be walking into a trap that Slothen's had laid for fifteen years! You don't know what her trigger might be or what she's designed to do! You can't count on her for anything!"

Cole drummed his fingers on the table. "We think we've got the cues that set her off figured out. If we can just keep her sane and rational—"

"And what if Slothen gets on the com to welcome her home and taps her trigger? Huh! What are you going to do then?"

Cole gave him a penetrating stare. "She'll be bound at all times—"

"Yeah, and she broke your ribs when she was—"

"*And* we'll be ready for anything. We're not walking into this blind, Kopal."

Rudy ran a hand through his damp brown curls. "What about getting off Palaia? Even if she can get you in—"

"Jossel will still be our hostage," Jeremiel said quietly. "So long as she's alive, she'll be leverage. I don't think Slothen will sacrifice his star captain just to keep Carey. Because . . ." his voice floundered and Rudy clenched up inside. The internal war Jeremiel waged showed on his face, pulling every line tight. "Because if Carey was the officer who broke, by this time she'll have relinquished every bit of information she had."

Rudy sat back in his chair. *Goddamn, Jeremiel, you're fairly sure you're going to find a vegetable when you get there and you're going anyway?* He knew how much Jeremiel loved Carey. They'd been inseparable for twelve years and happier than any couple Rudy had ever known. But this—this "rescue" mission showed none of Jeremiel's brilliance with strategy. In fact, it had the feel of a thing done by a hair's breadth.

Rudy braced his palms on the table, glaring at Baruch. "This whole plan is ridiculous, Jeremiel, and you damned well know it! At least if you're going to do this, let me help you. With two battle cruisers, I might be able to keep the armada at Palaia off you long enough for you to succeed!"

Baruch's bushy brows lowered. "Horebian refugees are more important—"

"The number of survivors is lower than we thought! Two cruisers will be more than adequate to ferry them to Shyr! Let me help you," he pleaded. "Jeremiel, if you let me, I can—"

"No." Jeremiel shook his head slowly. "The ships that bear the civilians will need military backup in case of an attack. The starsails and freighters will never be able to stand up against a Magisterial assault without cruiser support. And we haven't much time, Rudy. You've got to get those people loaded and out of here before the cruiser that escaped reports back and Slothen dispatches a flotilla for Horeb." Jeremiel twined his fingers and gripped them so hard the nails went white. "If he hasn't already."

Rudy shoved his chair back, on the verge of that outburst he'd been controlling. "Jeremiel, for God's sake—!"

"Well," Tahn said nonchalantly. He got to his feet and headed for the door. "I've got some packing to do. Call me when the fighter's ready, Baruch."

Rudy couldn't help himself; that smug, this-discussion-is-over tone struck him like a fist. He lunged for Tahn, grabbed his black sleeves and slammed him against the wall. *"This is your doing, isn't it? You talked Jeremiel into it!"*

Jeremiel lurched to his feet, "Rudy, let him go."

Rudy shook his head and slammed Tahn against the wall again. Cole's muscular arms shook. He gripped Rudy's hands and brutally shoved him away, forcing Rudy to stagger backward two steps. Cole hurried past Rudy and struck the exit patch, then briskly strode into the corridor outside.

Jeremiel stepped from around the table and gripped the back of a chair. "It wasn't Cole's idea, Rudy. It was mine. What's the problem here? I've gone on plenty of clandestine missions alone before. Why are you so upset?"

Rudy swung around, breast heaving with impotent rage and concern for his friend. "Yeah. You have. And the last time half the fleet got wasted off Abulafia!"

Jeremiel pulled back slightly, as though shocked by Rudy's implication that the same thing might happen now. "We were all a lot younger then. The past twelve years have made seasoned war veterans out of every soldier over the age of eighteen in the fleet. Keep the ships bunched in defensive formations at all times and you'll be fine—within limits. Obviously you can't hold off twenty battle cruisers, but you can stand up to almost anything else." He extended a hand imploringly. "You don't need me or Cole to help you transport civilians to Shyr, Rudy. Tell me what's really bothering you? We're alone now. Talk to me."

Futility swept over Rudy. He couldn't tell Jeremiel that he loved him and couldn't bear the thought of losing him. The discussion that would have followed would have been an unproductive emotional malaise. Nor could he blurt out that he just "had a feeling" that the entire universe was about to come unraveled around them—that his gut had been tying itself in knots for days wondering what they'd do if they didn't get away from Horeb before the government arrived, wondering what they'd do if the Magistrates sent more than twenty cruisers. No matter how "seasoned" their crews, they couldn't stand up against that kind of firepower. But none of those arguments would have had the slightest impact on Jeremiel's decision to go or stay. And besides, he'd already made his decision.

Rudy headed for the door. He hesitated before the patch, wanting to embrace Jeremiel, not quite able to do so after the past few minutes. "Jeremiel, go. Come back if you can."

Rudy left before Baruch had time to respond.

* * *

Jeremiel and Cole sat in their ship in the landing bay, checking and rechecking the programming. The newest, hottest fighter in the fleet, it had a small oval cabin with a long rectangular forward portal and two small side portals. Five levels of computer screens displayed every conceivable type of data in the traditional synchronized color patterns to make it easier to read. The aft part of the ship held four tiny rooms with beds that pulled out from the wall and a communal latrine. They'd stuffed the spare sleeping quarters full of extra ammunition, rifles, food, and emergency equipment.

"I'm running the weapons check," Jeremiel informed.

"I'm ready." Cole bent over the copilot's console. His gaze darted over each programming sequence, double-checking the main system and the backup of the backup. "Looks good, Jeremiel. Try running the navigation program."

Baruch nodded and input the command. When it appeared on Cole's screen he took his time, scrutinizing every possible glitch. So many things could go wrong on other fronts, they hadn't the luxury of missing any ship errors.

"How are you feeling?" Jeremiel asked.

Eyes still riveted to the lines, Cole muttered, "Well enough."

"Your white count's still elevated."

"I'm fine."

"Doctor Kymot says you should stay in bed for at least another day."

"His name isn't on my birth certificate."

Jeremiel glanced reproachfully at him from the corner of his eye. "Neither's mine, but as your commanding officer—"

"I wouldn't try it if I were you. I'll just steal this ship and go to Palaia without you."

"Uh-huh." Jeremiel input a sequence to repeat a certain part of the program and leaned forward pensively, as though he'd found something amiss. "Every Magisterial officer I've ever known has been larceny minded."

"Including Carey?" Cole gibed and instantly regretted it. Jeremiel's face moved with the barest flicker of anguish. Baruch had been the epitome of controlled professionalism for the past three days, but Cole knew—as perhaps only he could—how difficult it was for Jeremiel to maintain that facade. Memories of Carey had been accosting him with fiery intensity as their departure neared. It must has been almost incapacitating for Jeremiel. Cole shook his head apologetically. "Sorry."

"Even Carey," Jeremiel answered, glossing over the emotions that tore at both of them. "You and Carey have always been two of a kind."

Cole looked back to the screen in defense. Lines continued to slowly scroll up until the com flashed, "end" in red, then he leaned back in his chair and swiveled around to gaze at Baruch. Jeremiel finished rechecking Cole's work and turned to face him.

"How are Rudy and Merle doing?" Cole asked.

"They're only a few hours from departure. They have another three or four loads of refugees to transport up. The remaining people, about two hundred, refuse to go."

"What? Who didn't want to leave?" Cole challenged in disbelief.

Jeremiel gazed at him steadily. "The elderly, for the most part. A few of those families have lived here for twenty generations. This is their home, no matter how dangerous. We're leaving them a healthy amount of supplies. We told them clearly that they'd have to fend for themselves when the Magistrates came looking."

Cole filled his lungs with air. At least a half dozen cruisers would "come looking." Already he could hear the pleas for mercy, the shrill whine of rifle fire, the cries of the children. "I hope they make it."

Jeremiel reached up to press the life systems patch and waited for the program to come up. "So do I. Our next priority is getting everybody else to Shyr."

"Rudy's and Merle's priority, you mean. You and I have to concentrate on staying alive for more than a week."

"I give us one in a hundred odds."

"Really?" Cole blurted. "You have a lot of confidence in us, don't you? I figured that for once Kopal was right and it was closer to one in ten million."

Jeremiel braced his elbows on his console as the life systems program began running. He studied it raptly. "You've always been a pessimist."

Cole grinned and turned his attention to the scrolling lines. Everything seemed to be in perfect order. But Jeremiel had programmed the ship himself. Cole would have expected no less. When the last line flashed, Cole grunted approval.

"You did a damn fine job, Baruch."

"Thanks for helping me run the confirming check. There's just one detail left to take care of."

"What's that?"

"Jossel. Do you want to escort her down or should I?"

Cole's breathing went shallow. Her seizures seemed to be getting worse. Even under sedation, she'd writhed and twitched as though possessed by a wicked demon. He knew. He'd gone to see her six times in the past twenty-four hours, and each time seeing her had hurt more. Jeremiel's theory about a "trigger" made too much sense to dismiss. "I will. Give me half an hour and I'll . . ."

The green com light flared on the pilot's console. Jeremiel's eyes narrowed as he reached for the patch. "Fighter *Yesod*. Baruch here."

Eli's voice boomed through the command cabin, "Commander, switch on your visual com. we've got a classified message coming in."

Baruch hit the patch. The foot-square screen that filled the space between Jeremiel and Cole flared to life. A little old man's face formed, withered, with spectacles resting low on his fleshy nose. Cole squinted in recognition at the same time that Baruch whispered, "What the hell is this?" He called, "Yosef? Where are you?"

Calas inclined his head and smiled affectionately. "Good evening, Jeremiel. You're looking well. We're aboard a cruiser called the *Sargonid*. We've captured Engineering. But we're not sure we can hold it long enough to—"

"You're on the *Sargonid*?" Baruch's mouth parted in shock. He stared unblinkingly for several seconds, then abruptly shifted to sit up straighter in his seat. "Who's there with you, Yosef?"

"We're holding the chief engineer, his name is Rad, and two of his technicians hostage."

Cole swiveled around to give Jeremiel an anxious look. "Ask him who 'we' is? Are Mikael and Sybil there?"

Jeremiel requested, "Yosef, where are Mikael and Sybil? Our information suggested they'd been taken aboard—"

"Oh, yes," Yosef's elderly face beamed. "They're right here. Sybil's feeling much better and Mikael's fine. He's been looking forward to talking to you."

The hair at the nape of Cole's neck had started to prickle. *Too neat. The timing's too perfect. The cruiser that escaped the Horeb attack has undoubtedly reported to Palaia. Is this some sort of ruse?* He felt as though an iron maiden had closed around his chest as he watched a tall, black-haired young man with a black beard walk in front of the monitor. He hadn't seen Mikael in a dozen years, but he would have known him anywhere.

"Jeremiel?" Mikael greeted. "You've no idea how good it is to hear your voice. We're in deep trouble. I—"

"Please hold on, Mikael," Cole announced and curtly doused the audio. He grimaced at Jeremiel. "What code level is this being sent on?"

Baruch's face tensed. He instantly input the request into his com unit. "Narrow beam."

"Not good enough."

"No." Baruch's expression hardened as he thought. "Not good enough. "If there's a Magisterial cruiser between us and them, the government now knows that the *Sargonid* has been compromised. Mikael could be in deeper trouble than he knows."

Cole exhaled tautly. "So could we, friend. What if this is a ruse of the Magistrates to get us to reveal data on the Underground's operations around Horeb? Or get us to go running to Mikael's aid?"

"And fall into a well-orchestrated ambush? Possible. Let's be careful what we say." Jeremiel switched the audio back on. "Mikael? Good work for sending this on narrow beam; however, we can't be certain how secure this dattran is. Give us the information on your status and needs quickly. That will lessen the chance of interception."

"Understood," Mikael responded guardedly. "Briefly, then, this is what happened: Yosef and Ari sneaked aboard in a crate of hypinitronium. They used the explosive to get into Engineering, then told Lieutenant Woloc they were part of the Underground, that they'd taken over the ship to rescue Sybil and me and wanted to make a trade: Us for Jossel."

"Hypinitronium?" Cole whispered. His eyes widened. Rad must have fainted when he saw the vials in the hands of two shaky old gents. "Why the hell wasn't it in gravitational stasis?"

"Unknown," Baruch murmured. Then, louder, to Mikael, "What's Lieutenant Woloc been doing in the meantime?"

"Everything possible to dislodge us," Calas informed bluffly. "We've already repelled two entry attempts by his forces, but we've got to have some reliable leverage soon to keep them at bay or we're going to lose Engineering."

Jeremiel bent forward over his white console, his blue eyes glittering with some conclusion that made Cole's stomach tighten. He whispered, "What are you thinking, Baruch?"

Jeremiel paid him no attention; instead, he said to Calas, "Mikael? The first thing you have to do is reroute all the major functions of the ship to Engineering. You have to incapacitate the bridge immediately."

"Just give me directions, Jeremiel," Mikael responded. "I've never seen controls as complex as these before."

Cole reached over and cut the audio again, then grabbed Jeremiel's shoulder hard and swiveled him around to glare questioningly. *"What are you doing?"*

Jeremiel gripped Cole's forearm. "We have to make this quick. The longer we prolong the conversation the more likely it is to be picked up. Trust me."

Cole vacillated, trying to figure the angle. A sudden light-headedness possessed him as details began falling into place. "Are you crazy? Even if they do have Engineering and we could miraculously get there before they lose it, there's no way we can—"

"Trust me!"

"All right. All right!" He threw up his hands. "Do it."

Baruch turned back to his com and input a new sequence, requesting locational data on the origin of Mikael's transmission. "Sector four, near the Mainz system." He shifted to peer sternly at the visual screen. "Mikael, it'll take us two days to get there. In the meantime, the first thing you must do is seal every deck. We don't want the *Sargonid*'s crew moving freely through that ship or they'll be able to lay countless traps for you and us—which they'll do anyway, but this way we can cut down their ability to mount forces and coordinate. Are you ready?"

"I'm ready."

"Put someone on the console next to you. Listen carefully. . . ."

When Baruch had finished and cut the transmission, he swiftly opened a line to the bridge. "Eli? Log this under Clandestine One and put on time-delay. I want you to tran it to Captain Kopal immediately after our departure. Understood?"

"Aye, Commander. Logging."

CHAPTER 35

Rachel stood uneasily beside Aktariel on the lip of the vortex overlooking the plains on Satellite 4. The fires of sunset sent waves of carnelian through the gathering clouds on the horizon and threw a sickly pink halo over the land below. Men and women walked barefoot through bloody battlefields, their clothing in shreds, eyes inflamed with hatred. Hoarse shrieks of rage and the pain of loss rang out as they searched the torn bodies littering the grassy fields.

Rachel watched a tiny dark-haired woman walk through the devastation. Her loose fitting white clothes bore old stains of blood; they shone as blackly as tar in the fading rays of sunset. The crowd dispersed, but the woman stayed, staring forlornly at heaven as though in silent prayer.

Rachel turned to look at Aktariel. His face gleamed like polished golden crystal in the darkness of the void, casting an amber shroud over his frost-colored cloak and Rachel's ivory robe. "Who is she?" she asked.

Aktariel sighed, "A zealot from a long line of zealots. She doesn't know it, but one of her distant ancestors was Iuedas o Makkabaios, or as your own people called him, Yehudah ben Mattathiah."

"Do we have to worry about her?"

"Arikha? No. She's on our side. At least, up to a point. Everything hinges on what the Mashiah will do."

Rachel started. She'd searched for years to find the alternate universe which showed the Mashiah freeing Gamants from the tyranny of the Magistrates—*or showed the end of Creation.* But she'd never been able to find either. Which meant they must exist in only one or two of the possible futures. That's why she'd taken steps with Nathan. . . .

"Is there really a Mashiah in this terrible universe, Aktariel?"

He turned glowing amber eyes on her. "Oh, yes, I assure you that there is. . . . Come, I want to show you the Pillars of Light and Dark."

He walked away before she could challenge him. His frost-colored cloak swayed, getting farther and farther ahead. Rachel followed, watching the darkness eddy beneath her sandaled feet. "Who is the Mashiah, Aktariel?"

He frowned at her and she noticed the way the breeze billowed in his silvered hood. "I can't tell you, Rachel. You've already jeopardized our success by saving Nathan. I can't risk—"

She started forward angrily and he shouted, *"Stop!"* and put out a hand to halt her progress. "I'm sorry. I almost took us too close. It's difficult to tell one blackness from another. Here, let me take your hand. We'll go forward slowly."

Rachel reluctantly twined her fingers with his and let him lead her ahead. She squinted into the darkness and thought she made out a different texture a few feet away—blacker than black, velvety smooth, not like the whirling funnel of the *Mea*.

Aktariel left her standing alone and carefully marched forward. After a short interim, he motioned for her to follow. "Come and stand by me, Rachel. Come and gaze upon the Foundations of Chaos."

She wet her lips nervously and cautiously stepped forward to gaze out across a narrow bridge of intervening stars to gaping ebony jaws that swallowed space-time.

"What is that?" she whispered.

"The Magistrates ironically call it Palaia Zohar. In a few days, they'll call it Accursed and pray to all the gods in history that they'd never put Palaia Station here."

She studied the singularity, noting the faint smoky haze that encircled it. "Is that the event horizon?"

"Yes, it actually has two. You can't see the inner one. But it's the interface of the two that creates a protective membrane which prevents the hole from losing its negative charge."

"And where is the Pillar of Light, Aktariel?"

He turned to gaze at her and she saw a terrible fear well in his glowing eyes. "I love you, Rachel. I've always loved you. The Pillar of Light, Jachin, is coming. Haven't I told you that only a man whose blood is Light will survive? *If one does not stand in the Darkness, he will not be able to see the Light.*"

CHAPTER 36

Amirah woke slowly, achingly, to find herself in a passenger chair in the rear of a cramped fighter. The effect of the potent drugs they'd given her in the brig had begun to wear off, leaving her nauseous and bleary. Out the long forward portal the deep blackness of light vault seemed to press down around them. How long had they been in vault? She wiggled her fingers. Her wrists and ankles sported EM restraints. Baruch was maintaining his hard-line, taking no chances, not even with her drugged. And he obviously still wanted her monitored, or she wouldn't be in the command cabin.

The room spread in a twenty foot white oval around her. Other than their uniforms, the only color in the entire ship came from the thirty computer screens that blanketed the wall before the pilot and copilot's seats. Shades of blue, green, violet, and red displayed critical information on the ship's systems. Baruch and Tahn hunched over the command consoles, speaking quietly to each other. Dressed in the crisp purple and gray uniforms of Magisterial security lieutenants, they looked obscene.

Baruch leaned back in the pilot's chair and rubbed his reddish blond beard. "Who should take the first watch?"

"I will. You get some rest," Cole responded.

Baruch nodded and got to his feet. "Wake me in four hours."

"I'll wake you in eight. We're in vault. There's nothing to do and no danger. Try to get a good night's sleep. It may be the last one you get for a while."

"*Four*. That's an order." Baruch gave Cole a stern glare, then swiveled around in his chair and stopped dead when he saw that Amirah was awake. "How are you, Captain?"

Cole instantly turned to look at her, too.

"Sick to my stomach. Foggy. What did you expect?"

Baruch ignored her question. He got to his feet and said simply, "Good night, Captain."

He walked toward his sleeping quarters and she heard his door close. Cole checked three of the screens over his head and swiveled back around in his chair to gaze at her. "I'm sorry I can't give you anything for the nausea—it would interfere with your wits. And I need you sharp."

He acted like a complete stranger and she hated herself for minding. "Why?"

"I brought some files I want you to look at."

Cole pulled his pistol and got up from his seat. He knelt in front of her, removing an EM key from his pants pocket. The restraints broke open into his waiting hand. Clutching them tightly, he stood up and backed away, then gestured her forward with the barrel of his pistol. "You're welcome to the copilot's seat."

She stood up on wobbly ankles and walked to the chair he indicated. Tahn rebound her ankles and took the pilot's seat; he cautiously reached down to the utility island that extended between the chairs and opened the top latch. He pulled two quarter-inch disks from the compartment and laid them in front of her.

Amirah skimmed the front code. "What are these?"

"Reports on Magisterial programs on Tikkun twelve years ago." Cole leaned back in his chair, propped a boot against the console and braced his pistol on his stomach.

Amirah's thoughts went to the reports on her grandmother. She'd reviewed the first ten pages before the security team had hauled her to the brig. She didn't know if she believed the stories there. But she couldn't fathom a *practical* reason for Baruch to have created them. As a result, questions had been nagging at her. Sefer truly had been a hero, a woman who would have sacrificed everything for her people—and almost did. If Calas hadn't won the war on the plains of Lysomia when he did, her grandmother would certainly have been killed by the guards she "belonged" to. The data on the camp atrocities and Sefer's wounds that the files had included, left a terrifying hate in Amirah. Those guards had used Sefer for every abominable task they could think of, from shoveling dead bodies into ditches to sexual perversities.

But she'd survived. *Good for you, Grandmama. If I ever find them, I assure you they'll pay.*

Amirah glanced at Cole. He was stroking his chin, watching her pensively. She said, "Let's get on with this, Tahn. Which com unit should I use?"

"The one on your right."

She turned her chair and shoved in the first disk. The file came up almost immediately.

NEUROPHYSIOLOGICAL RESEARCH: FILE 19118
Subject: Tikkun experiments. Planetary Commander: Johannes Lichtner.

. . . strange levels of metabolites in cerebrospinal fluid. Suspect . . . arousal systems . . . aggressive sensations seeking results in inability to accept peace . . . abnormally high number of receptors in basal ganglia . . . misfiring of circuitry sets brain's interpreter up for devising wrong methods . . . responds to endogenous events by delusional referents like journey though the *Mea* . . .

Amirah's chair squeaked as she leaned back. Over her shoulder, she tossed, "What is this?"

"What do you think it is?"

"Well, it . . . it looks an incoherency cover-up."

"Very good, Captain."

She waited for him to tell her more, but when he didn't, she gazed suspiciously back at the file. The government only initiated this sort of defensive measure on major projects of such strategic value that they couldn't risk any outside interference. Either that or they were frightened someone would find out what they were doing.

"Why would they cover this up?"

"Keep reading, Amirah."

For three hours she read. Her physical responses surprised her. First, her heart thundered, then sweat broke out beneath her arms, drenching her uniform until she felt she'd been standing in a misty rain. What had the government been doing? Developing new mind probe methodologies? The research scientists clearly believed they'd discovered an abnormal brain structure and identified a dangerous interrelationship between neurotransmitters which led Gamants to be irrationally aggressive.

The researchers had concluded that Gamant brain physiology naturally resulted in dangerous insanity. *And they recommended that the Magistrates learn to segregate the areas of the brain responsible, then harness and channel the insanity into a weapon to use against Gamant civilization. They wanted to try and turn Gamants against each other so they'd destroy themselves.* She rubbed stiff fingers over her tired face. So Cole believed Baruch's thesis about her "programming." Why else would he insist she read this particular file?

Her thoughts drifted and she saw Sefer Raziel hobbling toward her as though from a great distance, so prim in her traditional long Gamant robe of lilac wool, her gray hair knotted at the base of her skull. She and Grandmama used to play on those long winter days that so often infected the countryside. They'd sewn doll's dresses and Sefer had taught Amirah how to shoot a b-gun, taught her how to aim and squeeze the trigger instead of jerking it. Amirah recalled those days as warm and safe and timelessly wonderful. Her grandmother had been the kindest, most peace-loving human being she'd ever known. Amirah recalled the care with which Sefer had removed every spider from the house, grabbing their webs and hurrying for the door while the arachnids scrambled to get away. Yet, her grandmother did have a violent streak—the files Baruch had given her proved it. *You'd be violent, too, Amirah, if somebody threatened to erase from the universe everything you loved.*

She turned to glare at Cole. "This neuro file is preposterous. Gamants are no more aggressive than any other segment of humanity. If you were trying to convince me of Baruch's thesis about me, it won't work. These findings are absurd."

Cole let go of the pistol in his lap and brought up his fingers to steeple them over his lips. "Finish the file. Then we'll talk."

Angrily, she spun back to the screen.

When she got to the last line, she leaned forward abruptly. She didn't even realize she read it aloud: "Suggest massive sterilization of females over the age of. . . ."

Her voice drifted away with the words, but her eyes remained glued to the screen, her heartbeat pounding in rhythm with the flashing cursor. Swinging around in her chair, she fastened Cole with a threatening glare. "For the moment, let's grant that this file is authentic. Who wrote it?"

"I suspect Creighton or one of his cronies."

"Creighton?" She drummed her fingers on the control console. Cole watched her hands very carefully, lest she touch something forbidden. Had Tahn fabricated the file? He could have, but in that case, why the incoherency routine? To make it more believable? Certainly the Magistrates would have initiated such a cover-up if they'd performed those brutal experiments; what they'd done on Tikkun was against every treaty in civilized space. And knowing the government as intimately as Tahn did, he certainly could and *would* have scrambled the document to make it more convincing. But had he? While she concentrated on his handsome face, her thoughts silently examined the data.

He gripped his pistol again. "Let's begin. If I were you, my first conclusion would be that the file is a creative invention. Correct?"

Amirah lifted a shoulder. The command cabin seemed immensely more bright and white than an hour ago, as if the whole universe had gone stark. "Yes, and invented by someone with a thorough understanding of the government. Even the tiniest of details, the peculiar wording of policy and procedure that comes only to long-time servants, is exact."

"So, I'm your logical fabricator?"

"You or Halloway."

He nodded agreeably. "True. Carey could have done it easily. But she didn't."

"That leaves you, Cole."

He propped his pistol on his drawn-up knee. "Why would I have created it? The Underground has neither the leisure nor the facilities to mount propaganda campaigns. And, I assure you, we'd never release this kind of information to Gamant civilians. They'd go mad trying to find a hole to hide in."

Amirah rubbed the toe of her gray boot over the gray carpet. A soft swishing sound resulted, which seemed loud in the quiet.

"I didn't do it, Amirah."

"No," she said grudgingly. "I don't think you did.

Your lowest marks in Academy were in propaganda creation. And you were officially reprimanded twice for failing to employ the recommended Magisterial propaganda to ease tensions in war-ravaged areas. First, in the civil war on Kazant 9, and, second, in the dealings with the rebel leaders who'd captured the government on Sculptor 5."

"So, if not me, who?"

She glanced uncomfortably at his pistol. "I don't know. Creighton, probably. The writing style is consistent with other reports I've read by him—though the scramble makes it tough to tell for certain."

At the very thought that the report might be authentic, she dropped her arms to fold them tightly across her breast, struggling to hold in all the rising terror. Genocide? What would the Magistrates do to her if they found out about the blood that ran in her veins? Relieve her of command? Certainly. Then what? Put her in a hospital? A neuro center? Briefly, almost subliminally, images of a probe chair flitted through her mind.

Her stomach cramped viciously. *Blood . . . everywhere . . .* She bent forward, fighting the pain that shot through her. "Oh—no."

Cole's expression tensed. He automatically put his hand on her shoulder. "Amirah, are you all right?"

She looked up in agony, silently pleading for him or anyone to make it better, to make the flashbacks go away. She'd do anything if someone would just stop the pain! *Please, Grandmama, make the hurt stop! . . . Grandmama? Where are you? Why did you go away and leave me? I need you!*

. . . And suddenly she realized she was seeing through a child's eyes, vulnerable, desperate. *The most interesting part of the event was the sound of your voice . . . Maybe you and your grandmother were taken to Palaia . . . you were very young, very malleable . . . It's just going to get worse, Captain! Don't fool yourself!*

Confusion shredded her. She fought to remember. Remember! More flits of the probe chair. Stark room. *. . . Are we finished for today, Magistrate?"*

Convulsions of agony swept her, as though something were twisting the life out of her! Her identity vacillated between that of a child wild with fear and an adult struggling to logically defuse desperation. She screamed hoarsely and tumbled to the floor.

Cole jerked forward, stunned, wary. Amirah lay in a fetal position on the blue carpet, crying. A hand covered her eyes. "Amirah?"

She lifted both of her arms like a child begging to be picked up. In a little girl voice, she pleaded. "Hold me!"

Cole put his pistol within reach on the control console and took the EM restraints out of his pocket. He immediately bound her hands, then sat on the floor beside her and pulled her into his lap, holding her fiercely against him. Thudding steps sounded from the sleeping quarters. Jeremiel emerged running. Breathing hard, he stopped when he saw Cole and Amirah on the floor. Baruch pulled his pistol and aimed with deadly intent at Amirah.

Cole put up a hand to keep Jeremiel calm, then he slowly lowered it to stroke Amirah's sweat-damp hair. "It's Cole, Amirah. You're safe. It's not your fault. The government did this to you. Don't think about the images . . . let them go. Think about something else, anything else." She buried her face helplessly against his shoulder and wept, seemingly unable to find her own way out of the delusion. Cole paused, then gently reminded, "Remember in the caves on Horeb? I told you were beautiful. And you are, Amirah. A very beautiful woman of twenty-nine. Remember when we talked all night? We talked about places we'd been and flowers we loved. You laughed. I miss that Amirah, bring her back to me. Where is she, Amirah? She's in there somewhere. Can you find her?"

Her childish cries diminished to soft soundless sobs. She twisted the fingers of her bound hands into the front of his purple shirt, as though holding on for dear life.

Cole rocked her back and forth slowly. "It's Cole, Amirah. You don't have to be afraid. I'm here. Are you listening? Find your way out of those neural pathways. Follow my voice, come on, follow my voice to a time two weeks ago when you and I sat in front of the fire in the caves of the Desert Fathers and talked about military strategy. Remember? We discussed Antares Minor. You said I made a stupid error? You were right. Bet you never thought you'd hear me admit that, did you?" He forced himself to laugh warmly. "I'm not as bad as you think. Actually, I—"

"I—I know," she whispered feebly. Her frantic hands unfastened from his shirt and slid down his chest to his lap. She awkwardly patted his side.

He tightened his grip around her and braced his head on the top of hers so she could feel him nod. "Are you all right?"

"I need to . . . sleep."

"Let me help you to your quarters." He got into a kneeling position and slipped his arms beneath her shoulders and under her knees. He quietly carried her into her room and laid her on the narrow cot. While Cole pulled the blue blanket up over her, Jeremiel came to stand in the doorway, his pistol pointed at Amirah's chest.

"The restraints aren't enough. We have to sedate her."

Cole hesitated. He looked ruefully at Amirah, but a tangle of blond waves shielded her face. "Yes. Yes, I agree." He started to walk away and she frantically reached out and gripped his hand with both of hers. But she said nothing. She didn't have to. He knew she was afraid of his leaving—afraid the terror would return.

Cole looked at Jeremiel unhappily.

"I'll get it," Baruch said. He tossed Cole his pistol before he disappeared.

Cole gripped the gun and eased down onto the side of Amirah's cot. With his free hand, he drew her bound wrists into his lap. Her fingers felt small and frail in his grasp. He squeezed them tenderly. "I'm glad you're back, Amirah. Stay here. Stay with me."

He continued to talk softly to her until Jeremiel came back and gave her the shot and she fell deeply asleep.

CHAPTER 37

"Damn it, Merle! He didn't want us to know!" Rudy raged as he tramped around the first level conference room aboard the *Orphica*. The oval white table in the center had a stale cup of taza perched precariously on the edge of a stack of crystal sheets. Rudy glanced at it in annoyance, wishing he had the time to dump it and get another.

Merle ignored his outburst and finished watching the final scenes of the dattran run. She sat at the head of the table in front of a com monitor, one hand combing her long ebony locks back away from her round face. A petite woman, she had a pointed nose and dark graceful brows. When the file ended, Merle closed her eyes tightly and rubbed her forehead. "I don't believe it."

"Neither do I." Rudy propped his hands on his hips and paced furiously up and down the length of the table. "What the hell's he doing?"

"You know what he's doing." She fixed him with her dark serious gaze.

Rudy stopped and lifted a fist, wanting to slam it into something, unable to gather the anger to do it. He felt suddenly like crawling into a hole and refusing to ever come out again. "Why? *Why is he doing it!*"

Merle formed her mouth into a pout. "Because he's more desperate than he's ever been in his life."

"Oh, in the name of God, Merle! He's seen friends die before. Carey's loss is—"

"*Not the same, Kopal.*" One of her brows lifted reprovingly. "Halloway's not Pleroma—Carey's been his wife and best friend for a dozen years. He couldn't just leave her to the Magistrates' mercy. I'm amazed Jeremiel stayed through the strategizing and completion of the Horeb attack. It must have nearly killed him, knowing

341

every minute that Carey might be dying while he was arguing insignificant details about tactics."

Rudy stood unmoving. He'd noticed, too, the way Jeremiel's hands had clenched and unclenched during odd moments at the conference table, the way his voice took on a cutting edge when he discussed the Magistrates or what might happen to the Magisterial crew they put down on Horeb. "He can't do it, Merle. Nobody could. Not even with Tahn at his side. *Taking a battle cruiser out from under a crew of three thousand isn't possible anymore!*" He threw himself forward to brace his hands on the edge of the table near a mound of crystal sheets. The scent of stale taza rose up to him. "Merle, the latest battle cruisers have protective devices, secret passageways not on any schematics, alternative control centers, special tactics teams trained specifically to squelch takeover attempts. *He can't do it!*"

She quietly shoved her chair back and got up to pace. Strands of black hair clung wetly to her temples. "Baruch knows about the latest innovations in the cruisers. Even if none of us are exactly certain what they are or where they're installed—he knows what he's up against. And Tahn's brilliant at covert schemes, though I know you hate to admit that. Maybe together they can figure out some angle that you and I are missing."

Rudy folded his arms in frustration. "Maybe."

"And anyway, we can't worry about them. The last shuttles are on their way up. We've got to be ready to lead the fleet out of here within the hour."

"I know," Rudy responded hollowly. "I just . . ."

The com unit on the table flared suddenly, flashing blue alert, and Merle's navigation officer's frantic voice boomed through the room, *"Captain Wells, return to the bridge immediately! Enemy cruisers . . ."*

The first shot slammed the *Orphica* like the blast of God's fist. Rudy and Merle both tumbled to the floor in the quake that gyrated through the deck plates. The cold cup of taza toppled and spilled onto the floor in a dark torrent.

Rudy lunged to his feet and grabbed onto the chairs to steady himself while he scrambled for the door. *Too long—this is no ordinary attack. There must be three or more cruisers concentrating fire to shudder the bones of the ship this badly.* "Merle, I've got to get back to my ship!"

She crawled frantically along the other side of the table, making it to the door before him. She got to her feet and slammed a palm into the exit patch, panting. "There's no time, Rudy. Come with me to my bridge!"

CHAPTER 38

Carey walked silently at Zadok's side, her gaze wandering over the magnificent rolling hills of the fifth heaven. Late afternoon sunlight slanted down across the dirt path they followed, throwing a golden cloak over magnolia trees that burst with ivory blossoms everywhere she looked. A sweet citrus fragrance wafted on the warm breeze.

The archangel Michael had hastily led them through the last four gates. Before he vanished, he explained, "I must talk to Epagael before you get to the seventh gate." And he'd spread his wings and risen like a gorgeous white bird to soar away through the azure skies.

Carey knelt down in the lattice shadows cast by the branches over her head and picked up a fallen flower. Its broad white petals had turned brown on the tips, but it still glimmered waxily in the saffron light. Zadok watched her fondly, as though understanding how all this beauty and serenity must affect her horror-accustomed soldier's heart.

"Zadok?" she said. "Tell me about Rachel. I didn't understand that conversation you had with Sedriel. What role does she play in the future?"

Hunched and tired from their long walk, Zadok's ancient face seemed made of overused leather, wrinkled and dark. "There are legends," he answered, "about the Antimashiah. We always assumed the wicked being who would try to destroy the universe would be a man. But we were wrong."

He fixed Carey with eyes as black and glistening as ebony velvet. *"We were wrong."*

Carey frowned skeptically. How could anyone see Rachel as the Antimashiah? The woman had indeed suffered enormously at the hands of God, but would she destroy the universe to get back at Him? It didn't really seem like her style. "Why do you think she's the Antimashiah?"

"Oh, I know she is. I read her name upon the Veil. She has the letters AKT on her forehead."

"The Veil?"

"Yes. The cosmic curtain that shields the throne of God. On the Veil are written all the preexisting events of creation, including the identities of the true Mashiah and the famed Antimashiah. Rachel Eloel is definitely allied with the wicked angel, Aktariel."

Carey nodded, but she doubted the truth of it. Oh, not that she doubted the *appearance* that Rachel was working in concert with the Archdeceiver—but she remembered all too clearly the final hours before the *Hoyer*'s destruction when Carey herself had operated as a double agent. What could Rachel gain from pretending to be the Antimashiah? Time? An opening to destroy Aktariel?

Carey thoughtfully twirled the magnolia blossom in her hand. "And who does the Veil list as being the Mashiah?"

Zadok smiled, but an almost painful expression came to his face. "My great-grandson, Nathan."

"Mikael's son?"

"Yes."

"When was Nathan born?"

"Very recently, I think. It's been a long time since God let me see the Veil, over ten years, in fact, based on what you told me. But I recall that Nathan was supposed to be born in the middle of the year 5426."

Carey glanced disquietedly at the little patriarch. She prayed Mikael had survived the war on Horeb long enough to father the promised Redeemer. The clandestine information the Underground had been getting just before she'd left on the Kiskanu mission didn't make her hopeful.

The path led over a hill and down across a narrow plank bridge through a tree-shrouded swamp. The scents of moist grass and moss blanketed them as they entered the dark shadows. A froth of pink star-shaped blooms covered the bushes that crept alongside the sluggish water lapping at the planks of the bridge. Carey listened to the lyrical songs of the birds. Her boots pounded hollowly over the wood, providing a percussion accompaniment to the natural symphony.

When they climbed out of the cool shadows and up onto a meadowed terrace, Carey saw the sixth gate. Set against the green background of trees and undulating hills, it rose like an archaic curtained tabernacle. Two rows with seven gray marble columns each lined the approach. The tabernacle itself had an ornate gabled roof with a majestic red and green stained glass window over the door. Orange curtains shimmered as though aflame on either side of the door. And before the entry, the angel Gabriel knelt in prayer. His long golden curls brushed the shoulders of his crimson robe. The amber halo cast by his tall body gleamed with a fiery radiance in the stained glass, and cast a pastel reflection over his white wings.

As they approached Gabriel, a sudden thought struck Carey. "Zadok, who wrote the Veil? God?"

The elderly patriarch shook his bald head. "No, legends say that the wicked Aktariel wrote it just after Creation to show God the shapes that the chaotic patterns of the future would take."

"To warn God?"

"I don't know, Carey. I don't think anyone does. Perhaps to warn Him. Perhaps to persuade God to destroy the universe before things got out of hand. Aktariel had always been against the Creation."

"I'm intrigued," she said as they entered the dappling shadows of the row of gray columns.

"By what?"

"That you believe what the Veil says. If it's written by the Great Deceiver—"

"But I've never found it to be wrong, my dear. I'm sure Epagael watched over Aktariel's shoulder when he wrote it, assuring its correctness."

"Are you? You've more faith than I, Zadok. Fabricating the sequence of events at the end of time would seem to me just the sort of diversion the Archdeceiver would create to distract God from his final ploy, whatever that might be."

Zadok frowned up at her. "I know you'd rather believe Rachel isn't the Antimashiah, Carey, but I don't honestly see how Aktariel could deceive God. If that part of the

Veil had been wrong, I'm sure Epagael would have corrected it long ago."

Carey gazed up at the Tabernacle. The stained glass window flamed, throwing a geometric patchwork of rainbows over their path.

When they were about five feet away from the prostrate gatekeeper, Zadok gripped her arm lightly and tugged her with him to kneel on the ground. Her dusty black jumpsuit rustled as she got down on her knees at his side. Carey followed Zadok in forming her hands into the sacred triangle.

Quietly, Zadok prayed, "Please, Lord Gabriel, we stand at the door and knock. Let us enter."

As though shocked, Gabriel spun around and stared. His amber mouth parted slightly. "Zadok? What are you doing back? You're worse than the famines of Canaan!"

"It's been over a decade, Lord."

"That's only long to you, Patriarch."

"I know you weren't expecting us, Lord, but the Archistrategos led us through the first five heavens and promised to speak to Epagael about our request for an audience."

"Michael *led* you through?"

"Yes, Lord."

"That's most irregular." Gabriel got to his feet to loom over them like a crimson-robed pillar of fire. "But if Michael's interceding on your behalf, I'm certain Epagael will approve. Now . . ." He cast a curious glance at Carey. "Why are you here?"

Zadok braced a hand on Carey's shoulder and grunted his way to his feet. The orange curtains bracketing the Tabernacle billowed in the breeze like windblown flames. Bowing reverently, Zadok said, "It is not I, Lord Gabriel, who seeks Epagael, but this woman, Carey Halloway." He put a fatherly hand on Carey's auburn hair. "An angel plucked her from the horror chamber of the galactic Magistrates on Palaia Station and sent her—"

"*What angel, Zadok?*"

"She doesn't know. Neither do I."

Carey gracefully got to her feet and bowed as Zadok had. "Lord, the angel who came to me did not give me his name, but he guided me through a tunnel of light to the Void of Darkness where I met the Patriarch."

"He escorted you into Authades? That's more than incredible; it's bizarre." Gabriel ran a hand across his glowing face and, as though understanding had just dawned, his gaze darted over the verdant landscape. Casting a look over his shoulder, he leaned forward and whispered, "Did this angel perhaps have short hair, cut about here?" He ran a finger beneath his ear.

"Yes," Carey responded suspiciously. Did only certain angels have shorn hair?

"And did he wear a hooded cloak? Let me see, generally he favors velvets or satins. Blue or green?"

"Yes," Carey responded again. "Jade green velvet."

Gabriel leaned unsteadily against the door to the Tabernacle. He shook his head as though in astonishment.

"What's wrong?" Zadok demanded.

After a few seconds, Gabriel let out a low laugh. "Nothing, Zadok. Nothing I'm going to get involved in anyway. But I hope Michael knows what he's doing." He vented a troubled sigh and straightened up again. "Well, it seems I need to ask you some questions."

"That's the way it usually works, Lord," Zadok pointed out irritably. The old man had his head cocked like an eager dowager.

"Yes, indeed. Well, then, let me think." Gabriel fastened his glinting golden gaze on Carey in a way that made her muscles go tight. "Yes, maybe a question you'll need to know the answer to, eh, Halloway?"

Carey canted her body at a defensive angle. She'd no plans of attacking, but angels were unpredictable.

"Please get on with it, Lord. We're in a hurry," Zadok requested. He gripped Carey's black sleeve and pulled her closer to him.

Gabriel grinned sardonically, then shifted his attention to Carey again and laughed openly. "A hurry? Yes, I dare say that's true. Well, here goes. There is an ancient Koranic legend about the Golden Calf. It is said that at the end of the world, the Calf will come alive. How will that happen, Zadok?"

Trees waved in the wind, filling the air with a soft rustling sound. Zadok rubbed his smooth jaw, eyes focused on the hem of Gabriel's robe which flapped in the wind. "It is written, Lord, that when the angels ride down to seal the culmination, the hooves of their horses will kick dust into the mouth of the Calf and it will dance."

"Yes, very good, Patriarch." He lifted his brows as though greatly amused by the discussion. He chuckled. "Angels, however, come in many forms. It's all a matter of perspective, isn't it, Zadok?"

Calas frowned, puzzled. "I don't know what you mean, Lord."

"Well, I mean," Gabriel waved his arm and his crimson sleeve fluttered extravagantly. " 'Angel' is a later derivation from an ancient word: *mal'ak*, meaning messenger. Think about that, Zadok!"

"I don't understand, Lord."

"Don't you? Name the Angels of Vengeance, Patriarch."

"The Angels of Vengeance?" Zadok repeated. His ancient brow furrowed. He lifted a hand and began putting down fingers as he listed them: "You are one, Lord, Michael is another, Uriel, Satanel, Raphael, Suriel, Jehoel, Zagzagel, Metatron, Yefefiah, Nathanael, and lastly, the wicked Aktariel."

Gabriel nodded with an exaggerated pride. "Very good. But it's true, isn't it, that a rose by any other name is still a rose?" The angel lifted a hand and mimicked Zadok, putting down fingers as he said, "Baruch, Kopal, Wells, Tahn—"

"What does that mean?" Carey demanded loudly. She stepped forward like one of the Angels of Vengeance herself, eyes glowing. "Explain! What do Tahn and Wells—"

Gabriel cocked his head at her, but he spoke to Zadok. "You're certainly worthy to pass though the gate, Patriarch. Go."

Zadok bowed again and grabbed Carey's hand, dragging her forward with him to the door of the Tabernacle. Though she wanted to insist on an answer from Gabriel, she feared it might be her last chance to get through the gate. But fear fluttered in her stomach. Angels of Vengeance? Jeremiel and Cole and Merle. . . .

"Just a minute, Patriarch," Gabriel interrupted. "I said *you* could pass. Not Halloway."

Carey stopped and spread her legs, glaring up into the

huge creature's glowing face. Gabriel's mouth curled into a smile, but his eyes shone as coldly as frozen amber.

"Why can't I pass, Lord?" Carey asked.

"Because I have a question for you."

Carey's mouth tightened with foreboding. She'd known none of the answers Zadok had so easily rattled off. Was this arrogant angel trying to halt her journey to Arabot? "I'm not versed in the secrets of the Gamant patriarchs, Lord. I don't—"

"Oh, this is a different sort of question, Halloway. Yes, very different, indeed. Tailored especially for you."

"What is it?"

Gabriel walked in front of them to stand tall between the fluttering orange curtains. He opened his wings, spreading them until they blocked the entry completely. His eiderdown feathers shimmered blue, red, and green beneath the radiance of the stained glass.

He lifted his chin and his yellow curls cascaded down his back. "You know Maxwell's Constant for light, don't you, Halloway?"

"Of course."

"Are you also familiar with Epimenides' paradox?"

Carey searched her memories. "No. I'm sorry."

Gabriel laughed menacingly and lowered his gaze to study the square base of a gray column. "Well, let me grant you that part. Epimenides was a Cretan who postulated that 'All Cretans are liars.' He—"

"The *liar's paradox*. Yes, I know it now. Godel's famous Incompleteness Theorem in mathematics is based upon it. Go on."

Behind Gabriel, the sun set in a blaze of maroon, painting the hillsides and ivory magnolia blossoms with a wash of blood. The soothing warmth of the day faded into a faintly moist chill. Frogs in the swamp roused with the coolness of nightfall and croaked melodiously for a few seconds, then apparently thought better of it and hushed. Carey folded her arms to fight the ice that lanced the wind.

"I'm going to tell you the absolute truth, Halloway," Gabriel promised. "All angels tell the truth. And I say to you now, that the Archdeceiver, an angel of the highest status, has never lied. I ask you, how can that be?"

Carey's eyes narrowed unpleasantly. Obviously if angels

never lied, and the Archdeceiver was an angel, then he couldn't lie, but since he was the Archdeceiver he couldn't tell the truth. A paradox indeed.

She drummed her fingers on her folded arms. "What does this have to do with Maxwell's Constant, Gabriel?"

"Light by its very nature doesn't really exist in your universe. Isn't that true?"

"Yes. In an absolute sense, photons spend no time and cross no space, yet they—"

"Then why do we perceive light?" He waved his hand to the magnificent sunset that had turned the drifting clouds lavender.

"Because the photons strike our retinas, stop their Constant journey, and the electromagnetic energy is translated by our brains into an image."

"And some brains, Halloway, are better at that than others, particularly Gamant brains."

Dread welled in her breast, stinging like a herd of minuscule carnivores trying to gnaw their way out. Is that why the Magistrates had begun extensive experimentation on Gamant brain structures? What did they expect to find? What are we talking about?

Gabriel quietly scuffed the toe of his sandal in the fine sand that had blown up around the base of the Tabernacle. A gust of wind pressed his crimson robe tightly across his broad chest. "So, our brains are instruments of phase-change? Our observation actually creates the thing being observed, brings light from outside the universe into it?"

"What are you getting at?"

"God."

"I don't understand."

"Don't you? What do you think happens, my dear Halloway, when Epagael decides not to observe your universe?" He leaned forward, hanging breathlessly on her answer. Glowing golden curls fell to frame his majestic face.

"Well, if He were the only observer I'd say it ceased to exist, but since my universe has its own infinite number of individual consciousnesses—"

Gabriel laughed, a low, disparaging laugh that made her blood run cold. "Come, come, Halloway, try to see it from a higher perspective. All those consciousnesses

are 'contingent' realities. Yours, for example, is merely
an expression of a holistic universal consciousness spawned
by the *Reshimu*. If all the consciousnesses in your universe were taken together, they'd create nothing more
than a 'quantum wave function,' not a series of observables. That is, not without a fundamental canvas upon
which to appear. *What*, Halloway, is the single underlying principle which neither you nor any of the consciousnesses in your universe can directly observe?"

"I—I don't . . ." She struggled with herself. She was
a mathematician, for God's sake, she ought to be able
to figure this out. But what did it have to do with God
and the liar's paradox? "I don't know, Gabriel."

"No?" He smiled knowingly and extended a hand to
the benchlike bases of the pillars. A bat swooped and
soared in the darkness over the Tabernacle. "Why don't
you have a seat? You might be here a while."

* * *

Rudy hauled himself across the smoke-filled bridge of
the *Orphica* on his elbows. His mangled right leg left a
wide smear of blood on the carpet. "Merle?" he shouted.

He couldn't see her in the dense smoke. The three-
sixty monitors looked like hazy patches of color, but he
could tell that several had blanked. *Decks breached.* The
First Alert sirens had shut off sometime during the last
cruiser pass. They'd defended the starsails and freighters
for as long as they could. They had to get the hell away
from Horeb! He coughed raggedly and shouted, "Merle!
Merle, where are you?"

Vaguely, he saw someone move near the captain's
chair. A black smudge of battlesuit reared over the arm
and he made out her pale face.

"Kopal, take the nav console." She sucked in a wheez-
ing breath. "Jamice is dead." She pulled herself into her
seat and began checking damage reports on her chair
arm coms while Rudy made his way to the navigation
station.

He had to drag Jamice's bloody corpse out of the seat
before he could rise and slump into it. He quickly surveyed the intermittent incoming data. His eyes jerked to
the forward screen where thirty Magisterial battle cruis-

ers reconfigured, ten lining out for a head-on assault, fifteen swinging around and forming up into three flying wedges, five falling into flanking positions. . . .

"*Calculate and lay in vault coordinates, Kopal! Hurry!*"

"For where?" He spun around to stare openmouthed at her. "Where the hell are we going?"

Merle shook her head in panic.

"Merle, we can't go to Shyr—they'll follow us straight through! The *Hashomer*'s dead in space. The refugees aboard her will undoubtedly be taken to Palaia. Where else—"

"*Mainz system!*" she ordered. "Sector four! At least we might be able to warn Jeremiel and Tahn."

"We've got to tell the scattered starsails and freighters or they'll—"

"Then do it! Hurry!"

Rudy whirled around and sent the message under narrow beam, then input the request for vault coordinates. His hands shook while he waited for the numbers to come up. The lead Magisterial cruisers hurtled headlong at them, almost in firing range. . . . "Laid in. I'm initiating vault sequence!"

CHAPTER 39

Ornias stood before the open windows in his broad white office on Satellite 4. A cool breeze tousled his blue curtains and ruffled his sandy hair. An enormous black desk adorned the far wall, by the door. His purple general's uniform accentuated the breadth of his shoulders and narrowness of his waist. In his hands, he carried a cup of steaming taza.

"So, Rasch, your forces ran like scared rats when the Gamants attacked?" He turned to level a malicious stare at the bald-headed major who stood stiffly at attention in front of Ornias' desk.

Rasch's middle-aged face twitched. "No, sir. My forces fought valiantly. The Gamants came in wave after wave, they threw themselves at the cannons suicidally—until they broke through the perimeter and overran our positions. We must have killed at least three thousand in the first half hour."

"Yes," Ornias said coldly. "I've already been reprimanded by Slothen for your body count. Don't you realize, Major, that Gamants only work as a bargaining lever if they're alive?"

"Yes, sir, but my people have the right to protect themselves! I couldn't just tell them to sit there and—"

"Next time, Major. *I'll* relay information on casualties. Understood?"

"Yes, sir," he grunted.

"Who was the dissident who led the attack?"

"An unknown woman warrior, sir. Some of our soldiers claimed they heard her forces call her Arikha. Her second in command was definitely named Emon."

"Arikha . . . uh-huh. And your casualties, Major?"

"Seventy-five dead. Three hundred injured."

"I see," Ornias commented blandly, but his eyes had

a savage glitter. He paced lithely before the golden light streaming in through the window. "So now we have a wild pack of five thousand Gamants running free over the satellite. I understand they've discovered all the rents in the substructure that the Magistrates so carelessly left when they created these hunks of junk?" He sipped his taza and lifted a brow at Rasch. The major hadn't moved. He continued to stand rigidly at attention, his eyes focused on some distant point. "What do you suggest we do about it, Major?"

"Sir, I suggest we request the services of one of the battle cruisers at Palaia. Magistrate Slothen has ten cruisers in dock, sir, surely they can spare us one to help identify all the Gamant hiding places."

Ornias chuckled disdainfully. "You think we'll be able to find them, do you? You don't know much about Gamants, Major. They'll slither into every hole and rock crevice that exists on the satellite. Those gaps in the fabric provide perfect interconnecting passageways that lace this entire station."

"But it's worth a try, sir," Rasch insisted. His expression remained inscrutable, but his fists clenched at his sides.

"All right, Major. Make the request. I have to get to Satellite 6—the Gamants there have started wailing and tearing their hair, the fools. The claim that from their satellite they can see straight through the Horns of the Calf on Palaia to Zohar. They're afraid they're on the direct path to oblivion."

Rasch blinked thoughtfully. "The Horns of the Calf, General?"

Ornias shrugged disgustedly. Gamants were such imbeciles. In all the years he'd been forced to associate with them, he'd never grasped their fanatical attachment to obscure prophecies. Those ridiculous stories seemed to sustain them as surely as mother's milk. "Yes," he snapped tersely, "they call the Engineering Spires outside of Naas 'horns.' . . . Rasch, when you talk to the military advisory council tell them that I recommend mind-blanking for any rebel captured as a result of our search."

Rasch fell out of his stance, his head jerking quickly to stare at Ornias. "But, sir, that's excessive—"

"Tell them," he instructed. "We need to keep the total

numbers of Gamants high, to threaten the Underground, you understand. But mind-blanking will render the dissidents harmless."

"Aye, sir," Rasch said curtly. He saluted and strode for the door.

Ornias waited until he exited, then turned back to his view of the pleasant rolling countryside that spread in a green and yellow blanket for as far as he could see. The Magistrates did such a superb job recreating planetary environments. Birds soared high overhead. He leisurely sipped his taza. "Arikha . . . hmm."

* * *

Carey sat on the gray base of the pillar, her knees pulled against her chest, watching the stars emerge in a twinkling shawl from the charcoal blanket overhead. Zadok had slumped to the ground by the next pillar, bracing his back against the cold marble. Darkness grew up around them, and with it the sounds of a spring night. Owls let out lonely hoots from the towering trees; insects sawed like rusty hinges in the grass; frogs sang melodiously from the swamp.

Carey took a deep breath of the night-scented wind. The chill bit at her cheeks. Gabriel had gone into the Tabernacle and closed the curtains. They hung in sculpted copper folds beneath the stained glass window.

Zadok shifted to extend his ancient legs across the dirt path. In the starlight, his bald head gleamed as though frosted with silver icing. He'd spoken to her gently for the first hour, encouraging her, but then he'd fallen silent, letting her think. Carey had developed quite an affection for him. He had a charismatic strength of character that reminded her of Jeremiel.

"Zadok," she murmured. "I think we should be going."

He shifted against the pillar to look up at her. His black eyes shone like empty sockets in his withered face. "Have you figured out the answers?"

"Yes."

A look of delight lit his face. He gripped the base of the pillar and pulled himself to his feet. Dusting off his brown robe, he said, "You don't look happy about it."

"No. I'm not."

He waddled forward and tenderly put a hand on her shoulder, anxiously studying her face. As he analyzed her miserable expression, his lips pursed. He dropped his hand and sat on the pillar beside her.

"What is it, Carey? How can the Archdeceiver have never told a lie?"

"Oh," she sighed and waved a hand dismissively. "That one was easy. Over three thousand years ago, Einstein and Rosen came to the conclusion that parallel universes exist. We've never been able to access them, but we rely on that concept continually in our mathematics. If an infinity of parallel universes exist, Aktariel must have continuously told the truth in at least one of them. He must also have been a continuous liar in another. The question depends on which universe you're looking at." *Which also means, Zadok, that Rachel may be the Antimashiah in one, but she must also be the Mashiah in another.*

Zadok grimaced as though he'd been defrauded. "I see. And what about . . ." He blinked suddenly and his elderly face darkened. "Does that mean, my dear, that in some universes, the Veil that Aktariel wrote—"

"I don't know, Zadok. There may only be one Veil and one version of the seven heavens. But there may be more, too."

Zadok seemed to stop breathing. "I cannot believe that Epagael would allow us to fall into error. I have faith that there is only one Veil."

Carey slipped a hand beneath the auburn hair at the back of her neck and massaged the taut muscles. A tension headache pressed forcefully behind her eyes. She wished she had Jeremiel here—or Cole—either of them would be able to help her plan what to do if her suspicions about God were correct. Just seeing both men in her memory left her hurting. *How are you doing, Jeremiel? Cole? Are you all right?* Where would they be now? Far, far away from her, so far that it didn't mean anything to speculate.

Somewhere in the rolling hills, a coyote yipped. Then the entire pack joined in, creating a heartrending chorus. She felt almost as though they sang just for her. Odd that this heaven contained so many Earthlike animals.

The fourth had been filled with strange, odd creatures that she'd never seen before.

Zadok reached over and softly patted her knee. "What about the other question, Carey? What is the single underlying principal that no one can observe?"

"Time."

"Time? But whenever I watch the sun cross the sky I observe time."

"No," she said as she exhaled. "You infer time from movement. All that you're observing is motion."

He thoughtfully scratched his right ear. "So it's not possible to observe time?"

"I didn't say that. Theoretically, an observation of time would mean that the observer could go back and repeat his observation as many times as he wanted to— an infinite number, in fact."

"But I don't understand."

"I'm not sure I do either. Even if we could access parallel universes, our very presence as observers would change the experimental parameters so that we couldn't repeat the same observation an infinite number of times."

"But—"

"I suspect, Zadok, that an observer who exists outside the Void of Creation—one who isn't bounded by our physical laws—could conceivably repeat his measurements of time infinitely. And, thereby, *maintain its very existence.*" She ground her teeth softly. *What happens when God decides not to observe?*

As the darkness deepened, smears of galaxies fuzzed the sky, glimmering like halos over the treetops. Carey frowned. Was a timeless Observer, then, both necessary and sufficient for the existence of time? Without that observation being repeated continuously, did hard reality dissolve into its hazy realm of infinite possibilities? The universal quantum wave function? She shivered involuntarily and hugged herself. Inside the black box of the universe, the Observer became part of whatever he or she chose to watch. But what if the Observer existed outside? Had God trapped Himself in the mire of Creation? Or was He always free?

She eased off the pillar, dusted her black jumpsuit and

tramped quietly for the Tabernacle. When she stood before the closed orange curtains, she called, "Gabriel?"

Zadok ambled up behind her and patiently waited, his bald head shimmering in the starlight. The archangel ducked beneath the overhanging curtain and stepped out into the starlight. His glow splashed the land with a watery blanket of liquid gold, reflecting with a flaming intensity in the stained glass window.

Carey gazed up and answered, "Time, Lord Gabriel. That is the one thing we cannot directly observe. And the Archdeceiver must have told the truth continuously in some alternate universe."

"Very good, Halloway." Without another word, he pulled the curtain aside and made a sweeping gesture with his hand. "You may pass the gate."

Zadok, knowing the fickle ways of angels better than she, hurried forward and disappeared into the warm spice-scented darkness. Carey stopped beside Gabriel and narrowed her eyes. He lifted his amber brows questioningly.

"What is it, Halloway?"

"Your questions . . . time, multiple universes, the nature of the Observer. It's the cosmogonic starting point, isn't it? That's what Aktariel's seeking. He's trying to turn back the clock to erase all the observables in my universe?"

"Not just your universe, Halloway, but all adjacent ones, as well. Do you know who he is?"

"Yes, the angel who came to me. What role do I play in his plan, Gabriel?"

The archangel reached down and lifted her hand to gently kiss her fingers. His touch sent a flood of warmth through her. He responded, "A very fundamental one. Now, you'd better get going. Michael—gullible fool that he is—has already arranged for you to speak to Epagael."

CHAPTER 40

In the past hour, a leaden blanket of silence had fallen over Engineering. It terrified Mikael. Jeremiel had instructed him to incapacitate the ship by reducing it to running on "incremental power." Which meant that the cruiser had shut down almost every part of the ship except Engineering. Not even the food dispensers on board worked. The lights glowed with a dull sheen.

He sat in a chair beside Sybil's bed, watching her sleep, stroking her dark tangled hair to soothe himself. Touching Sybil had always eased his fears. She was fine when awake, but she still needed a great deal of sleep to keep up her strength. Rad and his two technicians slumped against the wall a few feet away, EM restraints securing their hands and feet. One of the techs snored softly.

Mikael gazed around the tri-level round chamber. Brilliant lustreglobes glared everywhere, hurting his eyes. He squinted up at the duty stations that perched like wire bird's nests on each level, fifteen in all. On the opposite side of the room, Ari sat with his feet propped on a control console, gleefully sipping a bottle of beer. The gun in his gnarled fist was aimed at Engineer Rad's barrel chest. Rad hadn't said a word in hours, but the collar of his purple uniform had darkened with sweat and his stubby black hair glistened as though studded with diamonds. His hands and ankles bore EM restraints. Yosef hunched over a panel on the other end of the long console, his spectacles propped beside his face while he slept. The constant hum of the ship sounded like the buzzing of insects on a summer night.

Mikael smoothed his callused fingers over Sybil's face. In their twelve years together, she'd rarely been ill, and then only with minor viruses or flus. Seeing her weak with pain and crying out for him the first few days had shredded his soul. He feared to be away from her for even a few seconds—feared she might awaken and find him gone. Even after the magic of the med unit, her shoulder still blazed with dark indigo and violet bruises and he knew she must be feeling as though demons had descended upon her with flashing swords.

Gently, Mikael lifted her hand and kissed the limp palm. She moaned something softly and her dark eyes fluttered open.

"Mikael?" she whispered groggily.

"I'm here, Sybil. I've been here all along."

She squeezed his hand. ". . . Love you."

"And I love you. Go back to sleep. I'm sorry I woke you."

"I had the strangest dream."

"About a thousand friendly soldiers with rifles appearing out of the air, I hope?"

She smiled faintly and it gladdened his heart. He pressed her cool hand against his cheek and nuzzled it tenderly. "No," she said. "It was a *funny* dream, Mikael."

A crawly sensation tormented his chest. She'd had strange, prophetic dreams since she'd been a child. "What dream, Sybil?"

"About a little boy. He was living with a community of men who wore white robes. They lived in caves on the shores of a green lake."

He bent down to kiss her warmly on the mouth, trying to stave off the inevitable discussion about their son. If he thought about Nathan now, he'd go mad trying to figure out what had happened, and he couldn't afford it. Not yet. There was no telling when Woloc would make his next assault.

She brushed black hair away from Mikael's eyes and examined his face. He knew he must look dead tired. "When was the last time you slept?" she whispered.

"I'll nap when I have the chance."

"What's happening, Mikael?"

"Nothing. That's what worries me. We've barricaded every possible entry we can find. But I have a terrible feeling that we've missed something."

"We just have to hold Engineering long enough for Baruch and Tahn to get here tomorrow."

"Tomorrow's an eternity, Sybil. While you've been sleeping for the past three hours, bangs and knocks have sounded all around us—Woloc's up to something. He's trying to figure another way in."

Sybil sank back and pulled the blankets up around her throat, peering at him through wide dark eyes. He tucked the edges of the blanket around her and kissed her.

"Try to sleep more, Sybil. There's nothing you can do. This is just a waiting game."

"No," she said and sat up. "Hand me my boots." While Mikael reached down to retrieve them from the floor, Sybil grabbed her gunbelt from the bedside table and fastened it around her waist. Mikael rose and handed her the boots. . . .

A soft resonance of breathing came from overhead and Sybil bolted off the bed and fell into a crouch as Ari screamed, *"Up there!"*

Mikael dove for the floor, rolling to come up firing. The entire second level swarmed with purple-uniformed soldiers. Mikael fired again and a man shrieked; his body slammed the white wall before tumbling over the railing; it bashed against the floor with a sickeningly dull sound.

Mikael scrambled back toward Sybil as Ari's pistol flared. The purple flash blinded Mikael for a second, but he kept crawling.

Yosef screamed, "I'll drop it!"

And Mikael whirled to see him holding a vial of hypini-tronium over his head. Yosef's elderly face pinched with intent and terror.

A familiar voice shouted, "Put it down, Yosef. We'll kill Mikael and Sybil!"

As though to make the point, a burst of fire slammed the floor in front of Mikael, separating him from Sybil. Bits of metal and debris showered his uniform. From the corner of his vision, he saw Yosef's elderly face wither.

Jason Woloc shouted again, "Stop! Lay down your weapons. We don't want to kill any of you!"

"Get out, Woloc!" Mikael responded, waving his arms emphatically. "Get out or this entire section of the ship is going up in a ball of flame!"

Standing on the second level, the lieutenant's honey blond hair had a silver sheen in the bright lights. Mikael sighted on him, his finger tightening on the trigger. The other fourteen or fifteen soldiers had positioned themselves around the balcony, rifles braced—just waiting for the order to open fire. Rad and his two technicians had scurried into the corner, trying to get out of the line of fire.

"I'll tell you one more time, Yosef," Woloc said, and as he did so he raised a hand over his head, ready to signal his forces to let loose a fiery apocalypse. "Put down that canister or Sybil Calas dies first!"

Yosef's old eyes misted. The canister swayed in his hand and Mikael felt a lump of ice lodge at the base of his throat.

Sybil shouted, "Drop it, Yosef. Do it!"

CHAPTER 41

Rev Amora sat and lectured:

"What is the meaning of the verse (Ps. 87:2): 'The lord loveth the gates of Zion more than all the dwellings of Jacob?' The 'gates of Zion'—these are the 'gates of the world'; for gate means an opening, as it is written (Ps. 118:19; 'Open to me the gates of righteousness.' Thus God said: I love the gates of Zion when they are open. Why? Because they are on the side of evil."

Book Bahir
1180 A.D. Stored in the
Museum of Antiquities,
France, Old Earth

Nathanaeus and Yeshwah gazed up at the huge stone walls of the Epitropos' palace that extended endlessly into the belly of the azure sky. The spring sun roasted their flesh, baking their faces a dark brown and sending sweat to stain their coarse white robes across their backs and beneath their arms. They each wore swords on their hips and quivers of arrows on their backs. Their bows were hooked on their belts. A low roar, like that of a stormy ocean, sullied the air. The crowd that had gathered milled around nervously, shaking fists in rage and shouting profanities. White poplars, tamarisks, mallow trees, and sweet licorice dotted the hillsides that cradled the city, scenting the hot wind like perfume.

Yesu—the affectionate Aramaic form of Yeshwah's name and the name by which Nathanaeus had come to call his best friend over the past fifteen years—looked fierce. He stood tall and dark, his brown hair clasped neatly at the base of his skull with a golden clip; his mahogany eyes focused like daggers on the palace balcony where they all hoped Lucius Pontius, the Epitropos, would emerge to answer their charges.

Nathanaeus moved to shift the weight of his one hundred and eighty pounds to his left foot. They'd been standing since dawn and weariness had afflicted them like a plague. People grumbled irritably, shoving at anyone who got too close in the confined courtyard.

Nathanaeus brushed long black hair over his ears. The searing breeze whipped his black beard over his broad chest. "This is foolish, Yesu. What if someone recognizes us? I think we should just go home."

Yesu shook his head patiently. "We can't go home, Nathan. He's gone too far this time."

"But if they find us here, you know what they'll—"

"You're afraid of death? I thought you'd gotten over that long ago. Didn't the *Paquid* teach you that life and death were all the same?"

Nathan heaved a sigh and folded his arms stiffly. "He taught me, just as he did you. But I'm still a weakling at heart, Yesu. The sight of swords and blood, especially my own, worries me."

As though he hadn't heard, Yesu squinted up at the balcony. "The great Pontius Pilatus must have lost what little mind he had. How could he seize the sacred Temple fund to finance the building of his aqueduct? Surely he knew it would fuel a revolt?"

"I'm sure that was his goal. That way he'll have an excuse to kill us by the thousands."

Yesu's mouth tightened. "I wouldn't doubt it. Did you hear the gossip this morning that Pilatus killed several Galileans and mixed their blood with their sacrifices? The old woman who told me claimed she heard it from that bastard prophet, Ben Panthera."

"Panthera? He's crazy. Why would anyone believe him?"

"Because, my friend, Panthera's madness lends him some strange sort of power."

Nathan breathed out ferociously through his nostrils. His black eyes narrowed. "Yes, I've seen him preach. I know what you mean. I was at his triumphant return to Natzaret last week. His own people, people he's known

since he was a boy, drove him out of the temple, screaming that he was possessed by demons."

Yesu shrugged and Nathan matched the gesture. Anyone who preached a different way eventually got accused
of black magic. A gust of wind swept the hillsides and
came roaring down into the city, peppering them with
sand. Their white sleeves crackled.

Yesu wet his dry lips. "When Ben Panthera starts sym-
pathizing with our *great leader* Lucius Pontius Pilatus,
then I'll worry about demonic influences. Right now he's
just an irritant."

"I hope you're right. Some people are saying he's the
Holy Serpent who will free us all."

"Ridiculous," Yesu insisted. "The Holy Serpent must
first descend into the depths of the Abyss before he can
subdue the Serpents of the Abyss. Ben Panthera has
never seen evil in his entire life. . . ."

His words faded as dozens of bronze-suited cavalrymen
rode from around the rear of the palace. Their raised
swords glinted like liquid silver in the bright sunlight.
The lead centurion's gravelly voice carried over the din
of surprised gasps and shuffling feet: "You pious imbeciles want to challenge the Procurator about the Temple
funds, *eh?* Well, he sends his answer!"

Screaming insults and shouts of rage, the soldiers
whipped their horses pell-mell into the crowd and began
slamming around indiscriminately with the flat edge of
their swords, using their weapons as clubs. The hideous
cries and cracks of shattering bone rent the air.

The crowd broke into a frenzy. Trying to get out of
the way, they ran over each other or pushed the weak
beneath the stamping hooves of the horses. A choking
storm of dust roiled up, hugging the impenetrable palace
walls like honey. The shrill wails of children pierced the
blazing day.

"Yesu, run!" Nathan blurted, grabbing him by the
arm.

They pulled their swords from their scabbards and
scrambled through the swarming horde of humanity,
leaping downed bodies, protecting each other's backs.
But as they dodged behind an empty chariot, Nathan saw
Pilatus arrogantly stride out onto the balcony and survey

the wailing crowd. A rich smile creased his cruel Spanish face.

Without even slowing his stride, Nathan unhooked his bow, grabbed an arrow from his quiver, and stopped just long enough to let it fly at the wicked Epitropos. The world seemed to die around him when he saw it strike home, piercing the man's breast. Pilatus shrieked and fell into a sprawling pile of purple cloak.

A cacophony of disbelief and satiated rage welled up with the power of a dozen Legions on the march. Nathan sucked in a sudden breath when a centurion pointed his shining sword and shouted, "Zealots! They've murdered Pilatus! Kill them! *Kill them!*"

Nathan vaulted a low clump of brush and spied a narrow opening in the crowd that led into the city. "No, this way, Yesu!" He lunged to grab Yesu's white sleeve, dragging him in the direction of salvation. Their legs pumped like those of hunted animals scurrying for the safety of their burrows.

Just before they scampered beneath the overhanging branches of a mallow tree, one of the soldiers spurred his horse forward, screaming, "You filthy rebels!"

Hooves thundered behind them, and Nathan caught the fiery glimpse of a sword blade as it arced up and came smashing down across Yesu's muscular back. Blood spurted hot and crimson across his white robe. His friend screamed raggedly and dove beneath the tree, crawling furiously for safety.

The centurion laughed and Nathan hefted his sword. He brutally swung it around to hack once and twice at the enemy's leg. The bone snapped under the impact and set the centurion to howling madly. Leveling his sword again, Nathan aimed higher. The sickening hollow-wood thunk of sword on skull sounded and the soldier fell out of his saddle, landing in a dead bloody heap on the ground.

In panic, Nathan lurched beneath the tree and crawled insanely, following the trail of Yesu's blood that splashed the sandy soil. *Please, Adonai, take me! Don't let Yesu die! Take me . . . take me. . . !* Shrieks swelled to a deafening climax around the palace. Nathan choked on the pungent scent of fresh blood.

The cool shadows of the squat whitewashed buildings

fell over him as he turned a corner and entered a shaded alley. A cry clotted his throat at the sight of Yeshwah. He lay in a heap of blood and white robe, propped against a stone wall.

"Yesu?" he shouted. Nathan tugged his friend to his feet and draped one of Yesu's arms over his shoulders, then half-carried, half-dragged him down the alleyway.

"Nathan," Yesu, groaned, face twisting in pain. "Leave me. They'll be coming!"

"Hold on, Yesu. It's not far."

Yesu gasped and moaned, trying to contain the wails that lodged in his throat. His dark brown hair had fallen out of its clasp to hang in grimy strings over his shoulders, tangling in his bushy beard. People watched openly from the windows on high, some screaming, *qana! qana!*—zealot—as though to shame them, to berate them for objecting to murder or the obscenity the Epitropos had placed in the sacred Temple! Nathan glared at them, casting profanities back. The fools, the pious Sebastian idiots! Lucius Pontius Pilatus had brought the Eagles of the Legion and the Imperator's Icon into Yerushalaim itself! He'd stolen the temple funds to build his aqueduct; he'd killed innocent Galileans to feed his ravenous appetite for blood. He deserved death a thousand times over!

"Help?" Nathan pleaded. "Help us! Somebody, please!"

He lugged Yesu around another corner and entered a dense residential section where the connecting apartments created a shadowed canopy. The scents of urine and stock animals permeated the gray stones. Ahead of him, a woman leaned alluringly in a doorway. She had long brown hair and huge blue eyes. Her full lips gleamed with rouge. Dressed in a bright scarlet robe shot through with silver embroidery, her profession wasn't hard to guess. She straightened up, a frown lining her face when she saw them.

"You!" Nathan shouted commandingly. "Is that your home? Open the door."

When she hesitated, Nathan rushed her, shoving her back against the wall with his free hand and hissing, "Do it now! If the decuria following us doesn't kill you, I will!"

She turned hastily and threw open the door. The stale musk of perfume and fornication drifted out. Nathan hauled Yesu inside and gently lowered him to the hard stone floor, then went back and jerked the woman inside before locking and barring the entry.

Hurriedly, Nathan returned to Yesu and carefully rolled him over on his side to check his back wound. The woman threw herself down on the floor beside him and peered at him through eyes enormous with fear.

"Are they after you?"

"I just told you they were," he answered sharply. Removing his dagger, he slit Yesu's robe and peeled the blood-soaked material back. The gaping gash that met his gaze made his knees go weak.

"What did you do?" she demanded.

"I killed a centurion," he said, knowing the whole truth would terrify her so badly she'd turn them in the first chance she got.

A sly cloying smile lit her pretty face. In the almost complete darkness, he could see a glint of amusement in her eyes. "I hope it was that *scortator,* Publius. He's been driving me mad with his slobbering caresses for months."

Nathan's heartbeat throbbed in his ears. "Get me some water and a towel. We have to clean this wound before it festers."

She lunged to her feet and ran for the pitcher beside her bed. Outside, the drumming sound of hooves on stone beat in the air like furious angels' wings. She stopped in mid-step, the pitcher trembling so that it spilled water across the floor. Raucous shouts and curses split the walls to seep into their sanctuary. Nathan held his breath. The woman stood rigidly. Both of them stared at the door as wide-eyed and silent as the dead.

But the soldiers passed by. The crack-thud of their passage echoed down the street until it vanished.

"What's your name, woman?" Nathan breathed.

"Miriam. Miriam of Migdal-Nunaya."

* * *

Council of the Synod of Bishops. Lakeside town of Nicaea, The Year of Gnosis, 4085.

Emperor Constantine rose in his seat, throwing back his red velvet cloak. Tall, with dark hair, he had a hooked nose and powerful eyes. The room quieted as the bishops turned in a wave to hear his words. They looked as worried as a flock of frightened birds. He smiled secretly to himself.

"My most reverend companions," he began, "I am a bishop of internal things. In the civil war of 4084, my military campaign was a crusade against corrupt Christianity. From this day forward, I tell you, my allegiances are to the blessed Teacher of Righteousness. Let no one doubt my resolve to make the Teacher's Truths the Truths of the entire world. For I believe that to change the religion of Byzantium is to change the world, forever and ever. Amen!"

CHAPTER 42

Amirah flexed her bound hands and feet, trying to relieve the ache. Cole had explained in great detail what had happened the night before, but all she remembered were flitting glimpses of a probe chair and a little girl asking: *"Are we finished for today, Magistrate?"* The pieces of the puzzle grew ever more frightening. A hazy picture had started to form: Grandmama screaming at her not to be a pawn; Baruch's notion of a trigger; the terror of the Devouring Creature of Darkness pursuing her; the curious words about the "holy serpent" and her horrifying delusion of being suffocated by the snake. But what did it all mean?

She carefully studied the multicolored computer screens in the oval command cabin. Baruch and Tahn sat riveted to their control consoles, murmuring softly to each other. Cold cups of taza sat languidly beside them; brown drink rings had formed around the lips. Despite their diligence in letting one another sleep as much as possible over the past two days, they both looked dead tired. She suspected they'd each spent most of their "sleeping" time in their quarters running calculations on every possible permutation of strategy. As Tahn scanned his console, his blue-violet eyes gleamed alertly. Baruch had his back to Amirah, so she couldn't see his face, but his blond hair shone darkly with sweat and the muscles of his shoulders bunched anxiously beneath his purple and gray uniform.

"We've got about fifteen minutes," Cole announced. "I think I'll pull out the suits."

"Good. I'll prepare the systems." Baruch spun around in his chair and began inputting data.

Amirah's eyes narrowed when the weapons screen began to pulse green for ready, then the emergency sys-

371

tems kicked on, the ship compartmentalizing to shield each section against decompression. *They expect a fierce battle. Why? Or perhaps they're preparing for the worst, just in case?*

Cole got up from his chair and went to the supplies closet beside Amirah. He gave her only a bare glance as he opened the door and pulled out three suits and helmets, then ransacked the compartment, removing two rifles and four new pistol charge packs.

Grabbing a suit, Cole called, "Jeremiel?"

Baruch turned and Tahn tossed him the garment. He caught it deftly and stood up. Unfastening his belt, he removed his pistols and slipped into the white jumpsuit before pulling his belt around his waist again.

Amirah's nervous gaze slid to Tahn. He stood tall and slim beside her, fastening up his suit. The white fabric shimmered like layers of opalescent satin in the harsh glare of the lustreglobes. Sweat dotted his straight nose. He looked at her and she saw the smooth line of his jaw tighten. The action told her more than he realized. The stakes, whatever they were, were too high for intimacy between them—and he regretted it.

"Cole?" she asked softly. "Why the vacuum suits?"

He slipped each of his pistols from their holsters and slapped in new charges, then he pulled the belt around his waist again. He tucked his Wind River fighting knife in his boot and adjusted the location so it didn't irritate his ankle. He gave her an insolent smile "Jeremiel and I are fussy. We don't even like surprise birthday parties."

He exchanged a grimly amused look with Baruch and it took every ounce of strength Amirah had to suppress the qualm of panic that rose in her. *What the hell's going on?*

"Coordinates for vault exit are in the system, Cole," Baruch informed. "Ready?"

"Just about. Give me another sixty seconds to help Captain Jossel into her suit."

Cole knelt down and removed her hand and ankle restraints. She rubbed her wrists furiously to get the circulation going again, watching him cautiously stand up and step back. Grabbing the last suit, he tossed it to her and quietly instructed, "Better hurry, Captain. You might need that sooner than you think."

Amirah stood on wobbling legs and stepped into the suit, fastening it all the way up. Were they expecting to be fired upon the instant they exited vault? *Who* would be firing? She tucked her long blonde hair into her collar and exhaled unsteadily. Cole observed her nervous movements and his face softened a little.

"Here," he said gently. He handed her a helmet. "Better put this on now, too. The last thing we want is to have you killed accidentally."

She took it from his grasp. "You'd rather have it happen on purpose, right? When it's most advantageous?" She'd meant it as a taunt, but the cold expression on his handsome face made her stammer, "Is–is that what you're—"

"You just tell your people to behave and we won't have any problems."

The helmet in her hand trembled. She almost dropped it. The *Sargonid?* "What do you mean, *my* people?" He didn't answer and a dark impenetrable fear blanketed her. "Cole, is the *Sargonid* out there?"

Tahn put on his helmet, and handed one to Baruch. Amirah stood like a sleepwalker while she watched them. Why wouldn't he tell her? She was impotent. She couldn't possibly affect their plans now! Was he afraid she might try something desperate anyway? *Just like he would have done?*

When Amirah hadn't moved after several moments, Cole came back and gently pushed her into her chair. She roughly shoved his hands away and reattached the restraints herself, fastening them around her ankles first, then her wrists. Cole scrutinized the action, then bent to double-check them. He gently settled her helmet over her head and clamped it down. She heard the muted clicks.

"I'm initiating exit," Baruch said. He hit several patches on his console and leaned back. The luminescent tunnel of yellow formed, wavering like windblown flames around the pointed nose of the fighter.

Amirah longed to scream or lash out in rage, but she only stared, waiting to see if a battle cruiser waited on the other side of vault.

Cole straightened up and caught the look on her face; he stopped. Hesitantly, he leaned forward to gaze through her visor into her anxious eyes.

"Just do what I tell you to," he instructed. "Don't be heroic. I don't want to hurt you, Amirah."

"I don't have a heroic bone in my body, Cole."

He cocked his head disbelievingly. "All those medals are for good looks, huh?"

"Pretty much."

He rose, then, almost as an afterthought, playfully bumped helmets with her before going back to the co-pilot's chair. An age-old symbol of camaraderie in space, the bump made Amirah's throat go tight with the urge to shout or cry out. Why had he done that? *Because he's a good soldier, Amirah—damn good. He knows you're terrified and on the verge of doing something crazy. He's trying to defuse your terror before you lash out. Sure. Right. It's not because he likes you and doesn't want you to feel so alone.*

The rectangular forward screen began to flare with more purple than yellow and the ship lurched when the stars burst to life, streaking the heavens. Amirah frantically searched the blackness, seeking the object of their concern, but she could only make out the known configurations of the Mainz galactic environment.

Tahn leaned sideways, scrutinizing one of the screens above Baruch's head. "On the money, Jeremiel. Good work. ETA is twenty minutes. No other ships on scanners."

Baruch nodded, but the motion reeked of tension so powerful it felt palpable in the narrow command cabin. "Run a gravity wave search. They might still be on their way in."

Cole's fingers danced over the console. "No. Nothing. Looks like . . ." he exhaled a relieved breath, "like maybe we've just got one to face."

"Affirmative. I'm magnifying. Maybe we can tell something from the ship's external appearance."

He input the commands. Through the portal, a battle cruiser appeared, its triangular wings gleaming silver in the pale starlight. The vessel sat quiet and unmoving. All its shields were down. It looked dead.

As they got closer, Amirah could read the numbers,

IOD-45. She fell back against the wall, praying Jason still lived and had organized a countermove. Her gaze riveted to her cruiser. But the longer she stared, the more certain she grew that something strange was happening. She studied the unnatural cant of the ship, the darkened bridge. *What is this, Jason?*

Baruch hit the communications patch, inhaled a deep breath and called, "Fighter *Yesod* to *Sargonid.* Do you read us, Mikael?"

They waited breathlessly, until finally a youthful voice announced, "Yes, Jeremiel. Thank God you're here. We almost lost Engineering yesterday."

Baruch glanced at Tahn, but Cole only glowered uncertainly at the com unit. "We're here, Mikael. Can you open bay twenty-three for us?"

"Hold on."

They all watched, Amirah sitting on the edge of her seat. *Who was Mikael? Mikael . . . Calas? Must be. Jason had captured the youth after all. How had Calas taken over Engineering?*

For another fifteen agonizing minutes, Amirah watched as they sailed in silence for her ship. The bay doors edged open as they approached, revealing a brightly lit expanse of white deck tiles. Baruch piloted the fighter toward the entry and Amirah saw Tahn grind his teeth, eyes squinted.

Abruptly, irrationally, Baruch pounded a fist into the reverse thrust patch on his console. The *Yesod* lurched, throwing Amirah backward so suddenly her helmet banged the wall.

Jeremiel swiveled around in his chair to face Tahn. "She's not ours—if she ever was."

"How do you know?"

Baruch glared out the forward portal at the cruiser. "The sound of Mikael's voice and the cant of the ship. Even on incremental power, Mikael would have had no problem keeping her upright. It's supposed to look like an inexperienced hand is at the helm."

Cole grimaced indecisively, then spun back around to take a hard look at the *Sargonid.* "Yes . . . maybe. This is too perfect. If I'd recaptured my ship and knew I had the chance to nab two top Underground leaders, I'd make it look like there wasn't anybody competent within parsecs."

Tahn leaned back in his chair and Amirah fought to keep her breathing even. Almost as though he sensed her effort, Cole gave her a deadly look. "Well, Amirah, what do you think? Are we flying into a trap?"

She forced a wry smile and shrugged. Tahn smiled back, but the gesture felt like a knife against her throat. While they stared each other down, Baruch accessed the com again. "Mikael, put Yosef on."

A few moments later, a feeble elderly voice responded, "Hello, Jeremiel."

"Hello, Yosef. I'm looking forward to seeing you. Things are not well on Gamant planets around the galaxy and it will be good to see a familiar face."

"What do you mean, things aren't well? Horeb was so isolated we heard very little." The old man's voice quavered.

"We'll discuss it tonight, Yosef. Suffice it to say that I heard from Nelda and the Magistrates have begun a major assault on Hinvoy."

"Nelda?" Yosef asked uncertainly.

"Yes, Zadok's wife."

A long pause ensued. The com unit crackled as though staticky. Baruch and Tahn exchanged a knowing look, as if they suspected Magisterial delaying tactics.

Finally, Yosef's voice came back. "Sorry, Jeremiel, we're having problems here with the communications systems. Zadok's wife has been dead for decades, I don't understand what—"

"Thank you, Yosef. Please hold on."

Baruch hit the patch to turn off the audio and pinioned Tahn with his blue eyes. Cole lifted a hand. "If Yosef had wanted to tip us off about a recent debacle, he could have simply played along."

Jeremiel smoothed a glove over his knee. "If he had a choice. Would he play along if Woloc's holding a gun to Mikael's or Sybil's head?"

Amirah watched the two men for a moment, then shifted to studying her cruiser. If Jason had managed to take the ship back, he'd have certainly set up something exactly like this. For the first time in fifteen years, she sent a prayer to Epagael begging Him to let it work.

"Let's think of something else to ask them," Tahn insisted. "Something more obscure."

Baruch bent over his control console and hit the com patch. "Yosef? Put Sybil on, please."

A long, long wait occurred, so long that Baruch's face contorted. Finally . . .

"Jeremiel?" a frail feminine voice called. "I was down the hall. How are you?"

Baruch tipped his chin toward the ceiling, focusing on the overhead panels. "I'm fine, Sybil. Are you all right?"

"So far. We're waiting for you and Captain Tahn to come and give us a hand. Lieutenant Woloc has attacked us three times. The last one was close. Without the hypi-nitronium vials, I'm sure we would have failed. Uncle Yosef threatened to drop one and Woloc backed off."

Baruch once again searched Tahn's face. Cole shook his head as though to say, "not good enough."

"I understand. Sybil, I need to ask you a question. Do you remember the night you had the nightmare and you came to my room in the subterranean chambers of the Desert Fathers?"

"Yes, Jeremiel." She laughed so sweetly, so fondly, that even Amirah reluctantly smiled. "You patted me to help me go to sleep. I haven't forgotten."

"Tell me again, what was your dream about that night, Sybil?"

A pause. A soft whisper of muted voices.

"I dreamed that my mom was in the Mashiah's palace, up in the light, and my dad was down in the darkness. My mom hunted and hunted for Daddy, but she couldn't find him. I remember in the dream, she was crying all the time. It scared me so badly I dove out of my bed and ran around for twenty minutes in the dark to find your room."

Still holding Tahn's eyes, Baruch replied, "I remember. You felt like ice when you climbed into bed with me. Stand by, Sybil."

Baruch hit the patch again and braced his elbows on his chair arms, steepling his gloved fingers. Inside his visor, Amirah could see that perspiration had glued his blond hair to his cheeks. "No one but Sybil would know that."

"And if they're holding a gun on Mikael?"

"She could lie easily and no one would know."

"Unless"—Tahn whispered ominously—"they have her attached to the probes and are monitoring truth or falsity, while simultaneously holding a gun to Mikael's head. I suspect in that case, she'd tell the truth no matter what it meant for you and me, old friend. How does she sound to you?"

"Within the range of normal, given the tense situation she's been enduring for days."

Cole flopped back into his chair. "Well, what do you think?"

Baruch laced his gloved fingers over his stomach and studied Cole intently. "I say we use Operation Shevirah."

Cole sat forward abruptly, his helmet no more than a foot from Baruch's. "I thought that was a last resort? I lean toward Operation Yacob."

Baruch said through a long exhalation, "In that narrow space, they could cut off the ends of the tube and box us tight with no effort at all."

Cole laughed, a low unpleasant sound. "If Woloc has his ship back, Jeremiel, he's going to box us anyway. He just has to mine all the approaches, get us inside, and we're dead, friend."

"Shevirah's a better plan."

Amirah could hear Cole's rapid breathing hissing through his helmet. Quietly, he informed, "My ardor for mind probes has dwindled over the years, Jeremiel."

"Mine's not exactly zesty, either, but at most, it would be two days' worth. We can hold out for that long."

Baruch glanced at Amirah and cupped a hand to Cole's helmet pickup. He lowered his voice so that she couldn't hear no matter how hard she tried. She caught the words, "Palaia," and "Carey," and "once we're in," then something about someone saying Slothen wanted Mikael badly, but she couldn't make any sense out of the connections. Tahn nodded occasionally, but he grew increasingly nervous as the low interchange continued, his glove tightening more and more over his knee.

Both men eased back into their chairs, gazes impaling each other. They sat like that until Cole vented a loud, "Goddamn it," and began fussing roughly with his helmet. He adjusted and readjusted it, as though his air supply had gotten pinched and he couldn't get quite enough oxygen. Baruch steepled his fingers over the base of his visor and watched.

"Well?" Baruch inquired calmly.

Tahn stopped manipulating his helmet and clenched a fist over his head. He let it hover in the air, as though he desperately wanted to slam it into something, but instead he slowly let it fall to the white control console. "It's insane, Jeremiel."

"Yes."

"It'll never work."

"Probably not."

Cole drummed his fingers manically. "You're supposed to be brilliant, why can't you think of something better?"

The reproachful tone made Baruch smile. "I'm working on it."

Cole's eyes narrowed in disgust. "Oh, I get it. You mean maybe something will come to you as we go along?"

"Hopefully."

"You inspire a lot of confidence, Baruch," Cole noted. He gave Amirah an imploring sideways glance, as though she somehow played a part in this plan. Without losing eye contact with her, he grabbed his taza cup, turned it over and shook out the last drops of brown liquid onto the gray carpet.

Amirah grimaced, seeing them splat to form a grimy starburst. Baruch lifted his brows. When Cole noted their responses, he leaned toward Jeremiel and whispered, "We're not coming back here anyway, are we?"

"Seriously doubtful."

Cole tossed his cup into the corner, listening to it land with a sharp crunching sound. He swung back to his console and hit the com patch, calling, "Mikael, this is Tahn, we're coming in through bay twenty-three. Stay in Engineering. We'll meet you there."

"Affirmative. We'll be waiting."

Amirah let out a long relieved breath as Baruch input the thrust commands and the fighter nosed downward, sliding smoothly toward the landing bay. When they eased inside and settled to the floor, Amirah's heart lurched. She'd been in this bay a hundred times. Two hundred feet square, three Magisterial shuttles sat along its right wall, gleaming like black isosceles triangles. On the other side, supply niches lined the walls.

Cole reached into the island compartment between the pilot's and copilot's seats and drew out a crystal sheet. He resolutely stood up and came across the floor to kneel in front of Amirah.

"Here. You're going to need this." He took the sheet, folded it, and slipped it into the side pocket of her vacuum suit.

"What is it?" she asked.

"A list of all the Magisterial files we're aware of that detail government atrocities against Gamants."

"Why would I want to review them?"

He passed the EM key over her ankle restraints. They broke open into his waiting glove. "You're a decent human being at heart, that's why."

Baruch hit a series of patches on his console and the side door slipped open, revealing the white-tiled bay lit with glaring lustreglobes.

Cole glanced outside and Amirah saw his breathing go shallow. He stood up and pulled out one of his pistols, then, with a medieval flourish, he bowed and presented it to her.

Her eyes darted over his face in confusion. Pillowed on his white glove, the weapon beckoned. "What are you doing, Cole?"

"Saving lives." He shoved the weapon closer, practically under her nose and sighed bleakly when she took it. Both he and Baruch unfastened their belts and let their guns down easy onto the gray carpet.

Amirah stared in utter disbelief.

Cole raised his hands over his head and grinned casually. "Come on, Captain. This ought to get you another Naassene Cross."

As though the words had triggered it, a shudder went through the *Sargonid*. Amirah clutched wildly for one of the wall braces. Her vision clouded, her balance wavered. For two haunting seconds the universe seemed to spin with no orientation. Everything went hazy, images jumping in and fading away at the same time, like standing on the canvas of a surreal painting when the artist splattered it with the brightest of colors. Then it stopped.

Baruch gave Tahn a look that made Amirah's blood

turn to ice. "Just like twelve years ago on the *Hoyer,* remember? It was like the very fabric of space heaved."

Tahn pulled himself straight. "I remember. *Phase change.*" In a low foreboding voice, he asked, "What the hell are we into?"

* * *

Fragrant river-scented breezes tousled Rachel's black hair. She huddled on a barren red hilltop, her face buried in the green robe over her drawn-up knees. The universe trembled around her.

"It's working, God," she whispered. "Can you feel it? *Can you?*"

And from somewhere far ahead of her in time and a long distance away, she *felt* Aktariel lift his hands to cover his ears so he couldn't hear the screams that vibrated through the fabric of the Void.

Calmly, she lifted her head and gazed at the goats grazing placidly in the green valley below. A few mud houses dotted the shores of the river. An old woman sat combing wool on her front step, laughing at the children frolicking in the dirt street.

Rachel let their happiness soak into her very tissues. Maybe, just maybe, Nathan could. . . .

In a burst of black and gold, Aktariel ran out of the whirling vortex, sprinting across the hilltop toward her. His blue cloak billowed out behind him. "Rachel? Rachel! Do you know what you've done?"

She serenely buried her face in her robe again, nuzzling her cheek against the soft silk. Like a wildfire, he'd said, it could *catch* across the voids. *Yes* . . . The heat from the blazing fire already roasted her soul. She could sense the strands flaming, shaking loose, reweaving.

As his sandaled feet pounded closer, Rachel lifted her head. He stopped, fists clenched tightly at his sides. He gazed down at her through bittersweet amber eyes, eyes that seemed to bear the entire weight of universal suffering in their gleaming depths.

"I've laid the first stone for the foundation of the Kingdom, Aktariel. That's what I've done."

CHAPTER 43

Jason grabbed his stomach when the *Sargonid* stopped shaking and the dizzying torrent of disorientation passed. He felt ill, his belly threatening to empty itself. He struggled to separate the dim lustreglobes from the blur of purple uniforms in Engineering.

"What the hell was that?" Rad demanded. His flat features seemed two-dimensional.

Jason shook his head emphatically and rushed back to bend over the visual com that monitored the landing bay. Had it been some Underground trick? No, the fighter still sat like a docile silver spear point. He whirled and waved at the four Gamant prisoners, "Get them out of here! Everybody else get into position for the ambush!"

Technicians scurried to inject the Gamants with sedatives to make them more manageable, then disconnected the probe units from their heads. Sybil Calas thrashed about wildly, but the men seemed quiet enough. Jason strode into the center of the room and stared up, surveying the preparations. Soldiers got into position on all three levels of Engineering, checking their rifles, licking lips nervously. A round of giddy laughter echoed. Tension hummed. Every man and woman aboard had dreamed of capturing Jeremiel Baruch and Cole Tahn. Long ago the Magistrates had ordered that both men be probed until their brains yielded no further information. The process would leave them vegetables, but after all the innocent people the Gamant Underground had slaughtered in the past quarter of a century, they deserved whatever they got. Tahn! The most infamous traitor in Magisterial history. If Jason could capture the man, the Magistrates might award him his own ship and then he wouldn't have to ache. . . .

"Lieutenant?" Engineer Rad said. Disbelief tinged his

voice. He peered steadily at the bay monitor. "You'd better take a look at this."

Jason ran back and braced a hand on the control console, gazing down. His mouth gaped as he watched two tall men, both in vacuum suits, step out of the fighter, their hands up. A smaller figure—a woman?—stepped out behind them, a pistol in her glove. She marched the men ahead of her to the bay exit and hit the wall com unit.

"Lieutenant Woloc?" Amirah's strong voice echoed all through the ship.

A cheer went up from the soldiers in Engineering, loud and exultant. Disbelieving voices chanted, "The captain captured Baruch and Tahn by herself!" "Good God, can you believe it? Jossel can do anything!"

Jason pounded the response patch. "Amirah! You're alive!"

"Alive and very tired," she responded wearily. "Could you and a security team meet me in the hallway and take these two prisoners off my hands? I could use a good dinner and ten hours of sleep."

"Yes, ma'am, Captain," he answered formally, but a softness invaded his voice. "We're on our way."

He cut the connection and ordered, "Sergeant Qery, gather your team and follow me."

"We're ready, sir," Qery announced.

Jason strode hurriedly out of Engineering and down the hall, pistol in his hand. His chest ached with emotion that he couldn't show. In the past few days, he'd worried so much about her safety that now he longed to run to her to make certain she really was all right, that no one had hurt her. But he couldn't do that. Duty obliged him to proceed in a cautious professional manner. He had to treat her return with the reserved joy that he'd accord any other shipmate.

They rounded a corner, heading down another long white hall to crowd into the transport tube. The tube descended smoothly, but for a moment, Jason felt as though a jolt of electricity had gone through him. He stiffened his knees. A nightmare feeling of futility and frustrated longing swept him up. *It would all begin again, now. All over again.* Anguish wailed through his heart like a wounded animal crying out in fear at the sight of the hunter.

When everything had settled down he'd . . . Yes, yes, he promised himself, he'd reapply for transfer. *This time, Amirah, please, let me go.*

The tube stopped and Qery and his team flooded out, dispersing down the corridor, lining the walls of the final approach. Jason brought up the rear. He gripped his pistol in a clammy palm before edging out in front and striding forward to peer around the corner.

Amirah and her two prisoners had removed their helmets. Blonde waves fluffed in luxurious disarray about her shoulders. Her turquoise eyes glistened with a combination of suspicion and curiosity. Baruch stood calmly, his face blank. But Tahn paced erratically, starting and stopping, whispering gruffly to Baruch, who simply nodded in response.

Jason signaled Qery to come forward and a sudden torrent of men washed around him. Charging down the hall, the security team slammed Baruch and Tahn up against the walls and searched them. Amirah stepped back and Jason hurried into the corridor. When she saw him, such relief came over her face that a fire of yearning raced through him.

"Good to see you looking so healthy, Captain," he said as he came up alongside her.

"You, too, Lieutenant."

She swayed slightly on her feet and Jason lunged to grab her elbow supportively. Her scent enveloped him; she smelled of sweat and some faint fragrance, like flowers after a rainstorm.

Quietly, he asked, "Are you all right?"

"Just exhausted."

"I'm sure." He squeezed her arm tenderly, more for himself than for her. Being this close salved some of his own desperate need to hold her. He cast a glance at Baruch and Tahn and his back crawled. Tahn stood watching him intently. When Jason lifted a condemning brow, Tahn gave him stare for stare, but an odd, almost pitying light glistened in the traitor's eyes. Jason reluctantly released Amirah's arm. "I can't wait to hear the story of how you captured the two most infamous desperadoes in the galaxy."

Her gaze went to Tahn—searching. Tahn stood passively as the security team clapped EM restraints on his wrists, but a bright savage glitter lit his eyes. Jason glanced back and forth between them. They seemed to be asking each other harsh, if silent, questions. Tahn broke the tug-of-war when he threw Amirah a smile so cavalier it felt like a slap in the face. She dropped her gaze and responded to Jason's earlier query, "I can't wait to tell you. Could we get together over drinks tonight? My cabin. Say 19:00 hours?"

Nervousness tightened his throat. "Yes, I'd like that. Why don't you go and get some rest. I'll send a dattran to Palaia telling them you're all right and that we have custody of Baruch and Tahn, then I'll get us into light vault and talk to Doctor Hilberg about setting up the mind probes so we can—"

"No!" Amirah blurted. Shock strained her beautiful face. "No, just . . . just put them in the brig until I can think more about it."

Jason's brows drew together. "Whatever you say, but it's standard operating procedure when you capture—"

"I'm well aware of that, Lieutenant," she said so sharply that the security team jerked their heads up, looking from their captain to their first lieutenant.

Jason spread his arms apologetically. "I meant no disrespect, Captain."

And then Amirah did something she'd never done. She frowned in self-reproach and walked forward to put a fond hand on Jason's shoulder. Her touch comforted him immeasurably.

"I'm very tired, Jason. Forgive me. I need to rest."

"I understand. I'll take care of the ship. Go and get some sleep. I'll see you tonight."

She patted his hand before walking away down the hall.

As the security team started dragging Tahn in the opposite direction, he struggled, shouting, "Amirah? *Amirah?*"

Jason opened his mouth to tell the prisoner to shut up, but he noticed how his captain's steps faltered. She stopped dead in her tracks as though she'd run into a brick wall. She didn't turn, but she lifted her face toward

the ceiling and seemed to be waging some inner battle.
"What is it, Cole?"

Startled at the first name usage, Jason stood
speechless.

In the gentlest voice he'd ever heard, Tahn said, "If
you need . . . anything . . . just send for me. *Understand?*"

Jason snorted incredulously at the implication that
Amirah needed anyone! But he stifled his outburst when
she turned. A worried expression ravaged her face.

She nodded at Tahn. "I understand. But I'm home
now, Cole. I'll be all right." She turned and marched
around the corner.

Jason tried to connect the sequence of events to figure
out what they'd been discussing, but gave up. "Qery,"
he ordered, "get the prisoners to the brig."

"Aye, sir." Qery waved a hand and his security team
lowered their rifles into firing position and herded the
prisoners down the hall. Jason stayed where he was,
watching their retreating backs. Baruch said something
inaudible and Tahn chuckled insolently. Then Tahn quietly added, "Well, at least we resolved our problem
about breaking through the defense net."

Jason frowned. An ominous feeling of disquiet plagued
him as he headed for the bridge.

Amirah entered her cabin and slumped back against
the wall. Her white vacuum suit felt heavy, pressing the
air out of her lungs. She bashed a fist into the patch to
close the door. A queasy sensation grew in her stomach.
Why had Tahn and Baruch given themselves up to her?
If they'd truly suspected that Jason had recaptured the
cruiser, they could have simply flown away. Why hadn't
they? Baruch had pushed for the surrender. Why?
Gamants were such strange. . . .

"*You're* a Gamant, goddamn you!"

She clenched her fists as she gazed around her cabin.
The familiarity soothed her a little. In the ten by ten foot
cubicle, a table and four chairs sat on her right. A small
bookcase depressed the wall over it. In the rear, her bed
crowded the narrow space, the white sheets and gray
blanket still rumpled—as she'd left them. A lattice
divider separated her bed from the main part of the

cabin. On the shelves that adorned the divider, precious knickknacks from all around the galaxy glimmered: tiny ruby-studded tapestries from Giclas 7, petite porcelain cups and saucers from Sculptor 3, rainbow wine glasses from Hevron on Old Earth. A pain lodged in her throat when she looked at them. Her grandmother had given them to her, so long ago she barely remembered the year. But she recalled the tender, loving look on Sefer's face when she'd helped Amirah wrap them in bright yellow paper to put in her hope chest.

Feebly, she repeated, "You're a Gamant, Amirah. The granddaughter of a great Gamant hero."

Madly, she flung off her vacuum suit and purple uniform, throwing them into a pile by her table. Bewildered, she put her hands to her head, squeezing, trying desperately to force the sound of Cole's voice out of her brain: *Someday you'll have to stop running away from yourself.*

She hurried into the shower and stood beneath the hot spray for a blessed twenty minutes, concentrating on the fragrant vanilla scent of her favorite soap. When she stepped out, her body tingled. She felt a little better. She fluffed her blonde hair and wandered naked around her cabin.

Being home engendered a deep feeling of warmth and security. The *Sargonid* throbbed with soundless virility, holding her like a lover. Her ship had always been her mate—for better or worse, in sickness and in health. She reached out and stroked the wall, projecting all the hope and affection she could, hoping it sank into the very hull.

"Now, get some rest. You're going to need it."

She walked to her bed and climbed in, tugging the covers up around her throat. Valiantly, she fought to sleep, but she kept tossing and turning, her thoughts returning to the cryptic conversation aboard the fighter. What had Baruch meant when he talked about going to Palaia? What could two, *two*, men possibly hope to do to help Gamant civilization on such a strictly guarded facility? They couldn't break through Palaia's security system—*even if they were free!* Which obviously they weren't.

After two more hours of endless flailing, she sat up. The lustreglobe over the table sparked in response to her movements, throwing a dim silver hue over the cabin.

Groggily, she got to her feet and crossed her cabin to retrieve her vacuum suit. Reaching into the pocket, she jerked out the sheet Cole had given her and squinted at the file listings. She'd expected five or six, not seventy-seven. Scrutinizing the titles, she selected a series on Tikkun that she hadn't read on the fighter.

Going to her com unit on the desk by her bed, she slumped down into the chair and input the request, directly accessing the main computer on Palaia. Minutes later, the com answered tersely: *"Files sealed. Please input clandestine authorization code."*

She railed, "What?"

Simple neuro files required a captain's security clearance to gain entry? She slammed a palm on the desk and input the numerical and alphabetical sequence. Out of fear, she used up half an hour with a request that all the files be transferred to the *Sargonid*'s data banks.

She hesitated, her fingers poised over the key patches. A wash of adrenaline made her breathing go shallow. She lowered her hands and requested all the data on *Amirah Malkenu Jossel, Captain, Serial Number: AZIZ-9151666*. Her hands quaked when a flood of information streamed in. Did they know so much about her? *How much?* Over four hundred files worth.

Pulling her blanket off her bed, she draped it over her bare shoulders and snuggled back in her chair, trying to decide which files to read first.

* * *

"If they're not here," Rudy demanded through gritted teeth, "where are they?" He held his injured leg as he made his way across the bridge of the *Orphica* to slump down into the navigation chair.

The ten other officers monitoring the consoles or conducting repairs on various units, stared worriedly at him.

Merle braced an elbow on the arm of her command chair and stared at the Mainz system stars depicted on the forward screen. Two dozen starsails and an odd number of freighters had begun arriving minutes ago. They dotted the black velvet blanket of space like fireflies. But no other cruisers had come through yet. "If they're not here, they're at Palaia."

Rudy felt like a hard fist had slammed him in the stomach. He hunched forward over the nav console and shook his head miserably. "What the hell are we going to do? If the Magistrates ambushed us at Horeb, Merle, the same is certainly waiting for Jeremiel and Cole at Palaia. Even if they managed to capture the *Sargonid*—"

Merle jerked up a silencing hand. Her eyes widened and Rudy spun to stare at the screen. Two cruisers streaked space like blue-violet tubes.

"Ours, Kopal?"

Rudy swiftly input the request into his com. "Yes," he sighed in relief. "Mass readings suggest the *Zilpah* and *Hammadi*."

Merle sank back in her chair, a stony look on her round face. "Kopal, let's find out their status. If they're both functional, maybe we can load all the surviving refugees onto one ship and dispatch it to Shyr. Then—"

"Yes!" Rudy shouted. He slammed an eager fist into his console. "With two cruisers and some starsails and freighters, we just damned well might be able to do it, Merle! Let's go for it!"

CHAPTER 44

Jason scrutinized himself in the mirror over the table. Straightening his purple uniform one last time, he combed his hair, retrieved the "confidential" dattran, books, and the necklace they'd taken from their Gamant prisoners, and stepped out into the hallway, briskly walking toward Amirah's cabin.

When he reached it, he lifted his hand and let it hover over the entry patch. Blood surged in his ears. She'd only invited him to her cabin once before, and it had devastated his personal life. Yet, he'd craved this—a chance to be alone with her again.

He hit the patch and called, "Amirah? It's Jason."

"Come in."

The door slipped open and he stepped inside. Oil lamps lit the room, scenting the air with the fragrance of rain-drenched forests. As his eyes adjusted, he saw Amirah standing over the com unit on her desk. Her uniform shone blackly in the dim light, but her hair shimmered like golden waves of silk. She held a half-empty glass of amber liquid in her hand. She turned to look at him and he tensed. She appeared sodden with fatigue. Her eyes looked more red than turquoise. Hadn't she slept in the past eight hours? He'd deliberately held back the spectacular news from Slothen, because he'd assumed she'd be resting. Shadows spawned by the lamps accentuated the hollows of her cheeks, bringing into prominence her button nose and heart-shaped mouth.

As she started across the floor, she swayed slightly and his brows lowered. Had she drunk so much, or was it just the exhaustion taking its toll? The latter, he assured himself.

"Please sit down, Jason," she said and gestured to the table. "What can I get you to drink?"

"Brandy." he said as he slid into a chair. He set the books and necklace down on the table. "We took these from the prisoners. I haven't had a chance to look at them, I thought you might—"

"We're in vault?"

"Yes, and have been for four hours. Our ETA at Palaia is forty hours."

She nodded and went to the refrigeration chest at the foot of her bed, removing a faceted crystal bottle and a glass. She brought them back to the table, along with her own glass. As she poured his full, he studied the way her hand trembled.

"Amirah? Are you all right? Did you get any sleep?"

She dropped into the chair opposite him. "No."

He glanced at her com unit, seeing the screen full of words. "You've been studying?"

"Yes, but let's not discuss it—yet. Tell me how the ship is. Did you contact Palaia?"

A surge of pride and happiness expanded his breast. He leaned across the table and smiled. "I did. When I first told Slothen about you capturing Baruch and Tahn, I thought he was going to faint. But he got hold of himself and acted almost giddy."

"Really?" She lifted her glass and drained it dry. "What did he say?"

Jason sifted through his pocket and found the dattran. He reverently handed it across the table and waited with quiet esteem. "Slothen wanted to make it public immediately," he informed her. "But I told him I thought it would be better to wait until you'd had time to absorb it."

Amirah's flesh paled so that her freckles stood out across her nose. She looked as stunned and offended as if she'd just been convicted of a crime she hadn't committed. In a violent move, she crumpled the sheet and threw it on the floor, then lurched to her feet to pace across the gray carpet.

Appalled by her response, Jason's mouth dropped open. "What's wrong? I thought you'd be so delighted you'd dance on the table. Only ten other people *in history* have been awarded the Magisterial Medal of Honor. I'm so proud of you I could burst!"

Her eyes flared. "Are you?"

"Yes!"

"Well, then, let me explain the glorious details of how I captured the two most wanted criminals in the galaxy."

He braced his elbows on the table and sipped his brandy. Though her face bore her typical captain's stoic mask, he could see her fists shaking. What had happened during her capture to tear her apart so? "I'd hoped you would."

She strode over to stand directly in front of him. Golden lamp glow danced across her captain's bars, catching in the silver threads adorning her epaulets. The diabolical gleam that flickered in her eyes made him flinch. "*They gave themselves up to me.* Tahn very politely handed me a pistol, then he and Baruch dropped their gunbelts and raised their hands over their heads."

For a moment, he was too shocked to respond. "They put up no resistance?"

"None."

"I don't understand."

"I don't either." The lamp spat and wavered, shimmering with a flaxen radiance over her taut face. "There were a thousand things they could have done. They could have used me as a bargaining chip to exchange for Calas, or kept a weapon and opened fire when you rounded the corner. They could have brought in explosives, mined the corridors and blown up half the ship. Their actions were totally irrational."

Jason smoothed his fingers over the beads of moisture that had formed on his cool glass. Amirah's confused voice lashed at him like a storm wind.

"Jason," she said adamantly. "Have you ever heard about Creighton's brain experiments on Gamants on Tikkun twelve years ago?"

"No."

Without taking her eyes off him, she lifted an arm and swung it around to point at her glowing com screen. "Slothen authorized the surgical mutilation of subjects, then ordered them 'disposed' of. *He murdered innocent people.*"

Jason's mind sought to find some framework to place the data into—but couldn't. He took another drink of his brandy. "What do you mean 'murdered'? The government would never—"

"The file on my screen now delineates the series of orders received by Major Johannes Lichtner, Block 10's commander, over a period of approximately sixteen months."

She drew a breath and met his gaze squarely. The wary look she gave him made his stomach roil. Did she fear he'd retreat to the classic "loyal officer" routine? No, she couldn't possibly. They'd seen too much horror together over the past few years to believe the quaint propaganda about the near-divine perfection of the Magistrates. But—murder? No, in her weariness she must have misunderstood the documents.

He stood up and extended a hand toward her com. "May I read what you've found?"

She gazed at him with such genuine gratitude that he had to fight his hands. They wanted to reach out and pull her into his arms to assure her he was, above all else, on *her* side.

"Yes," she said. "Thank you."

He went across the room and dropped into her desk chair. The opening line read: *GENERAL ORDERS RE-GARDING TIKKUN RESEARCH CENTER: Opened the 10th of Shebat, 5413. Closed the 15th of Nisan, 5414.*

Amirah brought both their glasses and the bottle of brandy over. She placed them on the desk, refilled their goblets and backed away with hers, sinking down on the edge of her disheveled bed.

"Thank you," Jason said and smiled.

She nodded obligingly and returned his smile, but a dark worry filled her eyes.

He forcibly tugged his gaze back to the green letters on the screen and concentrated. *General Order No. 1: Major Johannes Lichtner is ordered to assist, in any way requested, the needs of the neurophysiological team under the command of Colonel Jonathan Creighton for the entire duration of this project.*

"That's strange," Jason murmured.

"You mean the blanket authorization to do whatever Creighton said?"

"Yes." He swiveled around in the chair. "Have you ever seen an order before that didn't limit the authority of the officers involved based upon constantly updated progress reports?"

She took a long swallow of her brandy and hunched forward to brace her elbows on her knees. "No. I didn't know such orders were possible."

"Neither did I." He squinted back at the screen, considering the implications. "But they're convenient. In the event that something politically unpalatable occurs, such 'I wash my hands' orders give the Magistrates the ability to maintain they were not informed about the operations and therefore aren't responsible for any debacles."

"Keep reading, Jason. I *need* your input."

Bravely, he reached out and put a hand on her shoulder. Some of the tension went out of her back, her muscles relaxing beneath his fingers. He squeezed gently. "Do you want to try to sleep while I read? I have to be back on the bridge in five hours, but I'll be here until then, if you wake and want to talk."

Her usually hard expression softened, as though he'd just offered to guard her back against a thousand enemy soldiers. He smiled warmly and she reached up to grasp his hand. "Thank you. I think I will."

He winked confidently and watched her curl into a fetal position, facing him. Her hair spread like a pale veil of cornsilk across her white pillowcase. She closed her eyes and in only a few minutes, her breathing slowed to the deep rhythms of sleep. For the first time in their lives together, he let his gaze drift openly over the perfect contours of her body, lingering on the swell of her breasts and her long legs. The *Steel Woman*, as her crew affectionately called her, looked so vulnerable, so patently frail, that he had trouble turning back to his file.

But turn back he did.

He accessed the second file on Tikkun. A holo film taken in the camp began to roll, introducing the file. Jason's muscles contracted at the sickeningly sweet sound of the narrator's voice which explained, *"Eliminating useless subjects."* On the screen, a line of fifty or more people labored digging a deep ditch. Misty rain drenched the air, glistening like dew in the hair of the little children who struggled to lift their shovels high enough to throw dirt over the lip of the channel. A major, from his uniform, strode up, smiled smugly into the holo camera, and haughtily surveyed the channel, then ordered the people out.

"Hurry it up!" He shouted. *"You filthy Gamant swine are about to learn a new lesson in Magisterial mercy!"*

He lined them all up in front of the ditch, telling them to raise their hands over their heads and turn to face the deep gash in the crimson soil. People reluctantly complied, gazing fearfully over their shoulders. Ten soldiers marched up to stand behind them, braced their rifles, and opened fire. Jason twitched, watching the violet beams slash down mercilessly through men, women, and children. Screams rode the rain-soaked wind. A few brave souls tried to run, leaping their dead compatriots only to be sliced in half by soldiers further down the line. Most of the victims fell into the ditch, but those who didn't were casually pushed in by huge mechanical scoops.

Jason stopped the film and propped a fist on Amirah's desk.

"I can't believe . . ."

He shook himself out of his shock and entered the command to continue the film. The scene changed. A little boy dressed in a pancake hat and short pants stood with his hands up, tears streaking his five- or six-year-old face. He screamed, "No! No!" over and over as two guards took turns slamming him in the face and stomach with their rifle butts—cruel laughter split the sunny afternoon.

Jason clamped his jaw hard, hate rising like a hot wall of water to drown him. He pounded the patch to fast-forward the film. He stopped it randomly and gazed down on a group of emaciated, dead children lying in the rain. Their blood flowed in tiny channels down a slope toward a series of gray windowless buildings. The narrator noted simply, *"Useless subjects about to be buried."*

Hatred brought tears to Jason's eyes. He rubbed a callused palm over his face and glanced back at Amirah. She slept soundly, though her eyelids spasmed with dreams. Had she seen this file? He prayed she wasn't dreaming of the pitiful faces of the children.

Bracing himself, he forced his hand forward to hit the patch to continue the file.

Two hours later, he pushed away from the desk and stared agonizingly at Amirah's slumbering form. She hadn't even changed position.

He dropped his face into his hands and rubbed his forehead. A wretched headache pressed behind his eyes. But inside . . . inside he seethed. He felt betrayed by his own "beneficent" government—a ruling force that could at will suspend its own regulations, reinterpret policy to make it fit situational needs and discard its ironclad Ethics Directive without so much as blinking.

No wonder Amirah had been distraught. His own mind couldn't adjust to the brutal reality. He desperately wished Amirah were up so he could share his feelings, but he couldn't bear to wake her. Her beautiful face looked so peaceful, and she needed the rest so badly.

He toyed with the edge of the desk, thinking about the implications of the studies—about Gamant brain structure and Magisterial cruelty. His eyes darted over the room and he noticed, by accident, the folded crystal sheet that lay tucked beneath the corner of her com unit. Only the glittering white tip showed. Gingerly, he pulled it out and unfolded it, reading the awesome list of files. He glanced back up at the screen. Were they all like this one?

He swiveled back to the com and requested the file on the planet Jumes.

Three more hours swept by—hours of torment and despair that made him sick to his stomach. The clandestine project claimed to have isolated a genetic anomaly which caused dangerous abnormalities in the basal ganglia. In response to the discovery, fifteen thousand Gamant women had been forcibly ushered into the research installation and sterilized. And when the populace found out and rose up like a huge deadly beast in revolt . . . *Cole Tahn, then captain of the* Hoyer *had been ordered to scorch the planet.* Tahn had obediently complied. A level one attack, the entire central portion of Jumes had been devastated.

"How could you obey those orders, Tahn?" he whispered tautly to himself. "Didn't you know what was going on?"

Jason fumbled with his empty brandy glass, turning it so the lamplight danced in the facets. Is that why Tahn had committed treason? Had he finally realized what the government was doing and couldn't bear it?

Jason ran a silent calculation in his mind. How many

deaths had Tahn been responsible for because he loyally followed orders? A half million? A million? Had he finally balked at the level of punishment the Magistrates continually ordered him to inflict on innocent civilians?

A sudden sympathy for the "traitor" thumped in Jason's breast. If he'd been in Tahn's place, he might have done the same thing.

"Why don't cruiser officers ever research the history of the planets they're ordered to destroy?"

But he knew the answer. No one had the time. The Magistrates kept battle cruiser crews so busy they couldn't spare an extra day to sift through the vast array of clandestine files, or to decipher the infinite number of security classifications which made those files nearly impossible to find in the ocean of records.

He gazed at the com screen through half-lidded eyes. These files, for example, were not classified under the easy-to-find planet names—nor were they cross-referenced. If a captain didn't know the data would be under the obscure heading of: *Neurobiological anomalies in inferior species,* he or she would never think to pull up the file.

Jason swiveled around and curiously examined Amirah's serene and beautiful features. The soft lamplight landed like a golden scarf across her upper torso, playing wildly in the braid on her purple sleeves. A deep admiration and respect for her warmed him. How had she guessed where the Magistrates had hidden the information?

Out of curiosity, he instructed the com unit to list all the files she'd requested from Palaia this evening. A torrent appeared, many with strange foreign names, some with special code accesses required. He wondered what mysteries they held. He tried to access a file called: *Fideles*, but to no avail. He couldn't even get the com to respond. Next he tapped in a request for: *Peccavi*. Nothing. Searching through the array of peculiar files with classified codes, he at random selected: *Raziel*.

A brilliant flash lit the screen. Jason jumped. His heart pounded. The com flared a red warning and demanded: *IDENTIFY REQUESTER.*

He took a deep breath to steady himself and typed:

JASON MICHAEL WOLOC, FIRST LIEUTENANT:
EIN-9171676.

STATE REASON FOR REQUEST?

Jason scowled. "What the hell does that mean?" He
input: ON NEED TO KNOW BASIS—SECURITY OF
SARGONID.

STATE LEVEL OF EMERGENCY?

Jason subvocally cursed the machine. The com wanted
him to delineate whether it was a minor emergency: level
1, or extreme danger: level 5. No matter what he
answered, if he gained access as a result, the ship would
automatically log the entire com dialogue and shoot it to
Palaia the instant they exited vault. All level 5 com
entries went directly to Slothen's office.

*Of course, there are so many level 5 reports these days
that Slothen might not review this one for weeks.*

He took a deep breath and held it, bolstering his courage, then input: LEVEL 5.

The com fluttered and the red warning light faded. In
bold blue letters the com requested: *DEFINE STATUS
OF CAPTAIN AMIRAH M. JOSSEL? MENTALLY
INCOMPETENT OR DEAD?*

He glanced surreptitiously at her. The blue light from
the com cast an azure halo over her face. She did look
pretty pale. "You're being an idiot," he whispered to
himself. "This could get you court-martialed or worse."
He typed: DEAD.

The com fluttered and went blank, returning him to
the basic menu of files.

He shook his head incredulously. "That's a 'Request
Denied,' if I ever saw one."

He considered the ramifications, then began again.
This time when the com asked him to define Amirah's
status, he typed: MENTALLY INCOMPETENT.

CAPTAIN PRESENT IN ROOM?

AFFIRMATIVE.

*ENTER EMERGENCY BYPASS COMMAND
CODE.*

"Oh, this is too much!" He had to bypass the entire
com security system to gain entry? What sort of information did this file contain? Only captains possessed the
bypass code, but when Amirah had disappeared, he'd

been temporarily granted the privilege. He input: 81672-11673-ALKUM.

CODE ACCEPTED. INPUT CLANDESTINE CROSS-REFERENCE AND PROCEED.

"Clandestine cross-reference? Who the hell knows that?"

He abandoned the file and felt better. Since he hadn't actually gained access, the ship would discount the entry attempt.

Jason quietly got to his feet and retrieved Amirah's blanket from the floor. He longed to stay, but he'd pushed his time limit already, he had to get back to the bridge. He spread the blanket over Amirah as gently as he could, trying not to wake her.

Before he left, he found a crystal sheet and scribbled:

Please review the file on Jumes and numbers 2-3 on Tikkun. I'm on duty on the bridge in five minutes, but I'd like to talk to you when you wake up.

Thanks.
Jason

On the way out, he checked the thermostat. She always complained about being cold on the bridge. He threw her a fond look. More than once, he'd turned up the heat there, too—and heard about it in no uncertain terms from every male officer on duty.

He altered the temperature to a warm sixty-five and hit the patch to exit into the hallway.

* * *

Emon huddled in the warm petrolon guts of Satellite 4, gazing up at the tiny rip in the fabric overhead. The gray system of artificial tunnels formed a web around him. Soldiers filled the maze, their whispering echoing like the hissing of serpents in the confined spaces.

Emon glanced at Arikha. The little woman crouched beside him in the darkness, her dark hair gleaming as blackly as old blood around her pale face. She peered out at the night-clad plains where enemy campfires blazed. Beyond, General Ornias' military headquarters glittered, its mirrored buildings reflecting the streetlights so that it flared like a roaring wildfire.

"Arikha," Emon whispered. He reached over and gripped her frail wrist. "You don't have to do this anymore. We're close now. The gate to the dungeon is just over the next hill." He gestured to Palaia, floating in space beyond. "It's too dangerous for you to go out there!"

Arikha turned so that her face was silhouetted against the background of stars. Her eyes possessed an eerie calm. "I have to, Emon. God protects me. I'm not afraid."

Emon grunted something profane and pleaded, "Arikha, listen to me. We've scouted the area as best we can, but we're not really sure where that next tunnel comes up on the surface. It could be right in the middle of some blue beast's tent." He tightened his grip. "Don't do it. Not tonight. I have a bad feeling about this."

Arikha smiled and Emon felt that the sun had risen to shed its grace on him. His soul seemed to swell beneath that strong gaze. "Arikha, please. Not tonight."

"The Mashiah's coming, Emon. We have to prepare the way. No matter what happens to me, you have to lead our forces. You can do it, Emon. Just wait for the sign."

"What sign?"

Arikha's fingers trembled. She closed them into a fist and Emon could see the terrible fear on her face. "The skies, Emon. Look to the skies. Legend says the ship has the sacred shape. You have to wait until you see it to attack. And right now, tonight, we have to push these Magisterial dogs back, so that when the time is right, we can kill them all. I have to go." She patted Emon's hand and clasped her rifle before edging forward and scrambling out through the rent.

"Arikha, wait!"

Emon grabbed for her robe, but she slipped away. Emon watched her walk like a dark specter out into the midst of the enemy camp. Arikha's powerful voice wafted on the cool midnight wind, rising to roll over the camp. *"Now! Hurry! The Kingdom of Heaven has come!"*

Hearing her, Giclasian beasts rose from where they

warmed themselves by the fires, looming like huge black squid against the sky. A dark muttering of intergalactic lingua speared the night. Soldiers shouted and raced for her.

Arikha ran, preaching, leading her forces in a desperate battle to push the Giclasians back a few hundred feet off the hilltop.

Emon lifted his hand and furiously waved his soldiers forward. "Come on," he called. "Let's hit them hard this time. Harder than we've ever hit them! Arikha's got them running for us. Let's go!"

A wave of humanity crawled forward. They poured out over the face of the false alien world, firing blindly into the torrent of blue bodies that ran toward them.

Emon raced across the camp. All around him, screams rose to wails. The night ran with blood, both blue and red. Streams of it soaked Emon's boots and brown livery until it stuck like glue to his chilled flesh.

He fought and hacked his way throughout the night, until his arms ached and his head reeled. But they'd broken the resistance. Enemy soldiers flooded toward the military headquarters, their purple uniforms glowing in the gray rays of dawn.

Emon locked his trembling knees and squinted at the bloody battlefield. Most of his forces had already fled back into the hive of the substructure. Only a few hearty men and women wandered the abandoned encampment, collecting rifles, and charge packs. One man tugged relentlessly on the boots on a fallen comrade, tears streaming down his face.

But they had no choice. Supplies, including clothing, were in great demand. They could trust nothing the Magistrates dropped now. The food packages that had fallen from the sky weeks ago had been laced with some potent poison. The poor souls who'd consumed it, against his pleas, had died horribly. If only Arikha had been here then. She'd have. . . .

"Arikha?"

He ran for the nearest opening, shoving people out of the way to get down into the darkness. "Arikha? You! Yes, you. Have you seen Anpin? Where is she?"

The man's eyes went wide. "I haven't seen her."

Emon spun around and waved his arms frantically.

"Hurry. Everyone, start searching. We have to find Arikha!"

A new tidal wave of bodies rushed toward him, flowing down and around, people shouting and passing messages through the maze.

Arikha squirmed to tilt her head to watch the sunrise. The huge ruby ball lifted through a haze of lemon-colored mist over the distant Horns of the Calf on Palaia. The rocky prongs spiked the sky this morning—like a promise.

Arikha smiled.

The broken bodies of hundreds lay in twisted piles near her. The cardamom scent of Giclasian blood spiced the moist dawn air. From where she lay, she could see the hideous face of the beast who'd shot her in the early hours. Dead, the blue monster still seemed to grimace at her.

Arikha laughed—a dry rasping sound. She'd lain for hours feeling her blood soak into the wet dirt. She knew the wound in her back was fatal for it had severed her spine, low, near the base. She couldn't move her legs.

But it was all right. She . . .

"There's one!" a rough Giclasian voice shouted.

Arikha struggled to turn her head. A huge blue beast trudged toward her, sidestepping ruined tents and mounds of earth kicked up by mortar explosions. His azure face and ruby red mouth shone ghastly gray in the early morning light.

Arikha smiled up weakly. Behind the enemy soldier, the ball of the sun shaded pink, like a rose petal opening in the yellow mist. Another man, a human, strode up. And she knew him instantly. Dressed in his general's uniform, his cold lime green eyes bored into Arikha. She gathered all of her energy and spat at him.

"Yes," the general observed. "That's her." He waved over one of the Giclasian beasts. "Take her to Palaia. Creighton and Mundus will be waiting."

Arikha's body went limp as she felt cold alien hands slip beneath her shoulders and knees.

CHAPTER 45

Nathan stood in the cool shadows of the crowded court-yard before the gray stone Tower of Phaesel. Three entire legions of bronze-suited cavalrymen pranced around the area, spitting at the crowd or calling obscenities. Nathan kept his right hand hidden, tucked beneath his brown tunic, tightly gripping his knife. This day—*this blazingly hot day of Nisan the fourteenth!*—the fate of Yisroel would be decided.

Wisps of brown hair had fluttered lose from his raw-hide tie to dance over his face. He brushed them away, tucking them behind his ears. Hoots and shouts tore the world around him. The stench of dirty sweating bodies rode the wind like the breath of carrion birds. A thousand must have packed the Praetorium. Twenty feet in front of Nathan, the purple curtain which shrouded the door to the tower hung closed. A dais had been set up for the famed trial which had brought people flocking in from all over the region.

Nathan's whole body chilled with fear. He looked around him, noting the positions of his fellow zealots. The twelve of them formed a rough circle around the perimeter of the crowd. Most of his comrades lounged lazily back against the low stone walls near the numerous exits, making jokes with the yokels. He gave a slight nod to each as their glances met. Yeshwah, their leader and friend, had been captured the day before, tried and condemned for the murder of a Roman centurion. But today, on this searing spring day—the new Procurator, Herod Antipas, who'd been pulled from the province of Galeel to replace the murdered Lucius Pontius in Yudea, would have to make a choice. It was an established custom to free one condemned prisoner on the eve of Pesach.

Nathan and his comrades waited—for if Antipas made the wrong choice, they'd certainly kill everyone present if necessary to free their friend.

"Please Adonai," he prayed quietly. "Let Herod throw Yeshwah into our arms and we'll be on our way forever. I *hate* this cursed Romanized city. We'll never come back!"

The crowd shifted, moaning and shaking fists as one of the lay members of the Sanhedrin, Yohannan ben Zakkai, dressed all in white, marched haughtily into the court. He had a sharp nose and ears that stuck out. His black hair was primly knotted at the base of his skull. Guards dragged two men behind him, Ben Panthera—bastard son of a Roman soldier—and Yeshwah. Nathan's heart stilled as he gazed upon his lifelong friend. Yesu had been beaten badly. His right eye was a massive blue mound and dried blood still clotted the long strands of dark hair that draped over his dirty black livery. Yeshwah's good eye roamed the crowd, noting the positions of each of his men. A bare smile of gratitude and relief touched his bruised mouth. Desperation filled Nathan as he met Yesu's imploring gaze—he straightened, lifting his chin high in a silent promise he knew his friend would understand. Yeshwah nodded and Nathan's fingers tightened around the worn hilt of his knife.

They've hurt you, Yeshwah. They'll pay! I promise.

On this day, the Eve of Pesach, not a single pious man or woman walked the streets. They were all home, sacrificing lambs, making preparations for the great holy celebration which would begin at nightfall. Only the most filthy of the society's dregs populated the sun-drenched courtyard: slinking beasts from the Decapolis, Greek-speaking Syrians, some Canaanites and Idumaeans and a few, very few, derelict Yehudim.

Ben Zakkai, swine that he was, knelt on the dais and waited. In a few moments, the hideously fat figure of Herod pushed through the purple velvet curtains shrouding the door. A prolonged gasp went up from the crowd. Dressed in a regal purple robe which pulled tightly around his bulk, he looked like an obscenity. Another man, tall and rail thin with red hair, pushed through behind him. Nathan recognized the man, Herod's interpreter, Caius Jamaeus. Antipas waddled out onto the dais, sneering disdainfully at the groaning crowd.

"Great Epitropos, *Vale*, Caesar to be!" Ben Zakkai patronized. "I bring you the indictment for Yeshwah ben Yosef, who is blasphemously called the Mashiah."

The howling rabble's anger burst wide. Men shoved each other and women screeched. Everywhere, raised fists slashed the dry searing air. Herod slumped into his chair and took the rolled up scroll. He waved angrily to his centurions who dotted the walls, the gardens, the courtyard itself, and they rode forward on their horses, swinging their swords, shouting, "Shut up, you imbeciles! Shut up before we kill you all for the filth you are!"

The crowd quieted. Dark eyes went wide, staring expectantly at the dais and Antipas. But Nathan's eyes remained upon Yeshwah. His friend staggered, his knees too weak to hold him up. Two of the Syrian menservants rushed forward and gripped his elbows to support him.

Nathan's soul ached. He wanted to scramble up on that stage instantly and free his friend. But he'd be dead before he'd gone three paces. He forced his feet to be still. He had to wait . . . wait. . . .

Herod grumbled something inaudible to his interpreter and Jamaeus took the scroll from his hand and read it aloud. The indictment accused Yeshwah ben Yosef—known throughout the countryside as Ben Panthera—of being guilty of the crime of sedition, of stirring the people up against the Roman rulers, and of claiming to be a king, which constituted treason.

Herod shifted his bulk to a more comfortable position in his chair. Three servants with palm leaf fans assiduously blew his scraggly brown hair out of place. Herod lifted an authoritative fat hand and fluttered it about to quiet the crowd, then he bellowed, "You! Yes, you *amme kaddishe elyonim*, God's chosen bastards," he chuckled disdainfully. "Look at these men." He pointed to the two prisoners.

The crowd quieted and looked, their eyes almost bugging out as they compared Ben Panthera and Yeshwah. Panthera, dressed in white, gazed down over the crowd with a serene detachment, as though already forgiving them for condemning him to death—*mad, utterly mad*, Nathan thought. Yeshwah had his teeth gritted. His eyes darted with fiery contempt over everything Roman: Herod, the guards, even Ben Zakkai—a gutless romanized Yehud!

Nathan filled his lungs to bursting and watched in a frenzy, waiting, waiting. Matthya had edged in closer to Yeshwah, standing only ten feet away.

Herod lifted the scroll and slashed the air with it. "You know the way it works," he cried. "I give you your choice. Who shall I free?" A cruel grin came over his face. He turned to Ben Panthera. "*Yeshwah ben Yosef*— called Ben Panthera by you jealous fools—who declares himself Mashiah and King," his bloated hand moved down. "*Or Yeshwah Bar Abbas?*"

The crowd surged forward in a foul-smelling wave and had to be beaten back by the Roman soldiers. "We want Bar Abbas!" the assembly screamed and shrieked, shaking their fists. "*Bar Abbas! Bar Abbas! Bar Abbas!*"

Nathan almost wept with gratitude. He screamed along with them and carefully checked where his men were. They'd moved in, closer to the dais, just in case they needed to spring up on that platform and slit a few throats to free their friend. Yeshwah braced his legs to hold himself up. His eyes met Nathan's and they exchanged a silent communication of overwhelming relief.

Though the sun had been blightingly hot, a sudden wall of dark clouds rolled over Yerushalaim, blotting out all light. A subdued charcoal hue dimmed the world. Nathan licked his chapped lips, looking around uneasily. He felt almost as though God were watching, orchestrating this bestial proceeding.

Herod screamed shrilly, "And what shall I do with this madman who calls himself the Mashiah?" He thrust out an arm at Panthera.

The roar of the crowd was deafening. "*Crucify him! Crucify him! Crucify him!*"

Herod's extended hand trembled and his eyes grew wide with fear. Nathan blinked hard, shaking his head when he saw a dark shadow loom on the wall behind Herod. It seemed to swell, forming into a gigantic monster. Nathan caught his breath and fell back a step, his hand clutching his knife hilt as he glanced around—no one but him seemed to see it! No one screamed. No one pointed. The crowd's gaze was riveted solely on Herod.

For a long, inexplicable moment, Herod let his fist hover in the air, as though frozen in time. He cocked his head. Nathan tensed. *What's happening?* A soft whimper rippled through the assembly, then they went silent again.

The shadow rose over Antipas' fat head and dispersed down through the assembly like a watery plague of night. It seemed to linger around Nathan and he thought he felt . . . *what?* . . . some sense of love and concern. Then it vanished.

Herod suddenly lurched to his feet to sway like a drunken man. He stared wildly at his prisoners. Throwing out his barrel chest, he glared at Ben Panthera. "Are you a King?" he shouted.

Panthera gazed at him in a kindly way. "You say so."

Herod took a stumbling step forward, his eyes blazing with an unholy light. "What does that mean?" he shouted. He gestured to the frenzied crowd. "*They* say so, not *me!*"

Ben Panthera only bowed his head in silence.

Half-staggering, Herod went to glare up into the face of Yeshwah Bar Abbas. In a whisper that carried like smoke on the wind, he hissed, "Are *you* a King?"

Yeshwah's face was as still as stone when he replied, "No."

"Are you the Mashiah?"

"Every man who finds Truth is a mashiah."

Herod threw back his hideous head and laughed raucously, holding his blubbery belly. "Are you saying that every man has it in him to be the hand of God?"

Yeshwah straightened slowly. The hot wind blew his dark hair in veils over his face. "Oh, yes. Every one to the very last."

The smile on Herod's face faded like dust in the wind. He stared solemnly at Yeshwah. "What," he asked so softly he could scarcely be heard, "is truth?"

Yeshwah's nostrils flared. He moved his weight to his other foot. Boldly and loudly he answered, "Everyone who isn't deaf knows the Truth when he hears it! I came to bear witness to the Truth!"

Pride and fear welled in Nathan. But what was Yeshwah doing, shouting the teachings of the Qumran Dawn Bathers? These poor ignorant barbarians couldn't understand the depth of what he was saying! Why did he try? It just might get him killed!

Herod frowned and a look of pain and anguish came over his face. He stepped forward, getting closer to Yeshwah. *"What is . . . truth?"* he demanded again.

Yeshwah struggled to throw off the hands of the servants who held him. When they released him, he spread his legs and clenched his fists at his sides, daring the world to contradict him. "Truth?" he said in an orator's voice, "is Knowledge and Light! No one who follows your Law will be able to raise his eyes toward the Truth. It is impossible to serve two masters. Flee the Darkness! Look to the Light!"

Nathan's hands shook. The old *Paquid* had told them that, drummed it into their hard heads a thousand times sitting on the sunny shores of the Sea of Arabah—Truth was Knowledge. Knowledge was Light. Light was God. *Truth was God.* Yeshwah had just told all the impious swine in the audience to seek God. But none would understand. None!

Herod shuddered violently and gasped, "You, Yeshwah Bar Abbas, are an offensive rock in the way of Truth. You're a stumbling stone and a snare for all the citizens of Yerushalaim!"

Yesu's chin squared, but he didn't respond.

Herod's bloated face flushed. He swung around to the crowd, glaring through mad eyes. One of his quaking hands shot out to point at the prisoners. "Who," he croaked, "has committed the blasphemous, treasonous crime of *mesith*, claiming to have the powers of God?"

The crowd milled, weighing Ben Panthera's cryptic words about being a King and Yeshwah's words about Truth and Light.

A short, pudgy little Rab stepped forward, waving both fists. "Crucify Panthera!" he raged. "If you don't, you're no friend of Caesar's!"

Herod's flabby jaw shook. "You little worm! You despicable pious idiot! You *dare* suggest that I might betray the great and noble Caesar?" He whirled around and glowered at the prisoners, then his hand shot out like a dagger at Yesu. "Guards! Take this godforsaken philosopher, Yeshwah Bar Abbas, out and crucify him."

A ragged cry was torn from Nathan's throat. He ripped

his knife from its sheath and charged forward, slashing and hacking, fighting to get to Yesu.

Four guards in bronze breastplates ran forward to grab Yesu. Herod hurriedly staggered back through the purple curtains and the crowd went wild. Roman soldiers spurred their horses forward, trampling anyone who didn't move, to form a rearing, snorting barricade in front of the dais. Horses bashed with their hooves while soldiers chopped with their swords, murdering anyone who dared get close.

Nathan struggled against the wall of fleeing bodies that pushed around him. He saw two of his men go down beneath the swooping silver blades of the centurions—*and he saw Yesu hauled away, screaming, into the palace.*

"Oh, Lord, no, no!"

Matthya came rushing through the flailing crowd, shoving people out of his way to get to Nathan. He grabbed Nathan's arm. *"Wait!"* he shouted through gritted teeth. "Wait. We'll have another chance. At the crucifixion hill, Gulgolet. If we try now, they'll kill us all!"

They scrambled away, lashing out with fists and feet to get free. Nathan panted, "Did you see it, Matthya? The Darkness that hovered over Antipas' head?"

Matthya stared at him, his brown eyes glistening. "No, Nathan. No, I didn't see it. But I believe you. Today, Herod marks himself as everything dark in the world."

* * *

Ramadhan, Outside of Mecca, during the year of the Teacher, 4370.

Muhammed lay asleep in a cool cave in the mountains, dreaming of his beautiful wife, Khadija, when a voice intruded.

"Recite!" it commanded.

He frowned in his sleep, not understanding. "Recite what?"

"Recite in the name of the Pure Light!"

"But . . . what is that? God?"

"Abandon the search for God and the Creation! They are evil. Look for the Light by taking yourself as the starting point. Learn what it is within you that makes

everything its own and says, 'My God, my mind, my thought, my soul, my body.' Learn the sources of sorrow—and you will find the Light in yourself. Listen to these words, pass them down to the children that they may become Light in the Life of the Silence . . ."

When Muhammed awoke, he found the Teachings inscribed on his heart. He set to writing them down as fast as he could.

CHAPTER 46

Amirah propped herself against the lattice divider in her cabin and stared down at the remaining scenes in the Tikkun 5 file. She held a cold cup of taza in her numb hands. Jason sat in her desk chair, a hand cradling his chin, his face contorted.

When the file ended, Jason reached up and turned off the com unit. Amirah noticed that his hand quaked as he dropped it to her paper-littered desk. "I can't believe it. That file was worse than all the others combined."

"That's why I wanted you to see it."

Jason got up from the desk and went to slump into a chair at her table. He shoved the old books she'd been reading earlier out of the way. "Those were no neuro-physiological experiments, Amirah. It was genocide. All those 'eliminations' were authorized by the Magistrates." He rapped his knuckles quietly on the black petrolon top and shook his head. "The documents are clear. There's no getting out of it."

She felt so numb she could barely feel at all. Yet her mind and eyes had gone startlingly clear. Her cabin shimmered like cut crystal, every angle unsettlingly sharp; the chiaroscuro of light and shadow had a geometric quality. She'd skimmed every file that Cole had given her the name for, and discovered that the Gamant Project had begun long ago—almost forty years back. That was why her father had been so careful—so brutal in his insistence that no one know she was a Gamant. He'd tried to protect her. He'd worked in the records office. *Surely he must have known what the government was doing.*

Known . . . and done nothing.

Just as she was doing now.

She lifted her cup to take a sip, but it wobbled so badly she lowered it again and clutched it in both hands.

"Amirah?" Jason said quietly. "What are we going to do?"

"I don't know."

He slouched back in his chair. "I think . . ." He waved a hand futilely. "We should file ethics charges against the officers involved. The Magistrates themselves, if we have to!"

She fumbled with her cup. Tahn's words twisted in her stomach. . . . *I'd rather sell my soul to Aktariel than bargain with the Magistrates. At least I'd know the game plan with the Archdeceiver. The government changes policies so swiftly one can never be sure.*

Amirah took the chair beside Jason and gazed long and hard into his hazel eyes. All the love and respect he felt for her shone openly. She gave him a soft look. It was the first time he'd ever let himself be vulnerable with her and she wasn't certain how to handle it. She'd never been certain how to handle it—with anyone. "I don't know what I would have done without you the past five years, Jason. You've always been there when I needed you."

His eyes went over her face minutely. "I'll always be there—if you want me to be."

An ache built in her chest, for him and for her, for a relationship that could never be. If she filed ethics charges against the government, the Magistrates would conduct an in-depth study of Amirah Jossel, just as they had of Cole Tahn, and they'd discover her Gamant heritage. And she'd no longer be captain of the *Sargonid*. And God only knew what they'd do to Jason for being her accomplice.

Amirah stood up and went to the center of her cabin "Jason, I don't know what I'm going to do yet, but I don't want you involved."

"I'm already involved, Amirah. I can't just forget those files."

"No, I know that, I–I meant that whatever I do, I want you safe. I don't want you or the *Sargonid* contaminated by my actions. I need to think more about this. Then you and I, we'll talk again. I have to see Tahn first."

Jason got up from his chair and moved to stand very close behind her. "You can't bring him to your cabin. It

would look suspicious. Why don't you meet him in one
of the lower lounges? I'll escort him, if that meets your
approval."

"It does. Thank you, Jason."

The terrible weight of the future pressed down on her
and she started to shake visibly. She fought to stop the
tremor, but couldn't. Jason got a horrified look on his
face.

She held up a hand to let him know she was all right.
"It's just . . . just the frustration."

"I know. I feel it, too."

He swiftly stepped forward and took her in his arms.
She rubbed his broad back gently in gratitude. Only
Jason, who had known her in the worst of times, and
with whom she'd routinely argued the concepts of "right"
and "wrong" could understand how empty and frightened she felt now.

After several seconds, Jason boldly tightened his grip
around her. She considered backing away, but she was
too tired, and his arms felt so good, so strong—not a
fortress like Cole's arms, but soothing just the same. She
forced her thoughts away from Tahn and how deeply
she'd come to care about him. If she thought about that
tonight, it would tear her apart. When Jason leaned
down to kiss her, Amirah found herself kissing him back.
She felt too much gratitude for his support and understanding to tell him this was dangerous or that they had
no future together, for they might have no future at all.
After watching the atrocities on the holos, the latter
seemed most likely.

He kissed her very tenderly at first, as though afraid
she might pull away, but as the seconds swept by his lips
grew harder, more insistent. She felt the muscles of his
thighs pressing against hers and a sweet sense of oblivion
encompassed her. She let herself go, reveling in his
caresses until her body flamed and she found herself
responding hungrily. She pulled him tightly against her.

"Oh, Amirah," he whispered. "I love you. I'm sorry.
I know it makes things harder. But I—"

She covered his lips with hers, halting the words as she
reached up and started to unfasten his uniform shirt. The
thick mat of light brown hair on his chest brushed against
her fingers as she pulled the purple fabric back and sank

against his bare chest. "Jason, for tonight, lets pretend there's no *Sargonid,* no government, no Gamants. Just you and me, alone in a meadow somewhere high in the mountains."

He nuzzled his cheek against her hair. "That won't be difficult for me, Amirah. I've been dreaming it for over a year."

His muscles swelled against the fabric of his uniform as he swung her off her feet and into his arms, carrying her across the room to her bed.

Jason woke when Amirah rolled over onto her back. He yawned and blinked at the dark ceiling. Only the amber light from the bedside com unit lit the room, silhouetting the table and chairs and throwing their strange shadows across the far wall. Amirah whispered inaudibly, dreaming. He listened and smiled. *So you talk in your sleep? I'd like to get used to hearing that.* She shifted and groggily grabbed for the sheet, pulling it up over her bare breasts, then she lowered her arm and her fingers moved across the blanket, seeking the feel of his flesh. When she touched his forearm, she squeezed it weakly and relaxed again. Her hair tumbled across the pillow they shared. Jason lifted a lock and brushed it over his face.

The past year had been so agonizing that he could barely believe he was really here in her cabin. He felt as though a deep and aching wound had at last healed and he could breathe freely again without his chest constricting in pain. Tenderly, he touched her shoulder and whispered, "I love you, Amirah." He knew she couldn't hear, but he'd wanted to tell her for so long that just saying the words roused joy in him.

She moved slightly and muttered something incomprehensible. Then she said the word "sick," and a soft series of sounds escaped her parted lips, as though she might be crying.

Jason frowned and rolled onto his side. He touched her cheek. "Amirah?" he murmured. "You're dreaming."

"Sefer?" she whispered thickly. "Grandmama? Where are you. . . . Sefer Raziel? Grandmama. . . ."

"It's me, Amirah."

Her voice drifted into nothingness and she fell back into a deep sleep. Jason smiled fondly, but his expression turned stern almost immediately. Raziel. *Sefer?* It might be. A hot tide flooded his system. He carefully slid out of bed without waking Amirah and pulled on his uniform pants. Going to her com unit, he sat down and brought up the "Raziel" file again.

He went through the entire routine and when the com directed:

INPUT CLANDESTINE CROSS-REFERENCE AND PROCEED.

He typed: *SEFER.*

The screen instantly changed. Colors flickered. A holo began.

Jason eased back in the chair and folded his arms over his naked chest, watching.

A bright room appeared, a little girl slumping sideways in a probe chair. It had to be Amirah. Even at such a young age he'd recognize those dazzling turquoise eyes. Magistrate Slothen paced in front of her, four of his six legs carrying him across the floor.

The audio came up and Jason quickly reached over to turn it down. But Amirah seemed to hear. She made a soft sound and her hands started twitching on top of her gray blanket. Jason looked back to the holo. The hands of the little girl in the chair twitched, too.

Intrigued, he braced an elbow on the desk and turned the com screen slightly to the right, so he could watch the little girl and Amirah simultaneously. His Amirah seemed to be living the episode. When the child wrung her hands nervously, Amirah flinched. When the child cried out as the old woman was shoved through the door, Amirah moaned.

Jason's eyes shifted back and forth, watching both, listening in growing panic to the audio portion. *What the hell was Slothen doing?*

When the little girl's eyes went empty and she began struggling frantically with the old woman, Jason suddenly understood. Young Amirah saw something much different happening in the room than Sefer Raziel did. *Programmed.* He forced a swallow down his dust dry throat.

Fear soured in his belly. Did Slothen do this to all his top officers—or just to Amirah Jossel? The very thought made him go glacially cold inside. Every officer was mandated to undergo a psych evaluation annually. What did those neurobiologists do to them when they were under the probes?

On the bed beside him, his captain thrashed weakly, uttering soft suffocating sounds. Then she went stone still.

Jason looked back to the holo and saw Slothen enter the room and hand the child a pistol. In horror, he studied the way young Amirah lifted the weapon and aimed it like a trained war veteran.

Slothen's words about serpents mystified Jason, but he grasped the import when the child screamed and fell to the floor. *Part of the programming. But what's it mean? Where's the real life referent? There was always a referent.*

Then, in the midst of the fight, the child lifted the pistol . . .

Amirah sat bolt upright in bed.

Jason whirled to stare. Tangled blonde hair created a thick web over her face.

He jerked at the sound of the shot.

Amirah dove for him, knocking him out of the desk chair and shrieking like a madwoman. He hit the floor hard, struggling to throw her off without hurting her. She kicked and punched insanely, and *inexpertly*, screaming in a child's voice, *"No! No! NO! Grandmama?"*

Twisting out of his grip, she scrambled across the floor. *"No! Magistrate, no! Not my grandmama! NO, MAGISTRATE, PLEASE!"*

"Amirah!" Jason shouted.

He ran across the floor, trying to pick her up, but she fought him wildly, hysterically, clawing at his face and arms until blood ran down his hands. "Amirah! It's Jason! Wake up. You're aboard the *Sargonid*. You're not on Palaia Station. *Wake up!*"

She screamed unintelligibly and lunged. Jason blocked a punch aimed at his throat and grabbed her shoulders, then threw her sideways and rolled over on top of her to straddle her naked body. "Amirah? It's me, Jason! Do you hear me?"

Amirah sobbed, eyes wide and glazed with utter terror. Her limbs flailed like a dying spider's.

"Amirah," he said as calmly as he could. "Are you all right?"

After several minutes, her tears stopped, but her body still spasmed all over. In a husky voice, she whispered, "Jason? Get Tahn."

CHAPTER 47

Carey walked slowly across the seventh heaven, Arabot.
Michael had passed them hurriedly, which had shocked
Zadok to his bones. He panted along beside her, pushing
beyond his elderly endurance to hurry to the throne of
God. Grass clung to his brown robe from all the rest
stops they'd made because he could go no farther. Sunset
blazed like amethyst fire through the drifting clouds.
Cool grass stood tall and fragrant, lining the dirt path in
absinthe green walls.

Carey shortened her stride to match Zadok's and
walked in silence, listening to the birds in the trees. Their
melodious songs trilled through the coolness of the evening. The old patriarch had been giving her morose and
pitying looks for the past half mile and she couldn't
understand why. In a few more hours they'd reach the
throne of God and all the mysteries she'd ever enter-
tained would be answered—maybe. *If Epagael was
indeed God.*

They climbed a hill and emerged into a shadow-dappled vineyard filled with row after row of lush red grapes
on thick tangles of green vines. A tangy sweetness filled
the air, suffusing everything, the scattered trees dotting
the vineyard, the clouds shading crimson overhead, the
snowy mountain peaks in the distance.

"Carey? I've been wondering," Zadok called gravely,
"what will you do if you can't go back?"

She regarded him speculatively. "What do you mean?"

He reached out to link his arm comfortingly through
hers. "I mean what will you do if the Magistrates have
killed your body and you've no receptacle to return to?"

Strange that she'd never considered that possibility.
Somehow, she'd thought that if Aktariel specifically sent
her to heaven to talk to Epagael that she—like Zadok a

century ago—would be returned to reveal God's words to the Underground to help them stay alive. Why had she assumed that? Maybe her only duty was to go and enrage God and His actions thereafter would achieve Aktariel's desired effect? Maybe Aktariel didn't need her back in her universe. . . .

Carey clutched Zadok's arm tightly and continued through the vineyard.

A poignant hunger for Jeremiel welled up. Years began to drop away . . . the red grapes faded, blurring softly into red holly berries circling Pesach punch bowls. She could hear the gay holiday laughter as she and Jeremiel walked arm-in-arm amid the trees on Shaare. The white sunlight blazed in Jeremiel's blond hair. People danced around them, singing and shouting in joy. Jeremiel's deep voice soothed as he hugged her against him. *"I love you so much,"* he'd whispered into her ear. *"I can't remember a time when I didn't love you."* The ironic clashing of pistols against legs sounded as soldiers veered around them. No one went unarmed, not even on a holy day. She could hear her own careless laughter, feel her heart near to bursting with love for this tall, broad-shouldered man she'd tried to kill so many times in her life. As though to exacerbate the pain of her memories, old friends, men and women she'd loved and respected, came marching back, smiling and jeering as though they'd never been blown to bits in a hundred desperate battles: Phil Cohen grinned at her, telling a crude joke; Rich Macey threw her a disgusted look from across the bridge; and there was a soft touch and a blustering voice that was Cole's.

Carey's throat went tight. Would there be no more times like that? Would she never again be able to stand beside the people she loved?

"I don't know, Zadok," she answered.

They came to the end of the vineyard and entered an open meadow. Carey stopped in mid-stride. An intense electromagnetic aura filled this field. It made her hair stand on end. Wind swept through the wildflowers.

"What is this?" she asked.

Zadok's eyes widened. "The presence of Epagael. We're close." He pointed to the next swell in the land.

"Right over that hill is the seventh crystal palace of God."

Carey released his arm and broke into a trot. Auburn hair swirled over her face. When she reached the top, she stopped. At the foot of the snow-capped blue mountains, the seventh crystal palace sat like a sculpted work of art. Four towers jutted up into the sunset clouds, reflecting a rainbow of colors. A flock of round-faced cherubim laughed and tugged at each other's silver robes as they jauntily flew around the palace's turrets in a game of hide-and-seek. Wheels of fire swooped and soared at them, teasing playfully. And through all the magnificent beauty a stunning harmony of song rose and fell like the rush of waves on an ocean. It came from nowhere, everywhere, sweeping the land like a magic symphony.

The door to the palace opened and an angel stepped out. Clad in a cadmium yellow robe with a garish purple sash, he put a hand up to shield his eyes from the fading rays of sunset and looked in her direction. Amber curls hung down to his shoulders. His body glowed so brilliantly, it caused a fluttering golden halo to dance over the faceted surface of the palace. He lowered his hand and leaned lazily against the shimmering wall of the crystal palace. A smile curled his lips.

"Carey Halloway, isn't it?" he called. *"I thought you'd never get here."*

"Anapiel," she whispered to herself. She'd read about him in a hundred sacred Gamant religious treatises—the guardian of the final approach to God. The angel of the River of Fire.

Anapiel laughed softly, but it echoed from every tree and blade of grass. *"Yes, Carey. Come. Let's talk about your universe. Baruch and Tahn will be very glad to know you've finally arrived. They're not doing so well. In fact, they're on the brink of the Abyss."* He laughed again, low and cold, a sound that turned her blood to ice.

She lunged forward, racing down the hill with all her strength.

CHAPTER 48

Cole slouched over the table on the far side of the brig. He couldn't sleep. Even the vaguest effort made him angry with himself since he still hadn't the slightest notion what they were going to do once they got to Palaia.

On the far side of the white tiled room, Jeremiel lounged back in a chair, his eyes preoccupied, weaving strategy, no doubt—but they certainly couldn't discuss it here where every breath they took was recorded. Baruch looked dead tired; dark splotches stained the skin beneath his eyes and his blond hair hung in a stringy mass over his forehead. Everyone else slept in their narrow bunks. Mikael and Sybil huddled in each other's arms. Brigs were not designed for comfort, but the young couple seemed to be doing okay. Twenty beds slatted the aft wall and four tables with four chairs each lined the starboard. A drink dispenser stood like a silver trash receptacle in the center of the room. No other piece of furniture or adornment existed, except the chronometer that flashed 02:30 in blue over the door.

Cole clenched a fist and threw a quiet taunt out to Jeremiel. "You damn well ought to be sleeping. You've probably got twenty hours before doomsday."

Baruch shook his head mildly. "I've got it all figured out. It looks more like twenty-four."

"Yeah? Well, good, I feel better knowing it's a full day."

Cole absently fingered the too-tight cuff on the tan jumpsuit they'd brought him. When they'd roughly thrown him through the light-barred door, he'd immediately headed for the shower. The endless stream of hot water had revived him. In the Underground, they constantly attempted to save water, which meant that three-minute showers had become standard. The luxury of standing for fifteen and washing four times felt like a gift from God. He squinted back at Baruch. "You've got it figured out, huh?"

Jeremiel's blue eyes glittered. "I think so."

Goddamn, if we could only discuss it! "No *deus ex machina* endings, right? No bolts of lightning coming out of nowhere to destroy our enemies? I'm a pagan, remember."

"No lightning," Baruch promised. "What have you been thinking about?"

"Me?" Cole hunched farther over the table to loudly whisper, "The sound of the waves lapping against Charon's boat."

Baruch bowed his head to hide a smile. "I don't think. . . ."

Jeremiel's words faded as voices drifted through the door. They both looked up. The light bars vanished in a flash of gold, leaving the exit open. Alarm warmed Cole's veins at the sight of Jason Woloc. The young officer stood rigidly, his hands behind his back, while he gave clipped orders to the security staff, guarding the door. One sergeant quietly questioned him, obviously uneasy with the orders Woloc had issued.

Woloc said something terse and the sergeant saluted stiffly and backed away. Two purple and gray suited corporals entered the room and strode directly to Cole.

"Captain Tahn," the red-haired corporal asked. "Please come with us."

"What for?"

"Lieutenant Woloc wants to speak to you."

"About what?"

The corporal pulled his pistol and commanded, "Now."

Cole resentfully walked across the floor, his gaze never leaving Woloc. When he exited through the door into the crowded corridor, he stood awkwardly, waiting for instructions. Probes? Is that why the lieutenant had come to personally escort him—he'd talked Amirah into following standard procedures for handling enemy captives?

Tahn took a deep breath and glared because it made him feel better. Woloc met his harsh gaze almost frantically; something strange shone behind his eyes—curious, frightened.

"What's this all about, Lieutenant?" Tahn ventured.

Woloc pulled his pistol, aimed it expertly at Cole's broad chest, and responded, "Please march straight ahead, Captain."

"I'm marching."

Cole picked up his pace. Only Woloc followed him. No security team joined them. Cole scrutinized each intersecting corridor, waiting for the hidden soldiers that had to be monitoring the halls as an extra precaution.

When they reached the transport tube and stepped inside, Woloc hit the patch for level two and stared probingly at Cole as they ascended.

Conversationally, Cole remarked, "How's your crew, Lieutenant? Any signs of post-invasion disorientation?"

Woloc braced a shoulder against the wall. "Tell me something, Tahn? Do you know about these seizures? Is that why she called for you?"

A knot pulled tight in Cole's stomach. *Amirah* . . . "Yes, where is she?"

"Her cabin. That's where we're going."

"How is she?"

Woloc shook his head and let out a bewildered breath. "I don't know. I can't get her up off the floor."

Cole looked him over in detail. Woloc was almost shaking himself. His hair was matted to his head by sweat. "What triggered the seizure?"

Woloc pulled himself straight. "I'm not at liberty to say. That's classified—"

"Damn it, Woloc!" Cole shouted in rage. "Give me something to work with. I can't . . ."

The tube halted with a feathery touch and the door slipped back. Cole exited into the hall and Woloc followed.

"What cabin is it, Woloc?"

"210."

Cole picked up his feet and ran, heedless of the weapon Woloc held. He heard the lieutenant's steps pounding behind him. He veered around a corner and dashed headlong down the long white corridor. No one else walked the passageways. Had Woloc had the foresight to order them cleared so no one would see Cole go into Jossel's cabin? *A fine young officer, indeed.* Cole slid

to a stop in front of her cabin and struck the entry patch.
The door slid back.

Cole stepped inside and went to kneel by Amirah. She
lay in the middle of the floor, a gray blanket thrown
carelessly over her. Woloc entered and the door closed.

In the near darkness, Cole could tell that beneath the
blanket she was naked. He glanced at Woloc, and
noticed the lieutenant's uniform shirt was tucked haphazardly into his pants. Woloc's face tightened in defense,
as though he saw the line of Cole's thoughts. Not that
Cole was thinking anything particularly, except maybe
wondering why Amirah asked for him when she had
someone she trusted more closer at hand.

Cole sat on the floor and folded the blanket around
Amirah, then gently lifted her into his lap. She lay
limply, silently, her head against the shoulder of his tan
jumpsuit. She seemed tired to her bones, bled dry of
every ounce of vitality.

"Amirah?" Cole called. "Talk to me. Are you here?
Or somewhere else?"

As though barely able to get the energy, she murmured, "Cole, they made me kill her. . . . Slothen did."

"Who?"

Her body quaked uncontrollably and Cole held her
more tightly, crushing her securely against his chest.
"Who, Amirah?"

"Grandmama," she mouthed it more than spoke it.

Cole peered down at her haunted eyes. She appeared
to be staring back in time to that terrible day years ago,
but experiencing it as though it had happened only
moments before. What had occurred here tonight to
make her recall that? Woloc must have tripped the switch
somehow. Cole's thoughts wandered down unpleasant
pathways, wondering if Slothen would use a sexual cue?
He might. A chill empty feeling invaded Cole's gut. Jeremiel's notions about Jossel seemed even more likely now.
Sefer Raziel had vanished after her contacts on Rusel 3
claimed that Magisterial soldiers came to herd her and
Amirah into a ship and take them to Palaia. What had
Slothen done? Programmed Amirah and then tested his
trigger on Raziel? Who better to use than Amirah's own
beloved grandmother? If she could kill Raziel, she could
kill anyone. But *who* was Slothen's target?

"Lieutenant," Cole said amiably to Woloc. "The captain's all right now. Could you pull a robe out of her closet for her? She and I need to do some serious talking and I suspect she'd rather be warm for the duration."

"Yes."

While Woloc sprinted across the room, Cole called, "Amirah? Can you stand up?"

No response.

"Amirah?" He urgently put a hand under her chin, turning her beautiful face up. She appeared catatonic, as though her brain had simply shut off. "Amirah? Can you hear me?"

She didn't even blink. He smoothed blonde tangles back away from her cheeks and patted her hair. *Lord, what now? Is this part of the programming? A safety mechanism to keep her from lashing out at the government if she ever discovered the truth?* His stomach roiled. "Hold on, Captain. This won't take long."

Woloc hastily went through the uniforms and off-duty wear in the closet to find a magenta colored robe with tiny bands of white Orillian lace sewn over the bodice. He touched the garment almost reverently as he pulled it from the hanger. Cole watched the action with mild interest. Woloc walked back and handed it to Cole, but such reluctance pervaded the gesture that Tahn handed it back.

"Here," Cole said. "I'll take the blanket off and you put the robe around her shoulders."

"Yes, sir." Woloc knelt, ready to comply.

Cole hesitated, a little baffled by the "sir," and Woloc looked up. Their gazes locked. They stared at each other, evaluating. And a fragile bridge of trust grew between them. They both knew that something dangerous and deliberate had gripped Amirah, and she needed help. But how much did Woloc know about her programming? As Cole scrutinized those veiled hazel eyes, he figured it was more than Woloc would ever let on—unless Amirah directed otherwise.

Cole slipped an arm beneath the blanket and around Amirah's cool back, then pulled off the gray blanket, baring her muscular shoulders to the dim light. Woloc hastily draped the robe over her nakedness and tenderly smoothed his hands down her arms.

When Woloc lifted his eyes back to Cole's, fear shone in the depths. "Have you seen this happen to her before?" he asked tautly.

Cole shook his head. "No. I imagine that whatever triggered her memories of killing her grandmother also triggered a buried defense mechanism to keep her from acting on the knowledge."

"You mean Slothen—"

"That's exactly what I mean, Lieutenant. Slothen's taking no chance that he might lose her. I wager she won't even remember this episode—if she ever comes out of it."

Woloc shook his head in confusion. "But I don't understand. What's the programming for? What's she supposed to do?"

"You mean you don't know?"

"No!" Woloc asserted defiantly. He lurched to his feet and spread his arms helplessly. "I don't have any idea! Do you?"

Cole gently lifted Amirah and carried her across the floor to ease her down onto her bed. She looked as frail and willowy as a rag doll. From the corner of his eyes, Cole noticed that the com unit on the desk flashed: *END OF HOLO. REPORT ON LEVEL 5 ALERT STATUS.*

Cole turned around and glanced questioningly at Woloc. "What's going on? What level 5 alert?"

Woloc's face slackened. He ran to study the screen. "Oh, no."

"What is it?"

"I don't know. I . . ." He let the sentence dangle while he bent over the key patches and told the com unit to abandon the file. The com refused to respond. It continued to demand a report on the alert.

Woloc dropped into the desk chair and typed: LEVEL 5 TERMINATED.

STATUS OF CAPTAIN? HARMLESS OR DEAD?

Jason vented an astonished curse. "Was that file intended to render her harmless? What in the name of God is going on?" He input: HARMLESS.

Cole's brows drew together when the com responded: *STAND BY FOR MESSAGE FROM MAGISTRATE SLOTHEN.*

Woloc gritted his teeth and leaned forward, glaring

worriedly into the screen. Cole frowned when the screen blanked and a broad patch of white light flared. It began to shrink to a tiny pinpoint, changing color, darkening to a purple beam which . . .

Cole dove, grabbing Woloc by the shoulders and slamming him brutally to the floor as the coherent beam lanced through the back of the desk chair and pierced the far wall before shutting off. Woloc struggled to sit up and stared at the blast hole, panting. He wiped his mouth on his uniform sleeve and exchanged a panicked look with Tahn.

Cole got cautiously to his feet. He edged toward the unit and hit the patch to cut the power. The screen went a dull gray.

Through a long exhale, Cole observed, "Obviously the person who knew what was in that file was considered expendable, Lieutenant."

Woloc pulled himself to a sitting position. "I–I don't fully understand this. Slothen must have wanted to protect the ship in case Amirah's trigger ever went off accidentally. That's why I—"

"Yes, that's why you could get into the file at all. It was intended to send her into catatonia and then eliminate the person who knew about the trigger." Cole paced stiffly in front of Woloc. "Slothen's desperate to keep her in his power. *Goddamn it, what's he up to?*"

Woloc inhaled a shuddering breath. "After reviewing the Tikkun files, I suspect it relates to Gamants. Maybe . . ." he paused and squeezed his eyes closed as though trying to decide. "Maybe I'd better tell you what was in the file. Together we might be able to figure it out."

Cole studied Woloc quizzically. The young lieutenant met his gaze squarely. "Why? Why would you tell me?"

Woloc twisted his hands atop his knees. "Because Amirah trusts you. And after the assassination attempt, I'm afraid not to. We're going to be exiting vault in eight hours, Captain Tahn. Whatever we're going to do, we're going have to plan for it fast."

* * *

Slothen stood in the darkness before the windows of his office, gazing out over the nighttime city of Naas.

The triangular mirrored buildings reflected the sporadic rifle fire that lit the satellites. Fighters crisscrossed the skies, occasionally lancing the satellites when they could identify groups of Gamants. He twined the fingers of three of his hands together nervously.

"Do you see them?" Mastema asked from where he sat atop his antigrav gurney. "They're massing."

"I see them, and they're doing it despite our capture of that little female leader." Through his infrared vision, Slothen could make out a vast glowing crescent of human bodies ringing Satellites 4 and 6. "General Ornias' spies say they're waiting to attack."

"Waiting for what?" Mastema spat irritably. In the starlight, his blue face glimmered like wet slate. "They've got Ornias' soldiers bottled up tight within the military installation's walls. Why wait at all?"

Slothen lifted his twined fingers and held them over his ruby red lips while he thought. "They say the Mashiah is coming. They're waiting for him to lead them to victory."

Mastema opened his mouth, obviously to say something bitter, but he slowly closed it and turned back to gaze out the window at a violent explosion that fired a point on Satellite 6. A slack, haunted expression possessed the Master Magistrate. Very quietly, he whispered, "I pray to Milcom that they're wrong."

Slothen glanced at Mastema from the corner of his eye. Hadn't he heard that name before? Milcom . . . Milcom. . . . He methodically searched his tri-brain, trying to isolate the time and place. It had been years ago, more than a decade, hadn't it? On some backward world at the edge of the galaxy . . . *Horeb*. Yes. Yes, of course, that wild prophet on Horeb twelve years ago had preached about Milcom. Adom Kemar Tartarus had been his name.

Slothen surreptitiously examined Mastema. "Mastema, where did you hear of—"

Mastema lifted a hand abruptly, demanding silence. A fighter swooped erratically over the city, swerving around buildings to dive in low and sail down a major street. It listed suddenly and the nose struck the ground. It burst into a ball of fire and tumbled into a residential section. A thunderous rumble shook the government headquarters.

Slothen grabbed the windowsill to steady himself. "I can't believe . . . How could they have gotten weapons?"

Mastema turned his gurney around and somberly headed for the dark doorway where his guards waited. "How long until Tahn and Calas arrive, Slothen?"

"Six hours."

Mastema hesitated in the doorway, swiveling around to gaze blindly out the window. As the station's lighting deepened toward midnight, a gaping blackness swelled. Long stringers of light swirled down into the maw like silver threads. Ominously, Mastema whispered, *"Zohar."* Then he waved a hand emphatically. "You must take special precautions, Slothen. I don't care if you have to pull every soldier off the satellite battlefields to guard the spaceport on Palaia, we have to make certain that no one can rescue Tahn or Calas." He gazed back at the spinning darkness that blotted half the heavens. *"No one."*

CHAPTER 49

Sybil woke and pushed up in her bed in the brig. Her shoulder continued to ache a little when she moved, but the severe pain had gone. She silently observed the line of beds where Mikael, Ari, and Yosef slept. They looked serene, unaware of the hordes of enemies surrounding them.

Jeremiel continued to pace anxiously before the door, hands propped on his hips. Sybil had seen him there every time she'd opened her eyes in the past few hours. Cole Tahn had been gone when she'd awakened two hours ago. He was still gone. She'd tried asking Jeremiel what had happened, but Baruch had simply shaken his head and glanced significantly at the monitors surveying every inch of the room.

Mikael sensed Sybil's movements and rolled over on his side. He smiled drowsily at her, reaching out to grasp her arm and squeeze it.

"How are you?" he whispered. Black hair framed his pale face in a curly shroud, tangling in his beard.

"Mikael," she said. "I know where Nathan is."

He blinked his eyes open. "Where?"

She quietly told him of her dream and the names she'd heard mentioned. "The man with Nathan, Yeshwah, called the city *Yerushalaim*. It must be on a very backward planet. There was no technology at all, except for crude swords and horses for transportation. And the people were all dressed in coarse homespun robes."

Mikael shook hair out of his face and his eyes darted over the room while he thought, then he leaned forward and whispered, "Sybil, do you remember the old stories about the Fathers of the Gamant people? Avram, *Yeshwah*, and Sinlayzan? Wasn't Yeshwah killed in a city

430

called Yershulim. You know how pronunciation changes over time, maybe it's the same."

"Maybe." Sybil's mind ran wild with images of the metallic green water and the men in long white robes. What had it been called. . . ? She struggled with her memory of the Old Stories her father used to tell her. . . . *The shores of the Sea of Arabah?*

Sybil reached out and gripped Mikael's hand hard. "Old Earth?"

"Why would your mother take Nathan there?"

She started to answer, but halted when she saw Jeremiel stop pacing. He stood pensively, head tilted, listening to sounds coming from the hall beyond. He'd clenched his fists, as though on the verge of bursting through those light bars. And somewhere outside, Sybil heard Cole Tahn talking.

She quickly turned back to Mikael, trying to answer his question before the room burst to life again. "On the balcony, after the fight, Mama told me that she was *building the Kingdom of God*. I didn't know what it meant, but—"

Tahn strode swiftly into the room and the guards turned the light bars back on—a vague hum sounded. Sybil watched fearfully as Tahn gave Baruch a severe look and walked past him to the table. Cole used the toe of his black boot to pull out a chair, then propped his foot in it. He turned to peer at Jeremiel wryly. "You know, the Magistrates are a bunch of *nahash* sonsabitches.' "

Baruch nodded and walked thoughtfully toward Tahn. "I've known that for a long time. 'Snakes,' every one of them."

"Did you know that the word 'Naas' in Giclasian means snake? Fits, doesn't it?"

Jeremiel's steps faltered for the briefest of moments. "I didn't know that, but it does fit. You've been gone for four hours, Cole. What did the nahash sonsabitches do to you?"

"Oh, I spent a little time with Jossel and Woloc, then the lieutenant took me down to the med lab and left me under a probe unit for a couple of hours."

Baruch looked like he wanted to kill something. "Really? I thought—"

"She changed her mind. Just like a woman." Cole glowered and waved it off. He couldn't tell Jeremiel that Woloc had had no choice, that when he and the lieutenant had walked out of Amirah's cabin and straight into the arms of the ship's physician, Woloc had had to think fast.

Cole glanced around the room, surveying Mikael and Sybil's taut faces and the curious looks coming from Funk and Calas. He gave Baruch a nonchalant shrug. "Anyway, I'm all right. Just a little sick to my stomach."

"Well, sit down," Jeremiel instructed. He pulled out a chair for Cole which he gratefully dropped into. "They're snakes, all right."

Baruch took a chair beside Cole and tipped it back on two legs. "You'll find this interesting, Cole. There's an ancient Gamant legend about snakes. It says that the first man and woman were created of Pure Light and lived on a lush garden world. Their names were Adom and Hava. They were deceived by a serpent into taking off their garments of Light and clothing themselves in the skins of serpents. When Epagael found out, he punished them by throwing them out of the garden and condemning them to live in metal mountains for eternity. Which Gamant zaddiks have always interpreted as spiritual darkness. It's said that human beings will only awake from the darkness when the Holy Serpent descends into the Abyss and vanquishes it."

Cole chuckled disdainfully. "Metal mountains, huh? Like space stations? Palaia is certainly a center of spiritual darkness, I'll grant you that. But what the hell is a *holy* serpent? I thought all serpents were symbols of evil in Gamant mythology?"

"No." Mikael walked forward to hunch over the table, his dark eyes searching, as though he'd picked up something of what Cole and Jeremiel were up to. "Not all serpents are bad. The story Jeremiel was telling continues by talking about how the Spiritual Woman, the Mother of Life, who represents the female aspect of the Kingdom of Light, transforms herself into a serpent and appears to the sleeping Adom to wake him—to give him back his garment of Light."

"Why does she appear as a serpent? I'd think a god

could transform herself into something a lot less frightening."

Baruch waggled a finger. "It's a disguise, you see. That way, the serpents of the Abyss think she's one of them and . . ."

Jason Woloc's voice penetrated the room. Cole slowly turned to look at the young lieutenant. Woloc pretended ease as he chatted with the two corporals outside the door, but his right hand clutched his holstered pistol like a lifeboat.

The light bars vanished in a flash and one of the corporals hurried across the floor, pointing a gun at Cole's face. He grimaced and got up.

"What's this, Lieutenant?" he called belligerently to Woloc as he headed for the door. "Another torture session so soon?"

Woloc glowered and pulled his own pistol as Cole stepped into the corridor. "This way, Tahn. Your probe chair is still warm."

Cole caught himself doing a double take. Woloc sounded utterly serious. "I'm well aware of that, Lieutenant."

Woloc gestured down the hall with his pistol barrel. "You know the way to the tube, Captain."

When they got around the corner and into the transport tube, Woloc seemed to wilt. He sagged against the tube wall and hit the patch for level twenty. "She's waiting for you in the level twenty lounge, Tahn."

"She came out of it all right?"

"Perfectly. As though nothing ever happened. She didn't even remember . . ." Woloc stopped awkwardly. "Anything from last night."

"Did she ask about it?"

"Yes. I told her in great detail. It scared me to death. I didn't know what would happen to her when I got to the end of the holo story."

"And?"

"She didn't believe me at first. We talked. And she saw the laser hole in the chair. I think she believes it all now. She's started putting things together. She's deeply worried."

"Understandably. Why the level twenty lounge?"

"I thought it would be too dangerous for her to meet

you in her cabin again. Most of the engineering staff is in a division meeting in the 2010 conference room."

"I assume that's still at the other end of the deck?"

"Yes."

"Good."

The tube stopped and Woloc got out and checked the passageway. "Clear, hurry."

Cole broke into a trot, turning right at the intersecting corridor. When he got to the level twenty lounge, Woloc instructed, "It's sealed. Back up, Tahn."

Cole complied and Woloc input the code to open the door. When it whisked back, Woloc grabbed Cole's arm to stop him from entering. He dropped his voice to a conspiratorial whisper. "Take it easy on her, Tahn. She's still shaky. I don't know how stable she is."

"Thanks for the warning. I'll take it easy. Thank you, Lieutenant," Cole stepped into the lounge. The door snicked closed behind him and he noted the red flashing light on the patch which indicated the room had been sealed again. He couldn't get out—unless someone with authority decided to be beneficent.

He stood for a moment, letting his eyes adjust to the candlelit room. Odd, that he'd forgotten how pleasant the level twenty lounges on Magisterial cruisers were. Candlelight and violin music flitted over the small wooden tables that scattered the floor. Holos of different species of trees adorned the walls with green, red, and yellow splashes of color.

When he could finally see, he spotted Amirah. She sat alone in a booth on the far side of the lounge. A stack of ancient tattered books sat in front of her. Her form-fitting purple uniform glimmered with a brassy hue in the flickering gleam of the candles.

Jamming his hands in the pockets of his tan jumpsuit, Cole walked across the lounge and stood uneasily in front of the booth. Amirah's oval face shone golden, splotched here and there by faint dots of freckles.

"I understand you're feeling better."

She looked up through unsettled eyes. "Depends on what you mean. Physically I'm fine. Jason told me what you did last night. Thank you."

"My pleasure."

With a trembling hand, she gestured to the opposite

bench. "Please sit down, Captain. I've been doing some studying I thought you might find interesting."

He slid in on the bench across from her and cocked his head. "About what?"

"Grandmama used to say, 'Amirah, you must clasp the nightmare of your people's exile to your breast or you'll never be free.' "

Cole studied the way her mouth had pinched. "Sounds typically Gamant. What does it mean?"

She corraled the stack of old books with her hands and pushed them toward him. Faint remnants of gold lettering glittered on the bindings. "Ever seen these?"

He glanced speculatively at the volumes. "In your cabin, on the table. What are they?"

"Lieutenant Rad confiscated them from the old men who captured Engineering. He said he thought we ought to put them in stasis since they contained highly classified information."

"On what?"

Amirah pulled one of the volumes out of the stack, flipped through the brittle pages to find her place and remarked, "On the history and construction of Palaia Station. Come look at this, Cole."

The tightness in her voice made Tahn immediately rise and slide in on the bench next to her. She bent forward and pointed to something in the text. The strange diagrams on the ancient yellowed page shone starkly against the black tabletop.

He studied the symbols. "What are they?"

"These designs show the gradual development of the various structures of the sacred *Sefiroth*. My grandmother used to drill them into my head."

"And what are *Sefiroth?*"

"Spheres—vessels of light in the beginning—which burst to form the foundation of Creation. Together the Sefiroth create a realm of divinity which underlies all that we see and hear and touch; it's active in all that exists. The ancient Gamant mystics maintained that salvation lay in gathering up all the dispersed sparks and returning them to God."

Cole's heart fluttered as though his body knew something his mind hadn't quite put together yet. "Sparks?"

"In the context we're about to discuss, let's call them

primordial black holes—which because of the evaporation rate appear to be white holes, correct?"

"Yes . . . *sparks*." His heartbeat grew to a drumroll. "And how did these ancient mystics plan on gathering up all the sparks?"

"Through a complicated process known as *Tikkun*, which is where Baruch's home planet gets its name. The process sought to return everything to its original root."

"You mean the Big Bang?"

"No. Before. The mystics called it the Treasury of Light. It's a . . . a primordial ocean of pure energy."

Cole rubbed his chin. "Maybe I'd better take a closer look at these *Sefiroth* diagrams."

She gestured for him to do so and Cole braced his hands on either side of the ancient paper volume. A series of thirteen geometric designs crowded the page. As he studied them, a suffocating sensation gripped him as if a hard fist had knocked the wind out of him. It all fell into place—the connected diamonds, the vertical orientation, the two event horizons inclined at forty-five degree angles. He whispered, "*Sefiroth*, huh?"

"Uh-huh."

Their gazes held, hers severe, his astounded. "You know as well as I do that we're looking at the space-time map for an electrically charged black hole. Crude, but that's what it is."

Amirah nodded. "And that's only the beginning. Let me show you this other book." She reached across the table and slid another out.

While she searched for the right place in the text, an eerie feeling of premonition climbed Cole's spine. He shivered as his mind somersaulted backward in time. Twelve years ago, when he'd been locked in his cabin aboard the *Hoyer*, Rachel Eloel had come to visit him. She'd been in a panic, trembling. He remembered it as though it had happened yesterday. . . .

She stood in his open door like a beautiful apparition, silhouetted blackly against the nighttime corridor outside. "*I'm sorry to disturb you*."

"I wasn't exactly busy," he responded, wondering what she wanted. "Come in."

She stepped into his cabin hesitantly, her midnight eyes darting around the room. She fumbled unsteadily with a crystal sheet, crumpling it first in one hand then the other. Just watching her had made him fidget.

"I suspected you wanted in for a reason," he said congenially. "Was I wrong?"

After a few minutes of discussing the planet Tikkun, she stepped forward boldly and feverishly asked him, "Captain, would you help me with a physics problem?"

"It's not a calculation you're planning on using to blow up me or the Magistrates, is it?"

"No."

"Is it what you have in your hand?"

She gazed down at the crumpled sheet and cocked her head apologetically. "Yes. I hope you can still read it."

Quickly, as though afraid she'd lose her nerve, she handed it to him. Cole uncrumpled it and smoothed away the wrinkles. He went over the five equations in detail, growing more and more fascinated. Finally, he looked at her admiringly.

"You don't need any help from me. This looks perfect. My only questions are regarding your statistics for mass and charge. Are you sure they're correct?"

She looked confused. "I think so. Why?"

A handsome woman, those eyes held him riveted. She looked at him as though he knew more than God Himself—and damned well better give her the answers she needed or she'd kill him just because. "Come here. Let me show you what I mean."

She obliged, her long ebony hair draping over his arm as he pointed to the equations. "You see," he said, "you're correct here and here regarding the event horizons. Obviously charged black holes have two, one reflecting the mass and the other the charge. But here's where I'm a little confused. If you keep adding to the charge, as this series of five equations show, the inner event horizon will grow while the outer shrinks. You see what I mean?"

"Not exactly."

"Well, the maximum possible charge occurs when the inner and outer event horizons merge, correct?"

She nodded, but looked gravely uncertain. "Go ahead."

Though her forehead lined in concentration, Cole had the feeling that Rachel hadn't the slightest idea what he was talking about.

"What I'm trying to say is that if you execute this particular sequence, I'm afraid . . ."

Almost as though divinely inspired, Rachel's equations spun out across the lounge like silver runes, dancing over the candlelit walls, weaving a flashing web around Cole. He studied them, his pulse thundering. *I'm afraid you'll wind up with a naked singularity. . . .*

"Look at this, Cole," Amirah's soft voice intruded. "This section is on phase transition dynamics. It comes from a book entitled, *The Secret History of the Great Halls of Giclas*. It details the exact—did you hear me? *Exact* specifications for the containment vessel of Palaia Station. You understand what I'm suggesting? The holes inside Palaia have a negative charge. Zohar has a negative charge. The station will be reaching perihelion with Zohar in a matter of hours. I don't know the ratio or the formula, but—"

"I do." He sank back against the bench, his blood racing. "The only thing I can't be sure of is the current levels of mass or charge." He wiped his damp brow. "How soon is perihelion?"

"I'm not sure. Ten or twelve hours. It'll be close. I don't think we should try the main control room. The Engineering Spires on the outskirts of the city are less protected and almost invulnerable once we're inside."

"The Spires, huh?" he rubbed the back of his neck. Made to look like geological features, the Spires stood a good half mile from the edge of Naas. "I don't think the run across those open grassy hills to get there is going to be easy, Amirah. But it's an interesting idea. All we have to do is get into the control chamber, alter the frequency enough to make the containment vessel unstable, get off before it goes, then the *sparks* can go home to Zohar and . . ." He made a whirling gesture with his arms, "everything in the vicinity of Palaia gets sucked down the throat of the naked singularity. Oh, I like it. But how are we—"

"Who says we're getting off before it goes?" she asked with unnerving calmness. Her beautiful face had gone bland, as nonchalant as if she'd just told him she wanted catsup instead of steak sauce on her meat.

He smoothed his hands over the frayed edges of the

old book before him. They felt cool and ancient beyond years. He smiled at her, but it was a forced gesture. Inhaling a breath to bolster himself, he said, "You're right. Somebody's got to stay to manually work the controls, just in case the Magistrates have a bypass capability. Which they probably do. Do you know?"

"No. But I imagine they do."

"I do, too." He tapped a finger methodically against the top of the book and listened to the hollow thudding that resulted. Amirah watched him intently. "So . . ." he blurted uneasily. "Let's discuss your reasons for this." Carefully, he ventured. "Woloc said he told you about your grandmother."

Her turquoise eyes filled with dark emotion. She looked away, gazing out at the other candlelit tables, concentrating on the clear sweet notes of the violins. Tears sparkled on her lashes. "Yes. It makes sense. I just can't figure out what Slothen's goal is. What's inside me, Cole? *I can feel it growing, like some hideous creature!*"

He reached over and picked up her quaking hand and held it tightly between his. "We don't know. But as long as you're on our side, we can keep an eye on you and hopefully short-circuit the act before you can complete it." He stroked her fingers comfortingly. "Amirah. I need to talk to Baruch about this. Is there some place you can arrange—"

"It'll be dangerous. You know every cruiser is equipped with spies." She pursed her lips in a hard line. "But I'll try."

CHAPTER 50

Jeremiel walked briskly down the corridor, Cole in front of him and Jason Woloc behind. They rounded a corner and Jeremiel caught the gray glint of Woloc's drawn pistol. His skin crawled. Cole had gotten the message across in the brig that something might be happening soon, but Baruch had no idea how to paint the scenario—except that Tahn had unquestionably been talking to Jossel. That fact made his gut clench. *Jossel's unpredictable. Even if she were to take up the Gamant gauntlet, can we trust her?*

"Turn right," Woloc instructed tersely. "Get into the transport tube."

Cole bashed the entry patch with his fist and the door slid back. Jeremiel followed him inside. The narrow four by six foot room felt suffocatingly small when Woloc entered with his pistol and backed into the far corner.

When the door closed, Woloc hit the freight patch for level twenty, insuring the slowest descent, and blurted, "You've got three minutes, Tahn. Ninety seconds down, ninety up. Do it fast!"

Cole frantically stepped in front of Jeremiel, words tumbling one over another as fast as Tahn could say them. "I know the key to blowing the hell out of Palaia. I don't have time to explain the calculations, but suffice it to say that Zohar and Palaia are reaching perihelion in a few hours. The primordial holes in Palaia have a negative charge. Zohar has a negative charge. When we get to Palaia, Jossel and I are going to break away and head for the alternate control center stationed in the Engineering Spires outside of Naas. Once inside, we're going to alter the frequency of the containment vessel. If the mass and charge are right—"

"I get it, go on."

"In the meantime, I want you to find Carey and get her out of there, Jeremiel. In the melee that Amirah and I create, you should be able to grab a ship from the landing field adjacent to Naas—"

"Affirmative." Jeremiel's gaze went over Cole minutely, taking in his searching eyes, his labored breathing. "I didn't hear you delineate your escape plan."

Cole's smooth cheeks vibrated with his grinding teeth. "When I figure one out, I'll let you know. We've only got a few seconds, let's talk—"

"Tell me why Jossel would help us?"

"Woloc discovered a holo which shows Amirah killing her grandmother at Slothen's command. The government must have been testing the trigger to see—"

"Did you discover who the intended target of her programming is?"

"Negative," Cole shook his head vehemently.

"How's her mental stability. Can we trust her?"

Cole hesitated and cast a sideways glance at Woloc, as though he knew every word of this conversation would get back to Jossel. "Yes. I think so. I don't know how she'll respond under pressure, but I think so."

"What sort of diversion is she going to create to—"

"Unknown." Cole threw up his hands. The collar and sides of his tan jumpsuit already ran with sweat. "We all need to see what Slothen's got up his sleeve. She'll move at the first opening."

"Where are we going to get weapons? Will Jossel—"

"Yes. She and Woloc will both be carrying extra pistols. When the time comes—"

"So only you and I will have them."

"Yes, that's the best she can do. Now, I've got to show you the layout of the main neuro center on Palaia, the central control room and the setup of the Engineering Spires." Cole spun and extended a hand to Woloc. The lieutenant quickly took a folded crystal sheet from his shirt pocket and thrust it into Tahn's hands. Jeremiel scrutinized Woloc while Cole rushed to unfold the sheet. Why would the lieutenant help them? Because Jossel was helping? Didn't make sense. And he damned well didn't like things that didn't make sense.

Cole spread the sheet over the white wall of the tube, pointing hurriedly. "Look at this, Jeremiel. Our shuttle

should land at this field. This should be our route
through the main buildings complex. This is the neuro
center." He traced the corridors with his finger. "Carey
should be here somewhere." He circled a particular
locale. "Probably here. This is the security hospital.
Amirah and I will try to break away and follow this
route. We'll have a half-mile run over open country, but
I think we can make it. This is the arrangement of the
control facilities at the Spires—"

Woloc pulled his pistol again as the tube slowed.
"That's it for now, Tahn. Give me that sheet!"

Cole jammed it back into Woloc's hand and stared
angrily at the level number flashing in blue over the door.

Just before the door slipped back, Jeremiel lifted his
chin and asked Woloc. "Why you, Lieutenant? What's
your stake in this?"

The door pulled back to reveal a bright hallway filled
with six security guards. The soldiers turned to eye the
tube curiously and when they saw Woloc, hastily came
to attention.

"At ease," Woloc ordered. He frowned at a young
red-haired corporal. "Tuler, where's Lieutenant Rad?
He was supposed to be meeting me here."

The corporal's eyes widened. "I–I don't know, sir. He
told me he was going up to the probe room in the infirmary to meet you and interrogate Tahn and Baruch."

Woloc's mouth pursed disapprovingly and the crew
tensed, then the lieutenant amiably waved it away.
"Must have been a misunderstanding. I'll check the infirmary. Proceed with your duties."

"Aye, sir."

Woloc stepped back into the tube and sank against the
wall, obviously not practiced at lying to his crew. He
shifted his pistol to his left hand and wiped his clammy
right palm on his pants.

Jeremiel folded his arms and pressed, "You're the one
element I don't understand, Lieutenant. You've no
motivation for treason. Do you?"

Woloc lifted his eyes to meet Jeremiel's stern gaze. "I
think so. I saw the holos of Tikkun, Kayan, and Jumes.
And I saw the holo of what the government did to
Amirah. In fact, I almost died over it, but that's another
story we don't have time for." He glanced poignantly at

Cole. "Amirah may be a special case. I'm not sure. I don't think any officer required to undergo an annual psych exam at Palaia can be certain of his or her safety. I could never undergo one again." He wet his lips. "And more importantly, Baruch, *I'm going on this mission because my captain needs me.* "

Jeremiel gave Woloc a ruthless appraisal. Despite the fact that he instinctively liked the young officer, he couldn't afford to rely on someone whose motivations remained unclear. He wasn't even sure Woloc had fully thought out the consequences of his impending actions.

Stoically, Jeremiel demanded, "Is that because you love her, Lieutenant, or because you know your presence is strategically necessary to the success of the mission?"

Woloc glowered and straightened up, positioning himself like he wanted to level a lethal kick. He wasted a full two seconds glaring resentfully, then responded, "Either one would be enough, wouldn't it, Commander?"

From the locked confines of his memories, Carey's laughter wafted out, wry, affectionate. Jeremiel's hands quaked. He shoved them into the slanting pockets of his tan jumpsuit. "Depends. Do you love her enough to give up your ship, your crew, your very way of life? Dying for somebody's easy. Living on after the mission *without them* isn't. If Jossel dies and you survive this—which I'll grant is extremely doubtful—nothing of your old life will be left. It'll all be gone, Lieutenant. Are you ready for that? *What are you going to do without her or your world?*"

Woloc looked stunned and bewildered, as though he hadn't considered that dire possibility. The door slipped open and the astringent scents of the hospital drifted in to them, antiseptics, cleansers, pungent whiffs of anesthesia.

Jeremiel said, "Think about it, Lieutenant," and stepped out into the corridor. He knew the way to the probe labs on Magisterial vessels by heart, but his steps still faltered when he got close. Cole and Woloc exited behind him and he could hear them exchange a few vaguely hostile sentences.

Cole trotted to catch up with Jeremiel and walk at his side, while Woloc stayed behind them covering them with his gun. Cole gave Baruch a cockeyed look and muttered, "I've always been dumbfounded by your magnetic ability to sway people to our side. Do you have to practice to be that suave?"

Jeremiel tossed him an incredulous look. "Would you rather he started asking himself those questions when he's supposed to be guarding your back?"

Cole grimaced. "Not especially."

Jeremiel clamped his jaw and looked over at Cole. Tahn had a hard, preoccupied expression on his face, as though already living the next few desperate hours in his mind. Jeremiel asked softly, "You're not planning on leaving the Spires, are you?"

Cole glanced up and smiled faintly. "No."

* * *

Rachel sat at the connecting edge of two universal voids, tears blurring her eyes. Time was running out. She had to get to Palaia, to meet Aktariel, but fear choked her.

The darkness behind her had stopped its constant swirling as though stunned and waiting like an animal for its prey to move. She rocked back and forth to ease the pain that cramped her stomach.

On her left, the darkness of predawn blanketed Gulgolet. A dark-haired man hung on a huge cross, his legs broken, his face streaked with blood; at his feet, Nathan slammed a fist into the soft sand and choked down sobs.

To her right glared the brilliant light of the lustreglobes aboard the *Sargonid.* Sybil lay in bed reading. Brown curls fluffed around her daughter's face, accentuating her dark eyes and the unnatural paleness of her skin.

Rachel put her hands over her face to block the wrenching sights. "Get up. *Get up, damn you! You've done all you can. Go . . . go now and do what Aktariel needs you to—what you promised you would.*"

Wearily, she got to her feet.

CHAPTER 51

Amirah walked imperiously across the bridge of the *Sargonid*, feigning calm, though her heart beat so loudly she thought it would burst through her rib cage.

They'd just exited vault and on the broad forward monitor, Palaia loomed. From outside the EM shells, it looked like nothing more than a beautiful saffron-colored gas ball set adrift in the ebony ocean of space. Her crew worked industriously around her, charting their course, tending to last minute communications details, laughing about how nice a vacation would be, though none of them expected such a gift from the Magistrates.

Amirah walked in front of the reflective shielding over the transport tube door and stopped. She straightened the sleeves of her crisp dress uniform. The golden tassels on her captain's bars gleamed like gaudy bits of shredded tinsel. She'd braided her blonde hair and coiled it on top of her head. She looked too thin. Everything except her stony eyes seemed pale and tenuous. But those eyes . . . they could have belonged to the vengeful God she'd heard so many stories about in her youth. A divinity who could lift His hand and the bitter fire of His enmity would destroy worlds.

See, Grandmama, I remembered.

Pain clutched at her chest. She fought it down. *Oh, Grandmama, forgive me. Forgive me. . . .*

From out of her memories, Sefer's gravelly old voice admonished: *"Just believe, Amirah! That's all I ask. For on the Last Day, the heavens shall shudder and the planets shall be shaken from their places by the fury of the Lord of Hosts. On the sacred Mountain, the Lord will swallow up that veil that shrouds all the peoples and the oppressor will meet his end. Then the dead will live again!"*

Amirah went to ease down in her command chair. She

studied Jason's broad back. He bent studiously over the navigation console, but beneath the fabric of his purple uniform, she could see his shoulder muscles bunched like corded steel. A tingling, sinking sensation accosted her when she looked at him. She'd forced him to tell her in great detail about their night together, and her subsequent seizure. Since that time, flits of memory had come back to her—gentle, passionate. More than anything else, she'd recalled the timid love in his eyes and the reverent way he'd touched her. The knowledge left her off-balance. For years, she'd relied on him in the most dire of circumstances, but now she feared to. He wouldn't do anything misguided, would he? She'd been his lover—gladly—but in a battle situation she'd retreat to being his captain. Would he follow orders? *Would he leave her in the Spires' control room when she ordered him to?*

"Captain?" Jason called, breaking her out of her thoughts. "Something's not right here."

"Explain, Lieutenant."

Woloc's hands danced over his nav board. "I'm magnifying."

Palaia seemed to hurl toward them with dizzying speed. Amirah squinted at the image. Tiny silver lights circled the station. Strange, indeed. "Identify those objects, Woloc. I thought the satellites were inside the outermost energy shell."

"Aye, they are. Those aren't satellites, they're battle cruisers. From the spacing and speed, I'd guess they're on blue alert."

Amirah sat forward in her chair. *Blue alert?* "Lieutenant, please scan the galactic environment around Palaia. Any hint of enemy activity?"

"A moment, ma'am."

Amirah's breathing grew shallow and uneven. The thought of Underground cruisers nearby left her anxious—and traitorously hopeful.

Gever Hadash spun around in her chair and peered at Amirah. The golden com aura flared around her head, accentuating the lean weasel shape of her face and her green eyes. "Captain, I'm getting a flood of dattrans discussing the off-loading of captured Gamant civilians on

Satellite 4. Apparently the alert is simply a precaution against Underground attempts to rescue the captives."

"First Lieutenant? Your analysis?"

Jason lifted a hand and continued to study his com. "I suspect Gever's correct. There's no tangible threat out there and I'm getting no gravity wave fluctuations to indicate incoming vessels."

"Interesting," Amirah remarked. "One would think two cruisers would be enough to guard such a simple action. Twenty seems a little excessive."

"Yes," Jason muttered carefully. "Unless they've already had word of an impending attack." He looked at her over his shoulder and Amirah's eyes narrowed in thought.

"Possible. How long until we dock at Palaia?"

Jason accessed the chronometer on his console. "Our shuttle has been cleared to dock in forty minutes. Magistrate Slothen himself will meet us at the spaceport. He asked me to let you know that he's set up a celebration dinner for you tonight, so he can personally award your Medal of Honor."

His voice had been purely professional, just informing, but the words affected Amirah like a glacial breeze through her soul. The seven other members of her bridge crew turned to gaze at her, pride brimming in their eyes, and she felt physically ill. She got out of her chair and walked to stand behind Jason.

"Lieutenant, please assemble a security team and escort our prisoners to landing bay twenty-two. I'll meet you there in fifteen minutes."

"Affirmative, Captain."

Amirah lifted a hand to her communications officer. "Gever, you're in command. Establish standard orbit around Palaia. Take good care of the *Sargonid* until we get back."

"Aye, aye, Captain." Hadash got up from her console and dropped into the command chair. The rest of the bridge shifted in trained symmetry, Pirke taking Hadash's console, Reis taking Jason's, and on down the line.

Amirah hurried toward the transport tube and held the door for Jason. He trotted up and hit the patch for level two, saying, "I assume you're going to your cabin . . ."

The words: *one last time* hung bitterly.

"Yes," Amirah responded. "I need to get my dress cap. So do you, Lieutenant."

He nodded and slumped back against the wall, a forlorn expression on his handsome face. He looked as though he wanted to say something badly, but couldn't quite get the nerve.

Gently, she prompted, "What is it, Jason?"

When he glanced up, all the stoic professionalism he'd been working so hard to maintain vanished. His eyes shone with naked vulnerability and fear. "Amirah, there's a question I've been trying not to think about, but now that we're at Palaia, I–I'd like to ask you." He hastily amended, "You don't have to answer."

She smiled fleetingly. "I assume that means it's personal. Go ahead. You can ask me anything you want, Jason. I'll answer it as honestly as I can."

He held her gaze powerfully. "Amirah, when you—when you were *ill*, the only person you called for—"

"Was Tahn."

"Yes." He shifted uncomfortably to brace his other shoulder against the tube wall. "Are you . . . do you love him, Amirah?"

"No, Lieutenant." She said it quickly and decisively so she didn't have to think about what a lie it was, or how the question made her ache inside.

Jason examined her face in detail, trying to ascertain the truth of the assertion. After a few seconds, he quietly exhaled and the light came back to his hazel eyes. "Thank you for answering. I'd no right to ask, but—"

"You'd every right."

The door opened, revealing the long corridor on level two. Amirah put the heel of her hand over the patch to hold the door open. Jason watched her anxiously, as though waiting for her to say something intimate and reassuring. She railed at herself, *Can't you comfort the man, Amirah? Just for the briefest moment, can't you let him see the woman he loved last night? You're going on a suicide mission, what harm would it do?*

She shifted her palm to the patch to close the door. Jason didn't move a muscle, but she saw the swift rise and fall of his broad chest. The hum of the tube seemed to grow deafeningly.

"Forgive me, Jason. I know I've been acting aloof and cold." Spreading her arms in a gesture of futility, she vented a desperate laugh. "It's just that I'm scared to death."

A smile warmed his face. His hazel eyes softened. "I understand that feeling, Amirah."

She started to hit the "open" patch again, but her hand refused. Instead, she turned and wrapped her arms around Jason's shoulders, pulling him close in a frantic hug. His arms went tightly around her waist.

"Amirah," he murmured. "I know you don't remember what happened last night, but before we go down to Palaia, I want to tell you again that I love you."

She stared blindly at the white wall, feeling empty and aching. "Tell me again when we get out of this, will you? Right now, I'm too—"

"I'll tell you again." He assured. He embraced her so hard that she couldn't breathe, then he backed away suddenly. "Come on, we've got work to do."

"Yes. I'll meet you in the bay in ten minutes."

"Affirmative, Captain."

She stepped out of the tube and strode down the corridor. She heard the tube close just before she rounded the corner for her cabin. As though the soft click caused it, a sob lodged in her throat. She slumped against the wall and pressed her hot cheek to the cool tiles. *Don't feel, Amirah. Don't feel! You can't afford to. Not ever . . . not ever again.*

She shoved away from the wall and stolidly trotted to her cabin. Once inside, she wasted no time. She tramped to her closet and grabbed her purple dress cap from its hook. Pulling it down to the middle of her forehead—just as regulations required—she then strapped on two pistols and slipped Tahn's Wind River fighter into her black boot. He'd seemed irrationally fond of it—if she miraculously got the chance, she'd give it back to him. Finally, she clipped her communications unit to her belt and hit her exit patch.

She started for the door . . . but her steps faltered when she passed the divider and glimpsed the rainbow wine goblets. As though the years fell away, she saw Sefer's withered face. Grandmama gave her a tender, loving look as she wrapped another glass in the bright yellow paper they'd bought at the local stationery store that morning. *See these glasses, Amirah? They're made by the old Gamants on Earth. They say the swirling colors reflect the beauty of Epagael that pervades Creation. Remember that. The government can take everything away from you but that. God's beauty lives inside you. Don't forget. They can beat you and rape your mind and kill you—but they'll never take your Gamant soul. Not so long as you remember who and what you are.*

Amirah suppressed the cry that constricted her throat, but tears fell from her eyes to splat on the beautiful blue swirls of the goblet. "Grandmama, if you can hear me now, I want you to know that I've finally stopped running from myself. *And I'm going to make them pay for what they did to you.*"

She strode briskly to her table, picked up the curious necklace that Slothen had demanded they search Mikael Calas for, and sprinted out of her cabin to the transport tube. "Level twenty."

The tube descended. No one else got on. She rode alone through the dreadful silence. When the door snicked back, she stepped out into a group of four security officers. She spied Jason a short distance away. When he saw her, he shouldered through the crowd and saluted.

"The prisoners are already aboard the shuttle, Captain."

"Thank you, Lieutenant. The rest of the team is assembled?"

"Aye, sir."

Behind Jason, Amirah saw her security chief, Lilith Moab, straighten up and unsling her rifle. A very tall, heavily-muscled woman with short black hair and steely brown eyes, Moab was generally brusque and bad-tempered. The rest of the team milled nervously, glancing at their captain and first lieutenant, no doubt wondering about Woloc's hushed, urgent tone.

Amirah slapped Jason in the shoulder confidently. "Then let's go."

She led the way, and heard his steps pounding behind her. She greeted Moab and shoved through the doors leading out into bay twenty-two. The shuttle sat like a gleaming silver lance point on the white tiled floor. She strode purposely for it and her team followed obediently.

The two shuttle guards saluted as she walked up the gangplank. Amirah returned the gesture. When she stepped into the fuselage, Baruch's gaze pinned her. He sat in the last chair on the left side of the shuttle, wrists and ankles bound in EM restraints. Two long rectangular portals trimmed each side of the ship. A gleam lit Baruch's eyes—as though he were quietly speculating about her abilities.

I'm no Sefer Raziel, Baruch. You're right about that. She was braver than I am.

As she moved toward the command cabin, Amirah noticed that each prisoner had been provided with fresh clothing meeting their individual demands. Mikael Calas was dressed in traditional Gamant garb. His long red robe accented the black of his beard and hair. Sybil Calas wore an ivory robe. She glared fiercely at Amirah as she passed by. Funk and Yosef Calas had adopted matching gray robes. Tahn and Baruch wore official Gamant Underground black uniforms.

Amirah's gaze briefly touched Tahn's as she walked by—his expression struck her as hard as a stiff belt of whiskey on an empty stomach. Filled with dread and suspicion, he seemed to be silently pleading with her not to let him down—not to change her mind.

She ducked into the command cabin and eased down into the copilot's seat. Jason dropped into the pilot's chair and methodically struck all the patches to power up the shuttle. "Ready, Captain."

"As ready as I'll ever be," she teased lamely. "Initiate take-off, Lieutenant."

He threw her a fond look. "Yes, ma'am."

The bay doors slipped open to reveal the magnificence of space. Stars limned the heavens in twinkling lacy patterns. Below, the massive bulk of Palaia glowed. From this angle, through the layers of electromagnetic shells that shielded it, the station gleamed like a burnished copper coin. Amirah sat for several minutes, watching the station, and the huge gaping darkness that blotted the sky beyond.

Amirah noticed that Jason's gaze was riveted there,

too. "I'll input the secret dock codes if you'll reconfirm our approach, Jason."

"Affirmative."

Amirah keyed in the lengthy sequence and heard Jason call, "Shuttle *Theudas* to Palaia central control. We have been cleared for landing at dock C-A. We are on our final approach; please open a shoot through the shields."

Amirah watched numbly as a "hole" pierced the image of a hazy planet to reveal a transparent domed space station of enormous magnitude. On the satellites visible in the distance, garish flashes of purple erupted.

Amirah leaned forward, scrutinizing the gunfire through the rectangular forward portal. "Jason, ask central what's happening on those satellites? I don't like the looks of this."

"Hold on."

Jason hit the necessary patches, uttered the request, and waited. When the message came in, he struck the audio patch immediately. Amirah listened to a mechanical Giclasian voice explain, "Minor skirmishes are occurring on several satellites. They are contained and pose no threat. Please proceed toward dock C-A."

She and Jason exchanged a wary look. Almost inaudibly, Woloc inquired, "Where did the revolting Gamant population get weapons? Spoils of battle?"

"Probably." *Good for them.*

Out her side portal, Amirah saw the shuttle's wings gleaming with a golden fringe of fire, as though set aflame by the steep descent. A barrage of mortar fire exploded on one of the satellites. Several squadrons of fighters swooped down low, lancing the ground like fire-breathing dragons. The attacker's mortar barrage quieted. Closer, on Palaia, sunset radiated in carnelian blazes from the drifting clouds.

"Entering dock, Captain."

The receiving petrolon lock loomed out of the blackness like a siphon. The *Theudas* soared down it, slowing until the grapples attached and tugged the ship into a safe, brilliantly lit niche. A Giclasian maintenance team hurried out, their legs and arms rotoring in a blue blur.

Jason unfastened his seat restraints and peered intently at Amirah. "Ready, Captain?"

She lifted her face and said a silent good-bye to this shuttle and the life she'd known and loved for years.

"Captain?"

"Yes. I'm ready. Please assemble the security team and prisoners, Lieutenant."

"Aye, aye."

Jason saluted crisply and barreled through the entry to the passenger compartment. He uttered a few standard commands and a thudding of boots sounded. By the time Amirah entered to stand next to Tahn, all the prisoners were on their feet, ankle restraints removed, but hands bound in front of them.

The side door parted and two members of the security team raced down the gangplank to secure the bay. In the buzz of voices that began, Tahn leaned sideways and whispered, "What's all the fire on the satellites?"

"War."

His handsome face tightened. He swallowed hard when the entourage began to move, Mikael and Sybil down the plank first, then Funk and Calas, and finally Baruch. Tahn hesitated and Amirah saw him clamp his jaw. He peered out the doorway through pained eyes. She realized he was terrified. The possibility of being returned here must have stalked his nightmares for years.

"Relax," she whispered. "*If* you see a probe chair, I *guarantee* it won't be for long."

He threw her a tortured smile. "Right." And he marched out of the shuttle and down the plank into the huge white bay. Ten or twelve small silver fighters dotted the north wall, other than that the chamber was empty.

Moab spread her team in a diamond around the prisoners and herded them forward. Amirah brought up the rear, pistol drawn, heart echoing like thunder in her chest. Jason walked stiffly at her side. When they stepped into the long tube that would take them down to the planet's surface, she chanced a look at Tahn. His gaze darted recklessly—as though gauging his chances for escape if he tried to fight his way out.

The tube stopped and the door slipped open. The raw scents of rain-soaked vegetation and rich soil swirled in on the warm breeze. Outside, Amirah could see the blood red ball of the false sun hanging over the horizon.

She inhaled deeply, fighting the panic that reared like a raging bull inside her.

Moab began moving the prisoners out. "Come on, Calas! Walk straight ahead. The rest of you follow in single file."

Amirah waited until the tube stood empty before she, too, exited. Along the perimeter of the landing field, shuttles and fighters nestled side-by-side; their silver wings reflected the deepening colors of sunset. Heavily armed Giclasian guards stood before each one. Amirah scrutinized the blue aliens. Ordinarily Palaia sported an equal number of all species in its guard ranks. What had happened? Did the Magistrates only trust their own kind now?

"Captain?" Jason said in a low warning voice. "Slothen's ahead of us. You see him?"

Amirah braced herself, clutching her pistol grips tightly and looked up. She saw him. Standing atop a raised platform surrounded by dozens of guards, Slothen lifted two hands to her in greeting.

Amirah's soul screamed at her to run, to pull her pistol and kill everyone in sight, to *do* something. But she calmly lifted her hand and saluted.

They proceeded quickly to the dais. Amirah's security team waited at the base of the structure with their prisoners while Amirah climbed the stairs. She felt oddly as though she were ascending a gallows. Her blood throbbed so violently in her ears that a light-headed sensation tormented her.

Slothen greeted her with a bow. His blue face and red mouth both looked strained. His eyes kept straying to the satellites. "Welcome, Captain Jossel, and congratulations. We here at Palaia are deeply grateful for the valiant service you've rendered to the government."

"Thank you, Magistrate. I understand you requested that we search Calas to see if he wore a necklace. Here it is, sir." Amirah drew the gray ball on the chain from her pocket and handed it to Slothen. He took it gingerly, as though afraid of it.

"Actually, Captain, Master Magistrate Mastema requested it. Please, step forward and let me introduce you to him."

Amirah blinked in confusion. Slothen had disturbed

Mastema in his Peace Vault? Blessed God. Slothen
stepped aside to reveal a withered old Giclasian lying on
a mound of multicolored pillows.

She stepped forward.

"Master?" Slothen introduced. "This is Captain Jossel."

Amirah saluted perfectly. "I'm honored, Master."

Mastema barely looked at her. He reached hungrily
for the necklace. "Give it to me!" Slothen handed it over
and Mastema held it to his breast. "Let's get inside where
it's safe. I want Calas and Tahn under the probes immediately." He irritably shouted at his guards and they
shoved his gurney off the dais and toward a door that
led into the squat gray building to their right.

Amirah noted with relief that it was exactly the corridor they'd expected.

Slothen stepped around Amirah. "Please have your
security team escort the prisoners this way, Captain.
We've relocated the neuro research division into this
building. We'll be taking the prisoners directly into the
probe lab. From there, you and I and your first lieutenant will proceed to our temporary government headquarters near the main control room. A staff of military
advisers are awaiting our arrival."

Amirah felt a twinge of panic. She'd expected to have
more time . . . at least a half hour to find out . . . but
if Slothen wanted to separate her from Cole immediately
. . . she'd have to . . . oh, God. "You've evacuated the
old headquarters? Are things so bad here, Magistrate?"

"We'll discuss it inside, Captain. Please hurry."

"Aye, sir."

She trotted down the stairs to Moab and commanded,
"Escort the prisoners through the door that Magistrate
Slothen is taking."

"Aye, ma'am." Moab nodded, but her steely eyes
traced the string of satellites, noting the increased rifle
fire and activity of ᵗʰᵉ fighter ships. In the glare of sunset, the satellites seemed close enough to touch.

Amirah watched the Gamant prisoners begin to march
and led the way. When they got inside the gray building,
a new scent stung her nose: pungent, antiseptic. A long
hallway extended ahead of them. Slothen stood waiting
for her at the next door.

"Captain," the Magistrate informed stiffly. "We have

to go through one wing of the hospital to reach our head-quarters. I hope none of your security team members are squeamish?''

"I'm sure they've seen far worse in battle than your hospital has to offer, sir.''

Slothen scrutinized her team, then said, "Good. Please follow me." He struck the entry patch and the door opened. He lurched forward.

Amirah followed. A muted wail undulated from somewhere ahead. She turned and almost involuntarily her eyes sought out Jason's. He glowered as though already sickened by the place. Amirah passed through the next door and entered the first hospital chamber.

A wall of beds lined one wall. On those beds, people lay, eyes wide open, staring sightlessly at the white ceiling. No sound or sudden motion disturbed them. Their slack expressions never changed. One old woman wore a silver triangle around her wrinkled throat. *Gamants.* Helmets hung suspended over every bed.

"What is this?" Amirah whispered to herself.

But Jason responded, "Neuro *research.*" It sounded like a curse.

Amirah felt her team push through the door behind her. She stepped forward numbly. Some members of her team gasped, but Baruch's people only stared in deathly quiet. Amirah's feet seemed to walk by themselves toward the next door.

She glanced back at the old woman with the silver triangle and her heart did a triple-step. For the first time, she noticed that the woman had a tattoo on her forearm: 166TSEL. A relocation camp prisoner. Had this old woman known Sefer? They'd be about the same age if Sefer had. . . . Amirah's heart clutched up.

Epagael, how could you let her end up here on Palaia again?

She slammed a fist into the entry patch and stepped aside, gesturing for Moab to push the prisoners through first.

She propped her hand on her pistol as they filed passed. Funk and Calas. Mikael and Sybil. When Sybil stepped by and entered the new room, an urgent female voice begged, *"Are you the one?"*

"Who?" Sybil asked.

"The one we've waited so long for. God's Anointed. Or should we look for another?"

Amirah caressed her pistol grips as Baruch passed in a slight swish of black uniform. Tahn came next in line. He stopped a moment, but he didn't look at her. His gaze roved the beds as though seeing the fate of humanity writ large on the half-alive bodies. Finally, he turned and gave Amirah one look, a look that sent a jolt of frightened adrenaline through her. No amusement quirked his face now. Only a naked anger—as though he were asking her, *"When? WHEN?"* Then he lowered his eyes and stepped through the door.

Two security officers walked through behind Tahn and then Amirah and Jason entered the next room.

A sharp cry brought her up short. A little dark-haired woman with a long face extended a hand through the bright golden bars of her light cage, reaching out to Amirah pleadingly. "You're *her*, aren't you?" Her eyes blazed. "Aren't you?"

Amirah shook her head, puzzled. This room contained living Gamants. Men, women and children . . . children . . . huddled like beasts inside their cages, most oblivious to their environment.

A tumult broke out among the prisoners. From the edge of her vision, Amirah saw Baruch take three running steps toward one of the beds before Moab slammed him across the back with her rifle and he sank to his knees groaning. Tahn cried out hoarsely and threw himself at Moab, kicking, screaming, *"Let him go! That's his wife, damn it! Let him go. LET HIM GO!"*

A melee of shouts and flying fists blurred the opposite side of the room and Amirah spied the woman with auburn hair lying limply on the bed in the light cage. A chill swept her. *His wife. Carey Halloway.* Amirah would have known her anywhere.

"Amirah!" Tahn's voice lanced like an icy wind. Her security team had forced him back against the wall and surrounded him. His chest heaved. "Let Baruch see his wife. Let him see her! It can't possibly hurt anything."

"Moab," she ordered mildly. "Let Baruch go."

Moab's mouth puckered in stunned disapproval, but she released Baruch.

Baruch ran swiftly forward and braced his hands on

the light bars, staring down anxiously, trying to judge whether Halloway's chest moved.

Amirah marched to the control panel at the foot of the bed and switched off the field. When the light bars died, Baruch gave her a grateful look and sat on the edge of the bed. He gathered his wife in his arms and Amirah heard him softly murmur, "Carey. It's Jeremiel. I'm here. I love you, Carey."

Amirah turned away. Tahn had clenched his bound hands into fists. She could sense his frantic need to see Halloway himself. Grief ravaged his blue-violet eyes.

The door at the far end of the room burst open and four Giclasian guards flooded out. They quickly took in Baruch and the doused light cage, Tahn and his predicament, and brusquely inquired, "Why are you delaying? Magistrate Slothen is already in the temporary headquarters waiting for you!"

"We're on our way, Sergeant. Just give us a few more moments, then we'll—"

"The Magistrates want you there *now*, Captain. Slothen ordered us to bring you immediately and to help your team escort their prisoners to the main probe room where Master Mastema is waiting."

"All right, Sergeant," she said through a tense exhalation.

Tahn flinched visibly. Almost in slow-motion he sank back against the wall. Two of the Giclasians moved forward and herded the Gamant prisoners and her security team together; they pushed them through the door. Amirah caught the anguished look on Tahn's face as he cast one last glance at Halloway. Then he vanished into the next corridor.

The other two Giclasians whirled up to the bed. One of them kept a gun on Baruch while the other forcibly disentangled the Underground commander's arms from around Halloway and jerked him to his feet. For a moment, Amirah thought Baruch might lash out—but he willfully commanded his muscles to relax and tramped for the door.

One guard, a corporal, stayed with Amirah, standing silently, waiting. She stared again at Halloway who had fallen into a heap like a black crumpled scarf, her head at an awkward angle. Had she been conscious, it would have hurt. Amirah's hand ached as she straightened the woman's head and reached down to switch on the light cage again.

"Come on, Captain," Jason said. "We'd better be going."

She backed away from the bed. The guard followed.

She and Jason hurried to the next intersection of hallways. On her right, a long rectangular portal sat in front of a series of raised seats which looked down into a probe room. Mikael and Sybil, Ari and Yosef, were already locked into chairs and had probe units ominously secured over their heads. Baruch stood rigidly, studying the rifles aimed at his chest. A short distance away, Tahn struggled against two guards who tried to strong-arm him into a chair.

Barely visible on the far side of the room, Magistrate Mastema lay propped on his gurney. His eyes were wild. He held the necklace up to the lustreglobes, examining it as though terrified.

"Turn left," the Giclasian corporal commanded.

Amirah dragged her eyes away from the haunting scene and numbly proceeded down the corridor. But she couldn't get the image of Tahn's twisted face out of her mind. Maybe she should have pulled her pistol then? But there were so many guards.

Violent emotions threatened to rise. Amirah quickly walked forward, trying to still her panting lungs. *Soon,* she promised. *I just need to get an idea of what's happening on Palaia now. What the military set-up is.* At the end of the hall, five guards milled outside a broad open doorway. She and Jason walked between them and into the midst of Slothen and a frantic group of ten military advisers. An oval table stretched the length of the small room. Governor Ornias paced before a screen that took up one entire wall. Battle scenes blazed across the monitor. Dressed in a heavily tasseled general's uniform, he smiled at her condescendingly.

"Good evening, Captain," he greeted. His sandy hair and perfectly braided beard looked incongruous against the chaotic violence of the screen. He came over to her.

Amirah backed away from his scent. He smelled sweet, like a meadow of flowers. This was no soldier.

This was a prissy politician. "How the hell did you get to Palaia, Governor?"

"Not 'Governor' anymore, Captain," he corrected. "Now it's 'General Ornias.' I'm your commanding officer on Palaia."

She laughed disparagingly. "Then I'd better get back to my ship soon or you'll be filing charges of insubordination against me." She gestured to the screen to change the subject. "Where is that happening?"

"On Satellite 4. I'm afraid the Gamants went wild when they saw your shuttle descending. They're throwing themselves at the landing field in wave after wave. We're slaughtering them by the hundreds, of course."

She watched a group of fifteen people running insanely as two fighters dropped from the fiery heavens. Purple beams lanced out, exploding the ground and scattering their bodies like limp rag dolls. The military advisers in the room cheered triumphantly.

Slothen cut the com aura and waved a hand at her dismissively. "Captain Jossel, Magistrate Mastema apparently turned the probes up too high. He would like you to go to the probe room. Cole Tahn is dead and Mastema—"

A wretched cry escaped her throat. She ran with all her might. Jason's steps echoed behind her.

* * *

Emon waited until the last moment, then waved his troops forward. They flooded out of the rents in the substructure's fabric and ran through the sunset-painted hills around the spaceport.

"You saw the triangular shuttle!" he screamed. "It's the sign! We have to hurry!"

People rushed out behind him. On the opposite side of the port, Emon saw Sicarrii's soldiers leaking from the lattice, crawling over the surface like scampering ants.

They all rushed the photon fence.

And a spray of Magisterial fighters dove out of the heavens.

Purple beams panned the fence, killing fifty in a single sweep. Emon's heart lurched when he saw Sicarrii fall in a mound of blue shirt and blood. *Oh, no. No. No!* Some of Sicarrii's people broke and ran, racing back toward the lattice.

As the fighters swung around, Emon screamed in rage and terror at the remaining forces. "Get down! Focus your rifles on the same spot! We have to knock a hole in that fence or we'll never get through!"

He hit the dirt on his stomach and aimed. He heard others slap the ground around him and in a few seconds their combined fire caused the fence to flare like molten gold. As the fighters plunged down toward them, a wave of Giclasian soldiers ran across the landing field.

Emon and his troops kept firing. The wall overloaded and an entire section vanished. Emon scrambled up and shouted, "We have to capture the ships! Hurry! We have to capture the ships and get to the other satellites to load up people!"

A jubilant cheer tore the hot air as men, women, and children raced for the hole. The Giclasians hit the ground across the field and opened fire, but the onslaught of humanity kept going. Screaming, rushing, firing blindly at anything that moved in the compound.

Emon looked up just before he leapt for the hole. Despite the fact that sunset blazed like a marmalade wave through the lemon skies, a deep pitch blackness blotted the east, devouring the horizon.

CHAPTER 52

Rudy Kopal sat on the edge of the command chair of the *Hammadi*. He'd already sweated so much that his vacuum suit itched. His helmet sat on the floor beside him. Brown curls hung limply around his dirty face. They'd been working madly to patch the *Hammadi* back together over the past few hours. And now, as the ship hurtled through the yellow and purple flames of vault exit, he prayed she'd stay together in the attack. In front of him, his two chief officers licked their lips nervously. Marji Boyle, short with black hair and a triangular face, slouched wearily over the navigation console. Luther Calvin sat in front of the com console with a disheartened expression on his face. A skinny man with brown hair and a beak nose, he seemed to epitomize everything the crew felt: weary beyond exhaustion, desperate, afraid to hope, but willing to fight anyway.

The ship lurched slightly when they exited vault and Rudy called, "Get your helmets on, people. We don't know what we're going to be up against."

The clacking of helmets being fastened down clattered across the bridge. The *Orphica* streaked like lightning in front of them, diving for Palaia Station. Starsails and freighters emerged in a shotgun spray of light. They painted a hopscotch weave across the blackness of space. The vessels quickly veered, swinging around to form up into flanking position behind the *Hammadi* and the *Orphica*, awaiting further instructions about their place in the maneuver.

Rudy scrutinized the array of battle cruisers around Palaia. A black pit opened in his soul. *Twenty?* He'd been expecting a dozen. . . .

"*Captain!*" Boyle cried. "*They're forming up!*"

"The cruisers around Palaia separated into five groups

and swung wide, coming back around to reconfigure into flying wedges.

"How long to range, Boyle?"

"Sixty seconds, sir."

"Inform the commanders of the starsails to provide enfilading fire. Tell the freighters to fan out and cover the sails for as long as they can. Tell Captain Wells we'll lead the first pass." Rudy lightly pounded a fist into his knee. "And tell her—tell her good luck."

* * *

Rome. Cathedral of the Dawn Bathers, Annum 5384.

The entire crowd of white-robed devotees went silent when the elderly Patriarch hobbled into the arched cathedral. The old man clutched his precious book to his breast and looked around a little wistfully at the enormous size of the gathering. For twenty-five years the Church had supported and encouraged his odd scientific pursuits; he'd eaten its food, relied on its equipment and funding, warmed his hands by the fires his assigned monks had built to keep him from catching a chill. Not a man or woman there didn't love the wrinkled elder with all his or her might.

The Patriarch heaved a sigh and moved slowly down the aisle, heading toward the altar. The assembly rose to their feet with a shout that echoed through the church like the roar of a hundred lions.

The Patriarch smiled in embarrassment and forced his aged legs to climb the steps to the altar. When he stood at the top, he took his book in both hands and lifted it over his gray head.

In a voice thick with devotion and gratitude, he shouted, "Eppur si muove!"

CHAPTER 53

Breathing hard, Amirah ran around the corner and halted in front of the rectangular window overlooking the probe room. Mastema and his two guards hurried out of the room and pressed their faces against the window. The Master Magistrate screamed, "Bring him back! You fools! He can't die! Not yet. *He can't!*"

Inside, a Giclasian and a human lifted Tahn out of the probe chair and hurried him to a gurney. His muscular body had gone slack, legs and arms flopping unknowingly.

"Colonel Creighton!" Mastema raged. *"If Tahn dies—"*

"What happened?" Amirah shouted.

It was then that Amirah recognized Creighton. A qualm of horror rose. She could still hear his professional, cool voice narrating the atrocities on Tikkun. He'd gained weight and his hair and pointed beard had gone whiter since then, but his eyes still gleamed with that inhuman light.

"Captain?" Mastema questioned. "Tahn called for you just before. . . ."

Amirah shouldered by him and bashed the entry patch. She rushed inside just as Creighton moved a spiderlike revitalization machine over Tahn and hooked it up. She stood helplessly. Cole's blue-violet eyes were half-open, pupils dilated and fixed. Even in—in . . . death, his gaze hurled bitter accusations at her. Creighton and Mundus scurried around, whispering urgently, snapping commands back and forth. Jason quietly edged up beside her, his eyes darted, going over Baruch and the other Gamants under the probes, then shifted to the Magisterial personnel.

He whispered with near telepathic quiet, "Five of them, Captain. Only Mastema's two guards are armed."

Amirah's chest constricted as a hot rush of adrenaline fired her body. *Now!* her mind screamed. *It's your best chance!* But she hesitated and glared at Creighton, "What happened, Doctor?"

Creighton checked her captain's bars and squinted as though annoyed, "Surely you saw the fighting outside, Captain. Master Mastema wanted us to gain information as quickly as possible. Tahn wasn't being cooperative. Mastema turned the probes up to their highest intensity."

"*What!* No human can withstand that level! It's reserved for aliens with a much different brain structure." Her knees shook. *Oh, Cole, forgive me. . . .* "Did you damage his personality centers?"

"What does it matter?" Creighton casually replied as he attached a series of revitalization stimulators to Tahn's brain. "Slothen only cares about gaining information on Underground activities, Captain. Once we have that, the Magistrate has already ordered Tahn's tissue to be used as research fodder—if he lives."

Amirah stiffened her knees. They planned on keeping Tahn alive as long as possible? On methodically draining him of every shred of data, then using him for experiments? *Just like the old woman with the tattoo . . . and everyone else in that hideous room.*

She checked the status of Baruch and the other Gamants. Each writhed beneath the probes. Funk whimpered softly. On the screens over their heads bits and pieces of memories replayed. Amirah's soul withered. Baruch's memories were of Halloway. He went over and over the first moment he'd seen her on Palaia. Even as an outsider, Amirah could sense his terror. Sybil dreamed of a little boy in a white robe playing in the hot desert sun. Mikael and Yosef, oddly, were dreaming of each other a long time ago in a stark room aboard a cruiser. The *Hoyer*?

She glanced back at Cole. His fingers twitched beneath the revitalization stimulation. His pale face had contorted, as though he knew what was happening and was fighting it.

"Captain Jossel?" Mastema's scratchy voice penetrated the room. "I'd like to ask you some questions."

Her nerves hummed so tightly, she could barely force

her feet as far as the doorway. Jason stayed close to Tahn. "What is it, Magistrate?"

The withered alien fixed her with a penetrating stare. He held up Mikael Calas' glowing blue necklace. It swung like a pendulum in front of his face. "Do you know what this is? Did Calas tell you after you captured him?"

Amirah frowned at it. Somewhere in the oblivion of her childhood memories, she recalled Sefer speaking of a device like that, but she couldn't quite grasp the memory. "No."

Mastema's lavender eyes widened. "I think it's the Gehenna gate. It must be. Millions of Gamants have died protecting this, passing it down through the centuries." He laughed shrilly. "They thought we'd never get our hands on it!"

A sharp gasp sounded from the probe room and Amirah spun so suddenly she stumbled into the door. Creighton and Mundus had shoved Jason back; they hovered over Tahn, talking quickly. Amirah raced up behind them so she could see.

Cole's face had flushed. He blinked hard. When he finally figured out the nature of the huge machine encasing him, he let out a muffled cry of rage and began struggling to throw it off. He ripped the monitors from his head and flailed madly at the machine.

"Stop! Stop it!" Creighton demanded, trying to shove Tahn's hands away from his precious equipment. Tahn slammed him in the face with a hard fist. Creighton shouted in surprise and stumbled backward. "Mundus! Anesthesia!"

Mundus lunged for a syringe. Amirah's mouth gaped at the haphazard amount, and she grabbed Creighton by the shoulder. She brutally pulled him out of her way and stepped between Tahn and the hurrying Mundus. "Let me talk to him!"

"No. Get back!" Creighton demanded. "He's dangerous!"

Amirah ignored him and put her shoulder against the revitalization machine. She shoved it off so Tahn could see her face, but he didn't seem to know her. He continued to slam his fists into the machine. She clasped one of his frantic hands in a strong grip. "Cole! It's Amirah. Can you hear me? Calm down! You're all right!"

At the sound of her voice, he turned sharply to look at her. Recognition filled his panicked eyes. He clasped her hand back as hard as he could, and brought it to his chest. Beneath his black uniform, she could feel his heart thumping fiercely. He held onto her like a life raft in a stormy sea.

"You're all right, Cole," she soothed. "You're all right. . . . How are you feeling?"

He shook his head feebly. His gaze strayed to Creighton and Jason and . . . to Baruch. As though he'd been jolted with a current, he trembled and clutched her hand so hard it ached. His eyes begged her, *Now, Amirah. Now!*

She slowly straightened up and wiped her free hand on her purple pants. A gnashing like tiny teeth began in her chest.

Creighton strode haughtily over to Baruch and began turning up the intensity level on the silver probe unit. Jeremiel went rigid. His fists clenched and unclenched.

"While the Captain is handling Tahn," Creighton said caustically, "let's see what information we can gain from Baruch."

"Should I bring in his wife? She might be useful as leverage," Mundus suggested.

"Yes, do it."

Amirah started to object, but Mundus raced out of the room before she could open her mouth. In no time, he was back with two Giclasian technicians and Halloway on a gurney. He pushed her up in front of Baruch. She lay on her side. Auburn hair cascaded over her face. Her chest rose and fell so slowly beneath her black jumpsuit that it was barely noticeable. Creighton walked around and brought out a portable probe unit. Connecting it directly to Baruch's, he then placed it on Halloway's head.

Amirah had focused her attention so fully on the doctors' actions that she barely heard the muffled, enraged voices echoing through the halls outside. "What are you doing, Creighton?"

"Letting Baruch talk to his wife. If he can bring her

out of her catatonia, then we can use them against each other.''

Amirah watched in fascinated horror as Creighton went to the control panel on the table behind Jeremiel and stimulated first his mind, then Halloway's. Halloway's screen remained blank, but the screen above Jeremiel flared with happy scenes. He and Carey walked hand-in-hand down a dirt pathway shaded by towering cedars. She laughed and he put his arm around her, hugging her close. Shadows mottled their faces.

"Do you ever dream about running away, Carey?"

Amirah could barely stand the look in Halloway's eyes as she gazed up at her husband—filled with too much longing to be borne. *"No. Not me. You?"*

Jeremiel grinned wryly and patted her shoulder. *"Not me. I like constant battles and starvation."*

They shook their heads in unison and laughed.

Halloway's screen flickered suddenly. Amirah held her breath. Carey's body flinched. Memories flashed the briefest echo of Jeremiel's . . . trees and shadows . . . flits of conversation. Laughter.

Cole braced himself up on his elbows on his gurney. A terrible fear drenched his face. "No, Carey!" he shouted. "Don't do it. Don't come back!"

Amirah went ashen. Did he love her that much? So much that he'd rather she were dead than live through what the future held?

The images on Halloway's screen grew more coherent, the snatches of scenes longer . . . *"Do you believe in the coming of the Redeemer, Jeremiel?"* . . . a stern look from Baruch, uncertain . . . a river rushing over rocks . . . *"Yes, I believe . . ."*

Amirah tilted her head as the faint sound of voices in the hall outside came closer, like a hum increasing in intensity. Jason gave her look so penetrating, she turned to peer out the window, waiting.

"The fools," Creighton denounced sharply. "There is no Mashiah. . . ."

A blast like the fist of God slammed Palaia. Amirah clutched wildly for the door frame, but the force of the shock wave hurled her through the door. Jason crawled for her, pulling her back into the room as medical equipment cascaded to the floor in the observation room out-

side. The entire station heaved and seemed to list sideways
for a horrifying instant. Outside, Giclasian soldiers flooded
by, bellowing commands, staggering beneath the vibration
that pulsed through Palaia's bones.

Jason shouted to the forces, "What is it? What's
wrong?"

One of the soldiers yelled, *"It's the Underground!
They're attacking the station! Get to the subterranean shel-
ters. Hurry! Hurry!"*

The station's alert sirens snapped on, blaring piercingly.

Cole started to laugh hysterically. He rolled to his side
and glowered at the doctors. "No Mashiah, eh, Creighton?
That's the shofar, you sonofabitch! You hear me? *The
savior's coming!"*

Amirah's vision grew startling clear. Voices whispered
in her head. Anxious, terrified, *familiar.* She shook her
head violently, trying to quell them. When she looked
up, all Amirah could see were Cole's fiery eyes. Jason
was saying something to her, but she couldn't really hear
him. Everything in the room blacked out except Cole's
eyes. *His eyes, they . . . they looked so much like Grandmama's when . . . when . . .*

She fought it down! NO! *NO!*

Another blast pounded the station and the lustreglobes
flickered. Mundus spun and shrieked, then lunged for
the door. Creighton screamed for him to stay, but the
ugly Giclasian ran. In the turmoil, Cole dove off his gurney and scrambled on his stomach for Halloway. Mastema's guards lifted their rifles—

And Amirah rolled to her knees, pulled her pistol, and
fired.

The window shattered and spewed glass like twinkling
stars over the room. A hideous whine of Giclasian agony
rang out. Her next shot cut Creighton in half and sent
his lower torso flying against the revitalization machine.
Blood spattered Amirah's uniform and face.

"Amirah, get down!" Jason screamed. His body hit
hers with a jarring force, knocking her sideways as a shot
flashed through the room.

Jason's pistol flared. The blast shuddered the observation room. Amirah scrambled out from under him,
her pistol at the ready. From the corner of her vision,

she saw Cole brutally shove the probe helmet off Carey's head. He fleetingly touched her pale cheek before lunging for Baruch's helmet.

"Jeremiel, get up! Get up!"

Mastema's remaining guard stumbled through the probe room door, wounded, roaring like an animal, rifle aimed. Amirah's shot took him squarely in the chest. He toppled backward in a mutilated heap and she caught sight of Mastema's gurney disappearing around the corner.

"Hurry!" Jason demanded, grabbing her by the arm and jerking her to her feet. *"We've got to get out of here!"*

Baruch shook himself out of his daze and immediately grabbed for Halloway, dragging her off her gurney and onto the floor. He gently pulled her against the wall and sprinted for Mikael and Sybil, Ari and Yosef. All four woke shakily.

Another blast rocked the neuro center and Amirah's eyes widened. "That wasn't a shot hitting the EM shields," she whispered. "That was *on* the station!"

In the hallway, Giclasian screams pulsed jaggedly. Amirah shook off Jason's hand and ran for Tahn where he crouched on the floor. She jammed her extra pistol in his hand and stared him hard in the eyes. "Can you walk?"

His fist went tight around the gun. "Hell, yes."

Amirah gripped his forearm to help him to his feet. "Then let's get to the Spires!"

Tahn leaned on her, holding her back, looking at Baruch. "Jeremiel, get out of here! Take Carey and—"

Baruch came swiftly across the room. His voice was fast and deep. "I'm going to take everyone else to the landing field. If we can capture some of those fighters, we might just be able to hold off the station forces while you, Jossel, and Woloc get into the Spires."

"Jeremiel, goddamn it, no! I want you and Carey—"

"Shut up!" Baruch commanded authoritatively. *"That's got to be Rudy up there and if it is, he's vastly outnumbered! He's only got a half hour at most! Move, Tahn! GO!"* He slapped Cole hard on the shoulder and started for Halloway where she lay against the wall.

"Baruch?" Woloc called. Jeremiel turned and Jason tossed him his extra pistol. "Hope you make it."

Baruch smiled faintly. "Affirmative, Lieutenant."

Jason sprinted out of the room, his pistol aimed. Amirah followed, supporting Cole as they ran down the long corridor.

* * *

Arikha lay on her stomach, staring through her light bars at the bright green lamp on the bedside table. It had stopped flickering when the explosions died down. But it still gleamed with a sickly hue as though not on full power.

Or maybe it was just her eyes. They hadn't fed her in three days. She'd started feeling light-headed this morning, but it had grown to euphoria a few hours ago. Right now she seemed to be floating in a hot stormy ocean filled with sunlit dust. She absently waved her hand through the haze; it wavered like real dust.

Arikha blinked hard when she saw a woman enter the chamber. The stranger wore a long carmine cloak with the hood pulled up. Black hair fell in thick waves from her hood, spreading like a silken blanket over her chest. A beautiful woman, she had olive skin and a heart-shaped face. Her huge midnight eyes took in everything, going over each face in the beds. Finally, her eyes landed on Arikha and she walked forward, parting the sparkling dust like a ghost from the dark mists.

Her cloak swayed when she stopped beside the bed. "Have you seen General Ornias?"

Arikha croaked. "The guards . . . some of them said . . . all officers were going to . . . to take shelter in the Horns."

"The Horns?" Her eyes glowed with a frightening light that made Arikha huddle in upon herself.

"Yes. You know, the Spires." Arikha weakly extended a hand and pointed to the door that led out of the hospital.

The woman turned to leave.

"Wait! Please. Where is the Mashiah? Have you seen her?"

"No." The woman looked over her shoulder and wet her lips anxiously. "No. *Have you?*"

"I—I don't know. Maybe. She's here, you know."

"Yes," the stranger whispered forlornly and seemed to be struggling with herself. "I know." She swept for the door in a sibilant rustle of cloak, palmed the patch, and disappeared.

Arikha lay her head down and played with a fold in her blanket. The dust glimmered in the light of the lamp.

A few seconds later, the door where the woman had vanished slid back. The captain and lieutenant she'd seen earlier hurried out, the woman hauling the man in the tan jumpsuit.

When the captain looked at the room, she blurted, "Quickly, shut off all the light cages."

"Amirah!" the lieutenant shouted. "We haven't time!"

But the captain and the man she'd been supporting started running down the line of beds, hitting all the patches before they darted through the exit that led toward the landing field.

Arikha weakly sat up and threw her legs over the side of her bed. Every other prisoner who had the strength to follow rose and they coalesced into a weaving procession that stumbled for the door.

* * *

The First Alert sirens screamed in Rudy's ears as he hauled himself back into the command chair. Most of his bridge crew scrambled up from where they'd tumbled and crawled for their consoles. The next shot lanced out of the heavens, striking the *Hammadi*'s aft shields. The vessel hurtled sideways with such staggering g-force that three members of the crew passed out and toppled back to the floor.

Rudy gasped for breath, ordering, "Boyle! Hard right, we'll swing around—"

She'd slumped over her console, black hair glued to her face plate in bloody strands.

"*Boyle?*" He lurched out of his chair and took three bounds to jerk her back in her seat. Her head lolled aimlessly. *Dead.*

Rudy's soul chilled. He tugged her out of the nav chair

and sat down, inputting the sequence himself. "Ernist, take over auxiliary weapons and get ready!"

"Aye, sir!" the young lieutenant ran.

The crew shifted, rerouting functions to cover abandoned terminals. Rudy noted absently that a series of white dots lifted from Satellites 4 and 6 and sailed for Palaia. *Shuttles? What's Slothen doing? Reinforcing his ground troops in case we break through the shields?* He laughed morosely. They'd damned little chance of that.

The next blast came from the stern, spinning the *Hammadi* like a child's top. Surges of purple eddied across the forward screen like living flames.

Rudy pitched the vessel backward, spun around and soared headlong for the lagging ship in the Magisterial wedge. Wounded in their last pass, the cruiser hadn't enough agility to get out of the way before Rudy opened fire; its shields flared violet and vanished.

Rudy hit them again and sent the *Hammadi* plummeting out and away like a streak of lightning. Half his crew sprawled over their consoles, fighting to get back in their seats. On his mini-monitor, Rudy watched the Magisterial cruiser rupture. Ephemeral tongues of flame swept the wreckage before the hull exploded. Jagged fragments tumbled through a haze of congealed vapor.

"Sir?" Luther Calvin shouted. His eyes had narrowed painfully. *"They . . . they look like they're forming up for a Laced Star maneuver!"*

Rudy glanced up wildly. On the forward screen, five battle cruisers closed in from different directions, encircling the *Hammadi*, taking up the five points of a star.

A glacial sensation of folly filled his breast. He repressed the scream of angry despair that swelled up his throat. In a deathly quiet voice, he ordered, "Calvin, open a tran to Captain Wells—*Clandestine One.*

Calvin's hands flitted over the com console. "Open, sir. Go."

Rudy composed himself for a split second. "Merle. It's over for us. Take the first opportunity and back out of the maneuver. *Get out of here! You hear me?* There's nothing else you can do here. . . ."

His voice faded, gaze going back to the forward screen.

The cruisers had started their runs, following the lines of the star. When the first two ships reached the corners of the Star's interior pentagon, they opened fire simultaneously, slamming the *Hammadi* from both sides at once.

CHAPTER 54

Jeremiel gently released Carey into Sybil's arms and
glanced around at the rest of his motley entourage.
Mikael, Ari, and Yosef peered at him, awaiting instructions. The other nine Gamants who'd escaped their death
beds sank wearily against the walls. Several held guns in
weak fists. He'd been forced to kill a team of six soldiers
they'd encountered in the halls. They now had a total of
seven weapons among the fifteen of them. Not enough,
but it would have to do.

He eased out the door to examine the landing field.
Giclasians swarmed over it, guarding the fighters and
shuttles, arranging bulwarks. The pungent scents of seared
petrolon and burned flesh swelled the hot air. Blasted
carcasses, human and Giclasian, scattered the ground.

His gaze shot up to the sky. Dozens of shuttles
descended through the sunset-fired clouds, setting down
awkwardly in the hills beyond the boundaries of Naas.
The Giclasians on the landing field yelled shrilly to each
other as people streamed down the gangplanks, ragged,
dressed in bloody clothes, some clutching rifles, most
with makeshift weapons like clubs and rocks. *Gamants.*
Blessed gods.

Magisterial fighters soared suddenly overhead and cannon barrages ravaged the hills, exploding the shuttles.
People ran screaming, some fired at the fighters with
their rifles before racing away. Across the undulating
war-torn plains, Jeremiel could see hundreds of people
sprinting toward the Engineering Spires. He clinched his
teeth, not understanding why, but praying for them.
Praying for Tahn.

But not praying to Epagael. *Aktariel, it's now or never.*
I always believed you were on our side. Prove it!

Jeremiel clutched his pistol more tightly and got down on his stomach to crawl behind a toppled pile of crates.

Three small triangular shaped fighters sat no more than twenty long paces away. Jeremiel scanned the darkening skies. The sun had dropped below the horizon, but echoes of its light laced the heavens with a rusty saffron hue.

From behind, he heard a soft sound. He turned to see Sybil peering intently at him. Her dark eyes gleamed with a determination so powerful it felt tangible. He squinted out at the landing field again, noting the positions of the alien forces, then waved Sybil forward.

She and Mikael edged out, dragging Carey between them. Jeremiel's heart throbbed. Her head flopped aimlessly, beautiful auburn hair dragging in the dirt. Behind Mikael, everyone else emerged, crawling on their bellies.

When Sybil and Mikael got close enough, Jeremiel pointed to the three fighters arranged like an isosceles triangle in front of the crates. "You can both pilot ships, right"

Sybil licked her chapped lips and nodded. "Yes, Jeremiel. Just tell us what to do."

"We'll need to divide into three groups of five each. I'll create a diversion. When I do, you'll take your teams and run like hell for your fighters. Sybil, the one on the far left is yours. Mikael, yours in in the middle. I'll take the one on the right." His jaw hardened. "They may be sealed. I don't know. If so, forget about them. Get back to the building and try to find a hole to hide in until the shooting stops." *If it ever does.* He gestured to the Giclasian soldiers at the other end of the field. "Everyone with pistols should aim at those guards stationed at the southwestern edge of the field. They're the only ones who'll immediately have clear shots at you. You see the soldiers I mean?"

"Yes." Sybil peered malevolently out at the enemy. "And then what?"

Jeremiel smiled with a confidence he didn't feel. "And then we fly for the Spires and try to drive the Magisterial fighters away. Our goal is to give Tahn, Jossel, and Woloc enough time to get to the main auxiliary control room. Understand?"

"Yes." Mikael's nostrils flared. "Let's go."

Jeremiel reached over to caress Carey's cold frail hand. She felt like ice. "Choose up your teams. Tell whoever's left that they're to follow me."

Mikael and Sybil slithered away on their stomachs and quickly selected allies. Five people crawled forward and surrounded Jeremiel. They looked at him with wide, terrified eyes: four men and one women, all trembling from fatigue and lack of food. The leading woman had long stringy black hair and penetrating blue eyes.

"Commander Baruch," she whispered. "I'm Arikha Anpin. I was one of the leaders of the satellite rebellions before I got captured. I'm good with a gun. What do you need me to do?"

"I'm going to have to drag my wife, which means I'll only have one hand free—"

"No, I'll help you carry her. We'll support her between us. That way we'll both have a free hand to shoot—"

Screams shredded the air. The horde of Gamants racing for the Horns had reached the base of the mountain and started climbing frantically. And behind them, swarming herds of Giclasian soldiers pursued in a purple wave, swinging around in a wide circle, closing ranks. Jeremiel couldn't see the opposite side of the low mountain, but his gut tightened with the certain knowledge that Magisterial forces must be flanking those positions, too.

In the distance, six fighters broke out of formation and veered off, bringing their ships around.

"Ready, Arikha?" he called.

"Ready."

Jeremiel gently pulled Carey to her feet and draped her right arm over his shoulders. Arikha took her left arm. Carey sagged between them like a limp cloak. Jeremiel bent down and brushed his lips against her cold cheek.

When the next fighter barrage lanced the ground by the Spires, Jeremiel shouted, *"Now!"* He pulled his pistol and fired, panning the field as he ran for the fighter; Carey's legs scraped hideously over the dirt. Giclasian soldiers, confused and terrified by fire coming from the neuro building, jostled for new positions, plunging headlong for anything that offered cover.

Just before Jeremiel and Arikha reached the fighter, a

lance of purple split the ground asunder in front of him and he jerked Carey from Arikha's grip and locked his legs around her. He rolled desperately, trying to get behind the fighter's landing gear.

Arikha hit the ground on her stomach, firing in controlled, accurate bursts. An eerie luminescent web of purple zigzagged across the field. The world burst into a melee of wild shots, and screams as Jeremiel lunged for the entry console on the side of the fighter.

CHAPTER 55

Carey glared hotly at Anapiel. He'd closed the door to the seventh crystal palace and leaned against it, blocking her entry. In a haughty, nonchalant gesture, the angel smiled and flipped the ends of his purple sash. As the sun dipped lower, his yellow robe flared like molten flower petals. Zadok had been shouting and stamping around for hours, but it had done little good.

"When will Epagael see us?" Carey demanded. "Gabriel said that Michael had already arranged for our meeting. I have to talk to God and get home!"

Anapiel shook amber curls from his glowing face and laughed a low, cold laugh. "Rachel's been toying with things she doesn't understand. You'll be lucky if you can get home at all, Halloway. And if you manage that feat of magic, you'll be luckier still to find Tahn and Baruch alive."

Carey's chest tightened. "Why?"

"Because both of them have been captured by the Magistrates and are currently on Palaia—"

"No," she murmured. "No, not . . ."

As though from a great distance she thought she heard Cole call out to her—*frightened, panicked*. His wail echoed like mortar fire in her soul.

A responding cry was wrenched from the depths of her belly, *"Cole!"*

She lunged violently for Anapiel. *"Get out of my way, angel!"*

* * *

Every muscle in Cole's body ached. He had his arms braced over Amirah's and Woloc's shoulders. They dragged him headlong for the Spires, in the midst of a group of frenzied Gamants. People rushed and shoved, screaming orders, some crying. Many even dragged children by the hands as they climbed up the steep mountainside. The double doors to the subterranean control chambers loomed large, built into the earthen hillside.

Above, fighters veered, fell into formation, and headed back for them. Sailing over the tips of the lavender Spires, they blasted the group of rushing Gamants. The three men in front of Cole were hit. The hot spray of blood drenched Cole and Amirah. She cried out angrily, and rushed forward, dragging Cole forcefully as they tramped up the final stairs to the doors.

Amirah slid out from under Cole's arm, leaving Woloc to support him, and trotted forward to try the door. When it didn't yield, she bashed a boot into it repeatedly, then yelled, *"Get back!"* to the surging torrent of Gamants, turned her pistol to full power, and fired.

Chunks of the door flew off, spinning through the air and into the crowd, but the portal refused to crumble. Amirah let out a low guttural sound of rage and frustration, then shouted, *"Jason, Cole. Let's hit it together!"*

Woloc hauled Cole forward and he locked his knees and pulled his pistol. They lined out in front of the door and their eyes widened as two dozen more people moved up alongside them, each with a gun trained on the recalcitrant entry.

Amirah scrutinized the Gamants and smiled proudly. "On the count of three. Ready? *One, two . . . three!"*

They all fired. After several seconds, the door shattered . . . and a herd of distraught Giclasians rushed them, surging forward in a blue tidal wave. Screams of surprise and hatred tore the cool evening. Cole dove to the side, knocking Amirah out of the line of fire as a stampeding swarm of Gamants threw themselves at the Giclasian soldiers. Garish purple flames burned through the assembly. Cole covered Amirah with his own body and added his pistol to the onslaught. The Giclasians finally broke and ran back into the control center.

Amirah wriggled from beneath Cole and got to her feet to watch the human bombardment flood through the doors. Jason ran forward, shouldering through the crowd to stand beside them. When an opening occurred in the press, Amirah gripped Cole's arm and tugged it over her shoulders.

"Jason, you take point. Tahn and I will follow. He's the expert at singularity manipulation."

"Aye, Captain," Woloc sprinted inside.

Cole twined his fingers in Amirah's bloody purple sleeve and ran with all his strength.

From memory, they wound down the correct corridors, going deeper and deeper beneath the surface, sliding along the walls. The backup generators had kicked on, shedding a vague bluish light from the overhead panels. They could only see a few feet in front of them. Faint sounds of battle vibrated through the floor—mortar blasts, sections of building caving, racing feet.

"Amirah?" Woloc warned. "Wait."

Cole leaned a shoulder wearily against the wall as Amirah slipped out from beneath his arm. "What is it?"

The carpeted floor muted the thud of Amirah's boots as she moved forward.

Woloc whispered, "Do you hear it?"

"No, I . . ."

Cole did, a faint wailing, breathless, agonized; it swept down the corridors in the darkness. He gripped his pistol.

The suffocating screams came closer, accompanied by the shrill clacking of alien laughter. Amirah eased back, her hand moving along the wall until she touched Cole's shoulder.

"Back up," she whispered in his ear. "We can't let them catch us in the open."

Cole forced his exhausted body to retreat around the last corner they'd passed. Amirah and Woloc took the opposite side of the hall. They waited, their breathing hissing irregularly.

Cole wiped a hand over his brow. He didn't know why, but over the past fifteen minutes, a raging fever had possessed him. What drug had Creighton given him during the revitalization process? He felt on the verge of delirium.

Slithering steps sounded.

Three Giclasians bulled around the corner, dragging a human, a woman, between them. The creature in the lead had a blue lustreglobe implanted in his helmet. The constantly swaying light cast their images in monstrous multiple shadows across the white walls. The human was wounded, her blood streaked the gray carpet like a lurid trail of crimson paint. They'd obviously been toying with her, for wide triangular gashes were ripped in her yellow robe, slicing into the soft flesh of her breasts and legs. Triangles, in mockery of the Gamant sacred symbol?

"We'll take this human out onto the landing field," the leader said in his mechanical voice, "and cut her to pieces before the eyes of her filthy comrades."

The woman prisoner groaned in hatred and kicked out weakly. One of the Giclasians struck her in the face with his rifle butt and she sobbed.

Cole glanced at Amirah. Her beautiful face had gone rigid, turquoise eyes ablaze. She motioned for Woloc to back up further and get down. Jason complied, crouching in the darkness.

It seemed an eternity before the lead Giclasian rounded the corner and ran straight into Amirah's pistol.

She shoved her pistol into his throat and fired. The alien's balloon head burst. The second Giclasian shrieked as his cohort's blood sprayed him. Amirah waded into the fray, firing.

"Come on!" she shouted.

Woloc grabbed Cole and together they raced after Amirah. He felt at the edge of his endurance, hot, so hot and tired. He staggered erratically, unhappily forcing Woloc to physically haul him. Around the next corner, Amirah ran back.

She whispered roughly to him. "Stay on your feet! There're more coming."

As though just remembering, she reached into her boot and pulled out his Wind River fighting knife, then gruffly shoved it into his boot. "In case you need it for close-quarters combat," she hurriedly explained.

The weight of the ancient blade felt comforting. "Hurry, we haven't much time."

Amirah's arm went around his waist and she and Jason supported him down the dark hallway. He caught a glimpse of the wounded Gamant woman crawling around the corner before they dodged into an adjacent hallway.

The pounding of dozens of boots pummeled the floor. Alien voices clacked.

Cole blinked fiercely at the darkness. Tiny stars of

light flitted over the ceiling like wayward silver fireflies. *You can't pass out, goddamn you!* He leaned into Amir-ah's arm, praying that if worse came to worst, she could keep him from falling flat on his face at the feet of their enemies.

She understood instantly. "Jason! He's going to pass out!"

Amirah whirled around to catch Cole under the arms and press him back against the wall. He stood weakly, aware of her breasts pressing into his chest, of the pleas-ant scent of her sweat and the acrid smell of Giclasian and human blood staining her dress uniform, the warmth of her breath on his throat. Pale blue lights flashed from some nearby hallway and Cole tightened his hold around Amirah's shoulders and drew her against him with as much strength as he could muster. Woloc silently crouched, his pistol aimed down the corridor. They all stopped breath-ing when they heard alien movements—dozens of arms and legs slapping the walls, the pungent, nauseating scent of Giclasian sweat.

Cole nuzzled his chin against Amirah's hair. It felt good to hold her. She hugged him tightly as the onslaught of alien soldiers passed and the thudding of their boots died away.

In the fading remnants of light, Cole saw Amirah gaze up to study his face anxiously. She put a gentle hand against his drenched hair and felt his fevered flesh. A dark expression came over her. She looked like a hard-eyed goddess hewn from the palest of azure marble. Blonde hair dangled in blood-matted wisps around her cheeks.

"If you faint again," she informed. "I'm going to kick the hell out of you."

He laughed feebly, "You'll never make an angel of mercy, my dear. I'm not going to faint—at least not for another ten minutes. You think you and Woloc can get me to the control room before that."

Her eyes glittered with a frosty fire. "We'll get you there."

Jason trotted silently forward. "Captain, it's going to be close. Zohar has to be on its final approach. The attacks on the EM shields from the Underground have stopped. I think—I think we might be on our own."

Amirah swallowed hard. He meant the Underground cruisers had been killed. "You may be right."

Cole shook his head feebly. "No. I don't believe it, Amirah. It would take longer to kill both Kopal and Wells—no matter how outnumbered they are." His nostrils flared with fear for his friends.

"Then we'd better go. We might be able to help them."

For an indeterminate amount of time, they ran down one corridor, then another, until Cole had no idea where they were and he was so exhausted he was afraid Amirah might have to kick the hell out of him after all.

The building had gone unnaturally quiet. As quiet as a midnight graveyard. It frightened him. Where were the Gamant forces? He forced himself to think of all the times in his military career that he'd felt desperate beyond measure, when things had looked hopeless and he was sure he wouldn't make it. . . .

And his thoughts drew up Carey, the only friend he'd ever had who'd never let him down, coldly beautiful as she shoved him against the wall in the transport tube aboard the *Hoyer* and ripped open his shirt to stare at his bloody chest. *"Goddamn it, Cole! Stay alert! Run a count!* His memories jumbled, mixing, haunting.

Carey, oh my Carey. *Run a count, damn you.* "Ten, nine, eight, seven, six, fi . . ."

He felt his knees slam the floor. Blackness swallowed the world.

The next thing he knew, he was lying prostrate. The chill touch of the gritty tiles on his fevered face felt so soothing he longed to stay there forever. Scents of dirt and burning petrolon stung his nostrils and Amirah's terse voice ravaged, *"Get up, Cole! We're almost there. Get up or I'll shoot you myself!"*

He fought to slide his hands under his chest and push up, but dizziness swept him and he tumbled back to the floor. Pain eddied in scorching waves along his limbs.

Amirah's fingernails sliced into his arm and he felt Woloc's stern grip. He reeled drunkenly as they tugged him to his feet, shoved his pistol in his right hand, and ran again.

A human shriek of rage blared from the next intersection of corridors, and a rumble of assenting voices joined in. The floor beneath Cole's feet shook with the impact of dozens of pounding boots as people hurtled forward.

Amirah and Woloc dragged Cole to the floor and they slithered against the wall, pistols braced. His heart thundered as he blinked sweat out his blurry eyes and sighted down the length of his gray barrel. The walls oscillated wildly in his vision. *Stay conscious. For the sake of God . . . !*

Two Giclasians stumbled around the corner and toppled toward them. Cole triggered his pistol, blowing them to shreds before he realized they were already dead on their feet.

And Amirah and Woloc pulled him up and they were running again. Running, stumbling, running. . . .

They swung around another corner and Cole sucked in a breath. Six Giclasians swarmed toward them, arms and legs rotating, rifles leveled. Where had the Gamants gone? Didn't they realize this was the main control room? Cole raised his gun in sickening slow-motion and fired.

The lead soldier's head vanished in a blur of blood. Amirah and Woloc's pistols discharged, wiping out four in a single burst. Amirah screamed something unintelligible as she charged, hauling him forward with her.

The last Giclasian held his ground before the control room door and aimed.

Unthinkingly, Cole lunged in front of Amirah.

He didn't feel the blast that ripped his shoulder and sent him crashing into the wall and tumbling across the dirty floor. But when he heard Amirah scream raggedly and hideous flares of violet encircled him, he noticed that hot blood flowed across his chest in sticky surges.

Odd thoughts occurred to him. Not about his death. Thoughts about the *Sefiroth* and Rachel's curious equations and Jeremiel's comments about Woloc. And he wished he'd had just five minutes on the console which monitored Palaia's containment chamber so he could have tested his hypothesis about frequency variation and maximum singularity charge.

But he felt too weak to do anything but lie here against the cool dirty floor.

From the edge of his vision, he saw Amirah dart by and heard her brutally pounding agianst a wall. The entry patch? She let out a low desperate groan and then he heard her pistol discharge on full power. A shrapnel spray of burning petrolon spurted into the air and whined from the walls and ceiling, spattering him with melted flecks.

"Jason! Bring him!"

Then . . . *"Cole!"*

He jumped, startled. It wasn't Amirah's voice.

It was Carey. She sounded desperate, terrified.

"Carey," he whispered. "Where are you? Stay away, Carey."

Cole felt Woloc grab him beneath the arms and drag him headfirst into the control room. Dim silver light fell over the small hexagonal chamber, lighting dozens of computer screens. And faintly, very faintly, he heard someone laugh.

"Kind of you, Captain Jossel," an insidious, gloating voice, said, "to bring Tahn to us here."

CHAPTER 56

Carey shoved Anapiel away from the door to the palace. He laughingly stepped aside and made a broad sweeping gesture with his arm. "Take care, Halloway. The future is not as firm as it seems. You're walking on shifting sands."

She jerked open the door and stepped inside, waving curtly to Zadok. "Come on, Patriarch."

"No." Anapiel ordered as he stepped in front of Zadok to block his path. "From this moment forward, Carey, *dear,* you're alone."

She sprinted down the long hall. The walls glimmered with a marmalade light so fierce, it seemed Epagael had waved his huge hand and gleaned millions of orange stars from the heavens to use as the plaster of this structure.

She ran with all her might, racing past the curious statues that filled hidden niches. Her steps faltered when she saw the monstrous black whirlwind spin out of nothingness. It seemed a gigantic ebony wound—*like the vortex of a naked singularity*. In front of the wound, a long white Veil stretched endlessly. A broad River of Fire gushed in flaming molten braids to block her path from the Veil. The heat was suffocating.

Carey stood panting. The maw called to her in silent screams of rage and hope. Flashes of bizarre images twisted through her thoughts—light so brilliant no eye could ever perceive it, love beyond comprehension, a bitter well of darkness so black and abysmal it could only exist in the mind of God. Power pervaded the images, as though a thread of eternity connected them, spinning their souls together in a pattern Carey could barely grasp.

A gentle voice boomed from the gaping heart of the darkness. *"Did he make you come here?"*

"Aktariel? No, I came of my own free will."

"Why?"

She glared into the black pit. "What have you done to my friends?"

"Blame Aktariel. His wickedness is a blight upon your universe."

"*His* wickedness!" Terror for Cole and Jeremiel ate at her. Were they dead? Or just suffering? "Are you the Creator?"

"I am the Alpha and the Omega. The Beginning and the End. The Archigenitor and the Destroyer of Worlds."

She angrily swung around and pointed down the glittering orange corridor toward the general direction of the Void of Authades. "At this very moment, my friends, your Chosen People are dying by the thousands while they scream to you for help. Do something to save them, you bastard! What about all the promises you made to protect them? Who are you, Epagael? What are you? Are you God?"

Fiery sparkles lit the depths and of the black whirlwind and spiraled down into nothingness. "I am the Alpha—"

Carey shouted, *"Are you God? Or some—some form of alien species we know nothing about?"*

Epagael hesitated for a long, long time, until Carey wanted to run forward into the whirlwind and slam her fists into the amorphous Darkness.

Finally, He asked, "What is . . . 'alien'?"

Carey straightened. "Another species. A different sort of creature."

"The two are not mutually exclusive."

She slowly cocked her head as her heart started to pound. "What does that mean? Are you the only one of your kind? Or are you one of many 'gods'? Is there a creator beyond you—beyond all the gods? Did someone create you?"

"I am the Unborn."

"Are you eternal?"

"Only the Treasury is Everlasting."

The Treasury. . . !

Carey glanced around. The walls of the seventh crystal palace had begun to shimmer wildly, as though alive and waiting breathlessly for the final answer to this debate. "What is the Treasury?"

"The foundation of all."

"Including you?"

A pause. As though contemplating the question. "Is pure energy the foundation of your personality, Carey Halloway?"

"Yes. Ultimately."

"So it is of all things."

Carey's face slackened in understanding. A dozen years ago on Horeb an obscure prophet, Adom Kemar Tartarus, had preached something similar. She'd discussed it with Jeremiel often. Tartarus had believed that the idea of an eternal soul—in the sense of a person's distinct personality—was a quaint fiction. Only energy lasted forever. He'd believed that individual consciousnesses had an epiphenomenal basis, that *personality* was spawned by the interaction of the physiochemical processes in the brain. The old Gamant believers had always accused Tartarus of being influenced by Aktariel.

And maybe it was so.

Carey eyed the vortex inquisitively. Perhaps God's soul was nothing more than a macrocosmic example of the human soul, formed in the same way?

"Epagael?" she called. "Did you, like me, go through the stages of conception, birth, childhood, and adulthood?"

"Evolution occurs. Correct."

Carey folded her arms and rubbed her fingers over the old bloodstains stiffening the sleeves of her black jumpsuit. "Interesting."

The black whirlwind seemed to be spinning slower, as though listening. *What are you, Epagael? An alien parasite feeding upon the eternal sea of primordial Energy? . . . Perhaps all personalities were? Including her own?* Carey shivered suddenly. If God's personality evolved over billions of years, the current Epagael might not bear any resemblance to the deity who originally created the multiple universes. *Is that what you're doing, Aktariel? Trying to alter the personality of the being currently sprouting from the Treasury? Why?*

Lord, your gatekeeper, Sedriel, talked about Rachel. What's she done that has your angels so frightened?"

"Rachel, poor Rachel. She's the last of the *Sefirah*. She's trying to reconfigure the strands of light, to create a new refrain in the symphony of Chaos, to sweeten the melody."

"Will she succeed?"

"Unknown."

Carey's heart quickened. "If Rachel succeeds, how much of the Void will she kill? It won't just be my universe, will it?"

The River of Fire roared louder, almost deafening. Carey pressed her hands over her ears and glared at the black vortex.

"If Aktariel and Rachel succeed, Carey Halloway, all the universes in close proximity to yours will be sucked away."

A prickle of terror went up her spine. "Send me home, God. I want to go home."

No answer.

"I want to go home, God!"

"Why? You'll be going home to oblivion. . . ."

* * *

"Put down your weapons, Jossel and Woloc!" Ornias said as he squeezed the trigger of his pistol. His purple general's uniform clung wetly to his arms. Blood speckled his face and braided beard.

Amirah and Jason dragged Tahn through the door. It closed behind them. Blonde hair had fallen out of her clasp to drape in tangled curls around her cheeks. Computer screens glowed in the darkness, reporting information from across the station, and casting a rainbow over the hexagonal chamber. Slothen and Mastema crowded against the far wall, their blue faces pinched and hateful. Mastema lay atop his gurney with Mikael's curious necklace pressed against his bosom. Both Magistrates glared menacingly at her—but only Ornias had a gun.

A malignant rumble like a bestial growl went through the station. Amirah staggered.

"Zohar's getting closer!" Ornias wailed. "Drop your gun, Captain!"

Cole weakly took in the scene. "Do it, Amirah," he whispered.

Amirah hesitated, then reluctantly dropped her pistol and grabbed Cole's right arm with both hands. "Help me, Jason."

Woloc gripped Tahn's other arm and they dragged him into the center of the room by the main control console— a raised chair and semicircle of computer screens. Such a broad trail of blood marred the gray carpet that Amirah had started to tremble. The fragments of bone protruding from Cole's wounded shoulder shifted as she gently released him. When his handsome face twisted in pain, Amirah leaned forward and kissed his cheek, using it as an excuse to murmur in his ear, "Stay alert. We're not done yet."

He threw her an incredulous look.

She rose and wiped her bloody hands on her purple pants, then turned to face Slothen and Mastema. "Magistrates, I—"

"Shut up, Captain!" Ornias ordered. "Get Tahn up into that control chair. I thought Mastema would know how to run these controls, but the technology has changed so much since his day, that he's baffled. All of our other engineers and specialists are gone or dead, and we *must* have someone who knows how to keep this station out of Zohar's way."

Cole inhaled a difficult breath and laughed grimly. "What makes you think I'll do it, General?"

Ornias' jaw quivered with rage. "You will, Tahn! If I have to slice you apart piece by piece!" He took two steps toward Amirah and Jason. "Get him into that chair! Now!"

Amirah and Jason helped Cole to the chair where they let him down easy. Jason threw her a look of panic before he backed away.

Cole slumped forward over the console. . . . And his eyes suddenly sharpened as he took in the massive array of patches, levers, and com readouts. In a disturbingly amiable voice, he noted, "You're in deep trouble, gentlemen. I'm not sure there's anything I can do. Palaia is perched on the edge of Zohar's event horizon at this very moment."

Abject terror tensed Ornias' face. "Get us out of its path! I don't care how you do it—just do it!"

"But really, General, I—"

"*I'll kill Captain Jossel!*" he threatened and swung his pistol around to aim at Amirah's face. "If you don't do something Tahn, *she's dead!*"

Jason's breast heaved with impotent rage. He glanced at Ornias' pistol and Amirah's taut face.

Cole fixed Ornias with a lethal glare and swiveled around to the controls—his hand trembled as he lifted it to the console. An involuntary shudder went through his body. Amirah flinched. *He's going into shock. No, not yet!* Amirah walked back onto the raised platform and dropped a hand to squeeze his broad shoulder reassuringly. Cole seemed to rally; he closed his eyes and after a few moments the tremors stopped. He input a series of equations. Amirah counted them because she hadn't anything better to do: one, two . . . three . . . four, five.

Tahn waited and when an equation popped up in response to his query, he exhaled very quietly. It looked like a mass ratio to Amirah.

Cole casually input several more commands, grumbling inaudibly to himself as he shifted his wounded shoulder *to shield his console from Ornias' view!*

Amirah shot a glance at the screen and her heart throbbed agonizingly: WARNING! TAPPING SHIELDS AT LEVEL FIVE INTENSITY WILL RESULT IN FAILURE IN LESS THAN FIFTEEN MINUTES. PLEASE CANCEL COMMAND OR INSTRUCT REGARDING EXCESSIVE CHARGING OF SINGULARITIES?

Oh, God. The singularities in Palaia's hold don't have sufficient charge . . . he has to tap the shields.

Amirah stepped around to stand between Tahn and Ornias, to hide Cole's actions completely, even if for only a few precious seconds. Tahn understood. She heard him strike several patches in quick succession.

Ornias' malicious gaze riveted on her. "Move back to where you were, Captain?"

Amirah lifted her hands in surrender and gazed at Mastema and Slothen as though straining to hear what they were saying. The Magistrates spoke quietly, urgently to each other in low tones. Ornias followed her gaze. She caught Mastema's whisper: *But the ship is wait-ing . . . can't wait much longer.* Slothen responded: *. . . still fighting in halls . . . can't get out until . . .*

Ornias' eyes narrowed. He glanced fearfully at Amirah. "I said move back, Captain! My patience is run-ning thin!"

"Just how do you plan to get off this station, General," she taunted, delaying, "once we're out of Zohar's path? There are hundreds of Gamants on the plains of Naas. Maybe thousands by now." She laughed deprecatingly and noticed Jason take a deep breath. He nervously looked between her and Ornias.

Ornias gripped his pistol more tightly and glowered. "If you don't back up immediately, Captain, you won't live long enough to find out. Move!"

Amirah complied, stepping behind Cole's chair in time to see him hit the master override switch. His screen blanked. She braced a hand on the back of his chair to steady herself. In an intimate and comforting gesture Tahn lifted his good hand and twined his fingers tightly with hers. If they'd only had a few more days—oh, how she would have loved to spend time with him. She squeezed his hand fiercely.

"What's happening, Tahn?" Ornias demanded hysteri-cally. "Are you maneuvering us away . . ."

The station convulsed, lurching as though in the throes of death. The floor rose up to slam Amirah. Screams, Giclasian and human, swept the chamber and Amirah rolled, lunging for Ornias who lay stunned a few feet away—he saw her coming and crabbed backward, shout-ing, *"Don't try it! Don't try it, you little fool! Or I'll . . ."*

The door to the chamber rattled.

A moment later, a huge ebony whirlwind spun out of the wall near Cole. He lay in a crumpled pile of black uniform on the raised platform. Ornias shrieked and ran to stand beside Slothen and Mastema. In a splatter of brilliant gold, a woman appeared. She had waist-length black hair and the blackest eyes Amirah had ever seen. Her long carmine cloak fluttered as she gracefully walked toward Cole.

"Captain," she called gently as she knelt. Her cloak draped around her in deep blood-colored folds. An

expression of anguish creased her beautiful face when
she looked down at Tahn.

"Cole," the woman whispered.

He seemed to rouse at the sound of her voice. He
gazed up at her through mystified eyes. "Rachel, what
. . . what are you doing here? How did you—"

"Don't talk now. Save your strength. We haven't much
time." Rachel reached out and pulled back Cole's torn
black uniform then gently placed her hand on his wounded
shoulder.

He flinched against the pain.

Amirah watched in fascinated disbelief as the wound
began to heal. When Rachel removed her hand, Cole's
shoulder bore not the slightest trace of injury. He caught
Rachel's fingers as she tried to pull them back and held
them in a death grip. He fixed her with astonished blue-
violet eyes.

"How did you do that, Rachel?"

"It's very simple, really. You just have to refocus the
strands of the vortex. Adom used to do it effortlessly. It
took me time to learn."

"What's happened to you?"

She smiled as though speaking to a child she knew
would not understand. "The Serpent entered my soul."

"Serpent," Slothen whispered. His blue face twisted,
as though in abrupt understanding.

Rachel got to her feet and turned to peer evilly at
General Ornias. He shrieked and fired his pistol wildly.
The shot blasted a hole in the wall behind her. Jason
lunged. He kicked out brutally, bashing Ornias' hand and
sending his gun clattering across the floor.

Ornias bellowed in agony and grabbed his broken
wrist, but his eyes riveted on the strange woman.
"Rachel, what are you doing here?" he raged insanely.

Rachel knelt to retrieve the pistol. Amirah silently slid
toward Cole. She sat down and felt his shoulder in
amazement. His eyes blazed, and when she looked into
them Amirah knew that he'd accomplished what he'd set
out to do at those controls. Triumph shone. She patted
his side proudly, wondering how long they had before
the containment vessel exploded?

"I found you, Ornias," Rachel crooned in a chilling
voice. She circled the general, pistol aimed at his chest.

Jason backed away, moving to crouch beside Amirah.

"Rachel . . . what . . . what do you want? *What are you!*" The general screamed.

"I'm an old friend, remember? We have long-overdue business to take of." As though chanting words she'd memorized eons ago, words of horror and power, she lifted her voice. *"I remember, Ornias. I remember the cries of the children buried beneath the mound of dead in the square on Horeb. Children I knew would never see the next sun rise."*

She aimed her pistol with slow precision and fired. Two quick bursts burned out Ornias' eyes. He shrieked like a mad beast, sprawling across the floor and insanely clawing at his face.

Over his cries, Rachel shouted, "The pitiful whimpers of those children still fill my nightmares, Ornias! I hear them crying out to their parents, begging someone, anyone, to hold them."

She aimed again and slashed off his right arm. The dead meat thudded sickeningly to the floor. Ornias screamed and struggled to pull himself away—but Rachel followed.

"I remember, Ornias. You killed my husband. You destroyed my little girl's life." She tilted her head in a mad, insane gesture and her voice lowered to a whisper. *"You hurt my people."*

With agonizing slowness, Rachel aimed her gun at his chest. Ornias seemed to know. He sobbed and stiffened, preparing for the shot. But she hesitated and clicked her pistol down two notches before firing. Expertly, she cauterized Ornias' wounds. The blood stopped. The stench of burning human flesh reeked so fetidly in the air that Amirah's stomach rose into her throat.

"Did you think I'd kill you, Ornias " Rachel asked hoarsely.

He squealed, "Why are you doing this? Tell me what you want! I'll do anything!"

Rachel pulled on the golden chain that encircled her throat. A brilliantly glowing necklace—just like the one Mastema still held—fell out of her robe. She gripped it lovingly. "I've never had any intention of killing you, Ornias. On the contrary, I've spent years searching the voids, trying to find just the right home for you. You'll appreciate it. It's utterly dark and empty—just like your soul. And timeless. You'll never die, Ornias." She smiled. "Never."

Amirah's mind reeled. She could imagine Ornias crawling blindly through cold darkness for eternity, groping with his one arm, seeking a way out and never finding it.

Horror twisted Ornias' bloody face until he looked like a ghoul risen from a fresh grave. *"Rachel, no! Not that! Anything . . ."*

She lifted a hand and a gaping black maw spun into existence behind Ornias. He must have felt the brush of icy wind, for he desperately leaned back to grab for the steadying wall even as he fell.

His hideous scream echoed endlessly.

In the foray, Amirah crept on her hands and knees to the place by the door where she and Jason had dropped their guns. She retrieved hers and shouted, "Woloc!" then tossed him his. Jason fell into a defensive crouch.

No one breathed.

The maw spun closed and Rachel turned to give Slothen and Mastema frigid looks. "And as for you, Magistrates." She strolled toward Slothen. "You've tormented Gamants for millennia." She lifted her pistol again.

"Wait!" Slothen demanded. He threw out a trembling arm. "Are you . . . *are you the promised Mashiah?"*

Rachel stared into that blue alien face and laughed condescendingly. "It depends on your perspective."

And without even changing the half-amused expression on her face, she fired at Mastema, slicing through his breast. The Master Magistrate let out a small gasp before slumping to the floor. Blue blood pooled around him on the carpet. Rachel knelt and in a fearful gesture grabbed the *Mea* from the dead Giclasian's contorted hand.

Amirah got to her feet, watching in dread as Rachel swept across the room, her carmine cloak fluttering out behind her—*to hand the Mea to Amirah.*

Rachel extended it farther, until the gray globe swung over Amirah's heart. Eloel's eyes gleamed frighteningly. "Take it, Captain Jossel. For today, it belongs to Mikael Calas, but there will come a time when it will be your duty to pass it down to his son."

Amirah glanced oddly at Cole. He'd gotten weakly to

his feet and stood with a hand braced against the back of the command chair. "What's she talking about, Tahn? I don't—"

"Doesn't matter," he said. "Take it, Amirah."

She complied, accepting the device and slipping it around her neck. "But how can she know what the future holds?"

Slothen stepped out of the shadows, his lavender eyes wide and horrified. *"Because she's the Mashiah!"*

Rachel laughed, a low, cold-blooded sound and glowered at him over her shoulder. "You know so little about Gamants—"

"Mashiah!" Slothen hissed. He took another step and extended two of his arms, pointing at Rachel. *"That means serpent in the Gamant language, Amirah. Yes, do you understand? Serpent. Serpent!"*

Amirah gasped as a white-hot pain lanced her. She dropped to the floor on her knees. The earthquake began, shuddering through the floor, tossing her around like a rag doll. *The final battle!* The lights went out.

Smoke. She smelled smoke! She had to get out of here!

Amirah reeled to her feet. In the jet black corners of the room Darkness swelled. She could sense the hot breath of the Creature on her face. And outside, in the hall, Gamant voices spun an eerie web of horror. Terror gripped her by the throat. She screamed, *"Grandmama! Where are you? I can't see you in the smoke! Where are you?"*

Cole lunged off the dais and ran for her. "Woloc! Get her gun! She's—"

Jason dove for Amirah, knocking her to the floor. They struggled against each other, rolling over and over, fighting for the pistol. Cole screamed, *"Amirah! Stop it! Slothen's doing this to you! AMIRAH, DON'T!"*

Only the fiery azure glow of Rachel's *Mea* lit the room. As Rachel stumbled to keep her balance, it wavered over the walls and consoles like blue windblown flames. Cole threw himself into the struggle, trying to lock down Amirah's legs.

"Now, Amirah!" Slothen commanded. *"Hurry! They're all serpents, Amirah! Serpents!"*

Amirah screamed and fell into wild sobs, struggling

498   *Kathleen M. O'Neal*

with all her might against Cole and Jason. Cole tried to
grab for her flailing pistol hand, but she jerked it out of
his grip and aimed with deadly accuracy at Jason Woloc.
The lieutenant opened his mouth to shout, but Amirah
fired.

"*Serpents!*" Slothen hissed. "All of them!"

In the sudden purple flash Cole couldn't see anything
but the spinning blue aura around Rachel. He threw himself atop Amirah as she swung right and aimed at it. Her
pistol flared twice—quick bursts.

Cole cried out in shock as Rachel crumpled like a silk
scarf to lie in the tumbled heap of her carmine cloak.
Chest shot . . .

The station juddered violently beneath them, but
Amirah had gone limp. Cole pushed up on shaking arms
to stare at her. She lay on her side, gazing in horror from
Woloc's wide dead eyes to her pistol. Jason's face had
twisted miserably.

"Oh, my dear God," Amirah whimpered. She weakly
got to her knees and crawled over to Jason. She lifted
his hand and pressed it to her cheek. Silent sobs racked
her.

Cole wiped his dirty sleeve over his sweating forehead
and took in the room. Slothen stiffened when Cole's icy
gaze landed on him. The Magistrate took a step toward
Amirah.

"*You forgot one, Captain,*" Slothen whispered insidiously. He extended a blue arm toward Tahn. "*This one!
Serpent! Kill him!*"

Cole dove for the floor as Amirah picked up her pistol
and leveled it again . . .

But this time at Slothen.

Tears streaked her swollen face. "Magistrate," she
informed in a husky voice. "You've persecuted your last
Gamant."

Slothen thrust out four hands and screamed, "*No!
Amirah, don't you see? We had to do it. If there really was
a Mashiah we had to take precautions. We couldn't—*"

"You made me kill my grandmother!" Amirah raged.
"I remember now, Slothen! *I remember!*"

She fired and fired—and kept firing until nothing
moved. A ghastly purple halo engulfed the room. Blue
gouts spurted from the Magistrate's severed head and

mangled body, falling in huge spatters across Rachel's legs.

Cole scrambled on all fours for Rachel. Blood bubbled at her lips, but her chest still rose and fell. *Alive!*

He tenderly brushed the tangled strands of black away from her pale face and glanced at the chronometer that barely glowed the control console. "Go!" he shouted agonizingly at Amirah. "Get out, if you can! You've got three minutes!"

Amirah shook her head wearily. "No. I'm staying with you."

"Get out of here!" Cole commanded as he worked his way to the console and slumped down into the chair. He glanced hurriedly at the readings. The holes had reached maximum charge, Zohar verged on perihelion, Palaia's containment vessel was breaking up.

With unnerving calmness, Amirah said, "I'm staying, Cole. There's nothing left for me out there. You go!"

Cole spun around in his chair. "Don't be ridiculous! I'm the singularity expert. Only I—"

As though in a dream, Cole suddenly felt like he was floating—the shudder of the station ceased—he smelled the sweet scent of roses. He shook himself and spun around in his chair. Amirah leaned against the wall by the door, watching a huge maw of black whirl over Rachel's tumbled form.

A man of crystalline magnificence appeared, wearing a blue velvet cloak with the hood pulled up. He knelt gracefully at Rachel's side and anguish twisted his glorious face. He stroked Rachel's bloody cheek lovingly.

Cole couldn't move. Carey'd told him stories . . . about the bridge of the *Hoyer* just before the fiery apocalypse over Tikkun . . . an angel had descended, she'd said. *It was the angel who talked Dannon into taking the weapons console, Cole. It was the angel who saved me and what was left of the Underground fleet.*

When the crystalline being looked up at Cole, he felt the sorrow and despair in those kind eyes like a blow in his stomach.

The angel gracefully walked across the room to gaze down at Cole. "Captain Tahn. I'll give you as much time as I can, but you must go now. Hurry." He glanced forlornly back at Eloel. "Rachel spent a great deal of time preparing a place for you . . . I won't stop you from going."

"What place?"

"A good place. It may even stay that way. I don't know. The chaotic patterns are fluctuating too wildly for me to guess. If I have the chance, I'll try to—"

The shudder in the floor built to a crashing crescendo that made Cole's heart go cold and still.

The angel's amber eyes flamed. *"Get out, Captain. Now!"*

Cole lunged off the dais, racing erratically for Amirah. "I believe him. Come on!"

Together, they careened out the door and down the blood-spattered corridor, heading for the surface.

CHAPTER 57

A jolt like a cannon attack brutally threw Carey into her restraints and woke her. Her spirit seeped back into her flesh like a warm rush of water, aching in her glacially cold hands and feet. She shivered and sucked a sudden breath into her lungs.

"Carey?" Jeremiel's surprised voice demanded. A hard hand gripped her arm.

She blinked at the cramped interior of the fighter, noted the five Gamants in bloody rags huddled in the back and the instincts of twenty-five years of war kicked in. She straightened in her seat and scrutinized the weapons, power, and communications panels. "What's happening, Jeremiel?"

"Get on the weapons console! We've got six fighters on our tail!" He threw her a fleeting smile, before rushing to input data into his nav com. His blond hair and reddish beard bore a dusty shroud of tan dirt.

Carey spun around. Out the round side portal she could see the familiar landscape of Palaia, the Pharaggen Mountains, Naas and *Zohar*. The black hole rose like a malevolent whirling eye over the horizon. A tingle of terror wound through her. Red flashes caught her eyes and she glanced back at her weapons com, noting the positions of the incoming fighters. "Jeremiel, there are two fighters flanking the Magisterial line—"

"Ours! Mikael and Sybil."

Jeremiel's hands danced over the nav controls and their ship plunged and twisted sideways, ruthlessly slamming Carey back in her seat. She watched the hills blur into a mass of green and brown as they soared toward the Pharaggen Mountains on full thrust.

On her monitor, she saw the lead Magisterial fighter

swing around, coming to point-blank range on their port side. "Firing," she announced.

Purple lances shot out from their fighter, slamming the Magisterial ship. It hurtled sideways and five others dropped into formation around her and Jeremiel, boxing them. Mikael and Sybil swept by overhead, blasting the formation, killing one of the ships. It spun sickeningly and exploded.

"Firing again!"

Carey's shot arced across the closest fighter's shields as Jeremiel dove, then decelerated so shockingly that Carey's empty stomach heaved. As they swerved up and around, escaping the deadly formation, Carey fired again. The enemy fighter flared and exploded in a blinding flash of silver.

"Brace yourselves," Jeremiel coolly commanded. "We've got to get back to the mountains, before the Magistrates' ground forces trap the Gamant population that's gathered at the Spires."

"Affirmative." Carey wiped the sweat from her forehead and gazed out the portal at the mountains. Her mouth gaped. There had to be a thousand Gamants blanketing the green side of the eastern slope. And behind and all around them, purple-uniformed soldiers ran, firing in calculated patterns of devastation, picking off the most vulnerable segments of the fleeing masses. Purple flashes dusted the sunset drenched hills. In a desperate whisper, Carey murmured, "In the name of blessed . . . Aktariel. What are they doing there?"

Jeremiel glanced at her curiously. "Arikha says they've gathered to await the arrival of the Mashiah."

A hollow ache built in Carey's chest. *Who was the Mashiah in this universe? Was there one?*

A barrage of cannon fire came out of nowhere and struck them catastrophically, flipping them over. Their aft shields flared and died. Carey heard a woman behind her scream hoarsely when she saw a fighter swoop up from behind the cover of a rugged ridge. Jeremiel spun their ship frantically, trying to keep their forward shields to the attacker. Three more fighters emerged from the cover of the ridges. They swung up and around, then dove like hawks descending on a wounded mouse.

Carey fired again—missed—retargeted—fired. She sliced

off the starboard wing of the lead fighter and it heaved and gyrated as it slammed into the ground and tumbled in fiery fragments across the plains.

Two of the fighters joined up with one of the survivors from the last pass, lining out on either side of them. They fired simultaneously, pouring every erg into the forward shields. Another fighter sailed down from the heavens, dropping to fire point-blank at their vulnerable aft section.

The ship lurched and waffled violently. "We're hit!"

"I know," Jeremiel said calmly while he fought the helm to keep them from tumbling to their deaths. His eyes went stern. "Where are Mikael and Sybil, do you see them?"

Carey examined the tracker on her com. Nothing. "I don't know. Maybe they landed. Maybe they got hit."

Smoke boiled into the command cabin, blinding Carey. Flames licked around the edges of the door to the rear storage area. Lurching out of her seat, Carey weaved to the emergency equipment compartment, but instead of grabbing the fire control extinguisher, she tugged out five chutes and two jet packs. She threw the chutes at the terrified Gamants. "Do you know how to use these?"

The woman with long dark hair nodded. "Yes! I'm Arikha. I'll show the others."

Carey ran forward and awkwardly slipped the pack over Jeremiel's shoulders while he battled to keep the pitching ship in the air. He gave her a worried but warm look as she fastened the belt around his waist and pulled it tight, then hastily got into her own pack.

To the Gamants, Jeremiel called, "Arikha? Get ready. I'm going in low. You'll have to jump in quick succession."

"We understand, Commander." Arikha waved the other Gamants into the rear of the fighter by the side doors.

Carey watched the top of the Pharaggen Mountains heave up to meet them. The rocky plateaus loomed out like eager jagged teeth. The side doors parted and each Gamant jumped. Their chutes opened like blossoming flowers below.

"Ready, Carey?" Jeremiel asked tautly.

"Yes. Let's go."

She held her breath as Jeremiel hit the eject patch . . .

Carey tumbled end over end, the darkening yellow sky and tree-clad mountains swirling in a muddy smear around her. A savage roar exploded from somewhere below and a searing wall of heat rose to roast her face. Carey gasped and jammed her palm against the activation patch for her pack.

The jets kicked in with a ferocious jolt and she found herself flying like a hurled rock over the peaks. Their ship blazed below, pitching into rocks and disintegrating as it plunged down the western slopes.

Jeremiel? Carey frantically searched the skies, but saw only fighters forming up for another run and a few low-flying shuttles. On the plains below, either Mikael's or Sybil's fighter lay in a crashed, fiery heap. Another fighter sat intact beside it. Carey dove, skimming the ground, heading for the Engineering Spires where the Gamants had gathered. From her perspective the leveled out spaces appeared to form a huge animal of some sort, broad-shouldered and with horns. Trees passed below in green strips. She soared over the heart of the animal intaglio and decelerated.

Screaming people charged erratically out to meet her, waving their arms and cheering. And though Carey hadn't seen them in twelve long war-torn years, she recognized Mikael and Sybil standing hand-in-hand between the two prongs of the strange rock formation.

She landed in a burst of tan dust and frantically shoved through the swelling crowd, shouting in rage at them, *"Get back! Get back, damn it! I have to get to Mikael and Sybil!"*

The station shuddered turbulently under her feet. Carey ran, legs pounding as madly as possible over the reeling surface.

Mikael recognized her and threw down Sybil's hand to lunge for her. His black curls fluttered around his cheeks tangling in his beard as he ran. Dressed in a bright red robe streaked with dust and blood, he seemed a tattered pillar of flame.

"Lieutenant Halloway!" he called.

"Mikael! You're the leader of Gamant civilization! You've got to get these people off this mountain! The government forces are closing ranks! They've got you surrounded."

She grabbed him by the arm as they collided and bodily

hauled him back up to the high point overlooking the mumbling, shifting crowd, where Sybil waited. Brown hair draped in thick curls to Sybil's waist, accentuating the pale shimmer of her ivory robe.

As they climbed up between the two spikes, Sybil shouted, *"Look! It's Jeremiel!"*

Carey spun around to see Jeremiel racing up the northern slope, followed by a wailing crowd of ragged dirty soldiers with rifles clutched in their arms. He had a granite expression on his face.

"Carey!" he shouted. *"Get down! Get down! Fighters coming in!"*

She leapt for Mikael and knocked him flat as eight fighters swept over the peaks and blasted the mountaintop. People ran screaming, shoving, trying to find cover. Brilliant purple flares gouged the pastel colors of sunset and rippled through the clouds like lurid fire.

A hushed cry of astonishment began and swelled to crashing climax. A wave of people pointed at the doors to the subterranean control chamber. Carey rolled off Mikael's tall body and shaded her eyes. When she saw Cole and an unknown Magisterial captain running toward them, she lunged to her feet.

"Cole?"

* * *

Rudy rolled feebly to his side, coughing, gasping for breath. Blood smeared his face plate like thick pudding. He struggled to find a clear space so he could inspect the forward screen. His soul cried out at the sight that met his searching gaze. Bodies and debris had congealed into a spinning cloud around the *Hammadi*. Beyond the cloud, battle cruisers soared, still attacking stubborn starsails and freighters. Where was Merle? *Merle?* Palaia hung below, its orange bulk silhouetted against the looming blackness of Zohar. Purple splashes tormented the plains.

"Is that you down there, Jeremiel? Sorry we couldn't keep 'em off longer, old friend."

He shoved up on his elbows. Dead crew members sprawled hideously across the bridge. On the three-sixty monitors, he could see that decks two, five, and ten through twenty had breached.

He slammed a fist into the floor and suppressed the angry insanity that threatened to engulf him. "Do something, damn you. Do something!"

Rudy dragged himself back to the nav com and hoisted his injured body into the tip-tilted chair. He probed the few screens that worked and squinted at Palaia. The station's defense shells oscillated furiously.

"Breaking up. . . ?" Rudy peered pensively at the readings. Hope grew. He flexed his gloved hands over the controls and a low, desperate laugh took him. He struck a few patches, asking for updated information, then his smile faded to a miserable grimace.

"Forgive me," he whispered to all of the crew members with damaged suits who might still be alive on the contained decks. Methodically, he rerouted every shred of remaining power, including life support, to the weapons.

Flopping back in his chair, Rudy lifted a finger over the patch and let it hover . . .

Before striking it.

CHAPTER 58

A broad violet beam gored Palaia's shields, slashing the rolling hills with pulverizing force. Hope flared inside Carey. Six of the fighters swerved up and away, streaking toward the offending cruiser. *Kopal! It had to be! He was trying to draw the fighters' fire away from them.* "Move!" she shouted to the swarming Gamant multitude. "Get down!"

The Magisterial captain hauled Cole forward, partially supporting his weight. Overhead, three fighters swerved back through the twilit skies.

"Oh, God!" Carey heard Sybil Calas cry. "If we only had a *Mea*. In my dreams we always had a *Mea!*"

A Mea? Carey started to take off hers. . . .

But the blonde captain with Cole tore a *Mea* from around her throat and shouted, "Here!" She tossed it to Sybil.

Sybil's mouth dropped open, but she took the sacred device and pulled Mikael forward; in a tender gesture, she put the *Mea* between their foreheads and they kissed. . . .

Carey stumbled backward when the *Mea* ignited, burning with such a blinding blue light that the entire mountaintop erupted in screams and shouts of awe. Against the dwindling coral rays of sunset Mikael and Sybil seemed to merge, melding into a cerulean pillar of Pure Light. And over their heads, the tips of the rock spikes started to glow.

"The Horns!" Yosef Calas shouted. He staggered backward into Ari Funk's arms. "Look!"

The azure flame spread down the shafts and flooded forth like a watery carpet to drown every man, woman and child on the mountain. In awe, people frantically brushed at each other's fiery countenances.

507

A deep-throated growl percolated from somewhere in the depths of the station, rising to a rumbling roar that shook the foundations off the universe.

Carey's throat constricted as a huge spinning well of Darkness opened beside Mikael and Sybil. Like a slithering ebony serpent, it stretched endlessly into the flaming sky, twining out into space.

Blessed Aktariel, where does this go?

Shrill whines sounded as the fighters began their final run. Carey let out a jagged cry of rage. The fighters lined out into two wedges and hurled headlong for the Pharaggen Mountains.

A blinding flash of gold exploded near Mikael and Sybil. Carey spun breathlessly. As though in response to her cry, Aktariel walked gracefully forward and touched Sybil's forehead. Carey couldn't hear what Aktariel said to them, but Mikael nodded fervently.

When Aktariel lowered his hand and stepped back, Mikael and Sybil closed their eyes, as though concentrating harder. The cyclone of Darkness broadened, spreading like a sea of night into the heavens.

Aktariel turned to gaze forlornly at the terrified crowd, then he turned his attention to the blonde captain. She seemed dazed and uncertain as though some communication passed between them that left her reeling. Aktariel smiled sadly, lifted his hand, and vanished.

The captain stood rigid a moment, then glanced at Cole and shouted at the crowd, "What are you waiting for? Hurry it up!"

Cole desperately reached for her. "Amirah? What are you doing?"

The woman ignored Tahn, sprinting forward into the cerulean blaze that enveloped Mikael and Sybil. She climbed up the gritty side of one of the horns to wave frantically, shouting, *"Run into the Void! It's the only way to escape the cannons! RUN! RUN, OR YOU'LL ALL BE DAMNED."*

The hushed cry of *"Salvation . . . this is it . . . salvation . . ."* eddied forward through the assembly and a din of humanity raced forward in a flood that sounded like the crashing waters of an avenging sea swallowing up an enemy army. Male and female, young and old, they bravely lunged down the throat of the black serpent.

Carey charged headlong for Jeremiel. He stood, suddenly alone, on the downhill side of the Horns. He seemed barely aware of the enemy fighters that aimed straight for him. Jeremiel had a peculiar expression on his face as he watched the blonde captain: disbelief, awe.

"Jeremiel, hurry!" Carey demanded as she slid to a halt in front of him. "Run!"

The fighters opened fire. A din of whines like a herd of dying animals rose as the world vanished in a purple wash of light and flying debris. Carey dove for Jeremiel and together they rolled down the slope, tumbling head-first toward the edge of the dark Void Mikael and Sybil had opened. For the briefest of instants blackness enveloped them as they toppled over brush and rocks to land hard against an upthrust sandstone slab. Jeremiel threw himself over Carey, covering her protectively.

. . . But all the noise had stopped.

The whine of the fighters was gone. The screams had died away.

Only the rhythmic surging of Carey's heart gave voice to the ethereal quiet.

Jeremiel eased up and peered around. Blood coursed from the scratches on his left cheek and oozed from rips in his black sleeves.

He slowly pushed to his feet and his blue eyes darted over the landscape. "Carey, where are we?"

"I don't know," she whispered fearfully. She got up. They stood on a sandy hilltop overlooking a fortified village surrounded by high stone walls. Goats frolicked in the dirt streets, the bells around their necks jangling. Gamant refugees ran in a triumphant flood for the nearest gate.

Jeremiel put an arm around her shoulders and hugged her. On a hillside in the distance, a group of people had gathered beneath a series of standing crosses. An odd sensation of premonition made Carey feel hollow.

"Let's go ask somebody over there."

Jeremiel hesitated, his keen eyes scanning the hills. "Do you see Cole, or Mikael and Sybil?"

"No. But they may have been the last to come through."

CHAPTER 59

> From afar they come in joy of their God; from distant islands God has assembled them. He flattened high mountains into level ground for them. The hills fled at their coming.
>
> Yerushalaim, put on the clothes of your glory, prepare the robe of your holiness!
>
> **Psalms of Solomon**
> **Codex Sinaiticus.**
> **Circa 37 C.E. Document housed**
> **in Septuaginta archives on**
> **Josephus 4.**

Aktariel knelt on the floor and gently lifted Rachel's wounded body in his arms. She felt feather-light and as frail as a blade of grass. Her carmine cloak draped in sculpted folds over his legs. The hexagonal control chamber with its massive array of multicolored computer screens and consoles had gone utterly dark. But his golden glow and the combined effulgence of the *Meas* gave the chamber a greenish hue.

"Rachel?" he whispered. "I know you can hear me." He tenderly pushed the wealth of black waves away from her slack face. "I need you with me for the culmination. It'll be hard. Even afterward."

He felt her soul cower and he clutched her powerfully against him. "I can let you go if you want me to. Or . . ." he swallowed convulsively and nuzzled his cheek against hers. "Or I can let you go to Yisroel—with Sybil and Jeremiel. It's your choice."

She vacillated, mentally reaching out to him, then jerking away in fear. He gazed around the quaking room while he waited. Slothen's hideous body had gone stiff, his mangled arms thrusting up at odd angels. Mastema glared accusingly through wide dead eyes.

Finally, Rachel courageously reached out to him again. He smiled mournfully and put his hand over her wounded chest. His spirit flowed in and around her, pulling together the wavering strands of the vortex, mending the damage to her delicate human flesh.

She roused in his arms and looked up through dark somber eyes.

"Are you ready, Rachel. It's time."

"Yes, I–I'm ready."

He led her to the control console and waved his hand to call up the image of Zohar on one of the overhead screens. Rachel straightened beside him, standing bravely. Thick waves of black hair cascaded down the back of her carmine cloak.

She tilted her beautiful face up to gaze at him. In those midnight eyes he saw fear. "Are they all safely away, Aktariel?"

He bowed his head and nodded. "Yes, they're safe. Just as you wanted. I don't know the outcome of your actions. But I can't worry about it now."

In the golden glow of his face, he saw her mouth tighten. "I had to try."

Gently, he responded, "I know."

She fumbled aimlessly with the bloody starburst over her chest. "You let them go?"

"Yes."

Rachel touched his shoulder and he cautiously pulled her against him, letting himself drown for a few precious seconds in the feel of her body and fragrance of her hair.

"I'm sorry, Rachel. We must hurry."

On the overhead screen, he could see Zohar's black gaping mouth swell until it encompassed the screen.

Rachel pressed warmly against him. "Do you hear it?" she asked.

"I hear it."

It had started only moments ago—an unearthly music, like a glistening halo flitting around the edges of his consciousness. That soundless song of Light whispered to him in such sweet, high notes he wished he could dangle here on the edge of the two merging event horizons and listen to it forever.

"We need to get inside our own void," he urged and lifted his hand to draw out the spinning vortex. They stepped inside and stood on the very edge, still visually surrounded by the main control room with its flickering computer screens.

He braced himself—waiting—and finally Palaia Station broke up and its massive charge combined with that of Zohar.

The event horizons vanished in an actinic burst of such overpowering brilliance that Aktariel vented a small cry and threw up his arm to shield his eyes. Rachel buried her face in the soft folds of his blue hood.

"How much longer?" Rachel asked.

He shook his head and whispered. "I don't know."

The glittering shawl of music oscillated, growing deeper, changing into a wrenching wail that swept through Aktariel like a glacial wind. Despite the protective womb of their void, he could feel the dread and terror pervading Epagael as he absorbed this station with its few thousand tormented consciousnesses.

In the utter blackness, light flickered, then a long dagger shot out, stretching endlessly, widening like a river in flood as it streaked out of Zohar's throat and shot into the universe in a flaming silver wash.

Barely audible, Rachel said, "Jachin? The Pillar of Light?"

"Yes. Epagael's trying desperately to cleanse the universe before any more of the poison can enter His body. Which means—" he vented a soft sigh "—it's time for us to add our millennia of accumulated memories to the rush."

Aktariel took off his *Mea* and gestured for Rachel to do the same. She hesitantly complied and gently draped the golden chain atop his open palm. He closed his fingers tightly around both and gathered Rachel into his arms. He noticed with mild disdain that his muscles had started to tremble. What did he fear, he wondered? The possibility of failure? Or just the grief for all the small things he'd miss? Wildflowers and sunrises . . .

He caressed Rachel's long silken hair and closed his eyes, murmuring, "Stay close to me," as he tossed their *Meas* into the whirling darkness.

The void around them vanished in a flare of cold glittering glory. A deluge of misty rainbow fires swallowed them as they fell, and fell . . .

Their grip on each other strained until it felt as tenuous as a crystal thread.

"*Aktariel?* Rachel cried.

"*I'm here,*" he answered softly, comfortingly, and tightened his grip on her. "I'm here . . ."

. . . and they pierced the Treasury of Light and melted like prodigal sparks into the eternal blinding brilliance.

CHAPTER 60

Rudy laughed feebly when Palaia exploded. The *Hammadi* had been battered so brutally, the Magisterial cruisers had shoved the vessel out and away from the station. He lay on his back on the shattered bridge, equipment tumbling around him, pinning his legs to the floor. But on the forward screen, he saw chunks of the station hurtle outward at near light speed, streaming across the dark heavens like coherent beams of violet. They spurted around the blasted carcass of the *Hammadi* and streaked away into space.

Behind them, in the space where Palaia had been, a twinkling spray of white sparks coalesced out of the silver wash of light, growing in intensity.

"Singularities from Palaia's hold."

They moved as though animate, weaving toward each other in a gravitational dance of such sublime magnificence that Rudy's eyes blurred with tears. When the holes got too close to each other, white threads of mass shot out from each spark, tying to the other until the entire spray formed a gigantic glimmering net.

Rudy had to slit his eyes against the brilliance. Through the dark crescents of his blood-encrusted lashes, he watched the net condense against the background of Zohar and . . .

Vanish.

Debris, Magisterial cruisers, and a few of the starsails whirled down into the gaping naked singularity that blotted the sky like an ebony fist.

Rudy felt the tug on the *Hammadi* and a chill feeling of resigned acceptance pervaded him. He studied the ruined interior of the bridge, his eyes drifting over the toppled consoles and shredded walls to land painfully on the torn bodies of his crew. Dead. All dead.

Nothing mattered anymore. Palaia was gone.

And Jeremiel, and Tahn . . . and Merle.

His throat tightened chokingly and he closed his eyes briefly, wondering what it would be like? The oblivion of death? Would he sense it when the powerful electric fields of the charged hole tore apart every atom in his body?

He turned back to the forward screen to examine the instrument of his death. Rudy's eyes widened. A curious phenomena snaked around the edges of the naked singularity, like a whipping black elephant truck. It braised over several of the freighters and they vanished.

The trunk slithered toward the *Hammadi*.

CHAPTER 61

Nathan rolled onto his side beneath the scant shade of a
boulder and pounded a fist into the soft warm sand of
Gulgolet. He'd wept for so long and so hard that his
throat ached. He tried to swallow and had to force it
down while he gazed up at the line of crosses that stood
silhouetted against the lavender rays of sunset. Yesu's
head had lolled forward in unconsciousness minutes
before. His long hair draped like a brown sheath over
his naked chest. His loincloth and the ropes securing his
hands and feet to the cross were the only remnants he
wore to shield him against the coming chill of night.

That morning when the sun had edged above the horizon in a golden crescent, they'd launched their rescue
attempt—and failed. The Procurator had tripled his
forces around the hill. Matthya had been killed and
Nathan had escaped by sheer luck, disappearing in the
wild clash of horses and rush of fleeing people.

He squeezed his sun-ravaged eyes closed and listened
to the repentant voices that came from the crowd. All
day long people had been gathering, watching, some
gleefully cursing Yesu, others sobbing wildly.

"Lord," Nathan prayed in a gravelly voice. "Help,
Yesu. He's done nothing wrong. Nothing except try to
save his people from the injustices of the Romans.
Please, God, I'll do anything you ask. Just send me a
sign that you . . ."

Nathan opened his eyes when the earth began to
quake. He sat up and saw, as though in a hazy dream,
a great darkness well in the sky behind the crosses. Like
a funnel of the purest black, it spun outward to cover
the whole land—*and from its heart, angels, a man and a
woman dressed in strange clothes, emerged.*

The centurions, seeing them, spurred their horses in

fear and tried to gallop away, but the terrified animals sidestepped and ran in circles, shrieking and bucking. The angels shouted to each other in foreign words and drew swords of light from their belts, slashing the heavens with violet blades—as though in judgment!

"Oh," Nathan croaked as he staggered to his feet. "God sent me angels. Angels with swords of fire!"

The crowd on the hillside screamed and fled, racing away in a torrent of confusion and terror. Nathan knelt, trembling, as the angels trotted toward him. Tears streaked the woman's cheeks, creating a spiderweb of tracks in the dirt on her beautiful face. She glanced at Yesu and her eyes hardened. She said something soft and pulled a knife from her male companion's boot, then warily edged forward to slice the ropes that bound Yesu's feet. Peering anxiously at Nathan, she climbed the back of the cross and cut apart the ropes on Yesu's hands. She gripped Yesu tightly and helped him down to the warm sandy ground.

"Yesu?" Nathan called with tears in his hoarse voice. He dropped to his knees beside the woman angel and gripped Yesu's hot arm. "Yesu, don't die. Wake up." He gently shook Bar Abbas' shoulder. "Please, wake up?"

Nathan heard the running steps that swished in the sand behind him, but didn't look. He tenderly slapped Yesu's bearded bloody cheek and his friend's eyes fluttered and widened as he gazed over Nathan's broad shoulder. *Alive! Bless God!*

Nathan stared at the woman angel, then up at her male counterpart. "Thank you," he wept. "Thank you so much."

The man, who had brown hair and strange blue-violet eyes shifted uncomfortably. To the woman, he murmured, "Gamant?"

The female pushed spun gold hair away from her face and answered, "Similar. Let's see how much." She turned to Nathan and inquired in a heavy and odd Aramaic accent, "Who are you? What is the name of this city?"

Nathan prostrated himself before them and dug his fingers into the sand by their curious boots. "I am Nathanaeus, great angel, thank you. Thank you for com-

ing to help. I praise God that He sent you to the city of
Yerushalaim on this terrible day."

The golden-haired woman looked at the male angel
speculatively. Hostilely, she demanded, "Well, *historian*,
where the hell is that?"

Before the male could answer, a rush of people surged
up the hill, most of them covered with blood, and wearing rags. Nathan patted Yesu's chest soothingly and stood
up. He shielded his eyes from the last rays of sunset. A
man and woman led the way. Both young, his age, he
guessed. The man had black hair and wore a red robe.
The woman was small and thin and had long brown curls.
Beside them, two very old men hobbled, their ancient
legs barely carrying them through the deep sand of
Gulgolet.

"These are our friends," the woman angel explained.
She stepped aside and pulled her male companion back
with her.

Nathan swallowed anxiously, not certain what was happening, or why these supernatural beings treated him so
oddly.

When the young woman with brown curls got closer,
she looked up suddenly and her eyes widened in shock.
Her thin hand went to her throat, clutching it as though
in pain. The man with her stopped and gripped her elbow
steadyingly. "What's wrong, Sybil?"

A gust of hot wind swept the hilltop, salting them with
stinging grains of sand. Nathan threw up his arm to shield
his face, and when he slowly lowered it, he found one
of the old men staring from him to the dark-haired young
man and back again, as though weighing their similar
features.

The man waddled forward, short and pudgy, a bare
fringe of white hair surrounded his otherwise bald head.
A deep pattern of wrinkles wove across his round face.
He looked up at Nathan in a gentle way. His tall, gangly
friend followed cautiously, one step at a time.

"What's your name?" The little old man inquired in
that odd accent.

Nathan bowed respectfully, glancing at the people in
the gathering crowd. All of them dressed strangely, most
in curious shiny fabrics like nothing he'd ever seen. "I
am Caius Nathanaeus, elder. Who are you?"

"Nathanaeus?" the little man repeated softly. His eyes glowed suddenly. "I'm Yosef Calas. This is my friend, Ari Funk and . . ." he turned to the young man and woman standing awkwardly behind. "And this is—well, Mikael and Sybil Calas, my grandniece and nephew."

The young man, *Mikael*, stepped around Funk and gingerly approached Nathan. Beneath the sun-bronzed skin of the man's throat, Nathan could see his veins throbbing swiftly. Fear? No, that didn't make sense. These *beings* had nothing to fear from anyone in Yisroel, not even the Romans, he suspected.

Nathan bowed again, hesitantly. "Mikael," he said. "I am honored. I . . ."

Nathan stiffened slightly when Mikael gripped him by the shoulders and forced him to straighten up. He met Calas' dark probing eyes with bewilderment.

"Nathan?" the man whispered familiarly.

Nathan flinched slightly when Calas embraced him in a warm hug. He guardedly responded, slipping his arms around Mikael's waist. Over the head of Yosef, he could see "Sybil" watching him with tears in her eyes. Nathan smiled at her. She was a very pretty woman, indeed.

She cautiously stepped forward and put one arm around Mikael's back and one around Nathan's. She braced her head against Nathan's shoulder and her brown hair fell over his arm in a curly mass.

Nathan blinked contemplatively at the angels, not understanding this ritual. But, oddly, the embraces of these strangers filled some empty place that had always ached in his soul. He peered down questioningly, when he felt Sybil's warm tears soaking through his brown sleeve. He gently untangled one arm from around Mikael's waist and snugged it over Sybil's narrow shoulders, pulling her closer.

"It's all right, Sybil," he said reassuringly. "Now that you're here, everything's all right."

She started to respond, but a shout brought her up short.

Nathan looked up to see the male angel with the blue-violet eyes break into a run, shouting, *"Baruch! Carey!"* He charged across the hilltop, almost falling, as though weak, before colliding with the man and woman he'd called to. Their bright laughter made Nathan smile.

And in the darkening sky overhead, a dozen silver daggers pierced the drifting clouds like streaks of fire. Nathan gasped. Some were larger, some smaller, but all blazed like flame. "Mikael?" he asked with trepidation. "What are those?"

The angel with the blue-violet eyes burst into howls of joy, jumping up and down before he ran headlong out across the sandy hills, waving his arms and crying, *"They made it! Baruch, that's the* Orphica!*"*

CHAPTER 62

The Archistrategos Michael stood beside Zadok, staring across the boiling River of Fire into the darkness of God. An ominous current had shaken the heavens, sending cherubim, seraphim, and angels scurrying to the seventh crystal palace for guidance and protection. They huddled in wide-eyed flocks against the sparkling walls, afraid to breathe. Michael cast a taut look at Zadok. The elderly patriarch stood resolutely, fists clenched at his sides, as though he had a faint glimmering of the metamorphosis taking place before his eyes. Michael pitied him—humans had never understood. He dropped his gaze to study the sculpted hem of his yellow robe. In the marmalade light, it blazed with a crimson edge. Michael felt like an iron cage constricted the beating of his heart.

"What's happening?" Zadok whispered.

Michael's face contorted. Of all the angels, he was the most closely tied to Epagael—he could sense God's very thoughts. His amber nostrils quivered. "Pain. Shimmering haze. They're fighting a war of dominance."

"Who?"

"The Aktariel/Rachel androgyne and Epagael."

Michael cried out in pain and bent double, gasping. Epagael's deepest essence convulsed with agony. The spasms of silent terror streaked unbroken to the brilliant edges of His infinite awareness. Michael dropped to his knees unable to bear the brunt of it.

"What are you feeling?" Zadok pressed. He knelt on the floor beside Michael and put a withered hand on the angel's forearm, gazing up in fear.

"Disbelief. Epagael never seriously thought Aktariel could challenge him. . . . And guilt for the suffering. He knows now. He feels it writhing inside him like a tangle of poisonous serpents." Michael clutched his stomach

521

and rocked back and forth. *Yes, guilt so deep it bears the horrifying depth of Creation's Darkness on its wings.*

Michael jerked his eyes up to stare at the vortex. In the deep blackness across the River of Fire, stars coalesced into magnificent spots of awesome brilliance, then flickered and died. Galaxies pirouetted in cold graceful patterns. Universes spun hopes and dreams and denied them all.

Glorious. Majestic. Filled with bitterness.

And Michael knew what had happened. Aktariel had forced Epagael to slit His eternal eyes and gaze back at the patterns of the surviving multiple universes:

And He saw them naked for the first time. And knew them for what they really were:

Idols.

Empty.

Epagael had realized in agony that his infinite consciousness had been built upon those graven images. Just as surely as Aaron had carefully constructed an altar for his polished bull calf in the barren deserts of old, Epagael had gathered together his own idols and stacked them like stones around himself to form glittering fortress walls—and been blinded by the endless spinning maze of chaos. So blinded that his own altar to himself had begun to crumble and He'd barely noticed.

While He'd squandered his radiance on names and games the consciousnesses in the creation had cried out to Him—but he'd heard them not. For the tumbled rubble of those cold alien stones had covered his ears.

Michael ached with Epagael's self-hatred; it swelled and festered into a wound that could stand no touch.

God tried to forget it.

God tried to turn His head.

. . . But He could not.

Neither Aktariel nor Rachel would let Him.

Cold sorrow swept Epagael up and metamorphosed into blind terror.

Across the face of the vortex, a shadow crept, neither male nor female, and a splash of light burst forth, spilling into the seventh crystal palace.

The cherubim shrieked and flew to hover against the ceiling. The angels muttered fearfully amongst themselves as the effulgence showered them.

Michael smiled.

For beyond the cold barricade of voids that separated the heavens from the multiple universes, a cleansing sea of light rushed. Universes melted beneath that bright hot flood.

Michael glanced down at Zadok's bald head and worried face. "Do you feel it, Patriarch?"

"No, Lord. What?"

"The Redemption. It's begun."

EPILOGUE

*And the angels sounded the trumpets and said,
"Blessed are you, Lord, who has pitied your creatures." Then Seth saw the extended hand of the Lord
holding Adam, and he handed him over to Michael,
saying, "Let him be in your custody until the day
of dispensing justice at the last years, when I will
turn his sorrow into joy . . .*

> **Life of Adam and Eve.
> 1st Century, B.C.E. Old Earth
> Standard. One of the Lake of
> Acheron texts found on
> Philonian, 2728.**

Adam Kadmon sneaked through the brush on the
ridge top, grinning. His seven-year-old face bore streaks
of dust and his white robe was so filthy it looked like
he'd been tending mean-tempered goats all day. He put
a hand over his mouth and giggled while he peeked
around the thin arms of a tiny date tree. The sweet smell
of the plant filled his nostrils. Through the thin limbs,
he spied his friend, Halakhah, hiding in the cool shadows
of a tan boulder. She wore a long pale green robe covered with dirt. Adam stifled his laughter, thinking about
how Halakhah's mother always yelled at her when she
came home after playing with him. Halakhah's long black
hair draped down her back like a dark tangled curtain.
She eased up and peeked around the boulder, searching
for Adam, and he struck!

He rushed out from his hiding place and let out a
blood-curdling shriek of triumph. Halakhah spun more
quickly than he would have thought possible and dove
for him, knocking his legs out from under him. Adam

fought valiantly, wrestling, trying to throw her off, but she was bigger than him. She pinned his arms over his head and sat on his chest with a wide grin on her face. Adam squirmed like a marmot in a trap, but she kept him down.

"I got you!" she cheered and started laughing.

"You always get me!" he growled, but laughed, too, so hard that his stomach ached. Halakhah finally rolled off him and they lay side-by-side in the warm sand looking up at the clouds that sailed through the deep blue skies. Today, they all looked like dragons to him, large and small, long-tailed and short.

"You know what, Adam?"

He turned and squinted at her. "What?"

Over the top of her head he could see a herd of camels trotting down the side of the hill north of them. A haze of dust rose. The herder ran after them, a stick in his hand, driving them into the city below.

Halakhah licked her chapped lips and grinned. "I'm thirsty. Let's go to the city well and get a drink."

"Okay."

Adam craftily shot up and started running up the brush-covered hill.

"Hey!" Halakhah shouted.

He turned around, but kept walking backward. "Come on! We're racing."

"Why didn't you tell me?"

Girls. You had to tell them everything. He waved an arm frantically. "Come on!"

Halakhah got up and ran with all her might. She was a fast runner. Her green sleeves flapped out behind her as she sped up the sandy hill.

Adam anxiously waited until she got close then he grabbed her hand and dragged her to the crest of the hill. He drew a line with the toe of his sandal and grinned at her. "I'll count to four, all right?"

She pulled up the hem of her green robe and hunkered down. "Yes. I'm ready."

Adam took a bunch of deep breaths, getting himself ready. Below, the city spread like a glistening blanket of gold, the buildings shimmering as frostily as ice crystals. The fortress wall rose a hundred feet high and shone with the radiance of all manner of precious stones. The first level was garnished with jasper, the second, sapphire, the third chalcedony and the fourth, emerald. The twelve gates that dotted the high walls were made of pure white pearl. In the bright midday sun, they sparkled.

Adam opened his mouth to count, but stopped and pointed suddenly. "Halakhah . . . look! They're back!"

Halakhah glanced up and a wide smile came over her face. They both stared in awe when the angels shoved open the gates of the city and stood like tall pillars in the entries.

Dressed in shiny garments that reflected the light like mirrors, they lifted their arms and waved to the people on the hillsides.

"Hurry!" Halakhah said as she waved back. She raced down the hill with all her might. "Let's see what weird gifts they brought this time!"

Adam ran behind her, laughing. He loved the twelve guardian angels. They didn't come very often, but when they did, they brought things that made the crops grow bigger, the trees grow taller, the animals get fatter.

And they talked long into the night with the city elders, telling them how to keep the aqueducts flowing and the city water wells clean. Sometimes, they brought books with brightly colored pictures of animals that didn't live in Adam's world. His father, a respected Rab in the city, told Adam that those animals lived in heaven.

Adam eagerly raced through a grove of olive trees behind Halakhah, breathless to see the angels, his heart bursting with happiness that they'd come again.

He rounded the corner and let out a yip of delight, his favorite angel stood at the Valley Gate, his brown hair blowing in the wind. His strange shimmering robe clung to his muscular body, like a snake's shiny skin. The angel's gaze drifted caressingly over the city—as though the sight of the jeweled fortress walls and golden buildings made him ache almost too much to bear.

Halakhah reached the angel first. *"Colopatiron!"* she yelled and threw herself into his arms. The angel laughed and swung her around playfully.

"Halakhah," he teased. "You're growing up too fast. And you, too, Adam."

Adam slid to a halt by the angel and beamed up at

him. As always, Colopatiron wore a strange necklace that glowed like a blue star.

Adam reached out to pat the angel's knee affectionately. "I'm glad you came back," he said shyly. "My father said those books you gave him made his brain hurt."

"He did?" the angel's blue-violet eyes sparkled. "Well, gravitation isn't for everybody. I just thought it might help him with his next irrigation project."

Colopatiron looked out across the hills to the goats that frolicked in the distance and a deep breath expanded his chest. His eyes tightened with longing. "It's always so peaceful here," he said. Then he turned and hoisted Halakhah up on his left hip and extended a hand to Adam. The angel smiled broadly. "Why don't we go talk to your father about those books?"

Adam ran to take the hand. Somewhere in the distance, the haunting melody of the shofar blasted, twining around the jeweled walls like honey. Adam squeezed Colopatiron's big callused palm tightly as they walked down the narrow gold-paved streets of Yerushalaim.

DAW

Kathleen M. O'Neal

POWERS OF LIGHT

☐ **AN ABYSS OF LIGHT: Book 1** (UE2418—$4.95)

The Gamant people believed they were blessed with the gift of a direct gateway to God and the angels. But were these beings who they claimed—or were the Gamants merely human pawns in an interdimensional struggle between alien powers?

☐ **TREASURE OF LIGHT: Book 2** (UE2455—$4.95)

As war escalates between the alien Magistrates and the human rebels, will the fulfillment of an ancient prophecy bring their universe to an end?

☐ **REDEMPTION OF LIGHT: Book 3** (UE2470—$4.99)

The concluding volume of this epic science fiction trilogy by the bestselling author of *People of the Fire*. Will anyone be the victor when human rebels and alien Magistrates are caught up in the final stages of a war far older than either race?